PRAISE FOR
Portrait of an Unknown Woman

"Reading the latest Gabriel Allon is like visiting an old friend. Another tour de force by the master."

—Bob Woodward

"Silva can really write. The bastard." —James Patterson

"A smart summer escape."

—*Kirkus Reviews* (starred review)

"The scheme is a doozy, but the real draw here is the meticulously detailed look at the art of the forger."

—*Booklist* (starred review)

"A world-class practitioner of spy fiction."

—*Washington Post*

"With Silva's novels you find yourself being educated as well as being entertained. . . . Silva is that rarity of rarities, a writer whose stories just keep getting better."

—*Huffington Post*

"Of those writing spy novels today, Daniel Silva is quite simply the best." —*Kansas City Star*

"Hypnotic prose, well-drawn characters, and nonstop action will thrill Silva's fans and convert the uninitiated."

—*People* (starred review)

PORTRAIT OF AN UNKOWN WOMAN

ALSO BY DANIEL SILVA

PORTRAIT OF AN UNKOWN WOMAN

DANIEL SILVA

HARPER

NEW YORK • LONDON • TORONTO • SYDNEY

HARPER

A hardcover edition of this book was published in 2022 by HarperCollins Publishers.

HarperCollins books may be purchased for educational, business, or sales promotional use. For information, please email the Special Markets Department at SPsales@harpercollins.com.

FIRST HARPER PAPERBACKS EDITION PUBLISHED 2023.

Library of Congress Cataloging-in-Publication Data has been applied for.

ISBN 978-0-06-283498-0 (pbk.)

23 24 25 26 27 LBC 5 4 3 2 1

For Burt Bacharach

*And, as always, for my wife, Jamie,
and my children, Lily and Nicholas*

All that glisters is not gold.

—William Shakespeare, *The Merchant of Venice*

PART ONE

CRAQUELURE

MASON'S YARD

O N ANY OTHER DAY, JULIAN would have tossed it straight into the rubbish bin. Or better yet, he would have fed it into Sarah's professional-grade shredder. During the long, bleak winter of the pandemic, when they had sold but a single painting, she had used the contraption to mercilessly cull the gallery's swollen archives. Julian, who was traumatized by the project, feared that when Sarah had no more needless sales records and shipping documents to destroy, it would be his turn in the machine. He would leave this world as a tiny parallelogram of yellowed paper, carted off to the recycler with the rest of the week's debris. In his next life he would return as an environmentally friendly coffee cup. He supposed, not without some justification, there were worse fates.

The letter had arrived at the gallery on a rainy Friday in late March, addressed to *M. JULIAN ISHERWOOD*. Sarah had nevertheless opened it; a former clandestine officer of the Central Intelligence Agency, she had no qualms about reading other people's mail. Intrigued, she had placed it on Julian's desk along with several inconsequential items from the morning's post, the only sort of correspondence she typically allowed him to see. He read it for the first time while still clad in his dripping mackintosh, his plentiful gray locks in windblown disarray. The time was half past eleven, which in itself was noteworthy. These days Julian rarely set foot in the gallery before noon. It gave him just enough time to make a nuisance of himself before embarking on the three-hour period of his day he reserved for his luncheon.

His first impression of the letter was that its author, a certain Madame Valerie Bérrangar, had the most exquisite handwriting he had seen in ages. It seemed she had noticed the recent story in *Le Monde* concerning the multimillion-pound sale by Isherwood Fine Arts of *Portrait of an Unknown Woman*, oil on canvas, 115 by 92 centimeters, by the Flemish Baroque painter Anthony van Dyck. Apparently, Madame Bérrangar had concerns about the transaction—concerns she wished to discuss with Julian in person, as they were legal and ethical in nature. She would be waiting at Café Ravel in Bordeaux at four o'clock on Monday afternoon. It was her wish that Julian come alone.

"What do you think?" asked Sarah.

"She's obviously mad as a hatter." Julian displayed the handwritten letter, as though it proved his point. "How did it get here? Carrier pigeon?"

"DHL."

"Was there a return address on the waybill?"

"She used the address of a DHL Express in Saint-Macaire. It's about fifty kilometers—"

"I know where Saint-Macaire is," said Julian, and immediately regretted his abrupt tone. "Why do I have this terrible feeling I'm being blackmailed?"

"She doesn't sound like a blackmailer to me."

"That's where you're wrong, petal. All the blackmailers and extortionists I've ever met had impeccable manners."

"Then perhaps we should ring the Met."

"Involve the police? Have you taken leave of your senses?"

"At least show it to Ronnie."

Ronald Sumner-Lloyd was Julian's pricey Berkeley Square attorney. "I have a better idea," he said.

It was then, at 11:36 a.m., with Sarah looking on in disapproval, that Julian dangled the letter over his ancient metal dustbin, a relic of the gallery's glory days, when it was located on stylish New Bond Street—or New Bondstrasse, as it had been known in some quarters of the trade. Try as he might, he couldn't seem to let the damn thing slip from his fingers. Or perhaps, he thought later, it was Madame Bérrangar's letter that had clung to him.

He set it aside, reviewed the remainder of the morning post, returned a few phone calls, and interrogated Sarah on the details of a pending sale. Then, having nothing else to do, he headed off to the Dorchester for lunch. He was accompanied by an employee of a venerable London auction house, female, of course, recently divorced, no children, far too young but not inappropriately so. Julian astonished her with his knowledge of Italian and Dutch Renaissance painters and regaled her with tales of acquisitional derring-do. It was a character he had been playing to modest acclaim for longer than he cared to remember. He was the incomparable Julian Isherwood, Julie to his friends, Juicy Julie to his partners in the occasional crime of drink. He was loyal as the day was long, trusting to a fault, and English to the core. English as high tea and bad teeth, as he was fond of saying. And yet, were it not for the war, he would have been someone else entirely.

Returning to the gallery, he found that Sarah had adhered a fuchsia-colored sticky note to Madame Bérrangar's letter, advising him to reconsider. He read it a second time, slowly.

Its tone was as formal as the linenlike stationery upon which it was written. Even Julian had to admit she sounded entirely reasonable and not at all like an extortionist. Surely, he thought, there would be no harm in merely listening to what she had to say. If nothing else, the journey would provide him with a much-needed respite from his crushing workload at the gallery. Besides, the weather forecast for London called for several days of nearly uninterrupted cold and rain. But in the southwest of France, it was springtime already.

AMONG THE FIRST ACTIONS THAT SARAH HAD TAKEN AFTER coming to work at the gallery was to inform Ella, Julian's stunning but useless receptionist, that her services were no longer required. Sarah had never bothered to hire a replacement. She was more than capable, she said, of answering the phone, returning the emails, keeping the appointment book, and buzzing visitors upstairs when they presented themselves at the perpetually locked door in Mason's Yard.

She drew a line, however, at making Julian's travel arrangements, though she consented to peer over his shoulder while he performed the chore himself, if only to make certain he didn't mistakenly book passage on the Orient Express to Istanbul rather than the Eurostar to Paris. From there, it was a scant two hours and fourteen minutes by TGV to Bordeaux. He successfully purchased a first-class ticket and then reserved a junior suite at the InterContinental—for two nights, just to be on the safe side.

The task complete, he repaired to the bar at Wiltons for a drink with Oliver Dimbleby and Roddy Hutchinson, widely regarded as London's most disreputable art dealers. One thing led to another, as was usually the case when Oliver and Roddy were involved, and it was after 2:00 a.m. by the time Julian finally toppled into his bed. He spent Saturday tending to his hangover and devoted much of Sunday to packing a bag. Once he would have thought nothing about hopping on the Concorde with only an attaché case and a pretty girl. But suddenly the preparations for a jaunt across the English Channel required all of his powers of concentration. He supposed it was but another unwanted consequence of growing old, like his alarming absentmindedness, or the strange sounds he emitted, or his seeming inability to cross a room without crashing into something. He kept a list of self-deprecating excuses at the ready to explain his humiliating clumsiness. He had never been the athletic type. It was the bloody lamp's fault. It was the end table that had assaulted *him*.

He slept poorly, as was frequently the case the night before an important journey, and awoke with a nagging sensation that he was about to make yet another in a long series of dreadful mistakes. His spirits lifted, however, as the Eurostar emerged from the Channel Tunnel and surged across the gray-green fields of the Pas-de-Calais toward Paris. He rode the *métro* from the Gare du Nord to the Gare Montparnasse and enjoyed a decent lunch in the buffet car of the TGV as the light beyond his window gradually took on the quality of a Cézanne landscape.

He recalled with startling clarity the instant he had seen it for the first time, this dazzling light of the south. Then, as now, he was riding a train bound from Paris. His father, the German Jewish art dealer Samuel Isakowitz, sat on the opposite side of the compartment. He was reading a day-old newspaper, as though nothing were out of the ordinary. Julian's mother, her hands knotted atop her knees, was staring into space, her face without expression.

Hidden in the luggage above their heads, rolled in protective sheets of paraffin paper, were several paintings. Julian's father had left a few lesser works behind at his gallery on the rue la Boétie, in the elegant Eighth Arrondissement. The bulk of his remaining inventory was already hidden in the château he had rented east of Bordeaux. Julian remained there until the terrible summer of 1942, when a pair of Basque shepherds smuggled him over the Pyrenees to neutral Spain. His parents were arrested in 1943 and deported to the Nazi extermination center at Sobibor, where they were gassed upon arrival.

Bordeaux's Saint-Jean station lay hard against the river Garonne, at the end of the Cours de la Marne. The departure board in the refurbished ticket hall was a modern device—gone was the polite applause of the updates—but the Beaux-Arts exterior, with its two prominent clocks, was as Julian remembered it. So, too, were the honey-colored Louis XV buildings lining the boulevards along which he sped in the back of a taxi. Some of the facades were so bright they seemed to glow with an interior light source. Others were dimmed by grime. It was the porous quality of the local stone, his father had explained. It absorbed soot from the air like a sponge and, like oil paintings, required occasional cleaning.

By some miracle, the hotel hadn't misplaced his reservation. After pressing an overly generous tip into the palm of the immigrant bellman, he hung up his clothes and withdrew to the bathroom to do something about his ragged appearance. It was gone three o'clock when he capitulated. He locked his valuables in the room safe and debated for a moment whether to bring Madame Bérrangar's letter to the café. An inner voice—his father's, he supposed—advised him to leave it behind, concealed within his luggage.

The same voice instructed him to bring along his attaché case, as it would confer upon him a wholly unwarranted patina of authority. He carried it along the Cours de l'Intendance, past a parade of exclusive shops. There were no motorcars, only pedestrians and bicyclists and sleek electric trams that slithered along their steel tracks in near silence. Julian proceeded at an unhurried pace, the attaché case in his right hand, his left lodged in his pocket, along with the card key for his hotel room.

He followed a tram around a corner and onto the rue Vital Carles. Directly before him rose the twin Gothic spires of Bordeaux Cathedral. It was surrounded by the scrubbed paving stones of a broad square. Café Ravel occupied the northwest corner. It was not the sort of place frequented by most Bordelais, but it was centrally located and easily found. Julian supposed that was the reason Madame Bérrangar had chosen it.

The shadow cast by the Hôtel de Ville darkened most of the café's tables, but the one nearest the cathedral was sunlit and unoccupied. Julian sat down and, placing his attaché case at his feet, took stock of the other patrons. With the possible exception of the man sitting three tables to his right, none appeared to be French. The rest were tourists, primarily of the package variety. Julian was the café's sore thumb; in his flannel trousers and gray sport jacket, he looked like a character from an E. M. Forster novel. At least she would have no difficulty spotting him.

He ordered a café crème before coming to his senses and requesting a half bottle of white Bordeaux instead, brutally cold, two glasses. The waiter delivered it as the bells of the cathedral tolled four o'clock. Julian reflexively smoothed the front of his jacket as his eyes searched the square. But at four thirty, as the lengthening shadows crept across his table, Madame Valerie Bérrangar was still nowhere to be found.

By the time Julian finished the last of the wine, it was approaching five o'clock. He paid the bill in cash and, taking up his attaché case, moved from table to table like a beggar, repeating Madame Bérrangar's name and receiving only blank stares in return.

The interior of the café was deserted save the man behind

the old zinc-topped bar. He had no recollection of anyone named Valerie Bérrangar but suggested Julian leave his name and phone number. "Isherwood," he said when the barman squinted at the spidery lines scrawled on the back of a napkin. "Julian Isherwood. I'm staying at the InterContinental."

Outside, the bells of the cathedral were tolling once more. Julian followed an earthbound pigeon across the paving stones of the square, then turned into the rue Vital Carles. He realized after a moment that he was berating himself for having come all the way to Bordeaux for no reason—and for having permitted this woman, this Madame Bérrangar, to stir up unwanted memories of the past. "How dare she?" he shouted, startling a poor passerby. It was another unsettling development brought about by his advancing years, his recent propensity to say aloud the private thoughts running through his head.

At last the bells fell silent, and the pleasing low murmur of the ancient city returned. An electric tram glided past, sotto voce. Julian, his anger beginning to subside, paused outside a small art gallery and regarded with professional dismay the Impressionist-inspired paintings in the window. He was aware, vaguely, of the sound of an approaching motorbike. It was no scooter, he thought. Not with an engine note like that. It was one of those low-slung beasts ridden by men who wore special wind-resistant costumes.

The gallery's owner appeared in the doorway and invited Julian inside for a closer look at his inventory. Declining, he continued along the street in the direction of his hotel, the attaché case, as usual, in his left hand. The volume of the motorcycle's engine had increased sharply and was a half step higher in register. Suddenly Julian noticed an elderly woman— Madame Bérrangar's doppelgänger, no doubt—pointing at him and shouting something in French he couldn't make out.

Fearing he had once again uttered something inappropriate, he turned in the opposite direction and saw the motorcycle bearing down on him, a gloved hand reaching toward his attaché case. He drew the bag to his chest and pirouetted out of the machine's path, directly into the cold metal of a tall, immovable object. As he lay on the pavement, his head swimming, he saw several faces hovering over him, each wearing an expression of pity. Someone suggested calling an ambulance; someone else, the gendarmes. Humiliated, Julian reached for one of his ready-made excuses. It wasn't his fault, he explained. The bloody lamppost attacked *him*.

2

VENEZIA

IT WAS FRANCESCO TIEPOLO, WHILE standing atop Tintoretto's grave in the church of the Madonna dell'Orto, who had assured Gabriel that one day he would return to Venice. The remark was not idle speculation, as Gabriel discovered a few nights later, during a candlelit dinner with his beautiful young wife on the island of Murano. He offered several considered objections to the scheme, without conviction or success, and in the aftermath of an electrifying conclave in Rome, the deal was concluded. The terms were equitable, everyone was happy. Chiara especially. As far as Gabriel was concerned, nothing else mattered.

Admittedly, it all made a great deal of sense. After all, Gabriel had served his apprenticeship in Venice and had pseudonymously restored many of its greatest masterpieces. Still, the arrangement was not without its potential pitfalls, including the agreed-upon organizational chart of the Tiepolo Restoration Company, the most prominent such enterprise in the city. Under the terms of their arrangement, Francesco would remain at the helm until his retirement, when Chiara, who was Venetian by birth, would assume control. In the meantime she would occupy the position of general manager, with Gabriel serving as the director of the paintings department. Which meant that, for all intents and purposes, he would be working for his wife.

He approved the purchase of a luxurious four-bedroom *piano nobile* overlooking the Grand Canal in San Polo but otherwise left the planning and execution of the pending move in Chiara's capable hands. She oversaw the apartment's renovation and decoration long-distance from Jerusalem while Gabriel served out the remainder of his term at King Saul Boulevard. The final months passed quickly—there always seemed to be one more meeting to attend, one more crisis to avert—and in late autumn he embarked on what a noted columnist at *Haaretz* described as "the long goodbye." The events ranged from cocktail receptions and tribute-laden dinners to a blowout at the King David Hotel attended by espiocrats from around the globe, including the powerful chief of the Jordanian Mukhabarat and his counterparts from Egypt and the United Arab Emirates. Their presence was proof that Gabriel, who had cultivated security partnerships across the Arab world, had left an indelible mark on a region torn by decades of war. For all its problems, the Middle East had changed for the better on his watch.

Reclusive by nature and uncomfortable in crowded settings, he found all the attention unbearable. Indeed, he much preferred the quiet evenings he passed with the members of his senior staff, the men and women with whom he had carried out some of the most storied operations in the history of a storied service. He begged Uzi Navot for forgiveness. He dispensed career and marital advice to Mikhail Abramov and Natalie Mizrahi. He shed tears of laughter while telling uproarious tales about the three years he had spent living underground in Western Europe with the hypochondriacal Eli Lavon. Dina Sarid, archivist of Palestinian and Islamic terrorism, beseeched Gabriel to sit for a series of exit interviews so that she might record his exploits in an unclassified official history. Not surprisingly, he declined. He had no wish to dwell on the past, he told her. Only the future.

Two officers from his senior staff, Yossi Gavish of Research and Yaakov Rossman of Special Ops, were regarded as his most likely successors. But both were overjoyed to learn that Gabriel had chosen Rimona Stern, the chief of Collections, instead. On a blustery Friday afternoon in mid-December, she became the first female director-general in the history of the Office. And Gabriel, after affixing his signature to a stack of documents regarding his modest pension and the dire consequences he would suffer if he ever divulged any of the secrets lodged in his head, officially became the world's most famous retired spy. His ritual disrobing complete, he toured King Saul Boulevard from top to bottom, shaking hands, drying tear-streaked cheeks. He assured his heartbroken troops that they had not seen the last of him, that he intended to keep his hand in the game. No one believed him.

That evening he attended one final gathering, this time on the shore of the Sea of Galilee. Unlike its predecessors, the encounter was at times contentious, though in the end a kind of peace was made. Early the next morning he made a pilgrimage to his son's grave on the Mount of Olives—and to the psychiatric hospital near the old Arab village of Deir Yassin where the child's mother resided in a prison of memory and a body ravaged by fire. With Rimona's blessing, the Allon family flew to Venice aboard the Office's Gulfstream, and at three that afternoon, after a windblown ride across the *laguna* in a gleaming wooden water taxi, they arrived at their new home.

Gabriel headed directly to the large light-filled room he had claimed as his studio and found an antique Italian easel, two halogen work lamps, and an aluminum trolley filled with Winsor & Newton sable-hair brushes, pigment, medium, and solvent. Absent was his old paint-smudged CD player. In its place was a British-made audio system and a pair of floor-standing speakers. His extensive music collection was organized by genre, composer, and artist.

"What do you think?" asked Chiara from the doorway.

"Bach's violin concertos are in the Brahms section. Otherwise, it's absolutely—"

"Amazing, I think."

"How did you possibly manage all this from Jerusalem?"

She waved a hand dismissively.

"Is there any money left?"

"Not much."

"I'll line up a few private commissions after we get settled."

"I'm afraid that's out of the question."

"Why?"

"Because you shall do no work whatsoever until you've had a chance to properly rest and recuperate." She handed him a sheet of paper. "You can start with this."

"A shopping list?"

"There's no food in the house."

"I thought I was supposed to be resting."

"You are." She smiled. "Take your time, darling. Enjoy doing something *normal* for a change."

The closest supermarket was the Carrefour near the Frari church. Gabriel's stress level seemed to subside a notch with each item he placed in his lime-green basket. Returning home, he watched the latest news from the Middle East with only passing interest while Chiara, singing softly to herself, prepared dinner in the apartment's showplace of a kitchen. They finished the last of the Barbaresco upstairs on the roof terrace, huddled closely together against the cold December air. Beneath them, gondolas swayed at their moorings. Along the gentle curve of the Grand Canal, the Rialto Bridge was awash with floodlight.

"And if I were to paint something original?" asked Gabriel. "Would that constitute work?"

"What did you have in mind?"

"A canal scene. Or perhaps a still life."

"Still life? How boring."

"In that case, how about a series of nudes?"

Chiara raised an eyebrow. "I suppose you'll need a model."

"Yes," said Gabriel, tugging at the zipper of her coat. "I suppose I will."

CHIARA WAITED UNTIL JANUARY BEFORE TAKING UP HER NEW position at Tiepolo Restoration. The firm's warehouse was on the mainland, but its business offices were located on the fashionable Calle Larga XXII Marzo in San Marco, a ten-minute commute by vaporetto. Francesco introduced her to the city's artistic elite and dropped cryptic hints that a succession plan had been put in place. Someone leaked the news to *Il Gazzettino*, and in late February a brief article appeared in the newspaper's Cultura section. It referred to Chiara by her maiden name, Zolli, and pointed out that her father was the chief rabbi of Venice's dwindling Jewish community. With the exception of a few nasty reader comments, mainly from the populist far right, the reception was favorable.

The story contained no mention of a spouse or domestic partner, only two children, twins apparently, of indeterminate age and gender. At Chiara's insistence, Irene and Raphael were enrolled in the neighborhood *scuola elementare* rather than one of Venice's many private international schools. Perhaps fittingly, theirs was named for Bernardo Canal, the father of Canaletto. Gabriel deposited them at the entrance at eight o'clock each morning and collected them again at half past three. Along with a daily visit to the Rialto Market, where he fetched the ingredients for the family dinner, the two appointments represented the sum total of his domestic responsibilities.

Forbidden by Chiara to work, or to even set foot in the offices of Tiepolo Restoration, he devised ways of filling his vast reservoir of available time. He read dense books. He listened to his music collection on his new sound system. He painted his nudes—from memory, of course, for his model was no longer available to him. Occasionally she came to the apartment for "lunch," which was the way they referred to the ravenous sessions of midday lovemaking in their glorious bedroom overlooking the Grand Canal.

Mainly, he walked. Not the punishing clifftop hikes of his Cornish exile, but aimless Venetian wanderings conducted in the unhurried manner of a flaneur. If he were so inclined, he would drop in on a painting he had once restored, if only to see how his work had held up. Afterward, he might slip into a bar for a coffee and, if it was cold, a small glass of something stronger to warm his bones. More often than not, one of the other patrons would attempt to engage him in conversation about the weather or the news of the day. Where once he would have spurned their overtures, he now reciprocated, in perfect if slightly accented Italian, with a witticism or keen observation of his own.

One by one, his demons took flight, and the violence of his past, the nights of blood and fire, receded from his thoughts and dreams. He laughed more easily. He allowed his hair to grow. He acquired a new wardrobe of elegant handmade trousers and cashmere jackets befitting a man of his position. Before long he scarcely recognized the figure he glimpsed each morning in the mirror of his dressing room. The transformation, he thought, was nearly complete. He was no longer Israel's avenging angel. He was the director of the paintings department of the Tiepolo Restoration Company. Chiara and Francesco had given him a second chance at life. This time, he vowed, he would not make the same mistakes.

In early March, during a bout of drenching rains, he asked Chiara for permission to begin working. And when she once again denied his request, he ordered a twelve-meter Bavaria C42 yacht and spent the next two weeks preparing a detailed itinerary for a summer sailing trip around the Adriatic and Mediterranean. He presented it to Chiara over a particularly satisfying lunch in the bedroom of their apartment.

"I have to say," she murmured approvingly, "that was one of your better performances."

"It must be all the rest I've been getting."

"Have you?"

"I'm so rested I'm on the verge of becoming bored stiff."

"Then perhaps there's something we can do to make your afternoon a bit more interesting."

"I'm not sure that would be possible."

"How about a drink with an old friend?"

"Depends on the friend."

"Julian rang me at the office as I was leaving. He said he was in Venice and was wondering whether you had a minute or two to spare."

"What did you say to him?"

"That you would meet him for a drink after you were finished having your way with me."

"Surely you left the last bit out."

"I don't believe so, no."

"What time is he expecting me?"

"Three o'clock."

"What about the children?"

"Don't worry, I'll cover for you." She glanced at her wrist-watch. "The question is, what shall we do until then?"

"Since you're not wearing any clothing . . ."

"Yes?"

"Why don't you come to my studio and pose for me?"

"I have a better idea."

"What's that?"

Chiara smiled. "Dessert."

HARRY'S BAR

STANDING BENEATH A CASCADE OF scalding water, drained of desire, Gabriel rinsed the last traces of Chiara from his skin. His clothing lay scattered at the foot of their unmade bed, wrinkled, a button ripped from his shirt. He selected clean apparel from his walk-in closet, dressed quickly, and headed downstairs. As luck would have it, a Number 2 was nudging against the pier of the San Tomà stop. He rode it to San Marco and at three o'clock sharp entered the intimate confines of Harry's Bar.

Julian Isherwood was pondering his mobile phone at a corner table, a half-drunk Bellini hovering beneath his lips. When Gabriel joined him, he looked up and frowned, as though annoyed by an unwanted intrusion. Finally his features settled into an expression of recognition, followed by profound approval.

"I guess Chiara wasn't joking about how you two spend your lunch hour."

"This is Italy, Julian. We take at least two hours for lunch."

"You look thirty years younger. What's your secret?"

"Two-hour lunches with Chiara."

Julian's eyes narrowed. "But it's more than that, isn't it? You look as though you've been . . ." His voice trailed off.

"What, Julian?"

"Restored," he answered after a moment. "You've removed the dirty varnish and repaired the damage. It's almost as if none of it ever happened."

"It didn't."

"That's funny, because you bear a vague resemblance to a morose-looking boy who wandered into my gallery about a hundred years ago. Or was it two hundred?"

"That never happened, either. At least not officially," added Gabriel. "I buried your voluminous file in the deepest reaches of Registry on my way out the door of King Saul Boulevard. Your ties to the Office are now formally severed."

"But not to you, I hope."

"I'm afraid you're stuck with me." A waiter delivered two more Bellinis to their table. Gabriel raised his glass in salutation. "So what brings you to Venice?"

"These olives." Julian plucked one from the bowl at the center of the table and with a flourish popped it into his mouth. "They're dangerously good."

He was dressed in one of his Savile Row suits and a blue dress shirt with French cuffs. His gray hair was in need of a trimming, but then it usually was. All things considered, he looked rather well, except for the plaster adhered to his right cheek, perhaps two or three centimeters beneath his eye.

Cautiously Gabriel asked how it got there.

"I had an argument with my razor this morning, and I'm afraid the razor got the better of me." Julian fished another olive from the bowl. "So what do you do with yourself when you're not lunching with your beautiful wife?"

"I spend as much time as possible with my children."

"Are they bored with you yet?"

"They don't appear to be."

"Don't worry, they will be soon."

"Spoken like a lifelong bachelor."

"It has its advantages, you know."

"Name one."

"Give me a minute, I'll think of something." Julian finished his first Bellini and started in on the second. "And what about your work?" he asked.

"I painted three nudes of my wife."

"Poor you. Any good?"

"Not bad, actually."

"Three original Allons would fetch a great deal of money on the open market."

"They're for my eyes only, Julian."

Just then the door opened, and in walked a handsome dark-haired Italian in slim-fitting trousers and a quilted Barbour jacket. He sat down at a nearby table and in the accent of a southerner ordered a Campari and soda.

Julian was contemplating the bowl of olives. "Cleaned anything lately?"

"My entire CD collection."

"I was referring to paintings."

"The Tiepolo Restoration Company was recently awarded a contract by the Culture Ministry to restore Giulia Lama's four evangelists in the church of San Marziale. Chiara says that if I continue to behave myself, she'll let me do the work."

"And how much will the Tiepolo Restoration Company receive in compensation?"

"Don't ask."

"Perhaps I could tempt you with something a bit more lucrative."

"Such as?"

"A lovely Grand Canal scene that you could knock into shape in a week or two while gazing upon the real thing from your studio window."

"Attribution?"

"Northern Italian School."

"How precise," remarked Gabriel.

The "school" attribution was the murkiest designation for the origin of an Old Master painting. In the case of Julian's canal scene, it meant that the work had been produced by *some*one working *some*where in the north of Italy, at some point in the distant past. The designation "by" occupied the opposite end of the spectrum. It declared that the dealer or auction house selling the painting was certain it had been produced by the artist whose name was attached to it. Between them lay a subjective and oftentimes speculative series of categories ranging from the respectable "workshop of" to the ambiguous "after," each designed to whet the appetite of potential buyers while at the same time shielding the seller from legal action.

"Before you turn up your nose at it," said Julian, "you should know that I'll pay you enough to cover the cost of that new sailboat of yours. Two sailboats, in fact."

"It's too much for a painting like that."

"You funneled a great deal of business my way while you were running the Office. It's the least I can do."

"It wouldn't be ethical."

"I'm an art dealer, petal. If I was interested in ethics, I'd be working for Amnesty International."

"Have you run it past your partner?"

"Sarah and I are hardly partners," said Julian. "My name might still be on the door, but these days I am largely underfoot." He smiled. "I suppose I have you to thank for that, too."

It was Gabriel who had arranged for Sarah Bancroft, a veteran covert operative and overeducated art historian, to take over day-to-day control of Isherwood Fine Arts. He had also played a facilitating role in her recent decision to wed. For reasons having to do with her husband's complicated past, the ceremony was a clandestine affair, held at an MI6 safe house in the countryside of Surrey. Julian had been one of the few invited guests in attendance. Gabriel, who was late in arriving from Tel Aviv, had given away the bride.

"So where's this masterpiece of yours?" he asked.

"Under armed guard in London."

"Is there a deadline?"

"Have you another pressing commission?"

"That depends."

"On what?"

"How you answer my next question."

"You want to know what really happened to my face?"

Gabriel nodded. "The truth this time, Julian."

"I was attacked by a lamppost."

"Another one?"

"I'm afraid so."

"Please tell me it was a foggy night in London."

"Actually, it was yesterday afternoon in Bordeaux. I went there at the invitation of a woman named Valerie Bérrangar. She said she wanted to tell me something about a painting I sold not long ago."

"Not the Van Dyck?"

"Yes, that's the one."

"Is there a problem?"

"I wouldn't know. You see, Madame Bérrangar died in an automobile accident on the way to our meeting."

"And the incident involving the lamppost?" asked Gabriel.

"Two men on a motorcycle tried to steal my briefcase as I was walking back to my hotel. At least I think that's what they were doing. For all I know," said Julian, "they were trying to kill me, too."

IN THE PIAZZA SAN MARCO, a string quartet wearily serenaded the day's last customers at Caffè Florian.

"Are they incapable of playing anything other than Vivaldi?" asked Julian.

"What have you got against Vivaldi?"

"I adore him. But how about Corelli for a change of pace? Or Handel, for heaven's sake?"

"Or Anthony van Dyck." Gabriel paused before a shop window in the arcade on the square's southern flank. "The original story in *ARTnews* didn't mention where you found the painting. It didn't identify the buyer, either. The price tag, however, received prominent play."

"Six and a half million pounds." Julian smiled. "Now ask me how much I paid for the bloody thing."

"I was getting to that."

"Three million euros."

"Which means your profit was in excess of one hundred percent."

"But that's how the secondary art market works, petal. Dealers like me search out misattributed, misplaced, or undervalued paintings and bring them to market, hopefully with enough flair and panache to attract one or more deep-pocketed buyers. And don't forget, I had my expenses, too."

"Long lunches at London's finest restaurants?"

"Actually, most of the lunches took place in Paris. You see, I bought the painting from a gallery in the Eighth. The rue la Boétie, of all places."

"Does this gallery have a name?"

"Galerie Georges Fleury."

"Have you done business with him in the past?"

"A great deal. Monsieur Fleury specializes in French paintings from the seventeenth and eighteenth centuries, but he deals in Dutch and Flemish works as well. He has excellent relationships with many of France's oldest and wealthiest families. The ones who live in drafty châteaux crammed with art. He contacts me when he finds something interesting."

"Where did he find *Portrait of an Unknown Woman*?"

"It came from an old private collection. That's all he would say."

"Attribution?"

"Manner of Anthony van Dyck."

"Which covers all *manner* of sins."

"Indeed," agreed Julian. "But Monsieur Fleury thought he saw evidence of the master's hand. He called me for a second opinion."

"And?"

"The instant I laid eyes on it, I got that funny feeling at the back of my neck."

They emerged from the arcade into the fading afternoon light. To their left rose the Campanile. Gabriel led Julian to the right instead, past the ornate facade of the Doge's Palace. On the Ponte della Paglia, they joined a knot of tourists gawking at the Bridge of Sighs.

"Looking for something?" asked Julian.

"You know what they say about old habits."

"I'm afraid that most of mine are bad. You, however, are the most disciplined creature I've ever met."

On the opposite side of the bridge lay the *sestiere* of Castello. They hurried past the souvenir kiosks lining the Riva degli Schiavoni, then followed the passageway to the Campo San Zaccaria, home of the Carabinieri's regional headquarters. Julian had once spent a sleepless night in an interrogation room on the second floor.

"How's your old friend General Ferrari?" he asked. "Still pulling the wings off flies? Or has he managed to find a new hobby?"

General Cesare Ferrari was the commander of the Carabinieri's Division for the Defense of Cultural Patrimony, better known as the Art Squad. It was headquartered in a palazzo in Rome's Piazza di Sant'Ignazio, though three of its officers were stationed full-time in Venice. While not searching for stolen paintings, they kept tabs on the former Israeli spymaster and assassin living quietly in San Polo. It was General Ferrari who had arranged for Gabriel to receive a *permesso di soggiorno*, a permanent Italian residence permit. Consequently, Gabriel tried to stay on his good side, no easy feat.

Adjacent to the Carabinieri headquarters was the church for which the square was named. Among the many monumental works of art adorning the nave was a crucifixion executed by Anthony van Dyck during the six-year period he spent studying and working in Italy. Gabriel stood before it, a hand to his chin, his head tilted slightly to one side.

"You were about to tell me about the painting's provenance."

"It was good enough for me."

"Meaning?"

"It depicted a portrait that had been executed in the late sixteen twenties and had made its way over the centuries from Flanders to France. There were no glaring holes and no red flags."

"Did it require restoration?"

"Monsieur Fleury had it cleaned before he showed it to me. He has his own man. Not your caliber, mind you. But not bad." Julian crossed to the opposite side of the nave and stood before Bellini's majestic San Zaccaria Altarpiece. "You did a lovely job with it. Old Giovanni would have approved."

"You think so?"

Julian cast a glance of mild reproach over one shoulder. "Modesty doesn't suit you, my boy. Your restoration of this painting was the talk of the art world."

"It took me longer to clean it than it did for Giovanni to paint it."

"There were extenuating circumstances, as I recall."

"There usually were." Gabriel joined Julian in front of the altarpiece. "I assume that you and Sarah got a second opinion about the attribution after the painting arrived in London."

"Not just a second opinion. A third, a fourth, and a fifth as well. And all of our gold-plated hired guns concluded that the painting was the work of Anthony van Dyck and not a later follower. Within a week we had a bidding war on our hands."

"Who was the lucky winner?"

"Masterpiece Art Ventures. It's an art-based hedge fund run by one of Sarah's old contacts from her days in New York. Someone called Phillip Somerset."

"The name rings a distant bell," said Gabriel.

"Masterpiece Art Ventures buys and sells an enormous number of paintings. Everything from Old Masters to contemporary. Phillip Somerset routinely shows his investors twenty-five percent annual returns, from which he takes a substantial cut. And he can be quite litigious if he thinks someone has wronged him. Suing people is his favorite pastime."

"Which is why you went running to Bordeaux when you received a rather ambiguous letter from a perfect stranger."

"Actually, it was Sarah who convinced me to go. As for the letter, the men on the motorbike obviously thought it was in my briefcase. That's why they tried to steal it."

"They might have been ordinary thieves, you know. Street crime is one of the few growth industries in France these days."

"They weren't."

"How can you be sure?"

"Because when I got back to the hotel after being discharged from *l'hôpital*, it was quite obvious that my room had been searched." Julian patted the front of his jacket. "Fortunately, they didn't find what they were looking for."

"Searched by whom?"

"Two well-dressed men. They paid the bellman fifty euros to let them into my room."

"How much did the bellman get from you?"

"A hundred," answered Julian. "As you might expect, I passed a rather restless night. When I woke this morning, there was a copy of *Sud Ouest* outside my door. After reading the story about a fatal single-vehicle accident south of Bordeaux, I hastily packed my things and caught the first train to Paris. I was able to make the eleven o'clock flight to Venice."

"Because you were craving the olives at Harry's Bar?"

"Actually, I was wondering—"

"Whether you might prevail upon me to find out what Valerie Bérrangar wanted to tell you about *Portrait of an Unknown Woman* by Anthony van Dyck."

"You *do* have friends in high places in the French government," said Julian. "Which will enable you to conduct an inquiry with absolute discretion and thus reduce the chance of a scandal."

"And if I'm successful?"

"I suppose that depends on the nature of the information. If there is indeed a legal or ethical problem with the sale, I will quietly refund Phillip Somerset's six and a half million quid before he drags me into court and destroys what's left of my once glittering reputation." Julian offered Gabriel Madame Bérrangar's letter. "Not to mention the reputation of your dear friend Sarah Bancroft."

Gabriel hesitated, then accepted the letter. "I'll need the attribution reports from your experts. And photographs of the painting, of course."

Julian produced his smartphone. "Where shall I send them?"

Gabriel recited an address at ProtonMail, the Swiss-based encrypted email service. A moment later, secure mobile phone in hand, he was scrutinizing a high-resolution detail image of the unknown woman's pale cheek.

At length he asked, "Did any of your experts take a close look at the craquelure?"

"Why do you ask?"

"You know that funny feeling you got when you saw this painting for the first time?"

"Of course."

"I just got it, too."

JULIAN HAD BOOKED A ROOM FOR THE NIGHT AT THE GRITTI Palace. Gabriel saw him to the door, then made his way to the Campo Santa Maria del Giglio. There was not a tourist in sight. It was as if a drain had opened, he thought, and washed them out to sea.

On the western side of the square, next to the Hotel Ala,

was the entrance to a narrow, darkened *calle*. Gabriel followed it to the vaporetto station and joined three other passengers—a prosperous-looking Scandinavian couple in their late sixties and a world-weary Venetian woman of perhaps forty—waiting beneath the shelter. The Scandinavians were huddled over a map. The Venetian woman was watching a Number 1 crawling up the Grand Canal from the direction of San Marco.

When the vessel nudged against the jetty, the Venetian woman boarded first, followed by the Scandinavians. All three claimed seats in the cabin. Gabriel, as was his habit, stood in the open-air passage behind the pilothouse. There he was able to observe a single late-arriving passenger emerging from the *calle*.

Dark hair. Slim-fitting trousers. A quilted Barbour jacket.

The man from Harry's Bar.

5

CANAL GRANDE

H E ENTERED THE PASSENGER CABIN and lowered himself into a blue-green plastic seat in the first row. He was taller than Gabriel remembered, formidably built, in the prime of life. Early thirties, thirty-five at most. The malodorous trail he left in his wake indicated he was a smoker. The slight bulge in the left side of his jacket suggested he was armed.

Fortunately, Gabriel was in possession of a gun as well—a Beretta 92FS 9mm pistol with a walnut grip. He carried it with the full knowledge and consent of General Ferrari and the Carabinieri. Nevertheless, it was his intention to resolve the situation without having to draw the weapon, as an act of violence, even one in self-defense, would likely result in the immediate revocation of his *permesso*, which in turn would endanger his standing at home.

The most obvious course of action was to shed the man as quickly as possible. In a city like Venice, with its labyrinthine streets and gloomy *sotoportegi*, it would not prove difficult. It would, however, deprive Gabriel of the opportunity to determine why the man was following him. It was better to have a quiet word with him in private, he reasoned, than to lose him.

The Palazzo Venier dei Leoni, home of the Peggy Guggenheim Collection, slid right to left through Gabriel's field of vision. The two Scandinavians disembarked at the Accademia; the Venetian woman, at Ca' Rezzonico. San Tomà, Gabriel's stop, was next. He stood stock-still behind the pilothouse as the vaporetto alighted long enough to collect a single passenger.

As the vessel withdrew, he lifted his gaze briefly toward the soaring windows of his new apartment. They were aglow with amber-colored light. His children were doing their schoolwork. His wife was preparing dinner. Doubtless she was troubled over his prolonged absence. He would be home soon, he thought. He had one small matter to attend to first.

The vaporetto crossed the canal to the Sant'Angelo stop, then returned to the San Polo side and docked at San Silvestri. This time Gabriel disembarked and, leaving the platform, entered an unlit *sotoportego*. From behind him came the sound of footsteps—the footsteps of a formidably built man in the prime of life. Perhaps, thought Gabriel, a small measure of violence was called for, after all.

HE FELL INTO THE EASY, UNHURRIED PACE OF HIS AFTERNOON sojourns through the city. Even so, he twice had to loiter outside shop windows in order to keep his pursuer in the game. He was no professional surveillance artist; that much was obvious. Nor did he seem to be familiar with the streets of the *sestiere*, a shortcoming that would provide Gabriel with a distinct home-field advantage.

He continued in a northwesterly direction—across the Campo Sant'Aponal, along a succession of slender alleyways, over a humpbacked bridge—until he came to a *corte* bordered on three sides by apartment buildings. He knew with certainty that the dwellings had fallen into a state of disrepair and were unoccupied, which is why he had chosen the courtyard as his destination.

He moved to a darkened corner and listened to his pursuer's approaching footfalls. A long moment passed before the man blundered into view. He paused in a puddle of moonlight, then, realizing there was no way out, turned to leave.

"Looking for something?" asked Gabriel calmly in Italian.

The man wheeled around and reached reflexively toward the front of his jacket.

"I wouldn't do that if I were you."

The man froze.

"Why are you following me?"

"I'm not."

"You were in Harry's Bar. You were on the Number One. And now you're here." Gabriel stepped from the shadows. "Twice is a coincidence. Third time is the charm."

"I'm looking for a restaurant."

"Tell me the name, and I'll take you there."

"Osteria da Fiore."

"Not even close." Gabriel took another step across the courtyard. "Please reach for your gun again."

"Why?"

"So I won't feel guilty about breaking your nose, your jaw, and several of your ribs."

Wordlessly the young Italian turned to one side, raised his left hand defensively, and bunched his right fist against his hip.

"All right," said Gabriel with a sigh of resignation. "If you insist."

THE ISRAELI MARTIAL ARTS DISCIPLINE KNOWN AS KRAV MAGA is characterized by constant aggression, simultaneous offensive and defensive measures, and utter ruthlessness. Speed is prized above all else. Typically contests are short in duration—no more than a few seconds—and decisive in outcome. Once launched, an attack does not cease until the adversary has been completely incapacitated. Permanent injury is commonplace. Death is not out of the question.

No part of the body is off-limits. Indeed, practitioners of Krav Maga are encouraged to focus their attacks on vulnerable, sensitive regions. Gabriel's opening gambit consisted of a vicious kick to his opponent's exposed left kneecap, followed by a crushing downward heel strike on the instep of the left foot. Next he ventured north to the groin and solar plexus before directing several rapid elbows and side-handed blows to the throat, the nose, and the head. At no point did the younger, larger Italian manage to land a punch or kick of his own. Still, Gabriel did not emerge unscathed. His right hand was throbbing painfully, probably from a minor fracture, the Krav Maga equivalent of an own goal.

With the fingers of his left hand, he checked his fallen opponent for evidence of a pulse and respiration. Finding both, he reached inside the front of the man's jacket and confirmed that he was indeed armed—with a Beretta 8000, the standard-issue sidearm for officers of the Carabinieri. Which explained the credentials that Gabriel found in the unconscious man's pocket. They identified him as Capitano Luca Rossetti of the Venice division of Il Nucleo Tutela Patrimonio Artistico.

The Art Squad . . .

Gabriel returned the gun to its holster and the credentials to their pocket, then rang the regional headquarters of the Carabinieri to report an injured man lying in a *corte* near the

Campo Sant'Aponal. He did so anonymously, with his phone number concealed, and in perfect *veneziano*. He would deal with General Ferrari in the morning. In the meantime, he had to concoct a plausible cover story to explain his injured hand to Chiara. It came to him as he crossed the Ponte San Polo. It wasn't his fault, he would tell her. The bloody lamppost attacked him.

6

SAN POLO

FIVE MINUTES LATER, WHILE CLIMBING the staircase toward the door of the apartment, Gabriel encountered the tantalizing fragrance of veal simmering in wine and aromatics. He entered the passcode into the keypad and turned the latch, performing both tasks with his left hand. His right was concealed in the pocket of his jacket. It remained there as he entered the sitting room, where he found Irene stretched upon the carpet, a pencil in her fist, her tiny porcelain brow furrowed.

Gabriel addressed her in Italian. "There's a lovely desk in your room, you know."

"I prefer to work on the floor. It helps me concentrate."

"What sort of work are you doing?"

"Math, silly." She looked up at Gabriel with the eyes of his mother. "Where have you been?"

"I had an appointment."

"With whom?"

"An old friend."

"Does he work for the Office?"

"Wherever did you get an idea like that?"

"Because it seems like all your old *friends* do."

"Not all of them," said Gabriel, and looked at Raphael. The boy was sprawled on the couch, his long-lashed, jade-colored eyes focused with unnerving intensity on the screen of his handheld video console. "What's he playing?"

"Mario."

"Who?"

"It's a computer game."

"Why isn't he doing his schoolwork?"

"He's finished." With the tip of her pencil, Irene pointed toward her brother's notebook. "See for yourself."

Gabriel craned his head to one side and reviewed Raphael's work. Twenty rudimentary equations involving addition and subtraction, all answered correctly on the first attempt.

"Were you good at math when you were little?" asked Irene.

"It didn't interest me much."

"What about Mama?"

"She studied Roman history."

"In Padua?"

"Yes."

"Is that where Raphael and I will go to university?"

"You're rather young to be thinking about that, aren't you?"

Sighing, she licked the tip of her forefinger and turned to a fresh page in her workbook. In the warmth of the kitchen, Gabriel found Chiara removing the cork from a bottle of Brunello di Montalcino. Andrea Bocelli flowed from the Bluetooth speaker on the counter.

"I've always loved that song," said Gabriel.

"I wonder why." Chiara used her phone to lower the volume. "Going somewhere?"

"Sorry?"

"You're still wearing your overcoat."

"I'm a little chilled, that's all." He wandered over to the gleaming stainless-steel Vulcan oven and peered through the window. Inside was the orange casserole dish that Chiara used for preparing osso buco. "What have I done to deserve this?"

"I can think of one or two things. Or three," she added.

"How long until it's ready?"

"It needs another thirty minutes." She poured two glasses of the Brunello. "Leaving you just enough time to tell me about your conversation with Julian."

"We'll talk after dinner, if you don't mind."

"Is there a problem?"

He turned abruptly. "Why do you ask?"

"There usually is one where Julian is concerned." Chiara regarded him carefully for a moment. "And you seem upset about something."

He decided, with no small amount of guilt, that the wisest course of action was to blame his edgy mood on Raphael. "Your son failed to notice my return home because he was hypnotized by that computer game of his."

"I gave him permission."

"Why?"

"Because it took him all of five minutes to finish his math homework. His teachers think he's gifted. They want him to begin working with a specialist."

"He certainly didn't get it from me."

"Nor from me." Chiara offered him a glass of the wine. "There's a package in your studio. It looks as though it might be from your girlfriend Anna Rolfe." She smiled coolly. "Listen to a bit of music and relax. You'll feel better."

"I feel just fine."

Gabriel accepted the wine with his left hand and withdrew to the master bathroom suite, where he subjected the injured extremity to a thorough examination by the light of Chiara's vanity. The sharp pain produced by a gentle probe indicated at least a hairline fracture to the fifth metacarpal. Significant swelling was plainly evident, but as yet there was no visible bruising. At a bare minimum, immediate immobilization and icing were required. Given the circumstances, however, neither was possible, leaving Gabriel no treatment option other than alcohol and pain reliever.

He took down a bottle of ibuprofen from the medicine chest, shook several emerald capsules into his palm, and swallowed them with a mouthful of the Brunello. Repairing to his studio, he found the package. It had been sent to him by the publicity department of Deutsche Grammophon. Inside was a two-CD survey of Mozart's five remarkable violin concertos, notable for the fact that the soloist had recorded the pieces with the same instrument upon which they had been composed.

Gabriel placed the first disc onto the tray of his CD player, tapped the PLAY button, and went to his easel. There he gazed upon a beautiful young woman draped nude across a brocade-covered couch, her melancholy gaze fixed upon the viewer—in this case, the artist who had painted her. *Is there a problem?* No, he thought as his hand throbbed with pain. No problem at all.

GABRIEL MANAGED TO LISTEN TO THE FIRST TWO CONCERTOS before Chiara summoned him to the dining room. The meal arrayed upon the table looked as though it had been staged for a photo shoot by *Bon Appétit*—the risotto, the platter of roasted vegetables glistening with olive oil, and, of course, the thick veal shanks drenched in a rich sauce of tomato and herbs and wine. As always, they were fork tender, allowing Gabriel to eat with one hand, keeping the other cradled protectively in his lap. The Brunello-and-Advil therapy had worked its magic; he was only vaguely aware of the pain. He was certain, however, it would return with a vengeance the instant the drug wore off, probably sometime around three in the morning.

Chiara's eyes shone with candlelight as she guided the conversation. Diplomatically she raised the subject of Raphael's mathematical prowess, which in turn led to a discussion of how his gifts might be put to good use. Irene, the family environmentalist, suggested that her brother consider pursuing a career as a climate scientist.

"Why?" probed Gabriel.

"Did you read the new UN report about global warming?"

"Did *you*?"

"We talked about it at school. Signora Antonelli says Venice will soon be underwater because the Greenland ice sheet is melting. She says none of it would have happened if the Americans hadn't withdrawn from the Paris Agreement."

"That's debatable."

"She also says it's too late to prevent a significant increase in global temperatures."

"She's right about that."

"Why did the Americans withdraw?"

"The man who was president at the time thought global warming was a hoax."

"Who would believe such a thing?"

"It's a rather common affliction among Americans of the far right. But let's talk about something pleasant, shall we?"

It was Raphael who chose the subject. "What does *woke* mean?"

Gabriel directed his gaze toward his son and, to the best of his ability, answered. "It's a word that emerged from the Black community in the United States. If someone is woke, it means they care about issues involving racial intolerance and societal injustice."

"Are you woke?"

"Evidently."

"I think I'm woke, too."

"I'd keep it to myself, if I were you."

At the conclusion of the meal, the children volunteered to clear away the plates and serving dishes, a feat they accomplished with minimal conflict and no breakage. Chiara poured the last of the wine into their glasses and held hers to the light of the candles.

"Where shall we begin?" she asked. "Your meeting with Julian or the new tattoo on your right hand?"

"It's not a tattoo."

"That's a relief. What is it?"

Gabriel removed his hand from his lap and laid it carefully on the tablecloth.

Chiara winced. "It looks dreadful."

"Yes," said Gabriel gloomily. "But you should see the other guy."

7

SAN POLO

HAVE YOU TRIED TO HOLD a paintbrush?"

"I'm not sure I ever will again."

"How bad is the pain?"

"At the moment," said Gabriel, "I can't feel a thing."

He was perched on a stool at the kitchen island, his hand submerged in a bowl of ice and water. It had done nothing to reduce the swelling. If anything, it appeared to be growing worse.

"You really should have it X-rayed," said Chiara.

"And when the orthopedist asks how I broke it?"

"How did you?"

"I assume it was the knifehand strike."

"Where did it land?"

"I'd rather not say."

"Are you sure you didn't kill him?"

"He'll be fine."

"Will he?"

"Eventually."

With a sigh of dismay, Chiara took up Madame Valerie Bérrangar's letter. "What do you suppose she wanted to tell Julian?"

"I can think of several possibilities," said Gabriel. "Starting with the most obvious."

"What's that?"

"The painting was hers."

"If that were the case, why didn't she contact the police?"

"Who's to say she didn't?"

"Surely Julian checked the Art Loss Register before taking it to market?"

"No dealer ever acquires or sells a work of art without first checking to see whether it's been pinched."

"Unless the dealer doesn't want to know whether it's stolen."

"Our Julian is far from perfect," said Gabriel. "But he has never knowingly sold a stolen painting."

"Not even on your behalf?"

"I don't believe so."

Chiara smiled. "Possibility number two?"

"The work was seized from the Bérrangar family during the war and has been missing ever since."

"Do you think Valerie Bérrangar was Jewish?"

"Did I say that?"

Chiara set aside the letter. "Possibility number three?"

"Unlock my phone."

Chiara entered his fourteen-digit hard password. "What am I looking at?"

"A detail image from *Portrait of an Unknown Woman.*"

"Is there a problem?"

"What does the craquelure pattern look like to you?"

"Tree bark."

"And what does that tell you?"

"I will defer to your superior knowledge."

"Surface cracks resembling tree bark are typical of Flemish paintings," explained Gabriel. "Van Dyck was a Flemish painter, of course. But he worked with materials similar to those being used by his contemporaries in Holland."

"So his surface cracks appear more Dutch than Flemish?"

"Correct. If you look at *Lady Elizabeth Thimbelby and Her Sister* on the website of the National Gallery, you'll see what I mean."

"I'll take your word for it," answered Chiara, her thumbnails clicking against the surface of Gabriel's phone.

"What are you looking for?"

"The article in *Sud Ouest*." She dragged the tip of her forefinger down the screen. "Here it is. The accident happened yesterday afternoon on the D10, just north of Saint-Macaire. The gendarmes seem to think she somehow lost control of her car."

"How old was she?"

"Seventy-four."

"Married?"

"Widowed. Apparently, there's a daughter named Juliette Lagarde." Chiara paused. "Perhaps she'll agree to see you."

"I thought I was supposed to be resting."

"You are. But under the circumstances it's probably better if you leave Venice for a few days. With any luck, you'll be airborne before General Ferrari realizes you're gone."

Gabriel removed his hand from the ice water. "What do you think?"

"A splint should suffice. You can pick one up at the pharmacy on your way to the airport. But I would advise you to avoid striking anyone while you're in Bordeaux."

"It wasn't my fault."

"Whose fault was it, darling?"

It was Madame Bérrangar's, he thought. She should have simply telephoned Julian's gallery in London. Instead, she had sent him a letter. And now she was dead.

EXHAUSTED, GABRIEL CRAWLED INTO BED and, with his hand cradled gently against his chest, fell into a dreamless sleep. The pain roused him at four o'clock. He lay awake for another hour, listening to the barges making their way up the Grand Canal toward the Rialto Market, before padding into the kitchen and pressing the power button on the Lavazza *automatico*.

While waiting for the coffee to brew, he stirred his phone into life and was relieved to discover he had received no overnight correspondence from General Ferrari. A check of *Sud Ouest* confirmed that Valerie Bérrangar, seventy-four years of age, was still dead. There was a small update to the story regarding the arrangements for her funeral. It was scheduled for 10:00 a.m. on Friday, at the Église Saint-Sauveur in Saint-Macaire. Regardless of Madame Bérrangar's religious affiliation at the beginning of her life, thought Gabriel, it appeared as though she had ended it as a Roman Catholic.

He swallowed another dose of ibuprofen with his coffee. Then he showered and dressed and placed a few items of clothing into an overnight bag while Chiara, tangled in Egyptian cotton, slept on in the next room. The children spilled from their beds at half past six and demanded to be fed. Irene fixed Gabriel with an accusatory stare over her customary breakfast of muesli and yogurt.

"Mama says you're going to France."

"Not for long."

"What does that mean?"

"It means that your grandmother will be picking you up at school for the next few days."

"How many days?"

"To be determined."

"We like it when *you* pick us up," declared Raphael.

"That's because I always take you to the *pasticceria* on the way home."

"That's not the only reason."

"I like picking you up, too," said Gabriel. "In fact, it's one of my favorite parts of the day."

"What's your favorite?"

"Next question."

"Why do you have to leave again?" asked Irene.

"A friend needs my help."

"*Another* friend?"

"Same friend, actually."

She inflated her cheeks and stirred the contents of her bowl without appetite. Gabriel knew full well the source of her anxiety. Three times during his tenure as director-general of the Office he had been targeted for assassination. The last attempt had taken place on Inauguration Day in Washington, when he had been shot in the chest by a congresswoman from the American Midwest who believed him to be a member of a blood-drinking, Satan-worshipping cult of pedophiles. The two preceding attempts, though more prosaic, had both taken place in France. For the most part, the children pretended that none of the incidents, though widely publicized, had transpired. Gabriel, who still suffered from the unpleasant aftereffects, was similarly inclined.

"Nothing is going to happen," he assured his daughter.

"You always say that. But something *always* happens."

Having no retort at the ready, Gabriel looked up and saw Chiara standing in the doorway of the kitchen, an expression of mild bemusement on her face.

"She does have a point, you know." Chiara poured herself a cup of coffee and looked at Gabriel's hand. "How does it feel?"

"Good as new."

She gave it a gentle squeeze. "No pain at all?"

He grimaced but said nothing.

"I thought so." She released his hand. "Are you packed?"

"Almost."

"Who's taking Thing One and Thing Two to school?"

"Papa," sang the children in unison.

He returned to the bedroom and unlocked the safe concealed in the walk-in closet. Inside were two false German passports, €20,000 in cash, and his Beretta. He removed one of the passports but left the gun behind, as his arrangement with the Italian authorities did not permit him to carry firearms on airplanes. Besides, if circumstances warranted, he could acquire an untraceable weapon in France with a single phone call, with or without the connivance of his old service.

He deposited the bag in the entrance hall and at 7:45 a.m. followed Chiara and the children down the stairs of the palazzo. Outside in the street, Chiara set off toward the San Tomà vaporetto station. Then she stopped abruptly and kissed Gabriel's lips.

"You *will* be careful in France, won't you?"

"Cross my heart."

"Wrong answer, darling." She placed her palm on the left side of Gabriel's chest and felt the sudden pulse of his phone. "Oh, dear. I wonder who that could be."

BAR DOGALE

AFTER ENTRUSTING IRENE AND RAPHAEL to Signora Anton-elli, their environmentally conscious and reliably demo-cratic socialist teacher, Gabriel made his way through empty streets to the Campo dei Frari. The square remained in morn-ing shadow, but a benevolent sun had established dominion over the red-tile rooftops of the mighty Gothic basilica. At the foot of the bell tower, the second-tallest in Venice, stood eight chrome tables covered in blue, the property of Bar Do-gale, one of the better tourist cafés in San Polo.

At one of the tables sat General Ferrari. He had forsaken his blue uniform, with its many medals and insignia, and was wearing a business suit and overcoat instead. The hand he of-fered in greeting was missing two fingers, the result of a letter bomb he received in 1988 while serving as chief of the Cara-binieri's Naples division. Nevertheless, his grip was viselike.

"Something wrong?" he asked as Gabriel sat down.

"Too many years holding a paintbrush."

"Consider yourself lucky. I had to learn how to do almost everything with my left hand. And then, of course, there's this." The general pointed toward his prosthetic right eye. "You, however, appear to have come through your most recent brush with death with scarcely a scratch."

"Hardly."

"How close did we come to losing you in Washington?"

"I flatlined twice. The second time, I was clinically dead for nearly ten minutes."

"Did you happen to see anything?"

"Like what?"

"A brilliant white light? The face of the Almighty?"

"Not that I can recall."

The general seemed disappointed by Gabriel's answer. "I was afraid you were going to say that."

"It doesn't mean that there isn't a life after this one, Cesare. It just means that I have no memory of anything that happened after I lost consciousness."

"Have you given the matter any thought yourself?"

"The existence of God? An afterlife?"

The general nodded.

"The Holocaust robbed my parents of their belief in God. The religion of my childhood home was Zionism."

"You're entirely secular?"

"My faith comes and goes."

"And your wife?"

"She's a rabbi's daughter."

"I have it on the highest authority that the cultural and artistic guardians of Venice are quite smitten with her. It appears the two of you have a bright future here." The general's prosthetic eye contemplated Gabriel sightlessly for a moment. "Which makes your recent behavior all the more difficult to explain."

He entered the passcode into his smartphone and laid it on

the tabletop. Gabriel lowered his eyes briefly to the screen. The bruised and swollen face depicted there bore little resemblance to the one he had seen the previous evening.

"His jaw had to be wired shut," said General Ferrari. "For an Italian, a fate worse than death."

"He'd be sitting down to a nice long lunch later today if only he'd identified himself."

"He says you didn't give him much of a chance."

"Why was he following me in the first place?"

"He wasn't," answered Ferrari. "He was following your friend."

"Julian Isherwood? Whatever for?"

"As a result of that unfortunate business in Lake Como a few years ago, Signore Isherwood remains on the Art Squad's watchlist. We keep an eye on him whenever he comes to Italy. Young Rossetti, who was assigned to Venice only last week, drew the short straw."

"He should have walked out of Harry's Bar the minute he saw Julian with me."

"I ordered him to stay."

"Because you wanted to know what we were talking about?"

"I suppose I did."

"That still doesn't explain why he followed me onto the vaporetto."

"I wanted to make certain you arrived home safely. And how did you repay this act of kindness? By beating one of my best young recruits to a pulp in a darkened *corte*."

"It was a misunderstanding."

"Be that as it may, I am left with a most difficult choice."

"What's that?"

"Immediate deportation or a lengthy incarceration. I'm leaning toward the latter."

"And what must I do to avoid this fate?"

"You can start by showing at least a trace of remorse."

"Mea culpa, mea culpa, mea maxima culpa."

"Much better. Now tell me why Signore Isherwood came to Venice. Otherwise," said the general, glancing at his wristwatch, "you're liable to miss your flight."

OVER A BREAKFAST OF *CAPPUCCINI* AND *CORNETTI*, GABRIEL recounted the story as Julian had told it. Ferrari's artificial eye remained fixed on him throughout, unblinking. His expression betrayed nothing—nothing, thought Gabriel, other than perhaps mild boredom. The general was the leader of the world's largest and most sophisticated art crime unit. He had heard it all before.

"It's not so easily done, you know. Engineering a fatal car accident."

"Unless it was carried out by professionals."

"Have you ever?"

"Killed anyone with a car? Not that I can recall," said Gabriel. "But there's a first time for everything."

The general emitted a parched laugh. "Still, the most logical explanation is that the Bérrangar woman was running late for her appointment with Signore Isherwood and died in a tragic accident."

"What about the two men who tried to steal Julian's briefcase?"

Ferrari shrugged his shoulders. "Thieves."

"And the ones who searched his hotel room?"

"The search," acknowledged the general, "is harder to explain. Therefore, I would advise your friend to tell the French art crime unit everything he knows. It's a division of the Police Nationale called the Central Office for the Fight against Cultural Goods Trafficking."

"Catchy," remarked Gabriel.

"I suppose it sounds better in French."

"Most things do."

"I'd be happy to contact my French counterpart. His name is Jacques Ménard. He dislikes me only a little."

"Signore Isherwood has no wish to involve the police in this matter."

"And why is that?"

"An allergy, I suppose."

"A common affliction among art dealers and collectors. Unless one of their precious paintings goes missing, of course. Then we're suddenly quite popular." The general offered an approximation of a smile. "I assume that you intend to start with the daughter."

"If she'll agree to see me."

"Who could possibly resist the opportunity to meet with the great Gabriel Allon?"

"A woman who is mourning the death of her mother."

"What about the dealer in Paris?"

"Julian swears he's reputable."

"If you like, I can run his name through our database and see if anything turns up."

"I have contacts of my own in the Paris art trade."

"The dirty side of the trade, as I recall." General Ferrari expelled a lungful of air. "Which returns us to the topic of young Capitano Rossetti."

"Perhaps I should speak to him."

"I can assure you, Rossetti has no wish to see you. If the truth be told, he's rather embarrassed by the way things turned out last night. After all, you *are* half his size."

"And twice his age."

"That, too."

Gabriel checked the time.

"Going somewhere?" inquired the general.

"The airport, I hope."

"A Carabinieri patrol boat will collect you at San Tomà at ten o'clock."

"Ten is cutting it rather close, don't you think?"

"A representative from Alitalia will escort you through security and directly onto the plane. And don't worry about Chiara and the children," the general added as he ordered two more *cappuccini*. "We'll keep an eye on them while you're away."

10

VILLA BÉRRANGAR

IN THE MIDDLE AGES, WHEN English kings laid claim to all
of France, the picturesque village of Saint-Macaire was
designated a *ville royale d'Angleterre*. It seemed that little had
changed in the intervening centuries. A medieval tower stood
guard over the entrance to the old city, its clockface showing
half past five. Next to it was a café called La Belle Lurette.
Gabriel handed the waiter twenty euros and asked whether he
knew the address of Madame Valerie Bérrangar.

"She was killed in an auto accident on Monday afternoon."

Gabriel wordlessly handed over another banknote.

"Her villa is near Château Malromé. About two kilometers
to the east." The waiter slipped the money into the pocket
of his apron. "The entrance will be on your left. You can't
miss it."

The château stood on a broad hillside north of Saint-
Macaire, in the commune of Saint-André-du-Bois. Renowned

for the quality of its gravelly clay soil, the forty-hectare property was acquired in the late nineteenth century by Countess Adèle de Toulouse-Lautrec. Her son, a painter and illustrator who often found inspiration in the brothels and cabarets of Paris, had passed his summers there.

East of the château the road was dangerously narrow and lined on both sides with vineyards. With one eye on the instrument panel of his rented sedan, Gabriel drove two kilometers exactly and, as promised, glimpsed a dwelling on the left side of the road. Parked in the forecourt was a Peugeot estate car, metallic blue, Paris registration. Gabriel drew up next to it and switched off the engine. The instant he opened his door, a dog barked ferociously. But of course, he thought, and climbed out.

Warily he approached the entrance of the villa. As he stretched out a hand toward the bell push, the door opened to reveal a woman, dark in dress and demeanor, with the pale skin of someone who assiduously avoided the sun. She looked to be in her early forties, but Gabriel couldn't be sure. An Old Master painting he could reliably date to within a few years. But modern women, with their age-concealing balms and injections, were a mystery to him.

"Madame Lagarde?"

"*Oui*," she answered. "May I help you, monsieur?"

Gabriel introduced himself. Not with a work name, or one he plucked from thin air, but his real name.

"Have we met somewhere before?" asked Juliette Lagarde.

"I rather doubt it."

"But your name is very familiar." Her eyes narrowed. "Your face, too."

"You might have read about me in the newspapers."

"Why?"

"I used to be the chief of the Israeli intelligence service.

I worked closely with the French government in the fight against the Islamic State."

"Not *that* Gabriel Allon."

He offered her an apologetic smile. "I'm afraid so."

"What on earth are you doing here?"

"I'd like to ask you a few questions about your mother."

"My mother—"

"Was killed in an accident on Monday afternoon." Gabriel glanced over his shoulder toward the large Belgian shepherd berating him from the forecourt. "Would it be possible for us to talk inside?"

"You're not afraid of dogs, are you?"

"*Non*," said Gabriel. "Only dogs like that."

As it turned out, Juliette Lagarde didn't much care for the dog, either. It belonged to Jean-Luc, the caretaker. He had worked for the Bérrangar family for more than thirty years, looking after the house when they were in Paris, tending to the small vineyard. Juliette's father, a prosperous commercial lawyer, had planted it with his own hands. He had died of a massive heart attack while Juliette was still a student at the Paris-Sorbonne University. Having earned a useless degree in literature, she now worked in the marketing department of one of France's largest fashion houses. Her mother, unnerved by the jihadist terrorist attacks in Paris, had lately been spending most of her time in Saint-André-du-Bois.

"She wasn't an Islamophobe or a follower of the far right, mind you. She just preferred the countryside to the city. I worried about her being alone, but she had friends here. A life of her own."

They were standing in the villa's spacious kitchen, waiting for the water to boil in the electric kettle. The house around them was silent.

"How often did you speak to her?" asked Gabriel.

"Once or twice a week." Juliette Lagarde sighed. "Our relationship had been strained of late."

"May I ask why?"

"We were quarreling over the question of remarriage."

"She was involved with someone?"

"My mother? God, no." Juliette Lagarde held up her left hand. It was absent a wedding ring. "She wanted me to find another husband before it was too late."

"What happened to the first one?"

"I was so busy at work that I failed to notice he was involved in a passionate *cinq à sept* with a young woman from his office."

"I'm sorry."

"Don't be. These things happen. Especially in France." She poured boiling water from the electric kettle into a flowered teapot. "What about you, Monsieur Allon? Are you married?"

"Happily."

"Children?"

"Twins."

"Are they spies, too?"

"They're in elementary school."

Juliette Lagarde took up the tray and led Gabriel along a central corridor, into a sitting room. It was formal, more Paris than Bordeaux. The walls were hung with oil paintings in ornate French antique frames. They were works of high quality but moderate value. Someone had chosen them with care.

Juliette Lagarde placed the tray on a low wooden table and opened the French doors to the chill afternoon air. "Do you know who lived there?" she asked, pointing toward the distant silhouette of Château Malromé.

"A painter whose work I've always admired."

"You're interested in art?"

"You might say that."

She sat down and poured two cups of tea. "Are you always so evasive?"

"Forgive me, Madame Lagarde. But I've only recently traded the secret world for the overt one. I'm not used to talking about myself."

"Try it once."

"I was an art student when I was recruited by Israeli intelligence. I wanted to be a painter, but I became a restorer instead. For many years, I worked in Europe under an assumed identity."

"Your French is excellent."

"My Italian is better." Gabriel accepted a cup of tea and carried it to the fireplace. Photographs in handsome silver frames lined the mantel. One depicted the Bérrangar family in happier times. "You bear a striking resemblance to your mother. But then I'm sure you realize that."

"We were very much alike. Too much, perhaps." A silence fell between them. At length Juliette Lagarde said, "Now that we're properly acquainted, Monsieur Allon, perhaps you can tell me why her death is of any possible interest to a man like you."

"She was on her way to Bordeaux to meet a friend of mine when she had the accident. An art dealer named Julian Isherwood." He handed Juliette Lagarde the letter. "It arrived at his gallery in London last Friday."

She looked down and read.

"Is that your mother's handwriting?"

"Yes, of course. I have boxes and boxes of her letters. She was very old-fashioned. She loathed email and was forever misplacing her mobile phone."

"Do you have any idea what she might have been referring to?"

"The legal and ethical problems concerning your friend's painting?" Juliette Lagarde rose abruptly to her feet. "Yes, Monsieur Allon. I think I might."

She led him through a pair of double doors and into an adjoining sitting room. It was smaller than its neighbor, more intimate. It was a room where books were read, thought Gabriel, and letters to London art dealers written. Six Old Master paintings, beautifully framed and illuminated, adorned its walls—including a portrait of a woman, oil on canvas, approximately 115 by 92 centimeters, quite obviously Dutch or Flemish in origin.

"Does it look familiar?" asked Juliette Lagarde.

"Very," said Gabriel, and placed a hand thoughtfully to his chin. "Do you happen to remember where your father purchased it?"

"A small gallery on the rue la Boétie in Paris."

"Galerie Georges Fleury?"

"Yes, that's the one."

"When?"

"It was thirty-four years ago."

"You have a good memory."

"My father gave it to my mother on her fortieth birthday. She always adored this painting."

With his hand still pressed to his chin, Gabriel tilted his head to one side.

"Does she have a name?"

"It's called *Portrait of an Unknown Woman*." Juliette Lagarde paused, then added, "Just like your friend's painting."

"And the attribution?"

"I'd have to check the paperwork in my father's files, but I believe it was a follower of Anthony van Dyck. To be honest, I find the various categories of attribution rather arbitrary."

"So do many art dealers. They generally select the one that will earn them the most money." Gabriel drew his phone, snapped a photograph of the woman's face, and enlarged the image.

"Are you looking for something in particular?"

"The pattern of the surface cracks."

"Is there a problem?"

"No," said Gabriel. "No problem at all."

11

VILLA BÉRRANGAR

Together they lifted the painting from its hangers and carried it into the next room, where the natural light was more abundant. There Gabriel removed it from its frame and subjected it to a preliminary examination, starting with the image itself—a three-quarter-length portrait of a young woman, late twenties or early thirties, wearing a gown of gold silk trimmed in white lace. The garment was identical to the one worn by the woman in Julian's version of the painting, though the color was less vibrant and the subtle folds and wrinkles in the fabric were less persuasively rendered. The subject's hands were awkwardly arranged, her gaze vacant. The artist, whoever he was, had failed to achieve the lifelike penetration of character for which Anthony van Dyck, among the most sought-after portraitists of his day, was renowned.

Gabriel turned over the painting and examined the back of the canvas. It was consistent with other seventeenth-century Dutch and Flemish paintings he had restored. So, too, was the stretcher. It looked to be the original woodwork, with the addition of two twentieth-century horizontal reinforcements. In short, there was nothing out of the ordinary or suspicious. By all outward appearances, the painting was a copy of the original Van Dyck portrait that Julian had sold to Phillip Somerset, the New York art investor, for the sum of six and a half million pounds.

There was, however, one glaring problem.

Both works had emerged from the same gallery in the Eighth Arrondissement of Paris, thirty-four years apart.

Gabriel propped the Bérrangar family's version of the painting against the coffee table and sat down next to Juliette Lagarde. After a silence she asked, "Who do you suppose she was, our unknown woman?"

"That depends on where she was painted. Van Dyck maintained successful studios in both London and Antwerp and shuttled between them. The London studio was known as the beauty shop. It was a rather well-oiled machine."

"How much of the portraits did he actually paint?"

"Usually, just the head and face. He made no attempt to flatter his subjects by altering their appearance, which made him somewhat controversial. We think he produced about two hundred portraits, but some art historians believe the real number is closer to five hundred. He had so many followers and admirers that authentication can be a tricky business."

"But not for you?"

"Sir Anthony and I are well acquainted."

Juliette Lagarde turned to the painting. "She looks Dutch or Flemish rather than English."

"I agree."

"She was a rich man's wife or daughter?"

"Or mistress," suggested Gabriel. "In fact, she might well have been one of Van Dyck's lovers. He had a lot of them."

"Painters," said Juliette Lagarde with mock disdain, and

added tea to Gabriel's cup. "So let's say, for argument's sake, that Anthony van Dyck painted his original portrait of our unknown woman sometime in the sixteen forties."

"Let's," agreed Gabriel.

She nodded toward the frameless canvas. "So who painted that one? And when?"

"If he was a so-called follower of Van Dyck, he was someone who worked in Van Dyck's style but wasn't necessarily a member of his immediate circle."

"A nobody? Is that what you're saying?"

"If this piece is representative of his oeuvre, I doubt he was terribly successful."

"How would he have gone about it?"

"Copying a painting? He might have attempted to do it freehand. But if I were in his shoes, I would have traced Van Dyck's original and then transferred that image to a canvas of the same dimensions."

"How would you have accomplished that in the seventeenth century?"

"I would have started by poking tiny holes along the lines of my tracing. Then I would have laid the paper atop my ground and sprinkled it with charcoal dust, leaving a ghostly but geometrically accurate rendering of Van Dyck's original."

"An underdrawing?"

"Correct."

"And then?"

"I would have prepared my palette and started to paint."

"With the original close at hand?"

"It was probably on a nearby easel."

"So the artist forged it?"

"It would have only been a forgery if he had tried to sell his version as an original Van Dyck."

"Have you ever done it?" asked Juliette Lagarde.

"Copied a painting?"

"No, Monsieur Allon. Forged one."

"I'm an art conservator," said Gabriel with a smile. "There are some critics of our profession who claim that we restorers forge paintings all the time."

The room had turned suddenly cold. Juliette Lagarde closed the French doors and looked on while Gabriel secured the painting to its frame. Together they carried it into the adjoining room and returned it to its place on the wall.

"Which one is better?" asked Juliet Lagarde. "This one or your friend's?"

"I'll let you be the judge." Gabriel held his phone next to the painting. On the screen was a photograph of Julian's version of *Portrait of an Unknown Woman*. "What do you think?"

"I must admit, your friend's is much better. Still, it's rather unsettling to see them side by side like that."

"What's even more troubling," said Gabriel, "is that both paintings passed through the same gallery."

"Is it possible it's a coincidence?"

"I don't believe in them."

"Neither did my mother."

Which is why, thought Gabriel, she was now dead.

He slipped his phone into the breast pocket of his jacket. "Have the gendarmes returned her personal effects?"

"Last night."

"Did anything appear out of the ordinary?"

"Her mobile phone seems to be missing."

"She didn't have it with her when she was driving to Bordeaux?"

"The gendarmes say not."

"You've searched the house?"

"I've looked everywhere. The truth is, she rarely used it. She much preferred her old landline phones." Juliette Lagarde pointed toward the room's elegant antique writing table. "That's the one she used the most."

Gabriel went to the table and switched on the lamp. Stored in the phone's memory he found five incoming calls from Galerie Georges Fleury and three more from a Police Nationale number in central Paris. He also discovered, in Madame Bérrangar's desk calendar, a reminder for an appointment at four in the afternoon, on the last day of her life.

M. Isherwood. Café Ravel.

He turned to Juliette Lagarde. "Have you tried calling her mobile phone recently?"

"Not since this morning. I have a feeling the battery is dead."

"Do you mind if I give it a try?"

Juliette Lagarde recited the number. When Gabriel dialed it, the call went directly to voice mail. He severed the connection and held the unfaltering gaze of the unknown woman, certain for the first time that Valerie Bérrangar had been murdered.

"Did your mother have a computer?"

"Yes, of course. An Apple."

"It's not missing, is it?"

"*Non*. I checked her email this morning."

"Anything interesting?"

"On the same day my mother died in an automobile accident, she received a notification from her insurance agency that they intended to raise her rates. For the life of me, I can't imagine why. She was an excellent driver," said Juliette Lagarde. "Never so much as a parking ticket."

THE SKIES POURED WITH RAIN DURING THE DRIVE BACK TO Saint-Macaire. Gabriel checked into his hotel, then walked to La Belle Lurette for dinner, a book beneath his arm for company. After placing an order of *poulet rôti* and *pommes frites*, he rang Chiara in Venice. Their phones were Israeli-made

Solaris models, the world's most secure. Even so, they chose their words with care.

"I was beginning to get worried about you," she said.

"Sorry. Busy afternoon."

"Productive, I hope."

"Quite."

"She agreed to see you?"

"She made me tea," answered Gabriel. "And then she showed me a painting."

"Attribution?"

"Follower of Anthony van Dyck."

"Subject matter?"

"Portrait of an unknown woman. Late twenties or early thirties. Not terribly pretty."

"What was she wearing?"

"A gown of gold silk trimmed in white lace."

"Sounds like there might be a problem."

"Several, actually. Including the name of the gallery where her father purchased it."

"Do you think her mother was—"

"I do."

"Did you tell her?"

"I didn't see the point."

"What are your plans?"

"I need to go to Paris to have a word with an old friend."

"Do give him my best."

"Don't worry," said Gabriel. "I will."

BORDEAUX—PARIS

GABRIEL SLEPT POORLY, AWAKENED EARLY, and set out for Bordeaux before it was properly light. A kilometer north of the village of Sainte-Croix-du-Mont, his headlamps picked out the gray-white stain of a spent safety flare. The tire marks appeared a few seconds later, two black slashes across the opposing lane.

He eased onto the grassy verge and surveyed his surroundings. On the right side of the road, columns of vines marched down the slope of a steep hill. On the left, nearer the river, there were vineyards as well, but the land was tabletop flat. And largely treeless, observed Gabriel, with the exception of a coppice of white-barked poplar toward which the tire marks led.

He fished an LED torch from the glove box and waited for a cargo truck to pass before climbing out and crossing to the opposite side of the road. He didn't venture much beyond the broken white line at the edge of the tarmac; it wasn't necessary. From his vantage point, the damage was plain to see.

Two of the poplars had been snapped by the force of the collision, and the sodden earth was strewn with cubes of shattered safety glass. Gabriel reckoned that Valerie Bérrangar must have been killed instantly by the force of the impact. Or perhaps she had remained conscious long enough to notice the gloved hand reaching through the broken window. Not to render assistance but to seize her phone. Gabriel dialed the number, hoping he might hear a death rattle from amid the trees, but once again the call went straight to voice mail.

Killing the connection, he turned and examined the parallel tire marks. They crossed the southbound lane at roughly a forty-five-degree angle. Yes, he thought, it was possible that Valerie Bérrangar had been distracted somehow and unwittingly swerved to the left, directly toward the only stand of trees in sight. But the more likely explanation was that her car had been forced off the road by the vehicle behind her.

A car approached from the north, slowed briefly, and continued on toward Sainte-Croix-du-Mont. Two minutes elapsed before another appeared, this time from the south. It was not a busy stretch of road. At three fifteen on a Monday afternoon, it would have been quiet as well. Even so, the associates of the man who had forced Valerie Bérrangar's car into the trees had probably taken steps to contain the traffic in both directions so there would be no witnesses. General Ferrari was right; inducing a fatal accident was not easily done. But the men who murdered Valerie Bérrangar knew what they were doing. After all, thought Gabriel, they were professionals. Of that, he was certain.

He crossed the road and slid behind the wheel of his rental car. The drive to the airport was thirty minutes. His flight to Paris departed promptly at nine, and at half past eleven, having entrusted his bag to the bell staff of the Bristol Hotel, he was walking up the rue de Miromesnil in the Eighth Arrondissement.

At the northern end of the street was a small shop called Antiquités Scientifiques. The sign in the window read OU-VERT. The buzzer, when pressed, emitted an inhospitable howl. Several seconds elapsed with no invitation to enter. Finally the deadbolt snapped open with a thud, and Gabriel slipped inside.

ON THE MORNING OF AUGUST 22, 1911, LOUIS BÉROUD ARRIVED at the Musée du Louvre to resume work on a copy of a portrait of an Italian noblewoman, 77 by 53 centimeters, oil on poplar panel, that hung in the Salon Carré. The Louvre did not discourage the work of artists such as Béroud. In fact, it permitted them to store their paints and easels at the museum overnight. They were forbidden, however, to produce copies with the exact dimensions of the originals, as the European art market was awash with forgeries of Old Master paintings.

Formally attired in a black frock coat and striped trousers, Béroud strode into the Salon Carré that Tuesday morning only to discover that the portrait, Leonardo da Vinci's *Mona Lisa*, had been removed from its protective wood-and-glass case. He was disappointed but not unduly alarmed. Neither, for that matter, was Maximilien Alphonse Paupardin, the guard who kept watch over the Salon Carré and its priceless treasures, usually from atop a stool in the doorway. The Louvre was in the process of photographing its entire inventory of paintings and other objets d'art. Brigadier Paupardin was confident that Mona Lisa was merely having her picture taken.

But later that morning, after visiting the photography studio, a frantic Paupardin informed the Louvre's acting president that the *Mona Lisa* was missing. The gendarmes arrived at one o'clock and immediately sealed the museum. It would remain closed for the next week as the police scoured Paris for clues. Their investigation, such as it was, was a comedy of errors. Among the initial suspects were a brash young Spanish painter named Pablo Picasso and his friend, the poet and writer Guillaume Apollinaire.

Another was Vincenzo Peruggia, the Italian-born carpenter who had helped to construct the *Mona Lisa*'s protective case. But police cleared Peruggia of suspicion after a brief interview conducted in his Paris apartment. Which is where the *Mona Lisa* remained, hidden in a trunk in the bedroom, until 1913, when the humble woodworker attempted to sell the painting to a prominent art dealer in Florence. The dealer took it to the Uffizi Gallery, and Peruggia was promptly arrested. Convicted in an Italian courtroom of the greatest art crime in history, he received a one-year prison sentence but was set free after spending only seven months behind bars.

It was the remarkable tale of the *Mona Lisa*'s theft that inspired a restless Paris shopkeeper named Maurice Durand, in the drab winter of 1985, to steal his first painting—a small still life by Jean-Baptiste-Siméon Chardin that hung in a rarely visited corner of the Musée des Beaux-Arts in Strasbourg. Unlike Vincenzo Peruggia, Durand already had a buyer waiting, a disreputable collector who was in the market for a Chardin and wasn't worried about messy details such as provenance. Durand was well paid, the client was happy, and a lucrative career was born.

Two decades later, a fall through a skylight ended Durand's career as a professional art thief. He now operated solely as a broker in the process known as commissioned theft. Or, as Durand liked to describe it, he managed the acquisition of paintings that were not technically for sale. Working with a stable of Marseilles-based professional thieves, he was the hidden hand behind some of the most spectacular art heists of the twenty-first century. During the summer of 2010 alone, his men stole works by Rembrandt, Picasso, Caravaggio, and Van Gogh. With the exception of the Rembrandt, which hung in the National Gallery of Art in Washington, none of the paintings had resurfaced.

Durand ruled his global empire of art theft from Antiquités Scientifiques, which had been in his family for three generations. Its tastefully lit shelves were lined with antique microscopes, cameras, spectacles, barometers, surveyors, and globes, all meticulously arranged. So, too, was Maurice Durand. He wore a tailored suit, dark blue, and a striped dress shirt. His necktie was the color of gold leaf. His bald head was polished to a high gloss.

"I suppose it's true, after all," he said by way of greeting.

"What's that?" asked Gabriel.

"That men in your line of work never truly retire."

"Or yours, apparently."

Smiling, Durand lifted the lid of a varnished rectangular case. "Perhaps this might be of interest to you. An optician's trial lens kit. Turn of the century. Quite rare."

"Almost as rare as that watercolor you stole from the Musée Matisse a few months back. Or the lovely genre piece by Jan Steen you pinched from the Musée Fabre."

"I had nothing to do with the disappearance of either of those works."

"What about the sale?"

Durand closed the lid, soundlessly. "My associates and I acquired a number of valuable objects for you and your service over the years, including a remarkable terra-cotta hydria by the Amykos Painter. And then, of course, there was the job in Amsterdam. We caused quite a stir with that one, didn't we?"

"Which is why I have refrained from giving your name to the French authorities."

"What about General Cyclops, your friend from the Carabinieri?"

"He remains unaware of your identity. Or the identities of your associates in Marseilles."

"And what must I do to preserve this state of affairs?"

"You must provide me with information."

"About what?"

"Galerie Georges Fleury. It's on the rue—"

"I know where it is, Monsieur Allon."

"Are you in business with him?"

"Georges Fleury? Never. But I did foolishly agree to steal a painting from him once."

"What was it?"

"It was," said Durand, his expression darkening, "a disaster."

RUE DE MIROMESNIL

Aꜱᴇ ʏᴏᴜ ꜰᴀᴍɪʟɪᴀʀ ᴡɪᴛʜ Pɪᴇʀʀᴇ-Hᴇɴʀɪ de Valenciennes?"

Gabriel sighed before answering. "Valenciennes was one of the most important landscape artists of the neoclassical period. He was among the earliest proponents of working *en plein air* rather than in a studio." He paused. "Shall I go on?"

"I meant no offense."

"None taken, Maurice."

They had retreated to Durand's cramped rear office. Gabriel was seated in the uncomfortable wooden armchair reserved for visitors; Durand, behind his spotless desk. The light of his antique lamp was reflected in his rimless spectacles, obscuring his watchful brown eyes.

"A number of years ago," he continued, "Galerie Georges Fleury exhibited a stunning landscape said to have been painted by Valenciennes in 1804. It depicted villagers dancing around classical ruins at dusk. Oil on canvas, sixty-six by ninety-eight centimeters. Immaculate condition, as Monsieur Fleury's paintings always are. A collector of considerable expertise and means whom we shall refer to as Monsieur Didier entered into negotiations to purchase the painting. But the talks broke down almost immediately because Monsieur Fleury refused to budge on the price."

"Which was?"

"Let's call it four hundred thousand."

"And how much was Monsieur Didier willing to pay you to steal it for him?"

"The rule of thumb is that a painting retains only ten percent of its value on the black market."

"Forty thousand is rather small beer for you."

"I told him so."

"How much did he offer?"

"Two hundred."

"And you accepted?"

"Unfortunately."

From the cabinet behind his desk Durand removed a bottle of calvados and two antique cut-glass tumblers. Nearly everything in the room was from another age, including the little black-and-white video monitor he used to keep watch on his front door.

He poured two glasses of the brandy and offered one to Gabriel.

"It's a bit early in the day for me."

"Nonsense," said Durand after consulting his wristwatch. "Besides, a little alcohol at midday is good for the blood."

"My blood is just fine, thank you."

"No lingering effects from that unpleasantness in Washington?"

"Only an abiding concern for the future of American democracy." Gabriel reluctantly accepted the brandy. "Who handled the job for you?"

"Your old friend René Monjean."

"Any complications?"

"Not with the robbery itself. The gallery's security system was rather outmoded."

"Surely you didn't take just the one painting."

"Of course not. René grabbed four others to cover our tracks."

"Anything good?"

"Pierre Révoil. Nicolas-André Monsiau." Durand shrugged. "A couple of portraits by Ingres."

"Five pictures is quite a haul. And yet I don't recall reading about the robbery in the newspapers."

"Evidently, Monsieur Fleury never reported it to the police."

"Unusual."

"I thought so."

"But you went ahead with the sale nevertheless."

"What choice did I have?"

"When did things go sideways?"

"About two months after Monsieur Didier took possession of the painting, he demanded a refund."

"Also unusual," said Gabriel. "At least in your line of work."

"Unheard of," murmured Durand.

"Why did he want his money back?"

"He claimed the Valenciennes wasn't a Valenciennes."

"He thought it was a later copy?"

"That's one way of putting it."

"And another?"

"Monsieur Didier was convinced the painting was a modern forgery."

Of course he was, thought Gabriel. A part of him had known it was leading to this from the moment he spotted the incongruous Flemish-style craquelure in the photograph of Julian's painting.

"How did you handle it?"

"I explained to Monsieur Didier that I had fulfilled my end of our arrangement and that he should take his complaints to Galerie Georges Fleury." Durand gave a faint smile over the rim of his glass. "Fortunately, he didn't take my suggestion."

"You returned his money?"

"Half of it," answered Durand. "It turned out to be a wise decision. I've done a great deal of business with him since."

Gabriel raised the glass of calvados to his lips for the first time. "You wouldn't happen to have it lying around, would you?"

"The fake Valenciennes?" Durand shook his head. "I burned it."

"And the four other paintings?"

"I sold them at a steep discount to a dealer in Montreal. They covered René's fee, but barely." He exhaled heavily. "It was a wash."

"All's well that ends well."

"Unless one is a paying customer of Galerie Georges Fleury."

"The phony Valenciennes wasn't a fluke?"

"*Non.* Apparently, selling forgeries is the gallery's business model. Don't get me wrong, Fleury sells plenty of genuine paintings. But that's not where he makes his money." Durand paused. "Or so I have been reliably told."

"By whom?"

"You have your sources, I have mine. And they have assured me that Fleury has been selling worthless fakes for years."

"I have a terrible feeling a friend of mine might have purchased one."

"He's a collector, this friend?"

"A dealer."

"Not Monsieur Isherwood?"

Gabriel hesitated, then nodded slowly.

"Why doesn't he simply return it and demand his money back?"

"He sold the painting to a litigious American."

"Is there any other kind?" Durand eyed a window shopper in the video monitor. "May I ask you one other question, Monsieur Allon?"

"If you insist."

Durand made a face. "What in God's name happened to your hand?"

AFTER LEAVING MAURICE DURAND'S SHOP, GABRIEL WALKED south on the rue de Miromesnil to the rue la Boétie. He lingered for a moment outside the building at Number 19, then made his way along the elegant, gently curving street to Galerie Georges Fleury. Displayed in its window were three large oil paintings. Two were in the Rococo style. The third, a portrait of a young man by François Gérard, dated from the later period known as Neoclassicism.

Or so it appeared at first glance. But an inspection carried out by a trained professional—an art restorer, for example—might tell a different story. It could not be hurried, this appraisal. The restorer would have to take his time with each work in the gallery, engage in the time-honored tradition of connoisseurship. He might touch the paintings, examine their surfaces with a magnifying glass, even speak a few words to them in the hope they spoke to him. It would be advantageous if the gallery's owner—who was likely engaged in criminal conduct and therefore would be naturally vigilant—were not looking over his shoulder as he was conducting this ritual. Better still if he were distracted by the presence of someone else in the room.

But whom?

This was the question that Gabriel pondered as he made the short walk from the gallery to the Bristol. After checking into his room, he rang Chiara and described his quandary.

She replied by immediately forwarding him a list of upcoming performances by the Orchestre de Chambre de Paris.

"Your girlfriend is in town all weekend. Perhaps she has a few minutes tomorrow afternoon to serve as your distraction."

"She's perfect. But are you sure you don't mind?"

"If you spend the weekend in Paris with a woman you were once madly in love with?"

"I was never in love with her."

"Please remind her of that fact the first chance you get."

"Don't worry," said Gabriel before the connection went dead. "I will."

14

LE BRISTOL PARIS

SHE WAS STAYING AT THE Crillon, in the Leonard Bernstein suite. He was one of the few conductors, she added with a laugh, with whom she had never been romantically linked.

"Are you there now?"

"Actually, I interrupted my rehearsal to take your call. The entire Orchestre de Chambre de Paris is hanging on my every word."

"When will you be back at your hotel?"

"Not until four. But I have press interviews scheduled until six."

"My condolences."

"I plan on misbehaving terribly."

"How about a drink downstairs in Les Ambassadeurs when you're finished?"

"Let's have dinner instead."

"Dinner?"

"It's a meal that most people take in the early evening.

Unless one is Spanish, of course. I'll ask the concierge to book us a quiet table for two at the most romantic restaurant in Paris. With any luck, the paparazzi will find us, and a *scandale* will ensue."

Before Gabriel could object, the connection was lost. He briefly considered alerting Chiara to his new dilemma but thought it unwise. Instead, he dialed the number for Valerie Bérrangar's missing phone. Once again the call went straight to her voice mail.

He rang off and scrolled through his contacts until he arrived at the entry for Yuval Gershon. Yuval was the director-general of Unit 8200, Israel's formidable signals intelligence service. Gabriel had not spoken to him—or any of his old colleagues, for that matter—since leaving Israel. It was a momentous step, one that would invite future contact, perhaps unwanted. Still, Gabriel reckoned it was worth the risk. If anyone could locate Madame Bérrangar's phone, it was Yuval and his hackers at the Unit.

He answered instantly, as though he had been anticipating Gabriel's call. Given the Unit's extraordinary capabilities, it was not beyond the realm of possibility.

"You miss me, don't you?"

"Almost as much as the hole in my chest."

"So why are you calling?"

"I have a problem only you can solve."

Yuval exhaled heavily into the phone. "What's the number?"

Gabriel recited it.

"And the problem?"

"The owner was murdered a few days ago. I have a feeling the killers were dumb enough to take her phone. I'd like you to find it for me."

"It won't be a problem if the device is still intact. But if they smashed it to pieces or dropped it into the Seine—"

"Why did you mention the Seine, Yuval?"

"Because you're calling from Paris."

"Bastard."

"I'll send up a flare when I have something. And have fun at dinner tonight."

"How did you know about dinner?"

"Anna Rolfe just sent you a text message. Shall I read it to you?"

"Why not?"

"Your reservation is at eight fifteen."

"Where?"

"She doesn't say. But it must be close to the Bristol, because she's picking you up at eight."

"I never mentioned that I was staying at the Bristol."

"It looks to me as though your room is on the third floor."

"The fourth," said Gabriel. "But who's counting?"

THE FIRST TIME GABRIEL SAW ANNA ROLFE, SHE WAS STANDing on a stage in Brussels, delivering an electrifying performance of Tchaikovsky's Violin Concerto in D Major. He left the concert hall that night never imagining they might one day meet. But several years later—after the murder of Anna's father, the immensely wealthy Swiss banker Augustus Rolfe—they were formally introduced. On that occasion, Anna had offered her hand in greeting. Now, as Gabriel joined her in the back of a courtesy Mercedes-Maybach limousine, she threw her arms around his neck and pressed her lips against his cheek.

"Consider yourself my hostage," she said as the car drew away from the hotel. "This time escape is impossible."

"Where are you planning to take me?"

"Back to my suite at the Crillon, of course."

"I was promised dinner."

"A clever ruse on my part." Anna was casually attired in jeans, a cashmere sweater, and a car-length leather coat. Even so, there was no mistaking her for anyone other than the world's most famous violinist. "Did my publicist send you the new CD?"

"It arrived the day before yesterday."

"And?"

"A triumph."

"The reviewer from the *Times* said it displayed a newfound maturity." Anna frowned. "What do you think he meant by that?"

"It's a polite way of saying you're getting older."

"You wouldn't know it from the cover photograph. It's amazing what they can do with the click of a mouse these days. I look younger than Nicola Benedetti."

"You can be sure she idolized you when she was a child."

"I don't want to be anyone's *idol*. I just want to be thirty-three again."

"Whatever for?" Gabriel gazed out his window at the graceful Haussmann buildings lining the rue du Faubourg Saint-Honoré. "Where are we having dinner?"

"It's a surprise."

"I hate them."

"Yes," said Anna distantly. "I remember."

CHEZ JANOU

THE RESTAURANT TURNED OUT TO be Chez Janou, a bright and crowded bistro on the western fringes of the Marais. A low murmur passed through the dining room as they were escorted to their table. Anna took her time removing her coat and settling onto the red banquette. It was, thought Gabriel, a virtuoso performance.

When the commotion subsided, she leaned across the small wooden table and whispered, "I hope you're not disappointed it isn't more romantic."

"I'm relieved, actually."

"I was only joking, you know."

"Were you?"

"I got over you a long time ago, Gabriel."

"Two husbands ago, in fact."

"That was needlessly vindictive."

"Perhaps," said Gabriel. "But entirely accurate."

Both of Anna's marriages had been brief and unhappy, and

both had ended with spectacular divorces. And then there was the string of disastrous affairs, always with rich and famous men. Gabriel had been the exception to Anna's pattern. He had survived her mood swings and episodes of personal recklessness longer than most—six months and fourteen days—and with the exception of a single shattered vase, their parting had been civil. It was true that he had never quite loved her, but he had cared for her a great deal and was pleased that after an interregnum of some twenty years they had renewed their friendship. Anna was a bit like Julian Isherwood. She definitely made life more interesting.

As usual, her perusal of the menu was hurried and her selections decisive. They threw Gabriel onto the defensive, for he had intended to order the same items. His fallback— ratatouille followed by liver and potatoes—produced a sneer of mild rebuke on the famous face of his dinner companion.

"Peasant," she hissed.

The waiter removed the cork from a bottle of Bordeaux and poured a small measure for Gabriel's approval. For all he knew, some of the grapes used to produce the wine had come from the vineyard north of Saint-Macaire where Valerie Bérrangar's life had ended. He sniffed, tasted, and with a nod instructed the waiter to fill their glasses.

"What shall we drink to?" asked Anna.

"Old friends."

"How dreadfully boring." Her lipstick left a smudge on the rim of the glass. She returned it to the tabletop and rotated it slowly between her thumb and forefinger, aware that the eyes of the room were upon her. "Do you ever wonder how our lives would have turned out if you hadn't walked out on me?"

"That's not how I would describe what happened."

"You tossed your meager possessions into a duffel bag and drove away from my villa in Portugal as fast as you could. And I did not receive so much as a single—"

"Please let's not do this again."

"Why not?"

"Because I can't change the past. Besides, if I hadn't left, you would have thrown me out sooner or later."

"Not you, Gabriel. You were a keeper."

"And what would I have done with myself while you were on tour?"

"You could have come with me and kept me out of all the trouble I got into."

"Followed you from city to city while you basked in the adulation of your adoring fans?"

She smiled. "That about sums it up."

"And how would you have explained me? Who would I have been?"

"I always adored Mario Delvecchio."

"Mario was a lie," said Gabriel. "Mario never was."

"But he did the most wonderful things to me in bed." She sighed and drank more of her wine. "You never told me your wife's name."

"It's Chiara."

"What does she look like?"

"A bit like Nicola Benedetti, but prettier."

"She's Italian, I take it."

"Venetian."

"Which would explain why you're living there again."

Gabriel nodded. "She's managing the city's largest restoration company. Eventually, I'll go to work for her."

"Eventually?"

"I'm on administrative leave until further notice."

"Because of what happened in Washington?"

"And other assorted traumas."

"There are worse places to recuperate than Venice."

"Much," agreed Gabriel.

"I think I'll schedule a performance there. A night of

Brahms and Tartini at the Scuola Grande di San Rocco. I'll get a suite at that little hotel in San Marco, the Luna Baglioni, and stay there for a month or two. You can come by every afternoon and—"

"Behave, Anna."

"Will you at least introduce me to your family someday?"

"Don't you think that might be a bit awkward?"

"Not at all. In fact, I think your children might enjoy spending time with me. Despite my many faults and failings, all of which have been mercilessly chronicled in the tabloids, most people find me endlessly fascinating."

"Which is why I'd like to borrow you for an hour or two tomorrow."

"What did you have in mind?"

He told her.

"Is it really safe to visit an art gallery in Paris with you?"

"It was a long time ago, Anna."

"Another lifetime," she said. "But why me?"

"I need you to distract the owner while I take a careful look at his inventory."

"Shall I bring along my fiddle and perform a partita or two?"

"That won't be necessary. Just be your usual enchanting self."

"Eye candy?"

"Exactly."

She probed at the skin along her jawline. "I'm a bit old for that, don't you think?"

"You haven't changed a bit since—"

"The morning you walked out on me?" The waiter served their first course and withdrew. Anna lowered her eyes and said, "*Bon appétit.*"

RUE LA BOÉTIE

GABRIEL RANG THE GALLERY AT ten o'clock the following morning and, after a testy exchange with a male receptionist called Bruno, was connected to Monsieur Georges Fleury himself. Not surprisingly, the crooked French art dealer had never heard of anyone named Ludwig Ziegler.

"I advise a single client with a passion for Neoclassical paintings," Gabriel explained in German-accented French. "She happens to be in Paris for the weekend and would like to visit your gallery."

"Galerie Georges Fleury is not a tourist destination, Monsieur Ziegler. If your client wishes to see French paintings, I would suggest a visit to the Louvre instead."

"My client isn't here on holiday. She's performing this weekend at the Philharmonie de Paris."

"Is your client—"

"Yes."

Fleury's tone was suddenly more accommodating. "What time would Madame Rolfe like to stop by?"

"One o'clock this afternoon."

"I'm afraid I've already arranged to see another client at that time."

"Reschedule him. And tell Bruno to take a long lunch. I find him annoying, and so will Madame Rolfe. In case you were wondering, she drinks room-temperature mineral water. *Sans gaz*, with a slice of lemon. Not a wedge, Monsieur Fleury. A slice."

"Any particular brand of water?"

"Anything but Vittel. And no photographs or handshakes. For understandable reasons, Madame Rolfe never shakes hands before a performance."

Gabriel rang off, then dialed Anna's number. Her voice, when at last she answered, was heavy with sleep.

"What time is it?" she groaned.

"A few minutes after ten."

"In the *morning*?"

"Yes, Anna."

Swearing softly, she killed the connection. Madame Rolfe, Gabriel remembered, never rose before noon.

GABRIEL LEFT THE BRISTOL AT HALF PAST TWELVE AND WALKED beneath a leaden Parisian sky to the Crillon. It was one fifteen when Anna, in jeans and a zippered sweater, finally descended from her suite. Outside, they slid into the back of the Maybach for the short drive to Galerie Georges Fleury.

"Any last instructions?" she asked while appraising her face in the vanity mirror.

"Be charming, but difficult."

"Act naturally? Is that what you're saying?"

Anna glossed her heart-shaped lips as the car turned onto

the rue la Boétie. A moment later it stopped outside the gallery. Its owner and namesake was waiting on the pavement like a doorman. His hands remained rigidly at his side as Anna emerged from the back of the limousine.

"Welcome to Galerie Georges Fleury, Madame Rolfe. It is truly an honor to meet you."

Anna acknowledged the art dealer's greeting with a regal nod. Unnerved, he thrust a hand toward Gabriel.

"And you must be Herr Ziegler."

"I must be," said Gabriel evenly.

Fleury regarded him for a moment through a pair of rimless spectacles. "Is it possible we've met somewhere before? At an auction, perhaps?"

"Madame Rolfe and I avoid them." Gabriel glanced at the gallery's heavy glass door. "Shall we go inside? It doesn't take long for her to attract a crowd."

Fleury used a handheld remote to unlock the door. In the vestibule, a bronze life-size bust of a young Greek or Roman man stood atop a plinth of black marble. Next to it was an unoccupied receptionist's desk.

"As you requested, Herr Ziegler, it's just the three of us."

"No hard feelings, I hope."

"None at all." Fleury placed the remote on the desk and escorted them into a high-ceilinged room with a dark wooden floor and walls of garnet red. "My main exhibition room. The better pictures are upstairs. If you wish, we can begin there."

"Madame Rolfe is in no hurry."

"Neither am I."

Dazzled, Fleury led his internationally renowned visitor on a laborious tour of the room's collection while Gabriel conducted an unchaperoned survey of his own. The first work to catch his connoisseur's eye was a large Rococo painting depicting a nude Venus and three young maidens. The inscription at the bottom of the canvas suggested the work had been executed by Nicolas Colombel in 1697. Gabriel doubted that was the case.

He placed a hand to his chin and tilted his head to one side. A moment passed before Fleury noticed his interest in the work and joined him before the canvas.

"I acquired it a few months ago."

"May I ask where?"

"An old private collection here in France."

"Dimensions?"

Fleury smiled. "You tell me, Monsieur Ziegler."

"One hundred and twelve by one hundred and forty-four centimeters." He paused, then added with a disarming smile, "Give or take a centimeter or two."

"Very close."

Only because Gabriel had deliberately misstated the painting's actual dimensions. Any fool could see that the work measured 114 by 148 centimeters.

"It's in remarkable condition," he said.

"I commissioned the restoration after purchasing it."

"May I see the conservator's report?"

"Now?"

"If you wouldn't mind."

When Fleury withdrew, Anna approached the painting. "It's beautiful."

"But too large to transport easily."

"You're not thinking about buying something, are you?"

"Not me," said Gabriel. "But you certainly are."

Before Anna could object, Fleury reappeared, empty-handed. "I'm afraid Bruno must have misfiled it. But if Madame Rolfe is interested in the painting, I can forward you a copy by email."

Gabriel produced his phone. "Would you mind if I photographed her standing next to it?"

"Of course not. In fact, I would be honored."

Anna inched closer to the painting and, turning, adopted the smile she wore when acknowledging the applause of a sold-out concert hall. Gabriel snapped the photograph, then moved to the neighboring painting.

"A follower of Canaletto," declared Fleury.

"A very good one."

"I thought so, too. I acquired it only last week."

"From where?"

"A private collection." The Frenchman treated Anna to a watery smile. "In Switzerland."

Gabriel leaned closer to the canvas. "How certain are you about the attribution?"

"Why do you ask?"

Because the painting, at just 56 by 78 centimeters, was easily transportable. Especially if it were to be removed from its stretcher. "Do you think Bruno mislaid the condition report for this one, too?"

"I'm afraid the painting is already spoken for."

"Is there no way Madame Rolfe can make a competitive bid?"

"I've already accepted the buyer's money."

"Is he a dealer or a collector?"

"Why do you ask?"

"Because if he's a dealer, I'd be interested in taking it off his hands."

"I can't reveal his identity. The terms of the sale are entirely private."

"Not for long," said Gabriel knowingly.

"What do you mean, monsieur?"

"Let's just say I get a funny feeling when I look at this painting." He snapped a photograph of it. "Perhaps you should show us the good pictures now, Monsieur Fleury."

17

GALERIE FLEURY

FLEURY ESCORTED THEM UP A flight of stairs to the second-floor exhibition room. Here the walls were somber gray rather than red, and the paintings, by all appearances, were of a decidedly higher quality. There were several examples of Dutch and Flemish portraiture, including two works executed in the manner of Anthony van Dyck. There was also *A River Scene with Distant Windmills*, oil on canvas, 36 by 58 centimeters, bearing the distinctive initials of the Dutch Golden Age painter Aelbert Cuyp. Gabriel was doubtful the initials were authentic. In fact, after a moment of undisturbed reverie, he reached the conclusion, wholly unsupported by technical analysis, that the painting was a forgery.

"You have a very good eye," said Fleury from the opposite side of the room. He added a slice of lemon to Anna's mineral water and asked, "Something for you, Monsieur Ziegler?"

"The attribution for this painting would be nice."

"It has been firmly assigned by numerous experts to Cuyp himself."

"How do these experts explain the lack of a complete signature? After all, Cuyp generally signed the works he painted with his own hand and placed only his initials on paintings that were produced under his supervision."

"There are exceptions, as you know."

Which was indeed the case, thought Gabriel. "How's the provenance?"

"Lengthy and impeccable."

"Previous owner?"

"A collector of exceptional taste."

"French or Swiss?" asked Gabriel dryly.

"American, actually."

Fleury handed the glass of water to Anna and escorted her from painting to painting, leaving Gabriel free to carry out a second private inspection of the gallery's inventory. Eventually they all three convened before *A River Scene with Distant Windmills*, oil on canvas, 36 by 58 centimeters, by a forger of indisputable talent.

"Do you mind if I touch it?"

"I beg your pardon?"

"The painting," said Gabriel. "I'd like to touch it."

"Carefully," cautioned Fleury.

Gabriel placed the tip of his forefinger gently against the canvas and dragged it over the brushwork. "Did your man handle the cleaning?"

"It came to me in this condition."

"Are there paint losses?"

"Not extensive. But, yes, there is some abrading. Particularly in the sky."

"I assume the condition report contains photographs?"

"Several, monsieur."

Gabriel looked at Anna. "Does Madame Rolfe like it?"

"That depends on the price." She turned to Fleury. "What did you have in mind?"

"A million and a half."

"Come, come," said Gabriel. "Let's be realistic."

"How much would Madame Rolfe be willing to pay for it?"

"Are you asking me to negotiate with myself?"

"Not at all. I am merely offering you the opportunity to name your price."

Gabriel contemplated the worthless painting in silence.

"Well?" asked Fleury.

"Madame Rolfe will give you one million euros and not a euro more."

The art dealer smiled. "Sold."

DOWNSTAIRS IN FLEURY'S OFFICE, GABRIEL REVIEWED THE condition report and provenance while Anna, a mobile phone pressed to her ear, transferred the sum of one million euros from her account at Credit Suisse to the gallery's account at Société Générale. The final sale price included the cost of the frame and shipping. Gabriel, however, declined both. Madame Rolfe, he said, did not care for the frame. As for the shipping, he intended to see to it personally.

"I should have the export license in hand by next Wednesday at the latest," said Fleury. "You can pick up the painting then."

"I'm afraid Wednesday won't do."

"Why not?"

"Because Madame Rolfe and I are taking the painting with us."

"*C'est impossible*. There is paperwork to submit and signatures to obtain."

"The paperwork and signatures are your problem. Besides, something tells me you know how to acquire an export license for a painting that has already left the country."

The dealer did not deny the accusation. "What about proper packaging?" he asked.

"Trust me, Monsieur Fleury. I know how to handle a painting."

"The gallery accepts absolutely no liability for any damage once the painting leaves these premises."

"But you *do* guarantee the attribution, along with the accuracy of the condition report and provenance."

"Yes, of course." Fleury handed Gabriel a copy of the certificate of authenticity, which declared the work to be firmly attributed to Aelbert Cuyp. "It says so right here."

The dealer placed the sales agreement before Anna and indicated the line where she should sign her name. After adding his own signature, he photocopied the document and inserted it into an envelope, along with copies of the provenance and condition report. The painting he covered in glassine paper and bubble wrap, which was more protection than it deserved. At three fifteen it was resting on the backseat of the Maybach as it drew to a stop outside the Bristol Hotel.

"I thought I was only supposed to be eye candy," said Anna.

"What's a million euros between friends?"

"A great deal of money."

"It will be back in your account by Monday afternoon at the latest."

"What a pity," she said. "I was hoping you might remain in my debt a little longer."

"And if I were?"

"I would ask you to come to my performance tonight. There's a gala reception afterward. All the beautiful people will be there."

"I thought you hated those things."

"With a passion. But if you were standing at my side, it might be tolerable."

"And how would you explain me, Anna? Who would I be?"

"How about Herr Ludwig Ziegler?" She frowned at the object lying on the seat between them. "The esteemed art adviser who just spent one million euros of my money for a worthless forgery."

Gabriel carried it upstairs to his room and removed the canvas from its stretcher. One hour later it was wedged into the overnight bag he wheeled across the cavernous ticket hall of the Gare du Nord. His journey through passport control proceeded without incident, and at five o'clock he boarded a Eurostar train bound for London. As the banlieues of northern Paris slid past his window, he reflected on the shifting fortunes of his career. Just four months earlier he had been the director-general of one of the world's most formidable intelligence services. Now, he thought, smiling, he had found a new line of work.

Art smuggler.

18

JERMYN STREET

NOT SINCE THE OUTBREAK OF the pandemic, when the art world had slipped into something approaching cardiac arrest, had Sarah Bancroft endured such a dreadful week. It began with Julian's calamitous visit to Bordeaux and concluded, late that afternoon, with the collapse of a potential sale—a case of cold feet on the buyer's part and hard-nosed determination on Sarah's not to sell the painting in question, *Adoration of the Magi* by Luca Cambiaso, at a loss. To make matters worse, her new husband had left London on a business trip. Because his trade was espionage, he could not say where he was going or when he might return. For all Sarah knew, it would be Midsummer Day before she laid eyes on him again.

Which explained why, after engaging the gallery's security system and locking the front door, she made straight for Wiltons and settled into her usual corner table at the bar. A perfect three-olive Belvedere martini, Saharan dry, materialized a moment later, delivered by a handsome young waiter in a blue blazer and red necktie. Perhaps, she thought as she raised the glass to her lips, all was not quite as bad as it seemed.

At once there was a burst of uproarious laughter. It was Julian who had provoked it. He was explaining the hideous purple-red bruise on his cheek to Oliver Dimbleby and Jeremy Crabbe, the head of the Old Master department of Bonhams. According to Julian's version of the story, the collision with the lamppost had taken place not in Bordeaux but in Kensington, and was the result of nothing more malicious than a misguided attempt to send a text message while walking.

Mobile phone in hand, Julian reenacted the fictitious incident, much to the delight of the other dealers, curators, and auctioneers lining the bar. For his reward, he was kissed by the crimson lips of the stunning former fashion model who now ran a thriving modern art gallery in King Street. Watching the performance from her corner table, Sarah sipped her martini and whispered, "Bitch."

The kiss was little consolation; Sarah could see that. Julian was mortified by his appearance and distraught over the suspicious death of the woman who had asked him to come to France. So, too, was Sarah. Moreover, she was concerned about the painting she had sold to Phillip Somerset, a man whose acquaintance she had made while working at the Museum of Modern Art in New York. Her old friend Gabriel Allon had agreed to look into the matter. As yet, he had delivered no update on the progress of his investigation.

Amelia March of *ARTnews* detached herself from the bar and approached Sarah's table. She was a slender woman of erect carriage, with short dark hair and the unblinking, too-wide eyes of an Apple emoji. It was Amelia, with Sarah's anonymous help, who had broken the news about *Portrait of an Unknown Woman*. Sarah now regretted having leaked the information. If she had kept her mouth shut, the rediscovery and sale of the painting would have remained shrouded in secrecy. And Madame Valerie Bérrangar, she thought, would still be alive.

"I heard a naughty rumor about you the other day," Amelia announced.

"Only one?" asked Sarah. "I'm disappointed."

She could only imagine the sort of gossip that occasionally reached Amelia's ever-vigilant ears. After all, Sarah was a former covert CIA operative whose husband had worked as a professional assassin before joining the Secret Intelligence Service. She had also served briefly as the art adviser to the crown prince of Saudi Arabia. Indeed, it was Sarah who had convinced His Majesty to plunk down $450 million on Leonardo da Vinci's *Salvator Mundi*, the highest price ever paid at auction for a work of art.

None of which Sarah wished to ever see in print. Therefore, she made no objection when Amelia sat down at her table uninvited. Sarah reckoned it was better to hear the reporter out and, if possible, use the opportunity to make a little mischief of her own. She was in that sort of mood.

"What is it this time?" she asked Amelia.

"I have been reliably told—"

"Oh, for heaven's sake."

"*Very* reliably told," Amelia continued, "that you are planning to move Isherwood Fine Arts from its longtime home in Mason's Yard to, how shall we say, a less secluded location."

"Untrue," declared Sarah.

"You looked at two potential sites in Cork Street last week."

But not for the reason Amelia suspected. It was Sarah's ambition to open a second gallery, one that specialized in contemporary art and would bear her name. She had yet to broach the topic with Julian and was keen that he not read about her plans in *ARTnews*.

"I can't possibly afford Cork Street," she demurred.

"You just sold a newly discovered Van Dyck for six and a

half million pounds." Amelia lowered her voice. "Very hush-hush. Secret buyer. Mysterious source."

"Yes," said Sarah. "I think I read about that somewhere."

"I've been very good to you and Julian over the years," said Amelia. "And on numerous occasions, I have refrained from pursuing stories that might well have damaged the gallery's reputation."

"Such as?"

"Your exact role in the reemergence of that Artemisia, for a start."

Sarah sipped her drink but said nothing.

"Well?" probed Amelia.

"Isherwood Fine Arts will never leave Mason's Yard. Is now and ever shall be. World without end. Amen."

"Then why are you looking for a long-term lease in Cork Street?"

Because she wanted to cast a long shadow over the gallery owned by the former fashion model, who at that moment was whispering something into the ear of Simon Mendenhall, the mannequin-like chief auctioneer from Christie's.

"I swear to you," said Sarah, "as a friend and as a woman, that I will tell you when the time is right."

"You'll tell me *first*," insisted Amelia. "And in the mean-time, you will give me something juicy."

"Have a quick look over your right shoulder."

Amelia did as Sarah suggested. "The lovely Miss Watson and sleazy Simon Mendenhall?"

"Torrid," said Sarah.

"I thought she was dating that actor."

"She's shagging sleazy Simon on the side."

As if on cue, there was another eruption of laughter from the opposite end of the bar, where Julian had just concluded an en-core performance of the alleged incident in Kensington—this time for Nicky Lovegrove, art adviser to the vastly wealthy.

"Is that really how it happened?" asked Amelia.

"No," said Sarah, smiling sadly. "The lamppost attacked *him*."

AFTER FINISHING HER DRINK, SARAH WIPED THE SMUDGE OF lipstick from Julian's cheek and went into Jermyn Street. There were no taxis in sight, so she walked around the corner to Piccadilly and caught one there. As it bore her westward across London, she scrolled through the possibilities on Deliveroo, dithering between Indian and Thai. She ordered Italian instead and immediately regretted her choice. She had gained five pounds during the pandemic and another five after marrying Christopher. Despite thrice-weekly training runs on the footpaths of Hyde Park, the weight refused to budge.

As the taxi sped past the Royal Albert Hall, Sarah resolved to place herself on yet another diet. But not tonight; she was hungry enough to eat one of her Ferragamo pumps. After dinner, which she would consume while watching something mindless on television, she would crawl into her empty marital bed and remain there for the better part of the weekend, listening to "When Your Lover Has Gone" on repeat. Billie Holiday's classic 1956 recording, of course. When one was truly depressed, no other version would do.

She did her best Lady Day impersonation as the taxi turned into Queen's Gate Terrace and stopped opposite the elegant Georgian house at Number 18. It wasn't all theirs, only the luxurious maisonette on the lower two levels. Sarah was overjoyed to see a light burning downstairs in the kitchen. Environmentally conscious, she was certain she had not left it on by mistake that morning. The most plausible explanation was that her lover was not gone after all.

She paid off the driver and hurried down the steps to the maisonette's lower entrance. There she found the door ajar and the security system disengaged. Inside, lying on the kitchen island, was a canvas that had been removed from its stretcher—a riverscape with distant windmills, somewhere in the neighborhood of 40 by 60 centimeters, bearing what appeared to be the initials of the Dutch Golden Age painter Aelbert Cuyp.

Next to the painting was an envelope from Galerie Georges Fleury in Paris. And next to the envelope was an excellent bottle of Sancerre, from which Gabriel, wincing in pain, was attempting to extract the cork. Sarah closed the door and, laughing in spite of herself, shed her coat. It was, she thought, the perfect end to a perfectly dreadful week.

19

QUEEN'S GATE TERRACE

SARAH CHECKED THE STATUS OF her Deliveroo order and saw it was still open. "Tagliatelle with ragù or veal Milanese?"

"I wouldn't want to impose."

"My husband is away. I could use the company."

"In that case, I'll have the veal."

"Tagliatelle it is." Sarah placed the order, then looked down at the frameless, stretcherless canvas lying on her counter. "I'm sure there's a perfectly reasonable explanation for this. And for that swollen hand of yours as well."

"Where would you like me to begin?"

"Why not the hand?"

"I assaulted a plainclothes Carabinieri officer after meeting with Julian in Venice."

"And the painting?"

"I acquired it this afternoon at Galerie Georges Fleury."

"I can see that." Sarah tapped the envelope. "But how in the world did you pay for it?"

Gabriel removed the sales agreement from the envelope and pointed toward the practiced signature of the buyer.

"That was very generous of her," said Sarah.

"Generosity had nothing to do with it. She expects to be repaid in full."

"By whom?"

"You, of course."

"So the painting is mine? Is that what you're saying?"

"I suppose it is."

"How much did I spend on it?"

"One million euros."

"For that kind of money, I should have got a frame." Sarah tugged at the frayed corner of the canvas. "And a stretcher as well."

"The management of the Bristol Hotel might have found it odd if I had left an antique picture frame behind in my room."

"And the stretcher?"

"It's in a rubbish bin outside the Gare du Nord."

"Of course it is." Sarah sighed. "You should probably put it on a new one first thing in the morning to stabilize the image."

"If I do that, it won't fit in my carry-on luggage."

"Where are you planning to take it?"

"New York," said Gabriel. "And you're coming with me."

"Why?"

"Because that painting is a forgery. And I have a funny feeling the one you sold to Phillip Somerset for six and a half million pounds is a fake as well."

"Oh, hell," said Sarah. "I was afraid you were going to say that."

GABRIEL DREW HIS MOBILE PHONE AND RETRIEVED THE PHOTO-graph of the painting he had seen in Valerie Bérrangar's villa in Saint-André-du-Bois. *Portrait of an Unknown Woman*, oil on canvas, 115 by 92 centimeters, attributed to a follower of the Flemish Baroque painter Anthony van Dyck.

"That would explain the letter she wrote to Julian."

"Only partially."

"Meaning?"

"She called Georges Fleury first."

"Why?"

"She wanted to know whether her version of the painting was a valuable Van Dyck as well."

"And what did Monsieur Fleury tell her?"

"Given my limited experience with him, I can assure you it bore no resemblance to the truth. But whatever he said made her suspicious enough to contact the art crime unit of the Police Nationale."

Sarah swore softly as she pulled the cork from the bottle of Sancerre.

"Don't worry, I'm all but certain the police told Madame Bérrangar that they had no interest in pursuing the matter. Which is why she asked Julian to come to Bordeaux." Gabriel paused. "And why she is now dead."

"Was she—"

"Murdered?" Gabriel nodded. "And her killers took her mobile phone for good measure."

"Who were they?"

"I'm still working on that. I'm quite certain, however, that they were professionals."

Sarah poured two glasses of the wine and handed one to Gabriel. "What kind of art dealer hires professional assassins to kill someone in a dispute over a painting?"

"The kind who's involved in a lucrative criminal enterprise."

Sarah took up Gabriel's phone and enlarged the image. "Is Madame Bérrangar's painting a forgery, too?"

"In my opinion," replied Gabriel, "it is the work of a later follower of Van Dyck. Forty-eight hours ago, I told Valerie Bérrangar's daughter that I thought it was a copy of the painting you sold to Phillip Somerset. But I'm now convinced it's the other way around. Which would explain why the picture doesn't appear in Van Dyck's catalogue raisonné."

"The forger copied the follower?"

"In a manner of speaking, yes. And in the process, he made marked improvements. He's quite amazing. He truly paints like Anthony van Dyck. It's no wonder your five experts were deceived."

"How do you explain the paint losses and retouching that showed up when we examined the painting under ultraviolet light?"

"The forger artificially ages and damages his paintings. Then he restores them using modern pigments and medium in order to make them appear authentic."

Sarah glanced at the canvas lying on the countertop. "This one, too?"

"Absolutely."

Gabriel removed the painting's condition report from the envelope. Attached were three accompanying photographs. The first depicted the canvas in its present state: retouched, with a fresh coat of unsoiled varnish. The second photo, made with ultraviolet light, revealed the paint losses as an archipelago of small black islands. The last photograph presented the painting in its truest state, without retouching or varnish. The losses appeared as white blotches.

"It looks exactly like a four-hundred-year-old painting should look," said Gabriel. "I hate to admit it, but it's possible even I might have been fooled."

"Why weren't you?"

"Because I went into that gallery on the lookout for forgeries. And because I've been around paintings for a hundred years. I know the brushstrokes of the Old Masters like the lines around my eyes."

"With all due respect," replied Sarah, "that isn't good enough to prove the painting is a forgery."

"Which is why we're going to give it to Aiden Gallagher."

Gallagher was the founder of Equus Analytics, a high-tech art research firm that specialized in detecting forgeries. He sold his services to museums, dealers, collectors, auction houses, and, on occasion, to the Art Crime Team of the FBI. It was Aiden Gallagher, a decade earlier, who had proved that one of New York's most successful contemporary art galleries had sold nearly $80 million worth of fake paintings to unsuspecting buyers.

"His lab is in Westport, Connecticut," continued Gabriel. "If the forger made a technical mistake, Gallagher will find it."

"And while we're waiting for the results?"

"You'll arrange for me to have a look at the painting you sold to Phillip Somerset. If, as I suspect, it's a forgery—"

"Julian and I will be the laughingstocks of the art world."

No, thought Gabriel as he reached for his wineglass. If *Portrait of an Unknown Woman* turned out to be a forgery, Isherwood Fine Arts of Mason's Yard, purveyors of museum-quality Italian and Dutch Old Master paintings since 1968, would be ruined.

20

WESTPORT

THEY PASSED THROUGH HEATHROW SECURITY separately—Gabriel under his real name, with the forged Cuyp crammed into his carry-on—and reunited in the departure lounge. While waiting for the flight to be called, Sarah composed an email to Aiden Gallagher, informing him that Isherwood Fine Arts of London wished to hire Equus Analytics to conduct a technical evaluation of a painting. She did not identify the work in question, though she implied it was a matter of some urgency. She was scheduled to arrive in New York at noon and, barring a traffic disaster, could be in Westport by 3:00 p.m. at the latest. Could she deliver the painting to him then?

On board the plane, Sarah informed the flight attendant that she would require no food or drink during the eight-hour flight across the North Atlantic. Then she closed her eyes and did not open them again until the aircraft thudded onto the runway at John F. Kennedy International Airport. Armed with her American passport and Global Entry card, she glided through the rituals of the arrival process while Gabriel, his status reduced, spent an hour working his way through the maze of stanchions and retractable nylon restraints reserved for unwanted foreigners. His journey ended in a windowless room, where he was briefly questioned by a well-fed Customs and Border Protection officer.

"What brings you back to the United States, Director Allon?"

"Private research."

"Does the Agency know you're in the country?"

"They do now."

"How's your chest feeling?"

"Better than my hand."

"Anything in the bag?"

"A couple of firearms and a dead body."

The officer smiled. "Enjoy your stay."

A blue line directed Gabriel to baggage claim, where Sarah was pondering her mobile phone. "Aiden Gallagher," she said without looking up. "He's wondering whether it could wait until Monday. I told him it couldn't."

Just then her phone pinged with an incoming email.

"Well?"

"He wants a description of the painting."

Gabriel recited the particulars. *"A River Scene with Distant Windmills.* Oil on canvas. Thirty-six by fifty-eight centimeters. Currently attributed to Aelbert Cuyp."

Sarah sent the email. Gallagher's reply arrived two minutes later.

"He'll meet us in Westport at three."

EQUUS ANALYTICS WAS LOCATED IN AN OLD REDBRICK BUILDing on Riverside Avenue near the overpass of the Connecticut

Turnpike. Gabriel and Sarah arrived a few minutes after two o'clock in the back of an Uber SUV. They picked up coffee from a Dunkin' Donuts up the street and settled onto a bench along the sunlit bank of the Saugatuck. Fat white clouds flew across an otherwise spotless blue sky. Pleasure craft dozed like discarded playthings in their slips at a small marina.

"It almost looks like something Aelbert Cuyp might have painted," remarked Gabriel.

"Westport definitely has its charms. Especially on a day like this."

"Any regrets?"

"About leaving New York?" Sarah shook her head. "I think my story ended rather well, don't you?"

"That depends."

"On what?"

"Whether you're truly happy being married to Christopher."

"Deliriously so. Though I have to admit, my work at the gallery isn't quite as interesting as the jobs I used to do for you." She lifted her face toward the warmth of the sun. "Do you remember our trip to Saint-Barthélemy with Zizi al-Bakari?"

"How could I forget?"

"What about the summer we spent with Ivan and Elena Kharkov in Saint-Tropez? Or the day I shot that Russian assassin in Zurich?" Sarah checked the time on her phone. "It's nearly three. Let's go, shall we? I wouldn't want to keep him waiting."

They set out along Riverside Avenue and arrived at Equus Analytics as a black BMW 7 Series sedan was pulling into the parking lot. The man who emerged from the driver's seat had coal-black hair and blue eyes, and appeared much younger than his fifty-four years.

He extended a hand toward Sarah. "Miss Bancroft, I presume?"

"It's a pleasure to meet you, Dr. Gallagher. Thank you for seeing us on such short notice. And on a Saturday, at that."

"Not at all. Truth be told, I was planning to do a few hours' work before dinner." His accent, though faded, betrayed a Dublin childhood. He looked at Gabriel. "And you are?"

"Johannes Klemp," answered Gabriel, dredging up a name from his tangled past. "I work with Sarah at Isherwood Fine Arts."

"Did anyone ever tell you that you look a great deal like that Israeli who was shot on Inauguration Day? If I'm not mistaken, his name is Gabriel Allon."

"I get that a lot."

"I don't doubt it." Gallagher gave him a knowing smile before turning to Sarah. "That leaves the painting."

She nodded toward Gabriel's overnight bag.

"Ah," said Gallagher. "The plot thickens."

21

THE LOCKS ON THE OUTER door were museum grade, as were the security system and the equipment in Gallagher's laboratory. His inventory of high-tech gadgetry included an electron microscope, a shortwave infrared reflectography camera, and a Bruker M6 Jetstream, a sophisticated spatial imaging device. Nevertheless, he began his analysis the old-fashioned way, by examining the painting with the naked eye under visible light.

"It seems to have survived the flight intact, but I'd like to put it on a stretcher as quickly as possible." He cast a reproachful glance in Gabriel's direction. "As long as Herr Klemp has no objections, of course."

"Perhaps you should refer to me by my real name," said Gabriel. "As for the stretcher, a standard fourteen-by-twenty-two should work well. I'd use a five-eighths setback for the canvas."

Gallagher's expression turned quizzical. "Are you a painter, Mr. Allon?"

Gabriel's answer was the same one he had given to Valerie Bérrangar's daughter seventy-two hours earlier, in the commune of Saint-André-du-Bois. Aiden Gallagher was similarly intrigued, though for a different reason.

"It turns out we have a great deal in common."

"I'm sorry to hear that," quipped Gabriel.

"Artistically, I mean. I trained to be a painter at the National College of Art and Design in Dublin before coming to America and enrolling at Columbia."

Where he had earned a PhD in art history and an MA in art conservation. While working on the restoration staff at the Metropolitan Museum of Art, he specialized in provenance research and, later, scientific detection of forgeries. He resigned from the Met in 2005 and founded Equus Analytics. The *Art Newspaper* had recently christened him "a rock star" with no equal in the field. Thus the new BMW 7 Series parked outside his office door.

He directed his gaze toward the painting. "Where was it acquired?"

"Galerie Georges Fleury in Paris," answered Gabriel.

"When?"

"Yesterday afternoon."

Gallagher looked up abruptly. "And you already suspect there's a problem?"

"No," said Gabriel. "I *know* there's a problem. The painting is a forgery."

"And how did you arrive at this conclusion?" asked Gallagher dubiously.

"Instinct."

"I'm afraid instinct isn't good enough, Mr. Allon." Gallagher contemplated the painting again. "How's the provenance?"

"A joke."

"And the condition report?"

"It's a real work of art."

Gabriel fished both documents from his briefcase and laid them on the table. Aiden Gallagher began his review with the provenance and ended with the three photos. The painting in its present form. The painting under ultraviolet light. And the painting with the losses exposed.

"If it's a fake, the forger certainly knew what he was doing." Gallagher doused the overhead lights and examined the painting with an ultraviolet torch. The archipelago of black blotches corresponded with those in the photograph. "So far, so good." He switched on the overhead lights again and looked at Gabriel. "I assume you're familiar with Cuyp's work?"

"Very."

"Then you know his oeuvre has been plagued by confusion and misattribution for hundreds of years. He borrowed heavily from Jan van Goyen, and his followers borrowed heavily from him. One was Abraham van Calraet. Like Cuyp, he was from the Dutch town of Dordrecht. Because they shared the same initials, it can be difficult to tell the work of one from the other."

"Which is why a forger would choose a painter like Cuyp in the first place. Good forgers shrewdly select artists whose work has been subject to misattribution in the past. That way, when a new painting miraculously reemerges from a dusty European collection, the so-called art experts are more inclined to accept it as genuine."

"And if I conclude that the painting is the work of Aelbert Cuyp?"

"I'm confident you won't."

"Are you prepared to wager fifty thousand dollars?"

"Not me." Gabriel pointed at Sarah. "But she will."

"I require twenty-five thousand to begin an investigation. The rest is due upon delivery of my findings."

"How long will it take?" asked Sarah.

"Anywhere from a few weeks to a few months."

"Time is of the essence, Dr. Gallagher."

"When are you planning to return to London?"

"You tell me."

"I can have a preliminary report Monday afternoon. But there's a surcharge for rush jobs."

"How much?"

"Fifty thousand up front," said Gallagher. "Twenty-five thousand on delivery."

AFTER SIGNING THE RELEASE FORMS AND HANDING OVER THE check, Gabriel and Sarah hurried along Riverside Avenue to the Metro North station and purchased two tickets to Grand Central.

"The next train is at four twenty-six," said Sarah. "With any luck, we'll be sipping martinis at the Mandarin Oriental by six o'clock."

"I thought you preferred the Four Seasons."

"There was no room at the inn."

"Not even for you?"

"Trust me, I gave the head of reservations a piece of my mind."

"Where do you suppose Phillip Somerset is spending his weekend?"

"Knowing Phillip, he could be anywhere. Besides his town house on East Seventy-Fourth Street, he owns a ski lodge in Aspen, an estate on the East End of Long Island, and a large portion of Lake Placid in the Adirondacks. He flits between them on his Gulfstream."

"Not bad for a former bond trader from Lehman Brothers."

"You've obviously been reading up on him."

"You know me, Sarah. I've never been able to sleep on airplanes." Gabriel gave her a sideways glance. "What's the weather like in Lake Placid this time of year?"

"Miserable."

"What about Aspen?"

"No snow."

"That leaves Manhattan or Long Island."

"I'll call him first thing Monday."

"Get it over with. You'll feel better."

"Unless the Van Dyck turns out to be a forgery." Sarah opened a blank email and added Phillip Somerset's address. "What's the subject?"

"Catching up."

"Nice touch. Keep going."

"Tell him you're in New York unexpectedly. Ask him if he has a few minutes to spare."

"Should I mention the painting?"

"Under no circumstances."

"How should I describe you?"

"You're an art dealer who used to work for the CIA. I'm sure you'll think of something."

She completed the email as the train was drawing into the station. And at half past five, as they were climbing into a taxi outside Grand Central, Phillip Somerset rang her with his answer.

"Lindsay and I are having a few friends to lunch tomorrow at our place on Long Island. You're more than welcome to join us. And bring your friend," he suggested. "I'd love to meet him."

22

NORTH HAVEN

Sarah declined Phillip Somerset's offer of a car service and rented a premium European-made sedan instead. They collected it from a garage in Turtle Bay at half past ten the following morning and by noon were speeding through Suffolk County on the Long Island Expressway. To help pass the time, Sarah read aloud the quaint-sounding names of the towns and hamlets as they appeared on the faded green exit signs—first Commack, then Hauppauge, Ronkonkoma, and Patchogue. It was a silly game, she explained to Gabriel, that she had played as a child, when the Bancrofts had passed their summers in East Hampton with other rich Manhattan families like theirs.

"The new crowd is much richer than we were, and they're not ashamed to show it. Grotesque displays of wealth are now de rigueur." She tugged at the sleeve of the dark pantsuit that she had brought from London. "I only wish I'd had time to shop for something more appropriate."

"You look beautiful," said Gabriel, a hand balanced atop the steering wheel.

"But I'm not suitably attired for a weekend gathering at the North Haven estate of Phillip Somerset."

"How should one be dressed?"

"As expensively as possible." Sarah's phone chimed with an incoming text. "Speak of the devil."

"Have we been disinvited?"

"He's checking on our progress."

"Do you suppose he's contacting all his guests, or only you?"

"And just what are you implying?"

"That Phillip Somerset sounded inordinately pleased to hear from you yesterday."

"Our relationship is both personal and professional," admitted Sarah.

"How personal?"

"We were introduced by a mutual friend at MoMA's annual Party in the Garden fundraiser. Phillip was going through a messy divorce at the time. We dated for several months."

"Who ended it?"

"He did, if you must know."

"What on earth was he thinking?"

"I was in my late thirties at the time, and Phillip was looking for someone a bit younger. When he met lovely Lindsay Morgan, a yoga enthusiast and model twelve years my junior, he dropped me like an underperforming stock."

"And yet you remained invested in Masterpiece Art."

"How do you know that?"

"Lucky guess."

"I had already entrusted a small portion of my assets to Phillip before we began dating," said Sarah. "I saw no reason to demand a redemption simply because our relationship went awry."

"How small a portion?"

"Two million dollars."

"I see."

"I thought I made it clear the last time we were in New York that my father left me rather well off."

"You did," said Gabriel. "I only hope that Phillip has looked after your interests."

"My current balance is four point eight million dollars."

"Mazel tov."

"Compared to Phillip's other clients, I'm something of a pauper. He definitely has the Midas touch. That's why so many people in the art world are invested with him. The fund consistently delivers twenty-five percent annual returns."

"How is that possible?"

"A magical proprietary trading strategy that Phillip guards jealously. Unlike other art funds, Masterpiece doesn't reveal the paintings in its inventory. Its book is entirely opaque. And quite large, apparently. Phillip currently controls one point two billion dollars' worth of art. He buys and sells paintings constantly and earns enormous profits on the churn."

"By churn, you mean volume and speed."

"And arbitrage, of course," replied Sarah. "Masterpiece operates exactly like a hedge fund. It has a million-dollar minimum for new investors, with a five-year lockup. The fee structure is the industry-standard two-and-twenty. A two percent management fee and a twenty percent cut of the prof-its."

"I suppose the firm is domiciled in the Cayman Islands."

"Aren't they all?" Sarah rolled her eyes. "I must admit, I do enjoy watching my account balance go up and up each year. But a part of me doesn't like to think of paintings as a commodity to be bought and sold like soybeans and oil futures."

"You'll have to get over that if you're going to make it as an art dealer. Most of the paintings purchased at auction will never be seen by the public again. They're locked away in bank vaults or in the Geneva Free Port."

"Or in a climate-controlled warehouse operated by Chelsea Fine Arts Storage. That's where Phillip told me to ship the Van Dyck." Sarah pointed toward the sign for exit 66. "Yaphank."

THE EGG-SHAPED PENINSULA KNOWN AS NORTH HAVEN protrudes into Peconic Bay between Sag Harbor and Shelter Island. Phillip Somerset's weekend retreat, a thirty-thousand-square-foot acropolis of cedar and glass, stood on the eastern shore. His golden young wife greeted Gabriel and Sarah in the soaring entrance hall, dressed in a sleeveless linen pantsuit belted at her slender waist, her skin so smooth and flawless she looked like a filtered photograph on social media. When Gabriel introduced himself, he received a blank who-are-you stare in return, but Sarah's name Lindsay Somerset recognized instantly.

"You're the art dealer from London who sold my husband the Van Gogh."

"Van Dyck."

"I get them confused."

"It's a common mistake," Sarah assured her.

Lindsay Somerset turned to greet a new arrival, a prime-time television news anchor and his husband. Several more print and broadcast journalists were gathered in the luminous great room along with an assortment of hedge fund managers, painters, art dealers, fashion designers, models, actors, screenwriters, a renowned director of blockbuster motion pictures, an iconic musician who sang about the plight of Long Island's working classes, a progressive congresswoman from the Bronx, and a flock of young assistants from a New York publishing house. Evidently, it was a book party to which they had been invited.

"Carl Bernstein," whispered Sarah. "He was Bob Woodward's partner at the *Washington Post* during the Watergate scandal."

"Unlike you, Sarah, I was alive when Richard Nixon was president. I know who Carl Bernstein is."

"Would you like to meet him? He's right over there." Sarah snatched a glass of champagne from the tray of a passing waiter. "And there's Ina Garten. And that actor whose name I can never remember. The one who just got out of rehab."

"And there's a Rothko," said Gabriel quietly. "And a Basquiat. And a Pollock. And a Lichtenstein, a Diebenkorn, a Hirst, an Adler, a Prince, and a Warhol."

"You should see his town house on East Seventy-Fourth Street. It's like the Whitney in there."

"Not quite," said a baritone voice from behind them. "But you're welcome to visit anytime you like."

The voice belonged to Phillip Somerset. He greeted Sarah first—with a kiss on her cheek and a favorable remark about her appearance—before extending a sun-varnished hand toward Gabriel. He was a tall, physically fit specimen in his mid-fifties, with a boyish head of gray-blond hair and the confident, easy smile that comes naturally to the very rich. Strapped to his wrist was a colossal Richard Mille chronometer, a sporting model worn by wealthy men with pretensions of seamanship. His zippered cashmere sweater was vaguely maritime as well, as were his pale cotton trousers and electric-blue loafers. Indeed, everything about Phillip Somerset suggested that he had just stepped from the deck of a yacht.

Gabriel accepted the proffered hand and introduced himself, first name and last.

Phillip Somerset looked to Sarah for an explanation.

"He's an old friend," she said.

"And I thought I was going to spend the afternoon fending off questions about my trading strategy." Phillip Somerset released Gabriel's hand. "What an unexpected surprise, Mr. Allon. To what do I owe the honor?"

"I was hoping to have a look at a painting."

"Well, you've certainly come to the right place. Is there anything in particular you'd like to see?"

"*Portrait of an Unknown Woman.*"

"By Anthony van Dyck?"

Gabriel smiled. "I certainly hope so."

PHILLIP SOMERSET ESCORTED GABRIEL AND SARAH UP A FLIGHT of stairs and into a large, light-filled office with outsize computer monitors and a sweeping view of the whitecapped bay. A lengthy silence ensued as he regarded them speculatively from behind the no-man's-land of his half-acre desk. Then he looked directly at Sarah and said, "Perhaps you should tell me what this is all about."

Her answer was precise and lawyerly. "Isherwood Fine Arts has retained Mr. Allon to conduct a discreet inquiry into the circumstances surrounding the rediscovery of *Portrait of an Unknown Woman* and its sale to Masterpiece Art Ventures."

"Why was such an inquiry deemed necessary?"

"Late last week, the gallery received a letter expressing concerns over the transaction. The woman who sent it was killed in an auto accident near Bordeaux a few days later."

"Do the police suspect foul play?"

"No," answered Gabriel. "But I do."

"Why?"

"Her late husband purchased several paintings from the same gallery in Paris where Julian and Sarah acquired *Portrait of an Unknown Woman.* When I paid a visit to the gallery on Friday, I noticed three paintings that appeared to be forgeries. I purchased one of them and turned it over to Equus Analytics."

"Aiden Gallagher is the best in the business. I use him myself."

"He's hoping to have a preliminary report by tomorrow afternoon. But in the meantime—"

"You thought you'd have a look at the Van Dyck."

Gabriel nodded.

"I'd love to show it to you," said Phillip Somerset. "But I'm afraid it's not possible."

"May I ask why not?"

"Masterpiece Art Ventures sold it about three weeks ago. At a considerable profit, I might add."

"To whom?"

"I'm sorry, Mr. Allon. The transaction was private."

"Was there an intermediary?"

"One of the major auction houses."

"Did the house conduct a second review of the attribution?"

"The buyer insisted on one."

"And?"

"*Portrait of an Unknown Woman* was painted by Anthony van Dyck, almost certainly in his studio in Antwerp, sometime in the late sixteen thirties. Which means that, as far as Isherwood Fine Arts and Masterpiece Art Ventures are concerned, the matter is now closed."

"If you don't mind," said Sarah, "I'd like that in writing."

"Send me something tomorrow morning," replied Phillip Somerset. "I'll have a look."

23

GALLERY 617

ARLY THE FOLLOWING MORNING, SARAH rang her man at HSBC in London and instructed him to wire one million euros into the Credit Suisse account of the world's most famous violinist. Then she dialed Ronald Sumner-Lloyd, Julian's Berkeley Square solicitor, and together they drafted a letter shielding Isherwood Fine Arts against any and all future claims related to the sale of *Portrait of an Unknown Woman* by the Flemish Baroque painter Anthony van Dyck. Shortly before 9:00 a.m., she emailed the finished document to Phillip Somerset. He phoned her a few minutes later from his Sikorsky executive helicopter, which was bound from East Hampton to Manhattan.

"The language is rather aggressive, don't you think? Especially the clause regarding confidentiality."

"I have to look after our interests, Phillip. And if your sale goes sideways, I don't ever want to read the words Isherwood Fine Arts in the *New York Times*."

"I thought I made it clear that you have nothing to worry about."

"You also once assured me that you were interested in a long-term relationship."

"You're not still angry over that, are you?"

"I never was," lied Sarah. "Now do me a favor and sign the waiver."

"On one condition."

"What's that?"

"Tell me how you know Gabriel Allon."

"We met when I was working in Washington."

"That was a long time ago."

"Yes," said Sarah. "Lovely Lindsay must have been in elementary school at the time."

"She says you were rude to her."

"She doesn't know the difference between a Van Gogh and a Van Dyck."

"Once upon a time, neither did I," said Phillip before ringing off. "But look at me now."

THE DOCUMENT APPEARED IN SARAH'S IN-BOX FIVE MINUTES later, electronically signed and dated. She added her own signature and forwarded it to Julian and Ronnie in London. Then, after confirming two reservations for that evening's seven thirty British Airways flight to Heathrow, she rang Gabriel and told him that Isherwood Fine Arts was now legally and ethically in the clear.

"Which means that Julian and I get to keep our reputations, not to mention our six and a half million pounds. All in all," she said, "a rather fortunate turn of events."

"What are your plans for the rest of the morning?"

"First I'm going to pack my suitcase. Then I'm going to stare at my phone and wait for Aiden Gallagher of Equus

Analytics to tell me that you needlessly spent a million euros of my money on *A River Scene with Distant Windmills*."

"How about a nice long walk instead?"

"A much better idea."

It was a perfect spring morning, bright and cloudless, with a mischievous wind blowing from the Hudson. They walked along West Fifty-Ninth Street to Fifth Avenue, then turned uptown.

"Where are you taking me?"

"The Metropolitan Museum of Art."

"Why?"

"Its collection includes several important paintings by Anthony van Dyck." Gabriel smiled. "Real ones."

Sarah rang a friend who worked in the Met's publicity department and requested two complimentary admission tickets. They were waiting at the information desk in the Great Hall. Upstairs, they made their way to Gallery 617, a room dedicated to Baroque portraiture. It contained four works by Van Dyck, including his iconic portrait of Henrietta Maria, wife of King Charles I. Gabriel snapped a photograph of the queen consort's face and showed it to Sarah.

"Craquelure," she said.

"Do you notice anything unusual about it?"

"No."

"Neither do I. It looks exactly like Van Dyck's craquelure should look. But now look at this one." It was the face of the unknown woman, the version that Julian and Sarah had sold to Phillip Somerset. "The craquelure pattern is different."

"It's slight," said Sarah. "But, yes, there's a difference."

"That's because the forger is using a chemical hardening agent to artificially age the painting. It produces four centuries' worth of craquelure in a matter of days. But it's not the right *kind* of craquelure."

"Two separate reviews have declared our *Portrait of an*

Unknown Woman to be the work of Anthony van Dyck. Rome has spoken, Gabriel. The case is closed."

"But both reviews were based on expert opinion rather than science."

Sarah sighed in frustration. "Perhaps you're looking at this the wrong way."

"And what would be the right way?"

She gestured toward the portrait of Henrietta Maria. "Maybe that one is fake."

"It isn't."

"Are you sure about that?" Sarah led him into an adjoining gallery. "And what about that landscape over there? Are you absolutely certain that Claude Lorrain painted it? Or are you merely inclined to believe that because it's on display in the Metropolitan Museum of Art?"

"Your point?"

"My point," replied Sarah in a stage whisper, "is that no one really knows whether all the beautiful works of art hanging in the world's great museums are genuine or fakes. Least of all the learned curators and conservators employed by institutions such as this one. It's the dirty little secret they don't like to talk about. Oh, they do their utmost to guarantee the integrity of their collections. But the truth is, they get fooled all the time. By one estimate, at least twenty percent of the paintings in the National Gallery in London are misattributed works or outright forgeries. And I can assure you, the statistics for the private art market are much worse."

"Then perhaps we should do something about it."

"By putting Galerie Georges Fleury out of business?" Sarah shook her head slowly. "Bad idea, Gabriel."

"Why?"

"Because what starts in Paris won't stay in Paris. It will spread through the rest of the art world like a contagion. It will infect the auction houses, the dealers, the collectors, and the ordinary patrons of museums like the Met. No one, not even the most virtuous among us, will be spared its ravages."

"And if Aiden Gallagher tells us that the painting is a forgery?"

"We will pursue restitution quietly and then go our separate ways, never to speak of the matter again. Otherwise, we might shatter the illusion that all that glitters is actually gold."

"Glisters," said Gabriel.

Frowning, Sarah checked the time. "It is now officially afternoon."

They returned to the Mandarin Oriental and settled into the last empty table in the hotel's popular lobby bar. At two fifteen, as they were finishing their lunch, Sarah's phone shivered with an incoming call. It was from Equus Analytics.

"Maybe *you* should answer that," said Sarah.

Gabriel tapped the ACCEPT icon and lifted the device to his ear. "Thank you," he said after a moment. "But that won't be necessary. We're on our way now."

Sarah reclaimed her phone. "*What* won't be necessary?"

"Additional chemical analysis of the pigment."

"Why not?"

"Because Aiden Gallagher discovered several navy-blue polar fleece fibers embedded throughout the painting, including in places that had never been retouched. Since the fabric was invented in Massachusetts in 1979, it's safe to assume that Aelbert Cuyp wasn't wearing a fleece jacket or vest in the mid-seventeenth century. Which means—"

"Georges Fleury owes me a million euros."

Sarah switched their flights, then hurried upstairs to fetch her luggage. They would settle the matter quietly, she thought, and never speak of it again.

24

GALERIE FLEURY

THE NAVIGATION APPLICATION ON SARAH'S phone estimated the driving time from Columbus Circle to Westport, Connecticut, to be ninety minutes. But Gabriel, behind the wheel of their rented European sedan, managed to cover the distance in a little more than an hour. Aiden Gallagher's flashy BMW 7 Series was parked outside Equus Analytics, and *A River Scene with Distant Windmills*, adhered to a new stretcher, was lying on the examination table in the lab. Next to the painting was a two-page letter declaring the work to be a modern forgery. And next to the letter were three microscope photographs supporting Gallagher's conclusion.

"To be honest, I was a little surprised it was so cut-and-dried. Given the quality of his brushwork, I expected more of him." Gallagher pointed out the dark strands of polar fleece in the photographs. "It's a real amateur's mistake."

"Is there any other possible explanation for the presence of those fibers?" asked Gabriel.

"None whatsoever. That said, you should be prepared for Fleury to take great offense at my findings." Gallagher looked at Sarah. "In my experience, most art dealers become rather indignant when asked to part with a million euros."

"I'm quite confident Monsieur Fleury will see things our way. Especially when he reads your report."

"When are you planning to confront him?"

"We're leaving for Paris tonight. In fact," said Sarah, glancing at her watch, "we need to be on our way."

She made out a check for the final $25,000 of Gallagher's fee while Gabriel removed *A River Scene with Distant Windmills* from its stretcher and folded it into his carry-on bag. Their Air France flight commenced boarding at 6:45 p.m. At half past eight, they were over the East End of Long Island.

"There's North Haven," said Sarah, pointing out her window. "I actually think I can see Phillip's house."

"One wonders how he and Lindsay make do with only thirty thousand square feet."

"You should see the place in the Adirondacks." She lowered her voice. "I spent a long weekend there once."

"Kayaking and hiking?"

"Among other things. Phillip has lots of toys."

"He certainly didn't keep the Van Dyck for long."

"Some people flip houses. Phillip flips paintings."

Sarah accepted a glass of champagne from the flight attendant and insisted that Gabriel take one as well.

"What shall we drink to?" he asked.

"A disaster averted."

"I certainly hope so," said Gabriel, and left his glass untouched.

IT WAS A FEW MINUTES AFTER NINE THE FOLLOWING MORNING when the plane dropped from a cloudless sky and settled onto the runway of Charles de Gaulle Airport. After clearing passport control and customs, Gabriel and Sarah climbed into a taxi and headed for the center of Paris. Their first stop was Brasserie L'Alsace on the Avenue des Champs-Élysées, where, at 10:45 a.m., Gabriel placed his first call to Galerie Georges Fleury. It went unanswered, as did his second. But the third time he tried the number, Bruno the receptionist came on the line. Posing once again as Ludwig Ziegler, art adviser to the renowned Swiss violinist Anna Rolfe, Gabriel demanded to speak to Monsieur Fleury at once.

"I'm sorry, but Monsieur Fleury is with another client."

"It is imperative that I see him immediately."

"May I ask what this is regarding?"

"*A River Scene with Distant Windmills.*"

"Perhaps I can be of help."

"I'm quite certain you can't."

The receptionist placed the call on hold. Two minutes passed before he came back on the line. "Monsieur Fleury will see you at two o'clock," he said, and the connection went dead.

Which left Gabriel and Sarah with three long hours to kill. They drank coffee at Brasserie L'Alsace until noon, then walked up the Champs-Élysées to Fouquet's for an unhurried lunch. Afterward, they crossed to the opposite side of the avenue and, with their luggage in tow, window-shopped their way to the rue la Boétie. It was two o'clock exactly when they arrived at Galerie Georges Fleury. Gabriel stretched his injured right hand toward the intercom, but the automatic lock snapped open before he could place his forefinger atop the call button. He heaved open the glass door and followed Sarah inside.

THE VESTIBULE WAS UNOCCUPIED SAVE THE BRONZE LIFE-SIZE bust of a young Greek or Roman man perched atop its plinth of black marble. Gabriel called out Fleury's name and, receiving no answer, led Sarah into the ground-floor exhibition room. It was likewise uninhabited. The large Rococo painting depicting a nude Venus and three young maidens was gone, as was the Venetian scene attributed to a follower of Canaletto. No new paintings hung in their place.

"Looks as though Monsieur Fleury is doing a brisk business," said Sarah.

"The missing paintings were both forgeries," answered Gabriel, and headed for Fleury's office. There he found the art dealer seated at his desk, his face tipped toward the ceiling, his mouth open. The wall behind him was spattered with still-damp blood and brain tissue, the result of two recent point-blank gunshot wounds to the center of his forehead. The younger man lying on the floor had also been shot at close range—twice in the chest and at least once in the head. Like Georges Fleury, he was quite obviously dead.

"Dear God," whispered Sarah from the open doorway.

Gabriel made no reply; his phone was ringing. It was Yuval Gershon, calling from his office at Unit 8200 headquarters outside Tel Aviv. He didn't bother with a greeting.

"Someone turned on the dead woman's phone about one thirty local time. We got inside a couple of minutes ago."

"Where is it?"

"The Eighth Arrondissement of Paris. The rue la Boétie."

"I'm in the same location."

"I know," said Yuval. "In fact, it looks to us as though you might be in the same room."

Gabriel rang off and located the number for Valerie Bérrangar's phone in his directory of recent calls. He started to dial, but stopped when his connoisseur's eye fell upon the aluminum-sided Tumi suitcase, 52 by 77 by 28 centimeters, standing in the corner of the cluttered office. It was possible that Monsieur Fleury had been planning to embark on a journey at the time of his death. But the more likely explanation was that the suitcase contained a bomb.

A bomb, thought Gabriel, that would be detonated with a call to Madame Bérrangar's phone.

He did not bother to explain any of this to Sarah. Instead, he seized her arm and pulled her through the exhibition room to the entrance of the gallery. The glass door was locked, and the remote was missing from the receptionist's desk. It was, Gabriel had to admit, a masterpiece of planning and execution. But then he would have expected nothing less. After all, they were professionals.

But even professionals, he thought suddenly, make mistakes. Theirs was the bronze life-size bust of a young Greek or Roman man perched atop its plinth of black marble. Gabriel raised the heavy object above his head and, ignoring the searing pain in his hand, hurled it against the glass door of Galerie Georges Fleury.

PART TWO

UNDERDRAWING

25

QUAI DES ORFÈVRES

PERHAPS NOT SURPRISINGLY, THE FRENCH police assumed the worst when, at 2:01 p.m. on an otherwise pleasant spring afternoon, the elegant Eighth Arrondissement of Paris shook with the thunderclap of an explosion. The first units arrived at the scene moments later to find an Old Master art gallery engulfed in flames. Even so, the officers were encouraged by the fact that there appeared to be no large-scale loss of life of the sort associated with jihadist terrorist attacks. Indeed, at first glance, the only casualty appeared to be the life-size bronze bust of a young Greek or Roman man lying on the pavement, surrounded by blue-gray cubes of tempered glass. One veteran detective, after learning of the circumstances by which the weighty objet d'art exited the gallery, would declare it to be the first documented case in the annals of French crime that anyone had broken *out* of an art gallery.

The perpetrators of this most unusual act—a man of late middle age and an attractive fair-haired woman in her early forties—surrendered to police within minutes of the explosion. And at 2:45 p.m., after a series of hasty and incredulous phone calls between senior French intelligence and security officials, they were placed in the back of an unmarked Peugeot and delivered to 36 Quai des Orfèvres, the iconic headquarters of the Police Nationale's criminal division.

There they were separated and relieved of their personal effects. The woman's handbag and luggage contained nothing out of the ordinary, but her companion was in possession of several noteworthy items. They included a false German passport, an Israeli-made Solaris mobile phone, an Italian *permesso di soggiorno*, a painting without a frame or stretcher, documents from Galerie Georges Fleury and Equus Analytics, and a handwritten letter from a certain Valerie Bérrangar to Julian Isherwood, owner and sole proprietor of Isherwood Fine Arts, 7–8 Mason's Yard, St. James's, London.

At half past three, the items were arrayed upon the table of the interrogation room into which the man of late middle age was led. Also present was a sleek creature of about fifty clad in a banker's executive suit. Extending a hand cordially in greeting, he introduced himself as Jacques Ménard, commander of the Central Office for the Fight against Cultural Goods Trafficking. The man smiled as he lowered himself into his seat. It definitely sounded better in French.

Jacques Ménard opened the German passport. "Johannes Klemp?"

"A small man with a chip balanced precariously on his insignificant shoulder," said Gabriel. "Much loathed by hoteliers and restaurateurs from Copenhagen to Cairo."

"Do the Germans know you're abusing one of their passports?"

"The way I see it, allowing me to occasionally travel on one of their passports is the least the Germans can do."

Ménard took up the Solaris phone. "Is it as secure as they say?"

"I hope you didn't try to unlock it. I'll go blind reloading my contacts."

Ménard reached for the sales documents from Galerie Georges Fleury. "*The* Anna Rolfe?"

"She was in town last weekend. I borrowed her for a few hours."

"She has a fondness for Aelbert Cuyp?"

"It's not a Cuyp." Gabriel nudged the report from Equus Analytics across the tabletop. "It's a forgery. Which is why I purchased it in the first place."

"You can tell if a painting is a forgery merely by looking at it?"

"Can't you?"

"No," admitted Ménard. "I cannot. But perhaps we should begin here." He indicated the handwritten letter. "With Madame Bérrangar."

"Yes, let's," said Gabriel. "After all, if you had taken her complaint about *Portrait of an Unknown Woman* seriously, she'd still be alive."

"Madame Bérrangar was killed in a single-vehicle traffic accident."

"It wasn't an accident, Ménard. She was murdered."

"How do you know that?"

"Her phone."

"What about it?"

"The bomb maker used it to trigger the detonator."

"Perhaps we should start from the beginning," suggested Ménard.

Yes, agreed Gabriel. Perhaps they should.

GABRIEL'S ACCOUNT OF HIS INVESTIGATION INTO THE PROVENANCE and authenticity of *Portrait of an Unknown Woman* was chronological in sequence and largely accurate in content. It commenced with Julian's star-crossed visit to Bordeaux and concluded with the destruction of Galerie Georges Fleury and the brutal murder of its owner and his assistant. Absent from Gabriel's briefing was any mention of his visit to a certain antiques shop on the rue de Miromesnil or the assistance he received from Yuval Gershon of Unit 8200. Nor did he divulge the name of the wealthy American art investor who had purchased *Portrait of an Unknown Woman* from Isherwood Fine Arts—only that the painting had since been resold to yet another unidentified buyer and that the matter had been resolved to the satisfaction of all the parties involved.

"Is it a Van Dyck or not?" asked Ménard.

"The auction house that brokered the sale says it is."

"So your investigation was a waste of time? Is that what you're saying?"

"The death of Valerie Bérrangar and the events of this afternoon would suggest otherwise." Gabriel looked down at the forgery. "As would this painting."

"Did you really expect Georges Fleury to return the money based on the findings of a single expert?"

"The expert in question is regarded as the best in the world. I was confident that I could convince Fleury to accept the findings and refund the money."

"You were planning to threaten him?"

"Me? Never."

Ménard smiled in spite of himself. "And you're sure Fleury was dead when you and Madame Bancroft arrived at the gallery?"

"Quite sure," answered Gabriel. "Bruno Gilbert, too."

"In that case, who let you in?"

"The assassin, of course. He unlocked the door using the keyless remote that usually rests on the receptionist's desk. Fortunately, he waited fifteen seconds too long before calling Valerie Bérrangar's phone."

"How do you—"

"It's not important how I know," interjected Gabriel. "All that matters is that you now have the evidence to link her murder to the bombing of the gallery."

"The phone's identification number and SIM card?"

Gabriel nodded.

"Only if they survived the detonation. Still, it was rather reckless on his part, don't you think?"

"Almost as reckless as leaving that bronze bust next to the door. The man who hired him probably thought that I would be suspicious if it wasn't there. After all, I spotted three forgeries within a few minutes of setting foot in that gallery." Gabriel lowered his voice. "Which is why I had to die."

"Because you were a threat to a forgery ring?" asked Ménard skeptically.

"It's not a traditional ring. It's a sophisticated business enterprise that's flooding the art market with high-quality forgeries. And the man who's running it is making enough money to hire professionals to eliminate anyone who threatens him."

Ménard made a show of thought. "An interesting theory, Allon. But you have no proof."

"If you had listened to Valerie Bérrangar, you would have all the proof you need."

"I did listen to her," insisted Ménard. "But Fleury assured me there was nothing wrong with the painting he sold to Monsieur Isherwood, that it was simply a case of two copies of the same portrait."

"And you believed him?"

"Georges Fleury was a respected member of the Paris art

community. My unit never received a single complaint about him."

"That's because the fakes he was selling were good enough to fool the best eyes in the art world. Based on what I've seen of the forger's work, he could hold his own among the Old Masters."

"From what I hear, you're not too bad yourself, Allon. One of the world's finest art restorers. At least that's the rumor."

"But I use my talent to heal existing paintings." Gabriel tapped the surface of the forgery. "This man is creating entirely new works that appear as though they were executed by some of the greatest artists who ever lived."

"Do you have any idea who he might be?"

"You're the detective, Ménard. I'm sure you'll be able to find him if you put your mind to it."

"And who are you these days, Allon?"

"I'm the director of the paintings department at the Tiepolo Restoration Company. And I'd like to go home now."

MÉNARD INSISTED ON KEEPING THE FORGED PAINTING AND THE original copies of the documents, including Valerie Bérrangar's letter. Gabriel, who was in no position to make demands of his own, requested only anonymity—for himself and for Isherwood Fine Arts.

The French detective rubbed his jaw noncommittally. "You know how these things go, Allon. Criminal inquiries can be hard to control. But don't worry about the German passport. It will be our little secret."

By then it was approaching eight o'clock. Ménard escorted Gabriel downstairs to the courtyard, where Sarah waited in the backseat of the same unmarked Peugeot. It delivered them to the Gare du Nord in time to make the evening's last Eurostar to London.

"All in all," said Sarah, "a rather disastrous turn of events."

"It could have been worse."

"Much," she agreed. "But why is it that things always explode whenever I'm around you?"

"I just seem to rub certain people the wrong way."

"But not Jacques Ménard?"

"No," said Gabriel. "We got on famously."

"So much for handling the matter quietly. But I suppose that you got exactly what you wanted in the end."

"What's that?"

"A formal investigation by the French police."

"No one will be spared?"

"No one," said Sarah as she closed her eyes. "Not even you."

26

For the remainder of that glorious April, as French police and prosecutors sifted through the ruins of Galerie Georges Fleury, the art world looked on in horror and held its collective breath. Those who knew Fleury well were guarded in their comments, in private and especially to the press. And those who had done business with him said little if anything at all. The director of the Musée d'Orsay called it the most unsettled month for the arts in France since the Germans entered Paris in June 1940. Several commentators criticized the remark as insensitive, but few took issue with its sentiment.

Because *l'affaire Fleury* included a bomb and two dead bodies, the serious crimes division of the Police Nationale—the so-called Central Directorate of the Judicial Police—controlled the investigation, with Jacques Ménard's art sleuths reduced to a supporting role. Veteran crime reporters immediately sensed that something was amiss, as their sources at the Quai des Orfèvres seemed incapable of answering even the most basic questions about the probe.

Did the *police judiciaire* have any leads on the bomber's current whereabouts?

If we did, came the terse reply from the Quai des Orfèvres, we would have arrested him by now.

Was it true that Fleury and his assistant were killed before the bomb exploded?

The Quai des Orfèvres was not in a position to say.

Was theft the motive?

The Quai des Orfèvres was pursuing several leads.

Were others involved?

The Quai des Orfèvres had ruled nothing out.

And what about the man of late middle age and the attractive fair-haired woman who were seen smashing their way out of the gallery seconds before the bomb detonated? Here again, the Quai des Orfèvres was at its most elusive. Yes, the police were aware of the eyewitness reports and were looking into them. For now, they would have nothing more to say on the matter, as it was part of an ongoing investigation.

Gradually, the press grew frustrated and sought out greener pastures. The flow of new revelations slowed to a trickle, then dried up entirely. Quietly the inhabitants of the art world breathed a collective sigh of relief. With their reputations and careers intact, they carried on as though nothing had happened.

Such was the case, to a lesser extent, for the man of late middle age. For several days after his return to Venice, he tried to spare his wife the details of his most recent brush with death. He revealed the truth while attempting, with limited success, to accurately reproduce her honey-and-gold-flecked irises on canvas. His task was made more difficult by the late-afternoon light falling across the underside of her left breast.

"You violated every possible rule of tradecraft," she admonished him. "The field officer always controls the environment. And he never allows the target to set the time of a meeting."

"I wasn't debriefing a deep-penetration agent in the backstreets of West Beirut. I was attempting to return a forged painting to a crooked art dealer in the Eighth Arrondissement of Paris."

"Will they try again?"

"To kill me? I can't imagine."

"Why not?"

"Because I've told the French everything I know. What would be the point?"

"What was the point of trying to kill you in the first place?"

"He's afraid of me."

"Who?"

"You really must stop talking." He loaded his brush and placed it against his canvas. "It changes the shape of your eyes when you open your mouth."

She seemed not to hear him. "Your daughter dreamed of your death while you were away. A terrible nightmare. And quite prophetic, as it turns out."

"Why?"

"You were lying on a sidewalk when you died."

"She must have been dreaming of Washington."

"Her dream was different."

"How so?"

"You had no arms or legs."

THAT EVENING GABRIEL EXPERIENCED THE SAME DREAM. IT was so vivid he didn't dare close his eyes again for fear of its return. Repairing to his studio, he completed the painting of Chiara in a few fevered hours of uninterrupted work. In the broad light of morning, she declared it the finest piece he had produced in years.

"It reminds me of a Modigliani."

"I'll take that as a compliment."

"You were inspired by him?"

"It's hard not to be."

"Could you paint one?"

"A Modigliani? Yes, of course."

"I like the one that fetched a hundred and seventy million at auction a few years ago."

The painting in question was *Reclining Nude*. Gabriel commenced work on it after dropping the children at school and completed it two days later while listening to Anna Rolfe's new CD. Then he produced a second version of the painting, with a change of perspective and a subtle rearrangement of the woman's pose. He signed it with Modigliani's distinctive signature, in the upper-right corner of the canvas.

"Obviously, your hand suffered no permanent damage," remarked Chiara.

"I painted it with my left."

"It's astonishing. It looks exactly like a Modigliani."

"It *is* a Modigliani. He just didn't paint it."

"Could it fool anyone?"

"Not with a modern canvas and stretcher. But if I found a canvas similar to the type he was using in Montmartre in 1917 and was able to concoct a convincing provenance . . ."

"You could bring it to market as a lost Modigliani?"

"Exactly."

"How much could you get for it?"

"A couple hundred, I'd say."

"Thousand?"

"Million." Gabriel placed a hand reflectively to his chin. "The question is, what should we do with it?"

"Burn it," said Chiara. "And don't ever paint another."

CHIARA'S DIRECTIVE TO THE CONTRARY, GABRIEL HUNG THE two Modiglianis in their bedroom and then retreated once more to his quiet, unhurried life of semiretirement. He dropped the children at school at eight o'clock each morning and collected them again at half past three. He visited the Rialto Market to fetch the ingredients for the family's evening meal. He read dense books and listened to music on his new British sound system. And if he were so inclined, he painted. A Monet one day, a Cézanne the next, a stunning reinterpretation of Vincent's *Self-Portrait with Bandaged Ear* that, were it not for Gabriel's modern canvas and palette, would have set the art world ablaze.

He followed the news from Paris with mixed emotions. He was relieved that Quai des Orfèvres had seen fit to conceal his role in the affair and that his old friends Sarah Bancroft and Julian Isherwood had suffered no reputational damage. But when three additional weeks passed with no arrests—and no suggestion in the press that Galerie Georges Fleury had been flooding the market with paintings produced by one of the greatest art forgers in history—Gabriel reached the unsettling conclusion that a ministerial thumb had been laid upon the scales of French justice.

The arrival of the Bavaria C42 came as a welcome distraction. Gabriel took it on a pair of test runs in the sheltered waters of the *laguna*. Then, on the first Saturday of May, the Allon family sailed to Trieste for dinner. During their starlit return to Venice, Gabriel revealed that Sarah Bancroft had offered him a minor but lucrative commission. Chiara suggested he execute something original instead. He commenced work on a Picassoesque still life, then buried it beneath a version of Titian's *Portrait of Vincenzo Mosti*. Francesco Tiepolo declared it a masterpiece and advised Gabriel never to produce another.

He disagreed with Francesco's favorable assessment of the work—it was by no means a masterpiece, not by the mighty Titian's standards—so he cut the canvas from its stretcher and burned it. Next morning, after dropping the children at school, he repaired to Bar Dogale to consider how best to squander the remaining hours of his day. While he was consuming *un 'ombra*, a small glass of *vino bianco* taken by Venetians with their breakfast, a shadow fell across his table. It was cast by none other than Luca Rossetti of the Art Squad. His face bore only the faintest trace of the injuries he had suffered some six weeks earlier. He bore a message from Jacques Ménard of the Police Nationale.

"He was wondering whether you were free to come to Paris."

"When?"

"You're booked on the twelve forty Air France flight."

"Today?"

"Do you have something more pressing on your schedule, Allon?"

"That depends on whether Ménard intends to arrest me the minute I step off the plane."

"No such luck."

"In that case, why does he want to see me?"

"He wants to show you something."

"Did he say what it was?"

"No," said Rossetti. "But he said you might want to bring a gun."

27

MUSÉE DU LOUVRE

Jacques Ménard was waiting at the arrival gate at Charles de Gaulle when Gabriel emerged from the jetway, a bag over one shoulder, a 9mm Beretta pressing reassuringly against the base of his spine. After an expedited journey through passport control, they climbed into the back of an unmarked sedan and started toward the center of Paris. Ménard declined to disclose their destination.

"The last time someone surprised me in Paris, it didn't turn out so well."

"Don't worry, Allon. I think you'll actually enjoy this."

They followed the A1 past the Stade de France, then headed west on the boulevard Périphérique, Paris's high-speed ring road. Five minutes later, the Élysée Palace appeared before them.

"You should have warned me," said Gabriel. "I would have worn something appropriate."

Ménard smiled as his driver sped past the presidential palace, then turned left onto the Avenue des Champs-Élysées. Before reaching the Place de la Concorde, they dropped into a tunnel and followed the Quai des Tuileries to the Pont du Carrousel. A right turn would have taken them across the Seine to the Latin Quarter. They turned to the left instead and, after passing beneath an ornate archway, braked to a halt in the immense central courtyard of the world's most famous museum.

"The Louvre?"

"Yes, of course. Where did you think I was taking you?"

"Somewhere a bit more dangerous."

"If it's danger you want," said Ménard, "we've definitely come to the right place."

A YOUNG WOMAN WITH THE ELONGATED LIMBS OF A DEGAS dancer greeted Gabriel and Ménard outside I. M. Pei's iconic glass-and-steel pyramid. Wordlessly she escorted them across the immense Cour Napoléon and through a door reserved for museum staff. Two uniformed security guards waited on the other side. Neither seemed to notice when Gabriel set off the magnetometer.

"This way, please," said the woman, and led them along a corridor flooded with fluorescent light. After a walk of perhaps a half kilometer, they arrived at the entrance of the National Center for Research and Restoration, the world's most scientifically advanced facility for the conservation and authentication of art. Its inventory of cutting-edge technology included an electrostatic particle accelerator that allowed researchers to determine the chemical composition of an object without need of a potentially damaging sample.

The woman entered the passcode into the keypad, and Ménard led Gabriel inside. The cathedral-like laboratory was gripped by an air of sudden abandonment.

"I asked the director to close early so we could have a bit of privacy."

"To do what?"

"Look at a painting, Allon. What else?"

It was propped upon a laboratory easel, shrouded in black baize. Ménard removed the cloth to reveal a full-length portrait of a nude Lucretia thrusting a dagger into the center of her chest.

"Lucas Cranach the Elder?" asked Gabriel.

"That's what it says on the placard."

"Where did it come from?"

"Where do you think?"

"Galerie Georges Fleury?"

"I always heard you were good, Allon."

"And where did Monsieur Fleury find it?"

"A very old and prominent French collection," answered Ménard dubiously. "When Fleury showed it to a curator at the Louvre, he said it was probably the work of a later follower of Cranach. The curator had other ideas and brought it here to the center for evaluation. I'm sure you can guess the rest."

"The most advanced facility for the restoration and authentication of paintings in the world declared it to be the work of Lucas Cranach the Elder rather than a later follower."

Ménard nodded. "But wait, it gets better."

"How is that possible?"

"Because the president of the Louvre declared it a national treasure and paid nine and a half million euros to ensure it remain in France permanently."

"And now he's wondering whether it's a Cranach or crap?"

"In so many words." Ménard switched on a standing halogen lamp. "Would you mind having a look at it?"

Gabriel went to the nearest stainless-steel utility cart and after a moment of searching found a professional-grade magnifier. He used it to scrutinize the brushwork and craquelure.

Then he stepped away from the painting and placed a hand contemplatively to his chin.

"Well?" asked Ménard.

"It's the best Lucas Cranach the Elder I've ever seen."

"I'm relieved."

"Don't be," said Gabriel.

"Why not?"

"Because Lucas Cranach the Elder didn't paint it."

"How many more are there?"

"Three," answered Ménard. "They all emerged from Galerie Georges Fleury with a similar provenance and the same uncertain attribution. And the experts of the National Center for Research and Restoration, after careful evaluation, declared all three to be newly discovered works by the masters themselves."

"Anything good?"

"A Frans Hals, a Gentileschi, and the most delicious Van der Weyden you've ever laid eyes on."

"You're an admirer of Rogier?"

"Who isn't?"

"You'd be surprised."

They were sitting at a table at Café Marly, the Louvre's stylish restaurant. The declining sun had set fire to the glass panels of the pyramid. The light dazzled Gabriel's eyes.

"Are you formally trained?" he asked.

"As an art historian?" Ménard shook his head. "But four of my officers have advanced degrees from the Sorbonne. My background is in fraud and money laundering."

"Heaven knows, there's none of that in the art world."

Smiling, Ménard removed three photographs from a manila envelope—a Frans Hals, a Gentileschi, and an exquisite portrait by Rogier van der Weyden. "They were acquired by

155

the Louvre over a ten-year period. The Van der Weyden and the Cranach were purchased during the tenure of the current president. The Frans Hals and Gentileschi were acquired on his recommendation when he was the director of the paintings department."

"Which means his fingerprints are on all four."

"Evidently, he and Monsieur Fleury were quite close." Lowering his voice, Ménard added, "Close enough so that rumors are swirling."

"Kickbacks?"

Ménard shrugged but said nothing.

"Is there any truth to it?"

"I wouldn't know. You see, the Central Office for the Fight against Cultural Goods Trafficking has been ordered not to investigate the matter."

"What happens if the four paintings turn out to be forgeries?"

"The world's most advanced facility for the conservation and authentication of art has determined that they are genuine. Therefore, absent a videotaped confession on the part of the forger, the Louvre will stand by its findings."

"In that case, why did you ask me to come to Paris?"

Ménard drew another photograph from the envelope and placed it on the table.

28

CAFÉ MARLY

NOTHING ABOUT THE MAN DEPICTED in the photograph suggested he belonged anywhere near an Old Master art gallery in the elegant Eighth Arrondissement of Paris. Not the logoless cap pulled low over his brow. Or the wraparound sunglasses covering his eyes. Or the false beard adhered to his face. And certainly not the aluminum-sided Tumi suitcase, 52 by 77 by 28 centimeters, that he was wheeling along the pavements of the rue la Boétie. He was sturdy in manufacture, compact in size, confident in demeanor. An athlete in his day, perhaps a former soldier. He wore a drab overcoat against the cool early-spring weather, and leather gloves—presumably so that he would leave no fingerprints on the handle of the suitcase or in the taxi that was pulling away from the curb.

The time stamp on the photo was 13:39:35. Jacques Ménard handed Gabriel a second image, captured at the same instant. "The first shot came from the camera at the *tabac* across the street. The second one is from the Monoprix a couple of doors down."

"Nothing from your surveillance cameras?"

"This is Paris, Allon. Not London. We have about two thousand cameras in high-traffic tourist areas and around sensitive government buildings. But there are gaps in our coverage. The man in the photograph exploited them."

"Where did he get into the taxi?"

"A little commune east of Paris, in the Seine-en-Marne *département*. My colleagues at the Quai des Orfèvres haven't been able to determine how he got there."

"Did they manage to find the driver?"

"He's an immigrant from the Côte d'Ivoire. He says the customer spoke French like a native and paid the fare in cash."

"He checks out?"

"The driver?" Ménard nodded. "No problem there."

Gabriel lowered his gaze to the second photograph. Same time stamp, slightly different angle. A bit like his reworking of Modigliani's *Reclining Nude*, he thought. "How long did he stay inside?"

Ménard drew two more photographs from the envelope. The first showed the man leaving the gallery at 13:43:34. The second showed him sitting at a table at Brasserie Baroche. It was located about forty meters from the gallery, at the corner of the rue la Boétie and the rue de Ponthieu. The time stamp was 13:59:46. The assassin was looking down at the object in his hand. It was the remote unlocking device he had removed from Bruno Gilbert's desk.

"You and Madame Bancroft approached the gallery from the opposite direction." Ménard produced a photograph of Gabriel and Sarah's arrival, as if to prove his point. "Otherwise, you would have walked right past him."

"Where did he go next?"

"A taxi to the Sixteenth. A nice long walk in the Bois de Boulogne. And then, *poof*, he disappeared."

"Very professional."

"Our explosives experts were quite impressed with his bomb."

"Were they able to identify the phone he used to trigger the detonation?"

"They say not."

"I'm certain that Valerie Bérrangar's phone was inside that gallery."

"My colleagues at the Quai des Orfèvres have their doubts about that. Furthermore, they are inclined to accept the conclusion of the local gendarmerie that Valerie Bérrangar died as the result of an unfortunate road accident."

"I'm glad we cleared that up. What else has the Quai des Orfèvres concluded?"

"That the two men who tried to steal Monsieur Isherwood's attaché case were probably ordinary thieves."

"What about the men who searched his room at the Inter-Continental?"

"According to the hotel's head of security, they don't exist."

"Did anyone bother to check the internal video?"

"Apparently, it was erased."

"By whom?"

"The Quai des Orfèvres can't say."

"What *can* it say?" asked Gabriel.

Ménard drew a breath before answering. "It is the conclusion of the Quai des Orfèvres that the murder of Georges Fleury and the destruction of his gallery were the result of an embezzlement scheme by Bruno Gilbert and the man with the suitcase."

"Is there a shred of evidence to support this nonsense?"

"A few hours before you and Madame Bancroft arrived at

the gallery, someone transferred the entire balance of its accounts at Société Générale to the account of an anonymous shell company in the Channel Islands. The anonymous shell company then transferred it to the account of another anonymous shell company in the Bahamas, which in turn transferred it to the account of another anonymous shell company in the Cayman Islands. And then . . ."

"Poof?"

Ménard nodded.

"How much money are we talking about?"

"Twelve million euros. The Quai des Orfèvres is of the opinion the bomber wanted it all for himself."

"Clean and simple," said Gabriel. "And much more palatable than a scandal involving several million euros' worth of forgeries hanging on the walls of the world's most famous museum."

"Thirty-four million euros, to be exact. All of which had to be raised from outside sources. If it were to become public, the reputation of one of France's most treasured institutions would be severely tarnished."

"And we can't have that," said Gabriel.

"*Non*," agreed Ménard.

"But how do Sarah and I fit into this theory of theirs?"

"You and Madame Bancroft were never there, remember?"

Gabriel displayed the photograph of their arrival at the gallery. "And what happens if this becomes public?"

"Don't worry, Allon. No chance of that."

Gabriel placed the photograph atop the others. "How high does it go?"

"What's that?"

"The cover-up."

"Cover-up is an ugly word, Allon. So *américain*."

"*La conspiration du silence*."

"Much better."

"The director of the Police Nationale? The prefect?"

"Oh, no," said Ménard. "Much higher than that. The ministers of interior and culture are involved. Perhaps even *le Palais.*"

"You disapprove?"

"I am a loyal servant of the French Republic. But I have a conscience as well."

"I'd listen to your conscience."

"You never violated yours?"

"I was an intelligence operative," said Gabriel without elaboration.

"And I am a senior Police Nationale officer who is obligated to follow the orders of my superiors to the letter."

"And if you were to disobey?"

"I would be terminated. *Avec la guillotine.*" Ménard inclined his head toward the west. *"A la Place de la Concorde.*"

"How about a leak to a friendly reporter at *Le Monde*?"

"A leak of what, exactly? A story about a London art dealer who purchased a forged Van Dyck portrait from a Parisian art gallery and then sold it to an American investor?"

"Perhaps the leak could be a bit narrower in scope."

"How narrow?"

"A Cranach, a Hals, a Gentileschi, and the most delicious Van der Weyden you've ever laid eyes on."

"The scandal would be immense." Ménard paused. "And it wouldn't accomplish our shared goal."

"What might that be?" asked Gabriel warily.

"Putting the forger out of business." Ménard nudged the photographs a few millimeters closer to Gabriel. "And while you're at it, you might want to track down the man who tried to kill you and Madame Bancroft."

"How am I supposed to do that?"

Ménard smiled. "You're the former intelligence operative, Allon. I'm sure you'll be able to find him if you put your mind to it."

WHAT JACQUES MÉNARD PROPOSED NEXT WAS *UNE PETITE COL-laboration*, the terms of which he outlined for Gabriel while walking along the footpaths of the Jardin des Tuileries. Theirs was to be an entirely secret relationship, with Ménard playing the role of case officer and Gabriel acting as his informant and asset. It would be up to Ménard, and only Ménard, to determine how best to act upon their findings. If possible, he would resolve the situation quietly, without inflicting undue damage to the reputations of those who had been taken in.

"But if a few eggs need to be broken, well, so be it."

Gabriel made only a single demand in return, that Ménard make no attempt to observe his activities or monitor his movements. The Frenchman readily agreed to avert his eyes. He asked only that Gabriel avoid unnecessary violence, especially within the borders of the Republic.

"What if I'm able to find the man who tried to kill me?"

Ménard pulled his lips into a Gallic expression of indifference. "Do with him what you will. I'm not going to cry over a little spilled blood. Just make certain none of it splashes on me."

With that, the newfound partners went their separate ways—Ménard to the Quai des Orfèvres, Gabriel to the Gare de Lyon. As his train slithered from the station shortly after 5:00 p.m., he made two phone calls, one to his wife in Venice, the other to Sarah. Neither was pleased by his news or by his travel plans, Sarah especially. Nevertheless, after consulting with her husband on a separate line, she reluctantly agreed to Gabriel's request.

"How are you making the crossing?" she asked.

"The morning ferry from Marseilles."

"Peasant," she hissed, and rang off.

29

AT SEVEN FIFTEEN THE FOLLOWING evening, Christopher Keller was seated at a waterfront café in the Corsican port of Ajaccio, an empty wineglass on the table before him, a freshly lit Marlboro burning between the first and second fingers of his sledgehammer right hand. He wore a pale gray suit by Richard Anderson of Savile Row, an open-neck white dress shirt, and handmade oxford shoes. His hair was sun-bleached, his skin was taut and dark, his eyes were bright blue. The notch in the center of his thick chin looked as though it had been cleaved with a chisel. His mouth seemed permanently fixed in an ironic half-smile.

His waitress had presumed him to be a European from the mainland and had greeted him accordingly, with apathy bordering on contempt. But when he addressed her in fluent *corsu*, in the dialect of one from the northwestern corner of the island, she warmed to him instantly. They conversed in the Corsican way—about family and foreigners and the damage left by the springtime winds—and when he finished his first glass of rosé, she placed another before him without bothering to ask whether he wanted it.

It had done him no good, the second glass of wine, and neither had the cigarette, the fourth since his arrival at the café. It was a habit he had acquired while living under deep cover in Catholic West Belfast during one of the nastier periods of the Troubles. He now served in a clandestine operations unit of the Secret Intelligence Service sometimes referred to, incorrectly, as the Increment. His visit to Corsica, however, was entirely private in nature. A friend required the assistance of a man for whom Christopher had once worked—a certain Don Anton Orsati, patriarch of one of the island's most notorious families. As the friend's situation involved an attempt to kill Christopher's wife, he was only too happy to oblige him.

Just then the prow of an arriving Corsica Linea ferry nosed into the inner harbor, past the ramparts of the ancient citadel. Christopher slid a twenty-euro banknote beneath the empty wineglass and crossed the Quai de la République to the car park opposite the port's modern terminal. Behind the wheel of his battered Renault hatchback, he watched as the newly arrived passengers came spilling down the steps. Luggage-laden tourists. Returning Corsicans. Mainland French. A man of medium height and build dressed in a well-tailored Italian sport coat and gabardine trousers.

He tossed his overnight bag into the back of the Renault and dropped into the passenger seat. His emerald-green eyes stared with reproach at the cigarette burning in the ashtray.

"Must you?" he asked wearily.

"Yes," said Christopher as he started the engine. "I'm afraid I must."

THEY CROSSED THE BONY RIDGE OF HILLS NORTH OF AJACCIO, then followed the twisting road down to the Golfu di Liscia. The waves somersaulting onto the small crescent beach were unusually large, driven by an approaching *maestral*. It was how the Corsicans referred to the violent, unwelcome wind that blew in winter and springtime from the valleys of the Rhône.

"You arrived in the nick of time," said Christopher, his elbow protruding from the open window. "If you'd waited another day, you would have had the ferry ride from hell."

"It was bad enough as it was."

"Why didn't you fly from Paris?"

Gabriel removed the Beretta from its resting place at the small of his back and laid it on the center console.

"It's good to know that some things don't change." Christopher gave Gabriel a sideways glance. "You need a haircut. Otherwise, you're looking quite well for a man of your advanced age."

"It's the new me."

"What was wrong with the old you?"

"I had a bit of excess baggage I needed to lose."

"You and me both." Christopher turned his head to watch the waves rolling in from the west. "But at this moment, I am suddenly reminded of the man I used to be."

"The director of northern European sales for the Orsati Olive Oil Company?"

"Something like that."

"Does His Holiness know that you're back on the island?"

"We're expected for dinner. As you might imagine, excitement is high."

"Perhaps you should go alone."

"The last person who declined an invitation to dine with

Don Anton Orsati is somewhere out there." Christopher gestured toward the waters of the Mediterranean. "In a concrete coffin."

"Has he forgiven me for stealing you away from him?"

"He blames the British. As for forgiveness, Don Orsati is unfamiliar with the word."

"I'm not in a terribly forgiving mood myself," said Gabriel quietly.

"How do you think I feel?"

"Would you like to see a photograph of the man who tried to murder your wife?"

"Not while I'm driving," said Christopher. "I'm liable to kill us both."

BY THE TIME THEY REACHED THE TOWN OF PORTO, THE SUN was an orange disk balanced atop the dark rim of the sea. Christopher headed inland along a road lined with laricio pine and started the long climb into the mountains. The air smelled of the *macchia*, the dense undergrowth of gorse, briar, rockrose, rosemary, and lavender that covered much of the island's interior. The Corsicans seasoned their foods with the *macchia*, heated their homes with it in winter, and took refuge in it during times of war and vendetta. It had no eyes, went one often-repeated Corsican proverb, but the *macchia* saw everything.

They passed through the hamlets of Chidazzu and Marignana and arrived in the village of the Orsatis a few minutes after ten o'clock. It had been there, or so it was said, since the time of the Vandals, when people from the coasts took to the hills for safety. Beyond it, in a small valley of olive groves that produced the island's finest oil, was the don's sprawling estate. Two heavily armed men stood watch at the entrance.

They touched their distinctive Corsican caps respectfully as Christopher turned through the gate.

Several more bodyguards stood like statuary in the floodlit forecourt of the palatial villa. Gabriel left his Beretta in the Renault and followed Christopher up a flight of stone steps to Don Orsati's office. Entering, they found him seated at a large oaken table, before an open leather-bound ledger. As usual, he was wearing a bleached white shirt, loose-fitting cotton trousers, and a pair of dusty leather sandals that looked as though they had been purchased at the local outdoor market. At his elbow was a decorative bottle of Orsati olive oil—olive oil being the legitimate front through which the don laundered the profits of death.

Laboriously he rose to his feet. He was a large man by Corsican standards, well over six feet and broad through the back and shoulders, with coal-black hair, a dense mustache, and the brown-streaked eyes of a canine. They settled first on Christopher, inhospitably. He addressed him in *corsu*.

"I accept your apology."

"For what?"

"The wedding," answered the don. "Never in my life have I been so insulted. And from you of all people."

"My new employers might have found it odd if you had been there."

"How do you explain your eight-million-pound flat in Kensington?"

"It's a maisonette, actually. And it cost me eight and a half."

"All of which you earned working for me." The don frowned. "Did you at least receive my wedding gift?"

"The fifty thousand pounds' worth of Baccarat crystal? I sent you a rather lengthy handwritten note of gratitude."

Don Orsati turned to Gabriel and in French said, "I assume *you* were in attendance."

"Only because they needed someone to give away the bride."

"Is it true she's an American?"

"Barely."

"What does that mean?"

"She spent most of her childhood in England and France."

"Is that supposed to make me feel better?"

"At least she's not Italian," said Gabriel knowingly.

"At the end of many disasters," said Don Orsati, reciting a Corsican proverb, "there is always an Italian. But your lovely wife is definitely the exception to the rule."

"I'm confident you'll feel the same about Sarah."

"She's intelligent?"

"She has a PhD from Harvard."

"Attractive?"

"Stunningly beautiful."

"Is she good to her mother?"

"When they're on speaking terms."

Don Orsati looked at Christopher in horror. "What kind of woman doesn't speak to her mother?"

"They've had their ups and downs."

"I'd like to have a word with her about this as soon as possible."

"We're hoping to spend a week or two on the island this summer."

"He who lives on hope dies on shit."

"How eloquent, Don Orsati."

"Our proverbs," he said gravely, "are sacred and correct."

"And there's one for every occasion."

Don Orsati laid a granite hand gently upon Christopher's cheek. "Only the spoon knows the pot's sorrows."

"Mistakes are made even by priests at the altar."

"Better to have little than nothing."

"But he who has nothing will not eat."

"Shall we?" asked Don Orsati.

"Perhaps we should discuss our mutual friend's problem first," suggested Christopher.

"This business with the art gallery in Paris?"

"Yes."

"Is it true your beautiful American wife was involved?"

"I'm afraid so."

"In that case," said Don Orsati, "you have a problem, too."

30

VILLA ORSATI

GABRIEL LAID TWO PHOTOGRAPHS ON Don Orsati's desk. Same time stamp, slightly different angle. The don contemplated them as though they were Old Master paintings. He was a connoisseur of death and the men who dispensed it for a living.

"Do you recognize him?"

"I'm not sure his own mother would recognize him in that ridiculous disguise." The don glanced up at Christopher. "You would have never been caught dead looking like that."

"Never," he agreed. "One has to maintain certain standards."

Smiling, Don Orsati returned his gaze to the photographs. "Is there anything you can tell me about him?"

"The taxi driver said he spoke French like a native," answered Gabriel.

"The driver would have said the same about Christopher." The don's eyes narrowed. "He looks like a former soldier to me."

"I thought so, too. He certainly seems to know his way around explosive devices."

"Unless someone else built it for him. There are many fine bomb makers in this business of ours." Orsati once again turned to Christopher. "Wouldn't you agree?"

"Not as many as there used to be. But let's not dwell on the past."

"Perhaps we should," said Gabriel. Then he added quietly, "Just for a moment or two."

The don bunched his hands beneath his chin. "Is there something you wish to ask me?"

"There was a similar incident in Paris about twenty years ago. The gallery was owned by a Swiss dealer who was trading in paintings looted by the Nazis during the war. The bomb was delivered by a former British commando who—"

"I remember it well," interjected Don Orsati.

"As do I."

"And now you're wondering whether the man in these photographs works for my organization."

"I suppose I am."

Orsati's expression darkened. "You may rest assured, my old friend, that any man who offered me money to kill you would not leave this island alive."

"It's possible they thought I was someone else."

"With all due respect, I doubt that. For a man of the secret world, you have a rather famous face." Don Orsati looked at Christopher and exhaled heavily. "As for the former British commando, his fair hair, blue eyes, perfect English, and elite military training allowed him to fulfill contracts that were far beyond the skill level of my Corsican-born *taddunaghiu*. Needless to say, my business has suffered as a result of his decision to return home."

"Because you've turned down job offers where the risk of exposure was too high?"

"More than I can count." Orsati tapped the cover of his leather-bound ledger of death. "And my profits have fallen sharply as a result. Oh, don't get me wrong. I still get plenty of criminal and vengeance work. But my higher-profile clients have gone elsewhere."

"Anywhere in particular?"

"An exclusive new organization that offers white-glove concierge service to the sort of men who travel in private aircraft and dress like Christopher."

"Wealthy businessmen?"

"That's the rumor. This organization specializes in accidents and apparent suicides, the sort of thing the Orsati Olive Oil Company never bothered with. It is said that they're quite accomplished when it comes to staging crime scenes, perhaps because they employ several former police officers. They are also rumored to possess certain technical capabilities."

"Phone and computer hacking?"

The don shrugged his heavy shoulders. "This is your area of expertise. Not mine."

"Does this organization have a name?"

"If it does, I am not aware of it." Orsati looked down at the photographs. "The more important question is, who might have retained the services of this organization to kill you?"

"The leader of a sophisticated forgery network."

"Paintings?"

Gabriel nodded.

"He must be making a great deal of money."

"Thirty-four million euros from the Louvre alone."

"Perhaps I'm in the wrong line of work."

"I've often thought the same about myself, Don Orsati."

"What *is* your business these days?" he asked.

"I'm the director of the paintings department at the Tiepolo Restoration Company." Gabriel paused. "Currently on loan to the Police Nationale."

"A complicating factor, to say the least." Orsati made a face. "But please tell me how I can be of assistance to you and your friends from the French police."

"I'd like you to find the man in those photographs."

"And if I can?"

"I'll ask him a simple question."

"The name of the man who hired him to kill you?"

"You know what they say about assassinations, Don Orsati. The important thing is not who fired the shot but who paid for the bullet."

"Who was it who said that?" asked the don, intrigued.

"Eric Ambler."

"Wise words indeed. But in all likelihood, the man who tried to kill you in Paris doesn't know the client's name."

"Perhaps not, but he'll certainly be able to point me in the right direction. If nothing else he can provide valuable information on your competitor." Gabriel lowered his voice. "I would think that would be of interest to you, Don Orsati."

"One hand washes the other, and both hands wash the face."

"A very old Jewish proverb."

The don gave a dismissive wave of his enormous hand. "I'll put these photographs into circulation first thing in the morning. In the meantime, you and Christopher can spend a few days relaxing here on the island."

"Nothing like going on holiday with a man who once tried to kill you."

"If Christopher had actually *tried* to kill you, you would be dead."

"Just like the man who paid for the bullet," remarked Gabriel.

"Did Eric Ambler really say that about assassinations?"

"It's a line from *A Coffin for Dimitrios*."

"Interesting," said the don. "I never knew that Ambler was Corsican."

THE DISTINCTIVE SCENT OF THE *MACCHIA* ROSE FROM THE sumptuous feast that awaited them downstairs in Don Orsati's garden. They did not remain there long. Indeed, not five minutes after they sat down, the first knife-edged blast of the *maestral* arrived from the northwest. With the help of the don's bodyguards, they beat a hasty retreat to the dining room, and the meal resumed, though now it was accompanied by the howl and scrape of the much-despised intruder from across the sea.

It was after midnight when Don Orsati finally tossed his napkin onto the table, signaling that the evening had reached its end. Rising, Gabriel thanked the don for his hospitality and asked him to conduct his search with discretion. The don replied that he would use only his most trusted operatives. He was confident of a successful resolution.

"If it is your wish, I'll have my men bring him back here to Corsica. That way you won't have to get your hands dirty."

"It's never bothered me before. Besides," said Gabriel with a glance in Christopher's direction, "I have him."

"Christopher is a respectable English spy now. A man of distinction who resides at one of London's poshest addresses. He couldn't possibly get mixed up in a nasty business like this."

With that, Gabriel and Christopher went into the wind-blown night and climbed into the Renault. Leaving the estate, they headed eastward into the next valley. Christopher's secluded villa stood at the end of a dirt-and-gravel track lined on both sides by high walls of *macchia*. When the car's headlamps fell upon three ancient olive trees, he lifted his foot from the throttle and leaned anxiously over the steering wheel.

"Surely it's dead by now," said Gabriel.

"We'll know in a minute."

"You didn't ask the don?"

"And spoil an otherwise delightful evening?"

Just then a horned domestic goat, perhaps two hundred and fifty pounds in weight, emerged from the *macchia* and established itself in the center of the track. It had the markings of a palomino and a red beard, and was scarred from old battles. Its eyes shone defiantly in the glare of the headlamps.

"It has to be a different goat."

"No," answered Christopher as he applied the brakes. "Same bloody goat."

"Careful," said Gabriel. "I think it heard you."

The enormous goat, like the three ancient olive trees, belonged to Don Casabianca. It regarded the track as its private property and demanded tribute from those who traveled it. For Christopher, an Englishman with no Corsican blood in his veins, it harbored a particular resentment.

"Perhaps you could have a word with him on my behalf," he suggested.

"Our last conversation didn't go terribly well."

"What did you say to him?"

"It's possible I insulted his ancestry."

"On Corsica? What were you thinking?" Christopher inched the car forward, but the goat lowered its head and stood its ground. A tap of the horn was no more effective. "You won't mention any of this to Sarah, will you?"

"I wouldn't dream of it," vowed Gabriel.

Christopher slipped the car into PARK and exhaled heavily. Then he flung open his door and charged the goat in his bespoke Richard Anderson suit, flailing his arms like a madman. The tactic usually resulted in an immediate capitulation. But on this night, the first night of a *maestral*, the animal fought gamely for a minute or two before finally fleeing into the *macchia*. Fortunately, Gabriel captured the entire confrontation on video, which he immediately dispatched to Sarah in London. All in all, he thought, it was a fine start to their holiday on Corsica.

THE VILLA HAD A RED tile roof, a large blue swimming pool, and a broad terrace that received the sun in the morning and in the afternoon was shaded by laricio pine. When Gabriel rose the following morning, the granite paving stones were strewn with tree limbs and other assorted flora. In the well-appointed kitchen, he found Christopher, in hiking boots and a waterproof anorak, preparing café au lait on a butane camp stove. A local newscast issued from a battery-powered radio.

"We lost power around three a.m. The winds reached eighty miles per hour last night. They say it's the worst springtime *maestral* in living memory."

"Was there any mention of an incident involving an Englishman and an elderly goat?"

"Not yet. But thanks to you, it's all anyone's talking about in London." Christopher handed Gabriel a bowl of coffee. "Did you manage to get any sleep?"

"Not a wink. You?"

"I'm a combat veteran. I can sleep through anything."

"How long will it last?"

"Three days. Maybe four."

"I guess that rules out windsurfing."

"But not a hike up Monte Rotondo. Care to join me?"

"As tempting as that sounds," said Gabriel, "I think I'll spend the morning in front of a fire with a good book."

He carried his coffee into the comfortably furnished sitting room. Several hundred volumes of fiction and history lined the shelves, and upon the walls hung a modest collection of modern and Impressionist paintings. The most valuable piece was a Provençal landscape by Monet, which Christopher, through an intermediary, had acquired at Christie's in Paris. On that morning, however, Gabriel's eye was caught by the painting hanging next to it—another landscape, this one by Paul Cézanne.

He took down the painting and removed it from the frame. The stretcher appeared similar to those used by Cézanne in the mid-1880s, as did the canvas itself. There was no signature—not unusual, as Cézanne only signed works he considered truly finished—and the varnish was the color of nicotine. Otherwise, the painting appeared to be in good condition.

And yet . . .

Gabriel propped the painting in a rhombus of brilliant morning sunlight streaming through the French doors, then snapped a magnified detail image with his phone. With thumb and forefinger, he enlarged the photograph further and examined the brushwork. His reverie was so complete he failed to notice that Christopher, a gifted surveillance artist, had stolen into the room.

"May I ask what you're doing?"

"Looking for something to read," said Gabriel absently.

Christopher took down Ben McIntyre's biography of Kim Philby. "You might find this more interesting."

"Though somewhat incomplete." Gabriel looked down at the painting again.

"Is there a problem?"

"Where did you purchase it?"

"A gallery in Nice."

"Does the gallery have a name?"

"Galerie Edmond Toussaint."

"Did you seek the opinion of a professional?"

"Monsieur Toussaint gave me a certificate of authentication."

"May I see it? The provenance as well."

Christopher went upstairs to his study. Returning, he handed Gabriel a large business envelope, then slung a nylon rucksack over his powerful right shoulder.

"Last chance."

"Enjoy," said Gabriel as a gust of wind rattled the French doors. "And do give my best to your little caprine friend."

Steeling himself, Christopher went out and climbed into the Renault. A moment later Gabriel heard the blare of a car horn, followed by shouted threats of unspeakable violence. Laughing, he removed the contents of the envelope.

"Idiot," he said after a moment, to no one but himself.

THE *MAESTRAL* EASED AROUND ELEVEN, BUT BY LATE AFTERNOON it was blowing hard enough to loosen several tiles from Christopher's roof. He returned home at dusk and proudly displayed for Gabriel the 136-kilometer-per-hour wind reading he had taken on Monte Rotondo's northern face. Gabriel reciprocated by disclosing his concerns over the authenticity of the Cézanne, a painting that Christopher had purchased under a false French identity while working as a professional assassin.

"Thus leaving you with no legal recourse. Or moral recourse, for that matter."

"Perhaps one or two of the don's most terrifying men should have a word with Monsieur Toussaint on my behalf."

"Perhaps," countered Gabriel, "you should forget I ever said anything, and let it go."

The wind blew without relent the following day and the day after that as well. Gabriel sheltered in place at the villa while Christopher flung himself against two more mountains—first Renoso, then d'Oro, where his pocket anemometer recorded the winds at 141 kilometers per hour. That evening they dined at Villa Orsati. Over coffee, the don acknowledged that his operatives had no leads on the identity or whereabouts of the man who had carried the bomb into Galerie Georges Fleury. He then chastised Christopher over the tenor and tone of his recent confrontations with Don Casabianca's goat.

"He called me this morning. He's very upset."

"The don or the goat?"

"It's no laughing matter, Christopher."

"How does Don Casabianca even know that things have taken a turn for the worse?"

"The news has spread like wildfire."

"I certainly didn't mention it to anyone."

"It must have been the *macchia*," said Gabriel, and repeated the ancient proverb regarding the ability of the aromatic vegetation to see everything. At this, the don nodded his head solemnly in agreement. It was, he concluded, the only possible explanation.

The wind raged for the remainder of that night, but by dawn it was a memory. Gabriel spent the morning helping Christopher repair the damage to the roof and clear the debris from the terrace and the pool. Then, in late afternoon, he drove into the village. It was a cluster of sandstone-colored cottages huddled around the bell tower of a church, before which lay a dusty square. Several men in newly pressed white shirts were playing a closely fought game of *pétanque*. Once they might have regarded Gabriel with suspicion—or pointed at him in the Corsican way, with their first and fourth fingers, to ward off the effects of the *occhju*, the evil eye. Now they greeted him warmly, as he was known throughout the village as a friend of Don Orsati and the Englishman named Christopher, who, thank goodness, had returned to the island after a prolonged absence.

"Is it true he's married?" asked one of the men.

"That's the rumor."

"Has he killed that goat?" asked another.

"Not yet. But it's only a matter of time."

"Perhaps you can talk some sense into him."

"I've tried. But I'm afraid they've reached the point of no return."

The men insisted that Gabriel join the game, as they were in need of another player. Declining, he repaired to the café in the far corner of the square for a glass of Corsican rosé. As the church bells tolled five o'clock, a young child, a girl of seven or eight, knocked on the door of the crooked little house next to the rectory. It opened a few inches, and a small pale hand appeared, clutching a slip of blue paper. The young girl carried it to the café and placed it on Gabriel's table. She bore an uncanny resemblance to Irene.

"What is your name?" he asked.

"Danielle."

Of course it was, he thought. "Would you like an ice cream?"

The child sat down and pushed the blue slip of paper across the tabletop. "Aren't you going to read it?"

"I don't need to."

"Why not?"

"I know what it says."

"How?"

"I have powers, too."

"Not like hers," said the child.

No, agreed Gabriel. Not like hers.

32

HAUTE-CORSE

THE HAND THE OLD WOMAN offered Gabriel in greeting was warm and weightless. He held it gently, as though it were a cage bird.

"You've been hiding from me," she said.

"Not from you," he answered. "From the *maestral*."

"I've always liked the wind." Confidingly she added, "It's good for business."

The old woman was a *signadora*. The Corsicans believed that she possessed the power to heal those infected by the *occhju*. Gabriel had once suspected that she was nothing more than a conjurer and a clever teller of fortunes, but that was no longer the case.

She placed her hand against his cheek. "You're burning with fever."

"You always say that."

"That's because you always feel as though you are on fire." Her hand moved to his upper chest. The left side, slightly above his heart. "This is where the madwoman's bullet entered you."

"Did Christopher tell you that?"

"I haven't spoken to Christopher since his return." She lifted the front of Gabriel's dress shirt and examined the scar. "You were dead for several minutes, were you not?"

"Two or three."

She frowned. "Why do you bother trying to lie to me?"

"Because I prefer not to dwell on the fact that I was dead for ten minutes." Gabriel held up the blue slip of paper. "Where did you find that child?"

"Danielle? Why do you ask?"

"She reminds me of someone."

"Your daughter?"

"How is it possible that you know what she looks like?"

"Perhaps you're merely seeing what you want to see."

"Don't speak to me in riddles."

"You named the child Irene after your mother. Every time she looks at you, you see your mother's face and the numbers that were written on her arm in the camp named for the trees."

"Someday you're going to have to show me how you do that."

"It is a gift from God." She released the front of his shirt and contemplated him with her bottomless black eyes. The face in which they were set was as white as baker's flour. "You are suffering from the *occhju*. It is as plain as day."

"I must have contracted it from Don Casabianca's goat."

"He is a demon."

"Tell me about it."

"I'm not joking. The animal is possessed. Stay away from it."

The *signadora* drew him into the parlor of her tiny home. On the small circular table was a candle, a shallow plate of water, and a vessel of olive oil. They were the tools of her trade.

She lit the candle and sat down in her usual place. Gabriel, after a moment's hesitation, joined her.

"There's no such thing as the evil eye, you know. It's just a superstition that was prevalent among the ancient people of the Mediterranean."

"You are an ancient person of the Mediterranean as well."

"As ancient as it gets," he agreed.

"You were born in the Galilee, not far from the town where Jesus lived. Most of your ancestors were killed by the Romans during the siege of Jerusalem, but a few survived and made their way to Europe." She nudged the vessel of olive oil across the tabletop. "Proceed."

Gabriel returned the vessel to the woman's side of the table. "You first."

"You want me to prove that it's not a trick?"

"Yes."

The old woman dipped her forefinger into the oil. Then she held it over the plate and allowed three drops to fall into the water. They coalesced into a single gobbet.

"Now you."

Gabriel performed the same ritual. This time the oil shattered into a thousand droplets, and soon there was no trace of it.

"*Occhju*," whispered the old woman.

"Magic and misdirection," said Gabriel in reply.

Smiling, she asked, "How's your hand?"

"Which one?"

"The one you injured when you attacked the man who works for the one-eyed creature."

"He shouldn't have followed me."

"Make your peace with him," said the *signadora*. "He will help you find the woman."

"What woman?"

"The Spanish woman."

"I'm looking for a man."

"The one who tried to kill you in the art gallery?"

"Yes."

"Don Orsati hasn't been able to find him. But don't worry, the Spanish woman will lead you to the one you seek. Don Orsati knows of her."

"How?"

"It is not in my power to tell you that."

Without another word, the *signadora* took hold of Gabriel's hand and engaged in the familiar ritual. She recited the words of an ancient Corsican prayer. She wept as the evil passed from his body into hers. She closed her eyes and fell into a deep sleep. When at last she awoke, she instructed Gabriel to repeat the trial of the oil and the water. This time the oil coalesced into a single drop.

"Now you," he said.

The old woman sighed and did as he asked. The oil shattered.

"Just like the door of the art gallery," she said. "Don't worry, the *occhju* won't stay within me for long."

Gabriel laid several banknotes on the table. "Is there anything else you can tell me?"

"Paint four pictures," said the old woman. "And she will come for you."

"Is that all?"

"No," she said. "You didn't contract the *occhju* from Don Casabianca's goat."

Upon his return to the villa, Gabriel informed Christopher that Don Orsati's inquiries would bear no fruit and that Don Casabianca's goat was the devil incarnate. Christopher questioned the accuracy of neither assertion, as both had come from the mouth of the *signadora*. He nevertheless advised against telling the don to preemptively break off his search. It was far better, he said, to allow the wheel to spin until the ball had dropped.

"Unless the wheel continues to spin for another week or two."

"Trust me, it won't."

"There's more, I'm afraid."

Gabriel explained the old woman's prophecy regarding the Spanish woman.

"Did she say how the don knows her?"

"She said it wasn't in her power to tell me."

"Or so she claimed. It's her version of 'no comment.'"

"Did you ever run across a Spanish woman when you were working for the don?"

"One or two," said Christopher beneath his breath.

"How should we raise it with him?"

"With the utmost care. His Holiness doesn't like anyone rummaging through his past. Especially the *signadora*."

And so it was that two nights later, while seated beneath a cloud-draped moon in the garden of Villa Orsati, Gabriel feigned incredulity when told that the don's operatives had failed to locate the man who had delivered the expertly constructed bomb to Galerie Fleury. Then, after a moment or two of companionable silence, he cautiously asked Don Orsati whether he had ever encountered a Spanish woman who might have ties to the criminal art world.

The don's brown-streaked eyes narrowed with suspicion. "When did you speak to her?"

"The Spanish woman?"

"The *signadora*."

"I thought the *macchia* sees all."

"Do you want to know about the Spanish woman or not?"

"It was two days ago," admitted Gabriel.

"I suppose she also knew that I wouldn't be able to find the man you're looking for."

"I wanted to tell you, but Christopher said it would be a mistake."

"Did he?" Don Orsati glared at Christopher before turning once more to Gabriel. "Several years ago, perhaps five or six, a woman came to see me. She was from Roussillon, up in the Lubéron. Late thirties, quite composed. One had the impression she was comfortable in the presence of criminals."

"Name?"

"Françoise Vionnet."

"Real?"

Don Orsati nodded.

"What was her story?"

"The man she lived with disappeared one afternoon while walking in the countryside outside Aix-en-Provence. The police found his body a few weeks later near Mont Ventoux. He'd been shot twice in the back of the head."

"Vengeance was required?"

The don nodded.

"I assume you agreed to provide it."

"Money doesn't come from singing, my friend." It was one of the don's most cherished Corsican proverbs and the unofficial slogan of the Orsati Olive Oil Company. "Money is earned by accepting and then fulfilling contracts."

"What was the name on this one?"

"Miranda Álvarez. The Vionnet woman was confident it was an alias. She was able to give us a physical description and a profession, but little else."

"Why don't we start with her appearance."

"Tall, dark hair, very beautiful."

"Age?"

"At the time, she was in her mid-thirties."

"And her profession?"

"She was an art dealer."

"Based where?"

"Maybe Barcelona." The don shrugged his heavy shoulders. "Maybe Madrid."

"That isn't much to go on."

"I've accepted contracts based on less, provided the client agrees to confirm the target's identity once the target is located."

"Thus avoiding needless bloodshed."

"In a business like mine," said Don Orsati, "mistakes are permanent."

"I take it you were never able to find her."

The don shook his head. "Françoise Vionnet begged me to continue looking, but I told her there was no point. I refunded her money, excluding the deposit and the expenses for the search, and we went our separate ways."

"Did she ever tell you why her partner was murdered?"

"Apparently, it was a business dispute."

"He was an art dealer as well?"

"A painter, actually. Not a successful one, mind you. But she spoke highly of his work."

"Do you happen to remember his name?"

"Lucien Marchand."

"And where might Christopher and I find Françoise Vionnet?"

"The Chemin de Joucas in Roussillon. If you like, I can get you the address."

"If it's not too much trouble."

"Not at all."

It was upstairs in his office, said Don Orsati. In his leather-bound ledger of death.

33

LE LUBÉRON

THE NEXT MAINLAND-BOUND CAR FERRY departed Ajaccio at half past eight the following evening and arrived in Marseilles shortly after dawn. Gabriel and Christopher, having passed the night in adjoining cabins, rolled into the port in a rented Peugeot and made their way to the A7 Autoroute. They headed north through Salon-de-Provence to Cavaillon, then followed a caravan of tour buses into the Lubéron. The honey-colored houses of Gordes, perched on a limestone hilltop overlooking the valley, sparkled in the crystalline morning light.

"That's where Marc Chagall used to live," said Christopher.

"In an old girls' school on the rue de la Fontaine Basse. He and his wife, Bella, were reluctant to leave after the German invasion. They finally fled to the United States in 1941 with the help of the journalist and academic Varian Fry and the Emergency Rescue Committee."

"I was just trying to make conversation."

"Perhaps we should enjoy the scenery instead."

Christopher lit a Marlboro. "Have you given any thought to how you're going to make your approach?"

"To Françoise Vionnet? I thought I'd start with *bonjour* and hope for the best."

"How cunning."

"Maybe I'll tell her I was sent by a mystical Corsican woman who cured me of the *occhju*. Or better yet, I'll say that I'm a friend of the Corsican organized crime figure she hired to kill a Spanish art dealer."

"That should win her over."

"How much do you suppose the don charged her?" asked Gabriel.

"For a job like that? Not much."

"What does that mean?"

"Maybe a hundred thousand."

"How much was the contract on my life?"

"Seven figures."

"I'm flattered. And Anna?"

"You two were part of a package deal."

"Is there a discount for that sort of thing?"

"The don is unfamiliar with that word as well. But it warms my heart that you two have rekindled your relationship after all these years."

"There was no kindling involved. And we don't have a relationship."

"Did you or did you not borrow a million euros from her to buy that fake Cuyp riverscape?"

"The money was repaid three days later."

"By my wife," said Christopher. "As for your approach to the aforementioned Françoise, I suggest you fly a false flag. In my experience, respectable residents of the Lubéron don't hand over briefcases filled with cash to someone like His Holiness Don Anton Orsati."

"Are you suggesting that Françoise Vionnet and Lucien Marchand, an unknown painter with no established sales record, might have been involved in a criminal enterprise of some sort?"

"I'd bet my Cézanne on it, too."

"You don't own a Cézanne."

They rounded a bend in the road, and the Lubéron Valley revealed itself as a patchwork quilt of vineyards and orchards and fields ablaze with wildflowers. The brick-colored buildings of Roussillon's ancient center occupied a ridge of ocher-rich clay on the southern rim. Christopher approached the village along the narrow Chemin de Joucas and eased onto the grassy verge at the point where the slope of the hill met the valley floor. On one side of the road was newly plowed cropland. On the other, partially hidden from view behind an unkempt wall of vegetation, was a small single-level villa. From somewhere came the muted baritone bark of a large dog.

"But of course," murmured Gabriel.

"Better a canine than a caprine."

"Caprines don't bite."

"Wherever did you get an idea like that?" asked Christopher, and turned into the drive. Instantly a barrel-shaped dog with the jaws of a Rottweiler shot from the front door. Next there appeared a languorous barefoot girl in her early twenties. She wore leggings and a wrinkled cotton pullover. Her light brown hair swung long and loose in the Provençal light.

"She's too young," said Gabriel.

"What about that one?" asked Christopher as an older version of the girl emerged from the villa.

"She looks like a Françoise to me."

"I agree. But how are you going to play it?"

"I'm going to wait for one of them to get that dog under control."

"And then?"

"I thought I'd start with *bonjour* and hope for the best."

"Brilliant," said Christopher.

BY THE TIME GABRIEL OPENED HIS DOOR AND EXTENDED HIS hand, he was once again, in aspect and accent, Ludwig Ziegler of Berlin. But this version of Herr Ziegler was not an art adviser with a single famous client. He was a runner—a dealer without a gallery or inventory—who specialized in finding works by undervalued contemporary painters and bringing them to market. He claimed to have heard about Lucien Marchand through a contact and was intrigued by the terrible story of his disappearance and death. He introduced Christopher as Benjamin Reckless, his London representative.

"Reckless?" asked Françoise Vionnet skeptically.

"It's an old English name," explained Christopher.

"You speak French like a native."

"My mother was French."

In the villa's rustic kitchen, they all four gathered around a pot of tar-black coffee and a pitcher of steamed milk. Françoise Vionnet and the barefoot girl each lit a cigarette from the same packet of Gitanes. They had the same drowsy, heavy-lidded eyes. Beneath the girl's were puffy half-moons of unlined flesh.

"Her name is Chloé," said Françoise Vionnet, as though the girl were incapable of speech. "Her father was a struggling sculptor from Lacoste who walked out on us not long after she was born. Fortunately, Lucien agreed to take us in. We were hardly a traditional family, but we were happy. Chloé was seventeen when Lucien was murdered. His death was very hard on her. He was the only father she ever knew."

The girl yawned and stretched elaborately and then

withdrew. A moment later came the sound of a slender female body entering the water of a swimming pool. Frowning, Françoise Vionnet crushed out her cigarette.

"You must excuse my daughter's behavior. I wanted to move to Paris after Lucien's death, but Chloé refused to leave the Lubéron. It was a terrible mistake to raise her here."

"It's very beautiful," said Gabriel in Herr Ziegler's German-accented French.

"*Oui*," said Françoise Vionnet. "The tourists and rich foreigners adore Provence. Especially the English," she added, glancing at Christopher. "But for girls like Chloé who lack a university education or ambition, the Lubéron can be a trap with no escape. She spends her summers waiting tables at a restaurant in the *centre ville* and her winters working at a hotel in Chamonix."

"And you?" asked Gabriel.

She shrugged. "I make do with the modest estate that Lucien was able to leave me."

"You were married?"

"A civil solidarity pact. The French equivalent of a common-law marriage. Chloé and I inherited the villa after Lucien was murdered. And his paintings, of course." She rose suddenly. "Would you like to see some of them?"

"I'd love nothing more."

They filed into the sitting room. Several unframed paintings—Surrealist, Cubist, Abstract Expressionist—hung on the walls. They lacked originality but were competently executed.

"Where was he trained?" asked Gabriel.

"Beaux-Arts de Paris."

"It shows."

"Lucien was an excellent draftsman," said Françoise Vionnet. "But unfortunately he was never terribly successful. He made ends meet painting copies."

"I beg your pardon?"

"Lucien painted copies of Impressionist paintings and sold them in the gift shops of the Lubéron. He also worked for a company that sold hand-painted copies online. He was paid more for those, but not much. Maybe twenty-five euros. He produced them very quickly. He could paint a Monet in fifteen or twenty minutes."

"Do you happen to have one?"

"*Non.* Lucien found the work very embarrassing. Once the paintings were dry, he delivered them to his clients."

Outside, the girl extracted herself from the pool and stretched her body on a chaise longue. Whether she was clothed or not Gabriel could not say, for he was contemplating what was clearly the finest painting in the room. It bore a distinct resemblance to a work called *Les Amoureux aux Coquelicots*, by the French-Russian artist who had lived for a time on the rue de la Fontaine Basse in Gordes. Not an exact copy, more a pastiche. The original was signed in the bottom-right corner. Lucien Marchand's version had no signature at all.

"He was a great admirer of Chagall," said Françoise Vionnet.

"As am I. And if I didn't know better, I would have thought that Chagall painted it himself." Gabriel paused. "Or perhaps that was the point."

"Lucien painted his Chagalls purely for pleasure. That's why there's no signature."

"I'm prepared to make you a generous offer for it."

"I'm afraid it's not for sale, Monsieur Ziegler."

"May I ask why not?"

"Sentimental reasons. It was the last painting Lucien completed."

"Forgive me, Madame Vionnet. But I can't recall the date of his death."

"It was the seventeenth of September."

"Five years ago?"

"*Oui.*"

"That's odd."

"Why, monsieur?"

"Because this painting appears much older than that. In fact, it looks to me as though it was painted in the late nineteen forties."

"Lucien used special techniques to make his paintings appear older than they really were."

Gabriel took down the painting from the wall and turned it over. The canvas was at least a half-century old, as was the stretcher. The upper horizontal bar was stamped with a *6* and an *F*. On the center bar were the remnants of an old adhesive sticker.

"And did Lucien have special techniques for aging his canvases and stretchers as well? Or did he have a ready supplier of worthless old paintings?"

Françoise Vionnet regarded Gabriel calmly with her heavy-lidded eyes. "Get out of my house," she said through gritted teeth. "Or I'll sic the dog on you."

"If that dog comes anywhere near me, I'm going to shoot it. And then I'm going to call the French police and tell them that you and your daughter are living off the money that Lucien Marchand earned forging paintings."

Her full lips curled into a slight smile. Evidently, she didn't frighten easily. "Who are you?"

"You wouldn't believe me if I told you."

She looked at Christopher. "And him?"

"He's anything but reckless."

"What do you want?"

"I want you to help me find the woman who called herself Miranda Álvarez. I'd also like you to give me any additional forgeries you have lying around, along with a complete list of every fake painting Lucien ever sold."

"That's impossible."

"Why?"

"There are far too many."

"Who handled them?"

"Lucien sold most of his forgeries to a dealer in Nice."

"Does the dealer have a name?"

"Edmond Toussaint."

Gabriel looked at Christopher. "I guess that settles that."

WHY DIDN'T YOU SIMPLY TELL me the truth from the beginning, Monsieur Allon?"

"I was afraid you would skip the pleasantries and go straight to the part about setting the dog on me."

"Would you have really shot it?"

"*Non*," replied Gabriel. "Mr. Reckless would have shot it for me."

Françoise Vionnet eyed Christopher down her freshly lit Gitane, then nodded her head slowly in agreement. They had returned to the table in the rustic kitchen, though now it was a chilled bottle of Bandol rosé around which they were gathered.

"How much of the original story was true?" asked Gabriel.

"Most of it."

"Where did the fiction begin?"

"Chloé doesn't spend the winter in Chamonix."

"Where does she go?"

"Saint-Barthélemy."

"Does she work there?"

"Chloé?" She made a face. "Not a day in her life. We have a villa in Lorient."

"Lucien must have painted a lot of twenty-five-euro copies to afford a place like that."

"He never stopped painting them, you know. He needed some form of legitimate income."

"When did the fakes start?"

"A couple of years after Chloé and I moved in."

"It was your idea?"

"More or less."

"Which is it?"

"It was obvious that Lucien's copies were very good," she answered. "One day I asked him whether he thought he could fool anyone. A week later he showed me his first forgery. A reworking of *Place du village* by the French Cubist Georges Valmier."

"What did you do with it?"

She took it to Paris and hung it on the wall of a friend's chic apartment in the Sixth. Then she rang one of the auction houses—which one, she refused to say—and the auction house sent over a so-called expert to have a look at it. The expert asked a couple of questions about the painting's provenance, declared it authentic, and gave Françoise forty thousand euros. She gave two thousand to her chic friend from Paris and the rest to Lucien. They used part of the money to enlarge the villa's swimming pool and renovate the little outbuilding that Lucien used as his atelier. The rest they deposited in a bank account at Credit Suisse in Geneva.

"As for the reworking of *Place du village* by Georges Valmier, it recently sold for nine hundred thousand dollars at auction in New York. Which means the auction house made more in fees and commissions than Lucien was paid for his original painting. Who is the criminal, Monsieur Allon? Did the auction house *really* not realize that it was selling a fake? How is this possible?"

She sold several more forgeries to the same Paris auction house—all lesser-known Cubists and Surrealists, all for five figures—and in the winter of 2004 she sold a Matisse to Galerie Edmond Toussaint. The dealer purchased a second Matisse from Françoise a few months later, followed in short order by a Gauguin, a Monet, and a Cézanne landscape of Mont Sainte-Victoire. It was then that Toussaint informed Françoise that all five of the paintings she had brought him were forgeries.

"Which is why he had purchased them in the first place," said Gabriel.

"*Oui.* Monsieur Toussaint wanted an exclusive arrangement. No more independent sales through the Paris auction houses or other dealers. He said it was far too risky. He promised to take very good care of Lucien financially."

"Did he?"

"Lucien had no complaints."

"How much money did he earn?"

"Over the lifetime of the deal?" Françoise Vionnet shrugged. "Six or seven million."

"Spare me," said Gabriel.

"Maybe it was in the neighborhood of thirty million."

"Which side of the neighborhood? The north or the south?"

"The north," said Françoise Vionnet. "Definitely the north."

"And Monsieur Toussaint? What was his take?"

"Two hundred million, at least."

"So Lucien got screwed."

"That's what the Spanish woman told him."

"Miranda Álvarez?"

"That's what she called herself."

"Where did you meet with her?"

"Here in Roussillon. She sat in the same chair where you're sitting now."

"She was a dealer?"

"Of some sort. She was quite guarded in how she described herself."

"What did she want?"

"She wanted Lucien to work for her instead of Toussaint."

"How did she know that Lucien was forging paintings?"

"She refused to say. But it was obvious she knew her way around the dirty side of the business. She said Toussaint was selling more forgeries than the art market could absorb, that it was only a matter of time before Lucien and I were arrested. She said she was part of a sophisticated network that knew how to sell forgeries without getting caught. She promised to pay us twice what Toussaint was paying us."

"How did Lucien react?"

"He was intrigued."

"And you?"

"Less so."

"But you agreed to consider her offer?"

"I asked her to come back in three days."

"And when she did?"

"I told her we had a deal. She gave us a million euros in cash and said she would be in touch."

"When did the deal fall apart?"

"After I told Toussaint that we were leaving him."

"How much did he pay you to stay?"

"Two million."

"I assume you banked the million the Spanish woman gave you."

"*Oui*. And six months later Lucien was dead. He was working on another Cézanne when he was killed. The police never found it."

"I don't suppose you told them that Lucien was an art forger or that he had recently received a visit from a mysterious Spanish woman who called herself Miranda Álvarez."

"If I had, I would have implicated myself."

"How did you explain the thirty million at Credit Suisse in Geneva?"

"It was thirty-four million at the time," admitted Françoise Vionnet. "And the police never discovered it."

"What about the villa in Saint-Barthélemy?"

"It's owned by a shell company registered in the Bahamas. Chloé and I keep a low profile here in the Lubéron. But when we go to the island . . ."

"You live well on the proceeds of Lucien's forgeries."

She lit another Gitane but said nothing.

"How many are left?" asked Gabriel.

"Fakes?" She blew a stream of smoke toward the ceiling. "Only the Chagall. The others are all gone."

Gabriel laid his phone on the table. "How many, Françoise?"

OUTSIDE, CHLOÉ WAS STRETCHED LIKE A MODIGLIANI NUDE across the sunbaked paving stones next to the pool. "If only someone would pay her for doing that," said her mother judgmentally. "Chloé would be the richest woman in France."

"You were a front woman for a forger," said Gabriel. "You didn't exactly set a good example."

She led them along a gravel footpath toward Lucien's atelier. It was a small building, ocher in color, with a tile roof. The door was secured with a padlock, as were the wooden shutters.

"Someone tried to break in not long after Lucien was murdered. That's when I got the dog."

She unlocked the door and led Gabriel and Christopher

inside. The dank air smelled of canvas and dust and linseed oil. Beneath an overhead skylight stood an ancient studio easel and a cluttered old worktable with shelves and drawers for supplies. The paintings were leaning against the walls, perhaps twenty to a row.

"Is this all of them?" asked Gabriel.

Françoise Vionnet nodded.

"No warehouse or storage unit somewhere?"

"*Non*. Everything is here."

She walked over to the nearest queue of paintings and leafed through them as though they were vinyl record albums. Reluctantly she extracted one and displayed it for Gabriel.

"Fernand Léger."

"You have a good eye, Monsieur Allon."

She moved to the next row. From it she unearthed a pastiche of *Houses at L'Estaque* by Georges Braque. The next row of paintings produced a Picasso and another Léger.

"Surely the police searched this place after the murder," said Gabriel.

"Yes, of course. But fortunately they sent Inspector Clouseau." She removed another painting, a version of *Composition in Blue* by Roger Bissière. "I've always liked this one. Do I really have to give it up?"

"Keep going."

The next painting was a Matisse. It was followed by a Monet, a Cézanne, a Dufy, and, finally, by a second Chagall.

"Is that all of them?"

She nodded.

"Do you know what's going to happen if I find any more?"

Sighing, she produced two additional paintings—a second Matisse and a stunning André Derain. Twelve in all, with an estimated market value of more than €200 million. Gabriel photographed them with his phone, along with the Chagall in the sitting room. Then he removed all thirteen canvases from their stretchers and piled them on the grate. Christopher handed over his gold Dunhill lighter.

"Please don't," said Françoise Vionnet.

"Would you rather I give them to the French police?" Gabriel ignited the lighter and touched the flame to the canvases. "I suppose you'll have to make do with the thirty-four million."

"There's only twenty-five left."

"And you can keep it so long as you never tell anyone that I was here."

Françoise Vionnet saw Gabriel and Christopher to the door and waited until they were nearly inside the Renault before unleashing the dog. They made their escape without resorting to violence.

"Tell me something," said Christopher as they sped across the picturesque valley. "When did you realize that you were going to do that Herr Ziegler routine?"

"It came to me while you were needlessly lecturing me about the likelihood that Françoise Vionnet might have been Lucien's front woman."

"I have to say, it was one of your better performances. You did, however, make one serious tactical mistake."

"What's that?"

"You burned the bloody evidence."

"Not all of it."

"The Cézanne?"

"Idiot," murmured Gabriel.

35

LE TRAIN BLEU

THEY JETTISONED THE RENTED PEUGEOT in Marseilles and caught the two o'clock TGV from the Gare Saint-Charles to Paris. An hour before they were due to arrive, Gabriel dialed the number for Antiquités Scientifiques on the rue de Miromesnil. Receiving no answer, he checked the time, then rang a nearby shop that sold antique glassware and figurines. Its proprietor, a woman named Angélique Brossard, seemed slightly out of breath when she picked up the phone. She offered no expression of surprise or evasiveness when Gabriel asked to speak to Maurice Durand. Their longtime *cinq à sept* was one of the worst-kept secrets in the Eighth Arrondissement.

"Enjoying yourself?" asked Gabriel when Durand came on the line.

"I was," answered the Frenchman. "I hope this is important."

"I was wondering whether you might be free for a drink at, say, half past five."

"I believe I'm having open-heart surgery then. Let me check my schedule."

"Meet me at Le Train Bleu."

"If you insist."

The iconic Paris restaurant, with its garish gilded mirrors and painted ceilings, overlooked the ticket hall of the Gare de Lyon. At five thirty Maurice Durand was seated in a plush royal-blue chair in the lounge area before an open bottle of champagne. Rising, he hesitantly shook Christopher's hand.

"If it isn't my old friend Monsieur Bartholomew. Still caring for widows and orphans, or have you managed to find honest work?" Durand turned to Gabriel. "And what brings you back to Paris, Monsieur Allon? Another bombing in the works?" He smiled. "That's certainly *one* way to put a dirty gallery out of business."

Gabriel sat down and handed Durand his mobile phone. The diminutive Frenchman slipped on a pair of gold half-moon reading glasses and contemplated the screen. "A rather interesting reinterpretation of Braque's *Houses at L'Estaque*."

"Swipe to the next one."

Durand did as he was told. "Roger Bissière."

"Keep going."

Durand dragged the tip of his forefinger horizontally across the screen and smiled. "I've always had a soft spot for Fernand Léger. He was one of my first."

"How about the next one?"

"My old friend Picasso. Quite a good one, in fact."

"The Chagalls are better. The Monet, the Cézanne, and the two Matisses aren't bad, either."

"Where did you find them?"

"In Roussillon," answered Gabriel. "In the atelier of a failed painter named—"

"Lucien Marchand?"

"You knew him?"

"Lucien and I weren't acquainted, but I knew of his work."

"How?"

"We both did business with the same gallery in Nice."

"Galerie Edmond Toussaint?"

"*Oui.* Quite possibly the dirtiest art gallery in France, if not the Western world. Only a fool would buy a painting there."

Gabriel exchanged a glance with Christopher before returning his gaze to Durand. "I thought you dealt directly with collectors."

"For the most part. But I occasionally filled special orders for Monsieur Toussaint. He did a brisk trade in stolen art, but Lucien Marchand was his golden goose."

"Which is why Toussaint fought so hard to keep Lucien when the front woman from a rival forgery network tried to steal him away."

Durand smiled at Gabriel over the rim of his champagne glass. "You're getting rather good at this, Monsieur Allon. Soon you will no longer require my help."

"Who is she, Maurice?"

"Miranda Álvarez? That depends on whom you ask. Apparently, she's something of a chameleon. They say she lives in a remote village in the Pyrenees. They also say that she and the forger are lovers or perhaps even husband and wife. But this is only a rumor."

"Who are *they*?"

"People who toil in the dirty end of the art trade."

"People like you, you mean?"

Durand was silent.

"Is the forger Spanish, too?"

"That is the assumption. But, again, this is only speculation. Unlike some forgers who crave notoriety, this man is very serious about his privacy. The woman is said to be one of only two people who know his identity."

"And the other?"

"The man who runs the business side of the network. Think of them as an unholy trinity."

"What's the Spanish woman's role?"

"She oversees the delivery of the paintings to the galleries where they are sold. Most are midmarket pieces that quietly generate enormous amounts of cash. But every few months, another so-called lost master magically reappears."

"How many galleries are there?"

"I couldn't say."

"Try."

"One hears rumors about a gallery in Berlin and another in Brussels. One also hears rumors of a recent expansion into Asia and the Middle East."

"One wonders," said Gabriel pointedly, "why you didn't disclose any of this information during our last conversation."

"Perhaps if you had told me that you intended to purchase a painting from Galerie Fleury, I might have been more forthcoming." Durand smiled. *"A River Scene with Distant Windmills.* Definitely *not* by the Dutch Golden Age painter Aelbert Cuyp."

"How do you know about the sale?"

"Fleury was discreet in some matters, less so in others. He boasted of the sale to several of his competitors, despite the fact that he allowed Madame Rolfe's art adviser to remove the painting from France without an export license."

"He had no suspicions about me?"

"Apparently not."

"Then why was I targeted for assassination when I returned to the gallery four days later?"

"Perhaps you should ask the man who delivered the bomb."

Gabriel handed the Frenchman his phone a second time. "Do you recognize him?"

"Fortunately, no."

"I believe he murdered a woman in Bordeaux not long ago."

"The Bérrangar woman?"

Gabriel exhaled heavily. "Is there anything you *don't* know, Maurice?"

"Information is the key to my longevity, Monsieur Allon. And yours, I imagine." Durand looked down at the phone. "How else to explain the fact that you are in possession of this photograph?"

"It was given to me by the head of the Police Nationale's art crime unit."

"Jacques Ménard?"

Gabriel nodded.

"And what exactly is the nature of your relationship?"

"It's a bit like ours."

"Coercive and abusive?"

"Discreet and unofficial."

"Is he aware of our past collaboration?"

"*Non.*"

"I'm relieved." Durand returned the phone. "That said, I think this should be our last meeting for the foreseeable future."

"I'm afraid that's not possible."

"Why not?"

"Because I have an assignment for you."

"The names of those galleries in Berlin and Brussels?"

"If you wouldn't mind."

Durand removed his spectacles and rose. "Tell me something, Monsieur Allon. What happened to those paintings you found in Lucien's workshop?"

"Up in smoke."

"The Picasso?"

"All of them."

"A pity," said Durand with a sigh. "I could have found a good home for them."

AT HALF PAST TEN THE FOLLOWING MORNING, WHILE SEATED at the Louvre's Café Marly, Gabriel delivered his first report to Jacques Ménard. The briefing was thorough and complete, though evasive when it came to sources and methods. Like Christopher Keller, who occupied a nearby table, Ménard found fault with Gabriel's decision to destroy the forgeries he had discovered in Lucien Marchand's studio in Roussillon. Nevertheless, the French art detective was impressed by the scope of his informant's findings.

"I have to admit, it all makes a great deal of sense." Ménard gestured toward the gleaming glass-and-steel structure in the Cour Napoléon. "The criminal art world is a bit like *la pyramide*. There are tens of thousands of people involved in the illicit market, but it's controlled by a few major players at the top." He paused. "And it's obvious that you're acquainted with at least one or two of them."

"Aren't you?"

"*Oui*. Just not the right ones, apparently. Your ability to gather this much information so quickly is most embarrassing."

"Edmond Toussaint never popped up on your radar?"

Ménard shook his head. "And neither did Lucien Marchand. I don't care what sort of promises you made to the Vionnet woman. I'm going to open a case against her and seize those assets, including the villa in the Lubéron."

"First things first, Ménard."

"I'm afraid nothing has changed," said the Frenchman. "My hands remain tied."

"Then I suppose you'll have to force the issue."

"How?"

"By turning over my findings to one of your European partners."

"Which one?"

"Since we're looking for a Spanish woman who might or might not reside in a remote village in the Pyrenees, I would think the Guardia Civil might be the most logical choice."

"I don't trust them."

"I'm sure they feel the same about you."

"They do."

"How about the British?"

"Scotland Yard dismantled its Art and Antiquities Squad a few years ago. They treat art theft and fraud like any other property or financial crime."

"Then I suppose that leaves the Italians."

"They're the best in the business," conceded Ménard. "But what's the Italian connection?"

"At the moment, there isn't one. But I'm sure General Ferrari and I will think of something."

"He speaks very highly of you, the general."

"As well he should. I helped him crack an antiquities-smuggling ring a few years ago. I also helped him find a missing altarpiece."

"Not the Caravaggio?"

Gabriel nodded.

"The white whale," whispered Ménard. "How did you find it?"

"I hired a gang of French art thieves to steal *Sunflowers* from the Van Gogh Museum in Amsterdam. Then I painted a copy of it in a safe flat overlooking the Pont Marie and sold it for twenty-five million euros to a Syrian named Sam in a warehouse outside Paris." Gabriel lowered his voice. "All without your knowledge."

Jacques Ménard's face turned the color of the tablecloth. "You're not going to steal any paintings this time, are you?"

"*Non*. But I might forge a few."

"How many?"

Gabriel smiled. "Four, I think."

36

MASON'S YARD

LATELY, IT HAD OCCURRED TO Oliver Dimbleby that he was a very lucky man indeed. Yes, his gallery had endured its ups and downs—the Great Recession had been a rather close shave—but somehow the hand of fate had always interceded to save him from ruin. The same was true of his personal life, which was, by universal acclaim, the untidiest in the London art world. Despite his advancing years and ever-increasing girth, Oliver had encountered no shortage of willing partners. He was, after all, a glorified salesman—a man of immense charm and charisma who, as he was fond of saying, could sell sand to a Saudi. He was not, however, a womanizer. Or so he told himself each time he awoke with a strange body on the other side of his bed. Oliver loved women. *All* women. And therein lay the root of his problem.

Tonight he had nothing on his schedule other than a well-deserved drink—and perhaps a few laughs at Julian Isherwood's expense—at Wiltons. To reach his destination he merely had to turn to the left after leaving his gallery and walk one hundred and fourteen paces along the spotless pavements of Bury Street. His journey took him past the premises of a dozen competitors, including the mighty P. & D. Colnaghi & Co., the world's oldest commercial art gallery. Next door was the flagship store of Turnbull & Asser, where Oliver's deficit spending was approaching American levels.

Entering Wiltons, he was pleased to see Sarah Bancroft sitting alone at her usual table. He procured a glass of Pouilly-Fumé at the bar and joined her. The unexpected warmth of her smile nearly stopped his heart.

"Oliver," she purred. "What a pleasant surprise."

"Do you mean that?"

"Why wouldn't I?"

"Because I've always had the distinct impression that you find me repulsive."

"Don't be silly. I positively adore you."

"So there's hope for me yet?"

She raised her left hand and displayed a three-carat diamond ring and accompanying wedding band. "Still married, I'm afraid."

"Any chance of a divorce?"

"Not at the moment."

"In that case," said Oliver with a dramatic sigh, "I suppose I'll have to settle for being your sexual plaything."

"You have plenty of those already. Besides, my husband might not approve."

"Peter Marlowe? The professional assassin?"

"He's a business consultant," said Sarah.

"I think I liked him better when he was a contract killer."

"So did I."

Just then the door swung open and in came Simon Mendenhall and Olivia Watson.

"Did you hear the rumor about those two?" whispered Sarah.

"The one about their torrid affair? Jeremy Crabbe may have mentioned it. Or perhaps it was Nicky Lovegrove. It's on everyone's lips."

"A shame, that."

"I only wish they were saying the same about us." Smiling wolfishly, Oliver drank from his wineglass. "Sell anything lately?"

"A couple of Leonardos and a Giorgione. You?"

"Truth be told, I'm in a bit of a slump."

"Not you, Ollie?"

"Hard to believe, I know."

"How's your cash flow?"

"A bit like a leaky faucet."

"What about the five million I slipped you under the table on the Artemisia deal?"

"Are you referring to the newly discovered painting that I sold for a record price to a Swiss venture capitalist, only to find myself embroiled in a scandal involving the finances of the Russian president?"

"But it was great fun, wasn't it?"

"I enjoyed the five million. The rest of it I could have lived without."

"Fiddlesticks, Oliver. There's nothing you love more than being the center of attention. Especially when beautiful women are involved." Sarah paused. "Spanish women, in particular."

"Wherever did you hear a thing like that?"

"I happen to know that you've been carrying a secret torch for Penélope Cruz for years."

"Nicky," murmured Oliver.

"It was Jeremy who told me."

Oliver regarded Sarah for a moment. "Why do I get the feeling I'm being recruited for something?"

"Perhaps because you are."

"Is it naughty?"

"Extremely."

"In that case," said Oliver, "I'm all ears."

"Not here."

"My place or yours?"

Sarah smiled. "Mine, Ollie."

THEY SLIPPED OUT OF WILTONS UNNOTICED AND WALKED along Duke Street to the passageway that led to Mason's Yard. Isherwood Fine Arts was located in the northeast corner of the quadrangle, in three floors of a sagging warehouse once owned by Fortnum & Mason. Parked outside was a silver Bentley Continental. Its gleaming hood was warm to Oliver's touch.

"Isn't this your husband's car?" he asked, but Sarah only smiled and unlocked the gallery's door.

Inside, they climbed a flight of carpeted stairs, then rode the cramped lift to Julian's upper exhibition room. In the half-light Oliver could make out two silhouetted figures. One was contemplating *Baptism of Christ* by Paris Bordone. The other was contemplating Oliver. He wore a dark single-breasted suit, Savile Row, perhaps Richard Anderson. His hair was sun-bleached. His eyes were bright blue.

"Hullo, Oliver," he drawled. Then, almost as an after-thought, he added, "I'm Peter Marlowe."

"The hit man?"

"Former hit man," he said with an ironic smile. "I'm a wildly successful business consultant now. That's why I drive a Bentley and have a wife who looks like Sarah."

"I never laid so much as a finger on her."

"Of course you didn't."

He placed a hand on Oliver's shoulder and guided him toward the Bordone. The man standing before the canvas turned slowly. His green eyes seemed to glow in the faint light.

"Mario Delvecchio!" exclaimed Oliver. "As I live and breathe! Or is it Gabriel Allon? I often can't tell them apart." Receiving no answer, he looked at the man he knew as Peter Marlowe, then at Sarah. At least, he thought that was her name. At that moment he wasn't certain of the ground beneath his feet. "The retired chief of Israeli intelligence, a former hit man, and a beautiful American woman who may or may not have worked for the CIA. What could you possibly want with tubby Oliver Dimbleby?"

It was the retired Israeli spymaster who answered. "Your bottomless reservoir of charm, your ability to talk your way out of almost anything, and your reputation for cutting the occasional corner."

"Me?" Oliver feigned righteous indignation. "I resent the implication. And if it's a dirty dealer you want, Roddy Hutchinson is most definitely your man."

"Roddy lacks your star power. I need someone who can move the needle."

"For what?"

"I'd like you to sell a few paintings for me."

"Anything good?"

"A Titian, a Tintoretto, and a Veronese."

"What's the source?"

"An old European collection."

"And the subject matter?"

"I'll let you know the minute I finish painting them."

THE FIRST CHALLENGE FOR ANY ART FORGER IS THE ACQUISITION of canvases and stretchers of appropriate age, dimensions, and condition. When executing his copy of Vincent's *Sunflowers*, Gabriel had purchased a third-tier Impressionist streetscape from a small gallery near the Jardin du Luxembourg. He had no need to resort to such methods now. He merely had to ride the lift down to Julian's storerooms, which were crammed with an apocalyptic inventory of what was affectionately known in the trade as dead stock. He selected six minor Venetian School works from the sixteenth century—follower of so-and-so, manner of such-and-such, workshop of what's-his-name—and asked Sarah to express-ship them to his apartment in San Polo.

"Why six instead of only three?"

"I need two spares in the event of a disaster."

"And the other one?"

"I'm planning to leave a Gentileschi with my front man in Florence."

"Silly me," said Sarah. "But how are we going to explain the missing paintings to Julian?"

"With any luck, he won't notice."

Sarah instructed the shippers to arrive no later than nine the following morning and advised Julian to take the day off. Nevertheless, he wandered into Mason's Yard at his usual time, a quarter past twelve, as the crated paintings were being loaded into a Ford Transit van. The tragicomedy that followed included yet another collision with an inanimate object. This time it was Sarah's shredder, into which Julian, in a spasm of self-pity, attempted to insert himself.

Gabriel did not witness the incident, for he was in the back of a taxi bound from Fiumicino Airport toward Rome's Piazza di Sant'Ignazio. Upon arrival he took a table at Le Cave, one of his favorite restaurants in the *centro storico*. It was located a few steps from the ornate yellow-and-white palazzo that served as the headquarters of the Art Squad.

The palazzo's door swung open at half past one, and

General Cesare Ferrari emerged in his bemedaled blue-and-gold uniform. He crossed the gray cobbles of the square and without uttering a word of greeting sat down at Gabriel's table. Instantly the waiter delivered a frigid bottle of Frascati and a plate of fried *arancini*.

"Why doesn't that happen when I arrive at restaurants?" asked Gabriel.

"I'm sure it's only the uniform." The general plucked one of the risotto balls from the plate. "Shouldn't you be in Venice with your wife and children?"

"Probably. But I needed to have a word with you first."

"About what?"

"I'm thinking about embarking on a life of crime, and I was wondering whether you would be interested in a piece of the action."

"What sort of misdeed are you contemplating this time?"

"Art forgery."

"Well, you certainly have the talent for it," said the general. "But what would be my end?"

"A high-profile case that will shake the art world to its core and ensure that the generous funding and personnel levels of the Art Squad remain unchanged for years to come."

"Has a crime been committed on Italian soil?"

"Not yet," said Gabriel with a smile. "But soon."

37

BRIDGE OF SIGHS

Umberto Conti, universally regarded as the greatest art restorer of the twentieth century, had bequeathed to Francesco Tiepolo a magical ring of keys that could open any door in Venice. Over drinks at Harry's Bar, Francesco entrusted them to Gabriel. Late that evening he slipped into the Scuola Grande di San Rocco and spent two hours in solitary communion with some of Tintoretto's greatest works. Then he breached the defenses of the neighboring Frari church and stood transfixed before Titian's magisterial *Assumption of the Virgin*. In the deep silence of the cavernous nave, he recalled the words Umberto had spoken to him when he was a broken, gray-haired boy of twenty-five.

Only a man with a damaged canvas of his own can be a truly great restorer . . .

Umberto would not have approved of his gifted pupil's newest commission. And neither, for that matter, did Francesco. Nevertheless, he agreed to serve as a consultant to the project.

He was, after all, one of the world's foremost authorities on the Venetian School painters. If Gabriel could fool Francesco Tiepolo, he could fool anyone.

Francesco likewise agreed to accompany Gabriel during his nocturnal Venetian wanderings, if only to prevent another mishap like the one involving poor Capitano Rossetti. They stole into churches and *scuole*, roamed the Accademia and the Museo Correr, and even stormed the Doge's Palace. While peering through the stone-barred windows of the Bridge of Sighs, Francesco summarized the difficulty of the task ahead.

"Four different works by four of the greatest painters in history. Only a madman would attempt such a thing."

"If he can do it, so can I."

"The forger?"

Gabriel nodded.

"It's not a competition, you know."

"Of course it is. I have to prove to them that I would be a worthy addition to the network. Otherwise, they won't make a play for me."

"Is that why you allowed yourself to be dragged into this? For the challenge?"

"Wherever did you get the idea that this was going to be a challenge for me?"

"You don't lack for confidence, do you?"

"Neither does he."

"You're all the same, you art forgers. You all have something to prove. He's probably a failed painter who's taking his revenge on the art world by fooling the connoisseurs and the collectors."

"The connoisseurs and collectors," said Gabriel, "haven't seen anything yet."

He spent his days in his studio with his monographs and

catalogues raisonnés and photographs from past restorations, including several that he had conducted for Francesco. Together, after much debate, some of it conducted with raised voices, they settled on the subject matter and iconography for the four forgeries. Gabriel produced a series of preparatory sketches, then turned the sketches into four swiftly executed rehearsal paintings. Francesco declared the Gentileschi, a reworking of *Danaë and the Shower of Gold*, to be the finest of the lot, with Veronese's *Susanna in the Bath* a close second. Gabriel agreed with Francesco's assessment of the Gentileschi, though he was fond of his reinterpretation of Tintoretto's *Bacchus, Venus, and Ariadne*. His Titian, a pastiche of *The Lovers*, wasn't bad, either, though he thought the brushwork was a touch tentative.

"How can one *not* be tentative when one is forging a Titian?"

"It's a dead giveaway, Francesco. I have to *become* Titian. Otherwise, we're sunk."

"What are you going to do with that one?"

"Cremation. The others, too."

"Have you taken leave of your senses?"

"Clearly."

Early the following morning, Gabriel uncrated one of the paintings he had pillaged from Julian's storerooms, an early sixteenth-century Venetian School devotional piece of no value and little merit. Even so, he felt a stab of guilt as he scraped the unknown artist's work from the canvas and covered it in gesso and an *imprimatura* of lead white with traces of lampblack and yellow ocher. Next he executed his underdrawing—with a brush, the way *he* would have done it—and meticulously prepared his palette. Lead white, genuine ultramarine, madder lake, burnt sienna, malachite, yellow ocher, red ocher, orpiment, ivory black. Before commencing work, he once again reflected on the shifting fortunes of his career. He was no longer the leader of a powerful intelligence service or even one of the world's finest art restorers.

He was the sun amidst small stars.

He was Titian.

FOR THE BETTER PART OF THE NEXT WEEK, CHIARA AND THE children saw little of him. On the rare occasions he emerged from his studio, he was on edge and preoccupied, not at all himself. Only once did he accept an invitation to join Chiara for lunch. His hands left smudges of paint across her breasts and abdomen.

"I feel like I just made love to another man."

"You did."

"Who are you?"

"Come with me. I'll show you."

Wrapped in a bedsheet, Chiara followed him into the studio and stood before the canvas. At length she whispered, "You're a freak."

"Do you like it?"

"It's absolutely—"

"Amazing, I think."

"I see a touch of Giorgione in it."

"That's because I was still under his influence when I painted it in 1510."

"Who will you be next?"

Jacobo Robusti, the artist known as Tintoretto, was a learned and unsmiling man who rarely set foot outside Venice and allowed few visitors to enter his workspace. If there was one consolation, he was among the swiftest painters in the republic. Gabriel completed his version of *Bacchus, Venus, and Ariadne* in half the time it took him to finish *The Lovers*. Chiara nevertheless declared it superior to the Titian in every respect, as did Francesco.

"I'm afraid your wife is right. You truly are a freak."

Next Gabriel assumed the personality and remarkable palette of Paolo Veronese. *Susanna in the Bath* required the largest of the six canvases he had acquired from Isherwood Fine Arts and several additional days to complete—in large part because Gabriel intentionally damaged the work and then restored it. Luca Rossetti visited him three times during the painting's execution. Brush in hand, Gabriel lectured the young Carabinieri officer on the artistic merits and fraudulent pedigrees of his four forged masterpieces. Rossetti in turn briefed Gabriel on the preparations for their forthcoming operation. They included the acquisition of two properties—an isolated villa for the reclusive forger and an apartment in Florence for his front man.

"It's on the south side of the Arno, on the Lungarno Torrigiani. We've loaded it up with paintings and antiquities from the Art Squad's evidence room. It definitely looks like the home of an art dealer."

"And the villa?"

"Your friend the Holy Father called Count Gasparri. It's all arranged."

"How soon can you settle into the apartment and assume your new identity?"

"As soon as you say I'm ready."

"Are you?"

"I know my lines," answered Rossetti. "And I know more about the Venetian School painters than I ever thought possible."

"What was Veronese's name when he was young?" inquired Gabriel.

"Paolo Spezapreda."

"And why was that?"

"His father was a stonecutter. It was traditional for children to be named after their father's occupation."

"Why did he start calling himself Paolo Caliari?"

"His mother was the illegitimate child of a nobleman called Antonio Caliari. Young Paolo thought it was better to be named for a nobleman than a stonecutter."

"Not bad." Gabriel drew his Beretta from the waistband of his trousers. "But will you be able to recite your lines so confidently if someone points one of these at your head?"

"I grew up in Naples," said Rossetti. "Most of my childhood friends are now in the Camorra. I'm not going to fall to pieces if someone starts waving a gun around."

"I heard a rumor that an elderly Venetian School painter gave you a good thrashing the other night in San Polo."

"The elderly painter attacked me without warning."

"That's the way it works in the real world. Criminals don't often announce their intentions before resorting to violence." Gabriel returned the gun to the small of his back and contemplated the towering canvas. "What do you think, Signore Calvi?"

"You have to darken the garments of the two elders. Otherwise, I won't be able to convince Oliver Dimbleby that it was painted in the late sixteenth century."

"Oliver Dimbleby," said Gabriel, "will be the least of your problems."

By the time he commenced work on the Gentileschi, he was so exhausted he could scarcely hold a brush. Fortunately, Chiara agreed to pose for him, as the artist he was attempting to impersonate preferred the Caravaggesque method of painting directly from live models. He gave his Danaë Chiara's body and facial features, but turned his wife's dark hair to gold and her olive skin to luminous alabaster. Most of their sessions necessarily included an intermezzo in the bedroom—a hurried one, for Gabriel's time was limited. The end result of their collaboration was a painting of astonishing beauty and veiled eroticism. It was, they both agreed, the finest of the four works.

Like the other three paintings, it was unmarred by craquelure, a sure sign it was a modern forgery and not the work of an Old Master. The solution was a large professional oven. General Ferrari obtained one from the seized inventory of a Mafia-owned kitchen supplies firm and delivered it to the mainland warehouse of the Tiepolo Restoration Company. After removing the four paintings from their stretchers, Gabriel baked them for three hours at 220 degrees Fahrenheit. Then, with Francesco's help, he dragged the paintings over the edge of a rectangular work table, first vertically, then horizontally. The result was a fine network of Italianate surface cracks.

That evening, alone in his studio, Gabriel covered the paintings with varnish. And in the morning, when the varnish was dry, he photographed them with a tripod-mounted Nikon. He hung the Titian and the Tintoretto in the sitting room of the apartment, surrendered the Gentileschi to General Ferrari, and shipped the Veronese to Sarah Bancroft in London. The photos he emailed directly to Oliver Dimbleby, owner and sole proprietor of Dimbleby Fine Arts of Bury Street, upon whose rounded shoulders the entire venture rested. Shortly before midnight one of the images appeared on the website of *ARTnews*, beneath the byline of Amelia March. Gabriel read the exclusive story to his dark-haired, olive-complected Danaë. She made love to him in a shower of gold.

38

KURFÜRSTENDAMM

THE ARTICLE WAS PURPORTEDLY BASED on a single source who wished to remain anonymous. Even this was misleading, as it was Sarah Bancroft who had provided the initial tip and Oliver Dimbleby who had supplied the off-the-record confirmation and the photograph—thus making it, in point of fact, a two-source story.

The work in question was said to be 92 centimeters in height and 74 in width. That much, at least, was accurate. It was not, however, a lost work of the Late Renaissance painter known as Titian, and there had been no quiet sale to a prominent collector who wished to remain unidentified. Truth be told, there was no buyer, prominent or otherwise, and no money had changed hands. As for the painting, it was now hanging in a glorious *piano nobile* overlooking the Grand Canal in Venice, much to the delight of the wife and two young children of the newly minted art forger who had produced it.

The dealers, curators, and auctioneers of the London

art world greeted the news with astonishment and no small amount of jealousy. After all, Oliver was still basking in the glow of his last coup. In the salerooms and watering holes of St. James's and Mayfair, questions were raised, usually in conspiratorial whispers. Did this new Titian have a proper provenance, or did it fall off the back of a truck? Was tubby Oliver absolutely certain of the attribution? Did others more learned than he concur? And what exactly was his role in the transaction? Had he actually *sold* the painting to his unnamed buyer? Or had he merely acted as a middleman and pocketed a lucrative commission in the process?

For three interminable days, Oliver refused to either confirm or deny that he handled the work in question. Finally he released a brief corroboratory statement that was scarcely more illuminating than Amelia March's original story. It contained only two new pieces of information, that the painting had emerged from an old European collection and had been examined by no fewer than four leading Venetian School experts. All four agreed, without qualifications or conditions, that the canvas had been executed by Titian himself and not by a member of his workshop or a later follower.

That evening Oliver walked the one hundred and fourteen paces from his gallery to the bar at Wiltons and in keeping with neighborhood tradition promptly ordered six bottles of champagne. Much was made of the fact that it was Taittinger Comtes Blanc de Blanc, the most expensive on the list. Still, all those in attendance would later remark that Oliver seemed subdued for a man who had just pulled off one of the art world's biggest coups in years. He refused to divulge the price the Titian had fetched and feigned deafness when Jeremy Crabbe pressed him for additional details on the painting's provenance. Sometime around eight he pulled Nicky Lovegrove aside for a heart-to-heart, which gave rise to speculation that Oliver's unidentified buyer was one of Nicky's superrich clients. Nicky swore it wasn't so, but Oliver cagily declined comment. Then, after kissing the proffered cheek of Sarah Bancroft, he waddled into Jermyn Street and was gone.

It emerged the following day, in a lengthy article in the *Art Newspaper*, that the unidentified buyer had made a takeaway offer for the Titian after being granted an exclusive viewing at Oliver's gallery. According to the *Independent*, the offer was £25 million. Niles Dunham, an Old Master specialist from the National Gallery, denied a report that he had authenticated the painting on Oliver's behalf. Curiously, so did every other connoisseur of Italian School painting in the United Kingdom.

But it was the photograph of the painting that raised the most eyebrows, at least among the backbiting world of St. James's. For many years Oliver had utilized the services of the same fine art photographer—the renowned Prudence Cuming of Dover Street. But not, as it turned out, for his newly discovered Titian. Perhaps even more suspicious was his claim that he had taken the photograph himself. All were in agreement that Oliver could handle a tumbler of good whisky, or a shapely backside, but not a camera.

And yet no one, not even the unscrupulous Roddy Hutchinson, suspected Oliver of wrongdoing. Indeed, the general consensus was that he was guilty of nothing more serious than protecting the identity of his source, a common practice among art dealers. The logical conclusion was that it was only a matter of time before another noteworthy picture emerged from the same European collection.

When the inevitable finally happened, it was once again Amelia March of *ARTnews* who broke the story. This time the work in question was *Bacchus, Venus, and Ariadne* by the Venetian painter Tintoretto—deeply private sale, price unavailable upon request. Just ten days later, to absolutely no one's surprise, Dimbleby Fine Arts announced its newest offering:

Susanna in the Bath, oil on canvas, 194 by 194 centimeters, by Paolo Veronese. The gallery retained Prudence Cuming of Dover Street to make the photograph. The art world swooned.

WITH THE EXCEPTION, THAT IS, OF THE POWERFUL DIRECTOR of the Uffizi Gallery in Florence, who found the sudden appearance of three Italian Old Master paintings suspicious, to say the least. He rang General Ferrari of the Art Squad and demanded an immediate investigation. Surely, he shouted down the line to Rome, the canvases had been smuggled out of Italy in violation of the country's draconian Cultural Heritage Code. The general promised to look into the matter, though his fingers were firmly crossed at the time. Needless to say, he did not inform the director that the paintings in question were all modern fakes and that he himself was operating in league with the forger.

The forger's phantom front man—a collector and occasional dealer who called himself Alessandro Calvi—was currently living in an art-filled apartment within sight of the Uffizi, on the Lungarno Torrigiani. As it happened, General Ferrari had occasion to ring this disreputable character two days later on an unrelated matter. It concerned a piece of information the forger had received from a well-placed informant in Paris, an art thief and antiques dealer named Maurice Durand.

"Galerie Konrad Hassler. It's located on the Kurfürstendamm in Berlin. There's a coffeehouse on the opposite side of the street. Your associate will meet you there tomorrow afternoon at three."

And so it was that the phantom front man, whose real name was Capitano Luca Rossetti, left the luxury apartment on the Arno early the following morning and rode in a taxi to Florence Airport. His tailored Italian suit was new and expensive, as were his handmade shoes and his soft-sided leather attaché case. The watch on his wrist was a Patek Philippe. Like his collection of art and antiquities, it was borrowed from the evidence rooms of the Carabinieri.

Rossetti's travel itinerary included a stopover in Zurich, and it was approaching three o'clock when he arrived at the coffeehouse on the Kurfürstendamm. Gabriel was seated at a table outside, in the dappled shade of a plane tree. He ordered two coffees from the waitress in rapid German before handing a manila envelope to Rossetti.

Inside were two photographs. The first depicted three unframed paintings displayed side by side against the wall of an artist's workshop—a Titian, a Tintoretto, and a Veronese. The second was a high-resolution image of *Danaë and the Shower of Gold*, purportedly by Orazio Gentileschi. Rossetti knew the work well. At present, it was hanging on the wall of the apartment in Florence.

"When is he expecting me?"

"Three thirty. He's under the impression that your name is Giovanni Rinaldi and that you are from Milano."

"How do you want me to play it?"

"I'd like you to present Herr Hassler with a unique opportunity to acquire a lost masterwork. I would also like you to make it clear that you are the source of the three paintings that have resurfaced in London."

"Do I tell him they're forgeries?"

"You won't have to. He'll get the idea when he sees the photos."

"Why am I coming to him?"

"Because you're looking for a second distributor for your merchandise and you've heard rumors that he's less than honest."

"How do you suppose he'll react?"

"He'll either make you an offer or throw you out of his gallery. I'm betting on the latter. Make sure you leave behind the photo of the Gentileschi on your way out the door."

"What happens if he calls the police?"

"Criminals don't call the police, Rossetti. In fact, they do their best to avoid them."

The Carabinieri officer lowered his gaze to the photograph.

"When was he born?" asked Gabriel quietly.

"Fifteen sixty-three."

"What was his name?"

"Orazio Lomi."

"What sort of work did his father do?"

"He was a Florentine goldsmith."

"Who was Gentileschi?"

"An uncle he lived with when he moved to Rome."

"Where did he paint *Danaë and the Shower of Gold*?"

"Probably in Genoa."

"Where did I paint my version?"

"None of your fucking business."

CAPITANO LUCA ROSSETTI LEFT THE COFFEEHOUSE AT 3:27 P.M. and crossed to the opposite side of the elegant tree-lined boulevard. Gabriel tensed as the young Carabinieri officer reached his right hand toward the intercom of Galerie Konrad Hassler. Fifteen seconds elapsed, long enough for the dealer to have a good long look at his visitor. Then Rossetti leaned on the glass door and disappeared from view.

Five minutes later Gabriel's phone shivered with an incoming call. It was General Ferrari.

"Nothing exploded, did it?"

"Not yet."

"Let me know the minute he walks out of there," said the general, and rang off.

Gabriel returned the phone to the tabletop and directed his

gaze toward the gallery. By now the introductions had been made and the two men had withdrawn to the dealer's office for a bit of privacy. A photograph had been placed on his desk. Perhaps two. When viewed together, the images made it clear that a talented new forger had stepped onto the stage of the illicit art market. Which was exactly the message that Gabriel wished to send.

Just then his phone pulsed with another call. "What's going on in there?" asked General Ferrari.

"Hold on, I'll run across the road and check."

This time it was Gabriel who killed the connection. Two minutes later the door of the gallery opened, and out stepped Rossetti, followed by a well-dressed man with iron-gray hair and a crimson face. A few final words were exchanged, and fingers were pointed in anger. Then Rossetti ducked into a taxi and was gone, leaving the crimson-faced man alone on the pavement. He looked left and right along the boulevard before returning to the gallery.

Message delivered, thought Gabriel.

He dialed Rossetti's number.

"Looks as though you two really hit it off."

"It went exactly the way you said it would."

"Where's the photograph?"

"It's possible that in my rush to get out of the gallery I might have left it on his desk."

"How long before he sends it to our girl?"

"Not long," said Rossetti.

39

QUEEN'S GATE TERRACE

For the remainder of that week, the phone at Dimbleby Fine Arts rang nearly without cease. Cordelia Blake, Oliver's long-suffering receptionist, served as the first line of defense. Those with names she recognized—longtime clients or representatives of prominent museums—she transferred directly to Oliver's line. Those of lesser repute were asked to leave a detailed message and were given no assurance their inquiry would receive a reply. It was Mr. Dimbleby's ambition, Cordelia explained, to find a suitable home for the Veronese. He had no intention of selling the painting to just anyone.

Unbeknownst to Cordelia, Oliver delivered each of her pink message slips to Sarah Bancroft in Mason's Yard, and Sarah in turn forwarded the names and numbers to Gabriel in Venice. By the close of business on that Friday, Dimbleby Fine Arts had received more than two hundred requests to view the forged Veronese—from the directors of the world's greatest museums, from representatives of prominent collectors, and from a multitude of journalists, art dealers, and learned connoisseurs of the Italian Old Masters. With the exception of a curator from the J. Paul Getty Museum in Los Angeles, none of the names on the list was Spanish in origin, and none of the callback numbers began with a Spanish country code. Forty-two women wished to see the painting, all of whom were well-known figures in the art world.

One of the women was a reporter from the London bureau of the *New York Times*. With Gabriel's approval, Oliver allowed her to see the painting the following Monday, and by Wednesday evening her story and accompanying photographs were the talk of the art world. The result was another avalanche of calls to Dimbleby Fine Arts. Twenty-two of the new callers were women. None of their names or callback numbers were Spanish in origin. And none, according to Cordelia Blake, spoke with a Spanish accent.

Gabriel feared the worst, that the forgery network's front woman had no intention of attending the party he had so meticulously planned in her honor. Nevertheless, he instructed Oliver to prepare a schedule for the viewings. They were to last for one week only. The price band would be set at £15 million to £20 million, which would separate the wheat from the chaff. Oliver was to make it clear that he reserved the right not to sell to the highest bidder.

"And make sure you dim the lights in your exhibition room," added Gabriel. "Otherwise, one of your eagle-eyed clients might notice that your newly discovered Veronese is a forgery."

"Not a chance. On the surface, at least, it looks like Veronese painted it in the sixteenth century."

"He did paint it, Oliver. I just happened to be holding the brush at the time."

Gabriel spent Saturday sailing the Adriatic with Chiara and the children, and on Sunday, the day before the viewings were to begin, he flew to London. Upon arrival he headed for Christopher and Sarah's maisonette in Queen's Gate Terrace. There, arrayed on the granite-topped kitchen island, he found a surveillance photograph from Heathrow Airport, a scan of a Spanish passport, and a printout of a guest registration from the Lanesborough Hotel.

Smiling, Sarah handed him a glass of Bollinger Special Cuvée. "Tagliatelle with ragù or veal Milanese?"

SHE WAS TALL AND SLENDER, WITH THE SQUARE SHOULDERS OF a swimmer, narrow hips, and long legs. The pantsuit she wore was dark and businesslike, but the daring neckline of her white blouse revealed the fine curve of her delicate upturned breasts. Her hair was nearly black and hung long and straight down the center of her back. Even in the unflattering light of Heathrow's Terminal 5, it shone like a newly varnished painting.

Her name, according to the passport, was Magdalena Navarro. She was thirty-nine and a resident of Madrid. She had arrived at Heathrow aboard Iberia Flight 7459 and had dialed Dimbleby Fine Arts at 3:07 p.m. from her room phone at the Lanesborough. The call had bounced automatically to Oliver's mobile. After listening to the message, he had rung Sarah, who had prevailed upon her husband, an officer of Her Majesty's Secret Intelligence Service, to have an off-the-record peek at the Spanish woman's particulars. He had done so with the approval of his director-general.

"It took our brethren at MI5 all of twenty minutes to pull together the file."

"Did they have a look at her recent travel?"

"It seems she's a frequent visitor to France, Belgium, and Germany. She also spends a fair amount of time in Hong Kong and Tokyo."

Christopher ignited a Marlboro and exhaled a cloud of smoke toward the ceiling of his elegantly decorated drawing room. He wore a pair of fitted chinos and a costly cashmere pullover. Sarah was more casually attired, in stretch jeans and a Harvard sweatshirt. She plucked a cigarette from Christopher's packet and quickly lit it before Gabriel could object.

"Any other interesting travel?" he asked.

"She goes to New York about once a month. Apparently, she lived there for a few years in the mid-aughts."

"Credit card?"

"A corporate American Express. The company has a fuzzy Liechtenstein registry. She seems to use it only for foreign travel."

"Which would help to conceal the real location of her home in Spain." Gabriel turned to Sarah. "How did she describe herself in the message?"

"She says she's a broker. But she doesn't have a website or an entry on LinkedIn, and neither Oliver nor Julian has ever heard of her."

"Sounds like she's our girl."

"Yes," agreed Sarah. "The question is, how long do we make her wait?"

"Long enough to create the impression that she is of absolutely no consequence."

"And then?"

"She'll have to convince Oliver to let her see the painting."

"Could be dangerous," said Sarah.

"He'll be fine."

"It's not Oliver I'm worried about."

Gabriel smiled. "All's fair in love and forgery."

40

DIMBLEBY FINE ARTS

THE DIRECTOR OF THE NATIONAL Gallery arrived at Dimbleby Fine Arts at ten the following morning, accompanied by the infallible Niles Dunham and three other curators who specialized in Italian Old Masters. They sniffed, poked, prodded, kicked the tires, and examined the canvas under ultraviolet light. No one questioned the authenticity of the work, only the provenance.

"An old European collection? It's a bit gossamer, Oliver. That said, I must have it."

"Then I suggest you make me an offer."

"I won't get caught up in a bidding war."

"Of course you will."

"Who's next at bat?"

"The Getty."

"You wouldn't dare."

"I will if the price is right."

"Scoundrel."

"Flattery will get you nowhere."

"See you at Wiltons tonight?"

"Unless I get a better offer."

The delegation from the Getty arrived at eleven. They were young and suntanned and loaded with cash. They made a takeaway offer of £25 million, £5 million above the top end of the estimated price band. Oliver turned them down flat.

"We won't be back," they vowed.

"I have a feeling you will."

"How can you tell?"

"Because I see that look in your eyes."

It was noon when Oliver ushered the Gettys into Bury Street. Cordelia handed him a stack of telephone messages on her way to lunch. He leafed through them quickly before ringing Sarah.

"She's called twice this morning."

"Wonderful news."

"Perhaps we should put her out of her misery."

"Actually, we'd like you to play hard to get a little longer."

"Hard to get isn't my usual modus operandi."

"I've noticed, Ollie."

The afternoon session was a reprise of the morning. The delegation from the Metropolitan Museum of Art was smitten, their counterparts from Boston head over heels. The director of the Art Gallery of Ontario, a Veronese expert himself, was practically speechless.

"How much do you want for it?" he managed to say.

"I've got twenty-five from the Getty."

"They're heathens."

"But rich."

"I might be able to do twenty."

"A novel negotiating tactic."

"Please, Oliver. Don't make me beg."

"Match the Getty's offer, and it's yours."

"Is that a promise?"

"You have my solemn word."

Which is how the first day of viewings ended, with one final untruth. Oliver showed the Ontario delegation out of the gallery and collected the newest telephone messages from Cordelia's desk.

Magdalena Navarro had called at four fifteen.

"She sounded rather annoyed," said Cordelia.

"With good reason."

"Who do you suppose she represents?"

"Someone with enough money to put her up at the Lanesborough."

Cordelia collected her belongings and went out. Alone, Oliver reached for the telephone and dialed Sarah.

"How was your afternoon?" she asked.

"I have a bidding war on my hands for a painting I can't sell. Otherwise, nothing much happened."

"How many times did she call?"

"Only once."

"Perhaps she's losing interest."

"All the more reason I should call her and get it over with."

"Let's discuss it at Wiltons. I feel a martini coming on."

Oliver hung up the phone and engaged in the familiar ritual of putting his gallery to bed for the night. He lowered the internal security screens over the windows. He engaged the alarm. He placed a baize-cloth cover over *Susanna in the Bath*, oil on canvas, 194 by 194 centimeters, by Gabriel Allon.

Outside, Oliver triple-locked his door and set off along Bury Street. It should have been a triumphal march. He was, after all, the toast of the art world, the dealer who had stumbled upon a long-hidden collection of lost masters. Never mind that all of the paintings were forgeries. Oliver assured himself that his actions were in service of a noble cause. If nothing else, it would make for a good story one day.

Crossing Ryder Street, he became conscious of the fact that someone was walking behind him. Someone wearing a pair of well-made pumps, he thought, with stiletto heels. He paused outside the Colnaghi gallery and cast a leftward glance along the pavement.

Tall, slender, expensively attired, lustrous black hair hanging over the front of one shoulder.

Dangerously attractive.

Much to Oliver's surprise, the woman joined him and fixed her wide dark eyes on the Old Master painting displayed in the window. "Bartolomeo Cavarozzi," she said in faintly accented English. "He was an early follower of Caravaggio who spent two years working in Spain, where he was much admired. If I'm not mistaken, he painted this picture after his return to Rome in 1619."

"Who in the world *are* you?" asked Oliver.

The woman turned to him and smiled. "I'm Magdalena Navarro, Mr. Dimbleby. And I've been trying to reach you all day."

WILTONS WAS OVERRUN WITH AMERICAN AND CANADIAN museum curators, all divided into opposing camps. Sarah shook the hand of the Austrian-born director of the Met, then shouldered her way to the bar, where she endured a wait of ten minutes for her martini. The cocktail-party din was so deafening that for a moment she didn't realize her phone was ringing. It was Oliver calling from his mobile.

"Are you in this madhouse somewhere?" she asked.

"Change in plan, I'm afraid. We'll have to do it another time."

"What are you talking about?"

"Yes, tomorrow evening would be fine. Cordelia will call you in the morning and make the arrangements."

And with that, the call went dead.

Sarah quickly dialed Gabriel. "I could be wrong," she said, "but I believe our girl just made her next move."

41

PICCADILLY

W HERE ARE YOU TAKING ME?"

"Somewhere I can have you all to myself."

"Not the Lanesborough?"

"No, Mr. Dimbleby." She gave him a look of contrived reproach. "Not on our first date."

They were walking along Piccadilly into the blinding light of the sun. It was one of those perfect early-summer evenings in London, cool and soft, a gentle breeze. The woman's intoxicating scent reminded Oliver of the south of Spain. Orange blossom and jasmine and a hint of manzanilla. Twice the back of her hand brushed against his. Her touch was electric.

She slowed to a stop outside Hide. It was one of London's costliest restaurants, a temple of gastronomic and social excess beloved by Russian billionaires, Emirati princes, and, evidently, beautiful Spanish art criminals.

"I'm not quite posh enough for this place," protested Oliver.

"The art world is at your feet tonight, Mr. Dimbleby. You are, without a doubt, the poshest man in London."

They made quite an entrance—the corpulent, pink-cheeked art dealer and the tall, elegantly dressed woman with shimmering black hair. She led him down a swirling oaken staircase to the dimly lit bar. A secluded candlelit table awaited them.

"I'm impressed," said Oliver.

"My butler at the Lanesborough arranged it."

"Do you stay there often?"

"Only when a certain client of mine is footing the bill."

"A client who's interested in acquiring the Veronese?"

"Let's not rush things, Mr. Dimbleby." She leaned into the warm light of the candle. "We Spaniards like to take our time."

The front of her blouse had fallen open, exposing the inner curve of a pear-shaped breast. "Is it as nice as they say?" blurted Oliver.

"What's that, Mr. Dimbleby?"

"The Lanesborough."

"You've never been?"

"Only the restaurant."

"I have a suite overlooking Hyde Park. The view is quite lovely."

So was Oliver's. He nevertheless forced himself to lower his gaze to the cocktail menu. "What do you recommend?"

"The concoction they call the Currant Affairs is life-changing."

Oliver read the ingredients. "Bruno Paillard champagne with Ketel One vodka, red currant, and guava?"

"Don't mock it until you try it."

"I generally drink my champagne and vodka separately."

"They have an extraordinary sherry selection."

"A much better idea."

She summoned the waiter with a raised eyebrow and ordered a bottle of Cuatro Palmas Amontillado.

"Have you been to Spain, Mr. Dimbleby?"

"Many times."

"Business or pleasure?"

"A little of both."

"I'm from Seville originally," she informed him. "But these days I live mostly in Madrid."

"Your English is quite extraordinary."

"I attended a special art history program at Oxford for a year." She was interrupted by the reappearance of the waiter. After an elaborate presentation of the wine, he poured two glasses and withdrew. She raised hers a fraction of an inch. "Cheers, Mr. Dimbleby. I hope you enjoy it."

"You must call me Oliver."

"I couldn't."

"I insist," he said, and drank some of the wine.

"What do you think?"

"It's ambrosia. I only hope that your client is picking up the check."

"He is."

"Does he have a name?"

"Several, in fact."

"He's a spy, your client?"

"He is a member of an aristocratic family. His name is rather cumbersome, to say the least."

"Is he Spanish like you?"

"Perhaps."

Oliver sighed heavily before returning his glass to the tabletop.

"Forgive me, Mr. Dimbleby, but my client is an extremely wealthy man who does not want the world to know the true scale of his art collection. I cannot reveal his identity."

"In that case, perhaps we should discuss yours."

"As I explained to your assistant, I'm a broker."

"How is it that I've never heard of you?"

"I prefer to operate in the shadows." She paused. "As do you, it seems."

"Bury Street is hardly the shadows."

"But you have been, how shall we say, less than forthcoming about the origin of the Veronese. Not to mention the Titian and the Tintoretto."

"You don't know much about the art trade, do you?"

"Actually, I know a great deal, as does my client. He is a sophisticated and shrewd collector. Until he falls in love with a painting, that is. When that happens, money is no object."

"I take it he has a crush on my Veronese?"

"It was love at first sight."

"I already have two bids of twenty-five million."

"My client will match any offer you receive. Pending a thorough examination of the canvas and provenance on my part, of course."

"And if I were to sell it to him? What would he do with it?"

"It would be displayed prominently in one of his many homes."

"Will he agree to lend it for exhibitions?"

"Never."

"I admire your honesty."

She smiled but said nothing.

"How long are you planning to stay in London?"

"I'm scheduled to return to Madrid tomorrow evening."

"A pity."

"Why?"

"Because I might have an opening in my schedule on Wednesday afternoon. Thursday, at the latest."

"How about now instead?"

"Sorry, but my gallery is buttoned up for the night. Besides, it's been a long day, and I'm exhausted."

"A pity," she said playfully. "Because I was hoping you would have dinner with me at the Lanesborough."

"Tempting," said Oliver. "But not on our first date."

ON THE PAVEMENTS OF PICCADILLY, OLIVER OFFERED THE Spanish woman his hand in farewell but received a kiss instead. Not two Iberian air pecks but a single warm and breathy display of affection that landed near his right ear and lingered long after the woman had set off toward Hyde Park Corner and her hotel. The evening was made complete by the seductive final glance she gave him over one shoulder. *Silly boy*, she was saying. *Silly, silly boy.*

He turned in the opposite direction and, feeling slightly inebriated, fished his phone from the breast pocket of his suit jacket. He had received several calls and text messages since he had checked it last, none from Sarah. Curiously, her name and number had vanished from his directory of recent calls. Nor was there any record of a Sarah Bancroft in his contacts. Julian's numbers were likewise missing, as was the entry for Isherwood Fine Arts.

Just then the phone pulsed with an incoming call. Oliver didn't recognize the number. He tapped the ACCEPT icon and raised the device to his ear.

"Your car and driver are waiting for you in Bolton Street," said a male voice, and the connection went dead.

Oliver returned the phone to his pocket and continued on his present easterly heading. Bolton Street was a few paces ahead on the left. He rounded the corner and spotted a silver Bentley Continental idling curbside. Seated behind the wheel was Sarah's husband. Oliver lowered his rotund form into the passenger seat. A moment later they were headed west along Piccadilly.

"Is your name really Peter Marlowe?"

"Why wouldn't it be?"

"Sounds made up."

"So does Oliver Dimbleby." Smiling, he pointed out the tall woman with shimmering black hair walking past the entrance of the Athenaeum. "There's our girl."

"I never laid so much as a finger on her."

"It's probably better not to mix work and play, wouldn't you agree?"

"No," said Oliver as the beautiful Spanish woman disappeared from view. "I most certainly would not."

42

QUEEN'S GATE TERRACE

As PART OF HIS RETIREMENT package from the Office, Gabriel had been given a personal copy of the Israeli cell phone hacking malware known as Proteus. The program's most insidious feature was that it required no blunder on the part of the target—no unwise software update or click of an innocent-looking photograph or advertisement. All Gabriel had to do was enter the target's phone number into the Proteus application on his laptop, and within minutes the device would be under his complete control. He could read the target's emails and text messages, review the target's Internet browsing history and telephone metadata, and monitor the target's physical movements with the GPS location services. Perhaps most important, he could activate the phone's microphone and camera and thus turn the device into a full-time instrument of surveillance.

He had protectively installed Proteus on Oliver Dimbleby's Samsung Galaxy after his recruitment but had allowed the malware to remain dormant until 5:42 that afternoon. With the click of his laptop's trackpad—an action he undertook while drinking tea in Sarah and Christopher's kitchen in Queen's Gate Terrace—he established that his missing operative was at that moment walking westward along Piccadilly, accompanied by a sultry-voiced woman who spoke fluent English with a Spanish accent. Sarah hurried home from Wiltons in time to hear the final minutes of their conversation in the trendy bar of Hide.

"She's a worthy opponent, our Magdalena. And not to be taken lightly."

"All the more reason we need to keep tubby Oliver on a very short leash."

To that end, Gabriel dispatched Christopher to Mayfair to corral his wayward asset. It was approaching seven thirty when they arrived at the maisonette. The after-action debriefing, such as it was, began with an awkward admission on Gabriel's part.

Oliver frowned. "That would explain why Sarah and Julian vanished from my contacts."

"I deleted them as a precautionary measure after you agreed to have drinks with that woman without giving us any warning."

"I'm afraid she didn't leave me much of a choice."

"Why?"

"Because she's nearly six feet tall and shockingly beautiful. What's more, she seems to have left Madrid without packing a brassiere." Oliver looked at Sarah. "I think I'll have that drink now."

"The Currant Affairs or the Tropic Thunder?"

"Whisky, if you have it."

Christopher opened a cabinet and took down a bottle of Johnnie Walker Black Label and a pair of cut-glass tumblers.

He filled one of the glasses with two fingers of whisky and sent it across the kitchen island toward Oliver.

"Baccarat," he said approvingly. "Maybe you're a wildly successful business consultant after all." He turned to Gabriel. "Isn't Proteus the software that the Saudi crown prince used to spy on that journalist he murdered?"

"The journalist's name was Omar Nawwaf. And, yes, the Israeli prime minister approved the sale of Proteus to the Saudis over my strenuous objections. In the hands of a repressive government, the malware can be a dangerous weapon of surveillance and blackmail. Imagine how something like this might be used to silence a meddlesome journalist or prodemocracy advocate."

Gabriel clicked the software's PLAY icon.

"Because she's nearly six feet tall and shockingly beautiful. What's more, she seems to have left Madrid without packing a brassiere."

Gabriel paused the recording.

"Dear God," murmured Oliver.

"Or how about this?" Gabriel clicked PLAY again.

"How is it that I've never heard of you?"

"I prefer to operate in the shadows. As do you, it seems."

"Bury Street is hardly the shadows."

Gabriel clicked PAUSE.

"Aren't you going to play the part where I turned down a night of incredible sex in a suite at the Lanesborough?"

"I believe the offer was dinner."

"You need to get out more, Mr. Allon."

He closed the laptop.

"What now?" asked Oliver.

"At some point late tomorrow afternoon, you will invite her to see the painting on Wednesday at six p.m. You will also ask her for the number of her mobile phone. She will no doubt refuse to give it to you."

"And when she arrives at my gallery on Wednesday evening?"

"She won't."

"Why not?"

"Because you're going to call her Wednesday afternoon and reschedule the appointment for eight p.m. on Thursday."

"Why would I do that?"

"To let her know that she is the furthest thing from your mind."

"If only it were true," said Oliver. "But why so late?"

"I don't want Cordelia Blake to be around when you show her the painting." Gabriel lowered his voice. "It might spoil the mood."

"Is she really interested in buying it?"

"Not at all. She just wants to have a look at it before it disappears."

"And if she likes what she sees?"

"After examining the provenance, she will ask you to reveal the identity of the man who sold it to you. You, of course, will refuse, leaving her no choice but to extract the information by some other means."

"Music to my ears."

"It's possible she might try to seduce you," said Gabriel. "But don't be disappointed if she threatens to destroy you instead."

"I can assure you, she won't be the first."

Gabriel tapped a few keys on the laptop. "I just added a new name to your contacts. Alessandro Calvi. Mobile phone number only."

"Who is he?"

"My front man in Florence. Call him at that number in the Spanish woman's presence. Signore Calvi will take care of the rest."

THE FRONT MAN, WHOSE REAL NAME WAS LUCA ROSSETTI, LEFT Florence at ten o'clock the following morning and headed south on the E35 Autostrada. The car beneath him was a Maserati Quattroporte sedan. Like the Patek Philippe time-piece on his wrist, it was the property of the Arma dei Cara-binieri, Rossetti's employer.

He arrived at his destination, Rome's Fiumicino Airport, at half past one. Another hour elapsed before Gabriel finally emerged from the door of Terminal 3. He tossed his over-night bag in the trunk and dropped into the passenger seat.

"I was starting to get worried about you," said Rossetti as he accelerated away from the curb.

"I spent almost as much time trying to get through pass-port control as I did flying from London." Gabriel looked around the interior of the luxury automobile. "Nice sled."

"It belonged to a heroin trafficker from the Camorra."

"A childhood friend of yours?"

"I knew his younger brother. They're both down in Pal-ermo now, in Pagliarelli Prison."

Rossetti turned onto the A90, Rome's high-speed orbital motorway, and headed north. He took his eyes off the road long enough to glance at the surveillance photograph that Gabriel had placed in his hand.

"What's her name?"

"According to her passport and credit cards, it's Magdalena Navarro. She made a move on Oliver Dimbleby last night."

"How did he hold up?"

"As well as could be expected." Gabriel reclaimed the pho-tograph. "You're next."

"When?"

"Thursday night. A quick phone call only. I want you to

give her a time and a place and then hang up before she can ask any questions."

"What's the time?"

"Nine p.m. on Friday."

"And the place?"

"Beneath the *arcone* in the Piazza della Repubblica. You won't have any difficulty spotting her." Gabriel slipped the photograph into his briefcase. "What year did he go to England?"

"Who?"

"Orazio Gentileschi."

"He traveled from Paris to Rome in 1626."

"Was Artemisia with him?"

"No. Only his three sons."

"When did he return to Italy?"

"He never did. He died in London in 1639."

"Where is he buried?"

Rossetti hesitated.

"The Queen's Chapel of Somerset House." Gabriel frowned. "Does this sled of yours go any faster? I'd like to get to Umbria while it's still light."

Rossetti put his foot to the floor.

"Better," said Gabriel. "You're a criminal now, Signore Calvi. Don't drive like a cop."

43

VILLA DEI FIORI

THE VILLA DEI FIORI, A thousand-acre estate located between the Tiber and Nera Rivers, had been in the possession of the Gasparri family since the days when Umbria was still ruled by the popes. There was a large and lucrative cattle operation, an equestrian center that bred some of the finest jumpers in all of Italy, and a flock of playful goats kept solely for entertainment value. Its olive groves produced some of Umbria's best oil, and its small vineyard contributed several hundred kilos of grapes each year to the local cooperative. Sunflowers shone in its fields.

The villa itself stood at the end of a dusty drive shaded by towering umbrella pine. In the eleventh century, it had been a monastery. There was still a small chapel and, in the walled interior courtyard, the remains of an oven where the brothers had baked their daily bread. At the base of the house was a large blue swimming pool, and adjacent to the pool was a trellised garden where rosemary and lavender grew along walls of Etruscan stone.

The current Count Gasparri, a faded Roman nobleman with close ties to the Holy See, did not rent Villa dei Fiori or allow friends and relatives to borrow it. Indeed, the last unaccompanied guests of the property had been the morose art restorer from the Vatican Museums and his beautiful Venetian-born wife, an experience the four-member staff would not soon forget. They were surprised, then, to learn that Count Gasparri had agreed to lend the villa to an un-named acquaintance for a stay of indeterminate length. Yes, said the count, it was likely his unnamed acquaintance would have guests of his own. No, he would not require the services of the household staff, as he was intensely private by nature and wished not to be disturbed.

Accordingly, two members of the staff—Anna the fabled cook, and Margherita the temperamental housekeeper—departed Villa dei Fiori early on Tuesday morning for a brief and unexpected holiday. Two other employees, however, re-mained at their posts: Isabella, the ethereal half Swede who ran the equestrian center; and Carlos, the Argentinian cow-boy who cared for the cattle and the crops. Both took note of the unmarked blue-black Fiat Ducato van that came bumping up the drive shortly before noon. The two occupants unloaded their cargo with the swiftness of thieves stashing stolen loot. The plunder included two large metal crates of the sort used by touring rock musicians, provisions enough to feed a small army, and, curiously, a professional-grade studio easel and a large blank canvas.

No, thought Isabella. It wasn't possible. Not after all these years.

The van soon departed, and a tense calm returned to the villa. It was shattered at 3:42 p.m. by the appalling roar of a Maserati engine. A moment later the car streaked past the equestrian center in a cloud of powdery dust. Even so, Isabella managed to catch a brief glimpse of the passenger. His most distinguishing feature was the swath of gray hair—like a smudge of ash—at his right temple.

It was a coincidence, Isabella assured herself. It couldn't possibly be the same man.

The Maserati's engine note faded to a dull drone as the sedan sped toward the villa through the twin rows of umbrella pine. It stopped outside the walls of the ancient courtyard, and the man with gray temples emerged. Medium height, noted Isabella with mounting dread. Slender as a cyclist.

He collected an overnight bag from the backseat and spoke a few parting words to the driver. Then he slung the bag over his shoulder—like a soldier, thought Isabella—and walked a few paces across the drive toward the gate of the courtyard. The same forward slump to the shoulders. The same slight outward bend to the legs.

"Dear God," whispered Isabella as the Maserati shot past her in a blur. It was true, after all.

The restorer had returned to Villa dei Fiori.

NEXT MORNING HE SETTLED INTO HIS FAMILIAR ROUTINE. He led himself on a forced march around the property. He went for a vigorous swim in the pool. He leafed through a book about the Flemish Baroque painter Anthony van Dyck while sitting in the shade of the trellised garden. Carlos and Isabella watched over him from afar. His mood, they observed, was much improved. It was as though a great burden had been lifted from his shoulders. Carlos declared that he was a changed man, but Isabella went even further. He was not a changed man, she said. He was a new man entirely.

His work habits, however, were as disciplined as ever.

Wednesday's labors before the easel began after a spartan lunch and continued late into the night. In his previous incarnation, he had listened to music while he worked. But now he seemed to be engrossed in a dreadful play on the radio, something that sounded like the output of a butt-dialed mobile phone. The program featured a roguishly charming London art dealer called Oliver and his plucky assistant, Cordelia. Of that much, at least, Isabella was certain. The rest of it was a disjointed hodgepodge of traffic noise, toilet flushes, one-sided phone calls, and bursts of barroom laughter.

The episode that aired Thursday morning featured a conversation between Oliver and Cordelia over a seemingly trivial scheduling matter—a visit to the gallery by a woman called Magdalena Navarro. At the conclusion of the program, the restorer set off on a punishing hike around the estate. And Isabella, in contravention of Count Gasparri's strict instructions, set off toward the now undefended villa. She entered through the kitchen and made her way to the great room, which the restorer had once again converted into an artist's atelier.

The canvas rested on the easel, shimmering with a recent application of oil-based paint. It was a three-quarter-length portrait of a woman wearing a gown of gold silk trimmed in white lace. Isabella, who had studied art history before devoting her life to horses, recognized the style as Van Dyck's. The woman's face was not yet complete, only her hair, which was almost black. Lampblack, thought Isabella, with a magnificent sheen of lead white with touches of lapis lazuli and vermilion.

His pigments and oils were arrayed on a nearby table. Isabella knew better than to touch anything, as he left behind hidden telltales to alert him to intruders. His Winsor & Newton Series 7 sable-hair brush lay on his palette. Like the painting, it was damp. Next to it was a slumbering laptop. The device was connected to a pair of Bose speakers. Better to hear the travails of Oliver and Cordelia, thought Isabella.

She turned to the unfinished painting once more. He had made a remarkable amount of progress in so short a time. But why was he *painting* a painting and not restoring one? And where was his model? The answer, thought Isabella, was that he had no need of one. She remembered the remarkable painting that had flowed from his hand after he had suffered the terrible injury to his eye—*Two Children on a Beach*, in the style of Mary Cassatt. He had finished it in a handful of marathon sessions, with only his memory to guide him.

"What do you think of it so far?" he asked calmly.

Isabella swung round and laid a hand over her heart. Somehow she managed not to scream.

He took a step forward. "What are you doing in here?"

"Count Gasparri asked me to check on you."

"In that case, why did you come when you knew I was out?" He contemplated his pigments and oils. "You didn't touch anything, did you?"

"Of course not. I was just wondering what you were working on."

"Is that all? Or were you also wondering why I returned to this place after all these years?"

"That, too," Isabella conceded.

He took another step forward. "Do you know who I am?"

"Until a moment ago, I thought you were an art restorer who sometimes worked at the Vatican Museums."

"And you no longer believe that to be the case?"

"No," she said after a moment. "I do not."

A silence fell between them.

"Forgive me," said Isabella, and started toward the door.

"Wait," he called out.

She stopped and turned slowly to face him. The greenness of his eyes was unsettling. "Yes, Signore Allon?"

"You never told me what you thought of the painting."

"It's quite extraordinary. But who is she?"

"I'm not sure yet."

"When will you know?"

"Soon, I hope." He took up his palette and brush, and opened the laptop.

"What's it called?" asked Isabella.

"Portrait of an Unknown Woman."

"Not the painting. The program about Oliver and Cordelia."

He looked up suddenly.

"You've been playing it quite loudly. The sound carries well in the countryside."

"I hope it didn't disturb you."

"Not at all," said Isabella, and turned to go.

"Your phone," he said suddenly.

She stopped. "What about it?"

"Please leave it behind. And bring me your laptop and the keys to your car. Tell Carlos to bring me his devices as well. No phone calls or emails until further notice. And no leaving the estate."

Isabella switched off her phone and laid it on the table, next to the open laptop. As she slipped from the villa, she heard roguish Oliver tell someone named Nicky that his client would have to increase his offer to £30 million if he wanted the Veronese. Nicky called Oliver a thief, then asked whether he was free for a drink that evening. Oliver said he wasn't.

"What's her name?"

"Magdalena Navarro."

"Spanish?"

"I'm afraid so."

"What does she look like?"

"A bit like Penélope Cruz, but prettier."

44

DIMBLEBY FINE ARTS

IT WAS SARAH BANCROFT, FROM a table at Franco's Italian restaurant in Jermyn Street, who spotted her first—the tall, slender woman with almost black hair, dressed in a shortish skirt and a formfitting white top. She rounded the corner into Bury Street and instantly caught the attention of Simon Mendenhall, who was leaving Christie's after an interminable senior staff meeting. Simon being Simon, he paused to have a look at the woman's backside and was aghast to see her make a beeline for Dimbleby Fine Arts. Simon in turn made a beeline for Wiltons and informed all those present, including the dealer of contemporary art with whom he was rumored to be having a torrid affair, that Oliver's hot streak continued unabated.

At eight o'clock precisely, the raven-haired woman rang the gallery's bell. Oliver waited until she rang it a second time before rising from his Eames desk chair and unlocking the door. Stepping across the threshold, she pressed her lips suggestively against his cheek. During their weeklong game of cat and mouse, Oliver had sidestepped two offers of dinner and a thinly veiled sexual proposition. Only heaven knew what the next few minutes might bring.

He closed the door and locked it tightly. "Would you like a drink?"

"I'd love one."

"Whisky or whisky?"

"Whisky would be perfect."

Oliver led her through the half-light to his office and filled two tumblers with scotch.

"Blue Label," she remarked.

"I keep it for special occasions."

"What are we celebrating?"

"The impending record-shattering sale of *Susanna in the Bath* by Paolo Veronese."

"Where does the bidding stand?"

"As of this evening, I have two firm offers of thirty."

"Museums?"

"One museum," answered Oliver. "One private."

"I have a feeling that both of your bidders are going to be disappointed."

"The museum's offer is final. The collector made a killing during the pandemic and has money to burn."

"So does my client. He's anxious to hear from me."

"Then perhaps we shouldn't keep your client waiting any longer."

They carried their drinks to the gallery's rear exhibition room. The large painting was propped on a pair of baize-covered display easels. The tableau was only faintly visible in the semidarkness.

Oliver reached for the dimmer switch. As Susanna and the two elders emerged from the gloom, the woman raised a hand to her mouth and murmured something in Spanish.

"Translation?" asked Oliver.

"It wouldn't survive." She approached the painting slowly, as though trying not to disturb the three figures. "It's no wonder you have the entire art world at your feet, Mr. Dimbleby. It's a masterwork painted by an artist at the height of his powers."

"I believe those were the very words I used to describe it in the press release."

"Were they?" She reached into her handbag.

"No photographs, please."

She produced a small ultraviolet torch. "Would you mind switching off the lights for a moment?"

Oliver reached for the dimmer again and returned the room to darkness. The woman played the purple-blue beam of the torch over the surface of the painting.

"The losses are rather extensive."

"The *losses*," replied Oliver, "are exactly what one would expect to find in a four-hundred-and-fifty-year-old Venetian School painting."

"Who handled the restoration for you?"

"It came to me in this condition."

"How fortunate," she said, and switched off the ultraviolet torch.

Oliver allowed the darkness to linger for a moment before slowly bringing up the room lights. The woman was now holding a rectangular LED magnifier. She used it to examine the exposed flesh of Susanna's neck and shoulder, followed by the vermilion-colored robe she was clutching to her breasts.

"The brushwork is quite visible," she said. "Not only in the garments but the skin as well."

"Veronese became more overtly painterly in his brushwork later in his career," explained Oliver. "This work reflects the change from his earlier style."

She returned the magnifier to her handbag and stepped away from the painting. A minute passed. Then another.

Oliver cleared his throat gently.

"I heard that," she said.

"I don't mean to rush things, but it's rather late."

"Do you have a moment to show me the provenance?"

Oliver ushered the woman back to his office. There he drew a copy of the provenance from a locked file drawer and laid it on the desk. The woman reviewed it with justifiable skepticism.

"An old European collection?"

"Very old," replied Oliver. "And very private."

The woman pushed the provenance across the desktop. "I must know the identity of the previous owner, Mr. Dimbleby."

"The previous owner, like your client, insists on anonymity."

"Are you in direct contact with him?"

"Her," said Oliver. "And the answer is no. I deal with her representative."

"A lawyer? A dealer?"

"I'm sorry, but I can't reveal the representative's name or characterize his connection to the collection. Especially to a competitor." Oliver lowered his voice. "Even one as attractive as you."

She gave him a coquettish pout. "Is there really nothing I can do to change your mind?"

"I'm afraid not."

The woman sighed. "And if I were to offer you, say, thirty-five million pounds for your Veronese?"

"My answer would be the same."

She tapped the provenance with the tip of her forefinger. "Are none of your other potential buyers concerned about the flimsiness of the painting's chain of ownership?"

"Not at all."

"How can that be?"

"Because it doesn't matter where the painting came from. The work speaks for itself."

"It certainly spoke to me. In fact, it was rather talkative."

"And what did it say?"

She leaned forward across the desk and looked directly into his eyes. "It said that Paolo Veronese didn't paint it."

"Nonsense."

"Is it, Mr. Dimbleby?"

"I have spent the last four days showing that painting to the leading Old Master experts from the world's most respected museums. And not one of them has questioned the authenticity of the work."

"That's because none of those experts know about the man who visited Galerie Konrad Hassler in Berlin a few days after you announced the rediscovery of your so-called Veronese. This man showed Herr Hassler a photograph of the so-called Veronese side by side with the so-called Titian and the so-called Tintoretto. The photograph was taken in the studio of the art forger who painted them."

"That's not possible."

"I'm afraid it is."

"He assured me that the paintings were genuine."

"Signore Rinaldi?"

"Never heard of him," swore Oliver, truthfully.

"That's the name he used when he visited Galerie Hassler. Giovanni Rinaldi."

"I know him by a different name."

"And what name is that?"

Oliver made no reply.

"He deceived you, Mr. Dimbleby. Or perhaps you simply wanted to be deceived. Whatever the case, you are now in a very precarious situation. But don't worry, it will be our little secret." She paused. "For a small fee, of course."

"How small?"

"Half of the final sales price of the Veronese."

Oliver uncharacteristically chose the high road. "I couldn't possibly sell the picture after what you've told me."

"If you withdraw the painting now, you will be forced to return the millions of pounds you accepted for the Titian and the Tintoretto. And then . . ."

"I'll be ruined."

She handed Oliver a sheet of stationery from the Lanesborough. "I would like you to wire fifteen million pounds into that account first thing tomorrow morning. If the money doesn't appear by the close of business, I will telephone that reporter from the *New York Times* and tell her the truth about your so-called Veronese."

"You're a cheap blackmailer."

"And you, Mr. Dimbleby, don't know as much about the art world as you think you do."

He looked down at the account number. "You will receive the money *after* the sale of my Veronese. Which, I might add, is a genuine Veronese and not a fake."

"I insist on immediate payment."

"You can't have it."

"In that case," said the woman, "I will require a security deposit."

"How much?"

"Not money, Mr. Dimbleby. A name."

Oliver hesitated, then said, "Alessandro Calvi."

"And where does Signore Calvi live?"

"Florence."

"Please call Signore Calvi from your mobile phone. I'd like to have a word with him."

———————

IT WAS HALF PAST EIGHT WHEN OLIVER SHOWED HER INTO Bury Street. She offered him a hand in farewell. And when he refused it, she placed her mouth close to his ear and warned him of the professional humiliation he would suffer if he failed to send her the money as promised.

"Dinner at the Lanesborough?" he asked as she set off toward Jermyn Street.

"Some other time," she said over her shoulder, and was gone.

Inside the gallery, Oliver returned to his office. The scent of orange blossom and jasmine hung in the air. On the desk were two unfinished glasses of Johnnie Walker Blue Label whisky, a fictitious provenance for a fake painting by Paolo Veronese, and a sheet of stationery from the Lanesborough Hotel. Oliver returned the provenance to the file drawer. The sheet of stationery he photographed with his phone.

It rang a moment later. "Bravo!" said the voice at the other end of the connection. "I couldn't have done it better myself."

GENERAL FERRARI ARRIVED AT VILLA dei Fiori at two the following afternoon. He was accompanied by four tactical officers and two technicians. The tactical officers conducted a site survey of the villa and the grounds while the techs turned the dining room into an op center. The general, in a business suit and open-necked dress shirt, sat in the great room with Gabriel and watched him paint.

"Your girl arrived in Florence shortly before noon."

"How did she manage that?"

"A chartered Dassault Falcon from London City Airport. The Four Seasons sent a car for her. She's there now."

"Doing what?"

"Our surveillance capabilities inside the hotel are limited. But we'll keep an eye on her if she decides to do a bit of sightseeing. And we'll definitely have a couple of teams in the Piazza della Repubblica at nine o'clock."

"If she spots them, we're dead."

"This might come as a surprise to you, my friend, but the Arma dei Carabinieri has done this a time or two. Without your help," the general added. "The minute she purchases that painting, we'll have the grounds to arrest her on numerous art fraud and conspiracy charges. She will be staring down the barrel of a very long sentence in an Italian prison for women. Not a pleasant prospect for a frequent guest of the Lanesborough Hotel in London."

"I don't want her in a prison cell," said Gabriel. "I want her on the opposite side of an interrogation table, telling us everything she knows."

"As do I. But I am obligated under Italian law to provide her with an attorney if she desires one. If I do not, anything she says will be inadmissible at trial."

"What does Italian law say about art restorers taking part in interrogations?"

"Not surprisingly, Italian law is silent on that question. If, however, she were to consent to the restorer's presence, it might be permissible."

Gabriel stepped away from the canvas and appraised his work. "Perhaps the portrait will influence her thinking."

"I wouldn't count on it. In fact, it might be a good idea to put her in handcuffs before you let her see it."

"Please don't," said Gabriel as he loaded his brush. "I wouldn't want to spoil the surprise."

SHE SPENT THE AFTERNOON AT THE POOL AND AT 6:00 P.M. headed upstairs to her suite to shower and dress. She chose her clothing with care. Pale blue stretch jeans. A loose-fitting white blouse. Flat-soled suede moccasins. Her face was aglow from the Tuscan sun and required little makeup. Her raven hair she wound into a bun, with a few stray tendrils along her neck. Attractive, she thought as she evaluated her appearance in the mirror, but serious. There would be no flirtation to-night. No fun and games of the sort she had played with the art dealer in London. The man she was meeting in the Piazza della Repubblica could not be seduced or tricked into doing her bidding. She had seen a video of his visit to Galerie Hassler in Berlin. He was young, good-looking, athletically built. A dangerous man, she reckoned. A professional.

Downstairs, she crossed the lobby and stepped through the hotel's unassuming entrance into the Borgo Pinti. The midday crowds had retreated from the city, as had the heat. She stopped for a coffee at Caffè Michelangelo, then walked through the cool twilight to the Piazza della Repubblica. Its dominant architectural feature was the towering triumphal arch on the western flank. She arrived there, as instructed, at nine o'clock exactly. The Piaggio motor scooter drew along-side her a minute later.

She recognized the man at the helm.

Young, good-looking, athletically built.

Wordlessly he moved to the back of the saddle. Magdalena mounted the bike and asked for a destination.

"The Lungarno Torrigiani. It's on the—"

"I know where it is," she said, and executed a flawless U-turn in the narrow street. As she sped toward the river, his strong hands moved over the small of her back, her hips, her crotch, the inside of her thighs, her breasts. There was nothing sexual in his touch. He was merely searching her for a concealed weapon.

He was a professional, she thought. Fortunately, she was a professional, too.

The call arrived at Villa dei Fiori at 9:03 p.m. It was from one of the Carabinieri surveillance artists in the Piazza della Repubblica. The woman had appeared at the rendezvous point as instructed. She and Rossetti were now bound for the apartment. General Ferrari quickly relayed the information to Gabriel, who was still at his easel. He carefully wiped the paint from his brush and headed to the makeshift op center to watch the next act. The Oliver Dimbleby show had been a smashing success. Now it was Alessandro Calvi's turn in the spotlight. One mistake, thought Gabriel, and they were dead.

46

LUNGARNO TORRIGIANI

THE BUILDING WAS THE COLOR of burnt sienna, with a balustrade running along the length of the second floor. The apartment was on the third. In the darkened entrance hall, Rossetti relieved the woman of her Hermès Birkin handbag and emptied the contents onto the kitchen counter. Her possessions included an ultraviolet torch, a professional-grade LED magnifier, and a disposable Samsung phone. The device was powered off. The SIM card had been removed.

Rossetti opened her passport. "Is your name really Magdalena Navarro?"

"Is yours really Alessandro Calvi?"

He unsnapped her Cartier wallet and checked the credit cards and the Spanish driver's permit. All bore the name Magdalena Navarro. The cash compartment contained about three thousand euros and a hundred unspent British pounds. In the zippered compartment Rossetti found a few receipts, all from her visit to London. Otherwise, the wallet and bag were unusually free of pocket litter.

He returned her belongings to the bag, leaving a single item on the counter. It was a photograph of *Danaë and the Shower of Gold* by Gabriel Allon. "Where did you get this?" he asked.

"I happened to be in Berlin not long ago and had lunch with an old friend. He told me an interesting story about a recent visitor to his art gallery. Evidently, this visitor tried to sell my friend the painting in that photograph. He said it came from the same private collection as the pictures that have caused such a sensation in London. He showed my friend a photograph of those paintings as well. Three paintings, one photo. My friend found that odd, to say the least."

"The photograph was taken by my restorer."

"In my experience, art restorers make the best forgers. Wouldn't you agree?"

"That sounds like a question a cop would ask."

"I'm not a police officer, Signore Calvi. I am an art broker who connects buyers and sellers and lives off the scraps."

"Lives quite well, from what I hear."

He led her into the apartment's large sitting room. Three tall casement windows, open to the evening air, overlooked the domes and campanili of Florence. The woman, however, had eyes only for the paintings hanging on the walls.

"You have extraordinary taste."

"The apartment doubles as my saleroom."

She pointed out an exquisite terra-cotta Etruscan amphora. "You also deal in antiquities, I see."

"It's a major part of my business. Chinese billionaires love Greek and Etruscan pottery."

She trailed a forefinger along the curve of the vessel. "This piece is quite lovely. But tell me something, Signore Calvi. Is it a forgery like those three paintings you sold to Mr. Dimbleby? Or is it merely looted?"

"The paintings I sold to Dimbleby were examined by the most prominent Italian Old Master experts in London. And no one questioned the attribution."

"That's because your forger is the world's greatest living Old Master painter."

"There's no such thing as a *living* Old Master."

"Of course there is. I should know. You see, I work for one. He, too, can fool the experts. But your forger is far more talented than mine. That Veronese is a masterpiece. I nearly fainted when I saw it."

"I thought you said you were a broker."

"I *am* a broker. But the paintings I represent simply happen to be forgeries."

"So you're a front man? Is that what you're saying?"

"*You* are a front man, Signore Calvi. As you well know, I am in fact a woman."

"Why are you in Florence?"

"Because I'd like to make you and your forger an offer."

"What sort of offer?"

"Show me the Gentileschi," said the woman. "And then I'll explain everything."

Rossetti led her into the adjoining room and switched on the lights. She stared at the painting in silence, as though she had been struck mute.

"Shall I bring you the magnifier and ultraviolet torch?" asked Rossetti after a moment.

"That won't be necessary. The painting is . . ."

"Incandescent?"

"Incendiary," whispered the woman. "But also quite dangerous."

"Is that so?"

"Oliver Dimbleby behaved recklessly by bringing those

three pictures to market from your so-called old European collection. Already there are whispers in certain corners of the art world that the paintings might be forgeries. And then you compounded the mistake with your conduct at Galerie Hassler. It is only a matter of time before your ruse unravels. And when it does, there will be collateral casualties."

"You?"

She nodded. "The market for museum-quality Old Masters is a small one, Signore Calvi. There are only so many good pictures and so many collectors and museums who are willing to pay millions for them. Two major Old Master forgery rings cannot compete against one another and survive. One will inevitably collapse. And it will take the other one down with it."

"What's the alternative?"

"I am prepared to offer you and your partner the protection of a proven distribution network, one that will guarantee a steady stream of income for many years to come."

"I don't need your network."

"Your behavior in Berlin would suggest otherwise. The painting in the next room is worth thirty million if handled properly. And yet you were willing to let Herr Hassler have it for a mere two million."

"And if I were to entrust it to you?"

"I would sell it in a way that favors long-term security over short-term financial gain."

"I didn't hear a price."

"Five million," said the woman. "But I would insist on meeting with your forger in his studio before payment."

"Ten million," countered Rossetti. "And you will wire the money into my account before meeting with my forger."

"When would such a meeting take place?"

Rossetti pondered his Patek Phillipe wristwatch. "Shortly after midnight, I imagine. Provided, of course, that you have more than three thousand euros hidden in that Cartier wallet of yours."

"Where do you do your banking, Signore Calvi?"

"Banca Monte dei Paschi di Siena."

"I need the account and routing numbers."

"I'll bring you your phone."

SHE ENTERED THE NUMBER MANUALLY AND FROM MEMORY. The first time she dialed, she received no answer and rang off without leaving a message. The second attempt met with the same result. Call number three, however, found its intended target.

She addressed the person at the other end of the call in excellent English. There was no exchange of pleasantries, only the swift execution of a wire transfer of €10 million to an account at the world's oldest bank. Email confirmation arrived a few minutes after the call was concluded. With her thumb concealing the sender's name, she showed it to Rossetti. Then she carried the phone to the nearest window and hurled it into the black waters of the Arno.

"Where are we going?" she asked.

"A little town in southern Umbria."

"Not by motor scooter, I hope."

The Maserati was parked outside the building. Rossetti behaved himself in town but let it rip when they hit the Autostrada. He waited until they reached Orvieto before informing his forger—with a phone call placed in speaker mode on the car's Bluetooth system—that he was coming to see him on an important matter. His forger expressed disappointment at the intrusion on his privacy, as he was hoping to complete a painting that evening.

"Can't it wait until morning?"

"I'm afraid not. Besides, I have some good news."

"Speaking of news, have you seen the *Times*? Oliver Dimbleby announced that he sold the Veronese to a private collector. Thirty-five million. At least that's the rumor."

And with that, the call went dead.

"He doesn't sound pleased," said the Spanish woman.

"With good reason."

"It wasn't a consignment deal?"

"Straight sale."

"How much did Dimbleby pay you for it?"

"Three million."

"And the new painting?" asked the woman.

"It's a Van Dyck."

"Really? What's the subject matter?"

"I wouldn't want to spoil the surprise," said Rossetti, and put his foot to the floor.

SHORTLY BEFORE MIDNIGHT ISABELLA WAS AWAKENED FROM A pleasant dream by the frenzied barking of the dogs. Usually, the culprit was one of the wild boars that dwelled in the surrounding woods. But on that evening the source of the commotion was the two men traipsing across the moonlit pasture. They were part of a large all-male party of guests who had arrived that afternoon. Isabella was of the opinion that the *guests* were not guests at all, but were in fact police officers. How else to explain the fact that two of them were now strolling the pasture by moonlight, each armed with a compact submachine gun?

Eventually the dogs fell silent, and Isabella returned to her bed, only to be awakened a second time, at 12:37 a.m. Now the culprit was the wretched Maserati sports car. The same car, she thought, that had delivered the restorer to Villa dei Fiori earlier that week. It shot past her bedroom window in a blur and raced up the tree-lined drive toward the villa. Two figures emerged into the moonlit forecourt. One was an athletically built man, perhaps another police officer. The other was a tall, raven-haired woman.

It was the woman who entered the villa first, with the man a step behind. The shrieking began a few seconds later, a terrible anguished wailing, like the cry of a wounded animal. Surely it had something to do with the painting. *Portrait of an Unknown Woman* . . . Perhaps she had been mistaken, thought Isabella as she covered her ears. Perhaps Signore Allon was the same man after all.

PART THREE

PENTIMENTO

47

VILLA DEI FIORI

She did not surrender without a fight, but then they had not expected she would. Luca Rossetti attempted to subdue her first and was soon the target of a ferocious counterattack, leaving Gabriel no choice but to abandon his defense of the painting and come to his newfound friend's aid. He was joined a few seconds later by two of the tactical officers, who burst into the room with guns drawn like characters in a French farce. Next the techs entered the fray, and Gabriel wisely withdrew to safer ground to observe the end stages of the contest. It was Rossetti, with blood flowing from one nostril, who applied the handcuffs. Gabriel found the metallic crunch of the locking mechanism to be a most satisfying sound.

Only then did General Ferrari step unhurriedly onto the stage. After determining to his satisfaction that the suspect had not been injured, he commenced a review of the evidence against her. It included a €10 million wire transfer to the Banca Monte dei Paschi di Siena as well as the suspect's admission, preserved on video, that she was a key player in an international forgery network. At present, the Carabinieri were attempting to determine the origin of the payment. They were likewise working to identify the last three phone numbers dialed from the disposable Samsung now lying on the bottom of the Arno River. Neither task, said the general, would prove difficult.

But even without the information, he continued, there was sufficient evidence under Italian law to hand the suspect over to a magistrate for an immediate trial. Because she had been caught in flagrante delicto engaging in art fraud and related financial crimes, the outcome of such a proceeding would not be in doubt. She would likely receive a lengthy sentence in one of Italy's prisons for women, which, regrettably, were among Western Europe's worst.

"Upon your release, you will be extradited to France, where you will undoubtedly face charges for your role in the murders of Valerie Bérrangar, Georges Fleury, and Bruno Gilbert. I'm sure Spanish prosecutors will think of something with which to charge you as well. Suffice it to say, you will be an elderly pensioner by the time you are a free woman again. Unless, of course, you accept the lifeline that I am about to offer you."

Under the terms of the deal, the suspect would receive no prison time for her offenses related to the evening's sting operation in Florence. In exchange, she would provide the Carabinieri with the names of the other members of her network, a complete inventory of the forgeries now in circulation, and, of course, the identity of the forger himself. Any attempt at evasion or deception on the suspect's part would result in the withdrawal of the agreement and immediate incarceration. A second offer of immunity would be unlikely.

They had expected a declaration of innocence, but she made none. Nor did she request a lawyer or demand that General

Ferrari put his cooperation agreement in writing. Instead, she looked at Gabriel and posed a single question.

"How did you find me, Mr. Allon?"

"I painted four pictures," he replied. "And you walked straight into my arms."

At which point the mêlée resumed. Capitano Luca Rossetti was the only casualty.

SHE BEGAN BY CLEARING UP ANY LINGERING QUESTIONS AS TO the authenticity of her identity. Yes, she assured them, her name was in fact Magdalena Navarro. And, yes, she had been born and raised in the Andalusian city of Seville. Her father was a dealer of Spanish Old Master paintings and antique furniture. His gallery was located near the Plaza Virgen de los Reyes, a few paces from the entrance of the Doña Maria Hotel. It catered to Seville's wealthiest inhabitants, those of noble birth and inherited wealth. The Navarro clan were not members of that rarefied social stratum, but the gallery had given Magdalena a glimpse of the life led by those for whom money was of no concern.

The gallery had also instilled in her a love of art—Spanish art, in particular. She revered Diego Velázquez and Francisco de Goya, but Picasso was her obsession. She imitated his drawings as a young child and at the age of twelve produced a near-perfect copy of *Two Girls Reading*. She began her formal training soon after, at a private art school in Seville, and upon completing her secondary education she entered the Barcelona Academy of Art. Much to the dismay of her classmates, she sold her first canvases while still a student. An important writer from a Barcelona culture magazine predicted that one day Magdalena Navarro would be Spain's most famous female painter.

"When I graduated in 2004, two prominent art galleries

offered to show my work. One was in Barcelona, the other in Madrid. Needless to say, they were quite surprised when I turned them down."

They had placed her in a straight-backed chair in the great room's main seating area. Her feet were flat upon the terracotta tiles of the floor; her hands were cuffed behind her back. General Ferrari was seated directly opposite, with Rossetti at his side and a tripod-mounted video camera over his shoulder. Gabriel was contemplating the L-shaped tear, 15 by 23 centimeters, in the lower left corner of *Portrait of an Unknown Woman*.

"Why would you do that?" he asked.

"Turn down a chance to show my work at the tender age of twenty-one? Because I had no interest in being the most famous female artist in Spain."

"Spain was too small for a talent like yours?"

"I thought so at the time."

"Where did you go?"

She arrived in New York in the autumn of 2005 and settled into a one-room apartment on Avenue C, in the Alphabet City section of Lower Manhattan. The apartment was soon filled with newly completed paintings, none of which she was able to sell. The money she had brought with her from Spain quickly ran out. Her father sent what he could, but it was never enough.

A year after her arrival in New York, she could no longer afford painting supplies and was facing eviction. She found work waiting tables at El Pote Español in Murray Hill and at Katz's Delicatessen on East Houston Street. Before long she was working sixty hours a week, which left her too exhausted to paint.

Depressed, she started drinking too much and discovered she had a taste for cocaine. She fell into a relationship with her dealer, a handsome Dominican of Spanish descent named

Hector Martínez, and was soon acting as a courier and delivery girl in his network. Many of her regular customers were Wall Street traders who were making fortunes selling derivatives and mortgage-backed securities, the complex investment instruments that in three years' time would leave the global economy on the brink of collapse.

"And then, of course, there were the rock musicians, screenwriters, Broadway producers, painters, sculptors, and gallery owners. As strange as it might sound, being a cocaine dealer in New York was a good career move. Anyone who was anyone was using. And everyone knew my name."

The money she earned dealing drugs allowed Magdalena to stop waiting tables and resume painting. She gave one of her canvases to a Chelsea art dealer with a thousand-dollar-a-week cocaine habit. Rather than keep the painting for himself, the dealer sold it to a client for $50,000. He gave half of the proceeds to Magdalena, but refused to divulge the buyer's name.

"Did he tell you why?" asked Gabriel.

"He said the client insisted on anonymity. But he was also concerned I would cut him out of the picture."

"Why would he suspect a thing like that?"

"I was the daughter of an art dealer. I knew how the business worked."

The Chelsea art dealer bought two more canvases from Magdalena and immediately sold both works to the same anonymous client. The dealer then informed Magdalena that the anonymous client was a wealthy investor who admired her work greatly and was interested in becoming her patron.

"But only if I stopped dealing cocaine."

"I assume you agreed."

"I dropped my pager down a sewer on West Twenty-Fifth Street and never made another delivery."

And her new patron, she continued, lived up to his end of

the deal. Indeed, during the summer of 2008, he purchased four additional paintings through the auspices of the same Chelsea gallery. Magdalena earned more than $100,000 from the sales. Fearful of losing her patron's financial support, she made no attempt to discover his identity. But on a frigid morning in mid-December, she was awakened by a phone call from a woman claiming to be her patron's secretary.

"She wanted to know whether I was free for dinner that evening. When I said that I was, she said a limousine would collect me at my apartment at four p.m."

"Why so early?"

"My anonymous patron was planning to take me to Le Cirque. He wanted to make certain that I had something appropriate to wear."

The limousine arrived as promised and delivered Magdalena to Bergdorf Goodman, where a personal shopper named Clarissa selected $20,000 worth of clothing and jewelry, including a gold Cartier wristwatch. Then she escorted Magdalena to the store's exclusive hair salon for a cut and blow-dry.

Le Cirque was located a few blocks away, in the Palace Hotel. Magdalena arrived at eight o'clock and was immediately shown to a table in the center of the iconic dining room. In her mind she had sketched an image of her patron as a well-preserved blazer-wearing septuagenarian from Park Avenue. But the man who awaited her was tall and blond and forty-five at most. Rising, he offered Magdalena his hand and at long last introduced himself.

His name, he said, was Phillip Somerset.

48

VILLA DEI FIORI

ADMITTEDLY, IT WAS THE LAST name in the world that Gabriel had expected to come out of Magdalena Navarro's mouth. An experienced interrogator, he offered no expression of surprise or incredulity. Instead, he turned to General Ferrari and Luca Rossetti, to whom the name meant nothing, and recited a redacted version of Phillip Somerset's curriculum vitae. Former bond trader at Lehman Brothers. Founder and chief executive officer of Masterpiece Art Ventures, an art-based hedge fund that routinely returned profits of 25 percent to its investors. It was clear the general suspected there was more to the story. Nevertheless, he permitted Gabriel to resume questioning the suspect. He began by asking Magdalena to describe her evening at what was once Manhattan's most celebrated restaurant.

"The food was awful. And the decor!" She rolled her beautiful dark eyes.

"What about your dinner date?"

"Our conversation was cordial and businesslike. There was nothing romantic about the evening."

"Why the fancy dress and Cartier watch?"

"They were a demonstration of his power to transform my life. The entire evening was a piece of performance art."

"You were impressed by him?"

"Quite the opposite, actually. I thought he was a cross between Jay Gatsby and Bud Fox. He was pretending to be something he wasn't."

"And what was that?"

"A man of extraordinary wealth and sophistication. A Medici-like patron of the arts."

"But Phillip *was* wealthy."

"Not as wealthy as he claimed to be. And he didn't know the first thing about art. Phillip gravitated toward the art world because that's where the money was."

"Why did he gravitate to you?"

"I was young and beautiful and talented, with an exotic name and Hispanic heritage. He said he was going to turn me into a billion-dollar global brand. He promised to make me rich beyond my wildest dreams."

"Was any of it true?"

"Only the part about making me rich."

Phillip acquired Magdalena's paintings almost as quickly as she could finish them and deposited the money in an account at Masterpiece Art Ventures. The balance soon exceeded $2 million. She left her studio apartment in Alphabet City and settled into a brownstone on West Eleventh Street. Phillip retained ownership of the property but allowed her to live there rent-free. He visited often.

"To see your latest paintings?"

"No," she answered. "To see me."

"You were lovers?"

"Love had very little to do with what took place between us, Mr. Allon. It was a bit like our dinner at Le Cirque."

"Awful?"

"Cordial and businesslike."

Occasionally Phillip took her to a Broadway performance or a gallery opening. But for the most part he kept her hidden from view in the brownstone, where she spent her days painting, like Rumpelstiltskin's daughter at her spinning wheel. He assured her that he was arranging a splashy exhibition of her work, one that would turn her into the hottest artist in New York. But when the promised exhibition never materialized, she accused Phillip of deceiving her.

"How did he react?"

"He took me to a loft in Hell's Kitchen, just off Ninth Avenue."

"What was in the loft?"

"Paintings."

"Were any of them genuine?"

"No," said Magdalena. "Not a single one."

THEY WERE, HOWEVER, WORKS OF BREATHTAKING BEAUTY AND quality, executed by a forger of immense talent and technical skill. He had not copied existing paintings. Instead, he had cleverly imitated the style of an Old Master artist to create a picture that could be passed off as newly rediscovered. All of the canvases, stretchers, and frames were appropriate to their period and school, as were the pigments. Which meant that none of the paintings could ever be exposed as forgeries by a scientific evaluation.

"Did Phillip tell you the forger's name that night?"

"Of course not. Phillip has never told me his name."

"You don't really expect us to believe that, do you?"

"Why would he tell me such a thing? Besides, the forger's name wasn't relevant to what Phillip wanted me to do."

"Which was?"

"Sell the paintings, of course."

"But why you?"

"Why *not* me? I was a trained art historian and a former drug dealer who knew how to walk into a room with a quarter-ounce of cocaine and walk out with the money. I was also the daughter of an art dealer from Seville."

"A perfect point of entry for the European market."

"And a perfect place to take a few forged paintings out for a test drive," she added.

"But why would a wildly successful businessman like Phillip Somerset want to get mixed up in art fraud?"

"You tell me, Mr. Allon."

"Because the businessman wasn't so wildly successful after all."

Magdalena nodded in agreement. "Masterpiece Art Ventures was a bust from the beginning. Even when art prices were soaring, Phillip was never able get the trading formula right. He needed some sure bets to show his investors a profit."

"And you agreed to this scheme?"

"Not at first."

"What changed your mind?"

"Another two million dollars in my account at Masterpiece Art Ventures."

Magdalena returned to Seville a month later and took delivery of the first six paintings from New York. The shipping documents described them as Old Master works of minimal value, all produced by later followers or imitators of the masters themselves. But when Magdalena offered them for sale at her father's gallery, she inflated the attributions to "circle of" or "workshop of," which increased the value of the works substantially. Within a few weeks, all six paintings had been snatched up by her father's wealthy Seville clientele. Magdalena gave him a 10 percent cut of the profits and transferred the rest of the money to Masterpiece Art Ventures through an account in Liechtenstein.

"How much?"

"A million and a half." Magdalena shrugged. "Chump change."

After the initial test run, the paintings began arriving from New York at a steady clip. There were too many to sell through the gallery, so Magdalena established herself as a Madrid-based runner. She sold one of the canvases—a biblical scene purportedly by the Venetian painter Andrea Celesti—to Spain's most prominent Old Master dealer, who in turn sold it to a museum in the American Midwest.

"Where it hangs to this day."

But Phillip soon discovered that it was far easier for Magdalena to simply *sell* the paintings back to Masterpiece Art Ventures—at wildly inflated prices, with no actual money changing hands. He then moved the works in and out of Masterpiece's portfolio through private phantom sales of his own, using an array of corporate shell entities. Each time a painting supposedly changed hands, it increased in value.

"By the end of 2010, Masterpiece Art Ventures claimed to control more than four hundred million dollars' worth of art. But a significant percentage of those paintings were worthless fakes, the value of which had been artificially inflated with fictitious sales."

But Phillip was not content with the scale of the operation, she continued. He wanted to show explosive growth in the value of Masterpiece's portfolio and higher earnings for his investors. Meeting that goal required the introduction of additional paintings to the market. Until then they had limited themselves primarily to middle-tier works, but Phillip was eager to raise the stakes. The current distribution network wouldn't do; he wanted a premier gallery in a major art world hub. Magdalena found such a gallery in Paris, on the rue la Boétie.

"Galerie Georges Fleury."

Magdalena nodded.

"How did you know that Monsieur Fleury would be interested in going into business with you?"

"He acquired a painting from my father once and conveniently forgot to pay for it. Even by the reduced standards of the art world, Monsieur Fleury was an unscrupulous worm."

"How did you play it with him?"

"Straight up."

"He had no qualms about selling forgeries?"

"None whatsoever. But he insisted on subjecting one of our pictures to scientific analysis before agreeing to handle them."

"What did you give him?"

"A Frans Hals portrait. And do you know what Monsieur Fleury did with it?"

"He showed it to the future president of the Louvre. And the future president of the Louvre gave it to the National Center for Research and Restoration, which affirmed its authenticity. And now the forged Frans Hals portrait is part of the Louvre's permanent collection, along with a Gentileschi, a Cranach, and the most delicious little Van der Weyden you've ever laid eyes on."

"Not the outcome Phillip expected. But quite an accomplishment nonetheless."

"How many fakes did the two of you move through Galerie Fleury?"

"Somewhere between two and three hundred."

"How was Fleury compensated?"

"The first sales were consignment deals."

"And after that?"

"Phillip purchased the gallery through an anonymous shell

corporation in 2014. For all intents and purposes, Monsieur Fleury was an employee of Masterpiece Art Ventures."

"When did Galerie Hassler in Berlin come under your control?"

"The following year."

"I'm told you have a distribution point in Brussels."

"Galerie Gilles Raymond on the rue de la Concorde."

"Am I missing any?"

"Hong Kong, Tokyo, and Dubai. And all of it flows into the coffers of Masterpiece Art Ventures."

"The greatest scam in the history of the art world," said Gabriel. "And it might well have gone on forever if Phillip hadn't purchased *Portrait of an Unknown Woman* from Isherwood Fine Arts of London."

"It was your friend Sarah Bancroft's fault," said Magdalena. "If she hadn't bragged about the sale to that reporter from *ARTnews*, the Frenchwoman would have never known about it."

Which brought them, at half past two in the morning, to Madame Valerie Bérrangar.

49

VILLA DEI FIORI

THE FIRST TIME MAGDALENA HEARD Valerie Bérrangar's name, she was in her usual suite at the Pierre Hotel in New York. It was a cold and rainy afternoon in mid-March. A frustrated Phillip was lying next to her, annoyed that she had interrupted their lovemaking to take a phone call. It was from Georges Fleury in Paris.

"What were you doing in New York?" asked Gabriel.

"I pop over at least once a month to discuss the sort of things that can't be put in an email or encrypted text."

"Do you and Phillip always end up in bed?"

"That part of our relationship has never changed. Even during his brief infatuation with your friend Sarah Bancroft, Phillip was sleeping with me on the side."

"Does his wife know about the two of you?"

"Lindsay doesn't have a clue. About much of anything."

With General Ferrari's approval, Rossetti had removed the

restraints from her wrists. Her long hands were folded atop her right leg, which was crossed over her left. Her dark eyes tracked Gabriel as he slowly paced the perimeter of the room.

"I imagine Monsieur Fleury was rather nervous that afternoon in mid-March," he said.

"Panic stricken. A French policeman named Jacques Ménard had come to the gallery unannounced to question Fleury about *Portrait of an Unknown Woman*. He was afraid the entire house of cards was about to collapse."

"Why did he contact you and not Phillip?"

"I'm in charge of sales and distribution. Phillip owns the galleries, but he keeps the dealers at arm's length. Unless there's a problem, of course."

"Like Valerie Bérrangar?"

"Yes."

"What did Phillip do?"

"He made a phone call."

"To whom?"

"A man who makes his problems go away."

"Does this man have a name?"

"If he does, I'm not aware of it."

"Is he American?"

"I wouldn't know."

"What *do* you know?"

"That he is a former intelligence officer who has a network of skilled professionals at his disposal. They hacked into Madame Bérrangar's mobile phone and laptop, and broke into her villa in Saint-André-du-Bois. That's when they discovered the entry in her desk calendar. And the painting, of course."

"*Portrait of an Unknown Woman*, oil on canvas, one hundred and fifteen by ninety-two centimeters, attributed to a follower of the Flemish Baroque painter Anthony van Dyck."

"It was a dreadful mistake on Fleury's part," said Magdalena. "He should have told me that he had handled the original version of the painting. The truth is, it was so long ago it slipped his mind."

"How did the forger produce his copy?"

"Apparently, he used a photograph he found in an old exhibition catalogue. It was a minor picture produced by a nameless artist working in Van Dyck's style. The forger simply executed a more skillful version of it and, voilà, a lost Van Dyck suddenly reappeared after centuries in hiding."

"At the same Paris gallery where Valerie Bérrangar's husband purchased the original version thirty-four years earlier."

"The scenario wasn't out of the question, but it was suspicious, to say the least. If the French art squad had opened an investigation . . ."

"You would have been arrested. And Phillip Somerset's forgery-and-fraud empire would have unraveled in spectacular fashion."

"With disastrous consequences for the entire art world. Fortunes would have been lost and countless reputations ruined. Emergency measures had to be taken to contain the damage."

"Eliminate Madame Bérrangar," said Gabriel. "And find out what, if anything, she had told Julian Isherwood and his partner, Sarah Bancroft."

"I had nothing to do with the Bérrangar woman's death. It was Phillip who arranged everything."

"A single-car accident on an empty stretch of road." Gabriel paused. "Problem solved."

"Or so it appeared. But less than a week after her death, you and Sarah Bancroft showed up at Phillip's estate on Long Island."

"He told us that he had sold *Portrait of an Unknown Woman*. He also said that a second review of the attribution had determined that the painting was in fact a genuine Van Dyck."

"Neither of which was true."

"But why did he purchase his own forgery in the first place?"

"I explained that to you earlier."

"Explain it again."

"First of all," said Magdalena, "Masterpiece Art Ventures didn't actually pay six and a half million pounds for *Portrait of an Unknown Woman.*"

"Because Isherwood Fine Arts unwittingly purchased it from Masterpiece Art Ventures for three million euros."

"Correct."

"Nevertheless, Phillip handed over a substantial amount of money for a worthless painting."

"But it was other people's money. And the painting is far from worthless to a man like Phillip. He can use it as collateral to obtain bank loans and then sell it to another art investor for much more than he paid for it."

"And by routing the original sale through Isherwood Fine Arts," added Gabriel, "Phillip gave himself plausible deniability if it was ever discovered to be a forgery. After all, it was Sarah who sold the forgery to *him.* And it was Julian, a well-respected expert in Dutch and Flemish Old Masters, who concluded that the picture was painted by Anthony van Dyck and not by a later follower."

"Julian Isherwood's blessing increased the painting's value significantly."

"Where is it now?"

"Chelsea Fine Arts Storage."

"I suppose Phillip owns that, too."

"Phillip controls the entire physical infrastructure of the network, including Chelsea. And he was afraid that you and Sarah were going to bring it all down."

"What did he do?"

"He made another phone call."

"To whom?"

"Me."

WITH A SMALL PORTION OF THE MONEY THAT MAGDALENA HAD earned working for Phillip Somerset and Masterpiece Art Ventures, she had purchased a luxurious apartment on the Calle de Castelló in the Salamanca district of Madrid. Her circle of friends included artists, writers, musicians, and fashion designers who knew nothing of the true nature of her work. Like most young Spaniards, they usually ate dinner around ten and then headed off to a nightclub. Consequently, Magdalena was still sleeping when Phillip rang her at one o'clock on a Monday afternoon and told her to clean up the mess at Galerie Fleury.

"What sort of cleanup did he have in mind?"

"Destroy the forgeries in the gallery's inventory and, if necessary, return the million euros that you and the violinist paid for *A River Scene with Distant Windmills*."

"I was right about it being a forgery?"

She nodded. "Evidently, you told Phillip that you had given it to Aiden Gallagher for scientific analysis. Phillip was convinced that Aiden would be able to tell it was a fake."

"Because Aiden is the best in the business."

"The final word," said Magdalena.

"And when you heard the gallery had been bombed?"

"I knew that Phillip had once again misled me." She paused. "And that he had made a dreadful mistake."

For three weeks, she continued, she remained a prisoner of her apartment in Madrid. She followed the news from Paris obsessively, chewed her nails to the quick, painted a Picassoesque self-portrait, and drank far too much. Her suitcases stood in the entrance hall. One of them contained a million euros in cash.

"Where were you planning to go?"

"Marrakesh."

"Leaving your father to face the music for your crimes?"

"My father did nothing wrong."

"I doubt the Spanish police would have seen it that way," said Gabriel. "But please go on."

She instructed the network's remaining galleries to freeze all sales of forged paintings and reduced her telephone-and-text contact with Phillip to a bare minimum. But in late April, he summoned her to New York and told her to open the spigot.

"One of his largest investors had requested a forty-five-million-dollar redemption. The kind of redemption that leaves a mark on the balance sheet. Masterpiece needed to replenish its cash reserves in a hurry."

And so the forgeries flowed into the market, and the money flowed into Phillip's accounts in the Cayman Islands. By June the bombing of Galerie Fleury had receded from the head-lines, and the eyes of the art world were on London, where Dimbleby Fine Arts was preparing to exhibit a newly discov-ered version of *Susanna in the Bath* by Paolo Veronese. The painting had purportedly emerged from the same uniden-tified European collection that had previously produced a Titian and a Tintoretto. But Magdalena knew what the rest of the art world did not, that all three paintings were forgeries.

"Because the forger's front man," said Gabriel, "made quite a scene at Galerie Hassler in Berlin."

Magdalena looked at Rossetti. "I was suspicious about those paintings even before your front man tried to sell the Gentileschi to Herr Hassler."

"Why?"

"I know a provenance trap when I see one, Mr. Allon. Yours wasn't terribly clever or original. Still, I wasn't surprised by the reaction of the art world. It's the secret of our success."

"What's that?"

"The gullibility of collectors and so-called experts and connoisseurs. The art world desperately wants to believe that there are lost masterpieces just waiting to be rediscovered. Phillip and I make dreams come true." She managed a smile. "As do you, Mr. Allon. Your Veronese took my breath away, but the Gentileschi was to die for."

"You had to have it?"

"No," she answered. "I had to have *you*."

"Because the market for museum-quality Old Masters is small? Because two major Old Master forgery rings cannot compete against one another and survive?"

"And because Phillip's forger is unable to supply enough paintings to meet the demands of my distribution network," said Magdalena. "And because, for all his talent, he cannot hold a candle to you."

"In that case, I accept your offer."

"What offer?"

"To join the team at Masterpiece Art Ventures." Gabriel switched off the video camera. "Let's take a walk, shall we, Magdalena? There are one or two details we need to finalize before you call Phillip and give him the good news."

50

VILLA DEI FIORI

THEY MADE THEIR WAY DOWN the gentle slope of the drive, beneath the canopy of the umbrella pine. The first brush-strokes of dawn lay over the hills to the east, but overhead the stars shone brightly. The air was cool and still, not a breath of movement. It smelled of orange blossom and jasmine and the cigarette that Magdalena had charmed from Luca Rossetti.

"Where did you learn to paint like that?" she asked.

"In the womb."

"Your mother was an artist?"

"And my grandfather. He was a disciple of Max Beckmann."

"What was his name?"

"Viktor Frankel."

"I know your grandfather's work," said Magdalena. "But good genes alone can't explain talent like yours. If I didn't know better, I would have guessed that you were an apprentice in Titian's workshop."

"It's true that I served my apprenticeship in Venice, but it was with a famous restorer named Umberto Conti."

"And you were no doubt Signore Conti's finest pupil."

"I suppose I have a knack for it."

"Restoring paintings?"

"Not just paintings. People, too. I'm trying to decide whether you're worth the effort." He gave her a sideways glance. "I have a terrible feeling you're beyond repair."

"The damage is self-inflicted, I'm afraid."

"Not all of it. Phillip targeted you for recruitment. He groomed you. Preyed on your vulnerabilities. Got you hooked. I know his techniques. I've used them a time or two myself."

"Are you using them now?"

"A little," he admitted.

She turned away and expelled a slender stream of smoke. "And what if I told you that I willingly stepped into the trap Phillip set for me?"

"Because you wanted the money?"

"It certainly wasn't for the sex."

"How much is there?"

"In addition to the million euros in the suitcase in my apartment?" She lifted her gaze skyward. "I have another four or five scattered around Europe, but the bulk of my money is invested in Masterpiece Art Ventures."

"Current balance?"

"Maybe fifty-five."

"Million?"

"It's a fraction of what I deserve. If it wasn't for me, there wouldn't be a Masterpiece Art Ventures."

"It's not exactly a résumé enhancer, Magdalena."

"How many people can say they built a multibillion-dollar global forgery network?"

"Or brought one down," said Gabriel quietly.

She frowned. "How did you find me, Mr. Allon? The truth, this time."

"Your attempt to recruit Lucien Marchand gave me valuable insight into the way you ran your operation."

Magdalena took a final pull at the cigarette and with a flick of her long forefinger sent the ember arcing into the darkness. "And how is Françoise these days? Still living in Roussillon? Or has she settled permanently in Lucien's villa on Saint-Barthélemy?"

"Why did you try to hire him?"

"Phillip wanted to expand our inventory to include Impressionist and postwar works. His forger wasn't capable of it, so he asked me to find someone who was. I made Lucien a generous offer, which he accepted."

"Along with one million euros in cash."

She made no reply.

"Is that why you had him murdered? A lousy million euros?"

"I'm sales and distribution, Mr. Allon. Phillip deals with problems."

"Why was Lucien a problem?"

"Do I really need to explain that to you?"

"After Lucien and Françoise accepted the money and then reneged on the deal, Phillip was concerned that they posed a threat to you and Masterpiece Art Ventures."

Magdalena nodded. "Françoise is lucky that Phillip didn't have her killed, too. She was the real brains behind that network. Lucien was the brush and Toussaint the cash register, but Françoise was the glue that kept it together." She slowed to a stop before a small shrine to the Virgin Mary, one of several scattered about the estate. "Where in the world are we?"

"The villa was once a monastery. The current owner is quite close to the Vatican."

"As are you. Or so they say." She made the sign of the cross and set off again.

"Are you a believer?" asked Gabriel.

"Like ninety percent of my fellow Spaniards, I no longer attend Mass, and it has been more than twenty years since I last set foot in a confessional. But, yes, Mr. Allon. I remain a believer."

"Do you believe in absolution as well?"

"That depends on how many Hail Marys you intend to make me recite."

"If you help me take down Phillip Somerset," said Gabriel, "your sins will be forgiven."

"All of them?"

"A few years ago, I met a woman who ran a modern art gallery in Saint-Tropez. It was a money-laundering front for her boyfriend's narcotics empire. I got her out of the situation cleanly. Now she's a successful dealer in London."

"Somehow I doubt there's an art gallery in my future," said Magdalena. "But what did you have in mind?"

"A final face-to-face meeting with Phillip in New York next week."

"About the newest member of the team at Masterpiece Art Ventures?"

"Exactly."

"I imagine he's quite anxious to have a look at your Gentileschi."

"Which is why you're going to overnight it to Chelsea Fine Arts Storage."

"I hope your front man is covering the shipping costs."

"I'm afraid it wasn't included in the hammer price."

"I guess ten million euros doesn't go as far as it used to. But how are we going to get the painting through Italian customs?"

"I believe we're covered on that score." Gabriel handed her

a mobile phone. "This call is being recorded for quality assurance. If you try to pass a message to him, I'll hand you over to General Ferrari and wave goodbye."

She dialed the number and raised the phone to her ear. "Hello, Lindsay. It's Magdalena. I'm sorry to be calling at such a dreadful hour, but I'm afraid it's rather urgent. I promise not to keep Phillip long."

R OSSETTI DROVE MAGDALENA BACK TO Florence to collect her belongings from the Four Seasons and settle the enormous bill. By noon they had returned to Villa dei Fiori, and Magdalena, in sunglasses and a stunning white two-piece swimsuit, was stretched upon a chaise longue by the pool, a glass of chilled Orvieto wine in her hand. General Ferrari observed her disapprovingly from the shade of the trellised garden.

"Is there anything the staff of the Hotel Carabinieri can do to make her stay more comfortable?" he asked Gabriel.

"What would you have me do? Confine her to her room until we leave for New York?"

"Surely this place has a dungeon. After all, it was built in the eleventh century."

"I believe Count Gasparri converted it into his wine cellar."

Ferrari sighed but said nothing.

"Has the Art Squad never cut a deal with a thief or a fence to get to the next step of the ladder?"

"We do it all the time. And more often than not, the thief or the fence tells us only part of the story." The general paused. "Just like that beautiful creature lying comfortably next to the swimming pool. She's smarter than you realize. And quite dangerous."

"I'm a former intelligence officer, Cesare. I know how to handle an asset."

"She's not an asset, my friend. She is a criminal and a confidence artist who has millions of dollars stashed around the world and access to private airplanes."

"At least she doesn't have tattoos," remarked Gabriel.

"Her one and only redeeming quality. But I assure you, she is not to be trusted."

"I have enough leverage to keep her in line, including her videotaped confession."

"Ah, yes. A tragic tale about a once promising artist who was lured into a life of crime by the evil and manipulative Phillip Somerset. You realize, I hope, that perhaps half of it is true."

"Which half?"

"I haven't a clue. But I find it difficult to believe that she doesn't know the name of the forger."

"It's entirely plausible that Phillip kept it from her."

"Perhaps. But it is also entirely plausible that she was the one who took Phillip to that loft in Hell's Kitchen, and that the forger is now lying in the Umbrian sun with a drink in her hand."

"She doesn't have the training to paint Old Masters."

"So she says. But if I were you, I would revisit the matter."

"I'll boil her in suntan oil after lunch."

"Why don't you let me take her back to Rome instead? She can tell her tragic tale to the FBI legal attaché at the embassy. A prize like Magdalena would do wonders for my standing in Washington. Besides, it's an American problem now. Let the Americans handle it."

"And do you know what the FBI legal attaché will do?" asked Gabriel. "He'll call his superior at FBI headquarters. And his superior will call the assistant director, who will call the director, who will walk across Pennsylvania Avenue to the Justice Department. DOJ will assign the case to the US attorney for the Southern District of New York, and the US attorney will spend months gathering evidence before arresting Phillip and shutting down his company."

"The wheels of justice turn slowly."

"Which is why I'm going to deal with Phillip myself. By the time I'm finished, Masterpiece Art Ventures will be a smoldering ruin. The Feds will have no choice but to immediately make arrests and seize assets."

"A fait accompli?"

Gabriel smiled. "It definitely sounds better in French."

GENERAL FERRARI AND THE REST OF THE CARABINIERI TEAM departed Villa dei Fiori at two that afternoon. A unit from the Amelia station kept watch over the gate, but otherwise Gabriel and Magdalena were alone. She slept through the afternoon and insisted on preparing a proper Spanish dinner of tapas and a potato omelet. They ate outside on the villa's terrace, in the cool evening air. Magdalena's personal mobile phone lay between them, flaring with incoming message traffic and silenced phone calls, mainly from her circle of friends in Madrid.

"No man in your life?" asked Gabriel.

"Only Phillip, I'm afraid."

"Are you in love with him?"

"God, no."

"Are you sure about that?"

"Why do you ask?"

"Because it is my intention to leave you alone in his pres-

"My next redemption window isn't until September. I couldn't if I tried."

"I'm sure Phillip would make an exception in your case."

"Actually, he's quite strict when it comes to redemptions. He and Kenny fly rather close to the sun. If a handful of major investors were to simultaneously withdraw their funds, he would have to sell some of his inventory or secure another loan."

"Using a painting as collateral?"

"The art-backed loans," repeated Magdalena, "are the key to everything."

Gabriel downloaded Magdalena's account statements, then checked the tracking information for *Danaë and the Shower of Gold*. The painting was currently westbound over the Atlantic. It would spend the night in the air cargo center at Kennedy International and was scheduled to reach its final destination, Chelsea Fine Arts Storage, no later than noon on Monday.

A search of the flights from Rome to New York produced several options. "How do you feel about the ten a.m. Delta into JFK?" asked Gabriel.

"That would require awakening several hours before noon."

"You can sleep on the plane."

"I never sleep on planes." Magdalena reached for the laptop. "Can I pay for your ticket?"

"Phillip might find that suspicious."

"At least let me give you some miles."

"I have plenty."

"How many have you got?"

"The moon and back."

"I've got more." She booked their seats. "That leaves the hotel. Is the Pierre all right?"

"I'm afraid Sarah prefers the Four Seasons."

"Please tell me she's not coming with us."

"I need someone to keep an eye on you when I'm not around."

ence for several hours in New York next week. And I want to know whether you intend to live up to our agreement or run away with him."

"Don't worry, Mr. Allon. I'll get you everything you need to take Phillip down."

He asked where the meeting would take place.

"That's up to Phillip," said Magdalena. "Sometimes we meet at Masterpiece's office on East Fifty-Third Street. But usually we get together at the town house on East Seventy-Fourth. It doubles as Masterpiece's gallery. That's where Phillip receives potential investors and buyers."

"How does he handle the sales?"

"He prefers to deal directly with clients to avoid scrutiny and commissions. But if the client insists on an intermediary, he routes the sales through another dealer or one of the auction houses."

"How many other people work for the firm?"

"Three young female art experts and Kenny Vaughan. Kenny used to work with Phillip at Lehman Brothers. He's in it up to his eyeballs."

"What about the women?"

"They think the sun rises and sets on Phillip and that I'm a broker who buys and sells paintings on his behalf in Europe."

"General Ferrari is convinced that you're the forger."

"Me?" She laughed. "A Picasso, maybe. But not an Old Master. I don't have talent like yours."

Gabriel read late into the night and was relieved to find Magdalena still in her bed when he rose the following morning. After loading the *automatico* with Illy and San Benedetto, he unleashed Proteus on Phillip's personal smartphone, and within minutes the device was under his control. A scalable map depicted its current location and elevation: the eastern shore of an egg-shaped peninsula, twelve feet above sea level.

Gabriel downloaded Phillip's data onto his laptop and spent

the remainder of the morning wandering the digital debris of one of the greatest scam artists in history. It was half past twelve when Magdalena finally appeared. She wandered into the kitchen and emerged a moment later with a bowl of milky coffee. She drank it in silence, her eyes unblinking.

"Not a morning person?" asked Gabriel.

"Opposite of a morning person. A night stalker."

"Is the night stalker ready to do some work?"

"If you insist," she said, and carried her coffee to the pool.

Gabriel followed her outside with the laptop. "What were the first six paintings you sold through your father's gallery?"

"It was a thousand years ago," she groaned.

"The exact amount of time you'll spend in an Italian prison if you don't start talking."

SHE RECITED THE ARTIST, TABLEAU, AND DIMENSIONS OF EACH work, along with the name of the buyer and the price it had fetched. Next she listed the particulars of more than one hundred paintings that had passed through her brokerage in Madrid during the first year of the scheme. Most of the paintings she had simply sold back to Masterpiece Art Ventures. Phillip had then inflated their value with additional phantom sales before unloading the paintings onto unsuspecting buyers and cashing in on his investment. He also used the works as collateral to secure massive art-backed loans, money he used to acquire legitimate art and pay handsome returns to his investors.

"The loans," said Magdalena, "are the key to everything. Without leverage, Phillip and Kenny Vaughan wouldn't be able to make it work."

"So in addition to selling forged paintings, Phillip is committing bank fraud?"

"On a daily basis."

"Where does he do his banking?"

"Mainly, he deals with Ellis Gray at JPMorgan C he also has a relationship with Bank of America."

"How much debt is he carrying?"

"I'm not sure even Phillip knows the answer to that.

"Who does?"

"Kenny Vaughan."

The next ground they covered was Magdalena's expa into bricks-and-mortar retailing, beginning with her nership with Galerie Georges Fleury of Paris and conclud with the recent acquisition by Masterpiece Art Ventures galleries in Hong Kong, Tokyo, and Dubai. The total nu ber of forged paintings the network had unleashed on the a market exceeded five hundred, with a paper valuation of mor than $1.7 billion—far too many works for Magdalena to recal accurately. She was certain, however, that a significant percentage had passed through Masterpiece's opaque portfolio.

"How many does he currently control?"

"That's impossible to say. Phillip doesn't even reveal the genuine paintings in his possession, let alone the forgeries. His most valuable pictures are in his Manhattan and Long Island homes. The rest are in the warehouse on East Ninety-First Street. It's the equivalent of his trading book."

"Can you get inside?"

"Not without Phillip's approval. But a directory of the warehouse's current contents would tell you everything you need to know."

Over lunch, Gabriel logged into Magdalena's ProtonMail account and forwarded several years' worth of encrypted emails to his own address. Next they reviewed her personal finances, including her account at Masterpiece Art Ventures. Her balance was $56,245,539.

"Don't even think about trying to make a withdrawal," Gabriel warned her.

Magdalena reserved her usual suite at the Pierre and with a childlike frown returned to her chaise longue next to the pool. Her wounds, thought Gabriel, were definitely self-inflicted. Still, she was by no means beyond repair. After all, if a former contract killer like Christopher Keller was salvageable, then surely Magdalena was as well.

For the moment, she was merely a means to an end. All Gabriel required now was a reporter to turn her remarkable story into a weapon that would reduce Masterpiece Art Ventures to rubble. A reporter who was familiar with the worlds of finance and art. Perhaps one who had investigated Masterpiece in the past.

Only a single candidate fit the profile. Fortunately, the number for her cell phone was in Phillip Somerset's contacts. Gabriel dialed it and introduced himself. Not with a work name, or one he plucked from thin air, but his real name.

"Yeah, right," she said, and hung up the phone.

52

ROTTEN ROW

THE NEXT CALL GABRIEL PLACED that afternoon was to Sarah Bancroft. It found her on Rotten Row in Hyde Park, where she was attempting to dislodge the ten pounds that had settled astride her hips. The news from Italy came as a shock, so much so that she asked Gabriel to repeat it, just to make certain she hadn't misunderstood him. It was no less astounding the second time. Masterpiece Art Ventures, the art-based hedge fund where a portion of Sarah's inheritance was invested, was a $1.2 billion fraud propped up by the sale and collateralization of forged paintings. Furthermore, it seemed that Magdalena Navarro, she of the shimmering black hair and elongated body, had been sleeping with Phillip the entire time he had dated Sarah. For that reason alone, she leapt at the chance to travel to New York to take part in his destruction. Even if it meant staying at the Pierre.

"Shall I bring along Mr. Marlowe? I find that he comes in rather handy in situations like these."

"As do I. But I have another job in mind for him."

"Nothing dangerous, I hope."

"I'm afraid so."

Sarah left for New York early the following morning and arrived at JFK at midday. A Nissan Pathfinder awaited her at Hertz. She killed an hour in the cell phone lot and at two fifteen made her way to Terminal 1. Gabriel emerged a moment later, accompanied by the woman whom Sarah had last seen walking along the pavements of Jermyn Street.

Now, as then, she was wearing a shortish skirt and a form-fitting white top. Gabriel loaded their bags into the rear storage compartment and slid into the backseat. Magdalena climbed into the passenger seat, bringing with her the scent of orange blossom and jasmine. She crossed one long leg over the other and smiled. Sarah slipped the Nissan into DRIVE and set out for Manhattan.

THE PIERRE HOTEL STOOD AT THE CORNER OF EAST SIXTY-First Street and Fifth Avenue. Magdalena entered the ornate lobby alone and was received by the hotel's management as though she were returning royalty. Her suite, with its sweeping views of Central Park, was located on the twentieth floor. Gabriel and Sarah had been assigned adjoining rooms on the opposite side of the corridor. Like Magdalena, they checked in pseudonymously and instructed the woman at Reception to block all outside calls.

Upstairs, all three convened in the sitting room of Magdalena's suite. She opened a complimentary bottle of Taittinger champagne while Gabriel connected his laptop to the hotel's Wi-Fi network and logged in to Proteus. It appeared that Phillip had decided to remain in North Haven rather than return to the city. Gabriel increased the volume on the feed from the microphone and heard the clatter of a keyboard. The output from the camera was a rectangle of solid black.

Gabriel handed Magdalena her phone. "Let him know that you've arrived and would like to see him as soon as possible. And remember—"

"This call is being recorded for quality assurance."

Gabriel carried the laptop into the bedroom and closed the heavy internal door. Phillip answered Magdalena's call instantly. "How about one o'clock tomorrow afternoon?" he asked. "We'll have lunch."

"Will Lindsay be joining us?"

"Unfortunately, she's spending the week on the island."

"Lucky you."

"I'll send a car," said Phillip, and the connection went dead.

Gabriel listened to a minute or two of typing before returning to the sitting room. "Now the Gentileschi," he said to Magdalena.

The number for the warehouse was in her contacts. She tapped the screen and lifted the phone to her ear.

"Hello, Anthony. It's Magdalena Navarro calling. Did the painting arrive from Florence as scheduled? . . . Wonderful. Send it to Mr. Somerset's residence tomorrow morning . . . Yes, the town house, please. Place it on the easel in the gallery. And make certain it arrives no later than noon."

Magdalena killed the connection and surrendered her phone to Gabriel.

"Your wallet and passport as well."

She removed them from her Hermès Birkin handbag and handed them over.

"I need to run an errand, which means that you and Sarah will have a chance to get to know one another better. But don't worry," said Gabriel as he stepped into the corridor. "I won't be long."

Sarah chained the door behind him and returned to the sitting room. Magdalena was adding champagne to her glass. At length Sarah asked, "Is it true that Phillip was sleeping with you the entire time he was seeing me?"

"Only when I was in New York."

"Ah, that's a relief."

"If you must know," said Magdalena, "he was only using you."

"For what?"

"Introductions to rich benefactors of the Museum of Modern Art."

"And to think I gave him two million dollars to invest."

"What's your current balance?"

"Four and a half. You?"

"Fifty-six point two."

Sarah smiled without parting her lips. "I guess you were better in bed than I was."

53

LITERARY WALK

I N THE SPRING OF 2017, *Vanity Fair* magazine published an investigative profile titled "The Great Somerset." Twelve thousand words in length, the article chronicled its subject's rise from a working-class town in northeastern Pennsylvania to the pinnacle of Wall Street and the art world. No corner of his personal life escaped scrutiny: the instability of his childhood home, his youthful athletic prowess, his brief but meteoric career at Lehman Brothers, his ugly divorce, his peculiar penchant for secrecy. A source described only as a former friend said he had a dark side. An old colleague went further, suggesting he was a sociopath and a malignant narcissist. Both sources agreed that he was hiding something.

The article was written by Evelyn Buchanan, an award-winning reporter whose work for *Vanity Fair* had served as the intellectual property for two Hollywood films and a Netflix limited series. At present, she was seated on a bench along Central Park's Literary Walk. Robert Burns, feather pen in hand, eyes skyward in search of inspiration, loomed over her right shoulder. On the opposite side of the footpath, a sketch artist sat waiting for a subject.

Evelyn Buchanan was waiting, too. Not for a subject but a source. He had called her without warning the previous day—from where he refused to say. No, he had assured her, it was not a practical joke; he was in fact the man he claimed to be. He was coming to New York on an unpublicized visit and wished to meet with her. She was to tell no one that he had been in touch. He promised that she would not be disappointed.

"But national security isn't my beat," Evelyn protested.

"The matter I wish to discuss is related to the financial world and the art market."

"Can you be a bit more specific?"

"The Great Somerset," he said, and rang off.

It was an intriguing clue, all the more so because of the source. He had attended a book party at Phillip's showy North Haven estate that spring. Or so claimed Ina Garten, who insisted he'd had a hot little blonde on his arm. Evelyn, who had attended the same party, had found the prospect laughable. Now she had to admit it was possible after all. How else to explain why a man like Gabriel Allon would be interested in a creep like Phillip Somerset?

Evelyn checked the time. It was one minute before five o'clock. One minute before the world's most famous retired spy had promised to appear. The walkway was crowded with tourists, spandex-clad joggers, and Upper East Side nannies pushing strollers laden with the tycoons of tomorrow. But there was no one who looked as though he might be Gabriel Allon. Indeed, the only possible candidate was a man of medium height and build who was pondering the placard at the foot of the Walter Scott statue.

At the stroke of five o'clock, he crossed the walkway and

sat down on Evelyn's bench. "Please go away," she said quietly. "My husband will be back any minute, and he has anger-management issues."

"I thought I made it clear that you were to come alone."

Evelyn turned with a start. Then, regaining her composure, she stared straight ahead. "Who was the blonde?"

"I beg your pardon?"

"The woman you brought to Carl Bernstein's book party."

"She used to work at MoMA. Now she's an art dealer in London. I was helping her with a problem."

"What sort of problem?"

"The Great Somerset."

"You obviously read my article," said Evelyn.

"Several times."

"Why?"

"As you might imagine, the ability to read between the lines is an essential skill for an intelligence officer. Is the information accurate, or is my adversary trying to deceive me? Is my agent overstating his case, or is he playing it too safe? Has my source, for one reason or another, left critical information out of his report?"

"And when you finished reading my story about Phillip?"

"I had the nagging sense that you knew more about him than you shared with your readers."

"Much more," she admitted.

"Why wasn't the material included in the piece?"

"You first, Mr. Allon. Why Phillip Somerset, of all people?"

"Masterpiece Art Ventures is a fraud. And I'd like you to be the one to break the story."

"What have you got for me?"

"A whistleblower."

"An employee of the company?"

"Close enough."

"What does that mean?"

"It means that I'm going to impose some rather strict ground rules in order to protect the whistleblower's identity and to conceal my role in this matter."

"And if I refuse to accept those ground rules?"

"I'll find someone who will. And you and your magazine will be playing catch-up when Masterpiece crashes and burns."

"In that case, I'll listen to what you and your whistleblower have to say." She paused. "But only if you tell me where you got the number for my cell phone."

"I found it in Phillip's contacts."

Evelyn Buchanan smiled. "Ask a silly question."

HOW DID YOU FIND HER?"

"She was arrested in Italy last weekend after purchasing a forged Gentileschi from an undercover Carabinieri officer. I was a consultant to the Italian investigation."

"A consultant?" asked Evelyn dubiously.

"It's possible I might have painted the Gentileschi for them."

"A fake forgery painted by Gabriel Allon? This story is getting better by the minute."

They were moving at an unhurried pace along the foot-paths of Central Park. For the moment, Evelyn's notepad was tucked safely into her Chanel handbag. She was a petite woman of perhaps fifty, with short, dark hair and oversize tortoiseshell glasses. They were her trademark, the spectacles, like her razor-sharp prose, acerbic wit, and ruthless competitive streak.

"Where's the painting now?" she asked.

"A warehouse on East Ninety-First Street."

"Chelsea Fine Arts Storage?"

"That's the one."

"I remember when Phillip acquired it. I have to say, it made no sense to me at the time. Why would a tycoon like Phillip Somerset want to own a small-time art services company like Chelsea?"

"Because the tycoon needed the ability to ship and store forged paintings, no questions asked. He's flooded the art market with hundreds of fake paintings, including four that have ended up in the Louvre. But the best part of the story is that—"

"Phillip is using forged paintings as collateral to obtain massive bank loans."

"How did you know?"

"An educated guess." Evelyn smiled. "Did I mention that my husband works for Millennium Management. It's one of the world's largest hedge funds. Before that, he was a prosecutor in the US attorney's office for the Southern District of New York. When I was working on the profile of Phillip, Tom took a hard look at—"

"Your husband is named Tom Buchanan?"

"Do you want to hear the rest of the story or not?"

"Please."

"When Tom analyzed Masterpiece's annual returns, he was quite impressed. Envious, actually."

"Because Masterpiece had outperformed Millennium?"

"Easily. Tom being Tom, he started doing some digging."

"And?"

"He was convinced that Phillip was using borrowed money and money from new investors to pay off his old investors. In short, Tom believes that Phillip Somerset is the Bernie Madoff of the art world."

"He's running a Ponzi scheme?"

"Correct."

"How close did you get to proving it?"

"Not close enough for my editors. But Phillip definitely knew that I was on to him."

"How?"

"He employs a man named Leonard Silk to watch his back. Silk is retired CIA. When he left the Agency, he opened a one-man private security firm here in New York. He called me when I was working on my profile and threatened legal action if the piece alleged wrongdoing of any kind. I also received messages from a man who somehow knew that I liked to take long walks in the park. He warned me to be careful. He said bad things happen to women who walk alone in New York City."

"How subtle."

"Leonard Silk doesn't waste time on subtlety. That's Phillip's department. He was incredibly charming during our interviews. It's no wonder your whistleblower agreed to work for him."

"Actually, she saw through Phillip from the beginning."

"What was the original connection?"

"Drugs. When she couldn't sell any of her paintings here in New York, she earned a living dealing cocaine. Many of her clients were Wall Street types."

"Phillip snorted a mountain of blow back when he was at Lehman Brothers," said Evelyn. "It was just one of the reasons why they fired him. Even by Wall Street standards, he was out of control."

"Your article said he left Lehman on good terms."

"That was the public version of the story, but it isn't true. Phillip was practically frog-marched out of the building, and a do-not-resuscitate order went out on the street. When no one else would hire him, he started a hedge fund called Somerset Asset Management. And when the hedge fund collapsed, he hit upon a novel idea."

"He gravitated to the art world," said Gabriel. "Because that's where the money was."

Evelyn nodded. "Phillip started turning up at gallery openings and museum fundraisers, always with a beautiful woman on his arm and a pocketful of business cards. You have to hand it to him. The art-based hedge fund was an intriguing idea. Prices for blue-chip art were rising faster than equities or any other asset class. How could he possibly go wrong?"

"It never worked. That's why he started loading up his book with forged paintings."

They had arrived at Grand Army Plaza. "You never mentioned your whistleblower's name," said Evelyn.

"Magdalena Navarro."

"Where is she now?"

Gabriel glanced toward the Pierre Hotel. "It's her New York address. She has fifty-six million dollars invested in Masterpiece Art Ventures, all of which she earned selling forgeries for Phillip."

"So she says. But I can't accuse Phillip Somerset of the greatest art fraud in history based solely on the word of a former drug dealer. I need proof that he's knowingly selling forged paintings."

"What if you were able to hear it directly from Phillip's mouth?"

"Do you have a recording?"

"The conversation hasn't happened yet."

"When will it?"

"Tomorrow afternoon at one o'clock."

"What's on the agenda?"

"Me."

THEY THREADED THEIR WAY THROUGH THE GRIDLOCKED TRAF-
fic along Fifth Avenue and came whirling through the Pierre's
revolving door, into the refrigerated cool of the lobby. Upstairs, Gabriel knocked softly on the door of Magdalena's
suite. Sarah confirmed his identity before opening the door.

"How's the prisoner?" he asked.

"The prisoner is resting in her room." Sarah offered Evelyn
her hand, then turned to Gabriel. "Do we need to clarify the
ground rules before we begin?"

"Ms. Buchanan has agreed that your name and the name of
your highly regarded gallery in London will not appear in her
copy. She will describe you only as an art world insider." Gabriel glanced at Evelyn. "Isn't that correct, Ms. Buchanan?"

"And how will I describe *you*?"

"This story isn't about me. It's about Phillip Somerset and
Masterpiece Art Ventures. Any information that I provide is
for background purposes only. You may not quote me directly.
Nor are you to say where this interview is taking place."

"An undisclosed location?"

"I'll let you choose the words, Ms. Buchanan. I'm not the
writer."

"You're just the consultant to the Italian police who painted
a fake forgery?"

"Exactly."

"In that case, perhaps it's time for me to meet the prisoner."

Gabriel knocked on the door of the bedroom, and a moment later out stepped Magdalena.

"My goodness," said Evelyn Buchanan. "This story is getting better by the minute."

THEY WENT THROUGH IT ONCE from the beginning. And then they went through it a second time, just to make certain of the relevant facts and dates. Magdalena's childhood in Seville. Her formal training as an artist in Barcelona. The years she spent dealing cocaine in New York. Her introduction to Phillip Somerset at Le Cirque. Her role in building and maintaining the most lucrative and sophisticated art-and-financial fraud scheme in history. There were no discrepancies between the version of the story she revealed under interrogation in Umbria and the one she recounted for Evelyn Buchanan of *Vanity Fair*. If anything, thought Gabriel, the Pierre Hotel edition was even more captivating. So, too, was the subject herself. She came across as cosmopolitan and sophisticated and, most important, credible. Never once did she lose her composure, even when the questions turned personal.

"Why would someone with your talent become a drug dealer?"

"At first, I did it because I needed the money. And then I discovered that I enjoyed it."

"You were good at it?"

"Very."

"Are there similarities between selling drugs and forgeries?"

"More than you realize. For some people, art is like a drug. They *have* to have it. Phillip and I simply catered to their addiction."

There was a gaping hole in Magdalena's account—namely, the precise set of circumstances by which she had ended up in Italian custody. Evelyn pressed Gabriel for details, but he refused to budge from his original statement. Magdalena had been arrested after purchasing a forged Gentileschi in Florence. The painting was now in an art storage warehouse on East Ninety-First Street. In the morning it would be moved to the gallery of Phillip Somerset's town house on East Seventy-Fourth Street. And at 1:00 p.m. it would be the subject of a conversation that would provide Evelyn with all the ammunition she needed to expose Masterpiece Art Ventures as a fraud.

"Will Magdalena be wearing a wire?"

"Her phone will be acting as a transmitter. Phillip's phone is also compromised."

"I don't suppose he gave his consent to being hacked."

"I didn't ask for it."

At nine o'clock they took a break for dinner. Sarah arranged for a round of martinis to be sent up from the bar while Magdalena ordered room service from Perrine, the hotel's acclaimed restaurant. At Gabriel's suggestion, Evelyn invited her husband to join them. He arrived as the waiters were rolling the table into the suite. Tom Buchanan was affable and erudite, the very opposite of the wellborn polo player who had lived grandly on the shoreline of East Egg and fretted about the decline of the white race.

Evelyn swore her husband to secrecy, then gave him a detailed briefing on the remarkable story that had landed in her lap earlier that afternoon. Tom Buchanan took out his anger on his Caesar salad.

"Leave it to Phillip Somerset to come up with something like this. Still, one has to admire his ingenuity. He spotted a weakness and cleverly took advantage of it."

"What weakness is that?" asked Gabriel.

"The art market is totally unregulated. Prices are arbitrary, quality control is virtually nonexistent, and most paintings change hands under conditions of total secrecy. All of which makes it the perfect environment for fraud. Phillip took it to the extreme, of course."

"How is it possible that no one noticed?"

"For the same reason no one noticed that mortgage-backed securities and collateralized debt obligations were about to take down the global economy."

"Everyone is making too much money?"

Tom nodded. "And not just Phillip's investors. His bankers, too. And they're all going to suffer enormous losses when Evelyn's story appears. Nevertheless, I approve of your methods. Waiting for the Feds to act isn't an option. That said, I wish you could give my wife an incriminating document or two."

"You mean the inner-office memo in which Phillip spells out his plan to create and maintain the largest art fraud in history?"

"Point taken, Mr. Allon. But what about the documents stored in that warehouse on East Ninety-First Street?"

"Phillip's current inventory?"

"Exactly. If Magdalena can say with absolute certainty that he has forged paintings on his book, it would be devastating."

"Is the former federal prosecutor suggesting that I clandestinely acquire a comprehensive list of paintings contained in that property?"

"I wouldn't dream of it. But if you do, you should definitely give it to my wife."

Gabriel smiled. "Any other advice, counselor?"

"If I were you, I'd think about putting a bit of pressure on Phillip's finances."

"By encouraging a handful of his important investors to take redemptions, you mean?"

"It sounds to me as though you already have a plan in place," said Tom.

"There's a man in London named Nicholas Lovegrove. Nicky's one of the most sought-after art advisers in the world. Several of his clients are invested with Phillip."

"We hedge fund types get very suspicious when investors pull their money. Therefore, it needs to be handled with discretion."

"Don't worry," said Sarah. "We art dealer types are nothing if not discreet."

56

GALERIE WATSON

THE DESTRUCTION OF MASTERPIECE ART Ventures commenced the following morning at 10:45 a.m. London time—5:45 a.m. in New York—when Christopher Keller presented himself at Galerie Olivia Watson in King Street. The small placard in the window read BY APPOINTMENT ONLY. Christopher hadn't made one, wagering that a surprise attack would prove more successful. He pressed the call button and, wincing, awaited a response.

"Well, well," breathed a sultry female voice. "Look what the cat left on my doorstep. If it isn't my dear friend Mr. Bancroft."

"It's Marlowe, remember? Now open the door."

"Sorry, but I'm all tied up at the moment."

"Untie yourself and let me in."

"I *do* love it when you beg, darling. Hold on, I can't quite seem to reach the button for the damn lock."

Several additional seconds elapsed before the deadbolt

thumped and the door yielded to Christopher's touch. Inside, he found Olivia seated at a sleek black writing table in the gallery's main exhibition room. She had arranged herself with care, as though posing for an invisible camera. As usual, her chin was turned slightly to the left, the right side of her face being the one that the photographers and advertisers had preferred. Christopher had never had a favorite. Olivia was a work of art, regardless of the vantage point.

Rising, she stepped from behind the table, crossed one ankle over the other, and placed a hand on her hip. She was clad in a fashionably cut jacket and matching slim-fitting trousers, suitably summer in color and weight.

"Marks and Spencer?" asked Christopher.

"It's a little something that Giorgio threw together for me." She lifted her chin a few degrees and stared at Christopher down the straight lines of her nose. "What brings you to my corner of the neighborhood?"

"A mutual friend needs a favor."

"Which friend is that?"

"The one who cleaned up your dreadful past and allowed you to open a respectable gallery here in St. James's." Christopher paused. "A gallery filled with paintings that were purchased with your boyfriend's drug money."

"Our mutual friend performed a similar service for you, as I recall." Olivia folded her arms. "Does your adorable American wife know what you used to do for a living?"

"My adorable American wife is none of your concern."

"Is it true she used to work for the CIA?"

"Wherever did you hear a thing like that?"

"Neighborhood gossip. There's also a nasty rumor going round that I'm involved in a flaming shag-fest with Simon Mendenhall."

"I thought you were dating a pop star."

"Colin is an actor," said Olivia. "And he's currently starring in the hottest play in the West End."

"Are you two serious?"

"Quite."

"So why are you shagging sleazy Simon on the side?"

"The rumor was started by your wife," said Olivia evenly.

"I find that difficult to believe."

"She also whispers the word *bitch* every time she sees me in Wiltons."

Christopher smiled in spite of himself.

"I'm glad you think it's funny." Olivia scrutinized his clothing. "Who's dressing you these days?"

"Dicky."

"Nice."

"I'll tell him you said so."

"I'd rather you tell your adorable American wife to cease and desist." Olivia shook her head slowly. "Honestly, I can't imagine why she would stoop to something so low."

"She's a bit jealous, that's all."

"If anyone has a right to be jealous, it's me. After all, Sarah's the one who ended up with you."

"Come now, Olivia. You don't really mean that. I was just a comfortable place for you to lay your head while you found your footing here in London. Now you're dating a pop star and your gallery is all the rage."

"All because of our mutual friend?"

Christopher made no reply.

"I thought he retired," said Olivia.

"It's a private matter involving a man named Phillip Somerset."

"*The* Phillip Somerset?"

"Friend of yours?"

"I sat next to Phillip and his wife at Christie's postwar and contemporary evening sale in New York a couple of years ago. The wife did some modeling before she hit the jackpot with Phillip. Laura is her name. Or is it Linda?"

"Lindsay."

"Yes, that's it. She's quite young and unspeakably stupid. Phillip struck me as a real operator. He asked whether I wanted to invest in his fund. I told him I wasn't in his league."

"Wise move on your part."

"Is there a problem?"

"Phillip is a bit like your old boyfriend. Shiny on the outside, dirty underneath. What's more, there's a rumor going around New York that his finances are rather shaky."

"Another rumor?"

"This one happens to be true. Our mutual friend would like you to whisper it into the ear of a prominent London art adviser whose client list includes some of the richest collectors in the world."

"How do you want me to play it?"

"A casual aside over an otherwise pleasant and businesslike lunch."

"When?"

"Today."

She glanced at her watch. "But it's nearly eleven. Surely Nicky has a lunch date already."

"Something tells me he'll break it."

Olivia reached for her mobile. "I'll do it on one condition."

"I'll have a word with her," said Christopher.

"Thank you." Olivia dialed and raised the phone to her ear. "Hello, Nicky. It's Olivia Watson calling. I know it's terribly short notice, but I was wondering whether you happened to be free for lunch today . . . The Wolseley at one? See you then, Nicky."

57

THE WOLSELEY

A ND SO IT BEGAN, WITH an apparently offhand remark, made over a costly lunch in one of Mayfair's finer dining rooms. The midday clatter of cutlery was such that Nicky leaned forward over his dressed Dorset crab appetizer and asked Olivia to repeat her statement. She did so in a confessional murmur, with the addition of a don't-quote-me-on-this disclaimer. The time was half past one o'clock. Or so claimed Julian Isherwood, who was dining well at a nearby table and noticed the ashen expression wash over Nicky's face. Julian's tubby tablemate didn't see a thing, for he was making a run at young Tessa, the newest addition to the Wolseley's waitstaff.

Nicky pressed Olivia to reveal the name of her source. And when she refused, he begged her pardon and immediately dialed Sterling Dunbar, a wealthy Manhattan real estate developer who bought paintings by the ton, always with Nicky looking over one shoulder. Sterling had been one of the first major investors in Masterpiece Art Ventures.

"Do you know my current balance?" he sniffed.

"I'm sure it's considerably larger than mine."

"A hundred and fifty million, a fivefold increase over my initial investment. Phillip assures me the fund is rock solid. Truth be told, I'm thinking about giving him another hundred."

The reactionary industrialist Max van Egan had parked $250 million at Masterpiece. He told Nicky he wasn't going anywhere. Simon Levinson—of the retailing Levinsons—was also inclined to stay put. But Ainsley Cabot, a collector of exceptional taste but only eight-figure wealth, heeded Nicky's advice. He rang Phillip at 9:15 a.m. Eastern time, as Phillip was stepping from his Sikorsky at the East Thirty-Fourth Street Heliport.

"How much?" he shouted over the whine of the rotors.

"All of it."

"Once you're out, there's no getting back in again. Do you understand me, Ainsley?"

"Spare me the bravado, Phillip, and send me my money."

Buffy Lowell reached Phillip at 9:24 a.m. as he was rolling up Third Avenue in his chauffeured Mercedes. Livingston Ford caught him eight minutes later, as he was crawling crosstown on East Seventy-Second Street. Livingston had $50 million in the fund and wanted out.

"You're going to regret this," warned Phillip.

"That's what my third wife told me, and I've never been happier."

"I'd like you to consider only a partial redemption."

"Are you suggesting there isn't enough cash in the till?"

"The money isn't sitting in an account at Citibank. I'll have to unload several paintings to make you whole."

"In that case, Phillip, I suggest you start unloading."

Which was how a seemingly offhand remark—made forty-five minutes earlier over a costly lunch in London—blew a $100 million hole in Masterpiece Art Ventures. The firm's founder, however, knew nothing of what had transpired. Desperate for information, he conducted a pair of hasty Internet searches—one for his own name, the other for the name of his firm. Neither unearthed anything that would explain why three of his largest investors had suddenly fled his fund. A search of social media likewise produced nothing damaging. Finally, at 9:42 a.m., he tapped the icon for Telegram, the encrypted cloud-based messaging system, and opened an existing secret chat thread.

I'm bleeding to death, he typed. Find out why.

WHEN PHILLIP SOMERSET PURCHASED HIS TOWN HOUSE ON East Seventy-Fourth Street in 2014, $30 million was considered a great deal of money. He had obtained the loan from his banker at JPMorgan Chase using several forged paintings as collateral, just one of the ways he had waved a magic wand and turned swaths of worthless canvas into gold. Several additional forgeries adorned the interior of the mansion, all to impress prospective investors and confer upon Phillip a patina of extraordinary wealth and sophistication. They were the elite of the art world, his investors. The ones with more money than sense. Phillip was a fraud and a clever forgery himself, but his investors were the fools who had made the elaborate scheme possible. And Magdalena, he thought suddenly. It would have never worked without her.

He entered the mansion's ground-floor foyer and was greeted by Tyler Briggs, his chief of security. Tyler was an Iraq War veteran. He wore a dark suit over a gym-hardened body.

"How was the ride in from the island, Mr. Somerset?"

"Better than the drive from the heliport."

Phillip's phone was ringing again. It was Scooter Eastman, a $20 million investor.

"Any scheduled deliveries today?" asked Tyler.

"A painting is supposed to arrive from the warehouse any minute."

"Clients?"

"Not today. But Ms. Navarro is supposed to drop by around one. Send her up to my office when she arrives."

Phillip dispatched Scooter Eastman's call to his voice mail and mounted the staircase. Soledad and Gustavo Ramírez, the Peruvian couple who ran his household, were waiting on the second-floor landing. Phillip absently returned their greetings while eyeing his phone. It was Rosamond Pierce. Midnight-blue blood. Ten million invested in Masterpiece Art Ventures.

"I'll be having lunch at home today. Ms. Navarro will be joining me. Seafood Cobb salads, please. One thirty or so."

"Yes, Mr. Somerset," replied the Ramírezes in unison.

Upstairs in his office, he listened to the new voice mails. Scooter Eastman and Rosamond Pierce both wanted out. In the span of thirty minutes, he had lost $135 million in investment money. Redemptions of that scale would threaten the most ethically run hedge fund. For a fund like Masterpiece Art Ventures, they were cataclysmic.

He relayed the news to Kenny Vaughan, the firm's chief investment officer, during their usual ten o'clock video call.

"Are you fucking kidding me?"

"I wish."

"A hundred and thirty-five million is going to hurt, Phillip."

"How long before we start to feel the pain?"

"Livingston Ford, Scooter Eastman, and Rosamond Pierce are all eligible for redemptions this month."

"Eighty million?"

"More like eighty-five."

"How much cash do we have on hand?"

"Fiftyish. Maybe."

"I could dump the Pollock."

"You owe JPMorgan sixty-five against the Pollock. Selling it isn't an option."

"How much do you need to make it work, Kenny?"

"Eighty-five would be nice."

"Be reasonable."

"Is there any chance you can lay your hands on forty?"

Phillip went to the window and watched two men in matching blue coveralls maneuvering a large rectangular crate from the back of a Chelsea Fine Arts Storage delivery truck.

"Yeah, Kenny. I think I might."

58

PIERRE HOTEL

Evelyn Buchanan arrived at the Pierre at half past twelve. Upstairs in Magdalena's suite, she informed Gabriel that her editors had signed off on an outline of her story. It would appear on *Vanity Fair*'s website immediately upon completion and would be included in the next print edition as well. The magazine's publicity department was putting in place a plan for a social media blitz. The *New York Times*, *Wall Street Journal*, Reuters, Bloomberg News, and CNBC had been alerted that a major story with far-reaching financial implications was forthcoming.

"Which means it will go viral within minutes of appearing on our site. There's no way Phillip will be able to contain the damage. He'll be dead before he knows what hit him."

"How soon can you publish?"

"If today goes as promised, I can have it ready by tonight."

"At the rate Phillip is going, he might not survive that long."

"Redemptions?"

"A hundred and thirty-five million and counting."

"He must be reeling."

"See for yourself."

Gabriel played a recording of Phillip's video call with Kenny Vaughan.

"*How much cash do we have on hand?*"

"*Fiftyish. Maybe.*"

"*I could dump the Pollock.*"

"*You owe JPMorgan sixty-five against the Pollock. Selling it isn't an option.*"

Gabriel paused the recording.

"Do you realize what you have?" asked Evelyn.

"It gets better."

Gabriel clicked PLAY.

"*How much do you need to make it work, Kenny?*"

"*Eighty-five would be nice.*"

"*Be reasonable.*"

"*Is there any chance you can lay your hands on forty?*"

"*Yeah, Kenny. I think I might.*"

Gabriel clicked PAUSE.

"Where is he going to get the money?"

"Unclear. But the timing would suggest he's thinking about putting my Gentileschi into play."

"If he does that—"

"We'll have irrefutable evidence that Phillip is engaged in bank fraud."

Just then the bedroom door opened and Magdalena emerged, wearing white stretch trousers, a loose-fitting blouse, and stiletto-heeled pumps.

Gabriel handed over her phone. "Keep it with you at all times. And whatever you do—"

"Where would I go without a passport, Mr. Allon? Staten Island?"

She dropped the phone into her handbag and went out. Her intoxicating scent lingered in the room after she had gone.

"Does she ever wear a bra?" asked Evelyn.

"Evidently, she forgot to pack one."

Gabriel switched the feed on the Proteus software from Phillip's device to Magdalena's. Then he rang Sarah, who was downstairs in the rented Nissan SUV.

"Don't worry," she said. "I won't let her out of my sight."

Two minutes later Sarah watched as Magdalena emerged from the East Sixty-First Street door of the Pierre and slid into the back of Phillip's waiting Mercedes S-Class limousine. The driver made three consecutive left turns and headed uptown on Madison Avenue. Sarah followed directly behind it—a violation of basic vehicle surveillance techniques, but a necessary one. The traffic was bumper-to-bumper, and Sarah had no backup other than the phone in Magdalena's handbag.

The traffic thinned at East Sixty-Sixth Street, and the Mercedes accelerated. Sarah was forced to run a pair of red lights to keep from losing it, but at East Seventy-Fifth Street she had no choice but to stop. When at last the light changed to green, the Mercedes was nowhere in sight. Two more left turns brought Sarah to the door of Phillip's town house on East Seventy-Fourth Street.

No Mercedes.

No sign of Magdalena.

Sarah drove to the end of the block and found a spot along the curb. Then she snatched up her phone and dialed Gabriel at the Pierre. "Please tell me she's inside that house."

"She's on her way upstairs."

Sarah killed the connection and smiled. Enjoy it while you can, she thought.

TYLER BRIGGS HAD INSTRUCTED MAGDALENA TO PROCEED DI-
rectly to Phillip's fourth-floor office. Instead, she had taken a
detour to the gallery. The Gentileschi was propped on a display easel. Magdalena snapped a photograph of the work with
her mobile phone. Then she took two wide-angle shots that
left little doubt as to the painting's current location—a room
that had been described in great detail in an unflattering *Vanity Fair* profile written by the woman who was at that moment
sitting in Magdalena's suite at the Pierre.

She realized suddenly that Tyler was watching her from the
gallery's doorway. He must have spotted her on one of the
security cameras. She reacted with the studied calm of a drug
dealer.

"Extraordinary, isn't it?"

"If you say so, Ms. Navarro."

"You don't appreciate art, Tyler?"

"To be honest, I don't know much about it."

"Has Mr. Somerset seen it yet?"

"You would have to ask Mr. Somerset. In fact, he's probably
wondering where you are."

Magdalena made her way upstairs. The door to Phillip's
office was open. He was sitting at his desk with a phone to his
ear and a palm pressed to his forehead.

"You're making a big mistake," he snapped, then killed the
call.

A frigid silence settled over the room.

"Who's making a mistake?" asked Magdalena.

"Warren Ridgefield. He's one of our investors. Unfortunately, several others are making the same mistake."

"Is there anything I can do to help?"

Phillip took her by the hand and smiled.

Phillip's shower was twice the size of the kitchen in Magdalena's old apartment in Alphabet City, an aquatic wonderland of marble and glass, the shower for the man who had everything. Magdalena could never recall which of the many brushed-chrome handles performed which function. She turned one and was blasted by water cannon on all sides. Frantically she tried another and was caressed by a gentle tropical cascade. She washed herself with Phillip's male-scented soap, dried herself with one of Phillip's monogrammed towels, and then contemplated her nude form in Phillip's gilt-framed mirror. She found the image unappealing and sorely in need of restoration. Portrait of a drug dealer, she thought. Portrait of a thief.

Portrait of an unknown woman . . .

In the master bedroom there was no sign of Phillip other than the stain he had left on the sheet. Their lovemaking had bordered on rape and had been accompanied by the constant tolling and chiming of his mobile phone. Magdalena's was tucked in her Hermès handbag, which lay at the foot of the bed, along with the clothing Phillip had ripped from her body. Aware that others were listening, she had endured his assault in muted silence. Her ravenous lover, however, had been in fine voice.

Dressed, she took up her handbag and went in search of him. She found him downstairs in the gallery, standing before the forged Gentileschi. He was wearing the expression of curatorial refinement he always donned for the benefit of his guileless investors. Phillip Somerset, patron of the arts. To Magdalena he would always be the uncultured philistine whom she had first encountered that night at Le Cirque. Bud Fox with a dash of Jay Gatsby. A forgery, she thought. And quite an obvious one at that.

"How good is it?" he asked finally.

"Better than the version at the Getty."

"Price?"

"All things being equal . . . thirty million."

"I need to unload it."

"I would advise against that, Phillip."

"Why?"

"Because the painting came from the same source as the ones that were sold by Oliver Dimbleby in London. If another picture emerges from the same so-called old European collection, it will raise red flags. The painting needs an entirely new provenance and sufficient time to cool off. We might also want to take the attribution down a notch or two."

"Attributed to Gentileschi?"

"Maybe circle of Gentileschi. Or even a follower."

"I'd be lucky to get a million for it."

"I didn't buy a painting in Florence, Phillip. I bought the greatest art forger in history. He'll pay dividends for years to come. Put the Gentileschi on ice in the warehouse and be patient."

Phillip stared at his phone. "I'm afraid patience is a virtue I can't afford at the moment."

"Who is it now?"

"Harriet Grant."

"What's going on?"

"I haven't a clue."

THEY ATE THEIR SEAFOOD COBB SALADS AT THE TABLE IN THE kitchen, with CNBC playing softly in the background. Magdalena drank Sancerre with hers, but Phillip, parched from his bedroom exertions, guzzled iced tea. His phone lay faceup at his elbow, silenced but aglow with incoming message traffic.

"You never told me his name," he said.

"I'm afraid I can't."

"Why not?"

"Parity, I suppose. You have your forger, and now I have mine."

"But you acquired your forger with ten million dollars of my money."

"You wouldn't have any money if it wasn't for me, Phillip. Besides, I went to a great deal of trouble to find him. I think I'll keep him all to myself."

He laid down his cutlery and eyed her without expression.

"Delvecchio," she said with a sigh. "Mario Delvecchio."

"What's his story?"

"The usual one. A failed painter who takes his revenge on the art world with a palette and a brush. He lives in an isolated villa in southern Umbria. He's extraordinarily well educated and trained. And quite beautiful, I must say. We became lovers during my stay. Unlike you, he's familiar with female pleasure centers."

"Is there something else I can do for you?"

"I'd love some more of this Sancerre."

Phillip signaled Señora Ramírez. "Does your lover have any other finished works lying around?"

"None that I'm inclined to introduce to the market at this time. I've asked him to cool it on the masterpieces for a while and concentrate on mid-level works that I can move under the radar."

"What are we going to do about his partner? This Alessandro Calvi fellow?"

"Now that Mario and I are sleeping together, I think I can convince him to part company with Signore Calvi."

"You're joking, right?"

"You know there's no one but you, Phillip." She patted the back of his hand reassuringly. "The truth is, I'm more worried about he who shall not be named than I am about Signore Calvi."

"Let me worry about him."

"How will he feel about having an Old Master stablemate?"

"I never promised him exclusivity."

Magdalena raised her wineglass to her lips. "Where have I heard that one before?"

Phillip adopted a new expression—caring friend and sexual partner. It was even less authentic than Phillip the intellectual and art world sophisticate. "What's got into you?" he asked.

"Besides you, you mean?" Magdalena laughed quietly at her own witticism. "I suppose I've just been thinking about my future, that's all."

"Your future is assured."

"Is it really?"

"Have you checked your balance lately? You could retire tomorrow and spend the rest of your life lying on a beach in Ibiza."

"And if I did?"

Phillip made no reply; he was staring at his phone again.

"Who is it now?"

"Nicky Lovegrove." He sent the call to voice mail. "Several of his clients are trying to cash out of my fund."

"My money is in that fund. *All* of it."

"Your money is safe."

"You also once assured me that you were going to turn me into a Spanish Damien Hirst. But it was nothing more than a clever ploy on your part to put a little cash in my pocket."

"It wasn't a little cash, as I recall."

"Where are they?" asked Magdalena suddenly.

"The paintings?"

She nodded.

"They're in the warehouse."

"I'd like them back."

"You can't have them."

"Why not?"

"Because they belong to me. And so do you, Magdalena. Never forget that."

His phone flared.

"Not another one."

"No. It's only Lindsay."

Magdalena smiled. "Do give her my best."

AFTER SPEAKING BRIEFLY TO HIS WIFE AND BIDDING FAREWELL to his business partner and mistress, Phillip Somerset returned to his office and rang Ellis Gray, head of art-based lending at JPMorgan Chase. Phillip and Ellis had bumped into one another in Sag Harbor over the weekend, rendering foreplay unnecessary. Phillip said he needed a bit of cash. Ellis, who had made millions dealing with Masterpiece Art Ventures, merely asked for the number Phillip had in mind and a description of the painting he intended to use as collateral.

"The number is forty million."

"And the painting?"

Phillip answered.

"A *Gentileschi* Gentileschi?" asked Ellis.

"It's newly discovered. I'm planning to keep it under wraps for a year or two before putting it on the market."

"How's the attribution?"

"Bulletproof."

"And the provenance?"

"On the thin side."

"Where did you purchase it?"

"A Spanish dealer. That's all I can say."

Ellis Gray, who made his living lending money against paintings, was well acquainted with the opacity of the art world. Nevertheless, he was not prepared to fork over $40 million of JPMorgan Chase's money on a picture without a past, even for a client as important and reliable as Phillip Somerset.

"Not without a full scientific evaluation," added Ellis. "Send it to Aiden Gallagher up in Westport. If Aiden says it's kosher, I'll expedite the loan."

Phillip killed the connection. Then he video-called Kenny Vaughan and told him that no emergency infusion of cash was in the offing.

"We might have to consider suspending redemptions."

"We can't. You have to make it work."

"I'll light a few candles and see what I can do."

Phillip dumped Kenny and accepted another call.

It was Allegra Hughes.

Allegra wanted out.

60

PIERRE HOTEL

GABRIEL HAD MADE THE REQUEST of Yuval Gershon early that morning. Yes, he realized it was an imposition and not altogether legal, as he had no official standing. And, no, he could not state with any degree of certainty that it would be the last time. It seemed he had become the first port of call for anyone with a problem, be they adulterous British prime ministers, supreme Roman pontiffs, or London art dealers. His current investigation, as was often the case, had included an attempt on his life. Yuval Gershon, of course, knew this. In fact, were it not for Yuval's timely intercession, the attempt might well have proven successful.

He gave the job to a new kid. It was no matter; in a field like theirs, the new kids were frequently better than the old hands. This one was an artist in the truest sense of the word. He made his first move at ten fifteen Eastern time, and by half past two he owned the place—the place being a Manhattan-based concern called Chelsea Fine Arts Storage.

As instructed, the kid headed straight for the database: insurance records, tax documents, personnel files, a dispatch log with a year's worth of pickups and deliveries, a master list of the paintings stored in a secure, climate-controlled warehouse on East Ninety-First Street near York Avenue. There were 789 paintings in all. Each entry included the name of the work, the artist, the support, the dimensions, the date of execution, the estimated value, the current owner, and the painting's exact location in the warehouse, by floor and rack number.

Six hundred and fifteen of the paintings were said to be owned directly by Masterpiece Art Ventures—which also happened to own Chelsea Fine Arts Storage. The remaining works were controlled by corporate shell companies with the sort of three-letter uppercase abbreviations beloved by asset concealers and kleptocrats the world over. The most recent arrival was *Danaë and the Shower of Gold*, purportedly by Orazio Gentileschi. The stated value of the work was $30 million, which was approximately $30 million more than what it was actually worth. As yet, the work was uninsured.

The warehouse also contained sixteen canvases by a once promising Spanish artist named Magdalena Navarro. At three fifteen that afternoon—following an incriminating luncheon with one Phillip Somerset, founder and CEO of Masterpiece Art Ventures—she returned to the Pierre Hotel. Upstairs in her suite she immediately surrendered her phone to Gabriel. He gave her a list of 789 paintings, and they went to work.

THEY FELL INTO A PREDICTABLE IF ALTOGETHER DEPRESSING rhythm. Magdalena would cast her eye down the list and call out when she spotted a painting she knew to be a forgery. Then, with Sarah and Evelyn Buchanan taking careful notes, she would recite the date and circumstances by which the work had found its way into the inventory of Masterpiece Art Ventures. The overwhelming majority of the canvases had been acquired through phantom sales conducted within Magdalena's distribution network, which meant no actual money had changed hands. But several had been routed through reputable dealers to provide Phillip with plausible deniability in the event the authenticity of the works was ever called into question.

Notably absent from the directory was Sir Anthony van Dyck's *Portrait of an Unknown Woman*, oil on canvas, 115 by 92 centimeters, which Masterpiece had recently purchased from Isherwood Fine Arts. According to the dispatch logs, the painting was moved to Sotheby's in New York in mid-April.

"A week after the bombing in Paris," Gabriel pointed out.

"Phillip must have unloaded it," replied Magdalena. "Which means some unsuspecting collector is now the proud owner of a worthless painting."

"I'll have a word with Sotheby's tomorrow morning."

"A quiet word," cautioned Sarah.

"Somehow," said Gabriel with a glance at Evelyn, "I don't think that's going to be an option."

By 5:00 p.m. they had twice scoured the list from top to bottom. The final tally was a breathtaking 227 forgeries with a declared valuation of more than $300 million, or 25 percent of Masterpiece's purported assets under management. When combined with the rest of the evidence that Gabriel and Magdalena had acquired in New York—including a recording of an attempt by Phillip Somerset to obtain an art-backed loan from JPMorgan Chase using a forged painting as collateral—it was irrefutable proof that Masterpiece Art Ventures was a criminal enterprise run by one of the greatest financial con artists in history.

At the conclusion of the review, Evelyn rang her editor at

Vanity Fair's Fulton Street headquarters and told him to expect her finished draft no later than 9:00 p.m. Then she sat down at her laptop and began to write.

"At some point," she informed Gabriel, "I'll have to ask Phillip for a comment."

Fortunately, they knew how to reach him. According to Proteus, his phone was presently near the corner of Fifth Avenue and East Seventy-Fourth Street, 134 feet above sea level. There were six missed calls, three new voice mails, and twenty-two unread text messages. The camera was staring at the ceiling. The microphone was listening to nothing at all. The damn thing was just sitting there, thought Gabriel. Like a paperweight with a digital pulse.

61

SUTTON PLACE

LEONARD SILK WAS WELL ACQUAINTED with the dark side of human nature. His clients, all of whom were sufficiently wealthy to afford his services, were a rogues' gallery of fraudsters, schemers, scammers, larcenists, embezzlers, insider traders, philanderers, and sexual deviants of every stripe. Silk never sat in judgment of them, for Silk was not without sin himself. He dwelled in a proverbial house of glass. He did not make a habit of throwing stones.

Silk's fall from grace had occurred in the late 1980s while he was serving in the CIA's station in Bogotá. Recently divorced, his personal finances under duress, he had entered into a lucrative partnership with the Medellín cocaine cartel. Silk had supplied the drug lords with valuable intelligence on DEA and Colombian efforts to penetrate their organization. In return, the drug lords had supplied Silk with money—$20 million in cash, all of it derived from selling cocaine in the country he was sworn to defend.

Somehow Silk managed to extricate himself from the relationship with both his ill-gotten fortune and his life, and retired from the Agency just days before the attacks of 9/11. He used a portion of the funds to purchase a luxury Sutton Place apartment. And in the winter of 2002, while his old colleagues were fighting the opening battle of the global war on terrorism, Silk went into business as a security consultant and private investigator. In a deliberate play on words, he called his one-man firm Integrity Security Solutions.

Silk offered his clients the usual array of advisory services but derived most of his income through illicit activities such as corporate espionage, computer hacking, blackmail, sabotage, and a product he euphemistically referred to as "reputational defense." He was renowned for his ability to make problems go away, or, whenever possible, to prevent problems from arising in the first place. He also possessed the capability, as a last resort, to make "problems" suffer fatal auto accidents or drug overdoses, or vanish without a trace. He had no operatives on his payroll. Instead, he hired freelance professionals as needed. Two recent operations had taken place in France, where Silk was well connected. Both had been carried out at the behest of the same client.

At 9:42 that morning, the client had asked Silk to ascertain why several investors had requested multimillion-dollar redemptions from his art-based hedge fund. With a few phone calls to his network of paid or coerced informants, Silk had discovered a possible explanation. It was not the sort of matter he liked to discuss over the phone, so he summoned his driver and headed uptown. Arriving at the client's residence on East Seventy-Fourth Street, Silk saw two workmen maneuvering a crated painting into the back of a delivery truck. A security man named Tyler Briggs was observing their efforts from the open doorway.

"Where's your boss?" asked Silk.

"Upstairs in his office."

"Is he alone?"

"He is now. He had company earlier."

"Anyone interesting?"

Briggs ushered Silk into the mansion's security control room. The art-filled residence was protected by an array of high-resolution cameras. At present, one was trained on Silk's client. He was sitting at his desk, a phone to his ear. He looked unwell.

Briggs sat down at a computer and wordlessly entered a few keystrokes. A moment later a tall, dark-haired woman appeared on one of the video screens. She was standing before a painting in the gallery. A Gentileschi, thought Silk. Quite stunning, but almost certainly a forgery.

"Why is she photographing it?"

"I didn't ask."

"Where did she go next?"

The security man played the recording.

"That's quite enough," said Silk after a moment.

The image froze.

"Walk upstairs to Mr. Somerset's office and quietly tell him to meet me in the garden."

The security man rose and started toward the door.

"One more thing, Tyler."

"Yes, Mr. Silk?"

"Tell Mr. Somerset to leave his phone behind."

SILK FOLLOWED A CORRIDOR TOWARD THE BACK OF THE TOWN house—past the wine cellar, the movie theater, and the yoga studio—and emerged into the walled garden. It was shaded by a large tree in midsummer leaf and overlooked on the north and east by elderly apartment buildings. Decorator outdoor furnishings stood forlornly on the spotless stonework. The splashing of the Italianate fountain silenced the rush of after-noon traffic on Fifth Avenue.

Five minutes elapsed before Phillip Somerset finally ap-peared. As usual, he was nautically attired. They sat down in a pair of low-slung wicker chairs. Silk delivered his findings without preamble or pleasantries. He was a busy man, and Phillip Somerset was in serious trouble.

"How bad is it going to be?"

"My sources haven't been able to uncover anything regard-ing the content."

"Isn't that exactly the sort of information I pay you for, Leonard?"

"The magazine's publicity department has contacted every business news desk in the city. They wouldn't have done that unless she had something big."

"Is it fatal?"

"Could be."

"And you're sure the story is about me?"

Silk nodded.

"Is the FBI involved?"

"My sources say not."

"So where is it coming from? And why did several of my investors choose today of all days to flee the fund?"

"It's possible that rumors are swirling in the art world about a damaging story in the works. But the more likely ex-planation is that you are under a coordinated attack by a de-termined and resourceful adversary."

"Any candidates?"

"Only one."

Silk didn't speak the name; it wasn't necessary. He had op-posed targeting a man like Gabriel Allon but had relented when Phillip offered him a payment of $10 million. Silk had given a substantial portion of that money to a French organi-zation known only as the Groupe, the same organization that had handled the Valerie Bérrangar job. He had also supplied the Groupe detailed information regarding Allon's travel plans—specifically, his intention to pay a visit to an art gallery on the rue la Boétie in Paris. Even so, the Israeli and his friend Sarah Bancroft had managed to escape the gallery alive.

"You assured me that Allon was no longer an issue," said Phillip.

"The video of Ms. Navarro's arrival here earlier this afternoon would suggest otherwise."

Phillip frowned. "Is Tyler Briggs on your payroll or mine, Leonard?"

Silk ignored the question. "She took several photographs of the painting that was on display in the gallery. Close-ups and wide shots. Looked to me as though she was trying to establish its location."

Phillip's expression darkened, but he said nothing.

"Did the two of you discuss business after you were finished in the bedroom?"

"In detail," answered Phillip.

"Was your phone with you?"

"Yes, of course."

"Where was hers?"

"I assume it was in her handbag."

"It was probably recording every word you said. You should assume your phone is probably compromised, too."

Phillip swore softly.

"I'm afraid to ask."

"I had two rather candid calls with Kenny Vaughan. I also tried to obtain an art-backed loan from Ellis Gray of JPMorgan Chase."

"Because several of your largest investors just happened to withdraw from your fund on the very day that Ms. Navarro was in your home taking pictures of a painting."

Phillip clambered to his feet.

"Sit down," said Silk calmly. "You're not going anywhere near her."

"You work for *me*, Leonard."

"Which is not something I'd like the FBI to know. Or Gabriel Allon, for that matter. Therefore, you will do exactly what I tell you to do."

Phillip managed a smile. "Did you just threaten me?"

"Only amateurs make threats. And I'm no amateur."

Phillip lowered himself into his chair.

"Where is she staying?" asked Silk.

"Her usual suite at the Pierre."

"I think I'll check in on her. In the meantime, I'd like you to go upstairs and pack a bag."

"Where am I going?"

"To be determined."

"If I leave the country now—"

"Your remaining investors will head for the lifeboats, and your fund will collapse within hours. The question is, do you want to be in New York when that happens? Or would you rather be lying on a beach with Lindsay?"

Phillip gave no answer.

"How much cash is on hand?" asked Silk.

"Not much."

"In that case, now might be a good time for you to settle your bill with Integrity Security Solutions." Silk handed over a phone. "Your outstanding balance is fifteen million."

"Rather steep, don't you think?"

"Now is not the time to quibble over money, Phillip. I'm the only thing standing between you and a cell in the Metropolitan Correctional Center."

Phillip dialed Kenny Vaughn and instructed him to wire $15 million into Silk's account at Oceanic Bank and Trust

Ltd. in Nassau. "I know, Kenny. Just do whatever you need to do."

Phillip killed the call and tried to return the phone.

"Keep it," said Silk. "Leave your personal phone on the desk connected to a charger and go to your place on the island. Don't make a move until you hear from me."

62

PIERRE HOTEL

URING THE THIRTEEN-BLOCK RIDE FROM Phillip Somerset's town house to the Pierre Hotel, Leonard Silk made a series of hurried phone calls. The first was to Executive Jet Services at MacArthur Airport on Long Island; the second, to a man who had run guns to the Contras and cocaine for the cartels. Lastly, Silk called an old friend from the Agency named Martin Roth. Marty was a supplier of cyber-and-surveillance specialists and, if circumstances warranted, muscle and firepower. His private security business was based in a warehouse in Greenpoint. Silk was a regular customer.

"When do you need them?" asked Marty.

"Twenty minutes ago."

"The traffic in Midtown is a bitch. And I'm stretched pretty thin as it is."

"Do what you can," said Silk as his Escalade drew to a stop outside the Pierre's Fifth Avenue entrance. "My client will be grateful. And so will I."

Inside, the hostess in the Two E Bar & Lounge greeted Silk by name and showed him to a corner table. A glass of single malt appeared a moment later, followed soon after by Ray Bennett, a retired NYPD detective who now served as the Pierre's director of security. Nothing happened inside the hotel's walls that escaped Bennett's notice, which is why Silk paid him a substantial monthly retainer.

Bennett wasn't alone. There were others like him at every high-end hotel in town, all feeding Silk a steady stream of dirt, most of it accompanied by receipts and security video. Information about the private lives of reporters was a priority. Bennett had once given Silk the means to kill a *New York* magazine exposé about one of his most important clients. Silk had rewarded his asset with a $25,000 bonus, enough to take the financial sting out of his divorce settlement and pay for his kid's tuition at Holy Rosary.

Hotel regulations forbade Bennett to sit down with a customer, so he remained on his feet while Silk made his request. "There's a woman staying in a suite on the twentieth floor. She's acquainted with an important client of mine. The client is concerned she might be in danger."

"What's her name?"

"She checked in under Miranda Álvarez. Her real name is—"

"Magdalena Navarro. She's a regular."

"Have you noticed anything unusual?"

"Unless I'm mistaken, she's only set foot outside the hotel once since she arrived."

"What's she been doing with herself?"

"She had a dinner party last night."

"Really? With whom?"

"Her friends from across the hall. They checked in at the same time. False names. Just like Ms. Navarro."

"I need their real names," said Silk.

"How badly?"

"Ten thousand."

"Twenty."

"Done," said Silk.

RAY BENNETT RETURNED TO HIS OFFICE, CLOSED THE DOOR, and sat down at his computer. As director of security, he had unlimited access to guest information, regardless of their demands for privacy. He called Leonard Silk a moment later and read him the names.

"Sarah Bancroft and Gabriel Allon."

Bennett's iPhone pinged with a text message.

"Look at the photograph I just sent you," said Silk.

Bennett enlarged the image.

"Recognize her?"

"She's that reporter from *Vanity Fair*."

"Has she been in Ms. Navarro's suite?"

"I believe she's there now."

"Thanks, Ray. The check's in the mail."

The connection died.

Bennett looked at the two names on his computer screen. One of them was familiar. *Gabriel Allon* . . . Bennett was certain he had seen it before. But where?

Google gave him the answer.

"Shit," he said softly.

OUTSIDE, LEONARD SILK SLID INTO THE BACK OF HIS ESCAlade and dialed the burner phone he had given to Phillip.

"Did you speak to her?" he asked.

"I couldn't. She's rather busy at the moment."

"Doing what?"

"Telling Evelyn Buchanan everything she knows about

Masterpiece Art Ventures. Gabriel Allon and your friend Sarah Bancroft are with her. It's over, Phillip. Your charter leaves MacArthur at ten fifteen. Don't be late."

"Maybe I should take the Gulfstream instead."

"The point of this operation is to get you and Lindsay out of the country without leaving any footprints. When you arrive in Miami, a car will run you down to Key West. By the time the sun rises, you'll be halfway to the Yucatán Peninsula."

"What about you, Leonard?"

"That depends on whether you ever mentioned my name to your friend from Seville."

"Don't worry, she can't implicate you in anything."

Silk heard a chorus of car horns through the phone. "Why aren't you on the chopper yet?"

"Second Avenue is jammed."

"You won't have to worry about traffic where you're going."

Silk hung up the phone and lifted his gaze toward the upper floors of the hotel. *She can't implicate you . . .* Perhaps not, but Silk wasn't prepared to take that chance.

He rang Ray Bennett.

"I have another assignment, if you're interested."

"I'm listening."

Silk explained.

"How much?" asked Bennett.

"Fifty thousand."

"To go up against a man like Gabriel Allon? Get real, Leonard."

"How about seventy-five?"

"A hundred."

"Done," said Silk.

63

NORTH HAVEN

ALONE IN THE VAST, EMPTY house in North Haven, Lindsay Somerset sat in a simple cross-legged pose, her hands resting lightly on her knees. The floor-to-ceiling window before her overlooked the copper waters of Peconic Bay. Ordinarily the panorama filled her with a sense of contentment, but not now. She could find no inner peace, no *shanti*.

Her phone lay on the floor next to her mat, silenced, aglow with an incoming call. She didn't recognize the number, so she tapped DECLINE. Instantly the phone rang a second time, and once again Lindsay terminated the call. After two additional attempts to fend off the intruder, she lifted the device angrily to her ear.

"What the hell do you want?"

"I was hoping to have a word with my wife."

"Sorry, Phillip. I didn't recognize the number. Whose phone are you using?"

"I'll explain when I get there."

"I thought you were staying in the city tonight."

"Change in plan. We're scheduled to land at East Hampton at six forty-five."

"Wonderful news. Shall I make a dinner reservation?"

"I don't think I can face the mob scene tonight. Let's pick up something on the way home."

"Lulu?"

"Perfect."

"Any requests?"

"Surprise me."

"Is something wrong, Phillip? You sound down."

"Rough day. That's all."

Lindsay hung up the phone and, rising, pulled on a pair of Nikes and a Lululemon half-zip hoodie. Then she headed downstairs to the great room. *Rothko, Pollock, Warhol, Basquiat, Lichtenstein, Diebenkorn* . . . Nearly a half-billion dollars' worth of paintings, all controlled by Masterpiece Art Ventures. Phillip had carefully shielded Lindsay from the company's affairs, and her knowledge of how it functioned was limited to the basics. Phillip purchased paintings shrewdly and sold them at an immense profit. He kept a portion of those profits for himself and passed the rest on to his investors. Banks were eager to lend him capital because he never missed a payment and used his inventory as collateral. The loans allowed him to buy still more art, which produced still greater returns for his investors. Most saw the paper valuation of their accounts double in just three years. Few ever withdrew their money. Masterpiece was too sweet a deal.

Lindsay contemplated the Basquiat. She had been at Phillip's side the night he purchased it at Christie's for $75 million. In fact, it was their first real date. Afterward, he had taken her to Bar SixtyFive at the Rainbow Room to celebrate the acquisition with his employees. They were a small team—

three ponytailed young women with sensible shoes and Ivy League educations, and a guy named Kenny Vaughan who had worked with Phillip at Lehman Brothers. There was also a tall, beautiful Spanish woman named Magdalena Navarro. Phillip said she worked as a scout and broker for Masterpiece in Europe.

"Are you still sleeping with her?" Lindsay had asked during the drive to Phillip's town house.

"With Magdalena? Not anymore."

Lindsay posed the same question when Phillip proposed marriage—and when he insisted that she sign a prenuptial agreement guaranteeing her a payment of $10 million were they ever to divorce. In neither instance did she believe Phillip's denial. More troubling was her deeply held conviction that her husband and Magdalena remained lovers to this day. The sexual bond they shared was obvious in their every gesture and expression. Lindsay wasn't blind. And she wasn't as dumb as they thought she was.

I'll explain when I get there . . .

The sensation of disharmony returned. Whether it was their marriage or Phillip's business, Lindsay could not say. But something was amiss, off-kilter. She was certain of it.

Outside, she climbed behind the wheel of her white Range Rover and headed up the drive. As she passed the staff cottage, a security guard gave her a perfunctory wave and opened the gate. She turned left into Actors Colony Road, then dialed Lulu Kitchen & Bar in Sag Harbor. She greeted the hostess by name and placed her order: fried calamari, grilled octopus, two Bibb lettuce salads, grilled halibut, and a skirt steak. Phillip's credit card was on file, so there was no discussion of payment or even the size of the bill.

"Is seven fifteen all right, Mrs. Somerset? We're a bit busy tonight."

"Seven would be better."

She followed Route 114 down the length of the peninsula and into downtown Sag Harbor. The airport lay about four miles south of the village, on Daniels Hole Road. Once owned and operated by the town of East Hampton, it was now a fully private airfield that catered to people like the Somersets of North Haven. Phillip's Sikorsky was dropping from the clear evening sky as Lindsay turned through the entrance. The security guard allowed her to drive onto the tarmac, thus sparing Mr. Somerset the indignity of having to walk to the parking lot.

He settled into the passenger seat of the Range Rover while the ground staff loaded two large aluminum-sided Rimowa suitcases into the back. Both bags appeared to be unusually heavy.

"Dumbbells?" asked Lindsay as she kissed Phillip's lips.

"One contains two million dollars in cash. The other is filled with five-hundred-gram gold ingots."

"Why?"

"Because I'm not the man you think I am," said Phillip. "And I'm in trouble."

SHORTLY BEFORE TAKING OVER DAY-TO-DAY management of Isherwood Fine Arts, Sarah Bancroft had endured a brutal interrogation at the hands of a senior Russian intelligence officer, during which she was threatened with a deadly radiological toxin. Watching Evelyn Buchanan write her article was only slightly less torturous. Sarah offered guidance where she could, but mainly she kept her head down and tried to stay out of the line of fire, most of which was directed at Gabriel. No, he said time and time again, he had no desire to see his name included in the story. Ground rules were ground rules. There was no going back at the last minute.

"In that case," said Evelyn, "I have a few more questions I'd like to ask Magdalena."

"About what?"

"Oliver Dimbleby."

"Who?"

"Magdalena mentioned his name when she and Phillip were discussing your Gentileschi."

"Did she? I wasn't listening at the time."

"She also implied that all those newly discovered paintings were forgeries."

"That's because they were."

"Who painted them?"

"Who do you think?"

"Why?"

"To lure Magdalena into the open."

"Did anyone actually *buy* them?"

"Goodness, no. That would have been unethical."

"Please tell me the rest of the story."

"Finish the one in front of you, Evelyn. Your editor is expecting your first draft at nine o'clock."

By half past six Sarah could take no more. Rising, she announced her intention to go downstairs for a proper Belvedere martini. Magdalena requested permission to join her.

"Permission denied."

"If I was going to flee, I would have done it this afternoon while I was with Phillip. Besides, we had a deal, Mr. Allon."

She had a point. "One drink only," he said. "And no phone or passport."

"Two drinks," countered Sarah. Then she turned to Magdalena. "I'll meet you at the elevators in five minutes."

"Ten would be better."

Sarah headed to her room to freshen up. Magdalena did the same, leaving Gabriel alone with Evelyn.

"I'd like to ask you a few more questions."

"I'm sure you would," replied Gabriel absently. Then he checked the feed from Phillip Somerset's phone. The device had not moved in more than three hours. Fourteen missed calls, eight new voice mails, thirty-seven unread text messages.

No images.

No audio.

No Phillip.

WHEN IT WAS OVER, THERE WAS NEAR-UNIVERSAL AGREEMENT that it was all Christopher's fault. He rang Sarah from London as she was entering her room and kept her on the phone while she stripped off her wrinkled clothing and changed into something more appropriate. Putting her hair and makeup in order proved more of a challenge than she had imagined it would, placing her at the elevators two minutes behind schedule. Arriving, she breathed a sigh of relief. It seemed her new friend from Spain was running late as well.

But when three additional minutes elapsed with no sign of Magdalena, Sarah grew anxious. Her fear of impending disaster worsened when a press of the call button produced a glowing light but no carriage. Frantic, she snatched up the receiver of the house phone, explained her plight to the hotel operator, and was assured she would momentarily be lobby bound.

At last a carriage appeared. It stopped on a half-dozen floors, collecting a menagerie of annoyed hotel guests, before finally reaching the lobby. Sarah made straight for the bar, but Magdalena was nowhere to be found. She asked a waiter whether he had seen a tall, black-haired woman, approximately forty years old, quite beautiful. Unfortunately, said the waiter, he had not.

Sarah received a similar answer from the girl at Reception. And from the dark-suited security man standing nearby. And from the porters and valets at both of the hotel's entrances.

Finally she dialed Gabriel's number. "Please tell me that Magdalena is still upstairs with you."

"She left fifteen minutes ago."

Sarah's shouted obscenity reverberated through the Pierre's grand lobby. She had turned her back on Magdalena. And now she was gone.

MIDTOWN

MAGDALENA HAD RECOGNIZED THE MAN who greeted her elevator. She saw him each time she stayed at the Pierre. He was the hotel's head of security. A big guy with an Irish face and an outer boroughs accent. In her previous life, Magdalena would have avoided a man like him. It was obvious the guy was a cop. Retired, sure. But a cop all the same.

On that evening, however, the former police officer whose name Magdalena did not know had presented himself as her guardian. Quietly, his voice calm and assured, he had asked Magdalena whether she was expecting any visitors. And when she replied that she wasn't, he informed her that he had noticed two men loitering outside her suite earlier that afternoon. The same two men, he explained, were now drinking club soda in the lobby bar. It was his considered opinion that both were federal law enforcement agents.

"FBI?"

"Probably. And I think there might be a couple more outside."

"Can you get me out of here?"

"That depends on what you've done."

"I trusted someone I shouldn't have."

"I've done that once or twice myself." He looked her up and down. "Do you need anything from your suite?"

"I can't go back."

"Why not?"

"Because the man I trusted is there now."

With that, he took her by the arm and led her through a doorway. It opened onto a hallway lined with small offices, which in turn gave onto the hotel's loading bay. A black Escalade idled curbside on East Sixty-First Street.

"He's waiting for another guest. It's yours if you want it."

"I don't have any way to pay him."

"I know the driver. I'll take care of it."

The big former cop with an Irish face escorted Magdalena across the sidewalk and opened the rear driver's-side door. Seated in the back was a gray man in a gray suit. The former cop forced Magdalena inside and slammed the door. The Escalade lurched forward and made a left turn onto Fifth Avenue.

The gray man in the gray suit watched Magdalena without expression as she clawed at the door latch. Finally she capitulated and turned to face him. "Who are you?"

"I'm the man who makes Phillip's problems go away," he answered. "And you, Ms. Navarro, are a problem."

The driver had a neck like a fire hydrant and stubble-length hair. At the corner of East Fifty-Ninth Street and Park Avenue, Magdalena politely asked him to unlock her door. Receiving no response, she appealed to the gray man in the gray suit, who told her to shut her mouth. Furious, she tried to gouge his eyes from their sockets. Her attack ended when he seized her right wrist and twisted it to the breaking point.

"Are you finished?"

"Yes."

He increased the pain. "Are you sure?"

"I promise."

He reduced the pressure, but only slightly. "Why are you in New York?"

"I was arrested."

"Where?"

"Italy."

"How is Allon involved?"

"He was working with the Italian police."

"I assume you made a deal?"

"Doesn't everyone?"

"What were the terms?"

"He promised me that I wouldn't face charges if I helped him take down Phillip."

"And you fell for this nonsense?"

"He gave me his word."

"He used you, Ms. Navarro. And you can be sure that he was planning to hand you over to the FBI the minute he no longer needed you."

Magdalena tore her wrist from his grasp and retreated to the edge of the seat. They were inching across the intersection of East Fifty-Ninth Street and Third Avenue. On the other side of her blacked-out window was a traffic officer, arm raised. If Magdalena were successful in getting the officer's attention, she might extricate herself from her current circumstances. But she would also set in motion a chain of events that would lead inevitably to her incarceration. It was better, she reasoned, to take her chances with the solver of Phillip's problems.

"How much does Allon know?" he asked.

"Everything."

"And the reporter?"

"More than enough."

"When will the article appear?"

"Later tonight. Masterpiece will be toast by the morning."

"Will the story include my name?"

"How could it? I don't know your name."

"Phillip never whispered it into your ear while you were—"

"Fuck you, you bastard."

The blow came without warning, a lightning-fast backhand. Magdalena tasted blood.

"How chivalrous. There's nothing quite so attractive as a man who strikes a defenseless woman."

His phone rang before he could pose another question. He raised the device to his ear and listened in silence. Finally he said, "Thanks, Marty. Let me know if Allon makes a move." Then he returned the phone to his coat pocket and looked at Magdalena. "Evidently, Evelyn Buchanan's computer is about to have a serious malfunction."

"It won't stop the article."

"Perhaps not. But it will give you and Phillip plenty of time to get out of the country before the FBI issues warrants for your arrest."

"I'm not going anywhere with him."

"The alternative is a shallow grave in the Adirondacks."

Magdalena said nothing.

"Wise choice, Ms. Navarro."

Lᴵɴᴅsᴀʏ ɪɴsɪsᴛᴇᴅ ᴏɴ sᴛᴏᴘᴘɪɴɢ ɪɴ downtown Sag Harbor to pick up the food at Lulu. Phillip thought it an act of madness, like the suicide who slips into her wedding gown before swallowing an overdose of sleeping tablets. Now, as he stood at the end of the restaurant's handsome bar awaiting their order, he was relieved to have a moment to himself.

The din of the room was pleasant and midsummer in volume. Phillip's present circumstances notwithstanding, it had been a good day on Wall Street. Money had been made. He shook a few of the better hands, rubbed a couple of important shoulders, and acknowledged the discreet nod of a respected collector who had recently purchased a painting from Masterpiece Art Ventures for $4.5 million. In a few hours' time, the collector would learn that the painting was doubtless a forgery. In an attempt to conceal his embarrassment over being duped, he would assure his closest friends and business associates that he had always known that Phillip Somerset was a con artist and swindler. The collector would likely receive no restitution, as the available assets of Masterpiece Art Ventures would be limited and the line of claimants long. The talented Mr. Somerset would be unable to offer assistance to the authorities, for his whereabouts would be unknown. Lulu Kitchen & Bar on Main Street in Sag Harbor would be among the last places anyone would recall laying eyes on him.

He felt a hand on his elbow and, turning, found himself gazing into the terrier-like eyes of Edgar Malone. Edgar lived well on the fortune left to him by his grandfather, a substantial portion of which he had unwisely entrusted to Masterpiece Art Ventures.

"I hear you lost several investors today," he announced.

"All of whom profited handsomely from their association with my fund."

"Should I be worried?"

"Do I look worried to you, Edgar?"

"You don't. That said, I'd like to take some of my money off the table."

"Sleep on it. Call me in the morning with your decision."

The hostess informed Phillip that his order was delayed and offered him a glass of complimentary wine as recompense, as he was a valued customer and a prominent member of East End society—at least for a few more hours. He declined the glass of wine but accepted an incoming call to his burner phone.

"Send your helicopter back to Manhattan immediately," said Leonard Silk.

"Why?"

"To pick up the final member of your traveling party."

"Anyone I know?"

"Call your crew," said Silk. "Get that bird back to Manhattan."

FIVE MINUTES LATER, BAGS IN HAND, PHILLIP STEPPED FROM the restaurant's doorway into the warm evening air. He placed the food in the back of the Range Rover and settled into the passenger seat. Lindsay reversed out of the space without so much as a glance in the rearview mirror. Tires screeched, a horn blared. Phillip supposed it would one day be a part of the lore surrounding his disappearance—the near-collision on Main Street in Sag Harbor. Much would be made of the fact that Lindsay had been the one behind the wheel.

She jammed the transmission into DRIVE, and the Range Rover shot forward. "Explain how it worked," she demanded.

"There isn't time. Besides, you couldn't possibly understand."

"Because I'm not smart enough?"

Phillip reached for her, but she recoiled. She was driving dangerously fast.

"Tell me!" she screamed.

"In the beginning, it was a way to generate the extra cash that I needed to show a profit to my investors. But as time went on, buying and selling forgeries became my business model. If I had stopped, the fund would have collapsed."

"Because your so-called fund was nothing but a glorified Ponzi scheme?"

"No, Lindsay. It was a real Ponzi scheme. And a very lucrative one at that."

And it would have gone on forever, thought Phillip, if it wasn't for a Frenchwoman named Valerie Bérrangar. She wrote a letter to Julian Isherwood about *Portrait of an Unknown Woman*. And Isherwood asked none other than the great Gabriel Allon to investigate. Phillip might have been able to outwit the FBI, but Allon was a far more formidable adversary—a gifted art restorer who also happened to be a retired intelligence officer. What were the odds? It had been a mistake to let him leave New York alive.

Lindsay ignored the stop sign at the end of Main Street and swerved onto Route 114. Phillip seized his armrest as they flew across the narrow two-lane bridge separating Sag Harbor from North Haven.

"You really need to slow down."

"I thought you have a plane to catch."

"We both do." Phillip released his death grip on the armrest. "It leaves from MacArthur at ten fifteen."

"Bound for where?"

"Miami."

"I know I'm not as smart as you are, Phillip, but I'm fairly certain Miami is part of the United States."

"It's only the first stop."

"And after Miami?"

"A beautiful home overlooking the ocean in Ecuador."

"I thought rich criminals like you and Bobby Axelrod went to Switzerland to avoid arrest."

"Only in the movies, Lindsay. We'll have new identities and plenty of money. No one will ever find us."

She laughed bitterly. "I'm not going anywhere with you, Phillip."

"Do you know what will happen if you stay behind? The minute the fund collapses, the FBI will seize the houses and the paintings and freeze all the bank accounts. You'll be an outcast. Your life will be ruined. And no one will ever believe that you didn't know your husband was a criminal."

"They will if I turn you in."

Phillip unplugged Lindsay's phone from its charger and slipped it into his coat pocket.

"Surely you didn't do this all on your own," she said.

"Kenny Vaughan was the one who made the numbers work."

"What about Magdalena?"

"She ran sales and distribution."

"Where is she now?"

"On her way to the Thirty-Fourth Street Heliport."

Lindsay pressed the accelerator to the floor.

"If you don't slow down," said Phillip, "you're going to kill someone."

"Maybe I'll kill *you*."

"Not if I kill you first, Lindsay."

67

PIERRE HOTEL

WHEN MAGDALENA LEFT HER SUITE on the twentieth floor of the Pierre Hotel for the last time, she was clad in the same dark pantsuit she had been wearing the night she plucked Oliver Dimbleby from the pavements of Bury Street in London. She had her Spanish driver's permit and a single twenty-dollar bill, but no phone or passport. And no handbag, either. It was lying at the foot of her unmade bed, next to a Spanish-language copy of *Love in the Time of Cholera*. It was, in Gabriel's opinion, the clearest evidence of her intent. Of his many female friends and acquaintances, not one would take flight without a purse. Therefore, he was confident that there was some other explanation for Magdalena's sudden disappearance. An explanation that in all likelihood involved Phillip Somerset and Leonard Silk.

Whatever had happened, the hotel's surveillance cameras had been watching. Gabriel rang Yuval Gershon, explained the situation, and asked him to have a look at the recordings.

Yuval suggested that Gabriel have a word with hotel security instead.

"I have a terrible feeling hotel security was involved."

"What makes you think that?"

"The elevators mysteriously froze around the time she went missing."

"Describe her."

"Tall, long dark hair, dark pantsuit, no handbag."

"It looks to me as though you're on the nineteenth floor."

"Twentieth, Yuval."

"I'll get back to you when I have something."

Gabriel rang off. Sarah was anxiously pacing the room. Evelyn Buchanan was staring at her laptop with the shocked expression of someone who had just witnessed a murder.

"Is something wrong?" asked Gabriel.

"My article just disappeared from my screen." Evelyn dragged a forefinger across her trackpad. "And my documents folder is empty. All of my work, including my notes and the transcript of my interview with Magdalena, is gone."

Gabriel quickly disconnected his computer from the hotel's Wi-Fi network and instructed Evelyn to do the same. "How long will it take you to retype the piece?"

"It's not a matter of simply retyping it. I have to rewrite it from beginning to end. Five thousand words. Entirely from memory."

"Then I suggest you get started." Gabriel snatched up his phone and looked at Sarah. "Double-lock the door, and don't open it for anyone but me."

He went into the corridor without another word and headed for the elevators. An empty carriage appeared at once. He rode it down to the lobby and left the hotel via the Fifth Avenue entrance.

Outside, the sun had dropped below the trees of Central Park, but the twilight was abundant. Gabriel turned to the left and then made another left onto East Sixtieth Street. As he passed the entrance of the fabled Metropolitan Club, the private playground of New York's financial elite, he spotted two men sitting in a parked Suburban. Both were wearing earpieces. The one behind the wheel noticed Gabriel first. He said something to his partner, who turned his head to have a look at the legend as well.

The legend rounded the corner onto Madison Avenue and walked to East Sixty-First Street. The second team was parked directly opposite the Pierre's delivery entrance. They were three in number—the third member being the hacker who had penetrated the Pierre's Wi-Fi network and sucked the documents off Evelyn's laptop.

Gabriel was tempted to ask the hacker to return the purloined material. Instead, he crossed Fifth Avenue and entered Central Park. There he sat down on a bench and waited for his phone to ring, wondering, not for the first time, how his life had come to this.

Though Gabriel did not know it, Magdalena was at that moment pondering the same question. She was seated not on a park bench but in the back of a luxury SUV, next to a man who a few minutes earlier had threatened to kill her if she did not agree to flee the country with the financier whose art-based hedge fund she had exposed as a fraud. She had been given no information regarding their destination, though her lack of a passport suggested that their journey would be unconventional. It would begin, apparently, with a helicopter flight, as they were parked beneath the FDR Drive, near the pale-gray, boxlike terminal of the East Thirty-Fourth Street Heliport.

Magdalena glanced at her wristwatch, the Cartier tank that Clarissa the personal shopper had chosen for her at Bergdorf

Goodman that frigid December afternoon in 2008. What a waste, she thought suddenly, these costly trinkets. Art was all that mattered—art and books and music. And family, of course. It had been a mistake to involve her father in Phillip's fraud. Still, she was confident he would not be prosecuted. Art criminals never received the punishment they deserved. It was one of the reasons there was so much art crime.

A second SUV drew up beside them, and Tyler Briggs emerged from the passenger seat. Evidently, Magdalena would have a chaperone on the first leg of her journey into exile, lest she misbehave on board the aircraft and endanger the crew. She was considering one final act of insurrection before leaving Manhattan, a parting gesture to avenge her split and swollen lip.

Her seatmate was looking down at his phone. "Your ride is about to land," he informed her.

"Where am I going?"

"East Hampton."

"In time for dinner, I hope."

"It's only the first stop."

"And then?"

"Somewhere you'll be able to use that Spanish of yours."

"How's yours?"

"Fluent, actually."

"In that case, you won't have any trouble understanding what I'm about to tell you."

Calmly, she recited the crudest, vilest Spanish insult she could bring herself to repeat. The gray man in the gray suit only smiled. "Phillip always said you have quite a mouth on you."

This time it was Magdalena who lashed out without warning. Her blow opened a small cut in the corner of his eye. He wiped away the blood with a linen pocket square.

"Get on the helicopter, Ms. Navarro. Otherwise, there's a shallow grave in your future."

"Yours, too, I imagine."

Tyler Briggs opened Magdalena's door and escorted her to the waiting Sikorsky. Five minutes later they were headed across the East River. Before them stretched the working-class neighborhoods of Queens and the suburbs of Nassau and Suffolk counties. That slender riotous island, thought Magdalena.

She checked her Cartier. It was 7:50 p.m. At least she thought it was. The damn watch kept lousy time.

68

PIERRE HOTEL

Ray Bennett, the Pierre Hotel's head of security, was roughly the same size as Capitano Luca Rossetti. Well over six feet tall, at least 225 pounds. Most of that weight remained in reasonably good shape for a man of his age, which was mid-fifties. His hair was metallic gray and well groomed, his face was wide and square. It was a face, thought Gabriel, that had been made to take a punch. He asked its owner whether it would be possible for them to have a word in private. Ray Bennett said he preferred to speak in the lobby.

"That would be a mistake on your part, Mr. Bennett."

"And why is that, sir?"

"Because your colleagues will hear what I have to say to you."

Bennett contemplated Gabriel with a pair of all-seeing cop's eyes. "What's this about?"

"A missing guest."

"Name?"

"Not here."

Bennett led Gabriel through a doorway behind Reception and down a corridor to his office. He left the door open. Gabriel closed it soundlessly and turned to face the larger man.

"Where is she?"

"Who?"

Gabriel delivered a lightning-strike blow to Bennett's larynx, then raised a knee to his exposed groin, just to keep things sporting. After all, Gabriel was the smaller and older of the two combatants. A generous point spread was in order.

"You were standing at the elevator when she came downstairs. You told her something that put her mind at ease and escorted her to the delivery entrance. A black Escalade was waiting outside. You forced her into the backseat."

Bennett made no reply. He wasn't capable of one.

"I have a feeling I know who put you up to it, Ray. Nevertheless, I'd like to hear you say his name."

"S-s-s-s-s-s . . ."

"Sorry, but I didn't catch that."

"S-s-s-s-s-s . . ."

"Leonard Silk? Is that what you're trying to tell me?"

Bennett nodded vigorously.

"How much did he pay you?"

"H-h-h-h-h . . ."

"I beg your pardon?"

"H-h-h-h-h . . ."

Gabriel patted the front of Bennett's suit jacket and found his phone. It was an iPhone 13 Pro. He waved it before Bennett's face, and he was in. The same New York–based cellular number appeared three times in his RECENTS. One incoming, two outgoing. The last call was approximately an hour earlier, at 6:41 p.m. It was outgoing.

Gabriel showed the number to Ray Bennett. "Is this Silk?"

Bennett nodded.

Gabriel snapped a photograph of the screen with his Solaris. Then he handed Bennett the receiver of his desk phone. "Tell the valet to bring Ms. Bancroft's car to the Fifth Avenue entrance. Not the East Sixty-First Street doorway. Fifth Avenue."

Bennett pressed the speed-dial button and emitted an incomprehensible croak into the mouthpiece.

"Bancroft," said Gabriel slowly. "I know you can do it, Ray."

UPSTAIRS ON THE TWENTIETH FLOOR, GABRIEL FORWARDED Leonard Silk's phone number to Yuval Gershon before cramming his belongings into his overnight bag. In the room next door, Sarah packed with equal haste. Then she hurried across the hall and stuffed Magdalena's clothing and toiletries into her costly Louis Vuitton carry-on. At the writing desk, Evelyn Buchanan hammered away at her laptop without pause, oblivious, or so it seemed, to the commotion around her.

At 7:40 p.m. the phone in Sarah's room rang. It was the valet calling to say that Ms. Bancroft's car was waiting, as requested, outside the hotel's Fifth Avenue entrance. Evelyn Buchanan shoved her laptop into her bag and followed Gabriel and Sarah into the elevator. Downstairs in the lobby, there was no sign of Ray Bennett. Sarah informed the young woman at Reception that she and Mr. Allon were checking out earlier than expected.

"Is there a problem?" the woman inquired.

"Change in plans," lied Sarah effortlessly, and declined the woman's offer of a printed receipt.

A bellman relieved them of their luggage and loaded it into the Nissan Pathfinder. Evelyn Buchanan crawled into the backseat and immediately removed her laptop. Sarah settled into the passenger seat; Gabriel, behind the wheel. As he sped through the intersection of Fifth Avenue and East Sixtieth Street, he turned his head to the right, hiding his face from the two men sitting in the Suburban outside the Metropolitan Club. They made no attempt to follow them.

"Is kidnapping complimentary at the Pierre?" asked Sarah. "Or is there an extra charge?"

Gabriel laughed quietly.

"Where do you suppose she is?"

"I have a terrible feeling she's about to leave the country, whether she wants to or not."

"With Phillip?"

"Who else?"

"She doesn't have a passport."

"Maybe she won't need one where they're going."

"Phillip keeps his Gulfstream at Teterboro," said Sarah.

"He's too smart to use his own plane. He'll leave on a charter that someone has booked on his behalf." Gabriel paused. "Someone like Leonard Silk."

"Perhaps we should telephone Mr. Silk and ask him where his client is headed."

"I rather doubt that Mr. Silk would prove receptive to our advances."

"In that case," said Sarah, "we should probably contact the FBI."

"Could get ugly."

"For Magdalena?"

"And me."

"Better than the alternative, though."

"The FBI can't arrest Phillip without a warrant. And they can't obtain a warrant based on my say-so alone. They need credible evidence of criminal wrongdoing."

"They'll have it soon enough." Sarah glanced over her shoulder at Evelyn Buchanan, who was typing furiously on her laptop. Then she turned and gazed down the length of Fifth Avenue. "I hope you realize that none of this would have happened if we'd stayed at the Four Seasons."

"Lesson learned."

"And I never got my martini."

"We'll get you a martini after we stop Phillip from fleeing the country."

"I certainly hope so," said Sarah.

NOT SURPRISINGLY, RAY BENNETT CHOSE NOT TO INFORM Leonard Silk that the number for his personal mobile phone had fallen into the hands of the world's most famous retired spy. Consequently, Silk took no action to protect his device from attack. It came as he was headed uptown on First Avenue—a stealth zero-click invasion carried out by the Israeli-made malware known as Proteus. Like countless other victims before him, including numerous heads of state, Silk was unaware his device had been compromised.

Within minutes the phone was spewing a geyser of valuable information. Of immediate interest to Yuval Gershon were the GPS location data and the call history. On his own initiative, Gershon attacked a second device before calling Gabriel. It was eight fifteen in New York. Gabriel was barreling along Broadway through Lower Manhattan. The two men spoke in Hebrew to ensure that nothing was lost in translation.

"He left the Pierre at six forty-four. By the way, that was the exact time Ray Bennett led your girl out the service door. Something tells me it wasn't a coincidence."

"Where did he go?"

"East Thirty-Fourth Street Heliport. He was there until seven fifty-two."

"Where is he now?"

"Back in his apartment on Sutton Place. Number fourteen, in case you're wondering. Sixteenth floor, if I had to guess."

"Any interesting calls?"

"Executive Jet Services. It's a charter company based at MacArthur Airport on Long Island."

"I know where MacArthur is, Yuval."

"Do you know when Silk made the calls?"

"Maybe you should tell me."

"The first call was at four twenty-three this afternoon. He called again about twenty minutes ago."

"Sounds to me as if someone is planning to take a trip."

"Someone is. Silk called him twice. The last call was around seven o'clock. I lit him up a few minutes ago. There's no data on the phone, which means it's probably a burner. But I was able to get a fix on his location."

"Where is he?"

"The eastern shore of the North Haven Peninsula."

"Twelve feet above sea level?"

"How did you guess?"

"Message me if he so much as twitches."

Gabriel rang off and looked at Sarah.

"What did he say?" she asked.

"He said that we should probably charter a helicopter."

Sarah dialed.

THE OFFICES OF *VANITY FAIR* MAGAZINE WERE LOCATED ON THE twenty-fifth floor of One World Trade Center. Gabriel dropped Evelyn Buchanan on West Street near the 9/11 memorial, then followed the Battery Park Underpass to the Downtown Manhattan Heliport. He squeezed the Nissan into an empty space in the small staff parking lot, gave the attendant $500 in cash to keep the vehicle for the night, and led Sarah into the terminal. Their chartered Bell 407 waited at the end of the L-shaped pier. It departed at 9:10 p.m. and raced eastward, into the cooling twilight.

69

NORTH HAVEN

THE SOMERSETS OF NORTH HAVEN were owners of his-and-hers Range Rovers. Phillip's was a fully loaded 2022, black, tan interior. With the help of a security guard, he placed five aluminum-sided suitcases by Rimowa of Madison Avenue into the spacious rear storage compartment. Two of the suitcases contained cash; two, gold ingots. The largest was filled with clothing, toiletries, and a few personal mementos—including a collection of luxury wristwatches valued at $12 million.

Inside the house, Phillip found Lindsay where he had left her, seated at the island in the kitchen, the food properly plated and arrayed before her. She had lit candles, poured wine, touched nothing. The air smelled of lilies and grilled octopus. It turned Phillip's stomach. He checked the display screen of the hardline phone. Lindsay had made no calls during his brief absence.

"Shall I pack a bag for you?" he asked.

She stared silently into an emptiness of Phillip's making. She had not spoken a word since his ill-advised threat of violence. It was Lindsay who had drawn her sword first, but it had been reckless of Phillip to respond in kind. Almost as reckless, he thought, as divulging the name of the country where he planned to take refuge.

"You won't tell them where I am, will you?"

"The first chance I get." She gave him a counterfeit smile. "But not tonight, Phillip. I've decided it would be best if you simply disappeared. That way, I'll never have to look at your face again or, heaven forbid, visit you in prison."

Phillip returned to his office and executed a series of wire transfers, all designed to leave little if no trace of the money's final destination. Taken together, they had the effect of draining every cent from the accounts of Masterpiece Art Ventures. There was nothing left. Nothing but the real estate, the toys, the debt, and the paintings. The genuine works in the company's inventory were worth at least $700 million, but all were leveraged to the hilt. Perhaps Christie's would hold a special evening sale to auction the works off. *The Somerset Collection* . . . It had a certain ring to it, he had to admit.

Rising, he went to his window and for the last time surveyed his realm. The bay. His boat. His manicured garden. His blue swimming pool. He realized suddenly he hadn't used it once all summer.

A green light flared on the multiline desk phone. Phillip snatched up the receiver and heard Lindsay abruptly hang up downstairs. Evidently, she was still entertaining thoughts of turning him in. He switched lines and dialed East Hampton Airport. Mike Knox, the regular evening head of flight operations, answered.

"Your helicopter arrived about twenty minutes ago, Mr. Somerset. The passengers decided to stay on board."

"Any other inbound birds?"

"A Blade, a couple of privates, and a Zip Aviation charter from downtown."

"What's the ETA on the charter?"

"Twenty-five minutes or so."

"Is my helicopter fueled?"

"Finishing now."

"Thanks, Mike. I'm on my way."

Phillip hung up the phone and opened the bottom drawer of his desk. It was where he kept his unregistered firearm.

Not if I kill you first, Lindsay . . .

It would certainly guarantee a clean departure, he thought. But it would also saddle him with eternal infamy. If the truth be told, a part of him was actually looking forward to exile. Keeping the Ponzi scheme up and running all these years had been exhausting; he was sorely in need of a vacation. And now it seemed he would have beautiful Magdalena to keep his bed warm, at least until the storm blew over and it was safe for her to return to Spain.

Or perhaps not, Phillip thought suddenly. Perhaps they would live out their lives together in hiding. He imagined a Ripley-like existence, with Magdalena playing the role of Héloïse Plisson. With the passage of time, he might come to be viewed in a more favorable light—as an alluring figure of mystery, a villain protagonist. Putting a bullet into Lindsay would spoil that. The whole of the Upper East Side would be rooting for his death.

He closed the drawer, deleted his documents and emails, and emptied his digital trash. Downstairs, he returned Lindsay's phone. She stared through him as though he were made of glass. "Leave" was all she said.

THE BLADE COMMUTER HELICOPTER ARRIVED AT EAST HAMPTON Airport at ten minutes past nine o'clock. Six passengers,

Manhattanites all, spilled onto the tarmac and, after collecting their luggage, traipsed off toward the terminal. Magdalena watched them from the window of the Sikorsky. Tyler Briggs sat in the opposing seat, legs spread, crotch on full display. Magdalena calculated the odds of delivering a debilitating strike and then snatching the phone from his hand. They were reasonable, she reckoned, but retribution would likely be swift and severe. Tyler was ex-military, and Magdalena was already damaged from her skirmishes with the gray eminence. She'd had quite enough excitement for one evening. Better to ask nicely.

"May I borrow your phone for a moment, Tyler?"

"No."

"I just want to check a website."

"The answer is still no."

"Will you please check it for me, please? It's *Vanity Fair.*"

"The magazine?"

"Haven't you heard? They're about to publish a story about your boss. By tomorrow morning, the town house will be surrounded by camera crews and reporters. Who knows? If you play your cards right, you might be able to earn a little extra money. But I beg of you, don't sell those naughty videos you've saved on your computer. My poor mother will never get over it."

"Mr. Somerset ordered us to wipe the system this afternoon."

"That was wise of him. Now be a love, Tyler, and check the website for me. It's *Vanity Fair.* I can spell it for you, if that helps."

The phone rang before he could reply. "Yes, Mr. Somerset," he said after a moment. "No, Mr. Somerset. She was no trouble at all . . . Yes, I'll tell her, sir."

He hung up and slipped the phone into his jacket pocket.

"Tell her what?" asked Magdalena.

The security guard pointed toward the black Range Rover speeding across the tarmac. "Mr. Somerset would like a word with you in private before we leave."

HE BRAKED TO A HALT A FEW YARDS FROM THE SIKORSKY'S TAIL and popped the Range Rover's rear door. Magdalena took inventory of the cargo before climbing into the passenger seat. Phillip stared straight ahead, hands gripping the wheel. An unlocked cell phone lay on the center console. It was not his usual device.

At last he turned and looked at her. "What happened to your face?"

"Apparently, I said something that offended the sensibilities of your friend." Magdalena paused. "We were never properly introduced."

"Silk," said Phillip. "Leonard Silk."

"Where did you find him?"

"Smith and Wollensky."

"Chance encounter?"

"There's no such thing where Leonard is concerned."

"What was the occasion?"

"Hamilton Fairchild."

"Buyer?"

Phillip nodded.

"Which painting?"

"*Saint Jerome.*"

"Follower of Caravaggio?"

"Circle of Parmigianino. I dumped it on Hamilton in a private treaty sale arranged by Bonhams."

"I was always fond of that picture," said Magdalena.

"So was Hamilton until he showed it to an art dealer named

Patrick Matthiesen. Matthiesen told Hamilton that, in his learned opinion, the painting was the work of, how shall we say, a later imitator."

"I assume Hamilton wanted his money back."

"Naturally."

"And you refused?"

"Of course."

"How did the situation resolve itself?"

"Regrettably, Hamilton and his wife died in a single-engine plane crash off the coast of Maine."

"How many others were there?"

"Fewer than you might imagine. Leonard handled most of them with an envelope filled with naughty photographs or incriminating financial information. And not just buyers. Investors, too. Why do you think Max van Egan still has a quarter-billion in the fund?" Phillip took up the phone and refreshed the web browser. "How long before the story appears?"

"I'm surprised it hasn't already. When it does, Masterpiece will go up in flames."

"You're as guilty as I am, you know."

"Somehow I don't think your lenders and investors are going to see it that way."

Phillip tossed aside the phone in anger. "Why did you do it?" he asked.

"I was arrested an hour after I purchased the Gentileschi. It was an elaborate sting operation by Gabriel Allon and the Italians. They gave me a choice. I could spend the next several years in an Italian prison, or I could give them your head on a platter."

"You should have asked for a lawyer and kept your mouth shut."

"You wired ten million euros into a Carabinieri-controlled bank account. They would have eventually traced the money back to you, with or without my help."

"I suppose the redemptions were Allon's doing, too. He baited me into committing an act of bank fraud over a compromised phone."

"I told you to put the painting on ice," said Magdalena. "But you wouldn't listen."

"You put a rope around my neck and walked me to the gallows."

"I had no other choice."

"You were a drug dealer when I found you. And this is how you repay me?"

"But they were real drugs, weren't they, Phillip?" Magdalena took a long look over her shoulder. "I don't suppose Lindsay is in one of those suitcases."

"It's just the two of us."

"How romantic. Where are we off to?"

Phillip looked down at the phone; Magdalena, at her Cartier wristwatch.

It was half past nine.

70

DOWNTOWN

O<small>N THE TWENTY-FIFTH FLOOR OF</small> One World Trade Center, in a conference room overlooking New York Harbor, war had been declared. The combatants were five in number and were broken into three opposing camps. Two were senior editors, two were lawyers, and the last was a reporter with an impeccable track record for accuracy and click-generating copy. The piece under deliberation contained allegations of financial impropriety by a prominent figure in the New York art world. Complicating matters was the fact that the prominent figure's hired henchmen had deleted the only existing draft of the story. Furthermore, it appeared that the prominent figure was at that very moment attempting to flee the country.

Nevertheless, insisted the lawyers, certain legal and editorial standards had to be met. Otherwise, the prominent art world figure, whose name was Phillip Somerset, would have grounds to file a lawsuit, as would his investors.

"Not to mention his lenders at JPMorgan Chase and Bank

of America. In short, it has all the makings of a legal cluster-fuck for the ages."

"My source is a freelance employee of Masterpiece Art Ventures."

"With a rather dubious personal history."

"I have recordings."

"Provided to you by a former Israeli intelligence officer who was using a highly controversial cell phone hacking malware."

"New York is a one-party consent state. She knew she was being recorded when she met with Phillip."

"But neither Phillip nor Ellis Gray of JPMorgan Chase consented to being recorded. Therefore, their conversation regarding the art-backed loan is inadmissible, as it were."

"What about the paintings in the warehouse?"

"Don't even think about it."

With that, a temporary truce was declared, and work commenced. The reporter wrote, the editors edited, the lawyers lawyered—one paragraph at a time, at a pace more akin to an old-fashioned wire service than a storied cultural-and-current affairs monthly. But such were the exigencies of magazine publishing in the digital age. Even the staid *New Yorker* had been compelled to offer its subscribers daily content. The world had changed, and not necessarily for the better. Phillip Somerset was proof of that.

At half past nine they had a draft in hand. It was limited in scope but devasting in impact. The story appeared on *Vanity Fair*'s website at 9:32 p.m., and within minutes it was trending on social media. In the aftermath, much would be made of its final line. Phillip Somerset, it read, could not be reached for comment.

WHEN THE FIRST TEXT MESSAGES DETONATED ON LINDSAY's phone, she assumed they were from Phillip and ignored them.

There was a brief pause, followed by a second barrage. Then all hell broke loose.

Reluctantly Lindsay reached for the device and saw a stream of venom and threats, all sent by some of her closest friends. Attached to each of the texts was the same article from *Vanity Fair*. The headline read THE FAKE: INSIDE PHILLIP SOMERSET'S MASTERPIECE OF A PONZI SCHEME. Lindsay clicked on the link. Three paragraphs was all she could take.

She opened her RECENTS, found the number for Phillip's burner, and dialed. The background whir of the Sikorsky's turboshaft engines told her that he had not yet departed East Hampton Airport.

"Have you read the article?" she asked.

"I'm reading it now."

"I can't face this alone."

"What are you saying?"

"Don't leave without me," said Lindsay, and snatched her car keys from the kitchen counter.

THE CHARTERED BELL 407 WAS OVER THE WATERS OF LONG Island Sound when Evelyn Buchanan's article popped onto Gabriel's phone. He skimmed it quickly and was relieved to find that neither his name nor Sarah's appeared in the text. Neither, for that matter, did Magdalena's. Her allegations were attributed to an unnamed freelance employee of Masterpiece Art Ventures. There was no mention of her gender or nationality. For the moment, at least, she was in the clear. Phillip Somerset, however, was finished.

Voice calls were prohibited onboard the helicopter, so Gabriel shot a text message to Yuval Gershon and requested an update on Phillip's position. Yuval's reply appeared a minute later. Phillip was still on the tarmac at East Hampton Airport.

"Why hasn't he left yet?" asked Sarah over the drone of the Bell's engines.

"It seems Lindsay has had a change of heart. She called him two minutes ago and told him not to leave until she arrived."

"Perhaps it's time you had that chat with the FBI."

"I'm afraid there's a complicating factor."

"Only one?"

"Magdalena is there, too."

The helicopter remained over Long Island Sound until they reached the old Horton Point Light, where a turn to starboard carried them over the town of Southold and the waters of Peconic Bay. A ferry was crossing the narrow channel separating Shelter Island and North Haven. On the eastern shore of the peninsula, Phillip's now-abandoned estate was ablaze with light.

"It looks as though Lindsay left in a hurry," said Sarah.

They passed over Sag Harbor and commenced their descent toward East Hampton Airport. Directly beneath them, a white Range Rover was headed toward the airfield along Daniels Hole Road. It was Lindsay Somerset, thought Gabriel. And she was definitely in a hurry.

SHE MADE THE FINAL TURN INTO THE AIRPORT WITH DELIBerate care. Hand-over-hand on the steering wheel, a gentle acceleration mid-arc. Just the way her father had taught her when she was a girl of fourteen. The gate at the edge of the tarmac was open. The guard waved her through. Magdalena stood next to the Sikorsky; Phillip, at the open rear door of his Range Rover. He hoisted an arm in greeting, as though waving from the deck of his sailboat. Lindsay switched off the headlights, put her foot to the floor, and closed her eyes.

PART FOUR

UNVEILING

71

EAST HAMPTON

THE CALL CAME THROUGH ON the emergency line of the East Hampton Town Police Department at 9:55 p.m. Sergeant Bruce Logan, a twenty-year veteran of the department and lifelong resident of the East End, braced himself for the worst. It was Mike Knox calling from the airport.

"Helicopter or plane?" asked Logan.

"Actually, it was two Range Rovers."

"Fender bender in the parking lot?"

"Fatality on the tarmac."

"You're shitting me, Mike."

"I wish."

The department's headquarters were located on the southern edge of the airfield, on Wainscott Road, and the first officers arrived at the scene just three minutes after the initial call. They found the victim, a white male in his mid-fifties, lying on the tarmac in a bay of his own blood, his legs nearly severed, surrounded by several hundred carefully packaged five-hundred-gram gold ingots. The driver of the vehicle that had struck the man was an attractive, fit-looking woman in her thirties. She wore leggings, a Lululemon hoodie, and neon-green Nikes. She had no wallet and seemed unable to recall her name. Mike Knox supplied it for her. The woman was Lindsay Somerset. The dead guy with the nearly severed legs was her husband, a rich investor of some sort who owned a weekend palace in North Haven.

Death was formally declared, an arrest was made, a statement was issued. The news broke at midnight on WINS radio, and by nine the following morning it was all anyone was talking about. The real estate mogul Sterling Dunbar was in the shower when he learned that Lindsay Somerset had run down her scoundrel of a husband; the retailer Simon Levinson, still in his bed. Ellis Gray of JPMorgan Chase, having endured a sleepless night after reading the *Vanity Fair* story, was in his office overlooking Park Avenue. Two hours later he informed senior management that the firm was now on the hook for $436 million in loans issued to Masterpiece Art Ventures—loans that, in all likelihood, had been collateralized with forged paintings. Senior management accepted Gray's resignation, effective immediately.

By midday the FBI had assumed control of the investigation. Agents searched Phillip's homes, sealed his warehouse, and raided his offices on East Fifty-Third Street. The firm's three female art experts were taken to Federal Plaza and questioned at length. All denied any knowledge of financial or art-related impropriety. Kenny Vaughan, Phillip's wingman from his days at Lehman Brothers, was nowhere to be found. Agents seized his computers and printed files and issued a warrant for his arrest.

Phillip's crimes were global in scope, and so was the fallout. Two prominent European dealers—Gilles Raymond of Brussels and Konrad Hassler of Berlin—were arrested and their inventories seized. Dealers in Hong Kong, Tokyo, and Dubai were likewise taken into custody. Under questioning, all admitted that they were part of a far-flung distribution network that had been flooding the art market with high-quality forgeries for years. The French Ministry of Culture grudgingly acknowledged that four of those forgeries had found their way into the permanent collection of the Louvre. The museum's president abruptly resigned, as did the director of the esteemed National Center for Research and Restoration, which had declared all four works to be authentic.

But who was this master forger who had managed to deceive the world's most sophisticated art laboratory? And how many examples of his handiwork were now circulating through the bloodstream of the art world? Evelyn Buchanan, in a follow-up to her original exposé, reported that Phillip's warehouse likely contained more than two hundred forged paintings. Hundreds more, she wrote, had already been foisted upon unsuspecting buyers. When a partial list of those works appeared anonymously on a much-read industry message board, panic swept the art world. Collectors, dealers, curators, and auctioneers—having relied for generations on the pronouncements of connoisseurs—turned to the scientists to help them sort through the wreckage. Aiden Gallagher of Equus Analytics was so inundated with requests for evaluations that he stopped answering his phone and responding to emails. "Mr. Gallagher," wrote an art reporter from the *New York Times*, "is the scandal's only winner."

The losers, of course, were Phillip's well-heeled investors, the ones who had seen hundreds of millions of dollars in paper wealth wiped away in a matter of hours. Their lawsuits, countersuits, and public lamentations earned them little sympathy, especially from art world purists who found the very concept of a fund like Phillip's abhorrent. Great paintings, they declared, were not securities or derivatives to be traded among the superrich. They were objects of beauty and cultural significance that belonged in museums. Not surprisingly, those who made their living buying and selling paintings found such sentiments laughable. Without the rich, they pointed out, there would be no art. And no museums, either.

A federal judge appointed a trustee to sift through Phillip's assets and dole out the proceeds to those he had defrauded. Three hundred and forty-seven investors sought restitution. The largest claim was $254 million by the industrialist Max van Egan. The smallest was $4.8 million by Sarah Bancroft, a former curator from the Museum of Modern Art who now managed an Old Master gallery in London.

One of Phillip's investors, however, filed no claim at all: Magdalena Navarro, thirty-nine years old, a citizen of Spain who resided in the upscale Salamanca district of Madrid. According to documents seized from the offices of Masterpiece Art Ventures—and to sworn statements given to the FBI by the three cooperating employees of the firm—Navarro was a European-based freelance runner who purchased and sold paintings on Phillip Somerset's behalf. Her last recorded account balance was $56.2 million, a great deal of money to leave lying on the table.

As it turned out, the FBI knew more about Magdalena Navarro than it had revealed in public, which was nothing at all. It knew, for example, that the European art dealers Gilles Raymond and Konrad Hassler had identified her as the link between their galleries and Masterpiece Art Ventures. The Bureau also knew that Navarro had been in New York at the time of the hedge fund's spectacular collapse, having arrived on a Delta Air Lines flight from Rome and departed—less than twelve hours after Phillip Somerset's death—on a flight to London. Interestingly enough, she had been seated next to Gabriel Allon, the legendary former director-general of the Israeli secret intelligence service, on both legs of her journey.

The art dealer Sarah Bancroft, who also happened to be a former clandestine CIA officer, had accompanied Allon and Navarro on the flight to Heathrow.

Investigators also established that all three had stayed in separate rooms on the twentieth floor of the Pierre Hotel during their brief visit to New York. And that Magdalena Navarro was likely the source of the exposé in *Vanity Fair*. And that Navarro departed the Pierre Hotel shortly before the article's publication—without luggage or a handbag—and traveled to East Hampton Airport aboard Phillip Somerset's Sikorsky helicopter. And that she subsequently left East Hampton Airport, in the chaotic minutes following Somerset's grisly death, aboard a Bell 407 chartered by Allon and Bancroft. The pilot delivered them to JFK, where they spent the night in the airport Hilton. And by eight the following morning, they were gone.

All of which suggested to the FBI that a friendly chat with Allon was in order. Finding him proved less difficult than they imagined. The FBI's legal attaché in Rome simply rang the offices of the Tiepolo Restoration Company in Venice, and Allon's wife arranged a meeting. It took place in Harry's Bar—which was where, unbeknownst to the legal attaché, Allon's involvement in the affair began. While sipping a Bellini, he told the FBI officer about a private inquiry he had undertaken at the behest of an old friend whom he refused to identify. This private inquiry, he said in conclusion, led him to Magdalena Navarro and, ultimately, Phillip Somerset's $1.2 billion forgery-based Ponzi scheme.

"Where is she now?" asked the FBI man, whose name was Josh Campbell.

"Somewhere in the Pyrenees. Even I don't know where."

"Doing what?"

"Painting, I assume."

"Is she any good?"

"If Phillip hadn't got his hooks into her, she would have been a major artist."

"We'd like to question her."

"I'm sure you would. But as a personal favor to me, I'd like you to let her get on with her life."

"The Bureau isn't in the business of granting personal favors, Allon."

"In that case, you leave me no choice but to call the president directly."

"You wouldn't dare."

"Watch me."

And so Special Agent Josh Campbell returned to Rome empty-handed, but with a fascinating tale to tell. He wrote it up in a lengthy memorandum and fired it simultaneously to Washington and New York. Those who knew of Allon's past exploits were dubious as to the document's accuracy—and justifiably so. The report made no mention, for example, of a forged portrait by Anthony van Dyck. Or a recently deceased Frenchwoman named Valerie Bérrangar. Or a Parisian antiques dealer and art thief named Maurice Durand. Or the Swiss violinist Anna Rolfe. Or the notorious Corsican crime figure Don Anton Orsati. Or the lecherous but lovable London art dealer Oliver Dimbleby, whose fictitious rediscovery and record-setting sales of three Venetian School masterworks had recently set the art world ablaze.

By the end of July, all three canvases were hanging in the apartment of the forger who had created them, along with two versions of Modigliani's *Reclining Nude*, a Cézanne, a Monet, and a stunning version of Van Gogh's *Self-Portrait with Bandaged Ear*. On the easel in his studio was a painting with an L-shaped tear, 15 by 23 centimeters, in the lower left corner. After repairing the damage and retouching the losses, the forger shipped the work to a small gallery near the Plaza Virgen de los Reyes in Seville. Then, early the next morning, he disappeared.

72

ADRIATICO

FOR THE FIRST FIVE DAYS of the trip, the *maestral* prevailed. It was not the cold and blustery aggressor that had laid siege to the island of Corsica the previous spring, but a temperate and dependable companion that propelled the Bavaria C42 effortlessly down the length of the Adriatic. With the seas calm and the wind blowing across the stern of his spacious vessel, Gabriel was able to provide Irene and Raphael with a smooth and pleasant introduction to maritime life. No one was more relieved than Chiara, who had prepared herself for six sun-drenched weeks of moaning, groaning, and seasickness.

Their days lacked shape, which was their intention. Most mornings Gabriel awakened early and got under way while Chiara and the children slept in the cabins beneath him. Sometime around noon he would drop his sails and lower the swim platform, and they would enjoy a long lunch at the cockpit table. In the evening they dined in portside restaurants—Italy one night, Croatia or Montenegro the next. Gabriel carried his Beretta whenever they went ashore. Chiara never addressed him by his given name.

When they reached the southern Adriatic port of Bari, they spent the night in a comfortable boutique hotel near the marina, did a large load of laundry, and restocked their stores with food and plenty of local white wine. Late the following morning, when they rounded the heel of Italy, a warm and sultry *jugo* was blowing from the southeast. Gabriel rode it westward across the Ionian and arrived at the Sicilian port of Messina a day earlier than he had anticipated. The Museo Regionale was a short walk along the waterfront from the marina. In Room 10 were two monumental canvases executed by Caravaggio during his nine-month stay in Sicily.

"Is it true he used an actual corpse?" asked Chiara as she pondered *The Raising of Lazarus*.

"Unlikely," answered Gabriel. "But certainly not beyond the realm of possibility."

"It's not one of his better efforts, is it?"

"Much of what you see was painted by studio assistants. The last restoration was about ten years ago. As you can no doubt tell from the quality of the work, I wasn't available at the time."

Chiara gave him a look of reproach. "I think I liked you better before you became a forger."

"Consider yourself lucky that I didn't attempt to forge a Caravaggio. You would have thrown me into the street."

"I have to say, I rather enjoyed my afternoons with Orazio Gentileschi."

"Not as much as he enjoyed his time with Danaë."

"She would love to have lunch alone with you before this trip is over."

"Our cabin is too close to the children's."

"In that case, how about a midnight snack instead?" Smiling, Chiara directed her gaze toward the Caravaggio. "Do you think you could paint one?"

"I'll pretend I didn't hear that."

"And what about your rival? Is he capable of forging a Caravaggio?"

"He produced undetectable Old Master paintings from every school and period. A Caravaggio would be rather easy for him."

"Who do you suppose he is?"

"The last person in the world anyone would ever suspect."

Their midnight snack turned out to be a sumptuous feast several hours in length, and it was nearly ten in the morning by the time they set out for Limpari. Their next stop was a little cove along the Calabrian coast. Then, after an overnight sail that included a snack on the Bavaria's foredeck, they arrived at the Amalfi Coast. From there, they island-hopped their way across the Gulf of Naples—first Capri, then Ischia—before venturing across the Tyrrhenian Sea to Sardinia.

To the north lay Corsica. Gabriel charted a course up the island's western side, into the teeth of a freshening *maestral*. And two days later, on a cool and cloudless Wednesday evening, he guided the Bavaria into Porto's tiny marina. Waiting on the quay, their arms raised in greeting, were Sarah Bancroft and Christopher Keller.

THE SUN HAD SET BY THE TIME THEY REACHED THE WELL-guarded home of Don Anton Orsati. Clad in the simple clothing of a Corsican *paesanu*, he greeted Irene and Raphael as though they were blood relatives. Gabriel explained to his children that the large, expansive figure with the dark eyes of a canine was a producer of the island's finest olive oil. Irene, with her peculiar powers of second sight, was clearly dubious.

The don's walled garden was strung with decorative lights

and filled with members of his extended clan, including several who worked in the clandestine side of his business. It seemed the arrival of the Allon family after a long and perilous sea voyage was cause for celebration, as was the first visit to the island by Christopher's American wife. Many Corsican proverbs were recited, and a great deal of pale Corsican rosé was drunk. Sarah stared unabashedly at Raphael throughout dinner, entranced by the child's uncanny resemblance to his father. Gabriel, for his part, stared at his wife. She had never looked happier—or more beautiful, he thought.

At the conclusion of the meal, the don invited Gabriel and Christopher upstairs to his office. Lying on the desk was the photograph of the man who had tried to kill Gabriel and Sarah at Galerie Georges Fleury in Paris.

"His name was Rémy Dubois. And you were right," said Orsati. "He had a military background. He spent a couple of years fighting the crazies in Afghanistan, where he became quite familiar with improvised explosives. When he came home, he had trouble getting his life together." The don glanced at Christopher. "Sound familiar?"

"Perhaps you should tell him about Rémy Dubois and leave me out of it."

"The organization for which Dubois worked is known only as the Groupe. The other employees of this organization are all former soldiers and intelligence operatives. Most of their clients are wealthy businessmen. They're very good at what they do. And quite expensive. We found Rémy in Antibes. A nice place near the Plage de Juan les Pins."

"Do I have to ask where he is now?"

"You probably passed over him as you approached Porto."

"How much were you able to get out of him?"

"Chapter and verse. Apparently, the attempt on your life was a rush job."

"Did he happen to mention when he got the order?"

"It was the Sunday before the bombing."

"Sunday evening?"

"Morning, actually. He had to assemble the bomb so quickly that he didn't have time to buy a burner phone to use as the detonator trigger. He used a phone he picked up on another job instead."

"It belonged to a woman named Valerie Bérrangar. Dubois and his associates ran her car off the road south of Bordeaux."

"So he said. He was also involved in the murder of Lucien Marchand." Orsati inclined his head toward an unfinished Cézanne-inspired landscape leaning against the wall. "We found that in his apartment in Antibes."

"Who paid for the bullet?" asked Gabriel.

"An American. Evidently, he was a former CIA officer. Dubois didn't know his name."

"It's Leonard Silk. He lives on Sutton Place in Manhattan." Gabriel paused, then added, "Number fourteen."

"We have friends in New York." Orsati fed the photograph into his shredder. "Good friends, in fact."

"How much?"

"You insult me."

"Money doesn't come from singing," said Gabriel, repeating one of the don's favorite proverbs.

"And dew won't fill the tank," he replied. "But save your money for your children."

"Little children, little worries. Big children, big worries."

"But not tonight, my friend. Tonight we have no worries at all."

Gabriel looked at Christopher and smiled. "We'll see about that."

DOWNSTAIRS, GABRIEL FOUND RAPHAEL AND IRENE PROPPED against Chiara, their eyes glassy and unfocused. Don Orsati begged them to stay a little longer, but after a final exchange of Corsican proverbs he reluctantly acquiesced to their departure. He could not hide his disappointment, though, over Gabriel's travel plans. The Allon family intended to spend a single night at Christopher's villa, then set out for Venice first thing in the morning.

"Surely you can stay for a week or two."

"The children begin school in mid-September. We'll barely make it home in time as it is."

"To where will you sail next year?" inquired the don.

"The Galápagos, I think."

With that, they said their goodbyes and squeezed into Christopher's battered old Renault hatchback for the drive to the next valley. Gabriel and Chiara sat in back with the children wedged between them. Sarah sat in the passenger seat next to her husband. Despite the gaiety of the evening, her mood was suddenly tense.

"Have you heard from Magdalena?" she asked in the overbright voice of one who feared imminent disaster.

"Magdalena who?" replied Gabriel as the headlamps illuminated the enormous horned goat standing in the center of the track near the three ancient olive trees owned by Don Casabianca.

Christopher applied the brakes, and the car slowed gently to a stop.

"Would you mind awfully if I had a cigarette?" asked Sarah. "I feel one coming on."

"That makes two of us," murmured Gabriel.

Irene and Raphael, somnambulant a moment earlier, were suddenly alert and excited about the prospect of yet another adventure. Christopher sat with his hands upon the wheel, his powerful shoulders slumped, a picture of misery.

His eyes met Gabriel's in the rearview mirror. "I would prefer if your children didn't watch."

"Don't be ridiculous. Why do you think I sailed all the way to Corsica?"

"We've had a rough couple of weeks," explained Sarah. "Last night . . ."

"Last night *what*?" probed Irene.

"I'd rather not say."

Christopher said it for her. "He got a clean shot at me. It was like being hit with a pile driver."

"You must have provoked the poor thing," said Chiara.

"As far as that creature is concerned, my very existence is a provocation."

Christopher tapped the horn and with a cordial movement of his hand invited the goat to step aside. Receiving no response, he lifted his foot from the brake and inched the car forward. The goat lowered his head and drove it into the grille.

"I told you," said Sarah. "He's incorrigible."

"That's no way to talk about Christopher," interjected Gabriel.

"What does incorrigible mean?" asked Raphael.

"Incapable of being corrected. Depraved and inveterate. A hopeless reprobate."

"Reprobate," repeated Irene, and giggled.

Christopher opened his door, igniting the interior dome light. Sarah appeared stricken. "Perhaps we should all check into a hotel. Or better yet, let's spend the night on that beautiful boat of yours."

"Yes, let's," agreed Chiara as the car shuddered with the impact of another blow. Then she looked at Gabriel and said quietly, "Do something, darling."

"My hand is killing me."

"Let me," said Irene.

"Not a chance."

"Don't listen to your father," said Chiara. "Go right ahead, sweetheart."

Gabriel opened his door and looked at his beautiful wife. "If anything happens to her, let it be on your head."

Irene clambered across Gabriel's lap and leapt out of the car. Fearlessly she approached the goat and, stroking his red beard, explained that she and her family were sailing back to Venice tomorrow morning and needed a good night's sleep. The goat clearly found the story implausible. Nevertheless, he withdrew from the track without further contest, and the situation was resolved peaceably.

Irene squeezed into the backseat and rested her head against her father's shoulder as they resumed their progress toward Christopher's villa.

"Reprobate," whispered the child, and laughed hysterically.

73

BAR DOGALE

AGAINST ALL BETTER JUDGMENT, GABRIEL agreed to remain in Corsica through the weekend. He insisted, however, on spending Sunday night aboard the Bavaria, and by the time Chiara and the children awakened on Monday morning, he had put Ajaccio behind them. With the *maestral* at his back and his spinnaker flying, he reached the southern tip of Sardinia at sunset on Tuesday, and by late Thursday afternoon they were back in Messina.

That evening, while dining at I Ruggeri, one of the city's finer restaurants, Gabriel read with relief that prosecutors in New York's Suffolk County had dropped all charges against Lindsay Somerset in the death of her husband. Locked out of her homes, her bank accounts seized or frozen, she faced an uncertain future. There was speculation in a Long Island weekly that she intended to open a fitness studio in Montauk and settle permanently in the East End. The largely favorable local reaction suggested that Lindsay, with her act of madness at the airport, had emerged from the scandal untarnished by Phillip's fraud.

Three nights later, in Bari, Gabriel read that Kenny Vaughan, Phillip's fugitive chief investment officer, had been found dead of an apparent drug overdose in a New Orleans hotel room. Still unaccounted for was the money that Phillip had drained from the firm's cash reserves during the final hours of his life. According to the *New York Times*, any attempt to sell off the hedge fund's inventory of paintings would likely prove disappointing, as collectors and museums were skittish about acquiring anything Phillip had touched. A team of experts from the Metropolitan Museum of Art had conducted a survey of the warehouse on East Ninety-First Street in an attempt to definitively determine which of the 789 paintings were forgeries and which were authentic. Consensus had proven impossible.

Accompanying the article was a photograph of the last painting Phillip acquired before his death: *Danaë and the Shower of Gold*, purportedly by Orazio Gentileschi. The FBI had determined that it was shipped to New York from the Tuscan city of Florence, doubtless in violation of Italy's strict cultural patrimony laws. Whether it was a forgery or a genuine lost masterpiece the connoisseurs could not say—not without rigorous scientific testing of the sort conducted by Aiden Gallagher of Equus Analytics. Nevertheless, US authorities had acceded to an Italian demand that the painting be returned immediately.

Fittingly enough, it arrived in Italy the same morning that Gabriel, after a moonlit final run up the northern Adriatic, eased the Bavaria into its slip at the Venezia Certosa Marina. Four days later, after watching Chiara board a Number 2 at the San Tomà vaporetto stop, he escorted Irene and Raphael to the Bernardo Canal *scuola elementare* for the start of the fall term. Alone for the first time in many weeks—and having nothing else on his schedule other than a visit to the Rialto Market—he made his way through empty streets to Bar Dogale. Which was where, at a chrome table covered in blue, he found General Cesare Ferrari.

THE WAITER DELIVERED TWO *CAPPUCCINI* AND A BASKET OF sugar-dusted, cream-filled *cornetti*. Gabriel drank the coffee but ignored the pastry. "I've been eating nonstop for a month and a half."

"And yet you look as though you haven't gained a kilo."

"I hide it well."

"Like most things." The general was attired in his blue-and-gold Carabinieri finery. Standing upright next to his chair was a shallow portfolio case typically used by art professionals to transport drawings or small paintings. "Somehow you even managed to conceal your involvement in the Somerset affair."

"Not exactly. That FBI agent gave me an earful."

"It is my understanding that the interview was conducted over Bellinis in Harry's Bar."

"You were watching?"

"You don't think we let FBI agents wander around without an escort?"

"I certainly hope not."

"Special Agent Campbell gave me a good going-over as well," said Ferrari. "He was convinced the Art Squad was somehow involved in your shenanigans. I assured him that we were not."

"The swift return of *Danaë and the Shower of Gold* suggests he believed you."

The general sipped his cappuccino. "A rather remarkable development, even by your standards."

"Where is it now?"

"Still at the palazzo," said Ferrari, referring to the Art

Squad's Roman headquarters. "But later today it will be taken to the Galleria Borghese for analysis."

"Oh, dear."

"How long will it take them to conclude it's a forgery?"

"According to the *Times*, it passed muster in New York."

"With all due respect, we know a bit more about Gentileschi's work than do the Americans."

"The brushwork and palette are his," said Gabriel. "But the minute they subject the canvas to examination by X-radiography and infrared reflectography, I'm cooked."

"As well you should be. That painting needs to be exposed as a forgery and destroyed." The general exhaled heavily. "You realize, I hope, that your fictitious sales through Dimbleby Fine Arts of London have added new works to the oeuvres of three of the greatest painters in history."

"As of yet, none of the pictures that Oliver purportedly sold have found their way into the artists' catalogues raisonnés."

"And if they do?"

"I will immediately step forward. Until then, I intend to remain out of the public eye."

"Doing what?"

"I'm going to spend the next month cleaning crumbs and other assorted debris from my boat."

"And then?"

"My wife is considering allowing me to restore a painting."

"For the Tiepolo Restoration Company?"

"Given the perilous state of my bank account, I'm inclined to accept a lucrative private commission first."

The general frowned. "Perhaps you should just forge something instead."

"My brief career as an art forger is now officially over."

"And to think that it was all for naught."

"I brought down the largest forgery network in the history of the art world."

"Without finding the forger himself," the general pointed out.

"I would have if Lindsay Somerset hadn't ruined a perfectly good Range Rover killing her husband."

"Be that as it may, it's a rather unsatisfying conclusion to the story. Wouldn't you agree?"

"The guilty were punished," said Gabriel.

"But the forger remains free."

"Surely the FBI must have some idea who he is by now."

"Young Campbell says not. Clearly, your forger covered his tracks well." General Ferrari reached for the portfolio case and handed it to Gabriel. "But perhaps this might help solve the mystery."

"What is it?"

"A gift from your friend Jacques Ménard in Paris."

Gabriel balanced the case on his knees and popped the latches. Inside was *A River Scene with Distant Windmills*, oil on canvas, 36 by 58 centimeters, purportedly by the Dutch Golden Age painter Aelbert Cuyp. There was also a copy of a report prepared by the Louvre's National Center for Research and Restoration. It stated that the center, after weeks of painstaking scientific analysis, had been unable to render a definitive judgment as to the work's authenticity. On one point, however, it was certain in its findings.

A River Scene with Distant Windmills contained not a single fiber of navy-blue polar fleece fabric.

Gabriel returned the report to the portfolio case and closed the lid.

"Bon voyage," said General Ferrari with a smile.

74

SALAMANCA

CONTRARY TO THE STATEMENT THAT Gabriel made to Special Agent Josh Campbell of the FBI, Magdalena Navarro was not in hiding in a remote village in the Pyrenees. She was holed up in her apartment on the Calle de Castelló in the elegant Salamanca district of Madrid. At half past twelve the following afternoon, Gabriel thumbed the appropriate call button on the building's intercom panel, then turned his back to the camera. Receiving no answer, he pressed the button a second time. At length the speaker crackled into life.

"If you do that again," said a sleep-heavy female voice, "I'm going to come down there and kill you."

"Please don't, Magdalena." Gabriel turned to face the camera. "It's only me."

"My God!" she said, and unlocked the door.

Inside, Gabriel climbed the stairs to her apartment. She was waiting in the open doorway, wearing a gauzy cotton pullover and little else. Her raven hair was a tangled mess. Her hands were stained with paint.

"I hope I'm not intruding on something," said Gabriel.

"Only on my sleep. You should have warned me that you were coming."

"I was afraid you might try to flee the country." He looked down at the two matching Vuitton suitcases standing on the tiled floor of the entrance hall. "Which one has the cash?"

She indicated the bag nearest the door. "It's all the money I have left."

"What happened to the four or five million you had hidden in bank accounts around Europe?"

"I gave it away."

"To whom?"

"The poor and the immigrants, mainly. I also made a rather large donation to my favorite environmental group and another to my old art school in Barcelona. Anonymously, of course."

"Perhaps there's hope for you yet." Gabriel eyed her attire disapprovingly. "But not dressed like that."

Smiling, she padded barefoot down a corridor and reappeared a moment later in stretch jeans and a Real Madrid jersey. In the kitchen she prepared *café con leche*. They drank it at a table overlooking the narrow street. It was lined with luxury apartment buildings, designer clothing boutiques, and trendy bars and restaurants. Magdalena certainly belonged in a place like this, thought Gabriel. It was a pity she hadn't come by it honestly.

"Your skin is the color of Spanish saddle leather," she informed him. "Where have you been?"

"Circumnavigating the globe on my sailboat with my wife and children."

"Did you make any new discoveries?"

"Only the identity of the forger." He looked down at her paint-smudged hands. "I see you're working again."

She nodded. "Late night."

"Anything good?"

"A soon-to-be rediscovered Madonna and child attributed to the circle of Raphael. You?"

"I've turned over a new leaf."

"Not even tempted?"

"To what?"

"Forge a painting or two," said Magdalena. "I would be honored to serve as your front woman. But only if you agree to a fifty-fifty split of the profits."

"Perhaps I was mistaken," said Gabriel. "Perhaps you're a hopeless case, after all."

She smiled and drank her coffee. "I'm not a perfect person, Mr. Allon. But I've turned over a new leaf as well. And in case you're still wondering, I'm not the forger."

"If I thought you were, I would have arrived here with a contingent of Guardia Civil to take you into custody."

"I've been expecting them." She took up her phone and opened the web browser. "Have you read the news from Germany lately? Herr Hassler is now cooperating with federal prosecutors. It's only a matter of time before they request my extradition."

"I prevented a major terrorist attack on the Cologne Cathedral not long ago. If it becomes necessary, I can call in the chit."

"What about the Belgians?"

"Brussels and Antwerp are the organized crime capitals of Europe. I doubt the Belgian police will seek your extradition over a few fake paintings."

"Surely the FBI knows about me."

"And me as well," replied Gabriel. "For the moment, at

least, they're inclined to keep our names out of it." He looked up at the unframed painting leaning against the wall. "Yours?"

Magdalena nodded. "It's the one I painted after Phillip and Leonard Silk tried to kill you in Paris. Self-portrait of a front woman."

"It's not half bad."

"My new canvases are much better. I'd love to show them to you, but I'm afraid my studio is filled with half-finished forgeries at the moment."

There were no forgeries, of course—only wildly original works executed by an artist of immense talent and technical skill. Gabriel drifted from canvas to canvas, spellbound.

"What do you think?" asked Magdalena.

"I think Phillip Somerset's greatest crime was depriving the world of your work." Gabriel placed a hand thoughtfully to his chin. "The question is, what should we do with them?"

"We?"

"I would be honored to serve as your front man. I insist, however, on receiving no share of the profits."

"You drive a hard bargain, Mr. Allon. But how do you intend to bring the works to market?"

"With a show at a premier gallery, in a major art world hub. The kind of show that will turn you into a billion-dollar global brand. Anyone who's anyone will be there. And by the end of the night, everyone will know your name."

"For all the right reasons, I hope," said Magdalena. "But where will this show take place?"

"Galerie Olivia Watson in London."

Her face brightened. "Would you really do that for me?"

"On one condition."

"The forger's name?"

He nodded.

"It was me, Mr. Allon. I executed all those undetectable

Old Master paintings between shifts at El Pote Español and Katz's Delicatessen." She threw her arms around his neck. "How can I possibly repay you?"

"By allowing me to buy one of your paintings."

"Only if you promise never to sell it for a profit."

"Deal," said Gabriel.

Eｘactly forty-eight hours later—after yet another transatlantic flight to JFK and a brief stay at a Courtyard Marriott in downtown Stamford, Connecticut—Gabriel slid behind the wheel of a rented American-made sedan and drove into a blinding sunrise to Westport. It was a few minutes after seven when he arrived at Equus Analytics. Aiden Gallagher's flashy BMW 7 Series was nowhere in sight.

Gabriel lowered the portfolio case to the asphalt, drew his Solaris mobile phone, and dialed. Yuval Gershon of Unit 8200 answered instantly. "Ready?" he asked.

"Why else would I be calling?"

Yuval remotely unlocked the door. "Enjoy."

Gabriel slipped the phone into his pocket, picked up the portfolio case, and headed inside.

Tｈe laboratory was in darkness, the shades tightly drawn. Gabriel switched on his phone's flashlight and directed the beam toward the painting mounted on the Bruker M6 Jetstream spatial imaging device. A portrait of a woman, late twenties or early thirties, wearing a gown of gold silk trimmed in white lace. Any fool could see that the dimensions of the canvas were 115 by 92 centimeters. Gabriel snapped a photograph of the woman's pale cheek. The appearance of the craquelure gave him a funny feeling at the back of his neck.

He placed the portfolio case on an examination table and climbed the stairs to the second floor. There was a single room, identical in size to the lab below. At the end overlooking Riverside Avenue were some twenty wooden shipping crates, each containing a painting awaiting examination by the esteemed Aiden Gallagher. Only one of the crates had been opened, the one that had been used to ship the painting now secured to the Bruker. It had been sent to Equus Analytics by the Old Masters department of Sotheby's in New York.

At the opposite end of the room was an easel, a trolley, and a portable fume extractor. The drawers of the trolley were empty and spotlessly clean. The easel was empty, as well. Gabriel played the beam of the flashlight over the utility tray. Lead white. Charcoal black. Madder lake. Vermilion. Indigo. Green earth. Lapis lazuli. Red and yellow ocher.

Downstairs, he removed the riverscape from the portfolio case and laid it on the examination table. Next to it he placed two reports. One was from France's National Center for Research and Restoration; the other, Equus Analytics. Then he switched off the flashlight and waited. Two hours and twelve minutes later, a car drew up in the parking lot. They would settle the matter quietly, thought Gabriel, and never speak of it again.

THE MUSEUM-GRADE ALARM SYSTEM EMITTED EIGHT SHARP chirps, and a moment later Aiden Gallagher strode through the door. He wore khaki trousers and a V-neck pullover. He stretched a hand toward the light switch, then hesitated, as though aware of a presence in the laboratory.

Finally the overhead fluorescent panels flickered into life. Aiden Gallagher drew a sharp breath of astonishment and backpedaled. "How did you get in here, Allon?"

"You left the door open. Fortunately, I happened to be in the neighborhood."

Gallagher started to dial a number on his mobile phone.

"I wouldn't, Aiden. You'll only make things worse for your-self."

Gallagher lowered the phone. "Why are you here?"

"You owe my friend Sarah Bancroft seventy-five thousand dollars."

"For what?"

Gabriel lowered his gaze toward *A River Scene with Distant Windmills*. "You assured us that there were polar fleece fibers embedded in the surface paint, ironclad proof that it was a forgery. But a second analysis of the painting has determined that you were incorrect."

"Who conducted this review?"

"The National Center for Research and Restoration."

Gallagher offered Gabriel a half-smile. "Isn't that the same laboratory that mistakenly authenticated those four forgeries that ended up hanging in the Louvre?"

"Theirs was an honest mistake. Yours wasn't. And by the way," added Gabriel, "I knew that Cranach was a forgery the instant I laid eyes on it." He pointed toward the painting attached to the Bruker. "And I certainly don't need a spatial imaging device to tell me that Van Dyck is a forgery as well."

"Based on what I've seen thus far, I'm inclined to accept it as authentic."

"I'm sure you would. But that would be a miscalculation on your part."

"How so?"

"The smarter play is to take all of your forgeries out of circulation, one by one. You'll be the hero of the art world. And you'll get even richer in the process. By my calculation, the paintings upstairs alone will add a million and a half dollars to Equus's bottom line."

"Thanks to the Somerset scandal, my fee is now one hundred thousand for rush jobs. Therefore, those paintings represent two million in new business."

"I didn't hear a denial, Aiden."

"That I'm the forger? I didn't think one was necessary. Your theory is ludicrous."

"You're a trained painter and restorer, and a specialist in provenance research and authentication. Which means you know how to select works that will be accepted by the art world and, more important, how to construct and execute them. But the best part of your scheme is that you were in a unique position to authenticate your own forgeries." Gabriel looked down at *A River Scene with Distant Windmills.* "If only you had authenticated that one, you and Phillip might still be in business." He paused. "And I wouldn't be here now."

"I didn't authenticate that painting, Allon, because it's an obvious forgery."

"Obvious to me, certainly. But not to most connoisseurs. That's why you and Phillip decided that I had to die. You told us that you had found fleece fibers in the painting because it's the most common mistake made by inexperienced forgers. It's also something that could be discovered during, say, a hurried preliminary examination conducted over a weekend. When we collected the painting on Monday afternoon, you asked when we were planning to confront Georges Fleury. And Sarah foolishly answered truthfully."

"Do you realize how insane you sound?"

"I haven't arrived at the good part yet." Gabriel took a step closer to Gallagher. "You are a member of a very small club, Aiden. Its membership is limited to those lucky souls who have tried to kill me or one of my friends and are still walking the face of the earth. So if I were you, I'd stop smiling. Otherwise, I'm liable to lose my temper."

Gallagher regarded Gabriel without expression. "I'm not the man you think I am, Allon."

"I *know* you are."

"Prove it."

"I can't. You and Phillip were too careful. And the condition of your atelier upstairs suggests that you have gone to extraordinary lengths to conceal the evidence of your crimes."

Gallagher indicated the French report. "May I?"

"By all means."

He picked up the document and began to read. After a moment he said, "They weren't able to reach an opinion as to the authenticity." There was a trace of pride in his voice, faint but unmistakable. "Even their foremost expert on Golden Age Dutch painters couldn't rule out the possibility that it's real."

"But you and I both know it isn't. Which is why I'd like to borrow a laboratory knife, please."

Gallagher hesitated. Then he opened a drawer and laid an Olfa AK-1 on the tabletop.

"Perhaps you should do it," suggested Gabriel.

"Be my guest."

Gabriel grasped the high-quality knife by its yellow handle and cleaved two irreparable horizontal gashes through the painting. He was about to inflict a third when Gallagher seized his wrist. The Dubliner's hand was trembling.

"That's quite enough." He relaxed his grip. "There's no need to mutilate the bloody thing."

Gabriel sliced the painting a third time before ripping the swaths of canvas from the stretcher. Then, knife in hand, he approached *Portrait of an Unknown Woman*.

"Don't touch it," said Gallagher evenly.

"Why not?"

"Because that painting is a genuine Van Dyck."

"That painting," said Gabriel, "is one of your forgeries."

"Are you prepared to wager fifteen million dollars?"

"Is that how much Phillip got for it?"

Receiving no answer, Gabriel removed the painting from the Bruker and cut it to ribbons. Looking up, he saw Aiden Gallagher gazing at the ruined painting, his face bloodless with rage.

"Why did you do that?"

"The better question is, why did you paint it? Was it only for the money? Or did you enjoy making fools of people like Julian Isherwood and Sarah Bancroft?" Gabriel laid the laboratory knife on the examination table. "You owe them seventy-five thousand dollars."

"The contract specifically said that the money is nonrefundable."

"In that case, perhaps we can reach a compromise."

"How much did you have in mind?"

Gabriel smiled.

IT DID NOT TAKE LONG TO ARRIVE AT A FIGURE—HARDLY SURprising, for there was no negotiation involved. Gabriel simply named his price, and Aiden Gallagher, after a moment or two of sputtering remonstration, wrote out the check. The Irishman then requested reimbursement for the Van Dyck. Gabriel laid a five-euro banknote on the examination table and, check in hand, went into the sunlit Connecticut morning.

He took his time driving back to JFK but still managed to arrive four hours before his flight was scheduled to depart. He dined poorly in the food hall, purchased gifts for Chiara and the children in the duty-free shops, and then wandered over to his assigned gate. There he removed the check from the breast pocket of his handmade Italian sport coat—a check for the sum of $10 million, payable to Isherwood Fine Arts.

Included in the final settlement was $75,000 for the fraudulent report from Equus Analytics, $3.4 million for the forged Van Dyck, $1.1 million for the forged Albert Cuyp, $100,000 for the Old Master canvases that Gabriel used for his own forgeries, and $525,000 in assorted expenses such as first-class air travel, five-star hotel rooms, and three-olive Belvedere martinis. And then, of course, there was the $4.8 million that Sarah Bancroft had lost in the collapse of Masterpiece Art Ventures.

All in all, thought Gabriel, it was a rather satisfying end to the story.

He rang Chiara in Venice and gave her the good news.

"Reprobate," she said, and laughed hysterically.

AUTHOR'S NOTE

PORTRAIT OF AN UNKNOWN WOMAN is a work of entertainment and should be read as nothing more. The names, characters, places, and incidents portrayed in the story are the product of the author's imagination or have been used fictitiously. Any resemblance to actual persons, living or dead, businesses, companies, events, or locales is entirely coincidental.

Visitors to the *sestiere* of San Polo will search in vain for the converted palazzo overlooking the Grand Canal where Gabriel Allon, after a long and tumultuous career with Israeli intelligence, has taken up residence with his wife and two young children. The business office of the Tiepolo Restoration Company is likewise impossible to find, for no such enterprise exists. The Andrea Bocelli song playing in the Allon family's kitchen in chapter 6 is "Chiara," from the 2001 album *Cieli di Toscana*. I listened to the CD frequently while writing the first draft of *The Confessor* in 2002 and gave the name to the beautiful daughter of the chief rabbi of Venice, Jacob Zolli. Irene Allon is named for her grandmother, who was one of the early State of Israel's most important artists. Her twin brother is named for the Italian High Renaissance painter Raffaello Sanzio da Urbino, better known as Raphael.

The fictitious Umbrian estate known as Villa dei Fiori

appeared for the first time in *Moscow Rules*, a novel I conceived during an extended stay on a similar property. The staff took wonderful care of my family and me, and I repaid their kindness by turning them into minor but important characters in the story. Regrettably, several shopkeepers in the town of Amelia suffered the same fate in the novel's sequel, *The Defector*.

There is indeed a suite named for the conductor Leonard Bernstein at the Hôtel de Crillon in Paris, and Chez Janou is without question one of the city's better bistros. Nevertheless, the Swiss violinist Anna Rolfe could not have sent a low murmur through its brightly lit dining room, because Anna is the product of my imagination. So, too, are Maurice Durand and Georges Fleury, the owners of a disreputable art gallery in the Eighth Arrondissement. The art squad of the Police Nationale is in fact known as the Central Office for the Fight against Cultural Goods Trafficking—it definitely sounds better in French—but its personnel do not work in the historic building located at 36 Quai des Orfèvres.

Thankfully, there is no art-based hedge fund known as Masterpiece Art Ventures, and the crimes of my fictitious Phillip Somerset are entirely my creation. I included the names of real auction houses because, like the names of great painters, they are part of the art world's lexicon. It was not my intention to suggest in any way that companies such as Christie's or Sotheby's knowingly trade in forged paintings. Nor did I wish to leave the impression that the art-based lending units of JPMorgan Chase and Bank of America would accept forged paintings as collateral. Deepest apologies to the head of security at the Pierre for Gabriel's unconscionable behavior during his brief stay. The historic hotel on East Sixty-First Street is one of New York's finest and would never employ the likes of my fictitious Ray Bennett.

The madcap menagerie of London art dealers, museum

curators, auctioneers, and journalists who grace the pages of *Portrait of an Unknown Woman* are invented from whole cloth, as are their sometimes questionable personal and professional antics. There is indeed an enchanting art gallery on the northeast corner of Mason's Yard, but it is owned by Patrick Matthiesen, one of the world's most successful and respected Old Master art dealers. A brilliant art historian blessed with an infallible eye, Patrick never would have fallen for a forged Van Dyck, even one as skillfully executed as the painting depicted in the story.

The same cannot be said, however, for many of Patrick's colleagues and competitors. Indeed, in the past quarter century, the multibillion-dollar global business known as the art world has been shaken by a series of high-profile forgery scandals that have raised unsettling questions about the oftentimes subjective process used to determine the origin and authenticity of a painting. Each of the forgery rings utilized some version of the same hackneyed provenance trap—newly rediscovered paintings emerging from a previously unknown collection—and yet each managed to deceive the experts and connoisseurs of the commercial art world with remarkable ease.

John Myatt, a songwriter and part-time art teacher with a knack for mimicking the great painters, was raising two small children alone in a run-down farmhouse in Staffordshire when he made the acquaintance of a clever trickster named John Drewe. Together the two men perpetrated what Scotland Yard described as "the biggest art fraud of the twentieth century." With Myatt supplying the canvases and Drewe the counterfeit provenances, the pair foisted more than 250 forgeries on the art market—for which Drewe pocketed more than £25 million. Many of the forgeries were sold through venerable London auction houses, including several works, purportedly by the French painter Jean Dubuffet, that went under the gavel during a glamorous evening sale at Christie's in King Street. In the audience that night, feeling slightly underdressed, was the forger who had created them. The Dubuffet Foundation, caretaker of the artist's oeuvre, had declared the works to be authentic.

On the other side of the English Channel, two other forgers were simultaneously wreaking havoc on the art world—and making millions in the process. One was Guy Ribes, a gifted painter who could produce a convincing "Chagall" or "Picasso" in a matter of minutes. According to French police and prosecutors, Ribes and a network of crooked dealers likely introduced more than a thousand forged paintings into the art market, most of which remain in circulation. Ribes's German counterpart, Wolfgang Beltracchi, was similarly prolific, sometimes producing as many as ten canvases a month. It was Beltracchi's wife, Helene—not my fictitious Françoise Vionnet—who effortlessly sold a forged "Georges Valmier" to a prominent European auction house after only a brief examination.

Within a few short years, the Beltracchis were selling forgeries through all the major auction houses, all purportedly from the same hitherto unknown collection. In the process, they became fabulously rich. They traveled the world aboard an eighty-foot sailboat, cared for by a crew of five. Their real estate portfolio included a $7 million villa in the German city of Freiburg and a sprawling estate, Domaine des Rivettes, in the French wine country of Languedoc. Among their many victims was the actor and art collector Steve Martin, who purchased a fake Heinrich Campendonk for $860,000 through Galerie Cazeau-Béraudière of Paris in 2004.

One might have assumed that Knoedler & Company, the oldest commercial art gallery in New York, would have been resistant to the virus spreading through the European markets. But in 1995, when an unknown art dealer named Glafira Rosales appeared at the gallery with a "Rothko" wrapped in cardboard, Knoedler president Ann Freedman apparently saw no reason to be suspicious. In the decade that followed, Rosales sold or consigned nearly forty Abstract Expressionist works to Knoedler & Company, including canvases said to have been painted by Jackson Pollock, Lee Krasner, Franz Kline, Robert Motherwell, and Willem de Kooning.

As it turned out, Glafira Rosales was the front woman for an international forgery network that included her Spanish boyfriend, José Carlos Bergantiños Diáz, and his brother. The forger was a Chinese immigrant named Pei-Shen Qian, who worked out of his garage in Queens. According to prosecutors, Bergantiños Diáz discovered Qian selling copies on a street in Lower Manhattan, and recruited him. Qian was paid about $9,000 for each forgery, a tiny fraction of what they fetched at Knoedler. Besieged by lawsuits, the storied gallery closed its doors in November 2011.

With all due respect to the Abstract Expressionists, whom I revere, it is one thing to forge a Motherwell or a Rothko, quite another to execute a convincing Lucas Cranach the Elder. For that reason alone, a French judge sent shockwaves through the art world in March 2016, when she ordered the seizure of *Venus with a Veil*, the star attraction of a successful exhibition at the Caumont Centre d'Art in the southern French city of Aix-en-Provence. An exhaustive 213-page scientific analysis of the painting—the crown jewel of the enormous collection controlled by the prince of Liechtenstein—would later conclude that it could not have come from Cranach's workshop. Among the many red flags cited in the report was the appearance of the craquelure, which was said to be "inconsistent with normal aging." Representatives of His Serene Highness took issue with the findings and demanded the painting's immediate return. At the time of this writing, *Venus* was listed on the official website for the Princely Collections and on display in the Garden Palace in Vienna.

But it was the identity of the painting's previous owner—the French collector-turned-dealer Giuliano Ruffini—that so unnerved the wider art world. Several previously unknown works had recently emerged from Ruffini's inventory, including *Portrait of a Man*, purportedly by the Dutch Golden Age painter Frans Hals. Experts at the Louvre examined the painting in 2008 and declared it *un trésor national* that should never be allowed to leave French soil. Their counterparts at the Mauritshuis in The Hague were similarly rapturous, with one senior curator calling the painting "a very important addition to Hals's oeuvre." No one seemed overly concerned by the thinness of the provenance. The canvas, said the experts, spoke for itself.

For reasons never made clear, the Louvre chose not to acquire the painting, and in 2010 it was purchased by a London art dealer and an art investor for a reported $3 million. Just one year later, the pair sold the portrait to a prominent American collector for more than three times what they had paid for it. The prominent collector, after learning that *Venus* had been seized by the French, wisely subjected his $10 million "Frans Hals" to scientific testing and was told, in no uncertain terms, that it was a fake. Sotheby's quickly agreed to return the prominent American collector's money and sought restitution from the London dealer and the art investor. At which point the lawsuits began to fly.

As many as twenty-five suspect Old Master canvases, with an estimated market value of some $255 million, have emerged from the same collection—including *David with the Head of Goliath*, purportedly by Orazio Gentileschi, which was displayed at the National Gallery in London. It was not the first time the esteemed museum had exhibited a misattributed or fraudulent work. In 2010, the gallery aired its curatorial dirty laundry in a six-room exhibition called "Fakes, Mistakes, and Discoveries." Room 5 featured *An Allegory*. Acquired by the museum in 1874, it was thought to be the work of the Early Renaissance Florentine painter Sandro Botticelli. In truth, it was a pastiche executed by a later follower. More recently, a Swiss art research company utilizing a pioneering form of artificial intelligence determined that *Samson and Delilah*, one of the National Gallery's most prized paintings, was almost certainly *not* the work of Sir Peter Paul Rubens.

The National Gallery purchased the painting in 1980—at Christie's auction house in London—for $5.4 million. At the time, it was the third-highest price ever paid for a work of art. In today's market a sale of that size would hardly be newsworthy, as soaring prices have turned paintings into yet another asset class for the superrich—or, in the words of the late Manhattan art dealer Eugene Thaw, "a commodity like pork bellies or wheat." A. Alfred Taubman, the shopping mall developer and fast-food investor who purchased Sotheby's in 1983, cynically observed that "a precious painting by Degas and a frosted mug of root beer" had much in common, at least when it came to the potential for profit. In April 2002, Taubman was sentenced to a year in prison for his role in the price-fixing scheme with rival Christie's that swindled customers out of more than $100 million.

Increasingly, much of the world's most valuable art resides not in museums or private homes but in darkened, climate-controlled vaults. More than a million paintings are reportedly hidden away in the Geneva Free Port, including at least a thousand works by Pablo Picasso. Many collectors and curators are troubled by the degree to which paintings have become just another investment vehicle. But those who are in the business of buying and selling art for profit are just as likely to disagree. "Paintings," the New York gallery owner

David Nash told the *New York Times* in 2016, "are not a public good."

Most change hands under conditions of absolute secrecy, at ever-increasing prices, with little or no oversight. It is little wonder, then, that the art world has been beset by a succession of multimillion-dollar forgery scandals. The problem is doubtless made worse by the apathy of the courts and police. Remarkably, none of the forgers and their accomplices mentioned above received more than a slap on the wrist for their crimes. Front woman Glafira Rosales was sentenced to time served for her role in the Knoedler scandal. John Myatt and Wolfgang Beltracchi, after serving brief prison terms, now make their livings selling "genuine fakes" and other original works online. Beltracchi, during an interview with the CBS News program *60 Minutes*, expressed only one regret—that he had used the inaccurately labeled tube of titanium white paint that had led to his exposure.

The French forger Guy Ribes was likewise able to put his talent to legitimate use. It is Ribes, not actor Michel Bouquet, who mimics the brushstrokes of Auguste-Pierre Renoir in a 2012 film about the final years of the painter's life. Ribes also executed the "Renoirs" used in the film's production—with the assistance of the Musée d'Orsay, which granted him a private viewing of the Renoirs in its possession, including several not on public display. James Ivory lamented the fact that the notorious French art forger had not been available to work on the 1996 motion picture *Surviving Picasso*. Said the legendary director: "It would have been, visually, a different film."

ACKNOWLEDGMENTS

I AM GRATEFUL TO MY WIFE, Jamie Gangel, who listened patiently while I worked out the intricate plot and twists of *Portrait of an Unknown Woman* and then skillfully edited the first draft of my typescript. My debt to her is immeasurable, as is my love.

Anthony Scaramucci, founder of the investment firm Skybridge Capital, took time out of his busy schedule to help me create a fraudulent art-based hedge fund propped up by the sale and collateralization of forged paintings. London art dealer Patrick Matthiesen patiently answered each of my questions, as did Maxwell L. Anderson, who has five times served as the director of a North American art museum, including the Whitney Museum of American Art in New York. Not to be outdone, renowned art conservator David Bull—for better or worse, he is known in certain circles as "the real Gabriel Allon"—read my nearly 600-page typescript in its entirety, all while rushing to complete the restoration of a canvas by the Italian Renaissance artist Jacopo Bassano.

Legendary *Vanity Fair* writer-at-large Marie Brenner gave me invaluable insight into her work and the New York art world; and David Friend, the magazine's editor of creative development, shared harrowing stories of past investigations into the affairs of powerful men. I can say with certainty that there is a conference room in *Vanity Fair*'s newsroom on the twenty-fifth floor of One World Trade Center—and that it overlooks New York Harbor. Otherwise, the chaotic sequence of events depicted in the climax of *Portrait of an Unknown Woman* bears little resemblance to the way *Vanity Fair* reports, edits, and publishes consequential pieces of investigative journalism.

My Los Angeles super-lawyer Michael Gendler was, needless to say, a source of wise counsel. Louis Toscano, my dear friend and longtime editor, made countless improvements to the novel, as did Kathy Crosby, my eagle-eyed personal copy editor. Any typographical errors that slipped through their formidable gauntlet are my responsibility, not theirs.

I consulted more than a hundred newspaper and magazine articles while writing *Portrait of an Unknown Woman*, far too many to cite here. I owe a special debt to the reporters of *Artnet*, *ARTnews*, the *Art Newspaper*, the *Guardian*, and the *New York Times* for their coverage of the most recent Old Master forgery scandal. Five books were especially helpful: Anthony M. Amore, *The Art of the Con: The Most Notorious Fakes, Frauds, and Forgeries in the Art World*; Laney Salisbury and Aly Sujo, *Provenance: How a Con Man and a Forger Rewrote the History of Modern Art*; Noah Charney, *The Art of Forgery: The Minds, Motives and Methods of Master Forgers*; Thomas Hoving, *False Impressions: The Hunt for Big-Time Art Fakes*; and Michael Shnayerson, *Boom: Mad Money, Mega Dealers, and the Rise of Contemporary Art*.

We are blessed with family and friends who fill our lives with love and laughter at critical times during the writing year, especially Jeff Zucker, Phil Griffin, Andrew Lack, Noah Oppenheim, Esther Fein and David Remnick, Elsa Walsh and Bob Woodward, Susan St. James and Dick Ebersol, Jane and Burt Bacharach, Stacey and Henry Winkler,

Pete Williams and David Gardner, Virginia Moseley and Tom Nides, Cindi and Mitchell Berger, Donna and Michael Bass, Nancy Dubuc and Michael Kizilbash, Susanna Aaron and Gary Ginsburg, Elena Nachmanoff, Ron Meyer, Andy Lassner, and Peggy Noonan. Also, a heartfelt thanks to the team at HarperCollins, especially Brian Murray, Jonathan Burnham, Doug Jones, Leah Wasielewski, Sarah Ried, Mark Ferguson, Leslie Cohen, Josh Marwell, Robin Bilardello, Milan Bozic, David Koral, Leah Carlson-Stanisic, Carolyn Robson, Chantal Restivo-Alessi, Frank Albanese, Josh Marwell, and Amy Baker.

Finally, my children, Lily and Nicholas, were a constant source of inspiration and support. Nicholas, now a graduate student at the Security Studies Program at Georgetown University's School of Foreign Service, was once again forced to reside under the same roof as his father as I struggled to complete this, the twenty-fifth novel of my career. And one wonders why neither he nor his twin sister, a successful business consultant, has chosen to pursue a career as a writer.

ABOUT THE AUTHOR

DANIEL SILVA IS THE AWARD-WINNING, #1 *New York Times* bestselling author of *The Unlikely Spy, The Mark of the Assassin, The Marching Season, The Kill Artist, The English Assassin, The Confessor, A Death in Vienna, Prince of Fire, The Messenger, The Secret Servant, Moscow Rules, The Defector, The Rembrandt Affair, Portrait of a Spy, The Fallen Angel, The English Girl, The Heist, The English Spy, The Black Widow, House of Spies, The Other Woman, The New Girl, The Order,* and *The Cellist.* He is best known for his long-running thriller series starring spy and art restorer Gabriel Allon. Silva's books are critically acclaimed bestsellers around the world and have been translated into more than thirty languages. He resides in Florida with his wife, television journalist Jamie Gangel, and their twins, Lily and Nicholas. For more information, visit: www.danielsilvabooks.com.

"Inman's characters are totally alive and exuding energy, while the story is filled with mystery, sadness, and the exquisite beauty of youth."
— Larry Lawrence, *Abilene Reporter News*

"A grave and delicate story . . . slow and serene, making its point without fireworks. . . . The prose itself is graceful."
— Carolyn See, *Washington Post*

"The poignant, yet somehow exultant tale of a young boy dealing manfully with problems too big for him. . . . A complex story, masterfully plotted and told by a superb writer. . . . Another rich triumph for Inman."
— Barbara Hodge Hall, *Anniston* (Ala.) *Star*

"A novel with characters quirky enough to grab our interest but familiar enough that we may identify with their joys and sorrows. . . . Many readers will identify with *Dairy Queen Days* immediately, and remember it long afterward."
— Max B. Baker, *Fort Worth Star-Telegram*

"An amiable novel. . . . Robert Inman tells this story with humor, compassion, and a sense of baffling sadness at the ways relationships can go wrong. . . . He is a storyteller perched between the Old South and the New, a writer whose characters wrestle with tradition as they try to shape their futures."
— Linda Barrett Osborne, *New York Times Book Review*

"Inman shows his intimate knowledge of the region and an affection for the people who populate it. His characters are complex with eccentricities bred in the South."
— Ann Patterson-Rabon, *Spartanburg* (S.C.) *Herald Journal*

"Robert Inman's rich style, along with the plot and family of characters he creates in *Dairy Queen Days*, makes this a remarkable and profound novel. . . . A joyous addition to our Southern literature."
— Rick Tamble, *Nashville Banner*

DAIRY
QUEEN
DAYS

A Novel

ROBERT
INMAN

LITTLE, BROWN AND COMPANY
Boston New York Toronto London

For Chris and Larkin Ferris

I am leaving, I am leaving
But the fighter still remains.
— From "The Boxer"
Simon and Garfunkel

Life can only be understood backwards;
But it must be lived forwards.
— Søren Kierkegaard

Originally published in hardcover by Little, Brown and Company, 1997
First Back Bay paperback edition, 1998

Library of Congress Cataloging-in-Publication Data

Inman, Robert.
    Dairy Queen days : a novel / Robert Inman. — 1st ed.
       p.   cm.
    ISBN 0-316-41873-0 (hc)   0-316-41837-4 (pb)
    I. Title
  PS3559.N449D35   1997
  813'.54 — dc20   96-26258

10   9   8   7   6   5   4   3   2

MV-NY

Published simultaneously in Canada by Little, Brown & Company
(Canada) Limited

Printed in the United States of America

DAIRY
QUEEN
DAYS

ONE

TROUT MOSELEY WAS a day shy of sixteen when his father, Reverend Joe Pike Moseley, ran away.

Most people thought it started with the motorcycle. Maybe even before that, when they sent Trout's mother off to the Institute. But people thought Joe Pike had been handling that unpleasantness reasonably well — "keeping his equilibrium," as they said — until he showed up with the motorcycle.

It was an ancient Triumph, or at least what had once been a Triumph. Joe Pike found it in a farmer's barn, in pieces, and brought it home in the trunk of his car. Trout was standing at the kitchen window when he saw Joe Pike back the car down the driveway to the garage behind the parsonage. By the time Trout got out there, Joe Pike had the trunk open and was standing with his arms crossed, staring at the jumble of wheel rims, pitted chrome pieces, engine, handlebars, gasoline tank.

"What's that?" Trout asked.

"A once and future motorcycle."

"What're you gonna do with it?"

Joe Pike uncrossed his arms and hitched up his pants from their accustomed place below his paunch. "Fix it up. I am the resurrection and the life. Yea, verily." A trace of a smile played at his lips. *"Up from the grave He arose!"* he sang off-key. Joe Pike sang badly, but enthusiastically. In church he could make the choir director wince. He referred to his singing as "making a joyful noise."

"You know anything about motorcycles?" Trout asked.

"Not much."

"Need some help?"

Joe Pike stared for a long time at the jumble of metal in the trunk of the car. Trout wondered after a while if his father had heard the question. Finally Joe Pike said, "I reckon I can manage. It ain't heavy."

"I mean . . ." But then he saw that Joe Pike wasn't really paying him any attention. His mind was there inside the trunk among the parts of the old Triumph, perhaps deep down inside one of the cylinders of the engine, imagining a million tiny explosions going off rapid-fire. Trout studied him for a minute or so, then shrugged and turned to go.

"It's a four-cycle," Joe Pike said.

Trout turned and looked at him again. Joe Pike's gaze never left the motorcycle. "What?"

"You don't have to mix the gas and oil."

"That's good," Trout said. "You might forget."

When Trout looked out the kitchen window again a half hour later, the trunk of the car was closed and so were the double doors of the old wood-frame garage. But he could faintly hear Joe Pike singing inside: *Rescue the perishing, care for the dying!*

Over the next two months, Trout stayed away from the garage when Joe Pike was out there. But he followed the progress of the motorcycle by sneaking looks when Joe Pike was gone. At first it was a spindly metal frame propped up on two concrete blocks like a huge insect. Metal parts bobbed like apples in a ten-gallon galvanized washtub filled with solvent to eat away years of grime and rust. Before long, with the metal sanded smooth, the motorcycle began to take shape on the frame. Joe Pike took the fenders, wheel rims, gasoline tank, and handlebars to a body shop and had them repainted and rechromed. Replacement parts — headlamp, cables, speedometer — began to arrive by UPS.

Trout remained vaguely hopeful at first. Fifteen years old, almost sixteen, fascinated by the thought of motorized transportation. But he came to realize that Joe Pike had no intention of sharing the motorcycle.

Joe Pike worked on it in the garage deep into the night, showing up for breakfast bleary-eyed, smelling of grease and solvent, grime caked thick under his fingernails. That was uncharacteristic. Joe Pike was by habit a fastidious man. He took at least two baths a day — more in the summer because he was a prodigious perspirer — and changed his underwear each time. But this present grubbiness didn't seem to bother him. Neither did the state of their housekeeping, which got progressively worse. After Trout's mother went off to the Institute, the church had hired a cleaning woman to come once a week, but she was no match for the growing piles of dirty dishes and laundry. Trout finally took matters into his own hands and learned to operate the dishwasher and the washing machine and dryer. After a fashion. At school he endured locker-room snickers over underwear dyed pale pink from being washed with a red T-shirt. Joe Pike's underwear was likewise pale pink, but he didn't seem to notice, or at least he didn't remark upon it. Joe Pike's mind seemed to be fixed on the motorcycle, or whatever larger thing it was that the motorcycle represented. There was a gently stubborn set to his jaw, almost a grimness there. On Sundays his sermons were vague, rambling things, trailing off in mid-sentence. He didn't seem to be paying the sermons much attention, either. In the pews, members of the congregation would steal glances at one another, perplexed. *What?*

"How's it going?" Trout would ask.

"Okay."

"Don't you get cold out there?" It was March, the pecan trees in the parsonage yard still bare-limbed and gaunt against the gray morning sky.

A blank look from Joe Pike. "No. I reckon not." Then he would stare out the kitchen window in the direction of the garage, and Trout would know that Joe Pike wasn't really there with him at all. He was out there with the Triumph.

It worried Trout a good deal. It brought back all the old business of his mother's long silences, the way she went away somewhere that nobody else could go, stayed for days at a time, and finally just never came back. With Irene's silences, he had felt isolated, left out, wondering what of it, if anything, was his fault. Now, Joe Pike's preoccupation with the motorcycle gave him the same old spooked feeling. Joe Pike, like Irene, seemed unreachable. And Trout finally decided there was really nothing he could do but watch and wait.

So he did, and so did the good people of Ohatchee, Georgia — in particular, the good people of Ohatchee Methodist. They watched, waited, talked:

"What you reckon he's gone do with that thing?"

"Give it to Trout, prob'ly. Man of his size'd bust the tires." (Hearty chuckle here. Joe Pike stood six-four, and his weight ranged from two hundred fifty to three hundred pounds, depending on whether he was in one of his Dairy Queen phases.)

"Well, it gives the Baptists something to talk about."

"Yeah. That and all the other."

"Damn shame."

"Was she hittin' the bottle?"

"Don't think so. Just went off the deep end."

"Poor old Joe Pike. And little Trout. Bless his heart."

Long pause. "Don't reckon Joe Pike had anything to do with it, do you?"

"Course not." Longer pause. "But it does make you wonder."

"Reckon they'll transfer Joe Pike at annual conference?"

"Prob'ly not. He's only been here two years."

"Hmmm. But folks sure do talk."

"Yeah. 'Specially Baptists."

They talked among themselves, but they did not talk to Joe Pike Moseley about his motorcycle. No matter how gracefully he seemed to have handled the business of his wife, there was in general an air of disaster about Joe Pike. People were wary, as if he might be contagious. Then too, a motorcycle just didn't seem to be the kind of thing you discussed with a preacher. At least it didn't until Easter Sunday.

Ohatchee Methodist was packed, the usual crowd swelled by the once-a-year attendees, the ones Joe Pike referred to as "tourists." They were crammed seersucker to crinoline into the oak pews and in folding chairs set up along the aisles and the back wall. It was mid-April, already warm but not quite warm enough for air conditioning, so the windows of the sanctuary were open to the spring morning outside and the ceiling fans went *whoosh-whoosh* overhead, stirring the smell of new clothes and store-bought fragrances into a rich, sweet stew.

When everyone was finally settled into their seats, the choir entered from the narthex singing "Up From the Grave He Arose!" They marched smartly two by two down the aisle, proclaiming triumph o'er the grave, and the congregation rose with a flurry and joined in, swelling the high-ceiling sanctuary with their earnestness. The choir paraded up into the choir loft, everybody sang another verse, and then they all sat down and stared at the door to the Pastor's Study to the right of the altar, expecting Joe Pike to emerge, as was his custom. They sat there for a good while. Nothing. They began to look about at one another. *What?* After a minute or two, they heard the throaty roar of the motorcycle, faintly at first, growing louder as it approached the church and stopped finally at the curb outside. Trout — seated midway in the middle section with his friend Parks Belton and Parks's mother, Imogene — looked around for a route of discreet escape. Joe Pike had spent all night in the garage. He was still there when Trout left for Sunday school. And now he had ridden the motorcycle to church. *Maybe if I crawl under the pew.* But he sat there, transfixed. They were all transfixed.

After a moment, the swinging doors that separated the sanctuary from the narthex flew open and Joe Pike swept in, huge and hurrying, his black robe billowing about him, down the aisle and up to the pulpit. He stopped, looked out over the congregation, gave them all a vague half-smile, and then settled himself in the high-backed chair behind the pulpit. He slouched, one elbow propped on the arm of the chair, chin resting in his hand, one hamlike thigh hiked over the other, revealing a pair of scuffed brown cowboy boots. Trout stared at the boots. Joe Pike had bought them in Dallas years ago when he played football at Texas A&M, but they had been gathering dust in various parsonage closets for as long as Trout could remember. He had never seen Joe Pike wear the boots before.

The choir director, seated at the piano, gave Joe Pike a long look over the top of her glasses. Then she nodded to the choir and they stood and launched into "The Old Rugged Cross." As they sang, Joe Pike sat staring out the window, the toe of his boot swaying slightly in time to the music, his brow wrinkled in thought.

The last notes faded and the choir sat back down. Joe Pike remained in his seat, still staring out the window, out where the motorcycle was. The choir director gave an impatient cough. Then Joe Pike looked up, shook himself. He stood slowly and moved the two steps to the pulpit. He picked up the pulpit Bible. It was a huge thing, leatherbound with gold letters and gilt edging and a long red ribbon to mark your place. Joe Pike held it in his left hand as if it weighed no more than a feather. He opened it with his right hand, flipped a few pages, found his place, and marked it with his index finger.

His eyes searched the words for a long time. Then his brow furrowed in dismay, as if someone had substituted a Bible written in a foreign tongue. He looked up, his gaze sweeping the congregation. His mouth opened, but nothing came out. Sweat beads began to pop out on his forehead. He opened his mouth again and made a little hissing sound through his teeth.

Trout had known for a good while that Joe Pike was really two people — the big man you saw and another, smaller one who was tucked away somewhere inside. Trout didn't know who the small man was. Maybe Joe Pike didn't either, actually. But he gave little evidences of himself in tiny movements of eye, hand, mouth — such as this business of hissing through his teeth — mostly when agitated. You had to be quick to catch it. Most people didn't. But Trout had formed the habit of watchfulness. You had to be watchful in a house where your mother said nothing for long stretches and your father was two people. So now, watching Joe Pike carefully, he saw this hissing through the teeth and read it as trouble, pure and simple.

"What's he doing?" Parks Belton whispered to Trout.

Trout shrugged. "I don't know."

Imogene Belton glared at them. "Shhhhhh!"

Suddenly, Trout felt a great urge to get up from his pew, go up to the pulpit and take the Bible from his father's hand, take him by the arm and say, "It's all right." He felt that the entire congregation, every last one of them, expected him to do just that. But he sat, as immobilized as the rest, all of them like morbid onlookers at the scene of a wreck. Finally, Joe Pike gave a great shuddering sigh and put the Bible back down.

There was a long, fascinated silence, a great holding of breath, broken only by the throb of the ceiling fans. And then Reverend Joe Pike Moseley said, "I'm sorry. I've got to go."

He closed the Bible with a thump. He drew in a deep breath. Then he walked quickly down from the pulpit and up the aisle, the black robe flapping about him, and out the door, looking neither left nor right. Not a soul inside the church moved. After a moment they heard the motorcycle cough to life out front. Joe Pike gunned it a couple of times, then dropped it into gear and roared away. They could hear him for a long time, until the sound finally faded as he topped the rise at the edge of town, heading west. They sat there awhile longer and then one of the ushers got up and went through the swinging doors into the narthex. He returned, holding Joe Pike's black robe. "I reckon he's gone for the day," the man said. With that, everybody got up and went home.

Trout woke the next morning in an agitated muddle, and for a moment he couldn't think of what was wrong. Then he remembered Joe Pike and the motorcycle.

Trout had slept badly, what little he had slept at all. He had assumed Joe Pike would return, certainly by nightfall. Apparently, so had the good people of Ohatchee Methodist, because none of them inquired, in person or by phone, during the afternoon. Whatever was going on at the parsonage or in the tortured soul of Reverend Joe Pike Moseley — best to let it marinate until Monday.

By dark Trout was getting worried. He pictured Joe Pike stranded somewhere, sitting morosely on a deserted roadside with a flat tire or a blown cylinder. Or worse. He thought at one point of sounding some kind of alarm. But two things deterred him and gave him some ease.

The first was the physical image of his father, massive and fearless. Joe Pike had played football for Bear Bryant. He was the only Georgia boy on the Texas A&M team when the Bear went there in 1954 and piled sixty of them onto buses and took them out in the desert to a dust-choked, heat-blasted camp and tried to kill them. Most gave up, some of them sneaking away in the night, dragging their weary bodies and their cardboard suitcases to the bus station at Junction so they could escape crazy Bear Bryant. But twenty-seven of them survived to ride the bus back to College Station, including Joe Pike Moseley. Trout had never been able to fully understand and appreciate why otherwise sane people willingly endured things like that, but it was enough to know that Joe Pike did. Joe Pike weighed two hundred fifty pounds at Texas A&M, even when Bear Bryant got through with him. He was very slow, but immovable and also brave. The Bear stuck him in the middle of the line and made the rest of the game take a detour around him. He once played three quarters against Rice with a broken wrist, until he finally fainted at the bottom of a pileup. All that was back before he became a preacher and a gentleman, of course. But even now — powerful of body, thunderous of voice — there was no question that Joe Pike was still immovable and brave. The good people of Ohatchee Methodist might think that Joe Pike was fleeing from something yesterday when he swept down out of the pulpit and roared off to the west. But Trout suspected just the opposite. He knew the look on Joe Pike's face, had seen it often enough before. Joe Pike was going to do battle. With what? The answer to that would have to wait for Joe Pike's return.

The other thing that kept Trout from calling for help was sheer embarrassment — both for Joe Pike and for himself. He imagined that by now, Joe Pike had probably fought whatever battle he was looking for and was laying low somewhere, considering how he might return to Ohatchee without the congregation or the Bishop doing anything drastic. Joe Pike was not a man to hurry to trouble. And for Trout's part — well, there would be snickers and whispers enough at Ohatchee High School tomorrow without sending out an alarm Sunday night.

So Trout fretted and kept his own counsel and finally drifted off into troubled sleep in the small hours of the morning. When he awoke, the house was still empty and quiet. Joe Pike, wherever he had gone, was still there.

As Trout lay in bed wondering what the hell to do, he could feel something else besides Joe Pike Moseley nibbling at the back of his brain. Then he remembered: it was his birthday. Sixteen years old. This was supposed to be something really special, wasn't it? But there was nobody here singing and prancing around, the way Joe Pike loved to do on birthdays and Christmas and Confederate Memorial Day and any other excuse he could find to be celebratory. For such a gentle man, he loved nothing better than a good celebration.

It occurred to Trout that maybe a lot of Joe Pike's celebrations had been an attempt to fill up Irene's silences. A kind of pitiful denial that never really worked. Since they had taken Irene away, Joe Pike had simply stopped trying. A final admission of defeat. And now, on what should have been the most celebratory occasion of Trout's young life, Joe Pike had gone away.

Trout mulled it over for a while longer, feeling a little brain-fevered. Then finally he got up and padded barefoot to the kitchen, where the clock on the stove read 8:30. Late for school. Nobody here to write him an excuse. What to do? He decided, for the time being, on inertia. He poured himself a glass of orange juice, sat down at the kitchen table, drank it slowly, and listened to the silence. In truth, he decided after a bit, the empty quiet was something of a relief after all that had happened. You could only put up with so much ridiculousness. Considering that, he felt better.

Then he thought, *I am alone in the house and I can do anything I want to do, as long as it's not permanent damage.* So he got up, took off his pajamas, dropped them in the middle of the floor, and stood there feeling the silence on his bare skin. He wandered buck naked through every room in the parsonage, ending up in the living room, where he checked to make sure the front door was locked; then he sat down in Joe Pike's favorite chair and finished the orange juice, celebrating the utter novelty of it.

Even when his mother had been here, mute and withdrawn, it hadn't been like this. A Methodist parsonage was a public accommodation. Church people would drop by at all hours of the day or night and march right in without knocking, as if they owned the place. Which, in fact, they did. A preacher might fill up the drawers and closets with his clothes and tack doodads to the wall, but he didn't own the place. The congregation considered the parsonage not so much the preacher's residence as an extension of the church itself. So there was always a lot of noise, coming and going, and you didn't wander around in your pajamas, much less buck naked. Over the years Irene had shrunk from that. Her own silence seemed in part a protest against invasion, the only way she could get any peace and quiet.

Now, as Trout sat doing what he darned well pleased, he considered that this, too, was a form of protest over being at the mercy of other people's silences and preoccupations. But enough of protest. Empty silence or not, it was his sixteenth birthday. Nobody could take that away from him. Even if he got run over by a truck at midmorning, the obituary would still read, "Troutman Joseph Moseley, 16 . . ." It was a marvelous thing, like having Christmas and the Fourth of July and Easter and Confederate Memorial Day all rolled into one. And even more marvelous was the fact that he was sixteen on a Monday, the only day of the week the state driver's license examiner would be in

Ohatchee. Trout Moseley didn't need anybody singing and prancing to get a driver's license.

He drove Joe Pike's car downtown himself and parked it across the street from the courthouse. He was waiting, first in line, when the examiner arrived at ten.

"Ain't you supposed to be in school, son?" the examiner asked.

"My daddy said it would be all right to skip this morning," Trout lied without blinking. "I've got band practice after school this afternoon, so I couldn't come then." *Band practice?* He admired his own inventiveness. The closest he got to music was church on Sunday and the Atlanta oldies station on the radio. But at five-ten, one hundred thirty pounds, he looked more like a band member than an athlete.

He produced his birth certificate and took the written examination. Trout had been studying for more than a year, had every word of the manual committed to memory. He sat quietly while the examiner checked his answers, and then they walked across the street to the car for his road test.

"How'd this car get here?" the examiner asked as they climbed in, Trout behind the wheel, the examiner holding a clipboard in his lap with a stub of pencil stuck under the metal clip.

"My daddy brought me and then walked home."

"Who's your daddy?"

"Reverend Moseley."

Eyebrows up. "Joe Pike Moseley?"

"Yes sir." Had the examiner heard about Joe Pike's Sunday escapade? Apparently not.

Wide grin. "I used to play football against Joe Pike. Lord, he was a grain-fed young'un. And rough as a cob." The examiner laughed, showing stained, uneven teeth. "Him and a long tall drink of water named Wardell Dubarry. Wardell would hit you low and then Joe Pike would get up a head of steam and come in high. They near about ruined our quarterback one year. You had to watch Joe Pike, or he'd take your head off with an elbow."

"Well, he's still grain fed," Trout said. He put his key in the ignition, started the car.

"Played for Bear Bryant."

"Yes sir. Texas A&M."

"Folks never could figure why Joe Pike went all that way to play football. He could've got a scholarship at Georgia. Or Georgia Tech." The examiner shook his head. "And then made a preacher to boot. You just never know about folks."

"No sir. I guess not."

"He doing okay?"

"Yes sir," Trout said. "He's just fine."

"Well, you tell him Will Dobbins from Thomson asked about him."

"Yes sir. I'll do that."

The examiner put his hand on the door handle. "Hell, turn the car off, son. I imagine you know how to drive just fine. You made a hundred on the written test. No sense in us wasting gas. Just make the Arabs richer. Come on in and I'll write you out a temporary license."

Trout drove out the highway a good way toward Valdosta with all the windows rolled down, filling the car with warming April and the smell of fresh-turned earth and blossom, feeling the novelty of being alone in the car, sixteen years old, legally licensed. It was heady stuff. Some-day, he thought, he might drive the car buck naked. That would be about as ridiculous as you could get. He thought fleetingly of going on to Florida. Decided against it. Thought about going to school. De-cided against that, too. And then he thought suddenly of Joe Pike and the motorcycle and his spirits sank. He turned around and headed home.

It was nearly noon when he got back to the parsonage. The phone was ringing, jarring the emptiness.

"Hello."

"Trout, it's me."

"Where are you?"

"Hattiesburg, Mississippi."

"What are you doing in Hattiesburg?"

"It's on the way to Junction."

"Junction what?"

"Texas. Listen, there's some chicken pot pies in the freezer."

Trout sat down at the kitchen table and stared at the refrigerator. Over the telephone line, he could hear the faint roar of traffic, the bleat of a semi's air horn.

"Trout?"

"Yes sir."

"You can fix 'em in the regular oven or the microwave. Directions on the package. Poke some holes in the top with a fork."

"Are you all right?"

"Yea, verily," Joe Pike said. "A little minor problem with the wiring, that's all. I got it fixed." There was a long silence from Joe Pike, broken by the dinging of a bell on a gas pump, a woman fussing at a child. Then he said, "I need you to hang in there with me, Trout. Something I've gotta do . . ." His voice trailed off. "Just hang in there, okay?"

"Okay."

"Love you, son."

"Love you, too."

Then there was a click on the other end of the line, and Trout was left with the silence and, after a moment, a dial tone. He hung up the phone, heard the rattling of the front door. He peered down the hallway and saw Imogene Belton through the door glass. She had a key and she was coming right on in.

Trout thought, *He didn't say anything about my birthday.* And then he thought, *But I didn't ask him when he was coming back, either.*

The Bishop came on Friday, after Trout had spent the week at the Beltons' house, clucked over by Imogene until he was sick to death of it.

"I feel like a freak," he told Parks.

"Well, what do you expect?" Parks answered.

What he did not expect was the Bishop. But he was waiting in the Beltons' living room when Trout and Parks got home from school. He was a trim, gray-haired man, about sixty, and he wore a black suit and clerical collar. He had good, strong gray eyes and a nice smile and a firm handshake. But Trout thought of what he had heard Joe Pike say one time: "When the Bishop shows up all of a sudden, it's most likely either death or embezzlement."

The Bishop politely but firmly shooed Imogene and Parks out of the living room, sat down on the sofa next to Trout and leaned forward, his elbows on his knees. Then he said, "Trout, your father's had a breakdown."

Trout shrugged. "It's an old motorcycle. He said he was having a problem with the wiring."

"You've talked to him?"

"Monday. He called from Hattiesburg."

"Did he sound all right?"

"Yes sir. I reckon so."

"Well," the Bishop said, "it's not just the motorcycle."

Trout sucked in his breath. "Is he okay?"

"Resting. A few days in the hospital . . ."

Trout stood, his schoolbooks clattering to the floor. "Where is he?"

The Bishop pulled him gently back to the sofa. "He's all right, Trout. I talked to him myself this morning. Joe Pike has . . ." — he fanned the air with his hands a bit, searching for words — ". . . he's been under a lot of pressure, and I think something just got out of kilter."

They sat there for a moment, Trout imagining Joe Pike huge and pale in a hospital bed . . . tubes and breathing apparatus . . . Trout felt sick. Orphaned at sixteen. Both parents gone batty.

Finally the Bishop said, "Your father needs a little time and space, I think. I've got some friends near Lubbock, and he's going to stay with them for a few days. And then" — he pursed his lips, musing — "I'm sending your father home, Trout. To Moseley. Maybe with his family, familiar surroundings, he can get his legs back under him. Your uncle Cicero will go out to Texas and fetch him and take him directly there. He and the minister at Moseley will simply swap pulpits. I think this is best for everybody concerned."

Trout thought about the Easter congregation at Ohatchee Methodist, staring slack-jawed as big solid Joe Pike Moseley, the most substantial of men, unraveled before their eyes. And then the curious stares of everybody at school, the hovering Imogene Belton, the half-whispers. He thought, with a rush of despair, *It won't do to stay here.*

The Bishop put his hand on Trout's knee. "I know this isn't easy for you, Trout. Moving, right here at the end of the school year."

Not just that. Unfair. Not just moving, but the whole business. Why should he, at sixteen, have to be the sane one in the family? At sixteen, you were supposed to be flaky, irresponsible, hormone-driven. Unfair. But there it was.

"No," Trout said. "It's okay. We'll manage."

The Bishop sat there for a moment, then rose from the sofa, smoothing the creased front of his black trousers. "Of course, there's the other thing, too. Moseley's just two hours from Atlanta."

Atlanta. The Institute. Irene. That's what the Bishop was getting at, of course, but he wouldn't come right out and say it. Nobody, including the Bishop, wanted to talk about Irene, not directly. When you got anywhere near the subject, folks started acting like boxers, bobbing and weaving and staying out of reach of a good left hook. Joe Pike had bobbed and weaved as long as he could, and then he lit out for Texas. Well, all right. Trout would pack up bag and baggage and move, unfair as it might be. But before long, somebody was going to have to sit still and talk to him about his mother.

TWO

HOME. MOSELEY, GEORGIA. Trout supposed it was as much home as anyplace else. He had never lived there, but compared with a series of four-year stays in various parsonages, Moseley was the one geographic constant in his life. It was a place of holiday visits, a day or two at a time in the big house across the street from the Methodist church. Never on the holiday itself, because a preacher had to be in his own pulpit for Easter or Christmas, but usually in the days after, when there was still the lingering smell of a roasting turkey or a spray of Easter lilies on a front hall table. Trout was never there for a long enough time to get much sense of the town. But you didn't have to be there for long to know that to be a Moseley in Moseley was something special. Trout remembered what Joe Pike had said in a moment of particular earthiness: "When a Moseley farts, everybody smells it."

It began with Trout's great-grandfather, Broadus Moseley. And it began with great promise in 1885 when Broadus moved with his wife and family from the North Carolina piedmont to what was then nothing but a quiet rural Georgia crossroads with a scattering of ramshackle houses. There had been some sort of unpleasantness in North Carolina, a family falling-out, the details of which remained murky. The family settled some money upon Broadus, but that was not its most important gift. Rather, it was an inbred business acumen and a knowledge of the burgeoning cotton mill industry.

There were three things to recommend the site he picked for his venture: it lay along the road from Augusta to Atlanta; the tracks of the Georgia Line were nearby; and the farm economy thereabouts was flat busted. It was exactly the combination Broadus was looking for: decent transportation, cheap land, hungry people. First he bought a great deal of land, far more than he needed for a mill. Then he built a railroad spur from the Georgia Line and erected a nondescript two-story brick building, powered it with coal-fired steam, and equipped it with looms, the latest European design. And the people came, ragged from the hardscrabble farms — reluctant to give up their independence, but desperate to survive.

Broadus intended it to be more than a mill town. He used the mill as a magnet to draw commerce. And since he owned the land, he shaped the growing town as he wished — parceling out tracts for business ventures and homes, laying out the streets to suit him. He named the town Moseley and the main street Broadus Street. ("Broad Street?" visitors would ask. "No, Broadus," the natives would answer, enjoying the quirk.) When it had progressed to a village of several hundred souls, he saw to its incorporation. And as its patriarch and principal wage payer, he saw to its politics. Broadus was a staunch Democrat who nevertheless admired certain Republican principles — chiefly, that men with sense enough to have money ought to call the shots.

By the time Moseley's main thoroughfare had become U.S. Highway 278, paved all the way from Atlanta to Augusta, the town was a thriving commercial center with a variety of retail businesses, a bank, schools, a newspaper, and a water and sewer system. The agricultural economy enjoyed something of a revival, and the town served as its hub and meeting place, its chief source of feed, seed, fertilizer, and loans. And Moseley Cotton Mill was the anchor, supplying steady employment and an economic base for the community. Broadus was careful not to repeat the mistake of so many in the southern textile business: getting too big in boom times and then having to scramble to stay afloat in bad. He kept the business prudently in check and kept plenty of reserves in the bank. He boasted of never having laid off a worker for economic reasons. Moseley Mill employees would never make a great deal of money, but as long as they behaved themselves, they wouldn't find themselves out on the street, either.

By the end of World War II, about a thousand people lived in Moseley in a residential area that radiated north and south along Broadus Street.

At the Augusta end of town was the mill building, and beyond it, a spiderweb of unpaved streets and small white frame houses — owned, tended, and ruled by Moseley Cotton Mill. Broadus kept the mill and mill village outside the city limits. It was his domain.

At the Atlanta end of town, separated from the mill end by the business district, the Moseleys and others of a certain stature lived. There were sidewalks here, canopied by oak trees that grew to great girth over the years. The houses were gracious if not particularly imposing, with wide banistered porches and a good deal of ornamental ironwork. Broadus Moseley's house was the only one with columns, but they were modest columns, one story high, supporting the porch that wrapped around the front and both sides of the house. Broadus believed in status but not ostentation.

As a buffer between the business district and his neighborhood, Broadus laid out and landscaped a small park — an acre of Saint Augustine grass and oak trees with a band shell in the middle.

There might be two ends to Broadus Street, but both were simply part of U.S. 278. In its best days, the mill end and the money end of town shared a certain vibrancy — the commonality of diesel fumes and the steady rumble of traffic that eased into town, stopped fitfully at the one traffic light at the center of the business district, and then ambled on. The Koffee Kup Kafe became a favorite lunchtime stopping place for Atlanta-to-Augusta travelers. *Southern Living* magazine lauded its sweet potato pie. And no right-thinking politician seeking statewide office would pass up the opportunity for a rally at the band shell in Broadus Moseley Park. It was unstated, but understood, that only Democrats were welcome. A Republican seeking the governorship ventured by in the late sixties, but only five people and a stray dog came to hear him, and three of the people were out-of-towners who wandered over after lunch at the Koffee Kup.

That was Moseley, Georgia, in its heyday. By the time Trout Moseley came to call it home, it had changed considerably. Now, most folks knew Moseley as a name on a big green sign on Interstate 20, which paralleled U.S. 278 a couple of miles from the center of town. Now, you could stand on the sidewalk in the middle of the business district at midafternoon and not see a car move for five minutes.

On one side of the street were City Hall and the next-door police station along with a few businesses that clung hopefully to life on the strength of local trade — a small grocery, a women's and men's ready-to-wear, the post office, the bank, and a former dry cleaners now occupied by the County Welfare Department.

The other side of the street was less fortunate. It boasted a hardware operated by Trout's uncle Cicero, who was also the police chief, and next door to Cicero, a struggling feed-and-seed. It sold more lawn and garden fertilizer and bug spray than farm supplies, most of the farmers in the county having given up on row crops and planted pine trees in the wake of the latest agribusiness downturn. Next to the feed-and-seed was a large weed-grown vacant lot where a furniture and appliance store had burned to the ground not long after the Interstate opened. People had taken it as an omen. It gave the business district a gap-toothed appearance. Beyond the lot were the Koffee Kup Kafe and a row of vacant storefronts. One had been home to the newspaper until it had gone out of business shortly after the opening of the Interstate and the furniture store fire. As business dwindled, there were no longer enough advertisers to support the weekly. And people who lived beyond the city limits didn't give a hoot about what happened in Moseley.

One thing that had not changed about Moseley was its reputation as a church town. There were six churches in Moseley proper, not counting the AME Zion for the black folks, which was two miles outside the city limits toward Augusta.

In the general vicinity of the mill were a Church of God, a Free-Will Baptist, and a Pentecostal Holiness. In his day, Broadus had referred to them as "sect" churches, full of shouting and carryings-on that kept his mill workers up all night during revival week. But he co-opted them all by subsidizing their physical facilities and their preachers' salaries, in return for which the preachers espoused thrift, hard work, loyalty to the Moseleys, and a disdain for liquor and unions.

Adjacent the business district at the Augusta end of town was a sturdy brick Baptist with a stubby white steeple, and on a back street a block away, a modest Presbyterian.

But the other end of town was reserved for Broadus Moseley's church. Moseley Memorial Methodist was directly across the street from Broadus's home, where he could keep an eye on it. Broadus built it as the mill and town grew and prospered. It was constructed of dark red brick with a cedar shake roof. It had twelve stained-glass windows — four on each side and two at the front and back — each depicting one of the Twelve Disciples. The parsonage was next door to the church so that Broadus could keep an eye on it and its occupants, too.

In the town's most prosperous days, it was a thriving church with a reputation and influence among Georgia Methodists far beyond its size. Young preachers who were marked by the Bishop for great things often pulled a tour of duty in Moseley on their way up the ladder of the church hierarchy. Back in the fifties there had been some talk about expanding the sanctuary, tearing down the parsonage next door and extending a wing in that direction. But the Moseleys vetoed that. Broadus Moseley was long in the grave by then and his son Leland, Joe Pike's father, was running Moseley Cotton Mill. Yes, Leland saw the need for more space. But it was the church Broadus Moseley had built, and his shadow still cast long across the community and the congregation. He had never taken kindly to folks' questioning his judgment. And he would not now, Leland said, take kindly to folks' meddling with his church and his stained-glass windows. Instead, they added an early-morning service, which became quite popular and was at the time a novelty among Georgia Methodists. That lasted until the early seventies, when I-20 took the starch out of the town. Not long thereafter, Moseley Memorial Methodist retreated to a single eleven o'clock service. It was all that was necessary.

Trout would learn all this over time. At the beginning there was only Aunt Alma, Joe Pike's older sister. She was enough.

Alma took care of everything. She sent a Moseley Cotton Mill truck and two men to the Ohatchee parsonage on a Friday morning, a week after the Bishop had broken the news to the congregation about Joe Pike's transfer. By noon the men had packed up and loaded everything Joe Pike's family owned. Imogene Belton had seen to the packing. There wasn't a great deal — hanging clothes on a bar the men had rigged across the back of the truck; a stack of boxes, including several from Joe Pike's study at the church; a few odds and ends, like Trout's bicycle and his mother's sewing machine and his father's old mahogany bookcase. Most of the furniture and furnishings in the parsonage belonged to the congregation, right down to the pots and pans, mostly bits and pieces donated over the years by its members as they updated their own homes.

The chairman of the Official Board of the Ohatchee Methodist Church came by at midmorning and stayed while the men from Moseley Mill packed and loaded. He tried to appear helpful, but Trout knew he was there to make sure the Joe Pike Moseley family didn't make off with anything they weren't supposed to. Trout decided not to take offense. After all, it was an altogether strange business. An air of doom hung over the parsonage and everything in it.

The last thing was the statue. Trout wrapped it in an old blanket and put it in the front seat of the car. Then he went back to the house and made one last check before the chairman of the Official Board locked up.

"Trout, I'm sorry things turned out the way they did," the chairman said, pocketing the key and offering Trout his hand. "But the Lord works in strange and mysterious ways, His wonders to behold."

Somewhere in the back of his mind, Trout could still hear the echo of the motorcycle pulling away from Ohatchee Methodist on Easter Sunday morning. Now, *that* was a wonder to behold. But it wouldn't do to say so to the chairman of the Official Board. So Trout said, "Yes sir."

"Your daddy's a fine man. He just needs a change of scene."

"That's what the Bishop said."

"You take care of him now, you hear. And give him my best."

"I'll do that."

Trout followed the truck from Ohatchee three hours north to Moseley, driving Joe Pike's green Dodge. It was midafternoon when they arrived. The May sun was still strong above the oak trees along Moseley's main street as Trout eased the car up to the curb between the church and the adjacent parsonage. He parked next to the Georgia State Historical Society marker dedicated to his great-grandfather: BROADUS MOSELEY. CIVIC VISIONARY AND TEXTILE PIONEER. 1861–1934.

There were several vehicles parked at the curb and in the parsonage driveway. A group of workmen clustered about an opening in the brickwork on one side of the house, peering into the dark underbelly. Another man was clipping the shrubbery in front. And two men were carrying a floral print sofa from a van with big letters on the side that read, BUCKLEY FURNITURE COMPANY, AUGUSTA, GA. Aunt Alma was standing on the porch directing traffic.

Alma was in her midfifties, tall and angular. She was rather attractive in a sharp-featured way, and Trout thought she probably had been something of a beauty as a girl. But now there was a sort of pinched severity about Alma. Her graying hair was close-cropped, almost boyish. She wore a plain gray dress with a lot of pleats at the waist, a little long at the hem, and glasses with plain gold rims. Trout thought she looked like someone who had stepped out of one of the old issues of *Life* magazine that Joe Pike kept in his church study.

She met Trout halfway down the sidewalk and gave him a hug. "Trout! Welcome home!" She smelled of flowers, something not quite perfume. Trout's mother, Irene, had never worn scents, or any makeup for that matter, and it always surprised him a bit when a woman had the smell of flowers about her.

"Hello, Aunt Alma. You smell good."

"Lilac water," she said. She released him, held him at arm's length, looked him up and down. "You look more like your grandfather Leland every day. He was a bit on the thin side, but he had nice blue eyes and a good chin. I think a good chin is important on a man. Your grandfather Leland looked like he knew what he was doing. And he could add columns of numbers in his head. You couldn't fool Leland Moseley when it came to numbers."

"I'm not much good at math," Trout said.

Alma shook her head and looked at him down the length of her nose. "You're not *all* Moseley. But I suppose you can't help that, can you?"

Trout shrugged. "No ma'am. I guess not."

"Well, come on in and let me show you what I've done."

The two men carrying the floral print sofa were in the living room, still holding it. "Over there," Alma ordered, and they set it against a side wall. Trout's gaze swept the room and he felt his eyes go wide. Everything was brand-spanking-new, with the rich smell of lacquers and pristine fabrics — sofa, two occasional chairs, love seat, coffee table (with copies of the *Methodist Christian Advocate* and *Southern Living* on top), fern stand (with artificial fern), knickknack shelf (with knickknacks, an assortment of porcelain stuff), brass fireplace set, Persian rug.

"I simply cleaned it out," Alma said with a sweep of her arm. "Took everything to the mill and stacked it outside the gate and told 'em to take what they wanted. It was all gone in thirty minutes, down to the wastebaskets. Then I went to Augusta and went shopping."

Trout looked at their image in the big mirror above the mantel and felt a little unclean, as if he had gone straight from mowing the grass to the Lord's Supper. He imagined sitting buck naked on the big floral print sofa. No. You would take great pains not to even break wind in a room like this. Alma was looking at him. She expected him to say something. "Gee," he said.

"That's just for starters," Alma said, and marched off. Trout followed her down a long hallway past two bedrooms, through the dining room, into the big kitchen, and finally to a third bedroom at the back of the house. Alma gave him a detailed inventory as they went along, ticking off items in her strong, clear voice. She seemed to have committed the bill of lading to memory. Everything was new, right down to the set of Corningware dishes in the kitchen cabinets and the oak seats on the commodes.

Trout's room had twin beds, a desk with a brass study lamp, a low bookcase, a five-drawer dresser — all in maple. The window curtains and bedspreads were a coordinated plaid — deep reds and dark blues, the same colors as the oval braided rug. Above the desk was a large framed picture of Jesus' hands, clasped in prayer. Trout went to the window and looked out at Moseley Memorial Methodist Church next door. This side of the building was shaded by pecan trees, and it appeared that every light in the sanctuary was on. He could see the stained-glass windows clearly, four of them on this side, each one a Disciple, each likeness with a name at the bottom. Simon the Cannanaean, Bartholomew, Judas Iscariot, James the son of Zebedee. Sort of the third-string disciples, Trout thought. He wondered how the artist knew what they looked like.

Trout turned back to Aunt Alma. She stood in the doorway, arms crossed. Watching him. Waiting. "It's real nice," he said. "We never had a place this nice." Then he heard some bumping about under the house.

"Central air," Alma said. "They're finishing up. The place had window units, but I took them all out. I put in a new heat pump, new ductwork. Everything." Trout noticed that she kept saying "I." Not "we" or "the church." She gave another sweep of her arm. She also seemed inclined toward sweeping gestures. "There's nothing," Alma said with a firm smile, "like starting over."

Trout thought about his father. Joe Pike liked to put his feet up on the furniture or throw one leg over the arm of a living room chair. He'd think twice about doing that here. But then, there was a lot Joe Pike Moseley would have to think twice about now. He was, indeed, starting over.

"When is Daddy gonna be here?" Trout asked.

Alma didn't say anything for a moment. Then she pursed her lips as if she were drawing on a straw. "When have you talked to him?"

"Last week."

"How did he sound?"

"Tired."

"Well," Alma said, "he hasn't talked to me. I've just had to handle everything on my own. But I *understand* that Joe Pike will be here tomorrow."

Alma turned around and walked out of the room, leaving Trout standing there staring at her back. He found her a few minutes later on the front porch, directing the men from the Moseley Mill truck who were carrying boxes up the front steps. "Put the clothes in the closets and take all the boxes to the kitchen. We'll unpack them there. Don't set anything down on the new furniture."

"Aunt Alma," Trout said.

She turned to him. "Yes?"

"I can unpack my things, but I think maybe the rest oughta wait till Daddy gets here. He's kind of peculiar about moving."

"Peculiar."

"Yes ma'am."

She nodded. "Yes. I suppose he is. Under the circumstances, who wouldn't be?"

Trout gave her an odd look, but he didn't say anything. Aunt Alma, as Joe Pike would have said, had a burr under her saddle. But Trout figured that until Joe Pike got here, it was best to keep his eyes and ears open and his mouth shut. Or as Joe Pike would have said: head up, fanny down. An old piece of Bear Bryant wisdom. Joe Pike was full of Bear Bryant wisdom. It had the ring of Scripture to it.

While the men emptied the truck under Alma's watchful eye, Trout wandered about the grounds taking stock. There was a single expanse of front lawn that took in both parsonage and church. The parsonage had the same dark red brick and cedar shake roof as the church, making them all of a piece. But the parsonage, being smaller, had room for a nice backyard, separated from the rear of the church by a low hedge. There was a brick barbecue pit, a swing hanging by chains from a big limb of a spreading pecan tree, a birdbath, a small frame garage that doubled as a storage shed, and a plot of broken ground where the previous occupant had been preparing a garden. Joe Pike would like that. He liked to dig, plant things, fuss over them, eat the fruits of his own labor.

For as long as Trout could remember, there had been a garden somewhere on the grounds of whatever parsonage they lived in. When Trout was a small child, Joe Pike had always set aside a corner of the plot where he could dig about, sifting the cool, damp earth through his fingers, while Joe Pike hoed and watered nearby. One year Joe Pike gave him a single tomato plant. It was his to care for. He cared for it too much, poking and prodding and watering and digging about the roots. It died. Joe Pike said the tomato plant was like a young'un. You had to know when to leave it alone.

There had been no garden at the Ohatchee parsonage this year. Joe Pike had been too busy with the motorcycle. But there was still time to plant, and here was the broken ground, waiting for him. If Joe Pike planted a garden, it would be a good sign.

Trout sat down in the swing and pondered that awhile. He was still there when Alma came around the corner of the house and sat down next to him.

"Do you need anything for the night?" she asked. "Toothbrush, pajamas?" Trout gave her a blank look. "You'll have to stay across the street with your Uncle Cicero and me."

"I'll be all right over here," Trout said. "I'm used to . . ." He broke off. He didn't want to say too much. Head up, fanny down.

"Yes," Alma said. "I know all about that."

"Well," Trout said agreeably, "I'll stay with you and Uncle Cicero." He stood up. "I'll just get some stuff . . ."

"Fine," Alma said. "Then I want to show you something."

Trout and Alma drove to the mill in her marvelous automobile, a 1934 Packard that Leland Moseley had bought when he took over management of Moseley Mill after Broadus's death. It was an important car — broad-shouldered and powerful, with gleaming chrome, huge whitewall tires, and a black finish so highly polished that it was like looking into a deep well. For as long as Trout could remember, it had hunkered under the porte cochere at the white-columned house across the street from the church, off-limits to children. As small boys, Trout and his cousin, Eugene, Alma's son, would stand well back and admire the car and talk about what it would be like to get it out on the highway at a hundred and twenty miles an hour. But they never touched it. Trout wouldn't have dared. He was by then an obedient child. Eugene would, but Aunt Alma had put some sort of terror into him about the car. Now, it was understood in the family that since Alma ran the mill, it was Alma's car. She drove it once a week, usually out toward Atlanta a few miles to exercise the engine, rarely to the mill. But on this May evening she said to Trout, "We'll take the Packard." It was the first time Trout had ever been inside the car. It had a cavernous interior and smelled of age and old leather. Like going for a ride in someone's parlor.

Moseley Cotton Mill was still in the two-story red-brick building that Broadus Moseley had built at the other end of town, surrounded now by a high chain-link fence with a padlocked gate. Alma handed Trout a key, and he unlocked the gate and swung it wide while Alma eased the car into the deserted lot and parked it next to the building. "Best lock it back," she called as she climbed out, and Trout closed the gate and joined her.

They went first through a small office area, an open space separated into cubicles by opaque glass partitions, each with a desk and file cabinets. Then down a hallway past a closed door with a brass plaque on it that read: ALMA MOSELEY, PRESIDENT. Finally, through another door and into the mill itself.

It was a long, narrow, high-ceilinged cave, crowded with row upon row of machines stretching back through shafts of late-afternoon light that danced with dust motes filtering through tall dingy windows. The machines were squat gray hulks, each with several small white cones on top, identical except for the bold black numbers stenciled on the side. Trout thought suddenly of war, the staging area for some giant battle. He stood there staring for a long moment, trying to imagine the mill in operation, the machines rumbling and clattering, people scurrying about. But there was only a hollow quietness, a dappled blend of light and shadow. Trout took a step toward the nearest machine, bent to peer at the white cones, saw that they were spools of thread.

"Cotton," Aunt Alma said quietly at his back, startling him. Trout turned with a jerk.

"One day, this will be yours," she said.

"Mine?" Their voices sounded hollow and distant in the great expanse of the room.

"Yours and Eugene's. You're the last of the Moseleys. And I don't believe there will be any more, not of your generation."

"What would I do with it?"

"Make cotton. That's what Moseleys do. You know all about that."

"No ma'am." And he didn't. Joe Pike didn't talk much about the family.

Alma's eyes swept the great room slowly. "Well, you will. Your great-grandfather came down from Carolina and built this mill and this town from scratch. For nearly a hundred years, this place has made the finest cotton yarn in the South." Her voice was soft, reverent. It had the ring of Scripture about it.

"The Moseley men . . ." she paused and gave a tiny impatient jerk of her head. "Well, most of the Moseley men . . ." Then she looked straight at Trout and fixed him with narrowed eyes. "We're going to get things back on track, Trout. At long last. We're going to start all over. Do you know what I mean?"

"Not exactly," he said.

"Well, you will." She started to go, then turned back to him suddenly. "There are three things I want you to remember, Trout. One, don't ever forget who you are. Two, be careful of these wild-as-a-buck young'uns out here in the mill village. And three, stay away from your Great Uncle Phinizy."

Trout woke abruptly in the night. The statue. It was still in the front seat of Joe Pike's green Dodge, parked now in the parsonage driveway. He sat up quickly and remembered that he was in the big four-poster bed in what had been Eugene's room on the second floor of Aunt Alma and Uncle Cicero's house. When they were growing up, Eugene was the only youngster Trout knew with a four-poster. Eugene was a good bit older and lived now in Atlanta. But the four-poster stayed behind. You didn't take things out of Broadus Moseley's house.

Trout swung his legs over the side of the bed, found the floor, flicked on a bedside lamp. He dressed quietly, then turned out the light, opened the door and padded barefoot down the carpeted stairs and out the front door, carrying his shoes.

He sat down on the top step and put on his shoes, then sat there for a moment, elbows on knees. Here, in late May, the night still had a bit of an edge to it, a breeze making the leaves dance, the outlines of objects still finely drawn in the light of the streetlamps — empty street, church and parsonage across the way. Another month and the night would blur with heat and haze, the concrete of the sidewalks warm to the touch long after midnight, the air still and close. In late May you could still feel a sense of expectancy. By late June whatever you were expecting had either come or it hadn't. A month. School would be out, Joe Pike would be settled into whatever he wanted to make of his ministry. *I'll give it a month,* Trout thought. And then . . . And then what? Did a sixteen-year-old near-orphaned preacher's boy have a lot of options? Hah. Anyway, he would give it a month.

He stood and started down the steps, and then the voice from the shadows of the porch grabbed him by the scruff of his neck.

"Where you going?"

"Shit!" He turned with a frightened jerk, the hairs on the back of his neck standing straight up.

"Shit?" the voice asked. "That's a mighty big word for a little old preacher's boy."

Trout stared into the shadows, and as his eyes adjusted, he made out the form slouched in one of the porch rockers, the glowing end of a cigarette. Then the tinkle of ice in a glass and the faint, sweet smell of whiskey. He thought for a moment it might be Uncle Cicero. But Cicero didn't smoke or drink. Out of respect for Aunt Alma, it was said. And besides, Cicero was in Texas, or at least on his way back. "Who are you?"

A low, rich laugh, like a diesel engine rumbling to life. Suddenly, Trout knew exactly who it was. Without ever having cast eyes on the man. And he heard some deliciously . . . what? . . . *wicked* quality in the voice that explained why Aunt Alma had said stay away from . . .

"Great Uncle Phinizy."

"You were expecting Basil Rathbone?"

Trout moved closer. "What are you doing here?"

"Why, I live here."

"I thought you lived in Baltimore."

"I *resided* for some time in Baltimore. There's a difference."

Trout felt his heart rise in his throat, his pulse quicken. Phinizy. The other son. Over the years, Trout had heard bits and pieces from Joe Pike. About the time of Broadus Moseley's death, there had been a falling-out of some kind. Leland took over the mill; Phinizy left. As far as Trout knew, he never came back. Joe Pike was the only one he kept in touch with. When Joe Pike spoke of Phinizy, it was usually with a laugh and a shake of his head. Something akin to awe there, but entirely different from the way it was with Bear Bryant.

Phinizy took a long drag on the cigarette, the end of it glowing bright orange, then flipped the butt into the bushes at the edge of the porch and exhaled a long stream of smoke. "I'm out back. Upstairs over the garage. Drop in when the notion strikes you."

Trout started to speak, but thought better of it.

"Did Alma warn you about me?" Phinizy asked. Trout nodded. "I would have been surprised if she hadn't." He took a long pull from his glass and smacked his lips appreciatively. "I'm rather infamous, I think. Black sheep. Embarrassment to the family, or at least Alma's notion of the family. But I rather like being infamous. If you're a nobody, you're just a nobody. If you're famous, they erect a statue of you and pigeons crap on your head. But if you're infamous, you're somebody without having to put up with pigeon crap."

Trout had a notion why Joe Pike Moseley had stayed in touch with Great Uncle Phinizy all these years. There was, in his raspy whiskey-and-smoke voice, a hint of some kind of hidden knowledge that he might, if he liked you, share. And without a lot of bullshit. Trout had the strange but inescapable feeling that he, too, had known Phinizy for a long time. Or maybe just wished he had.

"Alma's a pickle," Phinizy said. "She can't help it. Too much like her father."

Before he could stop himself, Trout blurted, "And who's my daddy like?"

The raspy laugh rumbled out of Phinizy's throat again. "I don't think he's figured that out yet. We'll see. Now go on about your business, whatever it is at three o'clock in the morning."

"And what's your business at three o'clock in the morning?" Trout asked.

"Waiting."

"For what?"

"To see what'll happen."

Trout stared for another moment, then shrugged, turned, and headed down the steps. He heard the click of the lighter and turned back for an instant to see the gnarled face in the brief flicker of flame, a grimace as Phinizy sucked air around the edges of the cigarette.

The statue was about eighteen inches high, heavy plaster, a boy and girl in peasant garb. They stood close together, the boy's mouth next to the girl's ear. It had a name: *The Secret*. Trout didn't know its origin, but it had been with them for as long as he could remember, as familiar as underwear. It was chipped in a couple of places and the plaster had broken on one of the fingers of the boy's hand, revealing a piece of wire underneath. That had been Trout's doing when he was perhaps three or four. In the parsonage where they lived then, the statue had resided on a tall fern stand, and Trout had reached for it one day and pulled it over. It barely missed his head, landing with a thud on the rug. He screamed with fright and Irene rushed in, grabbed him up, examined him frantically for damage. "What were you doing?" she cried. "You could have been killed!" And Trout blubbered, "I wanted to hear the secret." After that, the statue was always kept out of Trout's reach. When the Moseleys made one of their periodic moves, Irene would wrap the statue in a blanket and lay it carefully on the seat of the car between her and Joe Pike. And when they arrived, she carried it straightaway into the house and found a good spot for it. That meant they had taken proper possession, as much as you could possess a parsonage.

The front door of the parsonage was unlocked, as Aunt Alma's own door had been. Nobody seemed to lock anything around here except for the mill. Trout turned on the living room light, unwrapped the statue, and stood in the middle of the room holding it, looking for the place Irene might have chosen if she were here. He briefly considered the mantel, but it was filled with bric-a-brac, some lacquered plates, a Chinese bowl, a clock — all new stuff. The old statue would look out of place. So Trout took it to his own room and set it on top of the chest of drawers. Not perfect, but it would do. He stood looking at the statue for a moment; then on impulse he leaned close and put his ear next to the plaster girl's. Nothing. He straightened quickly, looked around, felt his face flush. Headline: BOY HEARS SECRET OF LIFE FROM STATUE. VISITS POPE TUESDAY.

Trout looked at his wristwatch. Three-thirty. He was wide awake. Might as well get a few things done. He found the church unlocked, too, and toted several boxes full of Joe Pike's preacher stuff to the study. It was empty except for a mahogany desk, an electric typewriter on a stand, a coatrack on which Joe Pike could hang his robe, two walls of built-in bookcases. Trout left the boxes in the middle of the floor, unopened. When Joe Pike got here, he would want to arrange and rearrange things to suit himself, filling shelves with books, moving furniture about, hanging framed certificates and photos on the wall (including an eight-by-ten of himself in his Texas A&M football uniform, massive and poker-faced in a three-point stance), fussing with everything until there was a comfortable, rumpled feel about it. Joe Pike was very territorial about his office. Church members might barge right on through the front door of the parsonage anytime they pleased, but they (and for that matter, Joe Pike's own family) would never think about entering the pastor's study without knocking. And if Joe Pike didn't want company at the moment, he might boom out, "I've got the Lord in here right now. We're transacting business. Come back later."

So Trout left the boxes unopened, then went back to the parsonage and unpacked his own things, stowing away clothes and books and personal items. He put his tennis racquet on top of the dresser along with his trophy from the Valdosta Junior Invitational. And he took down the picture of the praying hands from over the desk and replaced it with his Jimmy Connors poster. He put the praying hands on a high shelf in the closet. *Go ye into your closet and close the door and pray to the Lord which is in secret . . .*

Finally, he wandered into the master bedroom. The men from Moseley Mill had hung Joe Pike's and Irene's clothes in the two closets and left a stack of boxes on the floor next to the bed. These, too, would wait for Joe Pike.

Trout sat on the bed and began to think about all that had turned his life upside down. Losing both parents to one disaster or another, feeling the hot flush of embarrassment over being an oddity at the very time in life when you wanted to fit in, being uprooted from school and friends, driving up through Georgia into a past he knew precious little about. Standing in the great empty mill building, hushed like church except for Alma's voice. *We're going to get things back on track, Trout. Start all over.* What did that mean? Trout didn't want to start all over. He wanted to pick up where things had left off, when they had suddenly fallen off a cliff. He wanted his father back from Texas and his mother back from the Institute and the Atlanta oldies station playing on the radio in the kitchen and Joe Pike prancing about in some sort of celebration or another. It hadn't been all good back then, but it was better than now, better than empty stillness and yawning uncertainty. Better than all this strange newness, all these rules about who you could and couldn't talk to, all this mystic Moseley-ness. Better than having damn little you could count on. Better than this hollow feeling in the pit of his stomach that had been with him for a good while now.

He sat there for a long time, then looked up to see the bedroom windows beginning to gray with first light. He stared at the cardboard boxes. He wouldn't have opened them if he could. There might be things inside, things about Joe Pike and Irene, that he didn't really want to know. Having them back, damaged or not, would be enough.

THREE

THERE WAS A good-sized crowd gathered at the parsonage by the time Joe Pike got there at midafternoon on Saturday.

The ladies of the Parsonage Committee arrived first, bearing armloads of food and housewarming gifts. They made a big deal over Trout, and then they wandered through the parsonage, making a big deal over Alma's redecorating. Trout overheard one woman mutter, "The living room's a bit garish for a parsonage." And another replied, "She paid for it. She can be as garish as she wants."

The members of the Official Board of the church began trickling in, most of them men. The crowd swelled until there were thirty or so people, spilling out the front door of the house onto the porch and lawn, sipping punch in paper cups from a large bowl the ladies had set up on the dining room table.

They were, Trout came to realize, Joe Pike's distant past.

A man named Fleet Mathis was the longtime mayor and had been Joe Pike's scoutmaster before Joe Pike grew suddenly to great size and gave up the Boy Scouts for football.

"People been asking for years, when's the Bishop gonna send Joe Pike back home?" Fleet Mathis said.

"He'd have been here long ago, but Irene wouldn't stand for it," Aunt Alma said. She seemed unconcerned that Trout was right at her elbow when she said it. Aunt Alma seemed accustomed to saying exactly what she thought, whenever she thought it, and expecting everyone to agree with her.

Mostly, they did. But out of Alma's earshot, they appeared to say what they pleased. They regaled Trout with stories about his father's growing up. Garth Niblock was the barber who had given three-year-old Joe Pike his first haircut. He told how Joe Pike had screamed with indignation as his shoulder-length locks, his mother's pride, fell to the floor under Leland's watchful eye.

Miss Althea Trawick, now retired and shriveled, had been one of his elementary-school teachers in the years before Leland shipped Joe Pike off to Georgia Military Academy. Joe Pike didn't want to go, she told Trout, and later he rebelled and came home and caused a family uproar. Joe Pike, she said, seemed to keep the family in more or less constant uproar.

Charlie Babcock was the dentist who had filled Joe Pike's childhood cavities. Joe Pike had always had a sweet tooth, he said. He laughed and said he hoped Joe Pike would be a frequent customer at the new Dairy Queen, because Charlie sure needed some cavity business.

Tilda Huffstetler was the owner of the Koffee Kup Kafe who made Joe Pike's hand-decorated birthday cakes in her kitchen until he was a grown man. She told of shipping cakes by parcel post to Texas A&M when Joe Pike was off playing football, how he would always make a special phone call to thank her. This afternoon she had arrived with two of her famous sweet potato pies (famous, she said, because they had been featured in *Southern Living* magazine — "If it's in *Southern Living*, it's gospel") and insisted that Trout stop by any afternoon after school for a free slice.

Grace Vredemeyer was the church choir director, somewhat younger than most in the crowd and one of the few who wasn't a Moseley native. She had moved there with her husband twenty years earlier, only to lose him to cancer, and had stayed on. She had brought a copy of the weekly church bulletin for Joe Pike and showed Trout her column on church music entitled "Grace Notes." "I hope you can sing better than your daddy," she told Trout. "That man can't carry a tune in a bucket." To which Trout confessed that he couldn't either, but at least he was aware of the fact.

Judge Lecil Tandy was no longer a judge, but had been some years before and was still called "Judge" in the southern way. The name fit. He was tall and spare, with a lovely mane of soft white hair. He wore a three-piece seersucker suit, sagging a bit with age, and a watch chain from which his Phi Beta Kappa key dangled. Judge Tandy was the longtime Moseley family and Moseley Mill attorney and vice-chairman of the Official Board of the church. Aunt Alma was the chairman.

Trout guessed their average age at somewhere over sixty. They were sweet people, he thought, with soft, gentle rhythms of speech, in no particular hurry to say or do anything. They stood about on the porch and under the shade of the pecan trees on the lawn, drinking punch and trading bits of reminiscence and making Trout comfortable in their company. In their voices he could hear the echoes of Joe Pike's childhood, and he felt a tinge of wistfulness. To have grown up in a single place, to be able to say you were truly "from" somewhere . . . well, that might not be too bad. And he began to see how Joe Pike might find rest here for whatever troubled his soul. It would be, he thought, like drifting off to sleep under a soft, familiar blanket.

Just before three, a GMC pickup truck towing a U-Haul trailer pulled up at the curb in front of the parsonage. Uncle Cicero was at the wheel, Joe Pike riding shotgun. "Here he is!" somebody called out, and they all turned to look as Joe Pike threw open the door and hopped nimbly out of the truck and came hotfooting it across the parsonage lawn. "Good Lordy, looka here!" he called. The crowd surged out to meet him with Aunt Alma in the lead, and they gathered around him, hugging and shaking hands, all talking at once.

Trout hung back a bit, giving Joe Pike the once-over. His face was still ruddy from his motorcycle ride, but he looked fit and rested, big and solid and dependable, nothing like the man who had stood in the Ohatchee Methodist pulpit just weeks before, ashen-faced and sweating like a field hand.

Joe Pike was in his element now, never better than when he was in the middle of a crowd. Trout remembered how it was at Methodist Summer Camp years before: Joe Pike, one of the preacher-counselors, riding herd on a bunkhouse full of second-grade boys, Trout among them. Headed for the lake for an afternoon swim, Joe Pike draped with noisy, clambering kids, hanging from his shoulders, arms, legs. Trout, trotting along behind, watching. Joe Pike was the most popular guy at camp.

He was the most popular guy on the Methodist parsonage lawn this late-May afternoon, working this crowd like a master fisherman with a big bass on the line — reeling them in, drenching them with his smile, lifting them up.

"Lord, Miz Trawick, you ain't aged a day since I was in the second grade. I remember you in Vacation Bible School, saying, 'The Lord wants everybody to sit down and shut up.'"

"You never did," Miz Trawick shot back, hands on hips.

"No ma'am. I'm still on my feet, still talking." Big grin, sweeping them to him with his huge arms. "Mighty good to be back home . . . Mister Fleet, it's good to see ya . . . 'preciate y'all coming over . . . be over next week to get some of your sweet potato pie, Tilda . . . Hooooo-doggies!"

Then finally he looked out over their heads and his eyes lit on Trout and his face went soft. "Howdy, son."

"Howdy yourself."

The rest of them stood back a bit, and Joe Pike reached Trout in three big strides and threw his arms around him. He didn't say a word, just swallowed Trout up and held him for a long moment. Then he released him and held him at arm's length.

Trout looked up into Joe Pike's big brown eyes and saw what you would not see from a distance — a kind of opaqueness there, like a sheer curtain. There was a weariness around the edges, deep crow's-feet that hadn't been there before. He could tell that part of Joe Pike was still off someplace else, maybe out there on the road to Junction. That was the thing about Joe Pike. There was so much of him, he could be two places at once. For such a big man, he was a quick, moving target.

"You okay?" Joe Pike asked.

"Yes sir. How about you?"

Joe Pike worked his jaw for a moment. "I'm still vertical."

Trout thought he might have said more, but Aunt Alma was at Joe Pike's side now, taking hold of his arm. "Well, come on in and see the parsonage."

"Alma's been redecorating," Tilda Huffstetler said.

"I'll say she has," Fleet Mathis chimed in. "You better not let the Bishop see it, or he'll want to move in himself."

That drew a laugh from the crowd, and Joe Pike looked down at Alma. "Alma, what have you gone and done?"

Alma gave a wave of her hand. "Started all over."

Joe Pike nodded, then gave a little hissing sound through his teeth. "Sounds about right."

They started toward the house, and as they climbed the steps, Trout looked back toward the curb. Uncle Cicero's pickup truck was gone. The U-Haul trailer was still there, tilted forward on its tongue. Joe Pike, he realized with an uncomfortable lurch of his stomach, had brought the motorcycle home.

He was alone in the open gun turret, crouched in the bucket seat behind the quad-fifties, peering up into the fog, every nerve ending alive, as if he were wired directly into the ship's power plant. He heard the drone of engines high above. Germans. Or maybe Japs. He stared, trying to part the fog with his eyes, swinging the muzzles of the guns back and forth. They were getting closer, coming at him from every point on the compass, their nasty high-pitched roar closing in. *RUM-UM-UM-UM-ADN-ADN-ADN-ADN-RUM-UM-UM.* "Show yourself, you bastards!" he cried. He squeezed the trigger, and the guns bucked and roared, blotting out everything. A long fevered burst, every fourth round a tracer, evil red blips spitting off into the fog. He released the trigger. And still they came, even more of them now. Whole squadrons. An entire air force. *RUM-UM-UM-UM. . .ADN-ADN-ADN.* Then something about the sound caught his ear and he jerked his head up, straining to listen. *Damn! They're on motorcycles!*

Motorcycles. Trout sat bolt upright in bed. He was drowning in sweat, his pajama bottoms plastered to his legs, the bedsheets soaked. "Uggghhhh," he grunted.

He lay there for a moment, listening, trying to sort through the muck in his head. It was very early. The morning was the palest of gray around the edges of the window shade near his head.

Then he remembered. Moseley. The parsonage. Aunt Alma. The cotton mill. Joe Pike. The U-Haul trailer.

The door to the backyard garage was open and he could see the rear end of the motorcycle and next to it, Joe Pike's big rump. It occurred to him that Joe Pike had put on a little more weight during his trip. A grand tour of the Gulf states' Dairy Queens. He was crouched by the motorcycle, screwdriver in one hand, fiddling with the engine. Every so often he would reach up with the other hand and goose the throttle. *RUM-UM-UM-UM. . .ADN-ADN-ADN. . .RUM-UM-UM-UM.* Trout stood in the open doorway watching for a moment, and then Joe Pike seemed to sense he was there and looked back over his shoulder.

"Morning," Joe Pike said brightly.

"Daddy, for gosh sakes. It's five-thirty." *RUM-UM-UM-UM.* "You're gonna wake the neighbors."

Trout stepped out of the shed, feeling the cool wet grass on his bare feet, looked over at the house beyond the back fence. A light was on in the kitchen window, and a woman in curlers was peering out. She stared at Trout and he gave her a weak, embarrassed wave and she disappeared. He realized she must think he was the one out here playing with the motorcycle. Clad only in pajama bottoms. Crazy preacher's kid. Well, that was better than her thinking that it was the preacher himself over here making a ruckus at five-thirty. Joe Pike didn't need to get off on the wrong foot here.

Joe Pike was sitting on the motorcycle now, legs splayed out to the side, hands on the handlebars. He had on an old grease-smudged T-shirt and a faded pair of khaki pants. And the cowboy boots. He dwarfed the motorcycle, yet the man and the machine seemed to fit together in a strange way. He goosed the engine again, then cocked his head to one side, listening, and gave a tiny nod of satisfaction. He looked over at Trout. "You're up mighty early."

Trout shrugged. "I had this dream about guys on motorcycles."

"I never dream," Joe Pike said. "It's probably not healthy. They say you get rid of a lot of psychic waste matter when you dream."

Trout looked for a place to sit, spied an old Coca-Cola crate, turned it on end, and perched on it. "What're you doing?" he asked.

"Adjusting the idle. I took the carburetor apart and cleaned it and blew out the fuel line. It's been running a little rough. But I think I got it fixed. Must have been a piece of dirt or something." He reached down and turned off the ignition, and the motorcycle died with a cough. Trout crossed one leg over the other and wrapped his arms around his bare chest, huddled there on the Coca-Cola crate, watching, studying. Joe Pike hadn't known diddly about motorcycles when he brought the Triumph home in pieces in the trunk of his car. Didn't know a spoke from a piston. And here he was taking apart the carburetor.

"You been up long?" Trout asked.

"Never went to bed," Joe Pike said. He pulled a grimy handkerchief out of a back pocket and started rubbing on the glass face of the speedometer. "I couldn't sleep, so I've been nesting. Got all my stuff unpacked in the church study, put my name on the marquee out front. And today's sermon topic."

"What's your topic?"

"Bear Bryant and the Holy Ghost."

"Is that what you put on the marquee?"

"Yep."

"Aunt Alma said she planned a service without a sermon. Some extra hymns and stuff."

Joe Pike shrugged. "Preachers preach. Especially new preachers. Everybody wants to see if a new preacher can hold a congregation."

"Haven't you ever preached here before?"

"Not since I was ordained. My ordination service was in this church. You were just a baby. And I preached a sermon, sort of a call to arms, about the Disciples going out to witness. 'Go ye unto all the world . . .'" He smiled, remembering. "Young preachers tend to be full of piss and vinegar."

Trout took note of that. *Piss and vinegar.* Joe Pike's customary manner of speaking was colloquial, down-home, even mildly earthy at times. He had gained a reputation as a preacher whose choice of words raised eyebrows and kept the folks in the pews alert. Like the time in an Ohatchee sermon when he said Christians should get off their fatty acids. But *piss and vinegar?* This was something new. And it rolled easily off his tongue, the kind of thing Joe Pike Moseley the Texas A&M football player might have said. But then, Joe Pike Moseley was just back from Texas, wearing cowboy boots and taking apart a carburetor.

Joe Pike finished with the speedometer, then crammed the handkerchief back in his pocket. He climbed off the motorcycle, knelt on one knee next to it, reached for a ratchet wrench, and started removing the spark plug from the engine.

"How you been getting on with Alma?" he asked over his shoulder.

"Okay."

Joe Pike held up the spark plug, examined it closely. "She give you any instructions yet?"

"She told me not to forget who I am, be careful of the mill kids, and stay away from Great Uncle Phinizy."

Joe Pike turned with a jerk. "Phin?" He blinked, his face all puzzlement. "He's here?"

"Yes sir."

"Where?"

"He's living upstairs over the garage behind Aunt Alma's."

"I'll be doggoned," Joe Pike said softly.

"He says he's infamous."

"Yes, I imagine he is."

Joe Pike pulled out the handkerchief again, wiped off the spark plug, and studied it carefully, a smile playing at the corners of his mouth. Then he looked up at Trout. "Let me tell you about Uncle Phin. When I was playing football at A&M, he was the only member of the family who ever came to see me. We were playing Baylor, and when I walked out the door of the dressing room after the game, there he stood. Drunk as a lord, sucking on one of those Picayune cigarettes."

"Why was he the only one who went to see you?"

Joe Pike didn't appear to have heard the question. He turned back to the motorcycle, tightened down the spark plug, put the wire back on, then put the wrench and screwdriver in a cloth pouch and stored them in a compartment under the seat.

He stood, wiping his hands on his khakis, then finally looked down at Trout. "I'm sorry I missed your birthday."

Trout shrugged.

"It's not every day a guy turns sixteen," Joe Pike said.

"I guess not."

"I haven't gotten you a present yet. Thought I'd ask what you wanted."

"I got my license," Trout said.

"You did?"

"Yes sir. The examiner said he played football against you in high school. You and some fellow named Dewberg or something like that."

"Wardell Dubarry."

"That's it."

"Wardell and I used to do the old high-low on quarterbacks."

"Well, the examiner said y'all near about ruined his team's quarterback. He said y'all were rough as a cob."

"Yeah. I guess we were. Me and the mill kids. Wardell's still here. Still works at the mill. We'll go see him."

"Okay."

Joe Pike slung a leg over the motorcycle and eased down into the seat and reached for the handlebars. And then he seemed to forget for a moment that Trout was there. He stared off into the distance, far beyond the back wall of the storage shed, out past the edge of town, maybe beyond Atlanta. Maybe even all the way to Texas. And Trout realized that in some essential way, Joe Pike hadn't come back yet.

"Daddy . . ."

"You can still get there on two-lanes."

"What?"

Joe Pike turned and looked at him. "All the way from Ohatchee, Georgia, to Junction, Texas, and I never set foot on an interstate. Only a few four-lanes. Mostly just back roads where you can't see past the next hill. Lots of farm tractors and school buses. Folks wave at you when they pass. Figure you must be from somewhere around there or you wouldn't be on their back road in the first place. Never looked at a map, either."

"Didn't you get lost?"

"Hell, I was lost when I started. I just kept the nose pointed west, and I stopped and asked for directions every so often. It took a bit longer, but I wasn't in any hurry in the first place." Trout could hear the pride in Joe Pike's voice. *Hey, Ma! Look what I did!*

Joe Pike sat there for a moment, then shook his head, swung one leg over the motorcycle and sat sidesaddle looking at Trout.

"When is Mama coming home?" Trout asked.

He expected Joe Pike to duck this one, too. But instead, his eyes never left Trout. "Cicero and I stopped in Atlanta," he said. "Your mama's doctor didn't think it was best that we see her. Said she was resting, getting along okay."

"When, then?"

"The doctor was a little vague about that. He was a little vague about everything."

Instead, it was Trout who ducked his head. He thought at first that there was something false about Joe Pike's steady gaze. The appearance of dealing with things. But then he looked back up at Joe Pike and saw that that wasn't the case at all. If anything, it was too much honesty.

"Trout. . ." he said.

"Yes sir."

"I love you, son."

"I love you, too."

"Bear with me. And Mama. Give it all some time. One thing about it . . ."

"What's that?"

"It'll either work out or it won't."

"That's not much to go on," Trout said.

"No. I suspect not. Not much reassurance. But that's life, son."

Trout felt a rush of anger. Damn Joe Pike for leaving, and damn him for coming back empty-handed. He could understand the leaving, at least a little. Irene gone to ground, Joe Pike's faith — in himself and in God — shaken, his ministry gone sour. Okay, so he had gone out to do battle, smote his demons hip and thigh, vanquish devilment, whatever. But somewhere out there on the road to Texas, out on those rural two-lanes with the wind in his ears and the sun in his eyes and the heat phantoms on the pavement ahead, he seemed to have lost heart. And now he had returned from the journey weary and subdued — still vertical, as he said, but whacked off at the knees. And unsure of what was next. Trout, who needed desperately to be reassured about even some small thing, found that Joe Pike was reassured about nothing. There appeared to be no solid ground under either of them. *It will either work out or it won't. That's life.* Oh? Is that what life is? Well, if so, he thought, it truly sucks.

Trout realized that anger would serve no purpose here. It might even spook Joe Pike again. It was not a good sign that he was out here at six-thirty on a Sunday morning tinkering with the damned motorcycle. Better to watch and wait. He was getting quite good at it. So he gave Joe Pike a long look that he tried to shape into something like kindly forbearance. "Okay," he said. "Okay."

Aunt Alma seemed a bit disappointed that Joe Pike wanted to preach. She had indeed planned a Sunday morning service without a sermon — two anthems from the choir, Scripture readings and the like by various lay folk, Fleet Mathis giving a report on his and Eunice's recent trip to the Holy Land. Joe Pike could just take it easy, she said. But he insisted. He put on his robe and marched in behind the choir and sat patiently while everybody went on with the service Aunt Alma had planned.

Aunt Alma said it was the biggest crowd they had had in years, even bigger than Easter. But it truly wasn't very big, nothing like the regular Sunday turnout in Ohatchee. There were a lot of empty seats. And like the welcoming committee the day before, it tended toward older people, some of them downright ancient. There was a scattering of middle-aged and younger couples, only a handful of children. Three other teenagers, a boy and two girls who sat together on a back pew and didn't seem much interested in Trout.

It was a fairly small sanctuary: an arc of oak pews nestled close to the communion rail in front of the pulpit, all the wood stained dark; the cross and twin candles on the Communion table a burnished brass; deep burgundy carpeting on the floor; a sweep of stained glass along the walls where the Twelve Disciples looked down, bathing everything with softly fractured color. They sang old hymns — "Blessed Assurance" and "Rescue the Perishing" and "Take the Name of Jesus With You" — and the singing had a rich mellowness to it, aging voices with the pipe organ flowing beneath like an underground stream.

It was almost noon when Joe Pike finally rose to speak. It was absolutely still and expectant. The congregation waited. So did the Twelve Disciples, looking down from the windows, their bearded faces impassive. Joe Pike stood for a moment, leaning across the pulpit, his gaze taking everything in, resting finally on Trout, sitting with Aunt Alma and Uncle Cicero in the third row, directly in front of the pulpit. Their eyes met for an instant. *Pay attention. I'm gonna give it a shot.*

Then Joe Pike's gaze broke away and he raised up a bit, stood tall behind the pulpit, towering over it. "I've been in a fight," he said. Then he paused for a moment, cocked his head to the side, worked his jaw into a crooked grin. "I never knew but two folks who could whip me. That was Bear Bryant and the Holy Ghost. I ran into both of 'em in Texas."

He paused for a moment and ran his fingers through his hair, slicking it back on his head. There was dead silence in the sanctuary. *What's going on here?*

Joe Pike went on. "I like the phrase 'Holy Ghost.' Now I realize that the church, in its wisdom and an effort to be modern, has changed it to 'Holy Spirit.' But I like the thought, outdated though it may be, of God's ghost lurking about. Something we can't see but sometimes feel. An apparition that oozes through walls and appears in places we'd rather He not be." His eyes swept over the congregation again. "Have you ever been sitting alone in a room and all of a sudden felt there was somebody else there? And you looked up and there wasn't?" He raised his eyebrows, waiting. Trout saw a few heads nod among the congregation. "Well, that's the way I felt a few weeks ago. I was riding my motorcycle to Texas." He said it off-handedly, as if he were describing a trip to the grocery store. "And the Holy Ghost got on in Flatwoods, Louisiana. I had stopped at a traffic light, and when the light turned green and I pulled away, I thought to myself, 'There's somebody on this motorcycle with me.' Well, the Holy Ghost stayed on the back of that motorcycle all the way to Junction, Texas. I couldn't get a good look at Him, but I could feel Him back there, hanging on. And when I realized who it was, I got to asking questions. I'm talking really deep theology here. Everything from immaculate conception to papal infallibility. But every time I'd ask the Holy Ghost a question, He'd say, 'Uh-uh. Not important.' Now, I don't have to tell you, that gets mighty irritating after a while. And by the time we got to Junction, I'd had about enough. So I jumped off the motorcycle and yelled, 'Awright, dang it! Tell me what's important!'" Joe Pike smote the air with a massive arm. "But the Holy Ghost didn't say a word. Even though I couldn't see Him, I could feel Him pretty good, so I grabbed Him in a headlock and threw Him down on the ground, and we wrestled there for a good little while. And the Holy Ghost whipped me."

Joe Pike stopped suddenly, took a half-step back from the pulpit, and stood for a moment staring off above the congregation's heads, lost in thought. Trout stole a glance at Aunt Alma. She was staring at Joe Pike, mouth open. Then she closed her mouth and gave a tiny shake of her head. Joe Pike cleared his throat and stepped up again. "Texas ain't a good place to get whipped. It's hot and dry and you can get a mouthful of dirt when you waller around on the ground. And I did. It felt just like it did when Bear Bryant got through with me. I knew I'd been whipped. But I'm a stubborn fellow. So I asked the Holy Ghost one last time, 'What's important?' And this time, He asked back, 'What do you believe?' I thought about that for a good while, and then I said, 'I believe in the Father and the Son and the Holy Ghost. And beyond that, I'm pretty much open.' And the Holy Ghost said, 'That'll have to do for starters.' And then He told me to rest up and then get on back to Moseley, Georgia, and work on the rest of it. So here I am."

It was rather astonishing, Trout thought. He had sat through years of Joe Pike's preaching, and this was something entirely new. Joe Pike's sermons had always been heavy on Scripture and theology, spiced with anecdotes and snippets of humor — a clever phrase here, a nugget of scriptural wisdom there — all delivered in Joe Pike's rich, rolling voice that cascaded down over the congregation. He was a master of gesture — a quick jab of finger, a sweep of arm, a slow open-palmed beseeching. He was a huge, black-robed conductor, guiding the congregation through the symphony he had carefully crafted in the hours he spent behind the closed door of his study. When it was done, the supplicants might not be able to say in so many words exactly what the point was, but they spoke of Joe Pike's sermons with some satisfaction as "deep."

This, though — his first sermon in sixteen years in Moseley Memorial Methodist Church — was something altogether different. *Piss and vinegar.* Joe Pike looked out across the congregation as if to say, *Any questions here?* But nobody said a thing. Trout cut another quick glance at Aunt Alma. Her mouth was set in a thin, disapproving line. Everybody else looked simply perplexed. Joe Pike sat down.

Uncle Cicero had changed into his police chief uniform by the time they sat down to dinner in the dining room at Aunt Alma's house. Cicero explained that as the chief of a two-man police force, he felt it incumbent upon him to share weekend duty. He would be "on patrol" through the early evening. Cicero was short and a little beefy, mostly bald on top. But his tan uniform with dark blue piping and epaulets fit him nicely, and he wore it well. Little silver eagles were pinned to his collar points. His big leather belt with handcuffs, flashlight, billy club, and holstered .44 Magnum pistol was hanging on a coatrack out in the front hallway.

It was just the four of them, their voices a bit hollow in the high-ceilinged dining room with its massive mahogany furniture. The black woman named Rosetta who cooked for Alma and Cicero kept coming in from the kitchen with platters heaped with food, and Joe Pike kept taking portions while Rosetta beamed at him approvingly, and he and Cicero carried on a running discourse about the hardware business. Aunt Alma was unusually quiet. Perhaps, Trout thought, still taken aback by Joe Pike's sermon. Perhaps even offended. There was a prim set to her mouth, and she ate with small, precise motions.

Uncle Cicero liked talking hardware and he liked the word *your*. As in, "You've got your sand mix and then you've got your mortar mix and then you've got your concrete mix."

"So what do I need to pour a concrete floor in that storage shed behind the parsonage?"

"Your concrete mix. But before you do that, you'd want to put down your wire mesh."

"You mean like rebar?"

"No, you don't need anything as heavy-duty as your rebar, unless you're gonna keep something real heavy in there."

"Like an armored personnel carrier."

"Or a whiskey still." Uncle Cicero cackled. "Fellow come in my place back a few years ago, bought every sack of concrete mix I had and every inch of rebar. The state boys caught him with a two-thousand-gallon whiskey still in a barn on his proppity. It had your heavy-duty floor underneath it."

Aunt Alma roused herself then and let out a little forced laugh. "Good gracious, Cicero, couldn't you find something more uplifting to talk about at the Sunday dinner table than whiskey stills?"

Uncle Cicero nodded agreeably. "I could. I reckon."

Alma looked across the table at Joe Pike. "If you want a floor in the storage shed, just say so and I'll have the mill superintendent take care of it."

Joe Pike looked right back. "I'll take it up with the pastor-parish relations committee."

"There isn't one."

"Oh? And who takes care of pastor-parish relations?"

"I do."

"I see."

That was when Joe Pike took his third helping of roast beef, after Rosetta glided in from the kitchen and held the platter at his elbow. He took a couple of good-sized slabs and gave Rosetta a big smile. Everybody else passed, and Rosetta disappeared again into the kitchen. Joe Pike cut off a hunk of roast beef, shoved it into his mouth, chewed slowly, and swallowed. Trout picked at his plate, stealing glances at Joe Pike and Alma, waiting.

Finally, Joe Pike said, "I didn't come here to be a kept preacher, Alma."

Alma lifted her napkin from her lap, dabbed at her lips, then folded the napkin carefully and tucked it under the edge of her plate. Took a good deal of time doing it. Then she looked up at Joe Pike. "What *did* you come here for?"

"The Bishop sent me," he said simply.

"The Bishop's trying to save your ministry."

"It's a noble purpose, I suppose."

She shook her head. "Excuse me for saying so, Joe Pike, but you sound a little cavalier about it."

"I don't mean to, Alma. I think we could all use a little noble purpose in our lives."

Trout could hear something gently mocking in Joe Pike's voice, something faintly defensive in Alma's. Some ancient pattern of feint and jab between brother and sister, a ritual of sorts. It was a history Trout knew nothing about. Times past when he had sat at this table, there had always been a crowd — his mother, his cousin Eugene. Until her death ten years previous, Trout's grandmother, Lucretia Moseley. And family friends and retainers. It was a well-mannered crowd, the conversation genteel and polite. Feint and jab were not something you did at the Moseley dinner table.

"Well, I don't know what noble purpose you think you were serving with that business this morning," Alma said.

"You mean my sermon."

"I thought the thing about the Holy Ghost was right interesting," Uncle Cicero chimed in. "You reckon you could tell the Rotary Club about that?"

"Good Lord, Cicero." Alma laughed, and now it sounded even more forced. "The Rotary Club?"

"Well, it's hard to get good programs," Cicero said. "Last week Roscoe Withers got up and told about his trip to Augusta to the chiropractor."

Alma shook her head at Cicero. "Well, the Rotary Club is better off hearing about Roscoe's trip to Augusta than about some" — a flip of her hand — "trip to Texas on a motorcycle."

"Wandering in the wilderness," Joe Pike said. "It's an old biblical tradition." He put another piece of roast beef in his mouth and chewed thoughtfully.

Alma gave him a long, searching look. "I don't know what gets into you, Joe Pike. You've been more or less in a state of rebellion since you were two years old."

"You think maybe it's time I grew up?"

Alma pondered that for a moment. "I think whatever's ailing you, you need to handle it yourself. It has no place in the pulpit."

"Preachers have no right to ask questions?"

Alma leaned across the table toward Joe Pike, hands clasped as if in prayer. "People come to church on Sunday wanting to be told. They want answers. They want something they can depend on. They want some*body* they can depend on. Especially in your case."

Joe Pike looked a trifle amused. "Why especially in my case?"

"Because of who you are."

He gave a great sigh. "Ah, yes. There's always that."

"*Moseley* United Methodist. It wouldn't exist without this family."

A long silence, and then Joe Pike said, "Maybe it ought not to."

Alma flushed. "What do you mean?"

"Maybe the family has done too much. A church that doesn't have any initiative isn't much of a church."

"Initiative? Who's talking about initiative? I'm talking about money. I'm talking about half the budget. Half!"

"They don't have a pot to pee in," Uncle Cicero piped up.

"Cicero!" Alma warned.

"Don't look at me," Cicero said. "I'm Baptist."

"Well, you *attend* the Methodist Church."

"You Methodists are a lot more interesting," Cicero grinned, "running preachers in and out like it was a football game . . ."

"Then join!" she said. "Join, if you think it's so interesting."

"I'm Baptist," Cicero insisted. "What do you think, Joe Pike?"

"A fellow has to do what he has to do, Cicero. Yea, verily."

Alma gave a shake of her head, dismissing Cicero the Baptist. She reached across the table and took Joe Pike's hand. "I don't want to fuss, Joe Pike. Especially over the church. I'm glad you've come. I want you to be happy here, you and Trout. I want us to work together."

"Laboring in the fields of the Lord," Joe Pike said with a thin smile.

"Yes. Of course." She released his hand, then looked over at Trout. "I took Trout by the mill yesterday," she said. "I wanted him to see it. I told him it'll belong to him and Eugene one of these days."

There is something sadly desperate in her voice, Trout thought. If he knew more about her, he might know why. Watch and listen.

"That depends on Trout," Joe Pike said mildly.

"Actually," Trout said, "I've thought about being a tennis pro."

Alma laughed again, and this time there seemed to be a trace of genuine laughter in it. *Silly boy.* Trout felt a flash of irritation, but he kept his mouth shut.

Aunt Alma took a sip of her iced tea, dismissing Trout the Tennis Pro, then looked across the table at Joe Pike again. "Your old friend Wardell Dubarry is still at the mill, you know."

"It's been a good while since I've seen Wardell. We really haven't kept in touch. My fault, mostly."

"He's a troublemaker, Joe Pike."

Joe Pike nodded. "Wardell always did love a ruckus."

"Well, it's more than a ruckus. He's got people stirred up."

"How's that?"

"He's appointed himself as the plant conscience. Always agitating. Safety this, safety that. The temperature's too high, the pay's too low." She waved her hand and her voice rose an octave. "The light's too dim; there aren't enough exits. On and on and on! And I get *no help!*"

"Then why don't you sell it?" Joe Pike asked.

"What?!"

"Find a buyer. People buy and sell businesses all the time."

Alma looked stricken. "I can't believe you said that." There was a long, painful silence, and then she said quietly, "Yes, I suppose I can. You've never taken the slightest interest. Nobody but me."

Cicero chimed in again. "I heard Mister Leland say just before he died that not a damn one of his young'uns did what he wanted 'em to."

Alma's jaw tightened. "I don't believe my father ever used that word."

"What? 'Damn'? Why, Mister Leland was known to offer up your mild expletive every once in a while. Now, I never heard him give anybody what you'd call your dog-cussing, but —"

"HE NEVER USED THAT WORD!" Alma bellowed. The room rang with the echo of her outburst, like putting your head inside a bell while somebody struck it with a hammer. They all stared at her and she flushed with embarrassment.

The door from the kitchen swung open and Rosetta peeked into the dining room. "Y'all want something?"

"You got any more of that squash casserole?" Cicero asked. Alma gave him a murderous look. "Never mind," Cicero said. Rosetta disappeared.

"Papa was not a saint, Alma," Joe Pike said quietly.

Alma turned her gaze on Joe Pike. "I don't believe you have any right to judge," she said. Again, that sadly desperate quality in her voice. And Joe Pike didn't have any response to that.

They all sat there in silence awhile longer, and then Alma composed herself and sat back in her chair. When she spoke again, her voice was quite calm. "I don't expect you to have the same respect for the business I do, Joe Pike. But I don't ever remember you sending back a check." She waited for a response, got none. "And now with your extra financial burden, private care and all —"

"Alma!" Now it was Joe Pike's voice that shattered the air and stopped her dead cold. Trout looked up at his father, massive and bristling beside him, as angry as Trout had seen him in a long time. Then Trout looked across at Alma and saw how she recoiled from his anger.

"I didn't mean . . ." she began, then broke off. They both stared at their plates for a long moment.

And then Uncle Cicero said, "What's for dessert?"

Alma gave him a blank look. "Dessert?"

"I've sort of had a yen for some peach cobbler lately."

"We haven't had dessert in two years, Cicero. Not since your cholesterol flared up."

Cicero thought about that for a moment. "Well, it doesn't keep a fellow from having a yen for peach cobbler."

Alma stared at Cicero and gave a slow shake of her head.

Joe Pike stood up, pushing his chair back with a scrape. "Obliged for dinner," he said. Trout stood up, too.

Alma looked up at him. "I don't want to fuss," she said quietly. "We never used to fuss at this table."

Joe Pike looked down at her. "Maybe we should have. All we did was agree with Papa."

"I just wanted a nice dinner. To celebrate your being home. You and Trout."

"Sure."

"Dinner was real good, Aunt Alma," Trout said. And then something, he couldn't have said what, made him add, "Why didn't you invite Uncle Phinizy?"

Aunt Alma turned beet red. And Joe Pike hustled Trout out of there in a hurry.

As they were going down the front steps, Uncle Cicero called from the front door, "Joe Pike, Rotary Club meets Tuesday at noon in the back room at the Koffee Kup."

They were sitting in the car in front of the Dairy Queen, Joe Pike working on an Oreo Blizzard with crushed pecans on top and Trout, a cone of vanilla. Aunt Alma might not serve dessert with Sunday dinner, but there was always Dairy Queen. It was one of life's certainties. As Joe Pike would say, Yea, verily. They had the windows rolled down, the Atlanta oldies station on the radio. The Coasters: *He's a clown, that Charlie Brown. He's gonna get caught* . . . Trout had been raised on oldies. Most towns where they lived, you could get the Atlanta station. In Bainbridge Joe Pike had installed a special antenna on a tall utility pole next to the parsonage to bring it in. While Trout's friends were listening to Elton John, he got a steady dose of Clyde McPhatter, Elvis Presley, the Shirelles. Joe Pike and Irene danced in the kitchen, something called the Panama City Bop. They were good dancers. Joe Pike, for his size, was nimble and graceful. Tiny Irene whirled like a doll in his hands. Then one day Trout realized that Joe Pike and Irene didn't dance anymore. But Joe Pike kept the radio tuned to the oldies station. *Just in case,* Trout thought.

Joe Pike finished his Blizzard, scraping out the last morsel from the bottom of the cup with his red plastic spoon, reluctantly placing the empty cup on the dashboard. He had a look in his eye that told Trout he might go for another one with the slightest encouragement. Instead, he turned to Trout and asked, "Why did you do that?"

"What?"

"That remark about Uncle Phinizy."

Trout shrugged. "I don't know. It just popped out, I guess. Are you mad?"

"No."

"Aunt Alma likes to have her way, doesn't she."

"Yes. But it's not that simple."

Trout waited for Joe Pike to explain, but he didn't. Finally Trout asked. "What am I supposed to do about Aunt Alma?"

"I guess you'll have to decide that for yourself," Joe Pike said.

He sat there staring at the Blizzard cup while Trout finished his ice cream. Maybe he'll go for a chocolate shake, Trout thought. Or a banana split. Instead, Joe Pike said, "I guess I ought to be shot for what I did."

"What?"

"Running off like that."

Trout didn't know what to say. At a time like this, you could say too much. Or not enough.

"I just want you to know it didn't have anything to do with you, son."

Trout thought about that. He sort of wished it had.

"I'll tell you a piece of truth, Trout. God's got me by the short hairs." A long silence. "Last person did that to me was Coach Bryant."

"What did you do?"

Joe Pike's brow wrinkled, thinking back. When he talked about Texas A&M, about the Bear, he got an odd look at the corners of his eyes. You could see it if you knew where to look. Something like panic there, a nightmare made of heat, dust, agony. And pride, too.

"There were times I wanted to kill him," Joe Pike said finally.

"Why didn't you?"

"I was afraid to."

"You feel that way about God?"

Joe Pike pursed his lips, considering. Then he nodded. "Yep."

FOUR

JOE PIKE DROPPED Trout off in front of the high school shortly after eight the next morning.

"Aren't you coming in?" Trout asked.

"No. Just go to the office and ask for Mr. Blaylock. He's expecting you."

Trout had never started school alone before. Irene had always gone with him on the first day in a new town, even after he reached the age at which having your mother appear at school under any circumstance was something akin to contracting leprosy.

"Do I look okay?" he asked Joe Pike. He was wearing faded jeans, an old pair of Nike running shoes, a plain light blue T-shirt. He carried a half dozen dog-eared spiral binders, crammed with notes from his Ohatchee classes, and a couple of number-two pencils.

Joe Pike put on his mock-Scripture voice. "Give ye heed to the birds of the air and the fish of the sea, for they ask not, what shall I wear or what shall I eat . . ."

"But they weren't sixteen years old."

"You'll do fine, Trout. Play it by ear. It's just a week."

Trout stood at the curb watching Joe Pike's Dodge pull away. *Easy for Joe Pike Moseley to say.* In his day, Joe Pike had belonged here in this aging, nondescript red-brick building with its tall, sun-tainted windows. Joe Pike had never had to walk in cold turkey a week before the end of school with the kind of baggage Trout was toting these days. Trout felt like a man being paraded through town with a dead chicken around his neck.

He walked up the steps, past the squat columns guarding the entrance, into the front hallway. Straight ahead, through open double doors, the auditorium — rows of empty wood-backed seats, a heavy dark blue curtain across the stage with gold letters across the top: MHS. To his left and right, wide hallways — scuffed wooden floors, dingy pale green walls, flaking ceilings, open doorways from which he could hear the faint drone of voices. The place seemed weary.

So did Mr. Blaylock. Over sixty, bald, heavyset, with pale, watery eyes. Trout sat across the desk from Mr. Blaylock while he flipped through the manila folder full of records that Trout had brought from Ohatchee. The top of the desk was bare except for a small note pad and pencil. The pencil was freshly sharpened, the pad empty. Trout thought Mr. Blaylock looked like he wanted to be ready to go home as soon as the bell rang.

The room was sparse — the desk and two chairs, a Georgia state flag on a stand in one corner, a glass-front bookshelf full of old textbooks: *Algebra Made Easy, The American Century, Studies in Good Health.* And perched on the window air conditioner behind Mr. Blaylock's desk, a trophy — a football player in full stride atop four columns, ball tucked under his arm, running to glory; a tarnished brass plate at the base:

MOSELEY HIGH SCHOOL

2-A STATE CHAMPION RUNNER-UP

1953

"Well," Mr. Blaylock said. He closed the folder, opened a desk drawer, dropped the folder in, and closed the drawer. His wooden swivel chair creaked in protest as he leaned back, making a little tent with his fingers under his chin, looking at Trout expectantly.

Trout fidgeted. Finally he said, "I have trouble with math."

Mr. Blaylock gave a small flip of a hand, dismissing math. "Well, I wouldn't worry about it if I were you. Certainly not this close to the end of school. Anyhow, Einstein couldn't balance his checkbook."

"Yes sir."

The window air conditioner droned into the silence. Trout glanced up again at the trophy. Mr. Blaylock followed his gaze, turned with a squeak of the chair, and looked up at the trophy, then back to Trout. "I suppose you know all about that."

"No sir."

Mr. Blaylock gave him an odd look. "Joe Pike hasn't told you . . ." He reached out his hand toward the trophy, an almost reverent gesture. And then Trout understood. It was a sort of shrine.

"An extra point," Mr. Blaylock said.

"What?"

"Twenty-one to twenty. We missed the extra point. Best football game I ever saw in my life — high school, college, or pro. Except for that extra point."

"Well, it's a nice trophy."

Mr. Blaylock looked up at the trophy again, studied the brass plate for a moment, and frowned. "It says 'runner-up.'"

"Was that my daddy's team?"

"Yes. It was your daddy's team. That's exactly what it was. If it hadn't been, we woulda won maybe two games that year."

Then it dawned on Trout. "You were the coach?"

Mr. Blaylock stared up at the ceiling for a long time, and Trout wondered if he had heard the question. Then all of a sudden Mr. Blaylock stood up, banging the swivel chair against the wall. He leaned over the desk toward Trout, eyes lit up, nostrils flaring. "Sometimes you look back on something that happened years before, and you think, 'That was as good as it ever got.' But I knew it right then and there. Damnedest football game in history. Ass-busting, bone-crunching, gut-sucking football, the way it was invented. Kids being helped off the field, coming right back. Halfback from Bainbridge played most of the game with his nose mashed over to one side of his face, dripping blood down the front of his jersey. Coupla my boys didn't know their own names when it was over. I remember standing on the sidelines during that last quarter, thinking, 'Orzell Blaylock, this is it.'"

Then he stopped, blinked, sat back heavily in his chair, gave a huge sigh. "And we missed the extra point. If we'da made the extra point, we'da gone to overtime. And we'da whipped the sonsabitches in overtime. We had the momentum." He stopped, mouth open, breathing heavily. And then he repeated softly, "We had the momentum."

"I'm sorry," Trout said. It sounded pretty lame, but it was all he could think of.

"Yeah," Mr. Blaylock said. "Well . . ." They both sat there for a moment longer, and then Mr. Blaylock asked, "You and Joe Pike see many Falcon games?"

"Who?"

"The Falcons. Atlanta."

"Oh. No sir. They play on Sundays."

Mr. Blaylock nodded. "I reckon Joe Pike being a preacher and all . . ."

"It's not that. It's just that you can't leave Ohatchee after church and get to Atlanta in time for the game."

"Well, you're not in Ohatchee now."

"No sir."

"Moseley's not that far from Atlanta. Maybe you and Joe Pike can see some games this season."

"Yes sir."

"You do like sports, don't you?"

Trout glanced up at the trophy again. "I sure do like sports, yes sir."

"Which ones?"

"Well, actually . . . tennis."

"Tennis?"

"Yes sir." There was a long silence while Mr. Blaylock stared at the blank pad on his desk. Trout wondered if he might pick up the pencil and write something on the pad. But he didn't.

After a moment, Mr. Blaylock looked up at him again. "We don't want any trouble here, Trout."

"No sir," Trout said, feeling his face flush. *What in the hell is he talking about?*

"This ain't a good idea. Especially right now. And I told Joe Pike that. But he insisted. So let's just get through this the best we can, okay?"

"Yes sir."

"Any problems, you come see me."

"Yes sir."

"But I hope you won't have to."

"No sir," Trout said. His eyes went to the blank pad on the bare desk. "I can see that."

Trout vowed to keep his mouth shut and keep a low profile. Head up, fanny down. And by midmorning, he had decided it might be easier than he thought. The teachers seemed nice enough, but wary — as if they didn't quite know what to do with him. And as far as the students were concerned, Trout Moseley might as well have been invisible. They didn't so much ignore him as they looked right through him.

Until midmorning. They were changing classes, the hallway where Mr. Blaylock had assigned him a locker crowded and noisy with students. Suddenly, down the hall a piece, there was an explosion of sound and motion. "Outta the way! Comin' through!" Trout saw the mass of students parting; then she burst through — a flailing windmill of arms, legs, torso, crutches, flying hair, everything galloping off in a dozen directions at once. A big pad of some kind tucked under one arm, books under the other. Trout stared, transfixed. A wreck, happening before his eyes. Incredible.

"Move it! Move it! Comin' through!" She lurched to a halt in front of his locker, screwed up her face in a grimace and looked him straight in the eye. "Who the hell are you?"

"Trout Moseley," he said.

"I knew that."

"Then why did you ask?"

"I just wanted to see if you'd admit it."

"Admit it?"

A bell rang somewhere down the hall. Bodies swirled around them, giving both a wide berth. Invisible Trout Moseley and the human antigravity device.

"Meet me in the football stadium after school," she barked. And she lurched away, leaving him open-mouthed.

At first, he thought she wasn't there. Some kind of trick. The student body, hidden in the bushes next to the stadium, laughing their butts off. It had already been one of the strangest days of his life, ranking not far behind the day they took his mother off to the Institute and the Easter Sunday Joe Pike rode off on the motorcycle.

Then she waved and he saw her sitting in the shade by the concession stand behind one of the end zones. Back to the wooden side of the building, knees bent, the big pad open in her lap, crutches next to her on the grass. He walked the length of the field, feeling sweat trickling down his back and sopping his already-wet T-shirt. The only air conditioner in Moseley High School, it had turned out, was in Mr. Blaylock's office.

As he approached, he could see that she was drawing on the pad, making broad strokes with some kind of pencil, looking up at him and then back down. He stopped in front of her. "Hi. I'm Trout Moseley. I'm new here. What's your name?"

She concentrated on the pad for a moment longer, then looked up at him. "I know all about you."

"Oh?"

"I know your mama's in the Institute in Atlanta, your daddy flipped out and rode his motorcycle to Texas, and you play tennis."

"Well," Trout said, "I guess that about wraps it up." He craned his neck, trying to see over the top of the pad. "What're you drawing?"

She closed the pad with a slap, stuck the pencil behind her ear so that just the tip showed from her close-cropped brown hair. "None of your business. Sit down."

He sat a couple of yards from her, put his books down on the grass beside him and looked out across the hot green expanse of the football field. Twenty-one to twenty. It was just a ball game, wasn't it?

"You can forget tennis," she said.

"Oh?" Had Mr. Blaylock put out a memo to the student body? *This boy plays tennis. Watch him.*

"There's not a single tennis court in Moseley."

Trout thought about the Prince Extender racquet he coveted, hanging on pegboard in the pro shop at Ohatchee Country Club. Black graphite with white binding on the grip. A wicked-looking piece. Walk on the court with something like that and watch your opponent's eyes. *Uh-oh.* Two hundred and fifty dollars. He had been saving up for two years, and he was getting close. If he sent the money, they would ship it from Ohatchee, he was sure of that. It's not every day the pro shop at Ohatchee Country Club sells a two-hundred-fifty-dollar racquet.

"You want to know why?" she asked.

"Why what?"

"Why there's no tennis court in Moseley."

"Okay."

"Your grandfather wouldn't allow it." She waited for some response from him. He shrugged. "He thought it was frivolous," she said with a toss of her head. Trout searched her face. It seemed set in a perpetual scowl. She was rather pretty in a sharp-featured way, but the scowl undercut it. Was it indigestion? Or was she just generally mad at the world? He looked down at her crutches, lying on the grass between them.

"What are you looking at?" she demanded.

He nodded at the crutches. "Is that why you're pissed off? Or is it something else?"

She surprised him by giving him a crooked smile. "Hey, what have we here? 'Pissed off.' Pretty strong stuff for a preacher's kid."

Trout picked up his books, struggled to his feet. "Look. This hasn't been the best day of my life. Mr. Blaylock is fixated on a football game that happened thirty years ago. I've had to check myself several times today to see if I'm transparent, because you're the only kid who's spoken to me and you've got a snotty attitude and I don't even know your name. The lunch meat was inedible. Now you tell me there's no tennis court. I've never lived here before and I don't know what the hell it is about the Moseleys. I just know my dad said one time that when a Moseley farts, everybody smells it."

"Your daddy said that?"

"Yes."

"He's a preacher and he said that?"

"Yes."

She pursed her lips. "Hmmmm."

"Tell me something."

"What?"

"What's with the silent treatment?"

A tiny smile played at the corners of her mouth. But she didn't answer him directly. "Mill kids run this place," she said.

"And the mill kids are just shy, right?"

"No."

"Then what?"

"When you live over in the mill village and your mama and daddy don't make squat for money, there's not much to do for diversion."

"So I'm a diversion."

"You're a Moseley."

Trout looked away, studying the cloudless afternoon sky above the stadium press box, imagining the stands packed with people, the loudspeaker blasting. *Tackle by Joe Pike Moseley.* Joe Pike had made it here. Bet the mill kids didn't give *him* the silent treatment. Was it just Trout? Or had something changed? "What is it with you?" he asked.

"What do you mean?"

"Why did you talk to me when nobody else would?"

"I just don't give a damn."

"Oh. Well, that explains it." He turned on his heel and started walking away.

"Where are you going?"

"Dairy Queen."

He was at midfield before she called out again. "My name is Keats." He didn't look back.

There was a huge pecan tree next to the Dairy Queen, and a concrete picnic table underneath. Trout sat on one side with his Blizzard, Joe Pike on the other with a banana split, two extra scoops of strawberry ice cream.

There was an ancient woman at the window of the Dairy Queen. The man behind the counter was watching her, waiting for her order. The woman scanned the big menu in the window carefully, nodding at each item, silently mouthing their names. It had the appearance of a ritual, and she had the appearance of a regular. Trout could imagine her showing up every afternoon about this time, studying the menu at great length, then ordering the very same item. She never changed, and neither did the Dairy Queen menu. There was something comfortably predictable about a Dairy Queen, Trout thought. The menu, the regulars. The old woman. A couple of guys in an ACE PLUMBING truck with a jumble of pipes in the back. And now Joe Pike and Trout. It was their fourth trip to Dairy Queen since Joe Pike had arrived on Saturday. Joe Pike was working steadily through the menu.

"I've got an idea," Joe Pike said.

"Oh?"

"Jumping for Jesus."

"What's that?"

"An exercise class."

"Where?"

"The church. Did you get a good look at the congregation yesterday?"

"Sure."

"What did you notice about them?"

"Older."

"Moribund. If flies had lit on 'em, the flies would have gone to sleep."

The old woman at the Dairy Queen window finished scanning the menu and placed her order. A fifty-cent cup of ice cream with crushed pineapple on top. The man inside already had the cup ready. He handed it out the window, with a red plastic spoon stuck into the glob of pineapple.

Joe Pike sliced off a chunk of banana and strawberry ice cream from his split, lifted it to his mouth, savored it for a long moment, swallowed. "I stood in that pulpit years ago and delivered my first sermon as a kid preacher. You were one year old, fidgeting in your mama's lap. The congregation . . . It dawned on me this morning. Nothing's changed. The same people, give or take a handful, just fifteen years older. Sitting in exactly the same pews. In a church, when nothing changes, when people don't come and go, that's not good."

"Moribund," Trout said.

Joe Pike concentrated for a while on the banana split. Trout finished his Blizzard, took the empty cup to the trash can, returned to the table.

"It needs shaking up," Joe Pike said. "Something to get the older members' blood flowing, get some younger folks into the church."

"Jumping for Jesus."

"It might be the place to start. You like the name?"

"It has a ring to it, I guess."

"Marketing. Folks nowadays are part of the TV generation. You need a catchy phrase to get their attention. It's a little like selling Alka-Seltzer or Pepsi."

Trout thought about all those old folks, knobby knees and blue-veined legs, paunches and spreading behinds, twisting and bouncing in the assembly room of the education building to a strong rock beat. Maybe a little Four Tops. *Sugar pie, honey bunch . . . Ooga-chukka . . . ooga-chukka . . .* And Joe Pike up at the front, leading the pack. Well, that was a stretch. A test of the structural integrity of the building. Joe Pike in one of his Dairy Queen phases.

"How was it?" Joe Pike asked, interrupting the image.

"What?"

"First day at school."

Trout shrugged. "Okay."

"Just 'okay'?"

"No. Strange."

"In what way?"

"Mr. Blaylock said he didn't want any trouble."

"Was there any?"

"No. He said it wasn't a good idea, my being there. Especially now." He gave Joe Pike a long look, waiting. But Joe Pike didn't say anything. He finished off the banana split, placed the plastic spoon in the Styrofoam boat, wiped his mouth with a paper napkin, wadded it up and put it in the boat beside the spoon. "Will there be any Dairy Queens in heave-n-n-n-n?" he sang off-key, then grinned. "I sure hope so. It is one of life's great pleasures, and I can't imagine the Lord running the afterlife without it. How could you have the Sweet By-and-By without Dairy Queen?"

"Mr. Blaylock told me about the football game."

Joe Pike gave him an odd look. "What about it?"

"Twenty-one to twenty."

A cloud passed over Joe Pike's face then. Not so much pain as . . . what? Embarrassment? "What else?"

"That's about it."

"Well, there's not much more to tell. It was just a football game."

Joe Pike got up from the table and took his trash to the garbage can. Trout sat at the table, watching. When Joe Pike turned back to him, Trout said, "Did you know there's not a tennis court in this town?"

"I never thought about it. No, I guess there's not."

"Do you know why there's not a tennis court?"

"No."

"Grandaddy Leland wouldn't let 'em build one. He thought it was . . ." — Trout searched for the word — ". . . frivolous."

"Who told you that?"

"A girl at school. Where am I gonna play tennis if there's not a tennis court?"

Joe Pike sighed wearily. "I don't know, son."

"The State Juniors are coming up. I haven't practiced in more than a week."

"Maybe we can build a backboard at the end of the driveway," Joe Pike said hopefully.

"It's not the same." Trout knew he sounded petulant, but he couldn't help it. No tennis court, nobody to play tennis with. The only person who even acknowledged his existence all day was crippled. And pissed off at Trout's grandfather, to boot. No, make that pissed off at Moseleys in general. But at least she spoke.

"Yea, verily," Joe Pike said. "Out of the mouths of babes. You speak a profound truth, son. A backboard is not a tennis court."

"What's going on here, Daddy?" Trout asked.

Joe Pike pondered that for a moment, then made a little hissing sound through his teeth. "I'm not sure I know, son."

"When you find out, will you tell me?"

"Sure."

"When do you think that'll be?"

"Maybe tomorrow."

"What's tomorrow?"

"That's when we're gonna see Wardell Dubarry."

Trout woke deep in the night with his brain in overdrive — humming like a high-voltage line with the utter strangeness of it, the incredible twist his life had taken.

He thought of Ohatchee. Even with all that had happened there, it seemed so normal by comparison. He had had friends. A girlfriend. He had played tennis almost every day, even in the winter. He had delivered the *Atlanta Constitution* on his bicycle. He had almost lost his virginity.

The memory of it rushed back in a breath-catching, blood-pounding surge of heat. Cynthia Stuckey. A spring afternoon, the sweet smell of photinia blossoms drifting on the breeze through her bedroom window, parents gone. A flash of white thigh, her breast cool in his hand, her breath like hot wind in his ear. Cool and hot. Hot and cool. He had felt faint, as if he were about to be suddenly plucked from obscurity and made famous. And then . . .

He knew now that she had never entertained the slightest thought of letting him into her pants. She had teased him with breast and thigh and sent him home with an ache in his groin that made it difficult to walk upright, probably laughing her ass off as he limped down her front walk. But he had not known it then, not even suspected it. He had followed her around Ohatchee like a drooling puppy, hoping it would happen again. Just getting close, that was something. If he got close, even if he did more than that, he wouldn't tell his friends. Not even Parks Belton. He would be honorable. No smutty talk about Cynthia Stuckey. He was mad for her. A fool, but a fool gladly.

But then the other craziness had swallowed him — Irene, Joe Pike and the motorcycle, Easter Sunday — and Cynthia had dropped him cold, without warning. Not only dropped him, humiliated him.

Maybe it had been her mother, the chairman of the pastor-parish relations committee at Ohatchee Methodist. Or her father, who was on the school board and had voted to ban *Maggie, A Girl of the Streets* from the school library. They were both tight-asses. Maybe it was Cynthia herself. But she could have let him down easy. Instead, she gathered an audience in the hallway outside Plane Geometry the day he returned to school after Joe Pike's Sunday escapade. Trout could tell by the looks on all their faces that they were waiting for something. He touched her sleeve. That was all. Just touched her sleeve. And she spun on him, a nasty little smirk on her face, and said, "Go play with yourself, Trout. Leave me alone."

That had been two weeks ago, and it still made him writhe with embarrassment. And even worse was the fact that the other memory — breast, thigh, hot breath — could still reduce him to a gasping, fist-pumping pulp. To hell with Cynthia Stuckey! His fist was faithful. Always willing. Never an embarrassment.

So now, lying here in his new bedroom in this new parsonage in his strange new life, he kissed his fist and massaged the hot memory of Cynthia Stuckey from his mind, at least temporarily.

That done, he tried to go back to sleep. He would have to drag himself out of bed in the morning and face another day of near invisibility at Moseley High School. And the thought of that made him even more wide-awake. So he got out of bed and went to the front porch with his portable radio, sat in the porch swing, and tuned in the Atlanta oldies station. And thought about his mother.

Irene knew all the songs. The Shirelles, the Supremes, the Everly Brothers . . . *Here he comes . . . it's Cathy's Clown* . . . Elvis, Ruth Brown, Clyde McPhatter, Dee Clark . . . *Raindrops, so many raindrops* . . . Irene in a dishwasherless kitchen, hips swaying to Little Richard as she labored over a suds-filled sink. Joe Pike and Irene doing the Panama City Bop to Sam Cooke, blinds closed against parishioners who might not appreciate a preacher with rhythm. Big Joe Pike and tiny Irene, bear and bird, gliding and twirling. Watching them, Trout laughed and felt oh-so-fine. They taught him the steps, and they all laughed when he invented one of his own. *We're having a party* . . . The music. Keeping the world at bay, the world outside the parsonage. But then the time came when the music didn't work anymore, when Irene's silences grew and grew until they drowned out everything, even the music.

The Atlanta oldies station was playing Brenda Lee now. *I'm sorrreeee . . . so sorrree . . .* He wondered if Irene might be listening over there in Atlanta at the Institute. Did they allow people at the Institute to be up this time of night listening to the radio? Or did some guy come in at nine and give you a pill? Could you live in the past if you wanted? Or did some therapist keep insisting, "Now! Now!"

Was she lonely? There didn't seem to be much opportunity for company. Joe Pike and Trout were being held at arm's length for the moment. And the Troutmans, her own family back in Texas, were all gone except for some distant cousins. She was the antithesis of Joe Pike. She had no family to speak of. He had too much.

There was so much Trout needed to know from her. And about her. Her silences, and now her absence, had made her a stranger. When he finally got a chance to talk to her, would she know him? Would he know her? And would he even know which questions to ask?

The music drifted out of the radio, hung suspended in the hot quiet of the porch, and settled in that big hollow place somewhere between his stomach and his heart that Trout figured must be his soul.

I'm not gonna cry. Dammit, I'm not. You're not gonna make me cry, God!

But he did, while Brenda Lee sang.

And when she had finished and he had wiped away his hot tears, he looked across the street at Aunt Alma's darkened house. And he saw the light in the window of the garage apartment out back. Uncle Phinizy.

FIVE

THE GARAGE WAS at the back of the deep lot behind Aunt Alma's house, almost hidden from the house itself by pecan trees and a cane thicket, reached by a gravel driveway that curved around the edge of the lot from the porte cochere. There were three open garage bays on the ground floor. In the light of the half-moon, Trout could see the dim outline of lawn equipment and old bicycles in one bay. The other two were empty. The upstairs apartment had two dormers peeking from the roofline, open to the night air. In one of the windows, a light was on. Trout climbed the narrow outside stairs, hesitated for a moment on the small landing, knocked.

"Door's open, Trout."

He pushed the door open and looked inside. Phinizy was sitting deep in a Naugahyde recliner, legs up, floor lamp on at his shoulder, book in one hand, half-smoked cigarette between two fingers of the other. On the table at his elbow were a half-empty whiskey glass and an ashtray overflowing with cigarette butts. Phinizy marked his place in the book with his finger and closed it. He looked up at Trout, studying him. He took a deep drag on his cigarette and released a double stream of smoke through his nostrils that kept coming and coming, the streams breaking apart and curling back around his head, then disappearing as wisps of bluish haze into the lampshade. Trout stared. All that smoke coming out of this little bitty old man. Finally it ended and Phinizy said, "Well, don't just stand there. You'll let all the flies out."

Phinizy reminded him of a shriveled, wizened gnome from one of the folk tales Irene had read to him when he was a small child — leathery skin, beaked nose, gnarled hands. An ancient wreck of a man. But there was something else — a lively snap to the blue eyes, an odd way he cocked his head as if listening for some faint signal. An air of . . . what? Expectation?

"I saw your light on," Trout said, closing the door behind him. "How did you know it was me?"

"Well, Joe Pike left about an hour ago. And Cicero was here a little before that. I figured it was either you or Banquo's ghost."

"Who?"

"Haven't you read Shakespeare?"

"Yes sir. A little."

"Hmmmm. Yes sir. A young'un who says, 'Yes, sir.'"

"My mama taught me," Trout said.

"Ah, yes. Your mama."

"Why was Daddy here?"

"Same reason Cicero was. Same reason you are."

"Why is that?"

"You all think I know something."

"Do you?"

"Not much. Want a drink?" Trout looked at the whiskey glass. "I've got some ginger ale," Phinizy said. "Nobody around here drinks whiskey but me. It'd probably help Cicero and Joe Pike both if they'd tie on a good one every once in a while. But a man's got his obligations, I guess."

Phinizy turned down a corner of the page in his book and placed it on the table. Suddenly, he reached down and yanked the lever on the side of the recliner and sort of catapulted out of it — surprising Trout with the quick movement, the way he bounced on the balls of his feet, catlike — and disappeared through the door to the kitchen, flipping on the light as he went. Then Trout remembered. Rumpelstiltskin. The folk tale. A funny little man, a beautiful girl, gold spun from flax. Trout was struck again by a powerful sense of his mother. He could smell her, feel her. They nestled together on a sofa, the book with the curious illustrations open before them, the rise and fall of her voice reaching deep inside him. *And the little man stamped his foot . . .* It was so immediate, so real, it almost took his breath. Even more than the music from the oldies station.

He heard Phinizy in the kitchen, the tinkle of ice cubes in a glass. He looked around at the room. It was sparsely furnished: recliner, rickety breakfast table with two ladder-back chairs, an ancient sofa. The walls were bare except for one faded picture, an old lithograph — a man and a woman in a rowboat on a lake. He sat down on the sofa and waited.

Phinizy came back in a moment with Trout's ginger ale and a fresh drink for himself. He sat down again in the recliner, lit another cigarette, took a long sucking drag and let the smoke out lovingly, playing with it. Trout took a sip of his ginger ale. It was a little flat. Phinizy probably didn't drink much ginger ale.

"My father built this place," Phinizy said, looking about the room. "He hired a woman from Baltimore to come down here and teach Leland and me the social graces. She was young and rather attractive, and it wouldn't do to have her living in the big house. Father was very big on appearances. So he built this. Called it the guest house." Phinizy took a long pull on his whiskey, held up the glass for a moment and swirled the whiskey and ice around, squinting at it. Then he looked over the top of the glass at Trout. "If you can't hold up your end of the conversation, just say so. I'll try to go it alone."

Trout gave him a blank look.

"Either a question or a statement will be fine, as long as it has some remote connection to what has previously been said. The object here is to generally advance the topic."

"Well, ahhhh . . ."

"That'll do for starters. So, you ask, What am I doing here? Well, why not? I may have spent most of my life in exile, but I remain an heir to Broadus Moseley's vast fortune. I am content to let Alma run it. All I ask is this" — a grand sweep of his arm took in the apartment — "modest abode. I am content to live in the shadow of the big house and bask in its reflected glory."

Trout took another sip of the ginger ale. "Daddy said you've been away for a long time. Why did you come back now?" he ventured.

Phinizy thought about that for a moment. Then he said, "Tell you a joke. Two guys going to truck driving school. Joe and Charlie. Instructor's giving 'em a final oral examination. He says to Joe, 'Hypothetical situation, Joe. You're driving, Charlie's behind you up in the bunk asleep. You're going down a steep two-lane mountain road. Car just ahead in your lane. You suddenly discover your brakes are shot. You're coming up fast behind this car, so you pull out into the other lane. You're going faster and faster. All of a sudden another truck rounds a curve coming *up* the mountain right toward you. Whatcha gonna do, Joe?' And Joe says, 'I'm gonna wake up Charlie.' Instructor says, 'Why you gonna do that?' Joe says, ''Cause Charlie ain't never seen a real bad wreck before.'"

Trout laughed. But Phinizy didn't crack a smile. Trout felt stupid. And he thought that Phinizy was one strange duck. Finally he said, "Is there gonna be a wreck?"

"Ask you a question," Phinizy said. "Are you an optimist or a pessimist?"

Trout thought about that for a moment. "I'm just trying to get through adolescence," he said.

"Ask you another question. Are you a skeptic or a cynic?"

"What's the difference?"

"A skeptic asks questions. A cynic doesn't bother."

"I guess I'm a skeptic, then. What are you?"

Phinizy took a deep pull on the cigarette and held the smoke for a long time, then suddenly started coughing, blasting the smoke from his lungs. He bent double in the chair, shriveled body wracked with deep, wretched spasms. Trout started to get up, alarmed. Phinizy waved him away. The coughing went on for a long time before Phinizy finally began to get it under control. He sat there awhile longer, taking shallow, tentative breaths. He stared at the cigarette still clutched between two fingers, took a defiant drag from it and stubbed it into the pile in the ashtray.

"You oughta quit that," Trout said.

"No," Phinizy said, "I should have quit sixty years ago, right after I started. I was ten years old when I took my first drag off a coffin nail." He took a big drink of whiskey. And then he took off his glasses, pulled a handkerchief out of a pants pocket and wiped his watery eyes. Stuffed the handkerchief back in his pocket. Looked up, finally, at Trout. "Mark Twain used to say the reason he smoked was to have at least one bad habit in reserve, so he'd have something to give up in case of doctor's orders. It's as good an excuse as any, I suppose."

They both sat there in silence awhile, Trout staring at the floor, not knowing what to say.

"You're looking for some answers," Phinizy said quietly.

Trout looked up and shrugged. He didn't even know where to begin. "This place is weird," he said, making a vague gesture that took in town, school, mill, church, and house. And all that had transpired and been said since he arrived. "In school yesterday — nobody spoke to me but this one kid. And the principal said something about not having any trouble. And everybody seems to be ticked off about the Moseleys. But if Aunt Alma knows they're ticked off, she doesn't let on. She just sounds like she's preaching a sermon all the time. Moseley this and Moseley that. You'd think it was a religion or something."

"Did you ask Joe Pike?"

"Yes sir. He said something's going on, but he doesn't know what."

"Well, I don't either," Phinizy said. "I don't have any answers. But I know some history. And I've been around long enough to know that sometimes that's where you find some clues. You want to hear some history?"

"Yes sir."

And that was when Phinizy told him about Moseley, Georgia. About how Broadus Moseley created the town, lifted it up out of red clay and desperation and put his indelible mark upon it. And how he and his heirs, down to the present, claimed it as inviolable territory — a permanent and unchangeable shrine to its creator. It was, for Trout, an initiation into mystery — like Joe Pike in the pulpit, letting the big leather Bible fall open where it wished, reading at random a few verses of profound truth. Clues, portents, an intimation of all the rest. In it, an echo of Aunt Alma's voice: *Don't ever forget who you are.* He knew there was a great deal more, unseen and unknown. But it was a start.

There was the other, of course — the mystery of Joe Pike and Irene Moseley, of silences and escapes, the Institute and the motorcycle. The *why.* But Trout wasn't ready to get into all that with Great Uncle Phinizy. It was a private, personal mystery, and for the time being he would try to puzzle out that one for himself. Later, maybe . . .

And besides, when Phinizy had finished telling him about the town and his forebears, dawn was at the window.

Joe Pike was waiting behind the wheel of the car at the curb in front of the high school at midafternoon, arm slung out the open window. "You look like death warmed over," he said when Trout climbed in.

"I want to go home and go to bed," Trout said. He felt terrible —

drained, stupid with fatigue. All the air seemed to have leaked out of his lungs and puddled somewhere in the pit of his stomach.

Joe Pike started the car. "We've got a stop to make first. How'd it go today?"

"About the same. Where are we going?"

"I told you. To see Wardell Dubarry."

It was the first time Trout had ever been to the mill village. There had never been a reason. And there wasn't much to see. Just past the mill the road curved and the pavement ended and became dirt and gravel, lined on either side by houses, each exactly like its neighbor — white clapboard box on low brick piers, small porch, steep tin roof, door and two windows across the front, red-brick chimney on the right side, short gravel driveway along the left. Patches of grass were neatly trimmed at a uniform height, as if somebody had mowed them all at once. A few trees, an occasional shrub. Here and there, an attempt at individuality — a fern hanging at the edge of a porch, a splash of bright curtain at a window. But it was no match for the overwhelming sameness of the place.

"Why did they build 'em all the same?" he asked Joe Pike.

"They didn't build 'em. Grandaddy Broadus did."

Trout stared, thinking of all Phinizy had told him in the early-morning hours. History. At dawn, when he had finally gotten up to go, Phinizy had said, "Before you can know who you are, you have to know where you came from. Especially you. It's all there, Trout. Go take a good look at it. Then come back and tell me what you saw." The man talked in riddles. Or maybe, Trout thought now as they eased along the mill village street, gravel crunching under the tires, Phinizy just pointed out the riddles.

"They're all white," Trout said.

Joe Pike looked at the houses for a moment. "They get painted every other year whether they need it or not."

"Why?"

Joe Pike shrugged. "Because that's just the way it's always been done."

"Well, why don't they paint 'em something different?"

"Who?"

"The people who live in 'em."

"They don't own 'em."

"Who does?"

Joe Pike squinted at him. "They're mill houses, Trout. The mill built 'em. The mill owns 'em. The mill maintains 'em. Paints, cuts the grass, repairs the roof. Toilet gets stopped up, you call the mill."

"The mill," Trout repeated. "You and Aunt Alma."

Joe Pike shrugged. "I guess so. And you and Eugene and Phin and anybody else who has a stake in the business."

"Uncle Phin didn't tell me that."

"Phin?"

"He had a busy night last night."

Trout stared again at the houses, one after another. Beyond this street, on either side, he could see two more. There must be a hundred houses here. It reminded Trout of the long rows of looms inside the mill.

Then Joe Pike turned in one of the gravel driveways, just behind a faded red Ford, about the same vintage as Joe Pike's Dodge. The rear end was on jacks, hiked up in the air. A pair of legs stuck out from underneath. Faded jeans, almost white with age and washings. Dirty off-brand jogging shoes. No socks. Joe Pike and Trout got out of their car and walked over to the Ford.

"Hello, Wardell," Joe Pike said.

"Hello yourself, Joe Pike," the legs said back. Joe Pike and Trout stood there for a good while. From underneath the car, a clank of metal against metal. Then, "Shit." More clanking.

"Anything I can do to help?" Joe Pike volunteered.

"It ain't a motorcycle, Joe Pike." There was something about the voice that reminded Trout of fruit left on a tree too long, beginning to spoil.

More clanking. "Are you gonna come out and say hello?" Joe Pike finally asked.

"Depends."

"On what?"

"Whether Alma sent you or you come on your own."

"Well, a little of both."

A couple more clanks and then the legs began to wiggle out from under the car. And just kept coming. There was a great deal of Wardell Dubarry, at least lengthwise. When he finally stood up, wiping his hands on a greasy cloth, there was about six feet eight of him, incredibly thin with scarecrow arms and a head that looked like it had been

mashed sideways in a vise — great expanse of forehead, long sweeping jaw, deep-set eyes, unruly shock of gray-black hair.

"There ain't even a goddamn auto parts store in this town," Wardell
said. His voice was a deep, thick drawl, slow like a creek with little
eddies in it where it eased around rocks and roots. Trout stared up at
him, craning his neck. Wardell looked him over.

"This is Trout," Joe Pike said.

Wardell grunted. Trout realized his mouth was open, closed it.
Then Wardell turned to Joe Pike and gave him a long look. "Joe Pike,
you are one big hunk of preacher."

Joe Pike stuck out his hand. "How are you, Wardell?"

It was quick, barely a handshake. "I been better, I been worse."

"It's been a long time," Joe Pike said.

"It's been thirteen years since I laid eyes on you, Joe Pike. This
young'un here" — he gave a nod at Trout — "was still peeing in his
pants."

"Well, he's dry as a bone. And I'm back."

"And cut a deep furrow gettin' here, from what I hear." Wardell gave
a little twist to his mouth, not quite a smile. "How was Texas?"

Joe Pike folded his big arms over his chest. "Which time?"

"Either."

"About the same."

They just stood and looked at each other for a moment. Trout tried
to imagine them playing football together, about the same age as he
was now. Echoes. The driver's license examiner in Ohatchee: *They
near about killed our quarterback* . . . The trophy in Mr. Blaylock's
office at Moseley High: *Damnedest football game in history.* Now here
they were, middle-aged men, one gone to fat and the other to towering emaciation. But yet, oddly enough, almost young in each other's
presence. A bit of teenage swagger, the way they held themselves —
Joe Pike sucking in his massive gut, Wardell standing good and
straight. But there was something wary about both of them, too. They
stood a little back from each other now. Had they been rivals in some
way, back there at Moseley High School? Had they fought over a girl?
Thrown down a great dare? Trout realized with a jolt that Wardell
Dubarry was the first person he had ever met, outside the family, who
shared some sort of history with Joe Pike Moseley. But what of it?

"How's your family?" Joe Pike asked finally.

"Mostly growed," Wardell said. "Darrell's in the Army. Wardell Junior lives in New Orleans, works the oil rigs in the Gulf. Just me and Sue and the girl now."

"That's what you get marrying young," Joe Pike said.

Wardell looked at him for a long moment. "Wadn't nothing else to do. Get a job at the mill, get married. Go to work, raise kids." Something very close to anger there, Trout thought. But it was hard to tell. The drawl covered up a lot, like a coating of thick oil.

Joe Pike uncrossed his arms and stuck his hands in his pockets. "Yeah. I reckon."

They stood there a moment longer looking at each other and then Wardell turned to Trout. "My young'un's in the house. Go on up and say hello. Let me and your daddy talk, since he come on bidness." He indicated the house with a jerk of his head.

Trout looked up at the house, and then he saw her standing at the window, looking out at them.

"Her name's Keats," Wardell said.

"Yes sir."

"Why didn't you say something?" he asked after she had let him in the door.

"Say what?" She stood in the middle of the room, balanced on her crutches. She was wearing a Dairy Queen uniform — red jacket, white cap.

"Your daddy and my daddy . . ."

"So?"

"They went to high school together. They played football."

"So?"

"They played *The Game*."

If it meant a thing to her, she didn't let on. But then, Trout thought, she wasn't the one looking for answers. She seemed to know everything she needed to know. "How old are you?" he asked.

"None of your business."

"So?"

"Eighteen," she said. "Are you just gonna stand there all day? Sit down."

He looked around, spotted an overstuffed chair next to the front window, and sat down in it. She eased herself down on a sofa and laid her crutches on the floor beside her with a clatter. "You asked me if I'm pissed off because I'm crippled," she said. "I thought about that. I woke up in the middle of the night thinking about it. I haven't waked up in the middle of the night thinking about anything for a long time. Do I act like I'm pissed off?"

"You're . . . abrupt."

They sat there in silence for a moment. Trout looked about the room. It was small and cramped, just enough room for the sofa and overstuffed chair, a television set, a knickknack stand filled mostly with small framed photographs. A young man in uniform, another in cap and gown, a school photo of Keats in about the fifth grade, a snapshot of the whole family at a picnic table — Keats, about the same age as the school photo, crutches propped next to her on the bench. On the bottom shelf, a stack of library books. On the spine of one he could make out *Quo Vadis?* The fireplace had been bricked up and an oil heater stood on the hearth, vented with a flue that disappeared into the brickwork. There was an air conditioner mounted in a window next to the fireplace, but it wasn't on. On the opposite side of the room, a closed door. A bedroom, maybe. And through an open doorway at the back, he could see a small kitchen — sink, counter, refrigerator, cabinets, a chrome-and-Formica breakfast table. It was neat, everything spotless. A woman lived here.

"Is your mother home?"

"She works first shift." Trout gave her a blank look. "At the mill." Another blank look. "You know about shifts?"

"No."

"Good God. Your family owns the place."

"Look," he said irritably, "I've been here four days. I've only been in the mill one time in my life, and that was last Saturday." He had forgotten his fatigue for a while, but he could feel its ragged edge wearing at him again. He really ought to go home and go to bed. He looked out the window. Joe Pike and Wardell Dubarry were engaged in heated conversation next to the Ford. Wardell was waving his arms. Joe Pike stood there, red-faced, hands jammed in his pockets.

"The mill has two shifts," Keats said. He turned back to her. "It used to have three. First shift, eight in the morning until four in the afternoon. Second shift, four till midnight. Third shift, midnight till eight. They cut out third shift a couple of years ago. There wasn't enough work. They laid a lot of people off. Those that hung on to their jobs were glad to have 'em."

Trout looked at his watch. Three-thirty. "Your mother works first shift."

"Yeah. And Daddy works second. About the time Mama gets home, Daddy's going to work."

"Why do they do that?"

Keats snorted angrily, "Ask your Aunt Alma. It was her doing."

Trout didn't want to talk about Aunt Alma. So he said, "And you work at Dairy Queen."

Keats got up suddenly with a clatter of crutches. "Not if I don't get my fanny on over there." She headed toward the door, and Trout jumped up from his chair to open it for her. "Don't you dare!" she snapped.

He stopped in his tracks, stared at her, felt the anger scurrying up the back of his neck, whispering in his ear. "Yeah," he snapped back. "You're pissed, all right. You're not just abrupt, you're mad as hell about something. I bet you come home after school and beat your gerbil." He stepped in front of her, opened the door, walked out on the porch, left the door open behind him, stood at the edge of the porch smoldering.

Down in the yard, Wardell Dubarry was saying to Joe Pike, "I am damned tired of regimentation and standardization, Joe Pike!"

"Regimentation and standardization?"

"Ever'body's gotta think alike, act alike, kiss ass alike!" He waved his arms at the house. "Ever'body's *house* gotta look alike, for God's sake! Hell, I oughta paint the place red! And go over yonder and paint Dooley Bledsoe's house blue! And Faye Looney's pink!"

"Fine!" Joe Pike finally exploded. "Paint 'em! I'm not gonna get in the middle of all this, Wardell!"

And Wardell was saying to Joe Pike, "You're already in the middle of it, Joe Pike!"

Then Keats was standing next to him on the porch. "Daddy . . . ," she said. Wardell broke off and looked up at her, and all the anger went out of him. "I got to be at work in fifteen minutes," she said. "Darnella quit and Herschel says I got to be in early."

"Sugar, the car ain't fixed yet."

"Daddyyyy . . . ," her voice rose.

"We'll take her," Joe Pike said.

Wardell gave him a sharp look. "I'll get her a ride."

"Look, it's my fault your car's not ready. It's no trouble."

"No thank you, Joe Pike," Wardell said stubbornly.

Then Keats clambered down the steps, crutches and legs flailing, and the rest of them just watched. It was amazing. She careened off toward Joe Pike's Dodge. "I'm gonna ride with Reverend Moseley, Daddy," she shot back over her shoulder. "Y'all could stand there jawing all day, and I'd be out of a job. Herschel doesn't care how I get there. I can't see why you do."

Wardell Dubarry did a slow burn, but there didn't seem to be much he could do about it. Keats reached the Dodge, opened the front door, threw her crutches inside, vaulted into the seat, slammed the door behind her.

Trout walked down the steps, giving Joe Pike and Wardell a wide berth, and waited by the car for a moment; then he got in the back seat and rolled down the window. Keats didn't look at him.

Out in the yard, the two men stood glaring at each other. Trout wondered what he would do if they started fighting. Call Uncle Cicero? But the mill village wasn't even in the city limits. Never had been, never would be. As Phinizy had told him, Broadus Moseley had seen to that. *Maybe, if it comes to blows, I'll just lean over the seat and start honking the horn.* Or he might just let them go at it for a while. It might be a pretty good match. Joe Pike had a sizable weight advantage, but Wardell Dubarry looked a good deal faster. And he had long arms. But somehow, he couldn't imagine Joe Pike fighting. For his size and history, he was a gentle man. Wardell Dubarry — now there was a different story. He looked like he might fight you at the drop of a hat. Wardell Dubarry, in fact, looked downright nasty.

But they didn't fight. After a moment, Trout heard Joe Pike say, "Wardell, I can't help it if my name's Moseley. Call it a genetic defect if you want." Wardell just glared at him. So Joe Pike shrugged, turned on his heel, and got in the car.

They were halfway to the Dairy Queen before anybody said anything. Joe Pike said, "That's what I want to do when I grow up."

Keats gave him a strange look. "What?"

"Work at Dairy Queen." They rode on in silence a while longer. "Actually, I've always thought of Dairy Queen as a sort of religious experience. Anything that's good for the soul, that's a religious experience. And the taste of a spoonful of ice cream sliding down your throat is good for the soul. It may be what they had in mind when they talked about the Rapture."

"What's your favorite?" Keats asked.

"Oh, just the plain old vanilla. But I hasten to add there is not a loser on the menu. Sometimes I like a little crushed pineapple sundae or a chocolate shake. If you want to talk about a three-course meal, I'll go for two foot-long chili dogs and a banana split."

"Actually, the Blizzard is my favorite. Only sometimes I juice it up a little bit with some extra nuts or maybe even a splotch of butterscotch. You like butterscotch?"

"Yes ma'am," Joe Pike said. "I do dearly love butterscotch. Especially from Dairy Queen."

Good grief, Trout thought. *This is ridiculous. To hell with both of them.* And he put his head down on the seat and went to sleep.

Joe Pike banged on his door at six the next morning. "Trout, time to roll out."

"I'm not going," Trout said.

There was a long silence and then Joe Pike said, "Can I come in?" Joe Pike and Irene had both been good about that, asking before they entered. Especially the last few years. You never knew what a teenage boy might be doing alone in his room. But even if he wasn't doing anything he wouldn't want you to barge in on, it was his space. They both seemed to understand that. In fact, Joe Pike had said to him a couple of years ago, "Whatever you're doing in there, it's okay. You can't do it too much: you won't go blind, you won't grow black hairs on the palm of your hand. Later on, you'll move on to other things. When you're ready to do that, you come talk to me." It was the closest they had ever come to a birds-and-bees talk. It was enough for the time being. It had eased Trout's mind considerably. But later, when it seemed he might get into Cynthia Stuckey's pants, he didn't go talk to Joe Pike. It just didn't seem the thing to do.

"Come on in," Trout said now, "But I'm not going."

Joe Pike eased open the door and peeked into the room. Trout sat up in bed.

"Why aren't you going? Are you sick?"

Trout thought for a moment. "It's a holiday."

"What holiday?"

"Confederate Memorial Day."

Joe Pike shook his head. "Confederate Memorial Day was last month."

"But we didn't celebrate it."

Outside the open window, they heard a lawn mower start up. Joe Pike walked over to the window and looked out. "Morning," he called to whomever was outside. "Can I help you?"

"Miz Alma sent me," said a man's voice.

"That's quite all right," Joe Pike called out. "You tell Miz Alma I cut my own grass." The lawn mower engine coughed and died. "But I really appreciate it," Joe Pike said. "God bless you. And Miz Alma."

He closed the window. "I think we'll turn the air on today. Radio said it's gonna get up to ninety. And ain't even June yet. Of course, that's Atlanta. I was listening to the Atlanta station. Always hotter in Atlanta because of all that concrete. But still . . ." his voice trailed off. He stood next to Trout's bed. "So?"

"I'll stay home and cut the grass," Trout said.

"How about school?"

"I've enjoyed about all of Moseley High School I can stand for one year," Trout said.

"Two days?"

"There's only three left. School's out Friday."

Joe Pike shrugged. "I guess I'm thinking of the principle of the thing. I always like to see a fellow finish what he starts."

"Well, I'm finished," Trout said.

"Hmmmm. Well, come on and eat breakfast. It's on the table. We'll talk about it."

Joe Pike had fixed scrambled eggs, instant grits, slightly burned toast. It was a modest improvement. For a while after they took Irene away, the toast was inedible, the instant grits were watery, the eggs lumpy. So Trout had taken over cooking breakfast. Joe Pike seemed not to notice. He was working on the motorcycle at the time, and there was a lot he didn't notice.

Trout smeared blackberry jelly on the toast, and when he took the first bite, he discovered he was ravenous. He had gone straight to bed after they got home the previous afternoon and slept through the night. Now he cleaned his plate in silence. Joe Pike fixed him two more pieces of toast and he ate those and finally sat back in his chair.

"Is it that bad?"

"It was pretty good."

"No. I mean school."

Trout thought about it for a moment. "Nobody talks to me. They look straight through me, like I'm not there. Everybody but Keats Dubarry."

"Why Keats?"

"I think she thinks I'm some sort of freak. I don't know. She's weird. She's mad at the world."

"Hmmmm. I guess she comes by it honest."

"What's her daddy mad at?"

"The Moseleys. Life. Lack of an auto parts store."

"Was he always that way?"

"Pretty much. It made him a fairly decent football player. Wardell always acted like somebody was trying to take something away from him. He'd fight you. Wardell played left end and I played right tackle. Run one way, there was Wardell. Run the other, there was me. We did some damage."

"Were you friends?"

"I always thought so. With Wardell, it was hard to tell sometimes."

"Did he play football in college?"

"No. Actually, Wardell had an offer. Partial scholarship at a little junior college in Mississippi. But he didn't take it."

"Why not?" Trout asked.

"I don't know. 'Cause he's Wardell, I guess."

"What were you arguing about yesterday?"

Joe Pike's face clouded. "Nothing you need to worry about, son."

"Stop it!" Trout shouted before he could catch himself. Joe Pike's mouth dropped open. Trout couldn't ever remember yelling at his father before. He ducked his head and stared at his plate. But the anger didn't go away. It was a new thing, this anger. Strange and a bit frightening. And it seemed to insist on taking up residence.

"Trout?"

"You won't *talk* to me. Nobody *talks* to me. Nobody *tells* me anything. You all talk in riddles. You tell me what I oughta do, what I oughta think, how I oughta act. But you don't tell me why!" He looked up. "Why? What's going on here?"

Joe Pike took a long time to answer. Trout could see him wrestling with himself, and he realized that there was a lot maybe even Joe Pike didn't know. But dang it, he could tell him what he did know!

Finally, Joe Pike said, "There's trouble at the mill."

"I know that. Aunt Alma said so at dinner Sunday."

"To hear Wardell tell it, they're all riled up over there. Pay's abysmal; they think some of the working conditions are unsafe. Folks working off the clock —"

"What's that?"

"Everybody has a time card. You punch it when you go to work, again when you leave. They call it 'clocking in' and 'clocking out.' Only, some folks clock out and then have to turn around and go right back to work for another hour or so."

"Without getting paid?"

"Yes."

"Isn't that illegal?"

"Yes."

"Why do they do it?"

"Word gets around. Want to keep your job, you put in a few extra hours."

"What does Mister Dubarry want you to do about it?"

"Stop it."

"Can you?"

Joe Pike ran his fingers through his hair, wiggled his head from side to side for a moment, and looked out the kitchen window at the church building next door. Then back at Trout. "I don't run the mill. Alma does."

Then Trout said quietly, "But you're a Moseley."

"Yes."

"Mister Dubarry said you're in the middle whether you like it or not."

"Yes. That's what Wardell said."

They sat there awhile pondering that. And then Joe Pike said emphatically, "I don't need this. I just damned well don't need this."

"Are you sorry we came?"

"We didn't really have much of a choice, Trout."

"Because the Bishop said so?"

"Partly. Circumstances, you know . . ." He waved in the general direction of the storage shed out back. The motorcycle. All it represented.

"What happened in the game?" Trout asked.

"You mean *The Game?*"

"Yes. The extra point."

Joe Pike looked out the window, brows knitted, thinking back. "I fell down," he said finally.

"Fell down?"

Joe Pike looked back at him. "We scored with thirty seconds to go. Twenty-one to twenty. Coach Blaylock sent in twenty-five slant smash for the extra point."

"What's that?"

"A play. Quarterback hands the ball off to the left halfback, he slants across and runs behind the right tackle."

"Why didn't you kick the extra point?"

"In 1953 in Georgia high-school football, kicking an extra point was considered sissy."

"Why do they call the play 'smash'?"

A flicker of a smile played around the corners of Joe Pike's mouth. "Because I'm the right tackle and I'm the biggest, meanest sonofabitch on the line of scrimmage."

Trout was taken aback. He had never heard Joe Pike use the word before. But this was Joe Pike the football player, a person from the past, long before preaching, long before Trout. "And you . . ."

"Fell down. My feet got tangled up and I just fell flat on my face. The halfback climbed clear up my back, but he couldn't get over the top. Linebacker nailed him. Didn't gain an inch."

Trout thought about Orzell Blaylock, sitting there in the principal's office with the trophy gathering dust behind him on the air conditioner. Runner-up. "I think Mister Blaylock's still mad about it."

"I imagine they all are," Joe Pike said. "For most folks, it was the biggest thing that ever happened here, being in the state championship game. But for a Moseley, it might not be such a big deal, you see. The only Moseley in the whole stadium was me. I fell down, but I got up and went on with my life. Went places and saw things. Rest of 'em . . . well, they just stayed here."

"Didn't your mama and daddy come to the game?"

"No."

They sat there and mulled it over in silence. There didn't seem to be much more to say. Then Joe Pike heaved himself up out of his chair with a grunt and busied himself, stacking the breakfast dishes, carrying them to the sink where he added them to a growing pile. Aunt Alma had installed a brand-new dishwasher in the kitchen, but Joe Pike was wary of it. A man who could take apart a motorcycle and put it back together, buffaloed by a dishwasher. He turned to Trout, leaned against the counter. "So, what are we going to do about this incipient rebellion?"

"What?"

"Your refusing to go to school."

Trout shrugged.

"You want me to tell you something? Okay, I'll tell you something I've never told you before." Trout sat quietly, waiting. "You've surprised me, Trout. You were a terror as a little kid. Always into something. Testing the limits. When you were two, we used to sit down at the table for a meal and I'd say, 'Okay, Trout, turn over your milk so we can get started.' And you would. Or maybe you wouldn't. Just sit there and scrunch up your face and look at me." Joe Pike smiled, remembering. "I used to think, this is going to be one pain-in-the-butt teenager. But then all of a sudden you seemed to get over it. And the older you got, the easier you were to handle. It was like the hormones worked in reverse on you. You sort of mellowed out. "

Mellowed out? Damn, he really missed that one. There was no mellowing about it. If anything, just the opposite. There was that point a few years before when he had become aware of the growing tension in the house — of disappointment, dissatisfaction, even anger. He could *feel* it. And he began to feel it at approximately the same time he began to stumble into puberty. The two, he assumed, must at least in some part be connected — a noisy, messy, awkward kid underfoot, body changing alarmingly, voice squeaking, moods swinging wildly. Maybe they had taken a look at him one day and said to themselves, *What is going on here? We wanted a kid, but this little gawky freak?* He wanted to ask questions, but Irene was so quiet and distant, Joe Pike so preoccupied, he didn't know how to approach them. So he did the only thing he could think of. He tried to be good. He picked up his clothes, kept his room reasonably clean, tried not to slam doors or complain about the steady diet of oldies on the radio. When he had a wet dream, he was careful to wash out his pajamas in the bathroom lavatory before he put them in the laundry hamper. He even tried to like math and rutabagas. He was sure, somehow, that if he were truly good, if he made no mess and caused no uproar or embarrassment, Irene would get better and Joe Pike would come to himself and things would be right again. Instead, the silences deepened. So he tried harder than ever. And the harder he tried, the more the silences deepened until finally they took Irene away and left the great emptiness, left Trout baffled and exhausted. No matter how hard he had tried, it wasn't enough. But by then, he had formed the habit of being desperately good. He didn't quite know how to go about being bad. Marijuana made him throw up. Girls with bad reputations scared the hell out of him. The one time he would have willingly sinned, ached to sin, Cynthia Stuckey had stopped him. He was quite sick of all this goodness, but he felt trapped. And too, he was still a preacher's kid and that carried a certain aloneness with it. There was still Joe Pike to think of. But mellow? Horseshit.

"Your mother and I got real worried a couple of years ago," Joe Pike said. "We thought maybe you were on drugs."

"Drugs?"

"Did you ever mess around with drugs?"

"Well . . ." He shrugged, feeling both uncomfortable and irritated. This wasn't what he wanted — a psychoanalysis or a counseling session. He simply wanted to know what was going on. "I'm a preacher's kid," he said.

"Not easy, I know," Joe Pike said. "Not easy being a preacher, either, but at least I've got a pulpit to stand behind."

"Yeah. I guess."

"Well, anyway, we decided you weren't on drugs. You'd just gotten easy to deal with. We decided not to worry about it. Don't look a gift horse in the mouth, you know. But now . . ." He waved his hands and his voice rose dramatically. "Here we have rank disobedience. Open defiance. Rebellion! Anarchy! Domestic chaos!"

Trout considered it for a moment. He gave Joe Pike a careful look. "Why don't you punish me," he said.

"How?"

"Make me learn to ride the motorcycle."

They headed out U.S. 278 toward Atlanta about five miles, Joe Pike wearing his cowboy boots and a battered white helmet that made him look something like the Texas A&M football picture in his church study. Trout rode behind — bareheaded because there was only the one helmet, several sizes too big for him — holding on and craning his neck to see around Joe Pike's bulk. They turned onto a paved rural road, went another mile or so, and pulled off beneath a big oak tree in the bare yard of an abandoned farmhouse. It was a weathered, windowless ghost of a place with a high, sagging porch, vines creeping up the rock chimney, a riot of weeds around the sides and back of the house.

Joe Pike killed the engine. Trout slid off the back of the motorcycle; then Joe Pike let down the kickstand and got off and took off the helmet and tucked it under his arm. Trout climbed onto the seat, put his hands on the handlebars, gripped them, wiggled his fanny. It leaned to the left on the kickstand, so he put his feet on the ground and eased it upright. The cycle felt massive between his legs, warm leather and chrome, heat baking off the engine. He felt a vague stirring in his groin. *Gee. It's like . . .*

"A woman," Joe Pike said. Trout's ears reddened. He looked up at Joe Pike, who wiggled his eyebrows. Then he looked away, across the road to where rows of new corn were pushing up through the brown loam of a plowed field. It struck Trout. *It's been four months. No sounds behind the closed door late at night. What does he . . .* Trout's ears felt as if they might burst into flame.

"Start 'er up," Joe Pike said. He pointed. "Turn the key. Now, that pedal there is the starter. Stomp down on it." Trout stomped. The pedal barely moved. The engine coughed. "You're kinda light. Sort of jump on it." Trout stomped again, using the weight of his body, and the engine fired. "Now a little gas. That's the throttle over there." He goosed the throttle, the way he had seen Joe Pike do. The cycle vibrated under him, through him.

Joe Pike showed him the clutch and brake levers, the gearshift. Neutral and three forward gears. "Ready?"

Trout took a deep breath. It was a little scary. "I guess."

"Kickstand up." Joe Pike used the toe of his cowboy boot to raise the kickstand. "Okay. It's in neutral. Clutch lever in, drop it down into first gear." Trout heard a click as the gear engaged. "Now, it's just like driving a straight-stick car, except you got two wheels instead of four. Give it some throttle as you let the clutch out." Clutch and throttle. He raced the engine a bit, released the clutch. Too quick. The bike jumped a couple of feet, died, started falling to the left. Whoa! Trout struggled, toppling, losing it, panic racing through him. But then Joe Pike dropped the helmet and grabbed the cycle, wrestled it with his powerful arms like a cowboy bulldogging a steer and steadied it. "Okay?"

Trout's heart was pounding in his ears. "I guess."

"Want to call it a day? Try it another time? It's okay if you do."

"No." It was important to do this. It was the first thing they had done together for a long time. If he could pull this off, there might be something in it for both of them. And they both, he thought, needed a little something.

Joe Pike gave him a close look, then patted the handlebars as he would a horse he was trying to gentle. "This isn't a big bike as motor-cycles go. Two-hundred-fifty-cubic-inch engine. But still, you got a lot of weight here, son. And it can get away from you in a hurry, like just now. But you can control it as long as you keep moving forward. Momentum helps you keep your balance. A motorcycle's kinda like a person. Gotta keep moving. Stand in one place long enough, and sooner or later you'll topple over."

"Yes sir."

"All right. Try it again."

Trout went through the routine again. Gearshift in neutral. Stomp. *RUMMM-UM-UM-UM.* Clutch in, drop it into low. Throttle. *RUMMMMMMMMM-UM-UM.* Joe Pike stepped back and gave him room. Clutch out. He was moving!

"Little more gas! Not too much!"

Joe Pike ambled along beside him, keeping a hand on the rear of the cycle as Trout made a wide turn around the oak tree, wobbling a bit as the bike bumped across the uneven bare dirt. They made several slow, cautious circles of the yard, Trout's heart racing far faster than the engine, but after a while beginning to feel the bike steady underneath him.

"Little more gas," Joe Pike said. "Momentum."

Trout gave it a bit more throttle, and then suddenly Joe Pike wasn't there with him anymore. He was standing next to the steps of the old house, arms folded across his chest, watching. Trout circled several more times and finally eased up toward where Joe Pike stood. He called out. "Clutch in. Brake on. Ease to a stop. Get your feet down. Control it."

Trout stopped the bike and balanced it between his legs, both feet on the ground. He felt giddy. "Okay?"

"You look like you're about to go into labor. Relax."

"Okay."

"Now try the road."

"The road?"

"You wanta ride the thing, don't you?"

"Yes sir."

"Well, you're gonna get pretty bored making ruts in the yard here. Ain't but one way to learn how to ride a motorcycle, son. That's ride it."

"You think I'll be okay? I don't have a helmet."

Joe Pike looked out at the paved road and stared at it for a long moment. Then he looked back at Trout, put a big hand on his shoulder and squeezed ever so slightly. "Just take it easy. Respect the machine, keep your mind on your business, give everybody else lots of room. *Lots* of room. The minute you get cocky, that's when you get in trouble." He smiled. "Take your time. Have fun."

"What are you gonna do?"

Joe Pike picked up the helmet and turned away, walked over and sat down on the sagging bottom step of the old farmhouse, set the helmet down beside him, and hunched forward with his elbows on his knees. He clasped his hands. "I'll be deep in prayer and supplication. Yea, verily." He gave a tiny wave. "Go."

Trout went. Slowly, gingerly at first, keeping it in first gear several hundred yards up the road, getting the feel of the blacktop underneath the bike. Then he held his breath and dropped it down into second gear, gave it some gas and felt a shock of power as the bike leaped ahead. He looked down at the speedometer. Thirty. Then he topped a small rise and a bad thing happened. A small squat house on the left, a pickup truck in the yard. And a dog. Streaking for the road, yapping madly as he approached. "Shit!" he yelled in terror. The dog had an angle on him, a blur of black out of the corner of his eye, almost on him now, going for his leg! Headline: BOY, CYCLE EATEN BY MONGREL. Then — it was a reflex motion, an instinct for survival — he gunned the throttle with a vicious snap of his wrist, and the motorcycle almost jumped out from under him, engine screaming. AIYYYYHHHH! And suddenly he was past the farmhouse and the dog. A quick glance in the rearview mirror. The dog brought up short at the edge of the pavement, staring at his disappearing back, tongue lolling.

Trout flew! There was nothing now but the whine of the cycle, pavement flashing underneath, a rush of brown and green on either side. His heart was in his throat, eyes bugging. Third gear! He dropped it down, felt another jolt of power and then the bike settling beneath him, a marvelous streaking, growling cat gobbling up great lengths of asphalt. Another quick glance at the speedometer. Fifty. It felt like five hundred. The wind roared in his ears, whipped at his hair, teared his eyes. He was scared out of his wits and at the same time thrilled beyond anything he had ever experienced. *Godawmighty!* He leaned into the wind and rode in a state of grace for what seemed a hundred miles before he saw a stop sign ahead where the road dead-ended into another at the top of a hill. He realized it was the road that ran between town and the Interstate. He could see I-20 off to his right, cars and semis barreling along on the concrete. And off to the left, the Dairy Queen.

He rode down that way and turned around at the edge of the parking lot. It was midmorning, slack time. Only a Sheriff's Department car parked in front, a deputy lounging at the window, sipping coffee, talking to somebody inside, paying no attention to the fact that Trout was violating the Georgia Motorcycle Helmet Law. Next to the deputy, a HELP WANTED sign was taped to the plate glass.

He thought about Keats and the rest of them over at Moseley High School. Maybe wondering where the invisible kid was, maybe thinking they had scared him off. Well, to hell with them. He wasn't going back, not this school year. Three months until September. He would think of something. By September a giant meteor might have hit the earth. WHAM! Clouds of dust. A run on gas masks. Anything could happen. In the meantime, he could ride the motorcycle. On a motorcycle, you could outrun a lot.

He turned around and headed back. It wasn't a hundred miles after all. Maybe five. But he rode like a bat out of hell, and when he passed the house with the dog, the cur didn't make it halfway to the road before Trout had roared past.

Joe Pike was sprawled across the steps of the farmhouse, eyes closed. Prayer and supplication. Trout turned in, gunned the cycle, made another quick circle of the yard, stopped in front of Joe Pike, and killed the engine. Joe Pike finally opened his eyes. "Was it okay?"

"Yes sir. It sure was okay." And Trout saw then in Joe Pike's eyes a little of what it must mean to let go of something or someone.

But there was something else, a thing shared, a message passed and silently acknowledged. Trout understood a little bit about the motor-cycle. About Texas. It wasn't so much the getting there as it was the going. That was the thing.

Joe Pike was gone all afternoon. Trout hung around the house, lis-tened to some James Taylor . . . *in my mind I'm going to Carolina* . . . read a couple of articles in a tennis magazine, took a nap. Woke up in a state of excitement, thinking of Cynthia Stuckey. Gave in quite will-ingly to temptation. He was doing that a lot, he thought. But it was one of the few things he had much control over these days.

He wandered out to the storage shed in back of the parsonage and wiped down the motorcycle with the chamois cloth Joe Pike kept hanging on a nail. Then he threw a tennis ball against the side of the storage shed. *Thwock . . . thwock . . . thwock.*

He tired of that after a while, sat down in the backyard swing, and stayed there for a long time thinking about the morning, the motor-cycle. He could still feel the tingle through his body — vibration of the engine, rush of the wind — the precarious strangeness of it.

Then he thought about Joe Pike on the motorcycle, going all the way from Georgia to Texas with the Holy Ghost riding behind, whis-pering in his ear. Mile after mile disappearing under the wheels of the Triumph. One hill, one curve after another. The sun tracking his movement — rising at his back, setting in his face, disappearing over a horizon he could never quite reach.

It was a very unpreacherlike thing, riding a motorcycle. Trout knew of a Methodist minister over in Tennessee who was much sought after as a stand-up comic, renowned for his religious humor. An oddity, but not beyond the pale. Several in Joe Pike's own conference were pretty fair golfers; a good number were prodigious fishermen. Perhaps the most unusual was the one with the glass eye. He had been a counselor one summer at Methodist Summer Camp, in charge of a cabin full of fourth-grade boys including Trout. Bedtime the first night had been a rowdy affair until the preacher took out his glass eye, placed it on the window sill next to his bunk, and said, "Boys, I'm gonna be watching you all night," then turned over and went to sleep, surrounded by profound silence.

But not a single preacher Trout could think of had a motorcycle.

Joe Pike had always been a little unconventional — awesome in height and girth, a bit boisterous, given to occasionally nudging the limits of preacherly decorum. Nonetheless, a preacher who knew where the boundaries were, the way his son knew what a preacher's kid could and couldn't get away with. But now, Joe Pike had a motorcycle, gave no evidence of being the slightest bit uneasy about it, even after his escapade, and now had taken his hooky-playing son and taught him how to ride the darned thing. In doing so, he had cracked the door — intentionally or not — on an entire beyond-the-limits world. What was Joe Pike trying to tell him?

And how much of all that had to do with this *place* — this Moseley, Georgia, with its own set of strange and unsettling vibrations, undercurrents, mysteries? Its history, as Great Uncle Phinizy had recounted it, much of it bound up in who Joe Pike Moseley was, what he had been and become?

All of this caromed around inside Trout's head as he sat there in the swing, making him a little dizzy with the possibilities. He was thinking too much again, an old sin. He could hear the voice of his tennis coach back in Ohatchee: "Stop thinking, Trout! Just play!"

It was getting late, the shank of the afternoon falling on the backyard. He got up and went in the house, turned on the TV set in time for the six o'clock news from Atlanta. *President Carter, just back from a weekend with his top advisors at Camp David, says the nation is gripped by a great malaise . . .*

Then he heard Joe Pike pulling in the driveway in the Dodge. He turned off the TV and met Joe Pike at the door. He was carrying two boxes. One was white cardboard, rectangular. Trout could tell what was in that. A cake. The other box was square, gift wrapped.

When they had finished dinner, Joe Pike lit the sixteen candles on the cake with a flourish and pranced around the table and sang "Happy Birthday" with great off-key vigor. He was almost like the old Joe Pike Moseley, never happier than at a celebration of some sort, and Trout began to believe that things might turn out all right after all. He laughed until his sides hurt.

Then he opened the other box.

It was a motorcycle helmet. Red with a streak of gold lightning down each side.

SIX

THE REST OF the week passed uneventfully. Trout Moseley didn't go back to Moseley High, which ended the school year without ceremony at midmorning on Friday and graduated a class of thirty-five on Friday night in the football stadium. A lieutenant colonel from the Army post in Augusta gave the commencement speech, in which he espoused thrift, hard work, loyalty, and unyielding opposition to communism in all its forms. None of the Moseley family were in attendance. But when Trout and Joe Pike dined with Aunt Alma and Uncle Cicero on Thursday evening, Alma let it be known that Orzell Blaylock had called some time ago to solicit her opinion of the lieutenant colonel as a commencement speaker, and she had approved. Aunt Alma, on behalf of the family, had awarded a five-hundred-dollar scholarship to the top graduate, a girl who would be attending the Massey-Draughon Business College in Atlanta.

Aunt Alma did one other singular thing. Joe Pike happened to mention Trout's unhappiness over the lack of a tennis court in Moseley, and she arranged with friends in Augusta for Trout to play at the Augusta Racquet and Swim Club. "I want Trout to have every opportunity to fulfill himself," she said. "Papa didn't hold with tennis, and neither do I. But who says we all have to be the same?"

Joe Pike drove him to Augusta on Friday afternoon and Trout spent an hour with the club pro, who worked with him on his backhand.

Then Trout played a rousing match against the club's top sixteen-year-old, summoned especially for the occasion. He was a gangly young man with a wicked serve but little else, and once Trout got over his nervousness and figured out the boy's game, he won fairly easily. It felt good, having a racquet in his hands again, losing himself in the rhythm of competition.

After the match they retired to the veranda of the clubhouse overlooking the swimming pool — Joe Pike, Trout, his vanquished opponent, and the club pro — and talked about the State Juniors coming up. Both boys would be playing for the first time in the sixteen-to-eighteen division; neither would be seeded. But they all agreed that Trout might have a chance to pull off a surprise or two in the opening rounds. He had a decent serve-and-volley game and played the net as if he owned it. The backhand, that was the thing. Sometimes it was passable. Often it was as limp as a wet noodle. Only Trout knew how truly miserable it could be. He knew that if a savvy opponent caught him on a day when his backhand deserted him, he was a dead duck. But the club pro invited him back the next week for another session. They would work on it.

Sitting there at a table under a red-and-yellow-striped umbrella, sipping Cokes, kids splashing about in the sun-dazzled pool below, the *thwock-thwock* of smartly struck tennis balls echoing from the courts beyond, Moseley seemed worlds away. When he and Joe Pike climbed into the car for the drive back, Trout felt again like a pilgrim, going into a far, strange land.

On Sunday morning he awoke early and went out to get the paper from the driveway. That was when he noticed the sign on the church marquee next door: TODAY'S SERMON — THE GOSPEL ACCORDING TO ELVIS. He stood there and stared at it for a long time. *Uh-oh.*

Trout thought the crowd in the pews this Sunday seemed a smidgen larger than last week's. There was a scattering of unfamiliar faces sitting alongside the faithful who had been occupying the same places for years. Maybe the sign out front had something to do with it. Elvis. Dead for about a year now, drawing people into a church, of all places.

Trout sat with Aunt Alma and Uncle Cicero in their accustomed place, front and center. Aunt Alma gave him a curt nod when she and Cicero walked in and sat down, then crossed her legs, smoothed her dress, folded her hands primly in her lap. Cicero gave him a sly wink. Cicero the Baptist. *What are you crazy Methodists up to today?* Trout wondered if he ever attended the Baptist church on the opposite end of town. Probably not, he thought. Cicero seemed to do pretty much what Aunt Alma expected. Just before the choir marched in to start the service, Trout glanced back and saw Uncle Phinizy slip into a back pew. *Wake up Charlie. He ain't never seen a real bad wreck before.* Joe Pike ambled in behind the choir and took his seat behind the pulpit. Trout noted that Joe Pike was wearing plain black lace-up shoes. At least no cowboy boots.

They sang a couple of hymns, mumbled through the responsive reading, took up the collection, and sang the Doxology. Then Joe Pike got up and announced that he was starting a physical fitness group called Jumping for Jesus, in the spirit of keeping the Lord's Holy Temple (the body) fit and pure, starting with his own. He made a little joke about Dairy Queen being a religious experience, which drew a titter of laughter from the congregation. Aunt Alma's expression never changed.

Then Joe Pike delivered a long, rambling Pastoral Prayer and they sang the Gloria Patri and one more hymn. Joe Pike stood tall and massive behind the pulpit, waiting for the congregation to settle in the pews, arranged his notes on the big leather Bible before him. He looked out over the crowd, his gaze moving slowly from one side of the church to the other.

Then Joe Pike made the little hissing sound through his teeth and said, "I've come to realize in the past few weeks that we may find interesting things in unsuspected places if we're open to the possibility of doing that. The word for it, I think, is *serendipity.* It's not in the Bible, but I think it may have a religious connotation in a universe of uniqueness and wonder. Serendipity. A small boy walks along the sidewalk, looks down and finds a dollar bill. Or maybe a toadfrog. They're about the same to a small boy." He smiled, and the congregation smiled with him. "Serendipity. Messages come in all sorts of bottles, washing up on the shore of whatever ocean we happen to be walking along at the time. And there are all sorts of things we might loosely define as Scripture. So — " he took a deep breath " — today's Scripture comes from RCA Victor." He gathered himself up, clasped his hands in front of him like a small boy considering a newly found toadfrog, and sang:

"Are you lonesome tonight? Do you miss me tonight?
Are you sorreeee we drifted apaaaarrrt?"

Trout winced. It was awful. Joe Pike changed keys at least three times before he finished. At Trout's side, Aunt Alma said softly, "Sweet Jesus." Trout would have given a good deal of money to see the look on her face. But he contented himself with cutting a glance at her lap, where her knuckles were turning white around the handle of her purse. Trout expected to hear bodies falling out of pews onto the floor *THUD*, but it was stone-quiet in the church. Sort of like standing on the edge of a sheer cliff, looking off into nothing, your heart in your throat.

"Dear old Elvis," Joe Pike said. "Now, I don't want to appear blasphemous or anything, but have you ever thought about the similarities between Elvis and Jesus?" His gaze swept the congregation. No, they hadn't thought about that, Trout imagined. Not a single one of them had ever considered the possibility. Or suspected that anyone else would.

"Elvis and Jesus," Joe Pike went on. "Both of them born to humble beginnings, both powerfully influenced by their mothers. At a fairly early age, each came to realize in his own way that he wasn't ordinary. There was something special he was meant to do and be. Each became a messiah in his own way. Elvis, for his part, proclaimed a new American music. When he opened his mouth and sang, everything changed. A lot of disciples, a lot of false prophets came along later, but Elvis was the original."

There was some audible shuffling about in the pews now. Trout couldn't stand it any longer. He looked up at Aunt Alma. Her face was drained of color. There was a trace of panic around her eyes. He thought that any minute she might jump up and call out to Joe Pike, "Wait! Don't go there!" Trout looked back at Joe Pike, all alone up there behind the pulpit. All alone, way out on a limb, about to crank up the chain saw.

"I suppose the resemblance ends there. Elvis was a pretty good old boy from what you hear, had a decent raising and all. But fame got him. He couldn't stay away from those pills. Died on a cross of chemistry, and climbed up on it all by himself. But just because Elvis came to a bad end doesn't mean we can't learn something from him. In fact, I think God dearly loves a sinner. If He can't save him, He can use him as an example. We do the same thing: 'Looky there, young'uns. Mess around with that rock-and-roll music, you'll end up like Elvis. Or worse.'"

Joe Pike took a moment, shuffled his notes a bit, looked up again. "Now, what was it old Elvis was talking about when he sang, 'Are you lonesome tonight? Do you miss me tonight? Are you sorry we drifted apart?' Anybody want to hazard a guess?"

It was deathly quiet in the church. *What is this, Donahue? Class discussion? Preachers don't carry on a dialogue with the congregation. Preachers preach. Congregations listen.* Joe Pike waited. Trout remembered him standing before the Easter congregation in Ohatchee, sweating and miserable. Trout should have gone to him then. But instead, he had let Joe Pike ride off to Texas. Not again.

"A girl?" Trout blurted. Every head in the place turned to look at him. He could feel their eyes.

Joe Pike gave him a grateful smile. "Probably," he said. "Probably a girl. But" — he raised a finger, held it in midair — "what if he was talking about God. Is that possible?"

"I reckon," Trout said. Too late to stop now.

"Just for the sake of serendipity, let's consider that. Let's imagine that God is out there" — his arm swept toward the ceiling — "wherever it is we put Him. We say, 'God's in heaven.' Okay, heaven. We all know heaven, right? Lots of clouds, choir music, angels loitering about, maybe some biscuits and red-eye gravy for breakfast, a trip to Dairy Queen every evening. Good things happen in heaven. It's a good place to put God. Right?"

Joe Pike looked out across the congregation again and Trout, to his amazement, saw Tilda Huffstetler, in the next pew, nod vigorously. *Good for you, Tilda.*

"So God's up there in this place called heaven, 'cause that's where we put Him. And we can borrow Him on Sunday morning or when we think we need something. Meanwhile, all of us mere mortals are down here on earth. And we're just sort of rocking along. Get up every morning, shave our faces, put on our makeup, bolt down a little breakfast, dash off to work or school. Work all day, stagger to the car and drive back home. Wore out. Frazzled. Get home, the toilet's stopped up, the baby's got the croup, a delinquent payment notice in the mail. Eat supper, watch *Laugh-In* on TV, or maybe listen to a little Elvis on the stereo. Go to bed. Do it all over tomorrow. Most of the time, we just do it. What else, huh? That's life. That's what people do. Right?"

Another pause. This time, Tilda Huffstetler and her husband Boolie both nodded. Trout thought about Tilda down there at the Koffee Kup Kafe all day, making those sweet potato pies, watching folks eat them, making some more. Just feeding their faces, over and over. Pies come and pies go. After you've been in *Southern Living*, what is there?

"We just rock along," Joe Pike said. "But every once in a while, we let our guard down and this feeling creeps up on us. Like there's something missing. I don't know, maybe I'm the only one. But every once in a while, just before I drift off to sleep, I say to myself, 'What's wrong, Joe Pike?' Actually, I've been saying that a good deal lately. What's wrong? What's missing? What is this odd feeling I keep getting? Upset stomach?"

Joe Pike rubbed his ample stomach, felt his forehead.

"Maybe if I take some Maalox, it'll go away." He opened an imaginary bottle, poured imaginary Maalox into an imaginary spoon, drank it down, smacked his lips and made a face. A titter of laughter from the congregation, quickly stifled. "Nope! Still there!" He screwed the cap back on the bottle, set it on the edge of the pulpit and stared at it for a moment. "Then I hear old Elvis sing this song:

Are you lonesome tonight? Do you miss me tonight?
Are you sorry we drifted apart?

This time, he sang it softly, plaintively, and it didn't sound quite so off-key. It sounded . . . what? Small. Scared. *Lonesome*.

"Lonesome," Joe Pike said. "Maybe I'm just lonesome. But you say, 'Wait a minute, Joe Pike! How could you be lonesome? You've got Trout, and he's a fine young man and carries on a good conversation. And you've got the rest of your fine family. And all these good people here in Moseley who helped raise you and who are pulling for you now to get your act together. A whole town full. How can you be lonesome, Joe Pike?' Well, I don't know. Why aren't you" — he waved his arm across the congregation — "enough? Why do I, a minister of the gospel, feel so disconnected from God? Why do those things you taught me in Sunday school when I was a kid, those things they taught me in seminary, not seem to work anymore? Why do I feel lonesome?" He leaned across the pulpit, arms clasped, his gaze slowly sweeping the sanctuary. "And why do you?"

He waited a long time and let that sink in while he searched their faces. Trout looked up at Aunt Alma. Her mouth was ajar, and the look of panic around her eyes had been replaced by something that resembled sadness. Trout stared, unable to help himself. It was something he hadn't seen before, and he understood in that instant that there *was* something sad about Aunt Alma, something she usually kept so private you might never imagine. But here, in the midst of this gathering, it was naked in her face. Joe Pike had unmasked her, if only for an instant. Perhaps it was what he said. Perhaps it was because *he* was the one who said it. Trout could see that for some reason he couldn't yet fathom, it was a terrible burden to be Alma Moseley and that in her most unguarded moments, it made her terribly sad. Just now, was she about to cry? No, he couldn't imagine Aunt Alma crying. But now, and it startled him to know it, he could imagine her going completely to pieces under the right circumstances.

Then Alma looked down at Trout and saw that he saw. Her face flushed. The mask came down again. But Trout thought, *She will always know that I know.*

Up in the pulpit, Joe Pike did not see. He was immersed in his own agony. There was sweat on his upper lip, and he was making the little hissing sound between his teeth. The little man inside the big body, trying to . . . what? Alma and Joe Pike: *they are* both *two people.*

Joe Pike gave a great sigh, like a man who has misplaced something and despairs, for the moment, of locating it. Enough of this muddling about for now, he seemed to say. Out loud he said, "Let's think about all that this week. I don't want to speak for anybody else or put any false notions into anybody's head. Let's just think about it. Are we lonesome for God? With all our praying and hymn-singing and Bible-reading and churchgoing and hallelujah-shouting, do we sometimes in our darkest moments get the suspicion, 'Uh-oh! He ain't here. And He ain't paying attention.' And if He ain't, why?"

Then Joe Pike gathered up his notes and sat down. There was a long, astonished silence. Finally, Aunt Alma cleared her throat. Just that, nothing more. Up in the choir loft, Grace Vredemeyer took it as a signal. She got up and led the final hymn.

Aunt Alma didn't come right to the point at Sunday dinner an hour later, the way Trout had thought she might. They ate — she, Cicero, Joe Pike and Trout — in surprising good humor.

Alma talked about going to New York to shop for clothes. And that surprised Trout, too. He couldn't imagine Aunt Alma shopping for clothes. Everything she wore seemed so severe, plain-cut and solid-colored, unadorned. He tried to imagine her in a floral print with bangle earrings. No.

Uncle Cicero told a long, rambling story about the flimflam artist from Atlanta who had tried to bilk Miz Estelle Collier out of some money the past week. For a thousand dollars, he said, he would spray her roof with a substance that would extend the life of the shingles for twenty years. Miz Estelle Collier had let him get up on the roof with his sprayer, then took his ladder down and called Cicero, who arrived to find the con man hollering from the rooftop. Big-city crime, trying to invade Moseley, thwarted by local savvy. The bumpkins win again. Cicero, as was his Sunday custom, was in uniform, prepared for afternoon patrol. His gun belt was hanging, as was the custom, on the hall rack.

Joe Pike listened to everything, made an appreciative grunt or gave a nod at appropriate times, and ate five pieces of fried chicken.

When they were finished with the main course, Alma had a surprise: dessert. In honor of Trout, she said. Trout started to ask why, but thought better of it. Did he look like he needed dessert? Probably. Even his layoff from tennis, even the daily trips to Dairy Queen, had failed to add a pound to his thin frame. He had his mother's slightness. So, dessert — albeit, a fruit concoction out of respect for Cicero's cholesterol. They were well into it, Cicero holding forth at some length about the unsteady state of the local economy, when Alma broke in and said, "Jimmy's becoming an embarrassment."

Joe Pike looked up at her. "Jimmy?"

"Carter," she said.

"The President."

"We went to the inauguration, you know," Alma said.

Cicero chimed in. "At the inaugural ball, they stuck us in the basement of the Smithsonian right next to the McCormick reaper. With

Guy Lombardo. Some drunk from Delaware spilled his drink down the front of Alma's gown."

"We had nice seats for the parade," Alma said.

"About five blocks from the White House," Cicero added.

Alma's jaw tightened. "And when the parade was over, we went to a lovely reception at the White House."

"With about ten thousand other people," Cicero said. "Everybody that gave more than a hundred dollars."

"It was," she insisted, raising her voice a bit, "a very nice affair. Jimmy and Rosalynn were very gracious."

"You know President Carter?" Trout asked.

"Of course," she said, turning to him. "I've supported Jimmy ever since he ran for governor."

Cicero grinned. "Alma's the kind of supporter who'll give you a hundred dollars and take an hour telling you how to spend it."

"Cicero . . ."

"Yes, dear?"

"Have you ever run for political office or been involved in a political campaign?"

"No, hon. I do hold public office, I guess you could say."

"Appointive. Not elective."

"That's exactly right."

"Then you are speaking from a lack of knowledge."

Cicero smiled at her. "I've always left the politics to you, hon." He looked at Trout and Joe Pike. "It's an old tradition in the Moseley family, supporting worthy candidates. As long as they're Democrats, of course. A hundred dollars and lots of advice. My people, now, they always worked it from the other end. Graft and corruption. Give a politician a thousand dollars and tell him to spend it any way he wants to. And then go back later and help divide up the spoils. Shoot, my people even had truck with Republicans, of all things."

"Your people . . . ," Alma said with an almost imperceptible shake of her head.

Cicero's smile broadened. "We have mostly married above ourselves. With the notable exception of Cousin Flint. He took up with a hooker from Macon."

"Cicero!" Alma cut a glance at Trout.

"I know what a hooker is," Trout said.

"Well, we don't talk about . . ." — she waved her hand in the general direction of Macon — ". . . at the table."

"It is, after all, Sunday," Joe Pike said, taking another bite of dessert.

Alma stared at Joe Pike. "Not," she said after a moment, "that you could tell it by everything that has transpired."

Okay. Here it is.

"Let me venture a guess," Joe Pike said. "You're speaking of my sermon."

"If you want to call it that."

"You took offense, I fear."

"It was an exhibition," she said flatly.

Joe Pike put his spoon down, leaned back in his chair, crossed his arms and waited on Alma. Uncle Cicero helped himself to some more dessert. Methodist trouble. No place for a good Baptist to be.

Trout heard the telephone ring up in the front hall. He hoped nobody would get up to answer it, because things seemed about ready to get interesting here. But nobody at the table seemed to hear it. It rang again and he heard Rosetta pick it up.

"The congregation has just about had enough," Alma was saying.

"Enough what?" Joe Pike asked.

"Enough of your public hand-wringing."

"Is that what I'm doing?"

"First it's the Holy Ghost on a motorcycle. Now it's Elvis as the messiah. My Lord, Joe Pike!"

There was a long silence, and then Joe Pike said, "I take it you're not open to serendipity."

"Serendipity has no place in church."

"And what does, Alma?"

"Scripture. Eternal truth. Godly verities."

"On Christ the solid rock I stand."

"Yes!"

Joe Pike shook his head slowly. "Well, to tell you the truth, Alma, I don't know where the rock is right now. I'm trying to find it."

"Then find it somewhere else, Joe Pike. Not in my church."

"Your church."

"Our church."

"No, I think you had it right the first time. It's not the congregation that's had enough, it's you. Personally."

"Yes I have," Alma said. "I am personally mortified. Embarrassed, to tell you the truth. My brother, making a spectacle of himself in the pulpit of the church his family founded. It's appalling. I am being totally honest with you here."

Joe Pike nodded slowly and thought about it for a moment. Then he leaned toward Alma, elbows on the table. "Did you notice anything unusual about the congregation this morning, Alma?"

"No."

"Did you, Trout?"

"Yes sir."

"What?"

Trout felt himself his father's ally here. "There were a few more of 'em."

"Yes, there were," Joe Pike said. "Out there amongst the vast" — he swept his arm through the air — "reaches of the sanctuary, amongst the empty pews, sprinkled in with the small band of faithful, were a few *new faces*. And there may be a few more *new faces* next Sunday."

"Is that why you put on a show?" Alma demanded. "To draw a crowd?"

"It was an honest effort to be" — he waved his hand again, searching for a word — "honest. And I believe I struck a responsive note with some in the congregation. I saw a few heads nod." He turned to Trout. "Did you see any heads nod?"

"Yea, verily," Trout said.

"Don't mock me, son. I do that well enough myself."

"Yes sir."

Alma gave an impatient jerk of her head. "Well, if what you're after is filling up the pews, I suppose Elvis Presley or Godzilla or any other freak show will do just fine!"

Cicero spoke up. "I think if you'd serve coffee in the vestibule between Sunday school and church, you'd swell the crowd a little. Regular and decaf, and maybe your doughnuts on Communion Sunday . . ."

"Cicero, hush," Alma said. And then as an afterthought, "We Methodists refer to it as a narthex, not a vestibule. *Vestibule* is a Baptist word."

"I don't believe . . . ," Cicero started, then trailed off, deflating. He sat there for a moment, wrinkled his nose, furrowed his brow, stared down at his plate. Good old Cicero, just trying to grease the skids a little. Trout felt a pang of sympathy for him. Alma was drumming her nails on the table, paying Cicero no attention. *Did she pick him, or did he pick her? And whichever it was, why?*

Joe Pike looked at Alma for a long moment, then let out a breath and sat back in his chair. "You just don't see it, do you?"

"See what?"

"The church," he said quietly. "It's dying, Alma."

Now it was Alma's turn to look stricken.

"Those people who always show up," Joe Pike went on. "The terminally faithful. Judge Lecil and Mister Fleet and Eunice, Tilda and Boolie, Grace up there in the choir, all the rest with their perfect attendance records, sitting in the same places year after year until the cushions bear the permanent imprint of their rear ends."

Alma flushed. "Joe Pike!"

But Joe Pike plowed ahead, his voice growing urgent. "Did you ever notice how few cars there are parked at the curb on Sunday? They all *walk*, for God's sake. They all live *here* on this end of town. The Moseley end. It's like a little fiefdom. The Moseley manor house and the Moseley cathedral across the street and all the poor serfs trudging dutifully in the door when the bell tolls."

"They are our people!"

"I love 'em dearly, Alma. But we — our family — we have sucked the life out of them. We have turned them into Christian zombies."

"Stop it!" Alma cried out, banging her fist on the table. The dishes rattled. It scared the hell out of Trout. He jumped an inch or two in his chair. "Christ!" he blurted.

Just then, the door from the kitchen opened. Rosetta stood there staring at them. *My, my. White folks 'bout to come to blows in here. Fightin' over Jesus.*

At the table there was an embarrassed silence. Finally, Rosetta said to the blasphemers, "Fellow on the phone said to come quick. Wardell Dubarry's painting his house."

By the time they got there — all riding in Cicero's police cruiser — Wardell Dubarry was well along. It was a bright red, a shade that reminded Trout of Chinese New Year decorations. Wardell had already covered a good bit of one side of the house and was up on a ladder now at the peak of the roof, brush in hand, paint bucket hanging from the top rung. A middling crowd had gathered. On the other side of the street. *There's all kinds of wrecks,* Trout thought.

Cicero eased the police car to the edge of the street next to Wardell's house, and Alma was out of the car and up the yard before he could get the engine turned off. She stood there below the ladder for a moment, watching Wardell, while the others got out of the car and followed her. Wardell didn't seem to notice a thing. A portable radio, sitting in an open window below the ladder, was playing country music. Merle Haggard. *I'm proud to be an Okie from Muskogee!* Trout looked around for Keats. She was nowhere in sight. Probably working the afternoon shift at Dairy Queen. Did she know what was going on here? Did she care? Probably. Tweaking the noses of the Moseleys. She would get her jollies from something like that. Keats seemed to have a serious burr under her saddle about the Moseleys.

So, apparently, did her father. Wardell was having a grand time up there on the ladder, spreading on the red paint with sweeping flourishes of his brush. He didn't look down, just kept with the work.

"What do you think you're doing?" Alma demanded.

Wardell looked down and gave her an arch look. She could *see* what he was doing, couldn't she? Wardell went back to painting.

So Alma told him what he was doing. "You are painting *my house.*"

"Yes, as a matter of fact, I am. Painting the house," Wardell said.

Alma turned to Cicero. "Arrest him," Alma said.

Cicero looked pretty uncomfortable. He hitched his gun belt. Then he hitched his britches. Trout imagined that Cicero's underwear was probably creeping up the crack of his butt like ivy. "Hon, I can't do that," Cicero said in a low voice.

"What do you mean, you can't do that?"

"This" — he took in the neighborhood with a sweep of his hand — "is outside the police jurisdiction."

"That's ridiculous," Alma said.

"Well, that's what you Moseleys wanted."

"No, it's ridiculous that you won't arrest a man who's breaking the law."

"Which law?" Wardell asked from the top of the ladder.

"Damage to property," she answered.

Trout wanted to be helpful if he could. "You could take down the ladder, like Miz Estelle Collier did with the flimflam man," he said to Uncle Cicero.

"But Wardell's *on* the ladder," Cicero said. "The flimflam man was up on the roof."

Trout nodded. "Yes sir. I can see that."

Wardell added a few more brush strokes while they all watched, at a loss. Merle Haggard sang on: *We don't smoke marijuana in Muskogee.* Aunt Alma finally spoke up again. "Wardell, I'm going to tell you one last time. Stop painting my house and come down off that ladder. If you don't, you are fired. And you'll be out of this house by sundown if I have to put you in the street myself." She speared Cicero with a wicked look. "And given the level of support I'm getting, I may well have to do it myself."

Wardell paused in midstroke, then looked down at Alma. "I'm just doing what Joe Pike told me to do," he said.

"Hey," Joe Pike said, holding up his hands. "Leave me out of this."

"Joe Pike stood right yonder," Wardell said, pointing with his brush at the front yard, dripping red paint, "and said, 'Paint it red if you want to. I don't care.' Young Trout there was standing on the porch. He heard it."

There was a long silence while Alma stared at Joe Pike. "Yeah," he said finally with a shrug of his shoulders. "I did say that. But I didn't mean *paint* the house." He looked at Trout for confirmation.

"That wasn't the way you said it," Trout agreed. "You didn't say *paint* the house. You said . . ."

"Paint the house," Wardell filled in for them. "And I took it to mean 'paint the house.' You're a Moseley, ain't you? And the Moseleys own the house, don't you? And you said *paint* the house." Wardell went back to his painting.

Trout looked at Alma, Joe Pike, Cicero. *This is what a bad wreck looks like.* They all looked a bit dazed and slack-jawed, victims of collision with a man with a bucket of paint. Who wasn't even paying them any attention anymore.

Alma took one more step forward and gripped a rung of the ladder about a yard below Wardell's feet.

Wardell never looked down. "Take your damn hand off my ladder, Alma," he said. "It may be your house, but it's by God my ladder." He kept painting.

And then Joe Pike stepped forward, put *his* hand on the ladder just next to Alma's. He looked up at Wardell, and when he spoke, his voice sounded like barbed wire. "Wardell," he said carefully, "that will be enough of that. If you can't speak to my sister with a civil tongue, I'll come up there and haul your ass off that ladder myself."

Wardell's brush stopped in midstroke. Nobody moved. Nobody looked at anybody else. Nobody spoke. For once, Uncle Cicero seemed not to have the gift of words to grease the skids. It was as if they were frozen in tableau, not one of them having the foggiest notion how to extricate themselves from the situation.

Finally, Wardell said, "I reckon you won't have to do that, Joe Pike." He didn't sound like he really meant it, but he said it anyway.

It was Alma who finally moved. She slowly took her hand off the ladder, then turned and walked very deliberately back to Uncle Cicero's police cruiser. She got in, cranked it up, and drove away. Trout thought she carried it off quite well. The rest of them walked home.

Uncle Phinizy was reading Aeschylus, an old leather-bound volume with yellowed pages. He had found it, he said, in an antiquarian bookshop in Washington — had probably paid too much for it, but with Aeschylus, you wanted the heft of old leather in your hand.

Trout wasn't much interested in Aeschylus. He had come again in the middle of the night seeking answers, and Phinizy didn't seem at all surprised to see him. The door was open, only the screen keeping out the night. Bluish cigarette haze hung just below the ceiling and drifted upward through the shade of the lamp beside Phinizy's chair.

"The usual?" Phinizy asked when he had turned down the page of his book and placed it on the table at his elbow.

"I don't want anything," Trout said from the sofa.

"Well, you sure *look* like you want something."

Trout thought for a moment. "Why are they like that?"

Phinizy lit another cigarette from the one burning low in the ashtray, stubbed out the old one and took a drag on the new. "Did Joe Pike tell you what I did for a living?"

"No," Trout answered, remembering that Phinizy rarely spoke to anything directly. He was oblique. A riddler. It was aggravating, but if you wanted anything from him, you had to put up with the aggravation. He might eventually come to the point. Or he might not.

"I was a spy."

"What? You mean the Russians?"

"Among others."

"Gee."

"Oh," Phinizy said with a dismissive wave of his hand, "nothing glamorous. No parachutes, no submarines at midnight, at least not after the Big War. Most of the time I just read a lot."

"Read?"

"Spent most of my time in a cubbyhole reading newspapers, periodicals, things like that. Amazing what you can learn about people who don't want you to know anything about them, just by reading what they write. Not that they come right out and tell you in so many words. You pick up a piece here, a piece there, and before you know it you've got enough of the puzzle to tell what the whole thing looks like."

"You know Russian?"

"Like it was my mother tongue," Phinizy said.

Trout marveled at that for a moment, then let it go. Interesting, but not at all what he was after. He was bone-tired, head aching from all the space junk spinning wildly inside it, bouncing off one nerve ending and colliding with another. Phinizy was still being oblique. He appeared to tell you something, but he really didn't.

"You don't ever *say* anything," Trout accused.

"Who am I to say?" Phinizy shot back.

"A piece here, a piece there. How am I supposed to figure it out? I don't even know what I'm looking for." He stood up to go, disgusted. "You just want to stand around and watch the wreck. It's your entertainment. You're weird, Uncle Phinizy."

He was halfway down the steps when Phinizy opened the screen. "Trout." Trout stopped, but he didn't look back. Phinizy was seized by a fit of coughing, and Trout waited until he had finished. Then, "I'll come with you. I need some fresh air."

They walked through the downtown together, past the row of vacant storefronts, the Koffee Kup Kafe, the open lot where the furniture and appliance store had been, the feed-and-seed, Uncle Cicero's hardware.

Phinizy ticked off the names of now-departed businesses, ghosts from his youth: Grover's Sundries, where you could get a scoop of homemade ice cream for a nickel on a hot summer afternoon and savor it at a small round oak table beneath a paddle fan (in the back, behind a high counter, Dexter Grover dispensed condoms along with prescriptions, but children weren't supposed to know that); the Freewill Cafe, operated by a jackleg Pentecostal minister who dispensed Scripture with the stew and preached a sermon every afternoon from the sidewalk out front to whatever collection of human beings and stray animals was inclined to gather; *The Moseley Messenger,* a thin excuse of a newspaper that died from lack of advertising and interest; and Bob's Barber Shop, the main attraction of which was a lively penny-a-point pinochle game in the back room.

The town seemed to exist in Phinizy's memory as a vivid fixed point from which the rest of his life proceeded. He, who had lived so long away from it, was a walking compendium of Moseley's history — not just the major occurrences, but the trivia of everyday human commerce that made the place real.

"I loved this place," he said as they passed the last of the empty storefronts and crossed the street. "It was a good place for a boy to grow up."

"Why did you leave?" Trout asked.

"I grew up," Phinizy said. And then, "There was an unpleasant-ness."

"What?"

"Leland and I had different ideas about things. After our father died, Leland wanted the town to be a shrine to Broadus Moseley."

"And you wanted . . ."

"To let it breathe."

"So you left."

"Ran away, I suppose you could say if you wanted to be unchari-table about it."

They reached the other side of the street and started back in the direction they had come, back toward Broadus Moseley's end of town, past City Hall and the police department, the grocery store and the welfare office. Everything was dark except for a bare bulb dangling from the ceiling at the rear of the tiny police station. There was a padlock on the door. Law enforcement in Moseley went dormant at dark. A lone car with a sizable hole in the muffler rumbled along the street behind them, eased to a stop as the traffic light in front of City Hall turned red, sat there growling in idle for the minute it took the light to turn green, then moved on. Trout stopped and stood at the edge of the sidewalk staring at the traffic light, the street. There was no intersection here.

He turned to Phinizy. "There's no intersection."

"No."

"Why have a traffic light when there's no intersection?"

Phinizy smiled. "To stop traffic. Back in the fifties, Leland got powerfully exercised about traffic speeding through town. So he had the light put up. As you see, it stops traffic."

"But there isn't any traffic."

"No. I-20 took care of that."

"Then why don't they take the light down?"

Phinizy didn't answer. He turned and headed down the sidewalk. Trout followed, glancing back at the traffic light. Green. Yellow. Red. Since the fifties. Everything about the place was like being stuck in a time warp — not just the traffic light, but everything. Including people's lives. Including his own. He half expected a carload of teenagers out of an old black-and-white movie to round the corner — ducktail haircuts, bobby sox, pedal pushers, oldies on the radio. He was beginning to feel like one of them, suddenly thrust backward into a strange and distant and even forbidding time. And held there against his will.

They stopped at Broadus Moseley Park. Phinizy was badly winded by now, though they hadn't walked all that far or the least bit fast. They hunkered in silence for a long time on the steps of the band shell while Phinizy got his breath back. His face looked ghastly in the dim light that filtered through the trees from the lamp out on the street. The night was sultry and close around them, an army of crickets sending coded messages across the grass of the park. *Riddleit-riddleit.* After a while, Phinizy fished a cigarette out of the crumpled pack in his shirt pocket, lit it and sucked noisily.

Trout could feel despair settling in the pit of his stomach. It all seemed so incredibly screwed up and impossible and forbidding. Moseley, Georgia, might be Phinizy's place (or once had been), but it wasn't his. In the series of parsonages that had been home as far as memory took him, there was at least a sense of temporary permanence. A congregation, eager to make you a part of their little community. And inside the parsonage walls, the three of them. Three. But now with one gone, there seemed to be fewer than two. There seemed to be, at bottom, nothing here in this time and place you could count on, maybe even nothing you could really know. It was all smoke and myth.

It was almost as if Phinizy could read his mind. "I wish I had all the answers for you, Trout. But I can't tell you what I don't know," he said. He took another drag on his cigarette and flipped the glowing butt out into the grass. "I'm like you. Looking for bits and pieces."

"What about Aunt Alma and my daddy? At least you know about that."

"Do some thinking on your own, Trout. Form the habit of it."

"How?"

"All right. Alma and Joe Pike. Think about Alma. Try to imagine growing up as Alma. The girl in the family. Your father owns the mill — owns the town, for that matter. What does that mean?"

"Well," Trout said, "I guess you've got plenty of money."

"Money, prestige, social standing. You go off to get finished at a school for proper young ladies up east. You make your debut in Atlanta. The world's just waiting to kiss the hem of your dress. Then there's a younger brother."

"Daddy."

"What does the family expect his role to be?"

Trout thought for a moment. "The good son."

"Yes."

Phinizy waited. Trout searched his memory. "Uncle Cicero was talking about Grandaddy Leland at dinner the other Sunday. Grandaddy Leland said not a damn one of his children did what they were supposed to do."

Phinizy nodded. "And thereby hangs the tale. Joe Pike was supposed to . . ." He waited.

"Take over the business," Trout answered.

"And Alma was supposed to . . ."

"Be a lady."

"But what happened?"

"Daddy played football and became a preacher. Aunt Alma . . ." Trout waved his hand in the direction of the mill. "And she married Cicero."

"Don't sell Cicero short."

Trout thought about Cicero. "He's always saying something. Just when you think the lid's about to blow off."

"Uh-huh. Good work. Now, back to Alma and Joe Pike."

"I think . . ." Trout searched, trying to grab something that made sense. Put the bits and pieces together, enough to imagine what the whole thing looks like. "They both wish they were somebody else, don't they."

"It's a quite common human condition."

"Do you wish you were somebody else?"

Phinizy didn't say anything at first. Then finally, "Show me a man who doesn't have any regrets and I'll show you a man who died at birth. Trick is not to let your regrets run your life. Now, does any of that help?"

Trout shrugged. "Some, I guess."

"But not entirely."

"Is all that . . . what does it have to do with Daddy and Mama and everything?"

"Maybe nothing. I don't know a lot about your mama and daddy, Trout, at least about what went wrong. I'd tell you if I did. And it doesn't do any good to speculate, not on something like that. That's the thing about bits and pieces. Sometimes you put them together and they don't mean what you think they do. Sometimes they don't mean a goddamn thing."

"So what do you do?"

"Keep looking."

"I'm tired," Trout said. "I just want things to be fixed up. I just want to be . . ." He shrugged. What?

"Sixteen."

"Yes sir."

Phinizy looked at him for a moment, and the ancient crevices of his face seemed to soften a bit. Then he put his hand on Trout's knee and gave it a squeeze. It helped, at least a little. Phinizy said, "Something's going on here, Trout."

"What?"

"I don't know exactly. I'm like you. I listen, watch, keep my own counsel. Bits and pieces. But I haven't figured it out yet."

"Something with Aunt Alma and Daddy?"

"More than that. The town. The mill."

"Have you talked to Daddy about it?"

"Not yet. I figure Joe Pike's got his own load to tote just now."

"When?"

"Soon, I hope." Phinizy rose and stood on wobbly legs, gripping one of the posts of the band shell for support. "One piece of advice, Trout." Trout waited. "If all hell breaks loose, don't try to be a hero. Save your own ass."

SEVEN

TROUT LOST IN the first round of the State Juniors. Lost badly to the boy from Augusta. From the first volley, he exposed the nasty little secret of Trout's shaky backhand, and the longer they played, the worse it got. Trout lost the first set 6–4, and by the end of it, he was thoroughly unnerved. The second set was 6–0 and not even that close. Trout felt naked and humiliated, flailing away like a ten-year-old cutting brush with a machete.

When they met at the net at the end of the match, the boy offered his hand and said with a sly smile, "Get a backhand."

Trout shook his hand. "Get a life," he said. And then he thought, *I'm one to talk. He's got both. I've got neither.*

Trout and Joe Pike rode glumly back to Moseley — Trout slumped against the passenger door, letting Joe Pike drive, the hum of the tires on I-20 gnawing at the back of his brain. So much for tennis. After this, he wouldn't dare show his face at another tournament. Not until he got his backhand straightened out. That could take years, if ever.

"Oh ye who labor and are heavy laden," Joe Pike intoned after a while, keeping his eyes on the road.

"Daddy," Trout said, "I just don't need any Scripture right now. Okay?"

"I meant it as comfort. Balm of Gilead, all that stuff."

"He whipped my butt," Trout said.

"That he did," Joe Pike agreed. "Bad luck of the draw, getting the kid from Augusta."

"I wanted to crawl into a hole."

"I've had the feeling. TCU game in 1955 —"

Trout cut him off. He didn't need any Bear Bryant war stories, either. "There's not even a stupid tennis court in Moseley. How am I gonna work on my backhand if there's not even a stupid tennis court?"

"You could go to Augusta. They seem to know your backhand pretty well."

"Hey, come on!"

Joe Pike shrugged, but he didn't apologize. A few months ago, before all the trouble, Joe Pike would have carried on at great length — analyzing, pep-talking, putting a good face on things. Now, he didn't bother. His silence seemed to say, *You blew it, you chew it.*

They rode on. It was late afternoon and traffic had slacked off. They passed Social Circle, Rutledge, Madison. Towns that existed only as green exit signs, bypassed by the oblivious concrete ribbon of interstate in its rush to make Augusta by nightfall. Exit 52: Buckhead. Exit 53: Veazey. Exit 54: Crawfordville. And then Moseley, forced to share a sign with Norwood, insult added to injury. Trout couldn't even summon up the energy for a decent sigh. Air puddled at the bottom of his lungs like swamp muck. Summer stretched ahead of him like an endless, dust-choked road, and he trudged along it toward exile.

Joe Pike hadn't spoken for perhaps fifty miles. But as he flicked on the blinker for the Moseley exit, he said, "Maybe a job. Keep you occupied. Put some money in your pocket. I'll talk to Alma."

They stopped at the Dairy Queen for supper. When Trout went up to the window to place their order, he saw Keats on the other side. She slid the glass open. "I'm sorry," she said.

"About what?"

"The tennis thing."

Trout was stunned. "How . . ."

"Word travels fast."

Trout stared at her. *When a Moseley farts, everybody smells it.* "Want to take a few minutes to gloat?"

She stared back; then the tiniest trace of a smile played at the corners of her mouth. "The whole town was counting on you, Trout. We really had our hearts set on you winning that tournament. It would have put us back on the map."

To hell with her. "I'll have three foot-longs with chili, two chocolate shakes."

The smile faded. "I really am sorry," she said. She slid the glass closed and left him standing there.

The next morning Trout said to Joe Pike, "Maybe I'll go out for football."

"They'll kill you," Joe Pike replied.

"Thanks for the encouragement."

Joe Pike was making fresh-squeezed orange juice. He had sliced a dozen oranges in half and was standing at the kitchen counter, grinding away on a glass juice squeezer, an orange half lost in his massive hand. It made Trout wince, watching him. "Football's not a game for small people anymore." He put down the orange half, drained the juice from the squeezer into a pitcher, and turned to Trout. Joe Pike was huge, deep into one of his Dairy Queen phases now. If he kept going like this, Trout knew, he would pass three hundred pounds by midsummer, drinking fresh-squeezed orange juice and eating Lean Cuisine at home, then fleeing to Dairy Queen for sustenance. If habit held true, he would one day look at himself in horror and launch into grim dieting — salads, popcorn, gallons of water — terrible battles with himself that made Trout fearful. Throughout Trout's young life, Joe Pike had been, in turn, merely big, and huge — two people (at least) at war in the same body. It scared Trout, this going back and forth, kept him wary and off-balance. He wished Joe Pike would just stay put.

"In my day," Joe Pike was saying, "A little guy could play. Coach Bryant liked little guys. 'Agile, mobile, hostile,' he called 'em. But later on, after he'd been at Alabama for a while, he figured out he couldn't win with little guys. They just got busted up."

"Well, I'm not talking about playing for Bear Bryant."

"Soccer. Now there's a sport for a little guy. In fact, it helps to be little if you want to play soccer. Speed. Agility. Endurance." Joe did a little shuffle-step-kick, aiming an imaginary soccer ball through the legs of the table. Trout tried to imagine Joe Pike on a soccer field. No.

"They don't have soccer at Moseley High School. Or tennis."

"Oh."

"Of course, I could go somewhere else."

Joe picked up another orange half, cradled it in his hand and looked out the window for a moment. Then he said, "If you're gonna live in a place, Trout, you gotta *live* in it. Know what I mean?"

Trout didn't say anything. He worked on his scrambled eggs and instant grits, feeling Joe Pike's eyes on him.

"I want you to finish high school here," Joe Pike said.

Want? Or need? Trout thought. He didn't look up. "Like you did."

"Yes."

"Why did you?" No answer. "Miz Trawick said your family shipped you off to Georgia Military, but you ran away and came back home and caused an uproar."

Joe Pike smiled. "Sounds about right."

"Well?"

Joe Pike thought about it awhile. "I guess I just wanted to be regular, you know? Just one of the local kids. And that's what I want you to do."

"I'm not you. And it's different now."

"No," Joe Pike said, "I doubt it's much different at all, son. It wasn't easy for me, and it isn't easy for you. I know that. But it's what you make of it. Everything" — a wave of his hand took in the parsonage, the church next door, Aunt Alma, Moseley Mills, the universe — "is what you make of it."

And what, indeed had Joe Pike made of it — insisting on being one of the regular kids at Moseley High? He might have thought he was, but when he fell down on the extra point try in the state championship football game, it wasn't just a regular kid screwing up, it was Joe Pike *Moseley*. The only Moseley in the stadium, he had said. When a Moseley screws up, everybody knows it. And the stakes, Trout realized, were infinitely higher.

Trout put down his fork, pushed back his chair, stood up, looked down at the instant grits, and made a face. They were really terrible. They sat there in a gray lump on his plate, hardening like cement. Surely, after all these months, he should have the hang of instant grits by now. But they were either too runny or too lumpy. At the motel in Atlanta, the morning before his tennis match, they had had real grits. It was the best thing about the day.

He looked at Joe Pike. "If I'm gonna go out for football, I guess I need to get in shape. What should I do?"

Joe Pike gave him a sly grin, and there was some mischief in it, maybe an echo from Junction, Texas — flinty-eyed and remorseless Bear Bryant looking on as young men beat each other to a pulp in the heat and dust. "Go ye unto the football stadium and cast thine eye upon the grandstand and ascend and descend the steps thereof. Yea, verily."

By the third time he started up the grandstand steps, he had a great deal more appreciation for Bear Bryant. And Joe Pike Moseley the football player.

He could see the shabby wooden press box a great distance away, up there at the top of the stands, and he said to himself that he would never make it because his legs had stopped bending at the knee and his butt was bumping along the concrete steps and he had lost heart. He had passed mere pain on the first trip up, and by now everything was simply sweat-gushing, gut-churning, air-sucking misery. By the time he neared the top, he was barely moving. He thought that he could quit right there and never feel a pang of guilt, but he was afraid that if he did stop, he would tumble back down the steps and bash his head on the concrete. Headline: BOY DIES STUPIDLY IN FOOTBALL STADIUM. So he bent at the waist and gave a heave with the upper part of his body and somehow staggered up the last two steps. Then his legs buckled and he slumped against the wooden side of the press box, flaking paint raking his face. Down on his fanny now, legs splayed, chest heaving, eyes closed, white spots dancing in the grayness.

In his agony, he thought again of Joe Pike. He thought that he had none of his father's genes, that he was in truth too small and timid to play football. But he might try anyway if it would save him from being an invisible curiosity when school started again in late August. Maybe he would break something early in the season and wear a cast and be an object of admiration. Or maybe he would simply remain invisible.

After a while he opened his eyes and looked out across the brown-green sun-baked expanse of playing field, blinking in the great aching whitewashed June noontime. It was quiet except for the singing of crickets in the shady underbelly of the grandstand and the drone of a lawn mower off in the general direction of town.

"Hey!" she called, and he remembered suddenly that she was there, sitting in the shade of the concession stand down at the end of the field.

She had surprised him with her telephone call just before he left the parsonage. He was in his room, putting on shorts and T-shirt, when the phone rang back in the kitchen and Joe Pike picked it up. Trout heard the drone of Joe Pike's voice and assumed the call was church business. Or Aunt Alma. But when he emerged from his room a couple of minutes later, Joe Pike called down the hallway, "Trout. Phone for you."

It must be someone from Ohatchee, he thought. Maybe Parks Belton, inviting him to visit for the summer. Or the rest of his life. He would go, gladly.

"What's up?" she asked, and he recognized the voice immediately.

"What do you mean, 'What's up?'"

"Well, your tennis career is over, you've disgraced the town, school is out, and there's nothing for a rich kid to do in Moseley, Georgia."

God, she is a first-class female asshole.

"Actually," he said, "I was just going to the stable to give my polo pony a workout."

"Your daddy said you're going out for football."

"That's right."

"They'll kill you."

"That's what he said."

"I know. He told me. He's right, you know. Those mill kids, they'd love to get you on the football field."

"Well," he said, "I plan to add fifty pounds and some blazing speed before August, and I will kick their butts from here to Atlanta."

"Can I watch?"

"Sure," he had answered, but he hadn't imagined she meant right now, today, while he committed suicide on the grandstand steps. She was waiting when he got to the stadium. Joe Pike must have told her. Trout wondered if she had brought some of the other mill brats to hide in the bushes and snicker. But she was alone, sprawled in the shade of the concession stand. She gave him a wave, then watched while he made one magnificently vigorous ascent up the steps, bounced back down, started a second, faltered and nearly fell, made it to the top only by the grace of God, lurched slowly down, and damn near died on the third trip up. And now, all courage and fortitude gone from his frail body, he stood on wobbly legs, squinting at her in the brightness. Her aluminum crutches leaned against the side of the small white building. She had her legs crossed beneath her, Indian-style, and her drawing pad was open in her lap. She had a way of wrapping herself around the pad when she was drawing, shoulders slumped, back arched, mothering it, shutting out the rest of the world. But now she looked up at him, up here on the grandstand steps, barely alive.

"Take off your shirt," she called.

"What?" His voice was a dry croak.

Louder. "Take off your shirt."

"Why?"

She didn't answer. She just looked at him, waiting. So he pulled the sweat-soaked T-shirt over his head and stood there holding it, feeling the sun hot on his bare shoulders.

"Put it back on," she said after a moment. "You look like a plucked chicken."

"Kiss my fanny!" he yelled back.

"Show me!"

He turned his back to her, hiked down his shorts a bit, and pre-sented a sliver of bare rump in her direction.

He waited for reaction, got none, pulled up the shorts, and turned around again. She was deep into the drawing pad, paying him no mind. He put on his T-shirt. To hell with her.

Fifteen minutes later they wobbled toward home together in the noon heat, she on crutches, he following on rubber legs — following be-cause there wasn't room for both of them side by side on the sidewalk, and he was afraid if he walked ahead of her she would run over him. From behind, he could get a good look at her incredible, crazy gait — legs, hips, and body galloping off in several directions at once. There was a sort of crazy rhythm to it. Music. It needed music. Something with a strong, solid beat, lots of bass and drums. *Oooga-chuckka, oooga-chuckka.* Fats Domino, maybe. *I'm walkin', yes indeed, and I'm talkin'* . . . She tacked back and forth, taking up most of the sidewalk, and Trout began to get into the beat, doing a little juke motion with his hips, snapping his fingers, making jive sounds with his mouth.

"I hear that."

"Hear what?"

"That stuff you're doing with your mouth."

"What stuff?"

"That's the thanks I get. Sit out there in the hot grass with chiggers crawling up my butt while you run around like a crazy person."

"Hey," he protested, "I didn't ask you to come. I wish you'd stayed home."

"Well, I didn't. So shut up."

The sketch pad was tucked protectively under her left arm, pencils sticking out of her rear jeans pocket. The sketch pad was part of her, lurching along in counterpoint. *Oooga-chuckka, oooga-chuckka.* It bounced around inside his head, vibrating down into his spinal cord. Jive therapy. He could feel some of the strength returning to his legs, but the agony of the grandstand was still strong in his mind. He would have to give a good deal of thought to football.

"Want me to carry that for you?"

"What?"

"Your sketch pad."

"No," she said flatly.

"Aren't you afraid you'll get it sweaty?"

"I'm not afraid of anything," she snapped. And that, he thought, was probably the gospel truth.

A small kid on a bicycle approached, head down, elbows on the handlebars, just lazing along, paying no attention to anything but the cracks in the sidewalk. She waited until he was almost upon them and then she yelled, "Hey! Watch where the hell'ya goin'!" She raised a crutch menacingly, and the kid jerked his head up, eyes wide, and veered into the street, tires bumping off the curb. He struggled with the wobbling bike, almost losing it, finally gaining control. "Damn you, Keats!" He shot them a bird and pedaled off down the street. She launched out again down the sidewalk. The sketch pad had not moved a centimeter.

"You're afraid I'll see what's in it," Trout says.

"It's none of your business."

"Of course it's my business. I'm in it."

"No you're not."

"I saw you down there by the concession stand, watching me and scribbling on that thing."

"It's not scribbling. It's drawing."

"You give me the creeps."

They were at the corner where the street from the football stadium intersected with Broadus Street. She stopped dead in her tracks and turned on him with a flurry of arms, legs, crutches. It was amazing, watching her turn around like that. She pointed a crutch at him, holding it straight out. Her arms were very strong. The crutch didn't waver. "You'd better be nice to me," she said. "I'm the only non-Moseley under the age of eighty in this town who'll give you the time of day."

"Don't bother," he said mildly and made the *oooga-chuckka* sound with his mouth again.

She lowered the crutch and stared at him for a long time, and then her mouth curled in a sneer. "How'd it make you feel when they took your mother off to the loony bin?"

He could feel his jaw drop open.

"And how about when your crazy old man rode off on his motorcycle?"

"Screw you!" he blurted, flushing with anger.

Then her face relaxed into a smile, all wicked sweetness. "Aw, poor thing. Are you mad? Well, good. I never saw anybody that needed to be pissed off worse than you, Trout Moseley."

Then she turned with a disgusted shake of her head, dismissing him, and lurched away toward the east end of town, toward the mill village. Trout watched her for a moment, tried desperately to think of something brilliantly hateful to shout at her lurching back, and finally gave up with a shrug of defeat and headed west toward the parsonage.

Joe Pike was mowing the grass when Trout got home. He was intent upon it, stalking back and forth across the sun-hardened lawn of the parsonage. The lawn mower bounced ahead of him, rushing to stay out of Joe Pike's way. Joe Pike was clad in an ancient undershirt with the armpits eaten away, a pair of seersucker Bermuda shorts, a battered Texas A&M baseball cap, black wing-tip shoes, no socks. His massive belly cascaded over the frontside of the shorts like an avalanche. He was drenched with sweat, face flushed under the brim of the cap. And smoking a cigar.

He looked up as Trout turned down the walk toward the house, waved, stopped, and cut the lawn mower back to idle.

Trout looked down at Joe Pike's shoes. "You're gonna rub blisters on your feet like that."

Joe Pike stared at the shoes, then took the cigar out of his mouth. "I couldn't find my tennis shoes. I guess they're still in a box somewhere."

"Why didn't you . . ." Never mind. Instead, he said, "You don't smoke cigars."

"I used to," Joe Pike said. "Coach Bryant used to pass 'em out in the locker room after the game. When we won."

"What happened when you lost?"

"We tried to hide."

"Well, it stinks."

Joe Pike took a long look at the cigar. "There is something faintly spiritual about the combination of sweat and cigar smoke. I'll bet the Israelites smoked cigars when they got through smoting the Philistines hip and thigh. I'll bet God passed out cigars and said, 'Y'all went cheek to cheek and jaw to jaw, boys. So light 'em up.'" Then he jammed the cigar back in his mouth and gazed out across the lawn. The path left by the lawn mower looked like a snake, with splotches of uncut grass Joe Pike had left in his wake. When Trout mowed, he tried to keep his lines neat and straight, guiding the wheels of the mower along the indention left in the grass by the previous pass. "Looks like it was done by a drunk Meskin on a blind horse," Joe Pike said around the cigar. Not *Mexican*, *Meskin*. Something else he had brought back from Texas.

"Yeah," Trout said. Late in the afternoon, when it was cooler, he would get out the lawn mower and repair the damage. Neat lines and all that.

They both stood there and surveyed the mess for a moment and then Joe Pike reached down and cut the lawn mower off, and the engine died with a whimper. "Let's clean up and go get some lunch."

"The usual?"

"Sure."

Joe Pike ordered a foot-long hot dog with chili for Trout, three for himself. They sat in the car in front of the Dairy Queen and ate, watching the lunch crowd ebb and flow around them. When they had finished the hot dogs, Joe Pike went back to the window and brought Trout a huge tub of vanilla ice cream and a red plastic spoon.

"If you're gonna play football, you've gotta put some meat on your bones," he said.

Trout looked into the tub. There must be a gallon of it. The ice cream made a little curlicue at the top where the machine had cut off the flow. "Don't you want some?"

Joe Pike patted his belly. "Not me. I'm trying to watch it."

Trout spooned off a white glob of ice cream and let it slide down his throat, where it came to rest on top of the foot-long hot dog. He remembered the grandstand steps, the merciless sun. He felt sick, a little light-headed. "I can't eat that," he said, and put the tub of ice cream on the dashboard. Moisture beaded on the outside of the tub, trickled down onto the vinyl. They both stared at it for a moment. Then Joe Pike gave a great sigh and reached for it. "Waste is sinful." He looked at Trout and shrugged. "The starving children in China, you know."

Trout watched, mesmerized, as Joe Pike ate the whole thing, working the spoon around the inside edges of the tub where it was beginning to melt, carving like a sculptor and lifting it lovingly to his lips. He seemed lost in the ice cream, as if he were down inside the tub somewhere, an infant in its womb, doing forward flips and backward rolls, surrounded by its rich cold creaminess. He finished finally, scraped the bottom of the tub, licked the last drops off the plastic spoon, smothered a belch. Then he tidied up, gathering all their trash and taking it to the big barrel at the corner of the building. He came back to the car, slid under the wheel, cranked it up, rolled up the window, and turned on the air conditioner. There was a broad dark band of sweat down the back of his shirt and his collar was soaked. He would go home now and take another bath. Joe Pike took lots of baths in the summer. Trout realized they hadn't said a thing for perhaps ten minutes.

All the regulars were there at the Dairy Queen. The old woman ordering her cup of ice cream with crushed pineapple on top. The two guys in the ACE PLUMBING truck. Joe Pike and Trout Moseley in their old green Dodge.

"I got to thinking today, "Joe Pike said, "we should have some theological discussions, Trout. I don't believe we ever have."

"No sir. I don't remember any."

"Imagine that. Me a preacher and you sixteen years old, and we've never gotten beyond 'Jesus Loves Me.'"

"I guess not."

"Divine intervention, angels on the head of a pin, virgin birth — do you ever wonder about any of that stuff?"

"Well, it's not anything I'm worried about," Trout said. "It's not like acne or anything like that."

"If you were to ask me a theological question, what would it be?"

Trout shrugged. "I don't know."

"Come on. Something really profound."

Trout thought about it for a while. He really wanted to go home and take a nap and then sit in the swing in the backyard and think long and hard about this business of playing football. But Joe Pike seemed insistent. Maybe this was a game, too.

"Why are you a preacher?" Trout asked.

Joe Pike hung fire for a long moment, took a deep breath and let it out slowly. "Hmmmmmmmm," he said finally.

"Well?"

Joe Pike put the car in gear and started backing out of his parking place, craning his neck and making an intense thing out of looking out the back window of the car.

"Well?" Trout said again.

"Let me sleep on that one."

Trout drifted out of sleep the next morning to hear voices. Joe Pike. A woman. He jerked awake.

Grace Vredemeyer. They were sitting at the kitchen table, each with a coffee mug, the Mr. Coffee burbling on the counter, dripping a fresh pot. Grace Vredemeyer had a thin, tinkly laugh. Like cheap wind chimes. She was wearing a summer dress, bare at the shoulders, lots of flowers and vines. Trout thought of draperies. Her back was to Trout. Joe Pike looked up, saw Trout standing in the door, frowned, and made a little wave with his hand, shooing Trout away. Grace saw him, turned and stared at Trout, then giggled. "Oh, my."

"Trout, don't you think you should put some clothes on?" Joe Pike said.

Trout looked down at himself. Boxer shorts. His face flushed. He started to go, but then something — he couldn't say exactly what — stopped him. "What are you doing here?" he asked Grace Vredemeyer.

She didn't bat an eye. "I brought my column for this week's church bulletin," she said, holding up a sheet of paper. "Grace Notes."

"Trout . . . ," Joe Pike started.

"Can I read it?" Trout asked.

"Of course," Grace Vredemeyer said.

She held out the piece of paper, Trout took a couple of steps toward her and plucked it out of her hand.

GRACE NOTES
by Grace Vredemeyer
CHOIR DIRECTOR

You may have asked yourself from time to time how the hymns for each service are chosen. Well, there's more to it than just selecting a few numbers at random out of the hymnal willy-nilly.

First of all, I like to get the service off to a sprightly start with a good upbeat number. Something to get you "Jumping for Jesus," to borrow a phrase from Reverend Moseley's new aerobics program (Wednesday afternoons at five).

I like to think the second hymn should be slower paced, reverent and prayerful, coming as it does right after the Pastoral Prayer and just before the Offertory.

And then the third hymn, which precedes the sermon, should . . .

Trout handed the paper back to Grace Vredemeyer. "I'm going out for football," he said.

"Oh, that's nice." She threw Joe Pike a glance. "Another football player in the family."

"Yes ma'am."

He stood there for a moment longer looking at Grace Vredemeyer, definitely *not* looking at Joe Pike. Grace waited him out. She seemed to be a woman of infinite patience. Finally she said, "Have you found a girlfriend in Moseley?"

"Not yet," Trout said. "I'd really like to have one, though. Sometimes" — he took a deep breath — "I wish I were a brassiere." He cupped his hands and held them in front of his bare chest.

This time, Grace Vredemeyer didn't giggle. She snorted.

Joe Pike leaped out of his chair. "Trout!"

"Yes sir?"

"Apologize!" he thundered.

"Sorry, Miz Vredemeyer."

"Go to your room! Put some clothes on!"

"Yes sir."

He heard the front screen door bang shut a few minutes later, and then Joe Pike stood filling the doorway of his room, breathing hard, color high. "What in the hell was that?" he demanded.

"Grace Vredemeyer."

"Don't you smart-mouth me, buster!"

Trout ducked his head, stared at the floor. He might be pissed off, but he wasn't ready to be pissed off and look Joe Pike Moseley in the eye at the same time. "Why did she come here?"

"This is the parsonage, Trout. You know what a parsonage is. It's an extension of the church. People are in and out all the time."

"She could have taken it to your office."

"I wasn't *in* my office. But I'm going to my office now. And by the time I get back for lunch, I want you to have your attitude in gear. Understand me?"

Trout nodded.

Joe Pike surveyed the room. "Clean up. Put some pants on." Trout nodded again.

"I'm getting a little tired of your moping around, Trout. I can't help it if you lost the tennis match. I can't do anything about where we live. I'm trying to make the best of the situation. And I don't *need* you muddying the water." Trout looked up at him finally and Joe Pike's hard glare softened a little. "Just hang in there with me. Okay?"

And then Trout said, "Mama didn't like people coming to the parsonage all the time. It really bugged her."

Joe Pike looked as if he'd been hit hard in the stomach. Or maybe lower. He stood there for a moment, then turned and left. The back door slammed, and after a couple of minutes Trout heard the motorcycle start up back in the shed. Then it roared around the side of the house and took off down the street, heading out of town.

Trout spent a wretched hour, imagining Joe Pike growling along west on I-20, the nose of the motorcycle pointed again toward Texas. And all Trout's fault, for getting pissed off (as Keats had told him he should) and invoking the name that seemed to be Joe Pike's most implacable ghost-demon. Mention Irene, and Joe Pike went into a psychic three-point stance, the old defensive lineman digging in and waiting for onslaught. What was he so afraid of? She was such a small, quiet thing — especially now, sitting over there in the Institute in Atlanta, deep inside herself. Did she have any idea how she haunted this place and its inhabitants? Did she think of them? Did she think at all? Was she lost forever? Was she lost on purpose?

The silence, Irene's insistent silence, drove Trout out of the house, and he sat huddled in the swing on the front porch for a while. He thought of going to Phinizy's bare rooms. But what to say? *I ran Daddy off.* No, that didn't sound too good for either of them. Big old Joe Pike Moseley, he of stout body and mostly stout spirit, driven from his own home by a sixteen-year-old boy and the specter of a tiny, quiet woman? And Trout — consumed by his own miserable adolescent selfishness? Better to keep that to himself.

Then too, to air out your business was to invite advice, and he didn't think much of the advice he had gotten recently.

Keats: *You oughta be pissed off.* Well, see where that had gotten him just now. Joe Pike was gone and Grace Vredemeyer probably thought he was a smart-aleck pervert.

Alma: *Don't forget who you are.* Well, that's exactly what he'd like to do. She might like being a Moseley in Moseley, but to Trout, it was like having a dead chicken hung around your neck.

Phinizy: *Save your own ass.* Easy for Phinizy to say. He could say anything he damn well pleased, stir up all kinds of ruckus, and then beat a retreat if things got too hot. Trout was stuck, at the mercy of all the rest of them. No escape. He didn't even have a credit card.

So Trout sat there on the front porch of the parsonage, trapped between the dark silence of the house and the hot June morning, thinking despairing thoughts, mourning the loss of his father. Traffic passed in fits and starts: Uncle Cicero in his police cruiser, making his morning rounds, keeping Moseley safe from crime and communism; a Merita Bread truck headed for the Koffee Kup; a few cars and pickup trucks; an eighteen-wheeler loaded with live chickens, scattering feathers in its wake. And then he heard the motorcycle, coming in from the east, the unmistakable throaty rumble as Joe Pike geared down and stopped for the traffic light at the center of town. Trout stood, walked down the steps and waited in the yard next to the driveway. After a moment, Joe Pike turned in and stopped next to Trout, the engine throbbing beneath him. His hair was windblown and there were crinkly lines around his eyes from looking off into the distance, down the highway he had perhaps considered but not taken.

"You forgot your helmet," Trout said.

Joe Pike ran his hand across his head. "Yeah. I reckon I did."

"It's not safe, riding without a helmet. You said so."

"Yeah. I know."

"You get hurt, and I'm up a creek."

Joe Pike shrugged.

"I'm sorry," Trout said.

Joe Pike nodded. "It ain't easy."

"No sir. It ain't."

Joe Pike dropped the motorcycle down into first gear and eased off toward the backyard. Trout could almost see the rider on the back behind Joe Pike. Almost, but not quite. But he could see enough to realize that it wasn't the Holy Ghost at all. It was a tiny, quiet woman who used to love to dance.

At midmorning, Keats called. "Come get me," she said.

"What?"

"I need a ride to work."

"Call a cab."

"In Moseley? Are you kidding?"

"Call a friend."

"I just did."

"Oh? I'm your friend?"

"Not if you don't come get me and take me to work. And hurry up. I'm late."

"Look," he said, "you were truly shitty to me yesterday. And I could care less if you get to work or not."

"I'm sorry about that," she said quietly, sounding quite contrite.

"Oh?"

"Yes. I am. Really. I apologize."

"Okay."

"Now get your ass in gear, Trout. I'm gonna be late."

He went on the motorcycle. He didn't ask Joe Pike; he just went to the shed and cranked it up and took off. Joe Pike must have heard, but he didn't make an appearance at the door of his church office.

He found Keats fidgeting on her crutches next to the dirt street in front of her house, dressed in her Dairy Queen uniform. It was freshly starched and the heat of the morning hadn't taken the creases out of it yet. Very snappy, he thought. The yard was full of cars. One of them had an Avis Rental sticker on the back bumper. The front door of the house was open, and he could see people milling about inside.

"Why can't your Daddy take you to work?"

"He's busy," she said, eyeing the motorcycle.

"Doing what?"

"I don't know. I thought you'd bring the car."

"Well, I didn't."

"I've never ridden a motorcycle before."

"Can you get on by yourself?"

"Of course," she said. "You think I need a crane or something?"

It might have helped, he thought. It took her a while, much heaving of limbs, snorting and grunting, banging of crutches. "Don't look," she ordered. He held the bike steady, feet splayed, until she finally settled in behind him, tucked the crutches underneath his arm with the tips sticking out over the handlebars like twin machine guns. She held the crutches with one hand, put the other arm around his midsection and snuggled against him. "Giddy-up," she said.

Trout sniffed the air. "What's that smell?"

"White Shoulders," she said.

"You're wearing perfume?"

She didn't answer. It smelled very nice.

Herschel Bender was a retired Army sergeant. Keats said he had finished his military career running a mess hall at Fort Gordon in Augusta and used his savings to open the Dairy Queen. He was pasty-faced and paunch-bellied with thick arms and neck, dressed in short-sleeved white shirt and narrow plain black tie with a Dairy Queen cap covering his graying crew cut. He spoke in staccato, like a machine gun.

"Don't touch nothing," Herschel said. They were inside behind the counter, in the chrome and air-conditioned coolness. The Dairy Queen was spotless — machinery gleaming, counters scrubbed, floor pristine.

"Herschel hates dirt," Keats said. "He says if you gotta break wind, stick your fanny out the back door."

"You want a job?" Herschel asked Trout.

"I've never done anything like this . . ." Trout waved his hand.

"He's a Moseley," Keats said.

Herschel ignored her. "Not in here. Out there."

Trout looked out through the plate glass. The parking lot baked in late-morning emptiness. Too early for the lunch crowd.

"The tables need painting," Herschel said. There were three concrete picnic tables at the side of the building.

"I know a kid down the street that'll paint the tables," Keats said, her voice rising.

Herschel turned on her. "Keats, you got a problem?"

"He doesn't need a job," she said. "He's —"

"A Moseley," he finished.

"Yeah."

Herschel nodded slowly, thinking it over. "Okay, so I don't hire anybody named Moseley. And maybe I don't hire anybody on crutches."

She glowered at him, and Herschel raised his eyebrows, waiting for her to say something else. She kept her mouth shut. Trout felt incredibly awkward. "Look, I'll . . ."

"You want the job?" Herschel asked.

Trout glanced at Keats. She wouldn't look at him. "Yes sir," he said finally. "I sure do."

Herschel crooked his finger. "Come with me."

The tables were bare concrete, stained with grease and spilled food. Herschel gave them a disgusted wave. "I come out here every day, wash the damn things off, customers come right back and mess 'em up. Grown-ups as bad as the kids. If this place was a mess hall, I'd kick their butts. But you can't do that with a civilian establishment."

"Yes sir," Trout agreed.

"Word gets around you're kicking butts, it's bad for business."

"I guess so."

"So, we'll paint 'em. Won't stop people from making a mess, but it'll be easier to clean up. Capish?"

"What?"

"It's Italian for 'you readin' me?'"

"Yes sir."

"Had a lieutenant in Korea, little sawed-off Guinea, used to say that all the time. Capish? Capish? He'd roust me outta my fartsack all hours of the night, give me some stupid order. Capish? Capish? Hated his guts."

"Why do you say it, then?"

"Bad habit. Like standing over a hot griddle, cookin' food for people to feed their greedy faces. Shoulda taken my money and bought a boat and gone deep-sea fishing every day."

"Why didn't you?"

"I hate fishing."

Trout nodded, not at all sure he understood.

"Well, get to work," Herschel said.

From the storeroom around back, Trout had fetched, at Herschel's direction, a gallon plastic jug marked MURATIC ACID, a bucket, a stiff-bristled scrub brush and a pair of rubber gloves.

"What . . . how do you want me to do it?"

"Get the hose." Herschel pointed to a length of green garden hose, coiled and hung from a spigot on the side of the building. "Mix the muratic half and half. Scrub the tables with the mixture, then hose 'em down real good. By the time you finish the third one, the first one'll be dry. Then paint. Gallon of green enamel and a brush on the shelf in the storage room. Then clean up. Leave the brushes soaking in turpentine. Capish?"

"Yes sir. Capish."

Herschel turned to go. Then, "What'd you say your name is?"

"Trout."

"Like the fish."

"Yes sir."

"Who the hell named you after a fish?"

"It's short for Troutman. That's my mother's family name."

Herschel grunted, started away again, turned back. "Keats. It's amazing how she gets around like that."

"I guess so."

Herschel shook his head. "Sometimes you just wanna smack her in the mouth."

It took a good bit of the day. The first mistake he made was not using the rubber gloves. He put them on and worked for a while, but his hands got hot and sweaty so he took them off. By the time he had finished scrubbing down the tables, his hands were burning, splotched with angry patches of red, the outer layer of skin peeling off his fingertips.

Herschel brought him a foot-long hot dog and a Coke for lunch. "You ever take chemistry in school?" he asked.

"Yes sir."

"You study anything about acid?"

"Yes sir."

"Well, you'll probably die," Herschel said. "If you don't, you'll be disfigured for life and your children will be born deformed."

Trout's mouth dropped open.

"Not really," Herschel said. "Muratic ain't powerful stuff, but it's acid. Hose your hands down real good and put some ointment on 'em tonight."

"I shoulda kept the gloves on," Trout said.

Herschel left him there to eat his foot-long and drink his Coke.

The second mistake he made was taking off his T-shirt when he finished lunch. He thought he'd get a little sun while he painted the tables. When he finished at midafternoon, he tried to put his shirt back on, but he couldn't. His shoulders and back were scorched.

Herschel came out again and looked over the tables. Trout had done a neat job, taking care not to splatter paint on the concrete apron under the tables. They were a nice bright green, drying quickly in the sun. "Looks pretty good," Herschel said.

"Thanks."

"How much I owe you?"

Trout shrugged. "I don't know." He thought for a moment. "Ten dollars?"

Herschel fished in his pants pocket, pulled out a wad of bills and handed Trout a twenty. "Don't sell yourself short."

"Yes sir."

"You looking for summer work? Or are you spending full time developing your tan?"

Trout looked at his shoulder. It was beet red and it left a little yellow indention when he touched it with his finger. "I think I overdid it," he said. "And yes, I'm looking for a job."

Trout felt like his whole body was on fire. Hands burning from the acid, back and shoulders feeling like somebody was sticking him with a million pinpricks at once. Even the wind on his bare skin made him twitch. Keats sat well back on the seat, trying not to bump against him, holding on to the belt loops of his jeans. She didn't say much until they got back into town and stopped at the traffic light on Broadus Street. Then she said, "He offered you a job, didn't he."

"He told me to come back when I get out of the burn ward."

She didn't say anything else until they made a turn at the high school and started toward the mill village. Then she said, "Let me off."

"What?"

"I said, 'Let me off.'"

He rode on for several yards, and then she smacked him flat-handed in the middle of the back. "Owww! GodDAMN!" he bellowed, and almost lost control of the motorcycle. It wobbled, jumped the curb, crossed the sidewalk and came to a stop on the lawn of the school just short of the flagpole. He kicked down the kickstand with a vicious swipe of his foot, jumped off the cycle, grabbed Keats around the waist, hauled her off and dropped her on the grass with a thump. Then he picked up her crutches where they had fallen beside the motorcycle and shoved them at her.

"What in the hell is wrong with you? What in the living name of mother-of-God hell is the goddamn matter?" He was aware that he was screaming, that his eyes were bulging, but he couldn't stop. Sunburn and acid burn and tennis burn and general cruddy situation burn took utter control of his brain. "The man offered me a job! What's wrong with that? I need the money and I don't have a goddamn thing to do in this goddamn pissant town and I think I'm about to go fucking nuts! I can't help it if my name is Moseley! I didn't choose it!" He screamed at her like a madman, stomping around the spot where she sat on the grass, flailing his arms even though every movement hurt like hell. "I don't want to be a Moseley and I don't want to live here and I am tired of your smart-ass shitty attitude and your ragging on me and cutting my balls off for something I can't do a goddamn thing about! Do you hear? Do you hear? Go home and torture your goddamn gerbil or something. Just leave me the hell alone!"

The motorcycle was still idling. He turned and aimed a kick at the cycle, caught it in the gas tank, toppled it over. The engine died with a cough. "Shit!" he yelled. "Shit, shit, shit!" Then he picked up the motorcycle and climbed back on it and fired it up again.

"I'm sorry," Keats said. It was almost inaudible.

He looked down at her. "What?" he screamed.

"I said I'm sorry."

He sat there on the motorcycle for a moment staring at her. Then she made a little pained face, scrunched up her nose and looked down at the grass. They didn't say anything for a long time. Trout could feel the wrath draining out of his head, seeping down through his neck and chest and puddling in his stomach. He felt incredibly tired and a little light-headed. It had taken a lot out of him. All of it.

Finally she said, "Let's get out of the sun."

The school auditorium was dim and musty, with a storm of dust motes swirling in the late afternoon sunlight streaming through the tall windows, splashing across the rows of battered wooden seats. Trout hunched miserably, elbows on knees, in a seat down in front of the stage while Keats went looking for the first aid kit in the sickroom. She came back after a while with a can of spray something with a big red cross on it. She sprayed it on his back and shoulders and it felt wonderfully cool, taking the sting out of his flesh. Then she sat down in the seat next to him and propped her crutches against the armrest.

"Why?" he asked after a while. She didn't answer. "Why do you do that? Why don't you just leave me alone if you're so mad? I've never been around anybody who's as mad as you are. And you just turn it on and turn it off. It's like a damned ambush."

They heard the front door of the school building open and Trout froze. It was Mr. Blaylock. He could have looked through the open back door of the auditorium and seen them. *Hey! What the hell you young'uns doing down there? You with your shirt off . . .* But he passed by in the hallway without looking. They heard the door to the principal's office close and the drone of his window air conditioner as it started up. Trout eased his T-shirt on. It still stung, but the burn was a lot better.

They sat there a while longer and finally Keats said, "I got run over by a truck."

"What?"

"That's how . . ." She indicated the crutches. "The guy in the house next door got fired — drinking, I think — so the mill sent a truck and loaded up all their stuff to take it off. Joe and I were playing in the dirt behind the truck. Something slipped. It rolled back. And . . ." She shrugged.

"God," he said. "I'm sorry. I'm really sorry." He sat there for a long time, stunned. He had no idea what to say. He had assumed it was polio or something like that. There was still such a thing as polio, wasn't there? But no, it was a stupid truck. A Moseley truck. "Did anybody do anything?" He gestured at her legs. "I mean, to help?"

"I had a bunch of operations. The mill paid for all of it. The Moseleys."

"But . . ."

"Yeah."

Then he remembered something she had said just now. "Who's Joe?"

"My little brother."

"I didn't know you had a brother."

"I don't." She blanched, and then her face went all dull and lifeless. "The truck . . ."

"My God," he said softly. And for the first time, he truly felt the great crushing weight of being who he was. *Don't forget who you are,* Aunt Alma had said. It sounded so easy, so proud, so comfortable when she said it. Since she had said it to him that first afternoon in the mill, it had been mostly an irritation. People didn't speak to you at school, the principal was still upset because Joe Pike fell down in a football game. Everybody watched you, took careful note of every- thing you said and did, compounding the burden of being a preacher's kid. All that was a pain in the butt. But it wasn't anything he couldn't handle. This, though . . . Sweet Jesus. He could see that he was a product of a great aching history that stretched back farther than he could ever see. People with mills and trucks and money and power over other people's lives.

"I'm sorry," he said again. And he truly was. About more than the truck running over Keats and Joe Dubarry. He felt an overwhelm- ing hollowness, expanding and filling the empty space of the high-ceilinged auditorium and oozing out the doors and windows, sucking in an entire town and everything in it.

"It makes Daddy crazy," Keats said. "Every time he looks at me. Every time he sees these." She picked up the crutches with a clatter that echoed like gunfire in the auditorium's stillness, making the dust motes dance. "It's all I've ever heard. The damn Moseleys."

"I guess I understand —"

"No you don't," she snapped, suddenly angry again. "He named Joe for your father."

"Oh."

She picked up her crutches, planted them solidly on the floor, and vaulted up out of her seat. She had powerful hands and arms. She stood there with her back to him, and then she turned around. Her face was hard and sharp. He had seen it yield a little, every great once in a while. This morning when he picked her up, wearing her White Shoulders. But not now. It was a thing she allowed only in tiny pieces, like sloughing off old skin. Underneath, there seemed to be only the hardness.

"Yeah," she said. "Oh."

"Keats," he said quietly, "I didn't do it."

She just stared at him. Again, unyielding.

"I've got enough shit to tote around without all that."

She stared some more. Then she said, "You sure have a foul mouth for a preacher's kid."

"I don't . . . I try to be careful."

"Except with me?"

Trout heaved himself up out of his seat. *Sometimes you just want to smack her,* Herschel had said. Instead, he walked past her and started up the middle aisle toward the door.

"Aren't you gonna take me home?"

"I guess."

"One thing," she said.

He stopped, turned back to her.

"You finally got pissed off. Feel better?"

"No." He truly didn't. He felt as rotten as he had ever felt in his life. He wanted to go home and close the door and be by himself. Be very still. Not move a muscle. Not let a single sound intrude. He wouldn't even have to wait until dark because he thought you could probably create your own darkness if you let go of yourself. Then suddenly he thought, *Like Mother*. Was that it? Was that how it started? And what did she find when she got deep down inside herself — still and quiet and dark? It must be okay, because she had gotten very, very good at it.

"Keep trying," Keats said.

"What?"

"Being pissed off. It takes practice. Like anything worth doing."

EIGHT

WHEN TROUT PARKED the motorcycle in the shed behind the parsonage, he heard music coming from the church education building next door. Loud boogie music. Fats Domino. *Hello, Josephine . . . how do you do . . .*

He opened the door of the assembly room and peered in. Joe Pike, wearing ancient plaid Bermuda shorts, a faded green knit shirt, and jogging shoes. Grace Vredemeyer in pedal pushers and a loose-fitting upper garment, half-shirt and half-vest that wrapped around her bosom from both sides and tied in the back. *Say, hey, Josephine . . .* They faced each other, about ten yards apart, and they were doing jumping jacks. Trout remembered. Jumping for Jesus. The music thundered from Trout's boom box, set up on a table at one side of the room. All the folding chairs that usually filled the room had been stacked against a wall, leaving the expanse of linoleum floor clear for Jumpers. But it was just the two of them. Joe Pike was sweating profusely despite the air conditioning: hair matted against his skull, armpits and shirt front dark green, arms flailing the air, legs hopping out . . . back . . . out . . . back, belly bouncing up and down. Grace Vredemeyer was doing a pale, dainty imitation of Joe Pike's movements, like somebody making angels in snow. She sweated not at all; her hair and makeup were perfectly in place and undisturbed. She bounced a little under her upper garment, but it was like small animals burrowing furtively. She gave Trout a tiny wave without breaking stride. "Come join us," she called out.

Trout waved back, took a folding chair from a stack near the door, opened it, and sat down to watch for a moment until Fats Domino got through with them.

Jumping for Jesus. He hadn't given it much thought when Joe Pike had announced it from the pulpit the previous Sunday. Maybe he didn't think Joe Pike was really serious. He had never done anything remotely resembling it anywhere they had lived before. He was the sort of preacher who would golf with members of the congregation, have uproarious fun at an Easter egg hunt, dress in drag and dance in a chorus line at the Lions Club Follies. But church, to his way of thinking, had always been for, well, going to church. He hadn't had much truck with Boy Scout troops and sewing circles and literary societies, not in the church buildings. But now, everything was out of kilter. Elvis Presley in the pulpit and Fats Domino in the education building. And Joe Pike himself didn't seem to be having much fun with any of it. Look at him now: mouth set in a grim line, brow furrowed in concentration, arms and legs and belly shattering big chunks of air. *Josephine, Josephine . . .*

It troubled Trout on several counts. For one thing, it had the smell of another Dairy Queen phase coming to an end, the beginning of salad days, a body at war with itself. The little man trapped inside the big man, whoever he was, trying to claw his way to the surface. No, he didn't like it one little bit. And he liked this Grace Vredemeyer business even less. That had a smell to it, too, but nothing he dared try to put a name to. Not yet.

The music ended. Joe Pike gave out a big whooosh of air, arms collapsing at his side. "Lordy! That's too much like work!" He pushed the STOP button on the boom box before Fats Domino could crank up again. Trout knew the tape by heart. It was one of Joe Pike's favorites. The next song was "Blue Monday." Only this was Wednesday.

"Jumping for Jesus," Joe Pike said to Trout.

"Sure."

"Thought we'd have more of a crowd. But you've got to start somewhere," Joe Pike answered. "Folks hear about it, they'll come."

"We'll spread the word," Grace said. She did a couple of dainty torso rotations, keeping her eye on Trout. "Have you been exercising, Trout?" she asked.

"No ma'am."

"Your face is red."

"Oh. Yes ma'am. I reckon it is. I've been . . ." What to tell? What would Grace Vredemeyer even remotely understand about his day? Better still, would Grace Vredemeyer do the Christian thing and go away so he could talk about it with his father? He had a lot of questions. "I've been lifeguarding at the pool."

Grace gave him a blank look. It was another thing Moseley didn't have. A swimming pool.

"They needed a substitute. Just for the day," he said.

Joe Pike wasn't paying any attention. He was fumbling with the boom box, putting in another tape. He turned back to Grace. "Some alternate toe touches?"

"Sure," she said. She stood there bouncing lightly from one foot to the other.

Trout started for the door. He didn't want to see any more of this. He was exhausted, and his sunburn and his raw hands were beginning to sting again. He needed . . . What? A big vat of vanilla pudding. Naked.

"Your Aunt Alma wants to see you," Joe Pike said.

"What about?"

"Ask her."

"Now? I'm really tired. I thought I'd take a nap." Trout could hear the irritation in his voice and he didn't care.

"She's waiting for you. Get cleaned up first. She said she'd be at the mill until five-thirty."

Trout turned to go. He stopped, hand on the doorknob. "What's for supper?"

"Thought I'd fix us a salad," Joe Pike said.

"I thought so."

By the time he reached the parsonage, the boom box was thumping away again. The Bee Gees now. *Stayin' alive . . . stayin' alive . . .*

There was only a scattering of cars in the parking lot when Trout got to the mill. Second shift, he remembered, the one Wardell Dubarry worked. Trout imagined him now inside, tending looms and cussing the Moseleys. Alma's car was parked in front of the one-story office annex. It was her everyday car, a late-model gray Buick. Trout hadn't seen the old Packard in use since the day he arrived, the day she had brought him here and told him that one day, all this would be his. He stood beside the motorcycle for a moment, looking at the mill building: dull red brick, tall windows so sun-mottled, they looked like stained glass with the late-afternoon light hitting them just so. *Like a church,* Aunt Alma's other church. It had once operated twenty-four hours a day, six days a week, so Uncle Phinizy had told him. And the other church, the one where they were Jumping for Jesus just now, had had two services every Sunday morning to accommodate the crowd. What happened?

The door to the office annex was open. Trout stuck his head in, looked around, didn't see anybody. It was after five, the office staff gone for the day, their tiny cubicles with the wavy-glass partitions empty, desk-tops bare. Back in the mill area, he could hear the steady hum of machinery. He called out: "Aunt Alma?"

"Back here."

She was at the mahogany desk in her office, a big green-sheeted ledger spread open in front of her. "Be just a minute," she said, waving him into a chair. He sat, hunched a little forward. He had showered gingerly, found a tube of first aid ointment and smeared it on the places he could reach, then dressed in short-sleeved cotton shirt and khaki pants. If he didn't do too much moving around inside the shirt, it was bearable. He waited, trying to be still and quiet.

Aunt Alma looked up at him and frowned. "Do you have hemor-rhoids?"

"What? Oh, no ma'am. I just got a little sunburned."

"It runs in the family."

"Sunburn?"

"Hemorrhoids. All the Moseley men have them."

"Well, I never have, ah, had the problem."

"Your father had a terrible case when he was a teenager. Football aggravated his hemorrhoids."

"Maybe that's why he fell down," Trout said. Could you trip over a hemorrhoid?

Aunt Alma gave him an odd look and went back to her ledger. She consulted a pile of papers at her elbow and made entries in the book with a pencil, flipping pieces of paper as she went. "I'm almost finished," she said after a while.

"No hurry," Trout said. And waited some more.

She reached the bottom of the stack of papers, put them aside, then started to work with an old crank-handled adding machine — the index finger of her left hand moving down a column of figures on the ledger, her right hand jabbing keys, hauling on the crank. The paper tape curled out of the top of the machine, longer and longer, almost reaching the floor. Alma was very deft. She never took her eyes off the column of figures until she had finished and given the adding-machine handle a final pull. She squinted at the last figure on the tape and sat there for a long moment staring at it. She closed her eyes, opened them, looked again. Her lips moved silently. Then she ripped off the tape and started wadding it up until the long streamer of paper was just a small hard ball. She dropped it into a wastebasket at the side of the desk.

Trout stared. Alma looked up at him. Her eyes narrowed; then she broke into a perfectly hideous grin. "Now. How's it going?"

"Okay, I guess."

"I heard about your tennis tournament. That's too bad. I know you're disappointed."

"I played pretty badly," he said with a shrug. "I have this problem with my backhand."

She gave him a blank look. "I never played tennis."

"You know" — he demonstrated, wincing a little when the fabric of his shirt scraped across his back — "when you reach across your body to hit the ball. Backhanded. I don't do it very well."

"I see," she said.

"I have a pretty good serve," Trout went on. For some reason, it seemed important to explain this to Aunt Alma, who had grown up in a town where tennis was considered frivolous. Moseley could have used a little tennis, he imagined. Or maybe a drug culture. "In fact, my serve has been referred to as 'wicked.' Like a rocket. WHOOSH!" He made a rocket gesture with his hand, sending a ball screaming across Aunt Alma's desk. She flinched a little. "Usually, I can groove the sucker in there and knock the other guy back on his heels and never even have to bother with my backhand. I get a lot of aces."

"Aces?"

"Yes ma'am. That's where your opponent can't return your serve. But this kid from Augusta, he was *returning* my serve. Every time.

To my backhand. I had one ace the whole dad-burned match, Aunt Alma." Trout shook his head, remembering. "It was horrible. I feel like I let the family down. The whole town, in fact."

She shook her head, sympathetic. "It was just a tennis match, Trout."

"The State Juniors."

"Well, it's not the end of the world."

Trout stared at the floor. "I guess not."

"I'm sorry," she said. "Since I don't play, I suppose I can't fully appreciate what it means to you."

Trout looked up. "You could learn, Aunt Alma. I could teach you to play tennis. Everything — " he shrugged — "but the backhand, I guess."

"Oh no," she said with a dismissive wave of her hand. "At my age?"

"I had a friend in Ohatchee, his grandfather learned to water-ski when he was sixty. You're not that old."

Aunt Alma smiled. "No. Not quite."

Trout imagined Aunt Alma on the tennis court, maybe at the club in Augusta, dressed in a little white tennis skirt with her hair tied back. She had decent legs, what you could see of them. A little hippy, but that was from sitting here at the desk too much. She'd be stiff at first, but once she got the hang of it, she might play decently enough to enjoy the game. If she did, maybe she would build a tennis court. It would be a good way to get to know her better, teaching her to play tennis. If she'd just loosen up a little . . .

"I always wanted to go to Wimbledon," she said. "Not to play, just to watch. No, not even to watch so much as to just *be* there. It has a nice ring to it. Wimbledon. Very British, don't you think? The best people, on their best behavior. Some nice parties, I imagine."

"Well, why don't you go?"

Aunt Alma stared at him for a moment; then something wistful crossed her face. She looked away. "Maybe I should have," she said quietly. "But now? No, I don't imagine so."

Aunt Alma closed her ledger book with a bang, suddenly all business. "Enough about tennis. You've got the rest of your life to think about, Trout, and it's time you started learning."

"About what?" Trout squirmed in his chair. It sounded ominously permanent: *the rest of your life.*

"I'm going to start you off in shipping and receiving. It's hard work and it's not very glamorous, but it's a good point of view. Raw cotton comes in, white goods go out. A few weeks of that, then some time in the spinning and weaving operations. After school starts in the fall, you can work in the office. I want you to know the business top to bottom."

Trout felt his mouth drop open. Here? The mill? It was something he might have to think about in a zillion years, when Aunt Alma was dead from extreme old age and he and Eugene were the only ones left. And then they would hire somebody to run it and send checks every month. But now? Work here in this ancient beast of a building with all that machinery rumbling and growling, waiting to snatch you by the sleeve and chew you to a bloody pulp? He didn't even know how a pencil sharpener worked and didn't want to. He would screw something up horribly and the mill would explode and white stuff would float to earth for days. Headline: BOY PUSHES WRONG BUTTON. Joe Pike should be here. He should be the one running looms and shipping and receiving, maybe even running the whole mill — especially since he didn't seem to know why he had become a preacher. Instead, here was Trout, who had his mother's innate distrust — nay, outright fear — of all things mechanical, contemplating a career in textiles. *Dang it, Joe Pike Moseley, here I am cleaning up after you again.*

"Be here at eight," Aunt Alma said. "Cooley Hargrove is the shipping manager. He'll be expecting you. Now go home and get a good night's sleep. And for goodness' sake, get something for those hemorrhoids."

He was stopped at the traffic light in the middle of town when he heard Uncle Cicero hail him: "Trout! Yo, Trout!" Cicero was standing in the doorway of the hardware store, looking very snappy in his uniform and cap, gun belt circling his waist. "Need to talk to you, Trout."

Trout didn't much want to talk to Uncle Cicero just now. His back and shoulders were stinging again, and he wanted to go home and glop on some more ointment. But there didn't seem to be much of a way out of it. So he pulled over, parked the motorcycle at the curb, and followed Cicero into the store. It was a cavernous, high-ceilinged place, a single big room with shelves rising behind display cases along the walls, aisles lined with bins and more shelves, all filled with tools, nuts and bolts and nails, cans and cartons. Facing the front plate-glass window, a soldierly row of lawn mowers and garden tillers. Hanging from one pegboarded stretch of wall, Weed Eaters and chain saws. From another, brooms and mops. From still another, shovels and rakes and hoes. Along the back wall, sacks of mortar mix, rolls of fence wire, cases of motor oil, cans of paint. Near the front door, a long counter with a cash register and a big roll of brown kraft wrapping paper. It was well lit with low-hanging fluorescent fixtures, everything very orderly and neat, a rich stew of smells — leather and metal, wood and solvent. And color. Orange weed trimmers, green lawn mowers, oak-handled sledgehammers, bright red gasoline cans, even the grays and silvers and blacks of tools. Amazing how colorful hardware could be when you put it all together. Merchandise as decor.

Trout stood just inside the door, taking it all in, while Uncle Cicero leaned against the counter, arms crossed, cap tilted back on his head, lips pursed, watching. It struck Trout that Cicero didn't look at all like a policeman in a hardware store. He looked like a hardware man dressed in a policeman's uniform. The place fit him like a glove. He was perfectly at home. "Gee," Trout said. "It's a lot of stuff."

"I know where every item is, down to the last cotter pin," Cicero said. "Fellow comes in, wants a half-pound of your ten-penny galvanized nails, I take him right to 'em." Cicero pointed down one of the aisles where metal bins held a jumble of nails. "Another fellow comes in, says he needs a lawn mower. How much of a lawn mower? He doesn't know, just enough to cut the grass. How big's the lawn? Oh, about yea-by-yea." Cicero made a lawn with his hands. "What kind of grass you got? Bermuda in the front, Saint Augustine in the back. How often you cut it? Once a week." Cicero walked over to one of the lawn mowers, patted the silver handle. "Okay, what you need is your Lawn Boy Model L-250. Briggs and Stratton two-point-five horse engine, made in the good old U.S.A. Twenty-two-inch cut, self-propelled. On special this month for two ninety-five." Cicero knelt next to the Lawn Boy and pointed to the wheel height adjustment. "For the Bermuda in front, set 'er at one inch. You gotta show that Bermuda who's boss. For the Saint Augustine, pop 'er up to two inches. Cut Saint Augustine too close, you'll damage it. And keep the blade sharpened." He stood, gave Trout a direct look. "In the hardware bidness, you don't sell stuff to folks, you help 'em decide what to buy. And then you tell 'em how to use it. Now" — he stuck his finger in the air — "if the fellow says he's got two acres of zoysia sloping back to front with a stand of pine trees, I tell him to go to Augusta and get him a riding mower. You don't sell a fellow something he can't use, 'cause he'll be back in a week raising hell and you done lost a customer. Got that?"

"Yes sir."

"You come just in the nick of time, Trout."

"What for?"

Cicero tucked his thumbs in his gun belt. "I'm expanding."

"Oh," Trout said, looking around the store. "Where?"

"I've bought out Ezell." Cicero walked past him, out the front door and onto the sidewalk. Trout stood there, not sure what to do, and then Cicero motioned for him to come out. He stood next to Cicero on the sidewalk and followed his gaze to the feed, seed, and fertilizer store next door.

"I've been after Ezell for five years. And just this morning, he walked in here and said, 'All right, Cicero, you can have it.'"

"The store?"

"Yessirreebobtail."

"What are you gonna do with it?"

"Same thing Ezell's been doing. Him and me had sort of a gentlemen's agreement over the years. I didn't stock things like fertilizer and bedding plants and chicken feed and so forth. Somebody come into my store and want your twenty-five-pound sack of eight-eight-eight, I sent 'em to Ezell. Likewise, somebody walk into Ezell's place and want a hoe, he sent 'em to me. Only thing we never could agree on was your tree spikes."

"Tree spikes?"

"You know, those things you hammer in the ground around the base of a tree. Ezell contends that a tree spike is fertilizer. But I contend that anything you hammer is hardware."

Cicero walked back in the store. Trout followed. Cicero pointed to the side wall, the one he shared with Ezell. "I'm gonna knock out part of that wall right yonder, make about a ten-foot opening. And I'm gonna put my tree spikes and Ezell's tree spikes together on a rack right there."

"Sort of like a marriage," Trout said.

"That's it," Cicero laughed, enjoying the image.

"Well, that's nice. I guess."

"That ain't all," Cicero said, and led Trout out to the sidewalk again.

"Yonder." He pointed to the vacant lot just past Ezell's, the place where the furniture store had been. "Auto parts."

"You mean a store?"

"Not a store, Trout, a complex. Cicero's Do-It-All. I got a bulldozer coming in the morning to grade the lot. Then I'll put up a nice little building with skylights and a linoleum floor. And I'll knock a hole in the far wall of Ezell's place." Cicero gave a grand sweep of his arm, taking in the elements of his business empire-to-be. "Hardware. Feed, seed, and fertilizer. Auto parts. All connected."

Trout didn't quite know what to say. It was a little overwhelming. He could feel fatigue thick behind his eyes. He really would like to climb back on the motorcycle and go home and maybe revisit Uncle Cicero's grand design another day. But Cicero waited, beaming. "How about that," Trout said finally.

"It's the best thing that's happened to Moseley in a long time," Cicero said. "It'll draw from all over. Maybe even from Augusta."

"What does Aunt Alma think about it?"

"Well, I haven't told her yet. But anybody can see, all this town needs is a little shot in the arm, Trout. Get folks excited about coming to Moseley again. One-stop shopping." Cicero checked off items on an imaginary list. "Can of spackling paste, box of sixteen-gauge shotgun shells, ten pounds of azalea fertilizer, package of nasturtium seeds, radiator cap for a seventy-one Chevy Caprice, case of Havoline thirty-weight oil."

"And tree spikes," Trout added.

"You betcha." Cicero laughed again. "Don't forget your tree spikes. Then when you get through at Cicero's Do-It-All, go down the street yonder and eat lunch at the Koffee Kup. Pick up a pair of brogans at the dry goods. And shop the produce specials at the Dixie Vittles Supermarket."

Trout looked up and down the empty street. "What supermarket?"

"Oh, it'll come. This here" — he waved, taking in the hardware and Ezell's — "is the catalyst." They both stood there for a while, pondering it. And then Cicero said quietly, "I'd like to be known as a man of vision, Trout. The fellow who turned Moseley around."

Trout gave him a long look. And he saw that in his Uncle Cicero, there was not an ounce of guile or pretense or arrogant pride. Just a sawed-off little hardware man in a police chief's uniform with an honest, open face and the simple desire to do something right, whether it was fixing you up with the right lawn mower or fixing up a town with the right future. Trout liked his Uncle Cicero a great deal at that moment. "I think it's a great idea," he said.

"I hoped you would," Cicero said. "Can you be here at seven?"

"What?"

"First week or so, I want you to just wander around the store and look at things. Read all the labels, see what's where. You got to know your merchandise. I'll make up lists of items, just like I was a customer, and you fill 'em. By the end of the week, you'll pretty much be able to take over."

"Take over?"

"Of course, I'll be close by if you have a question or a problem. Supervising the construction."

Trout felt weak. He wanted to sit down on the curb and put his head between his legs. Cicero talked on, but his voice sounded hollow and far away. "I sure was glad to hear Joe Pike say you were looking for a summer job. But this could be a lot more than that, Trout. It's a chance to grow with the business. Build a career. Who knows —"

"Uncle Cicero," Trout interrupted, "I've got to go home now. I've had a long day. I got sunburned, and my back and neck are killing me. And I'm feeling a little light-headed. So I think I'd better just go."

Cicero looked at him, face scrunched up with concern. "You do look a little peaked, Trout. 'Scuse me for carrying on so and not noticing." He put his hand up against Trout's forehead. "You may even have a little fever there. Want me to drive you home?"

"No sir. I can make it."

"Well, you get a good supper in you, get a good night's sleep."

"Yes sir."

Cicero held out his hand. Trout stared at it for a moment, then realized Cicero wanted to shake. He did. Cicero had a nice firm, honest grip. A man of vision. "See you in the morning," he said.

"I can't eat this stuff," Trout said. He got up from the kitchen table, took the bowl to the sink, crammed all the leafy green and chopped-up red stuff and the crunchy little croutons and the imitation bacon bits into the disposal and turned it on. It roared in protest, digesting. Then he turned back to Joe Pike, who was shoveling a forkful of salad into his mouth, chewing it like a cud.

"What don't you like about salad?" Joe Pike asked after a moment.

"It grows in your mouth," Trout answered.

"Oh?"

"You put it in there and try to chew and it just keeps growing and you feel like you're gonna choke on it."

"You used to like salad. Mom fixed it all the time."

"That was different."

Joe Pike nodded. "Of course."

"I mean," Trout said, "she used different stuff."

"Same stuff."

"Well, she fixed it different."

Joe Pike ate some more salad. Trout watched him for a moment; then he went back to the table and sat down. "There's a chicken pot pie in the freezer," Joe Pike said. "And some sweet potato pie that Hilda brought from the Koffee Kup. And some of Grace's Jell-O fruit business."

"I've got three jobs," Trout said.

"Does that mean you don't have time to eat?"

"Uncle Cicero wants me at the hardware store at seven o'clock in the morning."

"And . . ."

"Aunt Alma wants me at the mill at eight."

"And . . ."

"Herschel wants me at the Dairy Queen at ten."

Joe Pike put down his fork and wiped his mouth with his paper napkin, then placed the napkin back in his lap. "Sounds like a full morning."

"Yeah."

"Are the positions incompatible?"

"What do you mean?"

"Well, you don't want to get lint in the ice cream or tacks in the looms."

"Daddy," Trout said angrily, "don't."

Joe Pike sat back in his chair and studied Trout for a while. "I'm sorry," he said finally. "I'm obviously not approaching your dilemma with the sense of gravity it deserves. Let's start over. You have three jobs — or, at least, job offers."

"Yes sir."

"An embarrassment of riches. Could you do more than one?"

Trout shrugged. "I don't think so. They're all the same hours, pretty much."

"Hmmmm," Joe Pike hummed gravely, furrowing his brow, twisting his mouth, and pondering — or at least appearing to ponder — the situation. Then he drummed a little cadence with his fingers on the edge of the table. Then he stared at a spot where the ceiling met the far wall, as if the answer to Trout's problem might be written there: ATTENTION! GO FOR THE MONEY! "How much do they pay?" Joe Pike asked finally.

"I don't know."

"You don't know?"

"Nobody said. That's not the point."

"What is?"

Trout shrugged.

"All right. Let me see if I can put this in perspective here. Preachers are supposed to be good at putting things in perspective. The hours are about the same. Money's no object. Sounds like it gets down to intangibles."

"Like?"

"Work environment, compatibility with colleagues, expectations for emotional and intellectual fulfillment. Coffee breaks."

Trout pushed his chair back with an angry scrape, got up and turned to go. "I can't even talk to you anymore."

"Sit down," Joe Pike ordered in his best no-nonsense voice. Trout sat down. Joe Pike gave him a long look, then reared back in his chair a bit, arms folded across his chest. "You want me to make up your mind for you? You want me to tell you what to do?"

Trout sat ramrod-straight in the chair and stared at his hands.

"What do *you* want to do, Trout? Which job do you want? Any, all, or none?"

"The Dairy Queen," Trout mumbled.

Joe Pike threw up his hands. "Touchdown!"

Trout stared at his hands some more, and then he finally looked up at Joe Pike. "Would you . . ."

"Nope."

"You don't even know what I was gonna say."

"Yes I do. You were about to ask me to square it with Alma and Cicero."

How does he do that? Does God whisper in his ear?

"Right?"

"I don't want to hurt Uncle Cicero's feelings and I don't want to make Aunt Alma mad."

"Well, there's a chance you will on both counts. But that's part of making a choice, son. I can't make your choice for you."

Joe Pike got up from the table, took his plate to the sink and rinsed off the few shreds of salad that were left. "I bought some wheat germ," he said over his shoulder.

"What?"

"I thought we'd have oatmeal for breakfast. With wheat germ on it."

Good grief.

Joe Pike put the stopper in the sink and started running dishwater.

"Daddy . . ."

"Huh?"

"Talk to me."

Joe Pike stood there for a moment longer with his back to Trout, then turned off the water, dried his hands on a dishtowel, came back to the table and sat down.

"Why are you mad at me?"

Joe Pike gave him a long look, his brow furrowing. "Son," he said finally, "I'm not mad at you. What makes you think that?"

"I don't know. You're just . . . not paying any attention."

Joe Pike sighed, rubbed his face with his hands, then folded them in front of him and leaned across the table toward Trout. "Trout, I'm sorry, son. I've got a lot on my plate right now. I'm worried about your mama, I'm worried about Alma and the mill . . ."

"And you're worried about why you became a preacher. You never did answer my question."

"Yes. That, too."

"Well, what am I supposed to do while you worry about all this stuff? I've got stuff to worry about, too."

"Most kids your age don't want their parents telling them what to do and how to think. I didn't. I wanted my father to just leave me alone."

"Is that why you ran away from Georgia Military Academy and went to school at Moseley High?"

"Yes."

"Is that why you went all the way to Texas to play football?"

"Mostly."

"Well, that's fine for you," Trout said. "I don't want you telling me what to do, either. But I want you there when I need you. And you're not there."

"I'm sorry," Joe Pike said quietly, looking at his hands. "I'll try to do better."

There didn't seem to be much else to say, so Trout got up to go. He was almost to the door when Joe Pike stopped him. "Practice one day when we were getting ready to play Baylor. We had wallered around and looked like a bunch of sandlot kids all afternoon, so Coach Bryant just all of a sudden stopped practice and sent everybody to the locker room. And we sat there and waited for him, scared out of our pants. Players, trainer, assistant coaches. Nobody moved. We waited, and the more we waited, the more scared we were. Finally, about a half hour later, Coach walked in. Didn't say a word, just stood there in the middle of the room. Then all of a sudden he hauled off and threw a block on an assistant coach that would kill a mule. Just slammed into this poor guy and knocked him into a row of lockers. Blam! Blam! Blam! Lockers come crashing down, the assistant coach is laid out on the floor half dead, eyes rolled back in his head, blood pouring out of a cut in his scalp. The rest of us just standing there with our mouths open. Horrified. I'm right at Coach's elbow and I'm about to pee in my britches 'cause I'm afraid I'm next. But then he puts his arm around my shoulder real gentle-like and says, 'You know, Joe Pike, sometimes it just helps to get things off your chest.' And he turns around and walks out. And on Saturday, we whipped Baylor pretty good."

Herschel was cleaning up when Trout got to the Dairy Queen about nine o'clock. There were a few late customers. A family in a pickup truck, mama and daddy in the cab, five kids in the back, all licking on ice cream cones. A station wagon with an "Illinois Land of Lincoln" tag towing a pop-top camper. The occupants, a man and woman and two teenage girls, were sitting at one of the concrete tables, munching on hot dogs. An elderly couple in a late-model Buick, the woman watching a small dog pee in the grass next to the parking lot while the man waited for his order at the window.

"Two cupsa vanilla with crushed nuts," Herschel said to Trout.

"What?"

"Don't just stand there. Fix the man's ice cream."

Herschel had stopped cleaning the griddle to take the man's order as Trout came in the back door. He pointed. "Cups there. Ice cream machine there. Just pull the lever down. Crushed nuts in the container. Anybody's eaten as much Dairy Queen stuff as you and the preacher oughta know what a cup of ice cream looks like. And wash your hands first."

Herschel went back to his work while Trout washed up gingerly at the sink in back. His hands were still a little raw from the acid he had used to clean the tables outside earlier in the day. Then he filled two cups with ice cream. He tried to finish them off with a little curlicue at the top, but it didn't work. The ice cream just flopped over. He found the mixed nuts, sprinkled a few on each. He eyed his work. Not bad for a start. He took the two cups to the front counter and slid the window open. Warm night air and the faint rumble of traffic on I-20 drifted in, mingling with the air conditioning.

"Spoons," Herschel said at his back. "Under the counter."

Trout took two red spoons out of a box and stuck them jauntily into the ice cream cups.

"Napkins," Herschel said.

Trout plucked two napkins out of the napkin holder on the counter and laid them beside the ice cream cups.

"Dollar fifteen," Herschel said.

"A dollar fifteen," Trout said to the customer. Then he recognized the man. Fleet Mathis. The mayor.

"Trout, that you?"

"Yes sir."

"Working at the Dairy Queen."

Trout looked over at Herschel. "I guess so, yes sir." Herschel grunted.

Fleet Mathis took a dollar bill out of his wallet and fished a nickel and dime out of his pants pocket, pushed them across the counter to Trout. "I'da thought you'd be working down at the mill with your Aunt Alma."

"Well . . ."

"Family business and all."

Fleet Mathis waited for a moment, but Trout didn't say anything, and finally he picked up his ice cream cups. "Too bad about the tennis tournament," he said.

"Yes sir."

"Your backhand, the way I heard it."

"That's it."

He started to turn away, but then he stopped and looked back at Trout. "Dairy Queen's our newest business."

"Huh?"

Fleet Mathis leaned over and peered through the open window at Herschel inside. "Sign of progress, that's what I tell folks, Herschel."

"Yes sir, Mayor," Herschel said. "A town that's got a Dairy Queen is an up-and-coming place."

Fleet Mathis looked at Trout. "Kind of ironic, Trout."

"What's that?"

"You working here at our newest business." He thought about that for a moment. "Well, good night, Trout. See you in church Sunday, if not before."

"'Night, Mr. Mathis. Hope you enjoy your ice cream."

He stood there at the counter watching Fleet Mathis walking back toward his car with the two ice cream cups. *He'll probably go right home and call Aunt Alma and tell her I'm working at the Dairy Queen. And then she'll have a fit and come storming over to the parsonage in the middle of the night.* Headline: BOY TRAITOR EXECUTED.

"It ain't an air-conditioned parking lot," Herschel said.

"What?"

"Close the window."

Trout slid the window shut. Then he leaned against the counter for a while and watched Herschel as he finished up at the grill. The muscles in his upper arms bulged against the tight sleeves of his shirt as he worked at the griddle with a spatula, scraping away the greasy brown residue of a day's worth of hamburgers and hash browns. He wore a stained apron, and his Dairy Queen cap was pushed back on his head, revealing a thinning patch of steel-gray crew cut. Herschel gave out a little snort. "Sign of progress, the man says. Next thing you know, they'll be announcing a Kmart and a Winn-Dixie. Maybe even a Lord and Taylor's."

"How long have you been open?" Trout asked.

"Two years next month. Before me, I think the last new business was a Laundromat. 1968. Stayed open a year, the way I heard it." He finished scraping, put down the spatula and turned to Trout. "You know what's wrong with this town?"

"The Interstate."

"No. The attitude. Folks just sitting around waiting for something to happen. Capish?"

"I guess so."

Herschel waved in the general direction of I-20. "Hell, the Interstate's no problem. Wasn't for folks coming in off the highway, I'd be a dead duck. You hungry?"

"Yes sir."

"You look it. Thirty years running a mess hall, I can tell a hungry man when I see one."

There were two weiners left on the little rotisserie cooker next to the griddle. Herschel took a foot-long bun out of the bun warmer, put it in a little paper boat, plopped the two weiners end-to-end in the bun and spread chili over the top. Trout's stomach rumbled in anticipation. He felt hollow.

"Tea?" Herschel asked.

"Sure. Great."

Herschel fixed a cup of iced tea and set everything in front of Trout on the counter. "Preacher ain't feedin' you?"

"We had salad."

Trout sat on a stool and ate while Herschel went back to cleaning up. He fought the urge to wolf it down, savoring every bite, filling up the hollowness. The crunch of the weiner nestled in the soft bread of the bun, overlaid with the tang of the chili. A religious experience, Joe Pike called it. Yea, verily.

When Trout finished, Herschel fixed him a cup of ice cream. "Here's how you do the curlicue," Herschel said. "A little twist of the wrist on the hand that's holding the cup, just as you're cutting off the flow. That's about the only trick I know to working Dairy Queen. Other than that, it's dish it up and dish it out. Clean place, good food, fair price."

Trout thought about it while he slowly ate his ice cream. Maybe that was why he chose the Dairy Queen. The thought of the mill gave him a dull, leadened feeling — all that clattering machinery, spinning bobbins of yarn, looms disgorging miles and miles of plain white cotton cloth, all of it going into the big ledger book on Aunt

Alma's desk. And the hardware store. He liked Uncle Cicero, but the idea of all that *stuff*. Nuts and bolts and loppers and tree spikes rattling around in his brain and banging into one another? There was too much rattling around in there already. He needed something cool and not too noisy and short on detail and long on routine. Dish it up and dish it out.

He scraped the last morsel from the bottom of the ice cream cup and let it slide down his tongue. Then he set the cup down on the counter, stood up, fished in his jeans pocket.

"On the house," Herschel said.

"Thanks."

"Ten to two tomorrow."

"Okay."

"Two-fifty an hour to start."

"That's fine."

Joe Pike and Phinizy were sitting on the front steps when Trout pulled into the driveway. The beam from the motorcycle's headlamp swept across them, but neither looked up. They seemed to be deep in conversation. Trout put the motorcycle in the shed and walked around to the front of the house. Joe Pike was wearing a short-sleeved dress shirt and tie. Had somebody died? Then he remembered. Wednesday night. Prayer Meeting. He felt an old familiar lurch in his stomach. There was something vaguely unsettling about the notion of Wednesday Night Prayer Meeting, something ancient and buried like an old bone turning to dust. He could not remember ever going, and maybe that was it. Guilt? Or something else?

Trout sat down beside Phinizy on the steps. "Hello," Phinizy said. He took a last drag off the stub of a cigarette he held between his thumb and first finger, pulled another out of the pack in his shirt pocket and lit it off the end of the stub.

"Hello yourself," Trout said. "Aren't you gonna offer me a cigarette?"

Phinizy sucked noisily on the new cigarette, then blew a double stream of smoke out his nostrils as he said, "No sir, I am not. Cigarettes make your breath smell bad and then you can't kiss girls."

"Don't you kiss girls?" Trout asked.

"Not anymore. At my age and stage, I'd rather smoke cigarettes."

Then he was shaken by an attack of wheezing and coughing, nasty wracking stuff that sounded like it was coming from somewhere down around his feet. Headline: MAN DIES, LUNGS FOUND IN AUGUSTA.

Joe Pike hadn't said a thing since Trout rounded the corner of the house. He sat hunched forward, elbows on knees, hands clasped, a massive silence. It was hard to see either man's face in the dim light filtering through the tree branches from the streetlamp out by the curb, but Trout could smell the aroma of argument in the air mingling with the pungency of tobacco. Phinizy gave a last hack, took a shallow breath, let it out easily. "Ahhhhh," he said. "A gentle habit, smoking." Then he tossed the glowing cigarette onto the walkway at the bottom of the steps and crushed it with his toe. "Your father and I were just discussing dichotomy."

"What's that?" Trout asked.

"Schism."

Trout gave him a blank look.

"Contradiction."

"Oh. That."

Phinizy looked over at Joe Pike. "A sixteen-year-old boy, and he understands the concept of dichotomy."

Joe Pike didn't say anything.

"Reverend Joe Pike Moseley here has been a rare study in dichotomy this evening," Phinizy went on.

"I just said —" Joe Pike started.

But Phinizy cut him off. "They tell me," he said to Trout, "that your father has always been a stickler for tradition when it comes to church business. The old tried-and-true hymns, real wine at Communion, even if it is watered down a bit, no Boy Scout troops or other such folderol. And good old-fashioned prayer meeting on Wednesday night. Praying and singing. A midweek infusion of the Holy Spirit to tide you over till Sunday. None of this 'Wonderful Wednesday' business they have in lots of churches where they study pop psychology and paint china and do book reviews. None of that in Reverend Joe Pike Moseley's church. Am I right?"

Trout fidgeted. He had learned from experience that the best course when a couple of adults got off on a tangent like this was to excuse himself and go to the bathroom. Or if escape was impossible, hunker down and disappear into the furniture. Anything to stay out of the line of fire. He had done a lot of that when Irene was around, when the tension got to critical mass — Joe Pike being excessively polite, Irene lapsing into what became longer and longer silences, but the air thick with conflict that politeness and silence only made worse. If they'd just *yell*. Explosions come and go. Silence creeps up your butt like a parasite and builds a nest.

But he decided to wait it out a bit and see what happened. There might even be an explosion. Joe Pike was the one hunkered down over there on the other side of the steps, keeper of the great silence. And there was a persistent, needling edge to Phinizy's voice. If he kept it up long enough, he might bring a rare burst of thunder and lightning. At least get a reaction, which was something Trout wasn't having much success at. He remembered Phinizy's joke about the two truck drivers. Another wreck about to happen?

"You're right," he answered Phinizy.

"So here you have a preacher conducting a good old-fashioned Wednesday Night Prayer Meeting. And he gets off on deodorant."

"Deodorant?"

A long moment. They all waited. Then Joe Pike's shoulders shook, and he sort of heaved himself into an upright sitting position. Trout held his breath, but when Joe Pike spoke, his voice was even. "I *said* . . ." He chewed on it a moment, then went on. "I said that *what if* the scientists made a mistake. They tested antiperspirant, and they say it's safe. So the FDA approves it and we buy antiperspirant and put it on our underarms every morning and go about our business. But what if there is some minuscule, hidden ingredient in antiperspirant that turns out, after many, many years of use, to be very, very bad. What if we wake up one morning and our underarms are rotting out? That's all I said."

"And that," Phinizy added, "is when Tilda Huffstetler started crying."

Trout stared. "She did?"

"She did." Phinizy nodded. "Tilda said she's been going to Wednesday Night Prayer Meeting for more than fifty years, and it's the first time she ever heard anybody talk about deodorant."

"Tilda's always been a little high-strung," Joe Pike said. "Maybe it's hormones."

"No," Phinizy said, "I think it's more like confusion. Or, to return to my original theme, dichotomy."

"Look," Joe Pike said, his voice rising a little now, "is there anything wrong with me introducing an idea? . . ."

"Which is?"

"Randomness. Uncertainty. The unknown."

Phinizy gave a wave of his hands. "If we can't be sure of our deodorant, what can we be sure of?" Joe Pike didn't say anything. "God?"

Joe Pike nodded. "That's the point."

"That's *your* point. I'm not sure it registered with Tilda Huffstetler." Phinizy pointed up in the trees. "You're up there in the theological stratosphere somewhere, trying to figure out the meaning of life, and Tilda's worried about her underarms. Or perhaps more precisely, she's worried about why *you're* worried about her underarms."

"I'm the preacher," Joe Pike said with a touch of bitterness. "I'm supposed to have it all down pat."

"To Tilda, you are. She wants to believe in God, her preacher, and her deodorant. You threw her a curveball, high and tight, and it near about took her head off."

Joe Pike snorted. "So what am I supposed to do, Phin? If I have doubts about something, am I just supposed to keep 'em to myself? Isn't that dishonest?"

"I don't get it," Phinizy said.

"Get what?" Joe Pike asked.

"First of all, why anybody — make that, why would a preacher — purposely introduce more chaos into an already chaotic existence?"

"Chaos is the essence of existence."

"Maybe the battle *against* chaos is the essence of existence. Else, why do we impose laws, record history, invent myths?"

"Habit," Joe Pike said.

"Self-defense. We blunder about, being as ornery and unreasonable and illogical as possible. But deep down, we want some rules. Something we can put in the bank."

"Okay, Phin. So we're just supposed to obey the rules. Ask no questions."

"I didn't say that, Joe Pike. You asked me why Tilda Huffstetler cried at Prayer Meeting. I'm playing devil's advocate here. Telling you what I think. You know, part of your trouble is that you're a Methodist."

"What do you mean?"

"Catholics got the Pope, Jews got Israel, Presbyterians got reincarnation, Baptists got biblical inerrancy. You Methodists take it all in.

Come on, everybody. Think what you want. Israelites, reincarnation-ists, inerrantists, probably even a few closet Papists on the back row. Inclusion becomes confusion. Then the other part of your trouble is that you think you deserve answers."

Joe Pike shrugged. "I'm just a poor wayfaring stranger."

"Always have been," Phinizy said. "I think you became a preacher because you thought God would whisper in your ear and tell you what it's all about. But He didn't. So you got on a motorcycle and rode off to Texas looking for Bear Bryant. And he wasn't there. If Bear knew you'd done that, he'd probably laugh his ass off."

"Maybe that's what God's doing," Joe Pike said.

"Maybe."

Joe Pike waved his hands, agitated. "But if I don't know, I've got to ask, Phin. And if it upsets folks, maybe it'll get 'em to thinking, get 'em out of their self-satisfied existence."

"Or, it may just bring the Bishop down on your fanny."

"Could be."

Phinizy stood, brushing ashes off his clothes. "Well, you do what-ever you want, Joe Pike. It's your business. I'm going home and have some bourbon and read Heidegger."

Joe Pike looked up at him. "Tell me something, Phin. Why did you come to Prayer Meeting tonight? You never have before. Why this time?"

Phinizy gave Joe Pike a long look. "Same reason I read Heidegger. You know Heidegger: 'Why is there something instead of nothing?' You and Heidegger are both wallowing in cosmic angst, Joe Pike. Chasing your theological tails like Little Black Sambo's tiger. It's inter-esting to watch." He shot a glance at Trout. "But I sure wouldn't want to live around it." He waited, but got no response. A trace of a smile played at his lips. "I am a cynical old sonofabitch. I don't believe in much of anything. But at least I'm consistent."

He turned then and shuffled off across the yard, lighting a cigarette as he went, the flame from his Zippo flickering in the darkness under the trees. Then he crossed the street — a thin, stooped figure in the dim light of the streetlamp — and disappeared into the long shadows cast by Aunt Alma's house.

After a while, Joe Pike said — to no one in particular — "That's what you get with a church that's been spoon-fed all its life. Put a little spice in the menu, everybody gets heartburn."

Since Joe Pike said it to no one in particular, Trout didn't feel any need to respond and wouldn't have known what to say anyway. So they just sat there for a long time. And finally Trout thought of the thing he *did* need to say. He was bone-tired and needed desperately to go to bed, but he had to say this one thing first: "Keats told me about getting run over by the mill truck," he said. "And her brother."

Joe Pike didn't say anything for a while. And then he took a deep breath and made the little hissing sound through his teeth. "Yeah," he said. "Too bad about that."

And that was all. When Trout realized that was all, he got up and left Joe Pike sitting there on the front steps with his theological angst and went to bed.

What woke him in the depths of the night was the sudden remembrance of what made him uneasy about Wednesday Night Prayer Meeting. It came back to him full-blown, as vivid as the replaying of a documentary.

A parsonage kitchen, a bit down at the heels as they sometimes were in small Georgia towns: scuffed green linoleum on the floor, shiny pale green walls, fluorescent fixture overhead, white metal cabinets. A calendar from an insurance company hangs next to the refrigerator with a parade of red X's halfway across the month of July. Each evening, Trout climbs up on a kitchen chair and, while Irene steadies him, marks off another day with a crayon.

Joe Pike stands now in the kitchen door. Short-sleeved white shirt and tie, Bible in hand. Irene at the sink, hands thrust into sudsy water.

"Time to go," Joe Pike says.

A long silence. Irene's hands thrash about under the water, scrubbing away at a skillet. She lifts it out, runs it under the rinse water, sets it aside on a drying rack. "I'm not going," she says.

"Aren't you feeling well, hon?"

"I feel just fine."

"Well . . ."

"I'm not going."

"Well. . ."

"I mean ever."

Trout doesn't know exactly where he is while this is going on, but he must be somewhere in the room because he can see and hear and even smell everything. It has a smell to it, like something left out of the refrigerator too long. And the look on Joe Pike's face — as if he had been slapped with a dead mackerel. And Irene's tiny back, absolutely rigid and unyielding.

"Irene, hon, you have to go."

"No I don't."

"You're the preacher's wife."

Irene doesn't say a thing, but she gives a tiny shudder, as if she's suddenly struck with a chill. After a moment, Joe Pike gives a shrug of his shoulders. "We'll talk about it later," he says.

He has turned and left the room before Trout hears Irene say, in a small but very firm voice, "No we won't."

Then there is a horrible sucking sound from the sink and Trout realizes Irene has pulled the plug. She stands there looking down as the dishwater runs out, and then she turns and walks away. She doesn't look at him, doesn't even seem to notice that he's there. Droplets of water and bubbles of suds drip from her hands, leaving a trail across the kitchen linoleum. Trout hears the door to her bedroom close. He's afraid to follow, so after a while he goes out the back door and around the side of the parsonage and climbs up in the pecan tree in the side yard and looks in the window. Irene is just sitting there on the side of the bed, facing the open window. Nothing separates them but the window screen and several yards of July night. He starts to raise his hand to wave to her, but then he realizes that she can't see him here in the tree, can't in fact see anything. She is so absolutely immobile that he doubts that she could hear him if he called out, or feel him if he climbed in the window and touched her arm. It is like watching a statue of his mother. Across the street at the church, he hears a piano start up and the thin, ragged chorus of the Wednesday Night Prayer Meeting singing "Blessed Redeemer."

That was all he could remember. Being in the tree, watching his mother, hearing the music. He didn't know what he did next, what he felt, even exactly how old he had been at the time. Five, maybe. Six.

What he did know with certainty is that on a July Wednesday, Irene Moseley had refused to go to Prayer Meeting and that she lapsed into what was the first of the great silences that grew and grew until finally she embraced them as she would a lover and disappeared into the void.

Trout thought, *She won. She never went back to Prayer Meeting.*

Then he remembered what Uncle Phinizy had said: "Save your own ass." Well, that was one way to do it.

NINE

TROUT WAS ON the front walk getting the morning *Atlanta Constitution* when the truck growled past the parsonage, belching diesel smoke, towing a big flatbed trailer with a bulldozer on the back. Joe Pike stuck his head out the front door and watched as the truck rumbled on down Broadus Street toward the middle of town. Trout opened the paper and scanned the headlines: AIDE SAYS REAGAN WILL RUN; ATLANTA COUNCIL TACKLES TRANSIT DILEMMA. Forecast: hot, humid, afternoon thundershowers, high 93. The air conditioning in the Dairy Queen would be a refuge. But first there were Cicero and Alma to deal with. An inert lump of dread weighted his stomach.

Down the street, the truck wheezed to a stop with a hiss of its air brakes. Trout looked up at Joe Pike. "Cicero's Do-It-All," he said.

"What?"

"You know about it?"

"No."

"Uncle Cicero's clearing the vacant lot where the furniture store used to be. He's gonna put up an auto parts store."

"Really?"

"And he's bought out Ezell. He's going to knock holes in the walls and tie the whole thing together and call it 'Cicero's Do-It-All.'"

"Alma didn't mention it."

"I don't think she knows. Unless he told her last night."

Joe Pike pursed his lips in a silent whistle. "How 'bout that old Cicero."

Trout gave Joe Pike a look-over. "That tie doesn't match." Joe Pike's belly cascaded over a pair of dark blue pants. The tie he was wearing with his freshly starched white shirt was decorated with green and yellow amoebas on an orange background. "Where did you get that thing?"

"Texas," Joe Pike said, fingering the tie.

Joe Pike had never had the foggiest notion of fashion. Once upon a time, Irene had checked him before he left the house every day to make sure he didn't have on one brown sock and one black one. Often, he did. Lately, cowboy boots and black robe had covered a multitude of Sunday sins. But this was Thursday.

Joe Pike wiggled the tie and fluttered his eyebrows. "Does it not work for you, sweetie?"

"It depends on what you're doing today."

"Visiting the sick and shut-in."

Trout grabbed his throat and stuck his tongue out. "Gaaaahhhh."

Joe Pike pretended to be wounded. He let the tie flop against his belly. "Well, if you don't like the tie, just say so."

"Maybe the dark blue with the red diamonds."

Joe Pike checked his watch. "Are you going to see Cicero?"

"I guess so."

"I'll drop you off. I want to get a good look at Cicero before Alma beats him up."

When Trout and Joe Pike got there, the flatbed trailer was pulled up next to the curb by the empty lot and the bulldozer, a hulking orange Allis-Chalmers, was backing down the ramp. Uncle Cicero, in uniform, was standing out in the street, directing traffic around the flatbed, waving his arms and giving directions to the bulldozer operator, who wasn't paying any attention to him. The operator played the big clanking machine like a church organist, hands and feet moving deftly over levers and pedals. Another man stood by the truck cab watching.

Joe Pike parked his car at the curb, and he and Trout walked over to Cicero. A Merita Bread truck approached and slowed. The driver peered out the window at the bulldozer.

"Keep 'er movin," Cicero called out.

"What's going on?" the bread truck driver asked.

"Progress! New business coming to town."

"Here?" The bread truck driver gave a snort, moved on down the street and pulled up in front of the Koffee Kup Kafe.

"Morning, Cicero," Joe Pike said.

"Joe Pike. How y'all?"

"Trout told me about your project."

Cicero's eyes danced with excitement. He looked as if he might break into a jig at any moment. "Yessirreebobtail. Profit and progress. Me and Trout are gonna have a busy summer."

Joe Pike looked at Trout. Trout looked at Joe Pike. Joe Pike shook his head. *Tote your own load, Bubba.*

The bulldozer cleared the trailer ramp, then did a neat ninety-degree pirouette and clanked up over the curb and onto the sidewalk. The concrete groaned and cracked under its weight. The operator cut the engine back to a deep-throated idle.

"Is that Grady Fulton?" Joe Pike asked Cicero.

"Yep."

"Hey, Grady!" Joe Pike yelled out.

Grady peered over at Joe Pike, grinned and waved. Then he climbed down from the seat and he and the other man slid the metal ramps onto the back of the flatbed. The other man climbed in the cab of the truck and pulled away, towing the empty flatbed. Cicero, Trout, and Joe Pike joined Grady on the sidewalk. Grady stuck out his hand and Joe Pike took it.

"Heard you was back," Grady said, looking Joe Pike up and down. "I believe you've growed some."

"Lord, Grady. It's been a long time," Joe Pike said. "This is my son, Trout."

Grady Fulton's hand was all callus and muscle. He was a little runt of a man, not much bigger than Uncle Phinizy, about sixty years old, with narrow eyes that squinted out from under the bill of an ancient, soiled Atlanta Braves cap with Chief Nok-a-Homa on the front. He looked Trout over, then Joe Pike, back to Trout. "You sure y'all kin?"

"I take after my mama," Trout said.

"Uh-huh." He gave a backhand to Joe Pike's belly. "I used to pick your daddy up for work every morning, and it'd take most of the bed of my pickup to carry his lunch."

"Grady and I worked construction during the summers when I was home from college," Joe Pike said to Trout.

Grady nodded. "Spent two of them summers four-laning two seventy-eight out of Augusta. That was about the time you was courting Alma, wasn't it Cicero?"

"Yep," Cicero said, giving a tug on his gun belt. "I remember how Mister Leland used to raise Cain every time he'd see that old truck of yours parked out in front of the house waiting for Joe Pike."

Grady Fulton lifted his cap, ran his hand through gray wavy hair and put the cap back on. "Mister Leland had a burr up his ass about that truck. He sure did." He clapped Joe Pike on the shoulder. "But then, Mister Leland always had a burr up his ass about *something* you was up to, didn't he."

"Yeah," Joe Pike said. "I reckon he did."

"Well," Grady Fulton said, "I got to get to work here. Clock's running, Cicero."

"How long you figure it'll take?" Cicero asked.

"Depends." Grady Fulton's gaze swept the vacant lot. It was waist-high in weeds, flourishing in the summer heat. As he studied the site, he pulled a pouch of Red Man chewing tobacco out of a back pocket of his ancient jeans, bit off a plug, worked it expertly into the corner of his jaw, and tucked the pouch away. "Ain't no telling what's in there. As I remember, they didn't do no clearing to speak of when the furniture store burned."

"No," Cicero said, "we was all just glad it didn't take the whole block. We just let it grow up and tried to forget about it."

Grady Fulton gave a short, dry laugh. "You may be digging up some old haints here, Cicero."

"Yeah, I may be."

"Okay," Grady said. "Let's see what we got. I'll scrape it all up; then I got a front-end loader and a dump truck coming next week to haul it off."

Cicero frowned. "Next week?"

"Or the week after."

"I was hoping maybe you could get it all done today."

"Today? Cicero, I got equipment tied up on two other jobs as it is." He pointed down the street where the flatbed had gone. "Kyle's headed over to Norwood now to pick up another dozer so we can do site preparation for a new Kmart in Thomson."

"I know you're doing me a favor . . ."

"What you in such an all-fired hurry for, anyhow?" He waved at the vacant lot. "It's been like this for ten years."

Cicero shrugged. And Trout thought, *Aunt Alma. He hasn't told her yet.*

Grady Fulton spat a well-aimed stream of Red Man juice into the weeds. He turned toward the rumbling bulldozer. And then Joe Pike spoke up. "Grady, you reckon I could . . ." He waved his arm toward the bulldozer.

Grady gave him a close look. "Been a long time, Joe Pike. You remember how? I can't have nobody tearing up my equipment."

Joe Pike grinned. "I was taught by the best dozer operator in the state of Georgia."

"At least," Grady said. "Well, come on."

Trout looked up at Joe Pike. "What . . ."

But he was already in motion, grabbing a handhold on the side of the bulldozer and pulling himself nimbly up onto the seat as Grady climbed up from the other side. Joe Pike settled himself in front of the controls and ran his hands over them, pointing to the black-knobbed levers and foot pedals, talking with Grady, who nodded and gestured. Trout couldn't hear them over the rumble of the diesel engine. He turned to Cicero. "Is Daddy gonna drive that thing?"

"I 'speck he is. Never saw him do it myself, but I hear he got pretty good at it when him and Grady was working together."

The diesel roared, belching black smoke from the stack above the engine. And then Joe Pike hunkered over the controls and pushed a couple of levers and the bulldozer lurched onto the vacant lot, jostling Joe Pike and Grady, who threw up his arms in mock horror. Joe Pike threw his head back, laughing. He pushed another lever and lowered the blade, and the bulldozer eased forward again. Trout stood there transfixed, mouth open in astonishment, as the blade bit into the earth, curling the weeds and laying them aside like a threshing machine, uncovering what the weeds had concealed — slabs of concrete, twisted lengths of rusty pipe, a fire-blackened water heater, a lot of unrecognizable rubble.

Trout pointed. Cicero smiled, winked. *Well, I'll be damned,* Trout thought. Another piece of Joe Pike's history, and this time something totally out of the blue. The Bear Bryant business — well, he at least knew a little about that. When Joe Pike went tearing off on the motorcycle in search of a past he had left in the heat and dust of Texas, it was at least a piece of history that Trout had heard about, however obliquely. But this? He hadn't the faintest idea what it was all about. And it wasn't so much the *thing*. It was the *surprise* of the thing. It was like seeing a rank stranger sitting up there on the high seat of the bulldozer, disguised somehow in Joe Pike Moseley's big body. Or maybe it was that little man tucked away inside the big one who was pushing and pulling those levers and stomping on the foot pedals as the bulldozer plowed through the weeds and debris toward the back of the lot.

Trout thought about Tilda Huffstetler, bursting out in tears at Wednesday Night Prayer Meeting. No wonder. Joe Pike Moseley kept opening his peddler's pack and pulling out stuff nobody suspected was there. Everything except what Trout really needed to know. He wanted to say, *Whoa! Wait a minute! Enough already!* Damn Joe Pike Moseley.

Down at the back side of the lot, the bulldozer clanked to a halt; then with Joe Pike pushing and pulling on the levers, it made an ungainly turn, wheeling on one churning track, and headed back toward the sidewalk, piling up debris and pushing it ahead of the blade. Joe Pike was all concentration. Beads of sweat stood out on his forehead, and the front of his white shirt was darkening with sweat. He had undone the top button of his shirt and slung his loosened tie back over his shoulder. So much for visiting the sick and shut-in.

"Is that Joe Pike yonder?" Trout heard at his back. He turned to see a crowd of gawkers gathering on the sidewalk behind them.

"It's Joe Pike, all right."

"Good Lord."

"Who's that up there with him?"

"Maybe it's the Bishop." Laughter.

"Cicero, what's going on?"

"Progress," Cicero said forthrightly. "The rebirth of Moseley, Georgia."

Beyond the crowd, Trout saw a gray Buick ease to a stop out on the street. The tinted passenger-side window slid down. Aunt Alma. She stared for a long time, taking it all in. Trout looked over at Cicero. Did he see? Yes. Cicero gave Alma a little wave. She didn't wave back. The window closed and the car moved on, heading toward the mill.

"Ahhhhh," he heard Cicero sigh.

"Did you . . . ?" Trout asked.

"Not exactly," Cicero said.

Headline: SHIT HITS FAN. "I've got to go," he said to Cicero.

He turned and started walking quickly down the sidewalk. Cicero caught up with him in front of the hardware store, jangling a fistful of keys. "I'll open up and you can get started," Cicero said. "You know how to work the cash register?"

Trout kept walking. "No sir."

"Well, I'll show you. Anybody comes in and needs something you can't find, I'll be right down yonder at the construction site." Cicero was at the door of the hardware store, putting the key in the lock.

Trout stopped. "Uncle Cicero . . ."

"Yeah."

"I, uh . . ."

Cicero turned and gave him a long, searching look. And then he knew. His face fell. Trout felt a rush of guilt. But then he thought, *No. I've got to get out of here.* "I'm sorry."

Cicero gave a little weak wave toward the store. "I was . . ."

"Aunt Alma offered me a job, too," Trout said. "I appreciate it. Really. But I'm gonna work at the Dairy Queen."

Cicero looked off down the street where it curved just before it got to the mill building. He looked for a long time, turning things over in his mind. Behind them, at the vacant lot, the bulldozer clanked and rumbled, traffic stopped, the crowd kept growing. It was, Trout realized, the biggest thing that had happened in Moseley in a good little while. He waited a while longer. Cicero kept looking down the street, searching for something just beyond the bend in the road. Trout waited. He thought he owed Cicero that much, not to just walk away. If Cicero wanted to yell at him a little, that would be okay.

Then Cicero turned back and Trout could see something in his eyes that looked very close to desperation. It was there, naked, unconcealed, terribly painful but exquisitely honest — more so than anything he had seen from Joe Pike Moseley in a long time, perhaps ever. Trout wanted to look away, but he couldn't do that, either. He saw, he knew for dead certain, that what was going on down there on the vacant lot with the bulldozer was this little chunky stump of a man in his terribly earnest police uniform trying to save his own ass. And knowing he might not be able, no matter what.

"You oughta do what's best for you," Cicero said. "We all got to get on about our lives, Trout. But" — he gestured again toward the hardware store — "it's always here if you want it."

"Thank you, Uncle Cicero," Trout said. He had a sudden urge to hug Cicero's neck. But he hesitated a moment too long, and Cicero turned and walked back down the sidewalk toward his construction project.

Aunt Alma came up like a shot from behind her desk when Trout told her. "The DAIRY QUEEN?" she cried out.

"Yes ma'am."

"That's the most ridiculous thing I ever heard in my life!"

"Aunt Alma —"

"Out there with trash people scooping up ice cream!" Alma's shrill voice shattered the air of the office. She picked up a stack of papers, waved them in the air and smacked them back on the desk. But Trout found himself, to his amazement, staying very calm. He stood before her desk, hands folded in front of him.

Aunt Alma pointed an accusing finger. "You are your father's son."

"Yes ma'am. I sure am."

"Don't sass me, Trout."

"I didn't mean to, Aunt Alma."

"Your father has been rebellious and defiant since he was in diapers, and he has caused this family untold grief and misery! Has and does! And if you keep going like you are, you're going to turn out the same way!" Her voice kept rising. She waved her arms. Her eyes bulged. Trout thought about what he might do if she popped a blood vessel. Pick up the telephone and call 911? Did Moseley even have 911?

"Aunt Alma, it's just a job."

"That's right!" she cried. "It's just a job! This" — she indicated the mill with a sweep of her hand — "is family! It's your future! Our future! Don't you realize that?"

Trout stood there for a long time, thinking about what he might say and do. He felt weariness settle over him. The easiest thing would be to just take the mill job, give himself over to this aging red building with its strange smells and vibrations and its ghosts of Moseleys past. The Dairy Queen, as he had just said, was just a job. It wasn't, despite what Joe Pike said, a religious experience. The mill, on the other hand, did seem like a Holy Crusade to Aunt Alma. There was a kind of come-to-Jesus fervor about the whole business — but not the abiding joy of a sinner saved. There was about her, as there was about Uncle Cicero, a kind of desperation. In fact, he thought now, the whole damn bunch was more than a little desperate: Joe Pike floundering in religious quicksand; Cicero trying just to *be* somebody besides Alma's husband; Alma herself, clutching her Moseley-ness to her breast like a shield against unnamed terror; even Phinizy, hunkered down behind his whiskey and his books, wry and watchful. And yes, he too was beginning to feel a little desperate. All this business about the future was making him a little crazy. He wanted to go away, find a quiet place where he could think and maybe figure out what to do, how to — as Phinizy had put it — save his own ass. And that was what finally made up his mind for him.

"I'm just sixteen years old, Aunt Alma," he said. "I'm going to work at the Dairy Queen. I'm sorry."

She stared for a moment, eyes narrowing. "Then go," she said, flipping her hand, dismissing him. "Go! Just go." She turned away from him with an angry jerk. Then she picked up the telephone receiver and started dialing. As he walked out he heard, "Put Cicero on the phone." He stopped in the hallway, imagined himself turning back, taking the receiver out of Alma's hand, replacing it in the cradle, and saying, *Leave the poor sonofabitch alone.* But of course, he didn't.

The mill village was teeming with midmorning life — women shelling peas on front porches, burning trash in backyard barrels, hanging wash from backyard clotheslines; men tinkering with automobiles; a pack of kids playing basketball on a bare-earth vacant lot. Keats was waiting on her front steps when Trout pulled up on the motorcycle and turned in the gravel driveway. The Avis Rental car, the one that had been there the day before, was still parked behind Wardell's old Ford.

"Your company's still here," he said as Keats danced toward him across the patch of grass.

"It's not company." She held her sketch pad tightly under her arm. She was wearing perfume again.

"What is it?"

She ignored the question. "How's your sunburn?"

"Better. But don't hold on too tight. Want me to hold your pad?"

"Of course not." She struggled onto the seat behind him, thrusting the crutches under his arms and across the handlebars. Then the pad slipped from her grasp, fell onto the ground next to the motorcycle and flopped open. Trout stared, eyes widening. "Whoooo," he said softly. A nude woman. High, arching breasts, narrow waist, slim thighs and legs, all soft lines and curves in thick pencil strokes. Trout felt himself stir.

"Give me that!" she barked.

He kept staring. "You're pretty good."

She rapped him sharply in the side with one of her crutches.

"Ow!"

"Stop looking. Pick it up and give it to me. Right now!" She rapped him again, harder this time.

"Awright! Damn!" He reached over, straining to keep the motorcycle balanced, and picked up the sketch pad by its spine, letting it close. She snatched it out of his hand. He twisted on the seat and looked back at her. Her face was beet red. "What —"

"None of your goddamn business!"

And it wasn't, he kept telling himself all the way to the Dairy Queen. But he couldn't help thinking about it. The nude woman hiding in the thick pages of the sketch pad had Keats's face. But the body was that of a woman who stood upright, proud and unfettered. A woman who had no need of crutches.

They said hardly a word all morning. Herschel showed him how to make a milk shake and a banana split and a Blizzard, how much chili to put on a foot-long hot dog, while Keats tended the window and kept her distance, closed-off and sullen. Then it was noon and the rush began, and it took all three of them to keep up with the crowd. He tried to help, but he was slow. She was impatient, snatching things away from him when he was half finished, fixing them herself. His irritation grew. Finally, she reached for a milk shake he was holding under the whirring blade of the stirrer.

"Give me that!" she barked.

"I can do it myself!" he shot back.

"People don't have all day waiting for you to fumble around!" She reached for it again, and he jerked it away from her, slopping some of it on the floor. "You're making a mess!" she cried. "Get out of the way!"

"Hey!" Herschel yelled. "Cut it out! You wanna fight, take it outside. Draw a crowd and sell popcorn."

"He's . . ." Keats started, but the look on Herschel's face cut her off. She turned with a huff back to the counter, slid open a window with a jerk. Joe Pike Moseley peered in, taking stock. "Morning. Y'all okay in there?"

"It's Amateur Hour," Keats snapped.

"Keats!" Herschel warned.

"Awright. Awright."

Herschel looked over at Trout. "You gonna fix the milk shake or not?"

"It's fixed," Trout said, seething, trying to keep his voice under control. He felt an urge to kick one of Keats's crutches out from under her. She was maddening. She made him feel like a kid with a wet diaper.

"Well, give it here," Herschel said.

Trout held out the milk shake. "Put a cover on it." Trout fitted a plastic cover over the shake, held it out again. "Straw and napkin," Herschel said. Herschel took the shake, straw, and napkin and passed them through the window to a woman who was waiting.

"Wanna wait on your daddy?" he asked Trout.

Joe Pike had on a fresh white shirt. He smelled like a bath. And he was wearing the amoeba tie again. Trout looked past him into the parking lot. Grace Vredemeyer was sitting in the front seat of Joe Pike's car. She waved to Trout. She, too, looked fresh from a bath, wearing another of her floral print summer dresses with a lot of neck and shoulder showing. "Visiting the sick and shut-in?" Trout asked.

Joe Pike glanced back at Grace in the car. "Grace sings to 'em; I bring glad tidings." Grace waved to Joe Pike.

"Daddy . . ."

Joe Pike turned back to him. "Uh-huh."

Don't you see . . . But he didn't, that was obvious. Finally Trout asked, "You want to order?"

"Two foot-longs, large order of fries, a chocolate shake, and a vanilla shake."

"What happened to salad?"

"Tonight," Joe Pike answered. "You can't visit the sick and shut-in on rabbit food."

"Glad tidings."

"Yea, verily."

Trout got up the order himself, took his time about it while several other customers came and went. He put everything in a cardboard carrier and delivered it to the window. Joe Pike was beginning to wilt in the heat. He pulled out a handkerchief and mopped his forehead. The collar of his shirt sagged. Out in the car, Grace Vredemeyer still looked perky. But she had rolled down both front windows. Trout opened the window and pushed the items through. "Three eighty-nine," he said.

Joe Pike fished in his pocket and pulled out a five. Trout handed it to Herschel, who rang up the cash register. "We're going to Augusta," Joe Pike said. "Grace's second cousin had open-heart surgery yesterday." Trout imagined Grace bursting into song in intensive care. Headline: MAN DIES WITH GRACE.

"Do you accept tips?" Joe Pike asked.

"No sir," he said as he handed over the change.

"See you for supper."

Keats snorted loudly as Trout closed the window. "Maybe he oughta put in tomorrow's order today. So you'll have it on time."

She glared at him, but Trout didn't say anything, and she turned back to the grill, where she was tending several sizzling hamburger patties. He looked at Herschel, who shook his head. Cool it. Trout took a deep breath and nodded. And he thought longingly of the hardware store.

The lunch crowd had barely cleared out when black clouds began to gather and the wind picked up, skittering bits of trash and dust across the parking lot. Herschel turned on the radio — the station over in Thomson — listening for a tornado warning. But it was just a nasty line of thunderstorms, the announcer said, barreling through on its way from Atlanta toward the coast. Marching to the sea like Sherman, the guy on the radio said. *War is hell, but y'all just keep listening to ol' Dan here 'cause we've got more Country Memories and a special on fryers at the Dixie Vittles Supermarket.*

Herschel stood next to Trout at the counter, peering out at the clouds. They were thickening fast — big, black nasty-looking things, boiling over the horizon from the west. A big truck pulling a flatbed trailer eased by on the road, slowing for the Interstate ramp. A blue tarpaulin covered the cargo and a loose corner of the tarp was flapping in the wind. "War," Herschel snorted. "Shit. What does that doofus know about war?"

"Maybe he was in Vietnam," Trout said.

"Naw. I know him. He's been over here trying to sell me some advertising."

"Did you buy any?"

"Hell, no."

"Why not?"

"You don't *advertise* a Dairy Queen. It's just *here*. You either want it or you don't."

Trout thought about that. Maybe Joe Pike was close to the truth after all. "My daddy says Dairy Queen is a religious experience."

Herschel shrugged. "Well, I don't know anything about that. I ain't religious, anyhow."

"What if you advertised and business got better?"

"What am I gonna do with it? Build another Dairy Queen next door? Then I got two of everything."

"You could add a drive-in window," Keats said. She was sitting on a stool over to the side, crutches propped against the wall, working away on her sketch pad. She didn't look up.

"I already got a drive-in window," Herschel said. "Folks drive in, come up to the window."

"Not when it rains, they don't," Keats said. "If you had a real drive-in window with a cover over it, they could order from the car and get what they want without getting wet."

"Rain don't last forever," Herschel said. "People oughta stay home when it's raining. Only doofuses get out in the rain."

"Like the Army," Keats said.

"Oh, hell yes. That's why I became a cook. It don't rain in a mess hall."

Keats sketched away, her hand making broad strokes on the pad. She glanced up and caught Trout watching her. He raised his eyebrows, questioning. Another nude? Keats stuck out her tongue at him, but there wasn't any malice in it. *God,* he thought, *she can turn it on and off. She could drive you plain crazy if you let her.* Keats went back to her drawing. "Is the Army a bunch of doofuses?" she asked Herschel.

"Only the majors."

"Why majors?" Trout asked.

Herschel smirked. "It's part of the job description. Enlisted men do most of the work in the Army. Lieutenants and captains do a little. Not much. Colonels and generals give the orders. And majors just, well . . ."

"Doofus," Trout offered.

"Exactly." He waved at the gathering storm. "Major sits around with his thumb up his butt until it rains. Then he says, 'Hey, it's raining! Let's get all the troops out and go for a hike, whattaya say!' Poor dumb grunts are slogging through the mud in full field pack, rain dripping down the backs of their ponchos. And where's the major?"

"Taking a nap." Trout offered, getting into the spirit of it.

"Going to the Dairy Queen," Keats one-upped him.

Herschel laughed, a kind of cackling explosion. It was infectious — laughing at laughter — and Trout and Keats joined in. Laughter bounced off the chrome and Formica like shards of light and settled about them, keeping the weather at bay. On the radio, ol' Dan was playing Country Memories and selling fryers. The wind whistled at the eaves of the building. An overhead fluorescent fixture hummed contentedly. Trout felt a rush of relief. It had been a tense morning — Joe Pike on the bulldozer, Uncle Cicero's disappointment, Aunt Alma's angry disgust, Keats's snarling impatience. He felt the hard knot in his stomach, the tightness around his shoulder blades, unwind. Then he thought that it had been a good while since he had laughed at anything much, a good long while since he had indulged in lazy, go-nowhere talk that made you feel like a cat stretching into sleep. The Dairy Queen, even with maddeningly unpredictable Keats sitting over in the corner stroking at her sketch pad, suddenly felt almost safe. A haven where laughter was possible. No theological angst, no industrial crisis, no grand plans for progress. A Dairy Queen should be a place that made people happy, if only just for the few moments that a banana split lasted. He could stay here, he thought. Maybe a cot in the back. He wasn't hard to please.

"Well," Herschel said. "I gotta go to the bank. Might as well do it while there ain't no customers."

Keats looked up. "You'll get wet. Doesn't that make you a doofus?"

Herschel took off his cap and apron, opened the cash register, and took a vinyl bank bag out of the cash drawer. "Nope," he grinned. "They got a drive-in window at the bank." He started toward the back door, then stopped and turned back to them. "I don't know what kind of burr you two have got under your saddles, but I want you to work it out while I'm gone. When I get back here, I wanna see smilin' faces. Happy campers. Capish?"

"Okay," Trout said.

Herschel looked over at Keats. She was deep into the sketch pad. Scratch-scratch. "Keats . . ." She waved one hand, kept working with the other. Herschel turned back to Trout. "There's a gun in the drawer under the cash register. If she doesn't get her fanny off her shoulder, shoot her."

The storm broke just as Herschel pulled out of the parking lot in his panel truck. One moment it was just dark clouds and skittering dust, and the next there was a terrible crack of thunder and the rain exploded — sweeping up in a shimmering wall from the Interstate, fierce and wind-driven, splattering the pavement like machine-gun fire, whipping under the overhang out front, spraying the plate-glass window. On the radio, ol' Dan was playing Johnny Cash: "Five Feet High and Rising." *We better get out in our leaky old boat. It's the only thing we got left that'll float . . .*

Trout leaned across the counter and stared out. The rain was so thick now, you could barely see the road. Then there was a brilliant flash of lightning and a thunderbolt so close, he could feel the hair on the back of his neck stand up. He jumped, then backed away from the counter, bumped into the ice cream machine, and felt the cold touch of chrome on his arm, eased away from that. He looked over at Keats. She was hunkered over the sketch pad, pencil poised in midair, looking at him. No, not really *at* him, the way you would look at a person's face if you wanted to make a connection. Her gaze was fixed on some point near his waistline, maybe a bit below. Her eyes were squinched in concentration and she seemed to be totally oblivious to the storm raging outside or to his nervous dancing about. Then all of a sudden she seemed to *see* him, standing there gawking at her. And she blushed furiously, her face turning the color of a ripe watermelon. She turned away with a jerk and looked out the window.

He realized suddenly that she did this a lot — looking at him when she didn't think he saw, head cocked to the side, eyes lingering on odd places. She was . . . she was . . . studying him. No. More than that. *Undressing* him. Good God! He felt incredibly vulnerable, as if he had stumbled naked onto a stage, blinded by footlights and hearing a sudden murmur of people out beyond in the darkness. Pointing.

Laughing. Blood rushed to his face and neck, pounded in his ears, swelled in his groin. He fought the urge to double over, covering himself.

The wind howled, the rain pounded the roof, the air exploded with one peal of thunder after another. There was a great yawning space between them there in the fluorescent-lit sanctuary of the Dairy Queen. And this sudden, unnerving knowledge that froze him in place and made escape impossible.

He took a deep breath. "If you're gonna draw pictures of me, the least you could do is let me see."

"They're not . . . they're not you," she stammered. He could see that she was rattled. Caught red-handed, like some Peeping Tom looking in his bedroom window. "You saw . . ."

"Just one," he said. His voice was a hoarse croak. "It was . . ."

"Yes."

"But there's lots of stuff in there. You're messing with that thing all the time. Looking at me. Like I'm on display or something." He took a step toward her, holding out his hand.

"No!" she cried, clutching the sketchbook to her. "I told you, you're NOT IN THERE!"

"Then why do you keep *looking* at me like that?"

There was a long, painful silence. She stared at the floor, wrapped around the sketchbook. Then she looked up at him. "I can't do men."

"What do you mean?"

"I don't know what men look like."

He laughed. "What the heck, Keats. Half the people in the world are men."

"I mean . . ." She shrugged. "Without any clothes on."

He stared at her. "What are you, some kind of nut?"

"No. I'm an artist."

"Naked men?"

"No. I just told you, I can't do men. I can't get it right." She rushed on in a torrent of words. "I know what a woman looks like. I can stand in front of a mirror and, ah, you know. See everything. The" — she caressed the air, making a curve with her hand — "way the lines go and all. But I've never seen a man. Without his clothes on."

"For God's sake, go to the library. They got pictures of statues."

"It's not the same."

Trout held his breath, then let it out with a whoosh. "Sheeez." He slumped down on a stool, looking at her huddled over there in the corner. She looked very small and a little desperate, not very dangerous now. He could imagine how it must be with her. She had some talent. She wanted to be an artist, maybe go off to school and study. But there were too many reasons why she never would. Never could. It just wouldn't ever happen, because there was just too much she couldn't escape. One part of him wanted to feel sorry for her. But another part was angry and indignant because of her foul attitude in general and what she was doing to him in particular. So she hunkered over there in the corner, looking a little pathetic and — he knew — hating that because she hated being thought of as pathetic.

Trout felt, for the very first time with her, that he had the upper hand. It gave him a sense of power, a feeling of being in control. And he hadn't felt that way in a good while. About anything. It was like a narcotic. "You give me the creeps."

"I'm just trying to imagine —"

"It's sick."

"No it's not! There's nothing sick about the human body."

"It's sick when you sneak around trying to undress people who don't want to be undressed."

"Look," she protested, holding up the sketchbook, "this isn't some filthy little girlie magazine like you guys hide under the mattress. It's art. This isn't the Dark Ages, for God's sake. And besides, I'm not sneaking."

"It's like you're stealing something from me. It's like . . . like . . . rape."

"Oh come off it, Trout," she said, her voice thick with disgust. "So, I imagine what you look like with your clothes off. What's the big deal!"

And suddenly she was in charge again, putting him on the defensive, making him feel like a naughty puppy. But she wasn't finished. "You could . . ." — she paused for a moment, and a smile flickered at the edges of her mouth — "you could pose for me."

"You mean . . ."

"Sure. Take all the mystery out of it."

"Oh, shit," he said softly. "You are truly nuts." This was, he thought, about the weirdest thing he had heard in a long string of weirdness. Not the idea of being naked with a girl. He had almost been back in Ohatchee with Cynthia Stuckey. But sitting there naked while she drew a picture of him? And that's all? That was entirely different. Interesting, maybe even more than that. But definitely different. It made him squirm with heat and strangeness all at once. He had no idea how to proceed from here.

And then, oddly, rescue came from the most unexpected source.

A car pulled into the parking lot, lights on, windshield wipers flapping furiously, and eased to a stop at the side of the lot near the picnic tables. The lights and wipers stayed on.

"Your Aunt Alma," Keats said.

Trout peered out. A gray Buick. The rain was beating against the windshield so hard, the wipers couldn't keep up with it. Then Aunt Alma rolled down the window about an inch and peered out. She and Joe Pike had the same eyes, he thought.

"I think she wants you to come out," Keats said.

He was thoroughly soaked in the few seconds it took him to dash from the back door around the side of the building to the car, snatch open the door, slide into the front seat and slam the door behind him. The engine was running — powering lights, wipers, air conditioner. Trout shivered as cold and wet collided with the confused knot in his belly. Aunt Alma didn't seem to notice. Her face was puckered up in thought, lips set in a grim line, hands gripping the steering wheel. The wipers went *thwock-thwock-thwock*. The rain was fierce, great driving sheets of it blowing against the car and making it shake. Trout stuck his hands between his legs and hunched forward, trying to stop the shivering, wondering what kind of craziness would bring Alma out in a driving rainstorm to the Dairy Queen. He doubted she had ever set foot on the Dairy Queen property before. It was not an Aunt Alma kind of place. Had she come to shanghai him and take him back to the shipping department? Right now, he didn't really care.

They sat there for a moment and then she said, "Trout, I'm sorry."

It was the very last thing on earth he expected. He opened his mouth, but nothing came out. *What is going on here?*

"I shouldn't put pressure on you," she went on. "I know you've had a tough time the past few months. Your mother, your father . . ." She shook her head. "It's not fair to put any extra burden on you, and I just want you to know I regret that I did."

"Aunt Alma . . ." He shrugged, still at a loss — in fact, astonished. This was Aunt Alma? Ten seconds ago, he would have doubted that she had ever apologized for anything in her whole life. And here she was, doing it as simply and easily as if she were ordering ice cream.

"I want your summer to be nice. Relaxed, no pressure. Is there anything I can do?"

He shivered again. "Could you turn off the air conditioner?"

"Oh," she said. She turned off the air but left the engine running. The wipers *thwock-thwocked*. Trout looked out through the windshield, saw Keats inside the Dairy Queen, up on her crutches now, peering out the window, watching.

"I didn't mean to rush. There's plenty of time for you to learn about the business." She turned toward him in the seat and pressed her hands together. "This is all going to work out." There was a bright snap to her eyes, something almost feverish. "It will work out just fine," she said earnestly. "I'm sure of it."

Trout's head spun. What on earth was she talking about? His future? Uncle Cicero's business expansion? Joe Pike's theological angst? Or was there more? Overpopulation? Air pollution? Headline: EVERY-THING TURNS OUT OKAY.

"All of it." She gave a little flip of her hand, bestowing all-rightness on the world.

"Look, Aunt Alma, if you want me to work at the mill . . ."

"No," she said firmly. "I think you've made the right choice, Trout." She waved at the Dairy Queen. "Enjoy yourself. No pressure. A little spending money in your pocket and nothing earthshaking to worry about."

No, he thought, *nothing but a girl trying to take my clothes off.*

"That's the Dubarry girl, isn't it?" She was leaning over the steering wheel, looking at Keats.

"Yes," Trout said weakly.

"Is she a friend?"

She said it very casually, but Trout was suddenly alert and wary. "Not really," he said.

"Just somebody who rides on your motorcycle."

Trout shrugged. "I've taken her to work a couple of times, I guess."

"Today?"

"Yes ma'am."

Alma looked at him now, very directly. "Did you notice anything unusual over there?"

"What kind of unusual?"

"Activity. Anything out of the ordinary."

He wanted to be careful. But he wanted to be helpful, too. After all, Aunt Alma had come all the way out here to tell him she was sorry. And she had let him off the hook about the mill. And he darned sure didn't owe weird Keats Dubarry anything.

"There was a rental car parked in the Dubarry's driveway," he said. "Yesterday and again this morning. The same car."

"Did you get a good look at it?"

"Pretty good."

"What kind of car?"

"Green. A Ford, I think. It had a rental car sticker on the back bumper. Avis."

"You didn't happen to get a tag number, did you?"

"No ma'am."

"Are you taking the girl home after work?"

"I guess so."

"If the car is still there, get the tag number."

"Okay."

The rain was letting up now. Aunt Alma turned off the wind-shield wipers. A few drops splattered on the glass, streaking it as they dribbled off. "I need you to keep an eye on things for me, Trout."

"Yes ma'am," he said. "I will."

When Trout dropped Keats off at home, the rental car was gone. "I see your company's left," he said as she struggled off the back of the motorcycle.

"Are you going back tomorrow?" she asked.

"Of course."

She shrugged, turned and started toward the house.

"Would you rather I didn't?" Trout asked.

"I don't care what you do," she said over her shoulder.

"I turned down two other jobs," Trout said.

That stopped her. She turned and looked back at him. "What?"

"Uncle Cicero's hardware store and Aunt Alma's shipping depart-ment."

"So what?"

"Aren't you going to ask why?"

"I don't care why. Maybe you're going through a late adolescence,

Trout." She turned again and headed back toward the house, bouncing along on the crutches across the grass. Then she froze suddenly, stayed stock-still for a moment, and turned back to him. To his great surprise, she looked sad. Small and sad and a little vulnerable. "I don't like being angry, Trout," she said quietly. "I see what it does to Daddy. Sometimes I can't help it."

"Does my working at the Dairy Queen make you angry?"

"I guess so," she said. "Up to now, it's been just mine. But it's okay." She paused, then added, "You're okay." And she gave him a tiny smile. She had a nice smile when she let herself, he thought.

"Thanks," he said.

She turned again toward the house. "Maybe I'll come to work naked tomorrow," he called out. She didn't act like she heard him.

As Trout headed home, he saw a fair-sized crowd gathered at the edge of the vacant lot downtown, the parking spaces along both sides of Broadus Street filled with cars. Among them, a Georgia State Trooper cruiser, a County Sheriff's Department car, and a plain blue sedan with an official-looking antenna on the back. As Trout passed on the motorcycle, he saw a length of yellow tape stretched across the front of the vacant lot, holding the crowd back. Over their heads, out in the middle of the lot, he could see the big orange bulk of the bulldozer.

He wheeled the motorcycle around and came back and parked in front of the hardware store. The front door was shut and a sign hung behind the glass: CLOSED. Trout walked quickly down the sidewalk to where the crowd edged up against the yellow tape. It was the biggest assembly Trout had witnessed since he arrived in Moseley — far bigger, for sure, than the Sunday morning congregation at Moseley Memorial Methodist. And it was abuzz with excited murmuring and gesticulating.

About half of the lot was scraped bare, down to red clay soil, puddled here and there by the afternoon downpour. There were several mounds of piled-up debris — chunks of concrete, twisted pieces of rusty pipe, charred timbers. The back side of the lot was still weed-grown, and the bulldozer was stopped at the edge of it — engine silent, seat empty, blade down. A knot of men stood around the front of the machine — a couple in uniform, two others in shirtsleeves. They were looking at something on the ground, and one of the men in shirtsleeves was snapping pictures with a big boxy camera. *An accident?* Trout thought with a rush of alarm of Joe Pike up on the bulldozer seat.

"What is it?" he asked a man standing next to him.

"Skeletal remains," the man said somberly.

"It's probably Cash Potter," said a woman, nodding knowingly.

"What makes you think that?" the man asked.

"Cash disappeared about the time the furniture store burned down," the woman answered.

"Naw," another man said. "Cash turned up in Chicago with a waitress from Augusta."

"Well," the woman huffed, "folks *said* Cash was in Chicago, but nobody I'd consider reliable has laid eyes on him."

Another woman spoke up. "Anyhow, what's to say it's somebody that burned up in the fire? Coulda been somebody that was murdered and buried over yonder."

"Best place in town to hide a body," the first man agreed.

"There was a bunch of Gypsies come through a couple of years ago," the other man said. "Coulda been one of them."

Trout edged away from the debate and looked out across the vacant lot again at the crowd around the bulldozer. Then he spotted Uncle Cicero, hunkering next to the blade with another man, pointing, his finger making a wide circle. Grady Fulton, the bulldozer operator, was standing next to him, hand jammed in the rear pocket of his jeans.

"Uncle Cicero," Trout called out. Cicero looked back and saw him. Cicero waved to him to come over. Trout hesitated, but Cicero kept waving, so he ducked under the yellow tape and started across the bare earth of the vacant lot, stepping around the puddles. He could hear the low irritated buzz of the crowd behind him. The freshly scraped dirt had a sour smell to it, like a stomach turned inside out.

Cicero met him at the rear of the bulldozer. "What is it, Uncle Cicero?" Trout asked.

"Skeletal remains," Cicero said. He sounded very official. His color was high. He took a hitch in his gun belt.

Trout looked back at the crowd. "A woman over there said it might be somebody named Cash Potter."

"No, I talked to Cash Potter on the phone last week. He's living in Chicago with a waitress from Augusta. Afraid to come home 'cause Emma Jean might kill him."

Trout peered around Cicero toward the front of the bulldozer. "Can I see?"

"Well, I don't want you to have no nightmares," Cicero said.

"Is it, like, gory?"

"Well, not exactly."

And it wasn't. It was just some bones sticking out of the dirt. The bulldozer had unearthed a large slab of concrete, and as one end of it angled up out of the dirt, it had exposed what was clearly the bones of a foot, mottled and yellow but quite intact.

"This here's Trout," Uncle Cicero introduced him to the circle of men in front of the bulldozer. "Joe Pike's boy." In addition to Grady Fulton, there was a state trooper, a deputy sheriff, two men from the Georgia Bureau of Investigation (one of them the man with the camera). They all seemed to know Joe Pike.

Trout stared at the foot. "Ever seen skeletal remains before, Trout?" the deputy asked.

"Yes sir," Trout said. "Biology class." The skeleton in biology class at Ohatchee High School had dangled from a wire contraption and was affectionately referred to as "Lubert," after the skin-and-bones principal of the school. But this — this bony foot poking through freshly turned earth, rudely disturbed from long, dark, quiet rest — there was something sad, even embarrassing about it. Like stumbling onto some terribly private act. Trout had a sudden urge to cover the foot with something — a sheet, a shirt, Grady Fulton's Nok-a-Homa baseball cap, anything.

"Is it a man or a woman?" he asked.

The deputy raised one foot, balanced on the other, placed the sole of his shoe next to the sole of the skeletal foot. "Man, I'd say. Size ten." The deputy lowered his foot and they all stood there for a moment, considering that.

Then Grady Fulton pulled his hands out of his back pocket, turned his head, and sent an expertly aimed stream of tobacco juice at the ground next to the bulldozer. "Well, God rest his soul and all that. But I got work to do if we gonna finish this up by dark, Cicero."

"You can't move the bulldozer, Grady," Uncle Cicero said.

"What do you mean, 'I can't move the bulldozer'?"

Uncle Cicero stuck his thumbs into his gun belt. "It's part of the crime scene."

"What do you mean, 'crime scene'?" Grady said, waving his hand at the foot. "It's just some poor old dead sonofabitch."

"Skeletal remains," Cicero said evenly. "Of unknown origin. Until I know who it is and how he got here, I have to make a presumption of homicide. And I'd appreciate it if you'd have a little more respect for the deceased."

"Awright, awright," Grady said, his voice rising. "Get Joe Pike down here and let him mumble a few words over the sonof . . . the deceased. But I got dirt to move."

Grady turned toward the bulldozer.

"If you get up on that bulldozer, Grady, I'll arrest you," Cicero said.

Grady turned slowly back to Cicero and stared at him for a moment, his jaw working like crazy on the chew. Then Grady looked at the Georgia Bureau of Investigation man, the one without the camera.

"Don't look at me," the man said. "This is Cicero's jurisdiction."

Grady stood there a while longer, then took off his Nok-a-Homa cap and scratched his head, put the cap back on, looked down at the ground, and scratched at the dirt with the toe of a boot. Finally he looked up at Cicero again and said, "How long?"

"Could be a couple of days," Cicero said.

"Shit," Grady said quietly.

"We got to get the Crime Scene Unit over here and" — Cicero waved his hand over the general area — "process the crime scene. It'll be at least tomorrow because they're tied up in Thomson. After that, it depends on them. Meantime, I intend to secure the crime scene, which includes any" — he waved at the bulldozer — "object in the general proximity which might have a bearing . . ."

"Shit," Grady said again, not so quietly this time. "So in the meantime, you're just gonna hold up my bulldozer."

"And you."

"Me?" Grady's voice rose a couple of octaves.

"To give a statement."

"I was running my dozer and I dug up a skeleton. That's my statement." Grady was yelling now.

"Tomorrow," Cicero said patiently. "I want you here when the Crime Scene Unit arrives. About eight should do it."

Trout marveled, mouth ajar. Cicero was . . . what? Cool, that's what. In charge, unflappable, professional. Talking law enforcement lingo.

Just like a real police chief. Aunt Alma should see him now. They all should see him.

Grady Fulton threw up his arms. "What am I gonna tell Kmart?" He didn't wait for an answer. He turned with a jerk and stalked away toward the crowd on the sidewalk behind the yellow tape.

"I'll write you an excuse," Cicero called out.

Then he looked at Trout. And winked.

TEN

"TELL ME ABOUT Cicero," Uncle Phinizy said.

"He was terrific," Trout said. "He just took charge of things. Like a . . ."

"Police chief," Phinizy finished. He took a long drag from his cigarette, held the smoke inside while he stubbed the butt in an overflowing ashtray, then finally exhaled, aiming at the open window. He picked up the whiskey and water from the table at his elbow, held the glass up to the light, and swirled its contents with a shake of his wrist, tinkling ice against the rim, admiring the amber color. Then he took a sip, swished it around in his mouth, swallowed, and made a satisfied clicking sound with his tongue against his palate. It was an art form, like his smoking.

Phinizy looked awful — the furrowed skin of his face gray, stretched tight and dry like parchment around his skull, white hair thin and wispy. He seemed to have shrunk in the stifling heat of the upstairs garage apartment. It was an oven, even here in the shank of the day with the sun disappearing toward Atlanta over the tops of the pecan trees at the edge of Aunt Alma's yard. The place had baked all morning and then steamed in the wake of the afternoon thunderstorm. A good bit of the storm seemed to have made its way inside through the leaky roof. Phinizy had placed a few pots and pans around to catch the worst of the drips, but there were puddles here and there on the floor. The thick heat assaulted Trout when he opened the screen door and stepped inside to find Phinizy reared back in his recliner, drink at hand, cigarette smoke curling about his head, reading a book: *Hugo Black and the Bill of Rights*. Phinizy paid him no attention. Trout hesitated in the open doorway.

"Damn a fellow who can't make up his mind whether to come in or stay out," Phinizy said from behind his book.

Trout stepped inside, navigated amongst the pots and puddles to the sofa, sat down, waited, sweated. Aunt Alma should fix the place up, Trout thought, at least put on a new roof. It was wretched — dingy, leaky, permeated with the smells of mildew and rotting wallpaper and the rank odor of gasoline and motor oil from the garage below. Alma might not be able to kick him out, but she wouldn't lift a finger to improve the accommodations, either. Phinizy could fix up the place himself, but he wouldn't give Alma the satisfaction. A Moseley standoff. Industrial-strength stubbornness. It seemed to run in the family.

After a while, Phinizy turned the book facedown in his lap. "Well, tell me about the ruckus." And Trout told him about Cicero and the skeleton in the vacant lot.

"You seem surprised about Cicero," Phinizy said. "How do you think he got to be police chief in the first place?"

"I figured . . . well, Aunt Alma . . ."

"Let me tell you about Cicero." Phinizy fished in the crumpled pack of Lucky Strikes on the table, lit another cigarette and took a drag. "He was a military policeman in the Army. Went to Korea, got shot, won some medals. Then came back here and married Alma." A smile played across Phinizy's face. "They eloped."

"You mean . . ." Trout's imagination conjured up a picture of Cicero climbing a ladder to Alma's second-story bedroom window, spiriting her away. No. Cicero might be the kind of person who would climb *up* a ladder, but Alma was not the kind who would climb *down* one. Still, the thought of Cicero and Alma running off to get married . . .

"Cicero came to the house and got her while Leland was at the mill one day. They stopped in Augusta and got a Baptist preacher to perform the vows, then called from Savannah that night to say they had gotten married."

"What did Grandaddy Leland do?" Trout asked.

"Threw a fit. I think it was the thought of the marriage being performed by a Baptist that made him the maddest."

"What did he do when they came home?"

"He ranted and raved for a while. Made life miserable for Cicero. The boy really put up with a lot. But then Alma went to Leland and told him if he didn't get his fanny off his shoulder, she and Cicero were going to leave. It scared the hell out of Leland. Joe Pike had already hightailed it off to Texas to play football, and Leland could stand just so much orneriness from his young'uns. So he set Cicero up in the hardware business."

"And the police chief job?"

Phinizy smiled again, savoring a thought. "Cicero did that on his own. The old chief, Max Cotter, fell dead as a wedge from a heart attack right in the middle of a town council meeting one night. Cicero was there, and he jumped up and said, 'I'll take it.' So with Max lying there bug-eyed on the floor, they made Cicero police chief. Nobody liked Max anyway."

"Gee . . . ," Trout said.

"Now, about the hardware store. How do you think Cicero's doing?"

Trout shrugged. "I don't know. He's got all these plans. Knocking out walls, clearing the lot and stuff."

"Uh-huh. And how do you think he's gonna pay for Cicero's Do-It-All?"

"Aunt Alma?"

"Why do you think that?"

"He acts kinda nervous about it. I don't think he told her what he was gonna do."

Phinizy nodded thoughtfully. He picked up the cigarette from the edge of the ashtray, took a drag, exhaled the smoke and studied it as it drifted toward the window. "Things are not always as they seem," he said after a moment.

"What do you mean?" Trout asked.

Phinizy stared at the smoke awhile longer until it was gone. Then he looked back at Trout. And he held up the book he had been reading. "Hugo Black."

"What?"

"You know who he was?"

"No sir."

"United States Senator from Alabama, elected with the help of the Ku Klux Klan. Then Roosevelt appointed him to the Supreme Court.

He became a champion of individual rights. I'll bet those Kluxers in Alabama thought he'd sold out on them. But old Hugo was just biding his time. He needed the Klan to get to the Senate, but when he got to the Court, he cut loose."

Trout stared at him. So?

"You see where I'm headed?" Phinizy asked. His voice was patient, like a teacher with a dull student.

"Not exactly," Trout confessed.

"Things are not . . ." He waited for Trout to finish.

Trout felt blank, his mind sucked dry by the heat. He tried to concentrate. Then the light came on. "Always as they seem."

"Bingo," Phinizy said. "Now, extrapolate."

"What?"

"Hugo Black." He held up the book. "Cicero." He pointed in the general direction of the hardware store.

Trout considered. "Is Cicero going to cut loose?"

"I believe that is exactly what he is doing."

"Can he? On his own?"

"Oh yes."

"Profit and progress." Trout repeated Cicero's mantra.

Phinizy nodded.

"He doesn't need Aunt Alma's money?" Trout asked.

"No."

"Then why is he so nervous about her?"

"Because he's in love with her."

It was an incredible thought, and it did a little ricochet number on the inside of his head. Aunt Alma was . . . Aunt Alma. It was as difficult to think of her as a, well, a love object as it was to imagine her climbing down a ladder to elope. Things are not always as they seem. *How do you ever know what is real?*

It was too much. He stood, propelled upward by confusion.

"You look a bit stricken," Phinizy observed dryly.

"I'm having a brain fart," Trout said. "I've got to go."

He was almost out the door when Phinizy stopped him. "Trout . . ." Trout turned back. Phinizy was lighting another cigarette. He took a short puff, spat the smoke impatiently. "Did you ever think about talking to your mother about any of this?"

Trout stared at him, dumbfounded. "Mother?"

Phinizy looked at him for a long moment, expressionless, then picked up his book and resumed his reading.

Trout lay awake for a long time, thinking about all that had transpired in the brief space of a day, piling in on top of a week, a month, a year, when things seemed to happen so fast that there wasn't time to keep up, much less make sense.

The thing was, people kept surprising him.

He had thought at the beginning that it would be enough to get some answers about his mother and father, and if he at least understood what had happened with them, he could make things right again. But then all these other people came crowding in, loud and insistent, muddling the picture. Instead of his just dealing with Joe Pike and Irene, there was this whole new cast of characters he had never considered, and even the ghosts of some who weren't around anymore. All of them, connected in ways he hadn't completely fathomed. And constantly revealing new quirks and secrets. Moving targets in a funhouse shooting gallery, changing shapes and colors before his eyes.

Aunt Alma. Eloping, for God's sake. With Uncle Cicero. For one thing, he couldn't imagine straitlaced Alma Moseley being that passionate about anyone. Uncle Cicero was a truly nice guy, but not the kind, he thought, that a woman would lose her head over, even years before when she was young and perhaps foolish. But she had. She had had the hots for Cicero. *Good grief. Aunt Alma?* Cicero had wooed her and won her and had spirited her away from right under Leland Moseley's nose. It cast both of them in an entirely new light — especially Aunt Alma. She might hold forth at length on "remembering who you are" and all that stuff, but somewhere deep in her soul there was a spark of rebellion, or there had been for at least one incredibly brazen moment.

It also made Trout smile to imagine Grandaddy Leland having a fit. He would have given a princely sum to have seen it.

Leland had died when Trout was six years old, and Trout's memory was of a tall, spare man with thinning gray hair and absolutely no sense of humor who always wore a vested suit, even when he played horseshoes.

Trout remembered a long-ago summer afternoon, he and Alma's son, Eugene, pitching shoes with Leland at the horseshoe pit Leland had set up. Two metal stakes, each surrounded by a broad bed of sand carved from the neatly trimmed grass of the backyard. Eugene was several years older than Trout, but still a young boy, barely able to toss the heavy iron shoe from one metal stake to the other. Trout couldn't reach the other one at all. Eugene protested: the boys should be allowed to move closer than Leland. But Leland would have none of it. Trout could remember him, all gray-pinstriped and vested, peering down from great height through his wire-framed glasses, saying, "That's the rule. Play by the rules or don't play."

So Eugene, who had a streak of rebellion himself, put down his horseshoe and went in the house. Leland never gave him a look. He and Trout played horseshoes by Leland's rules — Leland flinging the metal shoe with practiced ease, making several ringers; Trout, throwing with all his might but barely able to get his own shoe halfway to the stake. It wasn't much fun, but Trout was not the rebellious type.

After a while the back door opened and Aunt Alma shooed a pouting Eugene off the back porch and down the steps. "Eugene wants to play," Alma said to Leland.

"No I don't," Eugene said. "I don't *want* to play. Mama's *making* me play."

"He'll have to play by the rules," Leland said.

"Of course," Alma said.

And Eugene played. His defiance, at that point, had limits.

That early impression, and all Trout had heard since, added up to this: Leland Moseley was a tight-ass. He had, from all accounts, a rather severe notion of How Things Ought To Be and what it meant to be a Moseley in Moseley. But his daughter had chosen a man who was about as un-Moseley as you could get and, worse than that, run off with him. It was a kind of blasphemy. Trout wondered if it had contributed to Leland's demise. And if it had, did it haunt Aunt Alma? Would that explain a lot?

Aunt Alma was enigma enough. But there was also Cicero, still full of surprises. A successful and savvy merchant with the vision to imagine such a thing as Cicero's Do-It-All rising from the town's rubble. Moseley, Georgia, was dead for all intents and purposes, as dead as the poor soul whose bones had rested for so long beneath the weed-grown lot where the furniture store had once stood. But Cicero had, entirely on his own, decided to dig it all up and strike out boldly, much the same way he had seized upon the police chief's job. Cicero was, more than Trout had ever imagined, very much his own man. That was a very big thing. And more than that, he was — if you could believe Phinizy — still very much in love with Alma. It was bound to be a perilous balancing act for Cicero — being his own man and yet loving Aunt Alma, who seemed so desperately fierce in molding people and things to her expectations. How did Cicero manage it?

But at the very bottom, there was the basic question: What did all this mean to sixteen-year-old Trout Moseley, who was partly the product (through inheritance or influence) of all these people with their stubbornness and defiance and loyalties and visions, their rigidity and angst and despair. Things were indeed not as they seemed. There were all sorts of possibilities where none had seemed to exist. Other people took control of their own lives and saved their own asses, as Phinizy said Trout must do. And there appeared to be all sorts of ways of doing it. What was his?

Funny thing, the one person among the bunch he seemed to understand least was his mother. Fruit of her womb, yet stranger to the secrets of her mind. And odd that Phinizy had invoked her name this very evening in the face of Trout's puzzlement. *Did you ever think of talking to your mother?* What kind of cockeyed comment was that? Heck, they wouldn't even let him close to his mother. She could be a hostage of terrorists, for all the good it was doing Trout Moseley.

Trout sighed wearily. For the moment, it was too much. He was very tired — from all this thinking and from the long, eventful day. So he raised up and fluffed the pillow under his head and settled back into it and began to will himself to stop *thinking* and go to sleep.

He had just about drifted off when he heard Joe Pike prowling the house. He had on his cowboy boots. *Clump. Clump. Clump.* Out of his room, down the hall and into the kitchen. It was a noisy house, plaster walls and ceiling and hardwood floors. You could hear everything, especially if you were trying to go to sleep. After a moment, the refrigerator door slammed. *Clump. Clump. Clump.* Joe Pike strode back up the hall to the opposite end of the house, into the living room. The sofa creaked. Trout heard the tinkle of silverware against ceramic. Joe Pike was eating ice cream. A huge mound of vanilla, he imagined (vanilla was all they had in the fridge, and Joe Pike never ate a small portion of ice cream) topped with Hershey's chocolate syrup. After a while, the sofa creaked again. *Clump. Clump. Clump.* Back down the hall to the kitchen. Water running in the sink, rinsing out the ice cream bowl. Had he put the ice cream back in the freezer? He was as likely to leave it out as not. They lost a lot of ice cream that way. Should Trout get up and check? He threw back the sheet, considered, re-covered himself. To hell with it. A grown man who couldn't remember to put the ice cream back in the freezer . . . *Clump. Clump. Clump.* Back to Joe Pike's room. The door closed. The bed creaked. Did he still have on his cowboy boots? Then the radio, tuned as always to the oldies station in Atlanta. The Platters: *Yoo-hoo-hoo've got the magic touch . . .* Trout thought of Joe Pike and Irene dancing in the kitchen on some past evening when the Platters weren't quite as "oldie" as they were now. Perhaps Joe Pike thought of it too. He switched off the radio. A long silence. And then the bed creaked again. *Clump. Clump. Clump.* The door opened; Joe Pike walked back down the hall to the kitchen. But this time he didn't stop. The back door slammed. Trout waited, anticipating the rumble of the motorcycle's engine. Would Joe Pike remember to check the gas tank? There hadn't been much left in it when Trout arrived home in the early evening. He meant to gas up in the morning. If Joe Pike went out riding tonight, he would likely run out of gas and have to call Trout to come get him. Trout reached for the bedsheet again. But there was no motorcycle sound. Perhaps Joe Pike had gone for a walk. Where would he walk to this time of night? Oh, shit.

Trout waited for a long time, imagining the worst. He waited for perhaps fifteen minutes. *Long enough,* he thought. Then he got up and padded to the kitchen. The ice cream container was on the counter, beginning to ooze around the bottom, a puddle of melted vanilla spreading across the Formica. Trout wiped off the bottom of the box with a dishrag and put it back in the freezer. Then he picked up the telephone and dialed. She answered on the third ring, and she didn't sound like someone who had been asleep.

"Leave my daddy alone," Trout said. And he hung up.

Trout didn't sleep. He lay staring at the ceiling for another hour or so until he heard the back door open and Joe Pike came in. *Clump. Clump. Clump.* The door to Trout's room swung open, light spilled in.

Joe Pike stood there, massive, filling the doorway. His face was shaded by the hall light behind him, but Trout could tell that Joe Pike was powerfully agitated. He seemed to vibrate. Trout felt a sudden rush of dread. Headline: FATHER BEHEADS SON, BLAMES PHONE CALL.

"Think about the Second Coming," Joe Pike said, his voice a couple of octaves higher than normal.

Trout's mouth dropped open. He had no idea what to think about the Second Coming. So instead he asked, "Where have you been?"

"Over at the church," Joe Pike answered.

Trout turned on his bedside lamp. Even in its weak light, Joe Pike looked flushed and fevered. His hands gripped the door frame. Samson holding up the pillars of the temple to keep it from crashing on his head. "What about the Second Coming?" Trout asked.

"Imagine this," Joe Pike said, the words rushing out. "Imagine that someday we discover something really big out there." He swept one hand toward the heavens. "Some concept so complex and yet so pure and simple that it explains everything. What's smaller than small, what's beyond beyond. What if we wretched little human beings with our muddled minds and corrupted spirits suddenly stumble onto the big answer. And at that very instant of discovery God says, 'Okay, that's what I was waiting for. Curtain down. Come on home.' And that's the Second Coming. Not God coming to us, but us coming to God."

Good grief, Trout thought with a rush of something near panic. The Second Coming? It was something Joe Pike needed to talk to the Bishop about. Trout threw back the sheet and swung his legs over the side of the bed, then realized as his feet hit the floor that he really did, for a moment there, intend to call the Bishop. *Mister Bishop, sir, this is Trout Moseley. Could you hop in the car and run over and talk to my daddy about the Second Coming? I'll try to keep him calm until you get here.* But he didn't stand up; he just sat there on the side of the bed staring at Joe Pike, whose forehead was dotted with sweat, who made hissing sounds through his clenched teeth. No, the Bishop probably shouldn't see this after all.

Joe Pike released the door frame and took a big step into the room. The floor shook a bit under his weight. "Don't you see how logical it is?" he demanded. He was almost shouting now. His voice, his presence, filled the room, squeezing all the air out, making it hard to breathe. "What separates us from the rest of creation?" He rapped on his skull again. "Our minds! We can think! We can imagine! So doesn't it stand to reason that we can figure out the secret of creation and what the dickens we're all doing here?"

"I suppose," Trout said, not knowing what else to say.

"Yea, verily!" Joe Pike exploded. And then all the air seemed to suddenly go out of him with a whoosh. His arms fell to his sides, his shoulders slumped. He stared at the floor. "I'm failing," he said. He waved a hand weakly in the direction of the church building next door. "I've got all these questions. And when I ask 'em, folks just panic. They're good people. Good, Christian people. But they just want me to tell 'em everything's okay. And I can't do that. It's just playing games." He shook his head and his voice was heavy with despair. "Just playing games."

Trout could see that his father was in pain, real pain, and that he needed, at the least, acknowledgment. Back on Easter Sunday in Ohatchee, Trout should have gone to the pulpit and put his arms around Joe Pike. But he didn't. And Joe Pike had ridden off to Texas. It could happen again, Trout thought. And he just couldn't stand that. So he stood up and walked quickly to Joe Pike and put his arms around him, at least as far as he could reach. He held on for dear life, and he felt true fear for the first time. Not just unsettledness or uncertainty, but cold gnawing fear that what little he had left that was halfway sane was about to come completely unraveled.

On top of the dresser next to the door, Irene's statue stood still and mute. The boy, whispering in the girl's ear. The secret? *Hell,* Trout thought. *That kid doesn't know jack. Nobody does.*

Trout woke to the ringing of the telephone. It jangled several times, tugging him up from a deep well of troubled sleep. Then it stopped and he heard Joe Pike's rumbling voice, unintelligible, in the kitchen and he wondered if his father had ever gone to bed. He began to drift off again and then he jerked awake and looked at the clock on his bedside table. 6:15. Who would be calling at 6:15? Then he knew.

He heard the clack of the receiver as Joe Pike hung up, and he lay there, expecting to hear the clump of footsteps up the hall toward his bedroom. *Come on. Get it over with.* But he didn't. Trout stayed in the bed a few more minutes, examining the cold knot of dread in his stomach. And then he got up and went to face the music.

The back door was wide open, letting all the air conditioning out into the fast-warming day. Trout looked through the screen door and saw Joe Pike sitting at the bottom of the steps, his great shoulders hunched forward over the piece of sweet potato pie he was having for breakfast. Joe Pike heard the squeak of the screen door spring as Trout opened it, turned and looked up at Trout, then went back to his pie. Trout closed the door behind him. He sat down beside Joe Pike, stretching his legs and letting his toes wriggle for a moment in the grass. Joe Pike went on eating, finishing off the pie, wiping his mouth on his shirtsleeve. He sat there holding the plate, looking out across the backyard toward the garage where the motorcycle sat.

After a moment he said, "I understand you were busy on the phone last night."

Trout didn't say anything. He didn't look at Joe Pike, either, not directly. But out of the corner of his eye he could see the tiny movement as the muscles along Joe Pike's jawline tightened. His father was pissed. It didn't happen very often. He tried mightily to maintain an air of felicity, compassionate concern, even-tempered ministerial grace. Usually, he succeeded. But his eruptions, when they came, could be downright cosmic.

There was the indelible memory of Joe Pike flinging a cat out the second-story window of the parsonage in Moultrie, where they had lived before Joe Pike had been assigned to Ohatchee Methodist. Trout was ten at the time. The cat had climbed onto Joe Pike and Irene's bed in the middle of the night, pounced suddenly upon Joe Pike's face and dug in its claws. In his own room next door, Trout was blasted from sleep by Joe Pike's anguished bellow: "Sonofabitch!" Then an awful ruckus as Joe Pike sprang from the bed, dashed to the window and threw it open. And finally the howling screech as the cat flew through the air and landed in the backyard. For a long time, Trout could hear Joe Pike stomping and growling about the bedroom, wounded and mad. Trout huddled in his bed, terrified — both at the raw anger and at the thought that Joe Pike might bust his gizzard and fall dead on the floor.

Joe Pike's face was raked with angry scratches when he appeared at the breakfast table the next morning. He seemed fairly well composed, but there was a tightness around his eyes. Trout, at ten, had learned to look for the little signs, to watch and wait, sniff the breeze. He took a long look at Joe Pike, saw the tightness, remembered the explosion of his father's indignant rage that had shattered the night, the awful howl of the cat. And Trout started to cry.

Joe Pike softened. "Hey," he said, patting Trout on the shoulder, "I'm okay. Just a few scratches."

"Did you kill Lester Maddox?" Trout blubbered. The cat was a scrawny stray that Trout had befriended and named in honor of Georgia's governor.

"Good Godawmighty," Joe Pike thundered. "The damn cat almost killed *me!*" Then Joe Pike blanched, a flush of embarrassment spreading across his face, and ducked his head.

Irene had taken it all in, watching Joe Pike, expressionless. "Lester Maddox is just fine," she said to Trout. "I gave him some milk at the back door a few minutes ago." Then she turned to Joe Pike and looked at him for a long moment.

"Sorry," he said, chagrined. "I didn't mean . . ."

"Of course you did," she said. "The cat clawed the hell out of you."

"Irene . . ."

"Why shouldn't you be mad? Curse the cat. Curse God for making a cat act like a cat. Go downtown and stand on the corner in front of the newspaper office and yell, 'I hate cats!' Get really, truly pissed off, Joe Pike. It would do you a world of good."

Trout could feel his eyes widen. He had never heard his mother use a word like that before.

Joe Pike cut a nervous glance at Trout. "Irene, honey . . ."

"Stop trying to be Jesus," she said, her voice flat, tinged with disgust. And weariness. "It's exhausting."

Joe Pike stared at her for a moment; then he rose from the table and left the room.

Trout remembered it all clearly now as he sat with Joe Pike on the next-to-bottom step and felt his displeasure filling up the morning. Trout drew his legs up to his body, wrapped his arms around his knees. What to do? He could say he was sorry, but that wasn't really the case. He was sorry Joe Pike was pissed off; especially sorry that he, Trout, was the object of the anger. It was just not something he needed right now, not with all the other. But he wasn't sorry he had made the phone call. Okay, so Joe Pike hadn't been over there. But he could have been.

"Just who the dickens do you think you are?" Joe Pike asked. Trout didn't say anything for a few seconds, and Joe Pike turned and glared at him. "Huh?"

"She's always hanging around," Trout said.

"Grace Vredemeyer is the choir director," Joe Pike said stiffly. "I am the preacher. The preacher and the choir director are in business together. Church business. The Lord's business. That's all there is to it. Grace Vredemeyer is a fine Christian woman."

"Jumping up and down in the education building with her titties hanging out," Trout said, not making the slightest effort to hide his sarcasm.

"Watch your mouth, mister!" Joe Pike barked.

Trout felt a little thrill of perverse pleasure, and it emboldened him further. "And riding around all over the place in your car."

"Visiting the sick and shut-in," Joe Pike said.

Trout could hear a note of defensiveness creeping into Joe Pike's voice. He bore in. "There aren't any sick and shut-in at the Dairy Queen."

"No, just a smarty-pants young'un," Joe Pike shot back.

"People are talking," Trout insisted.

"Who?"

Trout shrugged.

"Well, they can dang well mind their own business." Joe Pike looked away, and his shoulders gave an angry shudder. He sat there for a while, fuming. Finally he said, "I've made all kinds of fool of myself at one time or another. Been an absolute damned fool on occasion. But" — he turned back and looked Trout straight in the eye — "I've never made a fool of myself over but one woman. Your mother."

Trout said, "I wish you'd make a fool of yourself over her again."

Joe Pike stared at him for several seconds and then his shoulders slumped. He seemed weary with the effort of argument. Joe Pike squeezed his eyes shut, shook his head slowly, opened his eyes again. When he spoke, his voice was dull, the fight gone out of it. "I can't, Trout." There was the same despairing resignation of the man who had clumped into his room in the middle of the night, ranting about the Second Coming and then saying how he had failed.

Again, Trout felt the grip of fear. And on its heels, a rush of anger. "I want her home, Daddy."

"So do I," Joe Pike said earnestly. "More than anything. I think if she were here, I could . . ." His voice trailed off.

What? Recover your faith? Lose weight? Comfort your son? Save the town? Come up with the answers? Stop lusting in your heart after Grace Vredemeyer?

"But she's not ready yet," Joe Pike finished.

"How do you know? Have you talked to her?"

Joe Pike thought about it for a moment, his brow furrowing. "No. They still don't want her to talk to us for a while."

"Why?"

"I believe she sees me as part of the problem." Joe Pike shrugged with resignation.

"How about me? Am I part of the problem?"

"No. Of course not." He shook his head, stared at his hands for a moment. "Just me."

Trout could hear in Joe Pike's voice a plea for sympathy. But Trout didn't sympathize. Not at all. His anger grew, like a headstrong animal straining at a leash, and he just let it go. "What *is* the problem? What's wrong with Mama? Nobody'll talk to me about what *is* the problem."

"She's depressed, son. I've told you that. I've told you everything the doctors have told me. I'm not trying to hide anything."

"Yes you are!" Trout cried. His voice rose an octave, and he knew he sounded like some shrill little kid, but it didn't matter. "You won't tell me what's really wrong! You won't tell me why!"

Joe Pike didn't say a thing. Maybe that was the great unanswerable question. Maybe even the great unaskable question. Why?

Suddenly, Trout felt himself smothering, as if Joe Pike had thrown his great bulk on top of him, every pound of it, squeezing the breath out of him. He wanted to scream, *Get off! Get off!* But the words wouldn't come. He felt a rush of panic. He had to break free or be crushed. Now! He gave a mighty heave and stood up with a jerk, took a couple of steps into the yard and spun back toward Joe Pike. His chest heaved as he gasped for breath and he felt his eyes bulging.

Joe Pike stared at him, alarmed. "Son . . ." He stood and held his hands out, reaching for Trout.

But Trout backed away another couple of steps. "What did you do to her?" he cried.

Joe Pike flinched, as if he had been slapped. "Do?" he said dully. "I didn't *do* anything."

"You . . ." What? What kind of name could you put to all those days and weeks and years of an invisible, deadly gas that filled the house — Joe Pike's forced jollity and Irene's lengthening silences and the growing knot of dread that started in the pit of Trout's stomach and grew like a cancer until it *became* him. They didn't yell, didn't fight, didn't even disagree about anything. It would have been so much easier if they had. But this *thing* between Joe Pike and Irene had no name that he knew. At twelve, thirteen, fourteen, fifteen years old, he didn't even know which questions to ask. So he remained silent, watchful, fearful. Toward the end, Irene didn't seem aware of anything, including Trout. And Joe Pike, his great body sagging with despair, grew remote. Both of them exhausted, disappointed, perhaps even ashamed. They hid their faces from Trout. And in doing so, for them — the once-secure center of his universe — he had ceased to exist. Then they had taken Irene away to the Institute, Joe Pike had ridden off to Texas, and Trout had been left alone and dumbfounded.

So now he faced his father here in the backyard of the parsonage and still he didn't know what questions to ask. He knew only that despair was turning to rage. That, too, frightened him. But he was beginning to see it as the only desperate defense he had left, and if he didn't stand and fight, he would sink beneath the same mire that had sucked in his parents.

"I'm sick," he yelled at Joe Pike. "I'm sick of Mama being gone. I'm sick of you being screwed up. I'm sick of being a Moseley. And I'm sick of this one-horse pissant town that doesn't even have a pissant tennis court."

Joe Pike's mouth dropped open. He started to say something, but instead he just made a sort of gargling sound in his throat. Then he closed his mouth and hissed between his teeth. He closed his eyes and nodded slowly, up and down. Then he opened his eyes and took a deep breath. "Well . . ."

Suddenly, the back door of the parsonage flung open with a bang and Aunt Alma stood there in the doorway, wrapped in a floral print dressing gown, hair wild from sleep, bug-eyed and livid. Trout and Joe Pike stared up at her in astonishment. "The sonofabitch is trying to start a union!" she cried.

ELEVEN

AUNT ALMA CALLED it a "war council." And she looked mad enough to fight. She towered over the living room gathering, enlarged by indignation. Joe Pike was there, Trout (she had insisted because "the day will come when you and Eugene will have to deal with subversives"), Cicero, Judge Lecil Tandy, the family's longtime legal retainer ("We'll take this thing all the way to the Supreme Court if we have to"), and even Uncle Phinizy. Aunt Alma must be dead serious, bordering on grim, if she had swallowed hard enough to include Uncle Phinizy.

It was barely seven o'clock. Judge Tandy looked dazed, his eyes watery and his skin sallow, roused unceremoniously from sleep and given no opportunity to bathe, shave, and don a seersucker suit appropriate to the occasion of giving considered legal advice. He was dressed instead in a flannel shirt, much out of season, and a rumpled pair of gray trousers. Between the cuff of one trouser leg and the black wingtip shoe below was a stretch of blue-veined bare skin and knobby ankle. The other ankle was covered by a black ribbed sock.

Joe Pike hunkered as far down as he could get in a stiff leather chair, a quizzical, distracted look on his face. Uncle Phinizy yawned broadly. It was his bedtime. Only Cicero looked fresh and awake. Cicero was habitually an early riser, and besides, he had human remains waiting for him down at the vacant lot. He was wearing a freshly starched uniform, creases razor-sharp, leather belt already strapped to his waist with pistol on one side and portable radio on the other. Cicero sat with his legs crossed, cap perched jauntily on his knee.

From the back of the house, they could hear Rosetta grumbling in the kitchen as she prepared coffee. Rosetta, too, had been rousted early. Metal and china rattled ominously.

They all sat, awaiting Alma's pronouncement. She stood in front of the fireplace, arms folded defiantly, color high. She too was in uniform: a defiant red summer suit, sensible pumps, hair pulled back in a tight bun, an amazing transformation from the wild-haired specter that had appeared at the back door of the parsonage an hour before. Trout thought she looked quite capable of addressing the State Democratic Convention if called upon. Or a White House conference. Perhaps her old friend President Carter would summon her to vanquish malaise. "Jimmy," she would say, "get a grip."

"Well, we can all thank Trout," Alma said.

Trout looked at her in surprise.

"The rental car parked in Wardell Dubarry's yard," she said. "Cicero traced it to the Augusta airport." She looked at Cicero, waiting for him to report.

Cicero fished a slip of paper out of his shirt pocket. He read: "1979 Ford. Green in color. Rented from Avis by one Sylvester DeShon. Washington, D.C., driver's license. Born eight twenty-two forty-three. Five foot eight, a hunnert and thirty pounds." He looked up at the others. "Scrawny fella." Then back down at his paper. "Hair, black. Eyes, gray. Wears corrective lenses. Picked up the car three days ago, turned it in yestiddy. Put on the registration form at Avis that he's employed by the Consolidated Textile Workers of America."

"Cah-TWAH!" Phinizy said suddenly.

"I beg your pardon," Aunt Alma said.

"Cah-TWAH," Phinizy repeated. "Consolidated Textile Workers of America. C-T-W-A. Cah-TWAH."

Alma fixed him with a withering look. Phinizy gave her a little flash of a smile. She didn't return it. "Do you have any information about the Consolidated Textile Workers of America, Phinizy?" she asked.

"No," he answered. "Just the acronym, Alma."

She continued to stare at him, jaw set, breathing rather forcefully through her nostrils. But she didn't say anything. Finally she turned back to Cicero. "Go on," she said.

"Well, that's about it, hon."

"A union organizer," Alma said slowly. "And black to boot."

"Well, that's no surprise," Phinizy said. "A goodly number of the mill workers are black."

"I know that," she snapped.

Trout stole a glance at the others. Phinizy studied Alma, bemused. Joe Pike studied a spot on the Oriental rug where two stylized deer frolicked amidst a leafy glen. Judge Tandy looked as if he might slip into sleep at any moment. Or die quietly.

Cicero folded the slip of paper, stuck it back in his shirt pocket, hitched up his gun belt, and hiked one leg over the other. The toe of his highly polished black shoe bobbed rhythmically.

From the kitchen, the sudden crash of crockery hitting the floor. Then, Rosetta: "Shit."

Joe Pike cut a quick glance over at Trout. They had been skirting each other warily since Trout's eruption in the backyard of the parsonage. It was hard to tell what Joe Pike was thinking. He had a befuddled look, and his face was slack from lack of sleep. But then, that was the way he looked most of the time these days.

"Thank you, Trout," Aunt Alma said.

"You're welcome," he answered without thinking. For what?

"A nice piece of intelligence," Phinizy said. And to Cicero, "Splendid detective work."

"Wadn't nothing to it," Cicero said. "First, I called your Atlanta airport because I figured anybody renting a car in this area had probably flew into Atlanta. Avis at Atlanta's got three green Fords, but one of 'em has a busted radiator, one was gone to LaGrange, and the other to Alabama. So then I called your Augusta airport and they didn't have but your one green Ford . . ."

"Thank you, Cicero," Alma cut him off.

Cicero gave her a nice smile. "No problem, hon." Then he stood up, plucking his cap from his knee, hitching his gun belt. "Well, I guess I'll be getting on downtown."

"Sit down, Cicero," Alma ordered.

"Hon, I got the state crime lab coming in" — he glanced at his watch — "fifteen minutes." He motioned in the general direction of town. Human remains waiting, perhaps even a murder mystery. A bulldozer held captive. Cicero's eyes fairly danced with anticipation.

"Cicero, we have a problem here," Alma said patiently. "Could you perhaps give us a few more minutes of your time?"

Cicero stood his ground. "The way I see it, hon, you got a legal problem. And you got" — he indicated Judge Tandy with a wave of his hand — "the finest legal mind in the state of Georgia here."

Judge Tandy struggled to his feet, gathering himself to emote.

"Just a minute, Judge," Alma said.

Judge Tandy sat, a bit deflated.

"We have a law enforcement problem," Alma said to Cicero.

"How's that?" Cicero asked. He remained on his feet, crossing his arms over his chest. Trout looked at him in surprise. Cicero seemed a little taller this morning. Maybe it was the angle of the light coming in the high window at the side of the room. Or the uniform.

"A subversive element is at work in the community," Alma said, trying to keep her voice even. "An outside agitator has come in here from Washington, D.C., and is attempting to stir up trouble."

"And now he's gone home," Cicero said.

"And left the radical element" — she shot a finger in the direction of the mill and her voice rose — "plotting God knows what. Wardell Dubarry and his crowd want to take over my business." She looked around at the others. "Our business."

"But hon," Cicero said patiently, "the mill and the mill village are outside the city limits. Outside my jurisdiction."

"They'll be marching in the streets!" Alma cried.

"They'll need a parade permit for that." Cicero looked down at Judge Tandy. "Judge, do we have a parade-permit ordinance in Moseley? I should know, but I confess I don't."

Judge Tandy frowned, considering it. "I don't recall," he said. "I don't know that we've ever had a parade."

"Well, get one!" Alma barked.

"A parade?" Judge Tandy asked.

"An ordinance!"

Just then the door from the dining room swung open and Rosetta backed through carrying a tray laden with silver coffee pot, cups and saucers, sugar and cream pitchers, and a crystal container full of spoons. "Y'all ready for coffee?" she asked.

"No!" Alma yelped.

Rosetta stared at Alma. It appeared for a moment that she might do something violent with the tray, but then she took a deep breath. "That be just fine, then," she said pleasantly. And she turned and went back the way she had come. Trout thought they all could have used a cup of coffee, but he didn't say anything.

The silence hung heavy in the room. Alma gathered herself, regained her composure. "All right," she said to Cicero after a while. "Go ahead. I thought you might be interested in the future of the family business, but you go ahead."

Cicero's gaze floated about the room, resting briefly on each of the others. "You're right. This *is* family business. And y'all are the family. Except the Judge here, who's mighty like family." Judge Tandy gave him an appreciative nod. "Besides, y'all got lots more sense than I have. I'm just an old police chief, doing his duty as he sees it. Anybody breaks the law, I'll take care of 'em." He gave a little wave of his cap to Alma. "See you for lunch, hon." And he left.

There was another long silence. Trout realized his mouth was hanging open. He closed it. Something Cicero had said echoed in his head. *Doing his duty as he sees it.* Then he remembered. General Douglas MacArthur, speaking to Congress. They had seen it on an old *March of Time* film in history class in Ohatchee. How about that, Trout marveled. Uncle Cicero quoting Douglas MacArthur. Did he know what he was doing? It was entirely possible. Just about anything was possible.

Finally, Alma said, "All right. We've got to get a handle on this thing."

"Nip it in the bud," Phinizy said.

"That's right. Judge Tandy, what do you recommend?"

Judge Tandy rose again, squaring his shoulders. He was a tall man, slightly stooped, with a shock of white hair, somewhat longish in the back. In his youth, Trout imagined, he had been something of a dandy. Now, well up in his seventies, he struggled to remain courtly and patrician. He cleared his throat. "In my considered opinion," he intoned, "there are several possible courses of action here, none of which are clearly preeminently advantageous and therefore worthy, in my estimation, of recommendation with complete certitude at this early juncture." He stopped for breath, looked around at what remained of the assemblage. Flannel shirt and bare ankle or not, Judge Tandy looked every bit the sage counsel, Trout thought, duly impressed. "We might, of course, consider the injunctive process. And then again, perhaps not." He nodded wisely. "Howsomever," he went on, "one should not in a situation such as this be predisposed to any particular proceeding, nor upon the other hand be prejudiced against any possibility. One should, in a manner of speaking" — he smiled benignly — "keep one's powder dry."

The words hung ponderously in the air. They waited for Judge Tandy to go on, but instead he sat down, folding his hands in his lap. Alma gave him a slightly vacant look.

"Judge Tandy," Phinizy spoke up. "Are you versed in labor law?"

"No sir," Judge Tandy said firmly. "I am not."

"Then perhaps," Phinizy said, "you should consult with someone who is."

"Splendid idea," Judge Tandy said. "I shall indeed do that." He inclined his head toward Alma. "If, of course, Alma approves."

"Yes," she said softly, a trifle disconcerted by Judge Tandy's discourse. Then she roused herself. "We can handle this by legal means, or by God, I'll shoot 'em."

"I don't think Uncle Cicero will let you do that," Trout blurted. They all looked at him. All except Joe Pike, who hadn't taken his eyes off the spot on the rug for several minutes now.

Alma dismissed the thought with a quick jerk of her head. "Moseley Mill will not have a union," she said through clenched teeth. "No matter what."

"I wouldn't be so sure about that," Phinizy said.

Alma glared at him. "Whose side are you on, Phin?"

He ignored the question. "Here's what will happen, Alma. If these people are serious about this, and you must assume they are, they will circulate a petition amongst the employees, calling for a union election. If they get a certain percentage of employees' names on the petition —"

"Damn their petition!" Alma barked. "I won't accept it."

"It's not your place," Phinizy said patiently. "The petition will go to the National Labor Relations Board, which will then set up the formal mechanism for a vote amongst all the employees."

"I won't allow it."

"You won't have any say in the matter."

"The hell you say!"

"Yes, the hell I say."

"How do you know so much?"

"I'm from Washington." He smiled. "Hotbed of unionism."

Alma turned to Judge Tandy. "Is that true?"

"I suppose," he said.

"Before the vote takes place," Phinizy went on, "you will have ample opportunity to make your case to the employees as to why they should reject the notion of a union. And the union will likewise have an opportunity to make theirs."

They all pondered that for a moment, and then Joe Pike looked up, shifting his gaze from the spot on the rug to one of the high windows where the morning was blazing in, the sun climbing above the trees to the east. Trout's gaze followed Joe Pike's, and he noticed for the first time how the windowpanes were mottled and wavy and how the thick curtains that hung at the edge of the window were faded from years of sunrises. He looked down again at the Oriental rug and saw that it was badly worn in several spots, thick brown threads showing through.

Alma said, "Joe Pike, I want you to go talk some sense into Wardell Dubarry."

Joe Pike started to speak, but Phinizy said quickly, "I don't believe that's a good idea. It might be considered tampering." He turned to Judge Tandy. "Isn't that the case, Judge?"

"I suppose," Judge Tandy said.

"They might win," Joe Pike said musingly, almost to himself.

"That's ridiculous. They wouldn't dare," Alma said.

Joe Pike continued to look out the window. "They might win because they're fed up with Moseleys."

"I repeat," Alma said, and there was pure steel in her voice, "there will be no union at Moseley Mill."

"Then," Joe Pike said, "there may be no Moseley Mill."

"You'd like that, wouldn't you," Alma spat.

Joe Pike turned and looked at her. "Why do you say that, Alma?"

Then Alma saw Judge Tandy peering up curiously at her, head cocked to one side, waiting. And she seemed to reconsider. "Let's not get into that now."

"Why not?" Joe Pike's voice had an edge of insistence.

She turned away and started for the door. "Why don't we have some coffee." She opened the door and called back toward the kitchen,

"Rosetta, you can bring the coffee now." She closed the door and resumed her place. "Judge Tandy —" she began.

"Alma," Joe Pike interrupted, "tell me something."

She stared at him. "What?"

"Why didn't Papa ever build a tennis court?"

Alma rolled her eyes, exasperated. "Joe Pike, for goodness' sake."

"I remember one time, sitting here in this very room. It was a Sunday afternoon, I believe, after dinner. I was about twelve at the time. That would make you fourteen. Papa was standing" — he pointed at the fireplace — "right about where you are now. Holding court. Do you remember?"

Alma said nothing. She just looked at Joe Pike, waiting him out.

"You had been reading a magazine article about a tennis player," Joe Pike went on. "I don't recall the name, but she had won at Wimbledon. And you asked Papa, 'Can we have a tennis court?' And do you remember what he said? He said, 'Tennis is not ladylike.' And then I spoke up and said, 'I'd like to play tennis, too.' And then Papa said, 'Tennis is a frivolous game.' Papa's idea of sport was pitching horseshoes." Joe Pike nodded slowly. "Horseshoes," he repeated.

"All right," Alma said after a moment, as if speaking to a dull-witted child.

But before she could continue, Joe Pike stood up abruptly. "Papa was a pickle, Alma. A sour dill pickle. I should have stayed here and told him so. But I ran off. I think I've been paying for it ever since."

He started toward the door, but stopped just for a moment at Trout's chair and touched Trout gently on the shoulder. Trout looked up into his father's face and saw the sadness there — an ancient thing, perhaps as old as Joe Pike himself. Trout opened his mouth to speak, but he couldn't think of anything to say. And then Joe Pike was gone. They heard his footsteps echoing in the hallway, and then the front door closed behind him. Trout thought for an instant to get up and follow, but again he was at a loss. Could anybody follow where Joe Pike Moseley was going these days? He looked over at Phinizy, who pursed his lips and gave an almost imperceptible shake of his head. *Don't ask me, boy.*

Aunt Alma looked unnerved. She was losing her audience and seemed suddenly fragile and vulnerable, standing there in front of the fireplace in her fierce red suit.

"Well," Phinizy said, breaking the silence, "there's nothing to be done at the moment."

"What do you mean?" Alma asked.

"If there is a union organizing effort, the ball's in their court. Don't you agree, Judge?"

"I suppose," Judge Tandy said.

"You mean we have to sit around and wait for that" — she waved impatiently, her voice rising again with indignation — "rabble to do something?"

It was clearly a foreign idea to Aunt Alma. Moseleys didn't wait for anything or anybody. Never had. Never would.

"I believe that is the case," Phinizy said calmly. "Wait, watch, and listen."

They sat there for a long moment — waiting, watching, listening. Smelling. They all seemed to smell it at once: something burning. As one, they all looked toward the dining room door, the one that led to the rear of the house and the kitchen. "Rosetta!" Alma called in alarm.

Trout was the first to reach the kitchen door, and when he threw it open, thick gray smoke billowed out. Alma was right behind him. "My God!" she screamed. "The house is on fire!" Trout took a deep breath and plunged into the room, arms flailing, trying to drive the smoke away. "Don't go in there!" he heard Uncle Phinizy shout behind him. Too late. Trout was lost now in the smoke, which was getting darker and thicker by the second, seizing his throat and stinging his eyes. Then he saw a flash of orange off to his right and stumbled toward it and saw the skillet blazing on the stove, belching the thick greasy smoke, the eye under the skillet glowing angrily. Next to it, a large pot of grits, also sitting on a red-hot eye, most of it already boiled out over the sides and dripping down the front of the stove. And smoke pouring from the open oven. Flames from the skillet were scorching the wall behind the stove, blistering the paint. Another minute, and the fire would race up the wall and reach the ceiling and then the whole house could go. He could hear shouts back behind him — Phinizy calling his name, Alma yelling at Judge Tandy to call the fire department. He reached for the skillet and then snatched his hands back, feeling the heat. He felt panic seizing him, tried to fight it. *Think! Think! Water! No, it's a grease fire! Got to get the skillet out of here!* He groped along the kitchen counter to his left. And then his hand touched a dishtowel. He grabbed it and wrapped it around the handle of the skillet and pulled it away from the stove. Flames leaped and heat blasted his face and grease spattered, stinging his arms. "Ow!" he yelled, and as he did so, he released the pent-up air in his lungs. Involuntarily, he sucked in a breath and with it, a great rush of smoke. He coughed violently, staggering against the counter, almost dropping the skillet. But somehow he held on, tried to force his mind onto getting his bearings. The back door would be somewhere to his left. He headed toward it, the smoke blinding him, filling his body. He retched violently. And he felt a searing pain in his hands, the handle of the skillet burning him through the dishtowel. *I can't hold it! I'm gonna die in here! Shit!* Then suddenly Uncle Phinizy was there, somewhere in front of him, holding the back door open. "Here, Trout!" he yelled. Trout staggered toward the rectangle of light and burst through the door and down the steps, sucking in great incredibly wonderful gulps of air and flinging the blazing skillet into the backyard, where it landed in an explosion of flaming grease and charred bacon strips.

"Rosetta!" Alma screamed from behind them in the house. "Where the hell are you? Rosetttttaaaaaa!"

And then, the fire siren on top of City Hall, beginning in a low, somber groan and growing to a keening wail.

Trout staggered onto the grass below the steps, lungs and throat on fire, legs rubbery, a great roaring in his head. Phinizy was right behind him, coughing violently, his frail body wracked with spasms. Trout grabbed for Phinizy, and they held on to each other for a moment and then sank to the grass. Phinizy lay on his back, hacking and wheezing desperately. Trout was on all fours. Dry heaves shook his stomach and gagged his throat, but nothing would come out.

The roaring noise in his head subsided a little and from inside the kitchen, he could hear Aunt Alma yelling, "The wall's on fire! Get some water!" And just then, Uncle Cicero dashed around the corner of the house, took a quick look at Trout and Phinizy, and then bolted up the steps and into the kitchen. "I'm coming, hon," he cried. In an instant, he was back down the steps, grabbing the garden hose coiled by the side of the house, turning on the water, dashing back up the steps with squirting hose in hand. Trout could hear the splash of water against the kitchen wall.

Suddenly, Phinizy stopped coughing. Trout looked over at him. He lay on his back, eyes closed, face deathly white. "Uncle Phin," Trout rasped, "are you okay?" No answer. Trout summoned enough energy from somewhere to yell, "Cicero! Help!"

It took the volunteer fire department ten minutes to get there and another twenty for the ambulance, which had to come from Thomson. The five members of the fire department who answered the call worked nearby — Fleet Mathis, the mayor; Earl Cobb, who owned the Texaco station; one of the foremen from the mill; Boolie Huffstetler, who helped his wife Tilda run the Koffee Kup Kafe; and Link Tedder, the city garbage collector. Uncle Cicero was also a volunteer fireman, but of course he was already there. Of the others, it was Link who arrived first, pulling up in front of the house in his garbage truck. The fire truck was right behind, siren wailing, Boolie at the wheel with the other three hanging on to the sides. By this time, Trout was somewhat recovered, though still woozy, and was standing anxiously on the sidewalk in front of the house watching for the ambulance. A crowd was gathered along the sidewalk and spilling over into the yards of the adjacent homes, but giving the Moseley place a wide berth.

The fire truck eased to a stop behind the garbage truck and next to a curbside fire hydrant. Count on the Moseleys, Trout thought, to have their own fire hydrant. The firemen scrambled down, dressed out in bits and pieces of uniform — Boolie wearing a helmet, Fleet Mathis a jacket, Earl a pair of rubber boots.

"Where's the fire?" Earl called to Trout.

"The kitchen," Trout called back.

He watched, fascinated, as Boolie grabbed a thick, short length of hose and attached one end to the side of the truck, the other to the hydrant. The engine of the truck rumbled throatily, changing to a deeper pitch as Boolie used a huge wrench to turn the valve on top of the hydrant. Fleet Mathis stood by a collection of gauges and levers on the side of the truck just behind the cab. "Pressure!" he cried out as Earl attached a big chrome nozzle to the end of the hose that lay neatly coiled in the back of the truck.

They were all quick and efficient, and Trout imagined that they had been through the drill more times than they could count. It would, he thought, pass for something to do in Moseley. The truck was a fairly new red pumper with CITY OF MOSELEY lettered in gold on the side of the door, and just below it, MOSELEY MILL.

Fleet Mathis stood by the truck, hand on one of the levers, while the others rushed past Trout, up the steps, and through the open front door, Earl in the lead, trailing hose behind them.

After a couple of minutes, Earl and Boolie came back, lugging the hose out the door and down the steps to the truck. "It's out," Earl said. He sounded disappointed.

"Well, that's good," Trout said.

Earl gave him a close look. "Are you okay, son? You look kinda peaked."

"I'm fine. Just a little smoke. I don't think Uncle Phin's doing too good, though. They've called the ambulance."

Earl got an oxygen bottle from the fire truck and followed Trout around the side of the house to the backyard. Phinizy was sitting in the grass, his back propped against the side of the steps, eyes shut, looking wretched. Cicero was kneeling beside him, fanning him with a folded section of newspaper.

Earl clamped the oxygen mask gently over Phinizy's mouth and nose. "Breathe deep, Mr. Moseley," Earl said. Phinizy took several shallow breaths; then he mumbled something, but they couldn't tell what he said because of the oxygen mask over his mouth. Earl took the mask off. "What's that?" But Phinizy didn't say anything else and Earl put the mask back on.

"Is he gonna be okay?" Trout asked.

"I imagine he'll be fine," Cicero said. "We'll get him over to the hospital at Thomson and get him checked out."

While they waited for the ambulance, Trout climbed the steps and peered into the kitchen. The windows above the sink were open, but the smoke was still thick and Trout felt a rush of nausea. He started to turn away, but then he noticed the peg just inside the back door where Rosetta always hung her coat and hat. She wouldn't have been wearing a coat on a hot summer day, but she never went anywhere without her hat. There was no hat on the peg now. But her apron was hung neatly.

Link Tedder came up the steps then, carrying a large fan. "'Scuse me," he said to Trout, and Trout stepped aside as Link set the fan just inside the doorway and disappeared inside with the plug. After a moment the fan hummed to life, drawing smoke out of the room, and Trout went back down the steps and stood looking down at Uncle Phinizy. Some of his color was beginning to return. And then Trout heard the siren of the ambulance — faint at first as it barreled down the road from the Interstate, and then louder as it turned at the intersection downtown and wailed to a stop in front of the house. Two medics hustled around the corner of the house with a stretcher, and the rest of them stood back as the medics fussed over Phinizy, checking his pulse and blood pressure and listening to his heart and lungs with a stethoscope.

"Is he okay?" Trout asked.

"Stable," one of the medics said. "But his lungs sound like a diesel truck with one cylinder misfiring."

They loaded Phinizy on the stretcher, and Cicero and Earl helped them carry it around front and load it into the back of the ambulance. "Any of y'all want to ride with us?" one of the medics asked.

"I'll go," Trout said quickly.

"No," Cicero said. "You don't look so hot yourself, Trout. You need to stay here and get your legs back under you." He looked around. "Where's Joe Pike?"

"He left," Trout said. "Before the fire."

"I'll go," Earl said. "Y'all come on when you can."

Cicero clapped him on the shoulder. "I 'preciate it, Earl."

Earl climbed into the ambulance with the stretcher and one of the medics, and the other one closed the rear doors and jogged around to the cab and climbed in. Then Cicero got out in the street and stopped traffic while the ambulance pulled into the driveway and backed up and roared away toward Thomson.

Trout and Cicero went inside. The whole house smelled of smoke, acrid and depressing. Alma was sitting alone in the living room, at one end of the sofa with the open windows at her back. She stared at her hands, folded neatly in her lap. "Are you all right, hon?" Cicero asked. She didn't answer, and he went on toward the kitchen.

Alma looked up then. "Trout," she said.

"Yes ma'am."

"Come sit with me."

He sat down next to her on the sofa and she took one of his hands in hers. "You saved my house," she said softly.

"Aw, I didn't . . ."

"Yes you did," she insisted. "Thank you." She looked at his arms then. "You got burned." The bare skin below his T-shirt was mottled with red splotches where the grease had spattered. He felt the stinging then. He hadn't even noticed. Alma rose. "I'll get some ointment. You sit right here."

She came back in a minute with a tube of ointment and sat beside him and spread it liberally on his arms, her fingers cool and gentle. Trout looked into her face. She seemed very close to tears.

"Thank you," she said again when she was done.

"I can't believe I did that," Trout said.

"This is your home," she said. "You saved your home." She put the tube of ointment on the lamp table beside the sofa, then wiped her hands absently on the skirt of her red suit, leaving a greasy mark. Trout stared at it, but Alma seemed not to notice. *My home?* What a strange thing to say. After a forgettable succession of parsonages, the thought of "home" as some specific physical place was foreign to him. Not this house, certainly. This was Aunt Alma's house.

Alma took his hand in hers again and they sat without speaking for a while. Out in front of the house, the crowd had thinned out, the first rush of excitement over, and those who remained talked in hushed tones, as if not quite comprehending that a disaster could actually strike the Moseleys. The engine of the fire truck throbbed on for a while, but then Fleet Mathis turned off the pump, and Trout could hear Fleet and Boolie stringing out the hose along the street, letting the water drain out before they coiled it neatly in the back of the truck. There were noises back in the kitchen, men walking about, the soft cadence of Judge Lecil Tandy's voice, the scrape of a piece of furniture being moved. But it was all a background. Here in the living room, it was still and quiet. And Aunt Alma seemed somehow . . . what? Softer, perhaps.

When she finally spoke, it startled Trout a bit. "Sometimes I feel all alone," she said. He looked up at her face, saw the tiny wrinkles around her eyes and mouth, more of them and deeper than he remembered. He realized it was the first time he had really *looked* at Aunt Alma. There was something about Alma that made you keep a wary distance, look just *beyond* instead of *at*. But now he looked. And he heard something almost childlike in her voice, something sad and wistful. He watched and waited. And listened.

"I didn't want this." She made a wide, slow sweep with her hand. And Trout understood that she meant more than the house. Much more. Perhaps everything. Her hand dropped back onto his. "I wanted . . ." Her voice trailed off and she looked away and shrugged. "But there was no one else. So I did what I had to do. Do you understand?"

"I think so," Trout said.

"It has been," she said, her voice barely above a whisper, "very, very hard. The others, gone. Papa dead, Joe Pike gone to preach, Eugene to Atlanta. And things changing. Beyond my control. I have done the best I could."

"I'm sure you have, Aunt Alma." Trout tried to be helpful.

She turned to him with a quick jerk and squeezed his hand. "And now it's yours."

"Mine?"

"I didn't know if you had it in you, Trout. I confess I had my doubts." Her voice was urgent now. "Until this morning. What you did . . . it was splendid. It's the way a Moseley behaves."

"It is?"

"Yes. Take charge. Get things done. It gives me strength to go on, Trout. To fight this union nonsense. To keep things under control until you're ready." She patted his hand. "I'm very proud of you, Trout." She gave him a lovely smile. "You're my hero."

Trout tried to feel a little heroic, but he didn't. Not in the least. Instead, he felt incredibly weary. It was just too much. He wanted to go somewhere and hide, but he couldn't for the life of him think where that might be. There seemed to be no refuge. Perhaps the best place would be home in bed. A quiet nap before he had to go to work at the Dairy Queen at three. Ah, the Dairy Queen. Whipping up a Blizzard or fetching a Dilly Bar from the freezer. It was so uncomplicated.

Alma sighed, interrupting his thought of sleep. "Good God, what a morning. Rosetta must have panicked when the fire broke out. Why on earth didn't she warn us?"

Trout started to say something about the apron hanging neatly on the peg by the back door, but he thought better of it. There would be plenty of time to get into that. Uncle Cicero would conduct a thorough investigation and no doubt come to the same conclusion Trout already had. *Et tu, Rosetta?*

The firefighters clumped through the hallway on their way out the door, trailed by Uncle Cicero, who stopped and looked into the living room. "Y'all all right?"

"Yes," Alma said. "We're all right."

She and Cicero looked at each other for a long time. Trout tried to fathom what passed between them, but he couldn't. Alma had a look of exquisite pain on her face. And Cicero looked thoroughly in charge of things. There was a firm, even set to his mouth. A reversal of roles? Or a reversion to old roles? Trout thought again of Cicero, spiriting Alma away from under Grandaddy Leland's nose. And again, it made him smile.

And then the portable radio at Cicero's hip crackled to life. "Cicero, this is Calhoun." Calhoun was Cicero's only police department employee, an excitable man in his early twenties with an unruly head of red hair. Just now, he sounded excited.

Cicero pulled the radio out of its leather holster and fingered the button on the side. "Calhoun, how many times have I got to tell you, observe proper radio procedure. What you say is, 'Unit Two to Unit One.'"

"Cicero," Calhoun said insistently, "you better get down here."

"Where?"

"The crime scene."

"Why, Calhoun?"

"The preacher's got the bulldozer."

TWELVE

UNCLE CICERO HEADED for his police cruiser, parked across the street in front of the parsonage, Aunt Alma and Judge Tandy right behind him. Trout set out at a dead run. By the time he covered the two blocks to downtown, Joe Pike was backing the bulldozer out of the vacant lot, ripping away the length of yellow tape Cicero had put up yesterday to cordon off the crime scene. The big orange machine eased between the van from the state crime lab and a Bronco with CHANNEL 5 EYEWITNESS NEWS emblazoned on the side, grinding the concrete of the curb beneath the treads.

There was a good-sized crowd: two men from the crime lab in white coats, the Channel 5 crew, Calhoun, and a lot of other local folk. They lined the sidewalks and milled about in the street — gawking, pointing, talking excitedly — but they were all staying well out of Joe Pike Moseley's way, including Calhoun. He was standing on the sidewalk in front of the police station, walkie-talkie in hand. The reporter and cameraman from Channel 5 were trying to interview him, but Calhoun seemed beyond words, mouth hanging open wide enough to let in a swarm of flies.

Joe Pike was playing the levers and pedals of the bulldozer — backing well out into the street, then wheeling neatly about and pointing the nose of the machine westward. The yellow crime-scene tape, caught on the rear of the machine, streamed out behind like the tail of a kite. Traffic in both directions came to a halt — a line behind the bulldozer, stretching back toward the mill end of town, several other vehicles stopping dead in the street as they approached from the opposite direction. Beyond the traffic in front, Trout could see Uncle Cicero's police cruiser, blue light flashing. And beyond that, in front of Aunt Alma's house, the fire truck and the garbage truck still parked at the curb. There were people on the sidewalk there, too, peering down the street to see what the commotion was all about.

Trout looked up at Joe Pike. He looked feverish and agitated, much as he had looked as he had stood in the doorway of Trout's room last night, babbling about the Second Coming. But there was a difference. Joe Pike looked quite resolute, as if he had come to some fairly significant decision. He had a cigar jammed in his mouth. Trout yelled over the rumble of the bulldozer engine, "What are you doing?"

Joe Pike took the cigar out of his mouth. "Come on up and you'll see," he yelled back.

He held out a hand. Trout hesitated, as he had in the church in Ohatchee and early that morning in Aunt Alma's living room. But then he thought, *Not this time.* He smelled another disaster, and he hadn't the foggiest idea what he could do about it, but he knew that he must not watch from the sidelines with his thumb up his fanny. So he reached up and Joe Pike's big hand swallowed his own and Joe Pike gave a tug, and Trout scrambled up the side of the bulldozer and settled onto the seat. He saw that Joe Pike was wearing his scuffed brown cowboy boots. They seemed to appear like apparitions whenever some kind of storm was about to break.

"Are you going to Texas?" Trout asked.

"Not quite that far." Joe Pike moved a couple of levers and stomped on a pedal. The big diesel engine roared and Trout could feel the vibration through his spine. Black smoke belched from the stack behind the cab. Traffic was piling up in front of them, and Trout could see Uncle Cicero, Aunt Alma, and Judge Tandy getting out of the police cruiser, heading toward them on foot. Cicero and Alma were walking fast, Judge Tandy bringing up the rear.

Joe Pike moved some more levers and the bulldozer lurched into motion. Trout lost his balance and almost tumbled off the seat, but Joe Pike grabbed him by the arm. "Hang on!" Trout grabbed a handhold on the edge of the seat, another on the metal cage covering the cab over his head.

The first vehicle in line just ahead of them was a grimy pickup truck. A woman was behind the wheel, peering through the mud-spattered windshield, her eyes growing wide as the bulldozer headed in her direction. Joe Pike waved, motioning her out of the way. She yelled something, then threw the truck into gear, backed up in panic, and smashed into the front of a Merita Bread delivery van. The bread van driver responded with an angry bleat of his horn, and the woman snatched the pickup into forward and cut hard right, leaping out of the way of the oncoming bulldozer just in time, lurching to the side of the street. The pickup shuddered to a halt with its front wheels up on the sidewalk. Through the window, Trout could see the woman screaming. But he couldn't hear her over the roar of the bulldozer engine. Joe Pike didn't seem to pay any attention. The bread van driver jumped out, surveyed the damage to the front of his truck, then jumped back behind the wheel and pulled over to the left in front of the Koffee Kup Kafe.

The bulldozer plowed ahead. Trout looked back to see the crowd falling in behind, led by Calhoun and the Channel 5 crew. The cameraman was running about, getting shots of the bulldozer and the crowd from all angles. They were all stepping over chunks of broken asphalt. The big steel treads of the bulldozer were chewing up the street. "You're tearing up the street," Trout shouted to Joe Pike.

"Yeah," he shouted back. "A dozer will do that."

Cicero and Alma were there now, Cicero out in the middle of the street, Alma standing on the sidewalk with a look of utter horror on her face. Joe Pike waved to her, but she didn't move a muscle. Judge Tandy came up beside her, badly winded. He saw Alma's expression, put his arm tentatively around her shoulders, then took it away.

"Stop, Joe Pike!" Cicero yelled up at the oncoming bulldozer.

Joe Pike cupped his hand behind his ear. "Can't hear you!" he yelled, although Trout had heard Cicero plainly.

"He said stop," Trout shouted to Joe Pike.

"Yeah. I know."

But he didn't. The bulldozer bore down on Cicero. He reached for his pistol. Trout's heart leaped to his throat as Cicero's hand tightened around the grip. Then he took it away, shook his head and stepped nimbly to the side as the bulldozer went past. Cars were pulling over to the side, backing into alleyways, fleeing in the opposite direction. Down at Aunt Alma's house, Trout could see the fire truck pulling away from the curb with everybody hanging on, turning into the parsonage driveway, backing into the street, and heading toward downtown. But it didn't go far. Traffic snarled, two cars bumped together and stalled. The street ahead was completely blocked. Trout looked at Joe Pike. Joe Pike shrugged.

It didn't matter. Because Joe Pike wheeled the bulldozer suddenly to the left and pointed it at the sidewalk. He didn't slow until it had lurched up over the curb and reached the edge of Broadus Moseley's park. Then he stopped. And lowered the bulldozer blade. *THUNK.* It landed in the grass just inside the sidewalk. Then Joe Pike shoved the bulldozer into gear again and plowed into the park, ripping up a wide swath of Bermuda grass and baring the earth so long ago covered at the behest of Moseley's patron saint.

Trout had a sense of pandemonium on either side of them — people running back and forth, arms waving, a flash of blue police uniform. But he was transfixed by what the bulldozer was doing to the park. He glanced up at Joe Pike, but he was intent on his work, arms and feet in motion as he shifted levers and mashed footpedals. They were headed now for a big oak tree. Trout flinched, preparing himself for impact. But Joe Pike wheeled neatly around the tree and took dead aim on the band shell. *Holy shit.* The blade hit the concrete sidewalk in front of the band shell first, scooped it up and tossed it aside as if it were Styrofoam. Then Joe Pike flicked a lever and the blade rose about a foot and the bulldozer hit the band shell with a crash of splintering timber. This time, Trout didn't even flinch. It seemed suddenly that nothing could stop Joe Pike Moseley and that no harm could come to him or his son sitting up here on the seat beside him. This might be senseless destruction or calculated purpose. Nothing to do but hang on and find out. Beams toppled, the roof collapsed, the flooring buckled and came up in big chunks of wood. The bulldozer never slowed. It crunched through and over debris; then the blade bit into the ground again, gouging up another swath of grass and earth.

Suddenly, Uncle Cicero was up there in the cab with them, hanging on to the metal cage next to Trout with one hand, pointing his pistol at Joe Pike's head with the other. Cicero yelled, "Joe Pike, you're under arrest!"

"No!" Trout screamed in horror.

Joe Pike looked over at Cicero, gave a huge sigh, and stopped the bulldozer. It idled for a moment. "Cut it off!" Cicero commanded. Cicero was mad as hell, face flushed and nostrils flaring.

Joe Pike switched off the diesel and it died with a rumbling cough. The crowd swarmed up around them, everybody yelling at once. "What's the charge?" Joe Pike asked Cicero.

Cicero lowered his pistol, then stuck it in the holster. "Disturbing a crime scene," he said without hesitation. His voice was steel-hard and unyielding. "Malicious destruction of town property. Malicious destruction of state property. Inciting a riot. Theft and unauthorized use of a vehicle. Failure to obey the order of an officer of the law. Failure to yield the right-of-way. Failure to give a proper turn signal. Reckless endangerment. Unauthorized use of a public facility." He stopped, thought for an instant, then added for good measure, "Failure to obtain a parade permit."

"Cicero," Joe Pike said quietly, "there wasn't nothing malicious about it."

"What in the hell do you think you were doing?" Cicero demanded.

Suddenly, Trout knew. He knew exactly. It was so obvious. "I know," he spoke up.

Cicero stared at him. Trout looked at Joe Pike, then back at Cicero. "Making a tennis court."

"That's right," Joe Pike said.

"Did you know about this?" Cicero asked icily. Trout felt as if he might be a candidate for the charge of accessory before, during, and after the fact.

"No he didn't," Joe Pike said. "It was all my idea and all my doing."

"Well," Cicero said between clenched teeth, "you have royally pissed me off, Joe Pike. And by God, you are going to jail."

He felt like a freak at the Dairy Queen as the afternoon wore itself out, the sole survivor of some terrible natural disaster. Herschel and Keats didn't have a lot to say to him, nothing at all about the events of the morning in town. But he could feel both of them cutting glances at him now and again, perhaps expecting him to come unglued and start screaming and throwing things. But he was quite beyond all that. He was simply numb. Burned out, like an electric motor run too long under too strenuous a load. He even imagined (surely, it was his imagination) the acrid smell of melted bearings and wires. It became so strong at one point that he went to the bathroom in back and checked the mirror to see if he had smoke drifting from his ears or a scorched look about his hairline. But there was only his own vacant stare looking back at him — hollow-eyed and slack-faced. But what could he expect? It had been a long night and an interminable day.

Joe Pike was in the city jail, or what passed for a jail — a one-cell cubbyhole at the rear of the police station. Uncle Cicero had hand-cuffed him (proper police procedure) and taken him straight there, leading him away from the bulldozer through the crowd that grew by the minute as word spread of the ruckus, every step dogged by the Channel 5 TV crew, shouting questions at Cicero and Joe Pike, none of which they answered. "No comment," Uncle Cicero kept saying grimly. "No damn comment." Part of the crowd stayed at the park to gawk at the wreckage of the grounds and band shell, but a good many followed Cicero and Joe Pike as they walked — Cicero with a firm hand on Joe Pike's arm — down the sidewalk to the police department and disappeared inside. Trout followed at a distance, not know-ing quite what to do or whom to ask. He looked around for Aunt Alma, but she was nowhere to be seen. He learned later that she had fled back to her house and had driven the Packard to the mill. Uncle Cicero was up to his ears in police business. And Uncle Phinizy was in the hospital in Thomson.

Trout stood for a while at the edge of the crowd that milled about in front of the police station, watching as people took turns pressing their faces against the plate-glass window to peer inside. Nobody said a word to him, but he could feel the breath of their whispers: *That's him. Joe Pike's young'un. Mama's at the Institute and Daddy's in jail.* There were even a few faces he recognized from his brief stay at Moseley High School. They stared unabashedly. Headline: INVISIBLE STUDENT SPOTTED. But they did not speak. After a while, Uncle Cicero came to the door of the police station and leaned out and said, "Y'all go on home. Ain't a thing here to see. Go on, now." As the crowd began to drift away, somebody pointed him out to the Channel 5 crew, and when they started in his direction, he slipped down an alleyway and took a circuitous route back to the parsonage. He locked the front door and took the phone off the hook and sat for a long time in one of the big overstuffed chairs in the living room, waiting for something to come to him. Nothing did.

About two o'clock he got on the motorcycle and headed down-town. The bulldozer was gone from the park, and so were most of the people. Instead, there were two stake-body trucks from the mill and several men at work, one group sweating profusely in the early after-noon heat as they cleaned up the splintered pieces of the band shell for hauling away, another group laying slabs of new green sod where the bulldozer had ripped up the grass. The downtown sidewalks were all but deserted. Trout parked in front of the police station and walked up to the door, above which a small air-conditioning unit throbbed, dripping water onto the sidewalk. Trout stepped around the puddle, opened the door and went in. Calhoun was sitting on the edge of a desk, thumbing through a copy of *Motor Trend*. He looked up and closed the magazine as Trout entered, but he kept his thumb in his place.

"I'm Trout Moseley," he said.

"Uh-huh," Calhoun answered.

"Can I see my dad?"

"Guess you'll have to talk to Cicero about that." Calhoun didn't sound unfriendly, just noncommittal.

"Where is he?" Trout asked.

Calhoun looked out through the plate-glass window. "Over yon-der." Trout looked and saw Cicero and the two men from the state crime lab in the middle of the vacant lot across the street. They had erected an open-sided tent over the crime scene to shade them from the sun. One of the men from the crime lab was in a shallow hole, handing up pieces of what Trout took to be skeleton to the other, who put them into a big plastic bag. Cicero watched, hands on hips.

"Could you ask him?" Trout asked Calhoun.

Calhoun shrugged, put the magazine down on the desk and started toward the door. "You could call him on the radio," Trout offered, trying to be helpful.

Calhoun went back to the desk, picked up the microphone of the police radio, and pressed a button. "Base to Unit One."

Across the street, Trout saw Cicero take his walkie-talkie out of its belt holster and hold it up to his mouth. "Whatcha want, Calhoun?" Cicero's voice came tinnily through the radio.

"Trout Moseley's over here. He wants to see the preacher."

"Well, let him," Cicero said. "I'll be over there in a minute."

Calhoun led him through a door and down a narrow hallway to the single cell where Joe Pike was propped on an old Army cot. It had a clean mattress but nothing else. It was stiflingly hot. This part of the police station wasn't air conditioned. And it was badly lit from a single overhead lightbulb and a small barred rectangle of window high on the back wall. Joe Pike didn't say anything as Calhoun unlocked the cell door, let Trout in, then locked it back and left. The springs of the cot creaked in protest as Joe Pike swung his legs over the side of the cot and made room for Trout to sit down.

"Are you okay?" Trout asked.

Joe Pike nodded at the wall opposite the cot, and Trout looked up and saw a large poster displaying traffic signs in reds and yellows with a word of explanation beneath each. "I've been studying," he said. "Cicero says most of the people he puts in here are charged with a traffic offense of some kind, so he put up the poster as a gesture toward driver education."

"Why did you do that?" Trout asked.

Joe Pike sighed wearily. He looked awfully tired, and the hot, cramped cell seemed to diminish him physically. He didn't say anything for a long time. But Trout waited. This time, he would get an answer if it took until next week.

Five minutes passed, perhaps more. And finally Joe Pike said, "It's your fault."

"What?"

"And I'm glad it is. This morning, sitting there on the steps. Or at least, me sitting and you jumping around yelling about this pissant town and no tennis court."

"Daddy, I didn't mean . . ."

"No," Joe Pike stopped him. "I know you didn't. But I got to thinking, sitting over there later in Alma's parlor, that's what I should have done. Way back yonder when my daddy and I used to get crossed up. I was way bigger than him, but I never thought of it that way. I always felt like a small, runny-nosed kid, especially after he got through cutting me down. He could use his voice like a switchblade." Joe Pike stopped and looked down at his hands, and Trout could see the exquisite pain in his father's face. "There were times," he went on softly, "there were times I should have stomped my foot and raised hell and said, 'Leland Moseley, you are dead wrong.' But" — he shrugged — "I never did."

Trout felt his heart wrench. He had never heard anything quite so nakedly honest from his father. He put a tentative hand on Joe Pike's arm.

"I guess that's what I was doing today," Joe Pike said. He turned and looked into Trout's eyes. "I love you, son. I guess I'm trying to make up for some things. For you, and for me." A wan smile then. "I guess I really tore up the pea-patch, huh?"

"Yeah," Trout said. "I guess you did."

And then Trout felt a flush of anger. It baffled him at first, but then he began to see where it came from. *Dang you, Joe Pike. Easy enough for you to jump on a bulldozer and go settle an old score, just like you jumped on the motorcycle and high-tailed it to Texas. My fault? No sirree. Don't try to put this monkey on my back.*

Trout asked, "When are you gonna get out?"

Joe Pike gave a big sigh. "I don't know."

"Can't you, what do they call it, post bond?"

"I can, but Cicero says I've got to have a bond hearing. Meantime, I guess I'll have to sit here and ponder the consequences of my transgression."

"And what am I supposed to do while you stay in here pondering your consequences? Fend for myself?"

Trout could hear his voice rising. So could Joe Pike. He leaned his head back against the wall and closed his eyes. He stayed that way for a long time, his only movement the rise and fall of his chest as he breathed. Out in the alley behind the jail, Trout could hear voices. Small boys, from the sound of it, giggling. Then a rock hit the bars of the high window with a *clank*. Trout stood up on the edge of the cot and looked out the window. "Cut that out or I'll whip your ass," he said without rancor. And the boys, three of them — barefoot and shirtless — fled. Then he sat back down. "I understand what you're saying about the bulldozer and all. But where does that leave me, Daddy? It may make you feel better to tear up the pea-patch, but for me, it's just one more piece of . . ."

"Shit," Joe Pike finished for him.

"Yeah."

"You need something solid. Something you can count on."

"Yeah."

Joe Pike opened his eyes now. If he took offense, he didn't show it. "I'm not a very practical man," he said. "I always depended on your mother for that."

"If Mama had been here, she would have told you to . . ." *What? Grow up? Stop trying to be Jesus? Something like that.* Big old Joe Pike — a Goodyear blimp of a man, tethered to earth by the firm hand of a tiny determined woman. Even in the months before they took her away, even in the depths of her great blank silences, her mere presence had kept him anchored. It was only when she left that he began to drift, finally fading into the distance on the motorcycle. *It all keeps coming back to Mama.*

Just then, the door down the hallway opened and Cicero walked toward the cell. He peered in. "How y'all?"

"Just great," Trout said.

"Trout, I'm sorry about all this. But I got to do my job. You understand, don't you?"

"Sure."

"Joe Pike," Cicero said, "I'm gonna go get us some lunch. I'll bring you a plate from the Koffee Kup."

Joe Pike didn't answer.

"Want something to read? Maybe something out of your study at the church?"

Joe Pike waved at the traffic signal poster on the wall. "I think I'll just ponder this, Cicero. It's all about figuring out how to get where you're going without running over anybody."

"Uh-huh," Cicero agreed.

"Things calmed down?" Joe Pike asked.

"Pretty much," Cicero said. "Too hot to be loitering around. And the Channel 5 bunch gave up and went back to Atlanta. I think they went over and interviewed Wardell about the union bidness before they left. They got their whole evening newscast out of Moseley tonight."

"Why were they here in the first place?"

Cicero waved toward the vacant lot. "Human remains. Ain't nothing excites your TV folks like human remains. Everything else just fell into their laps." Cicero shook his head, marveling. "Ain't it the damnedest thing. Not a thing worth telling has happened in Moseley since the furniture store burned down and now three stories in one day."

"Yes," Joe Pike agreed, "it has been an auspicious day. I feel honored to have been part of it."

Trout and Cicero looked at Joe Pike, and then they looked at each other. Cicero gave a little shake of his head. Was it history or random chaos? They wouldn't know for a good while. Trout had learned that much from listening to Uncle Phinizy. "Where historical significance is concerned," Phinizy had said, "it's hard to tell a volcanic eruption from a fart in the wind until a century or so has passed. A hundred years from now, Moseley, Georgia, may be just a fart in the wind." Thinking back on the events of the past eight hours, Trout understood. It was impossible to make any sense of it. A hundred years would do wonders for perspective. A good night's sleep would help.

Trout rose from the cot. "I've got to go to work. Can I get you anything?"

Joe Pike smiled and licked his lips. "A dollar cup of Dairy Queen vanilla." Cicero opened the cell door, and Trout stepped out into the hallway while Cicero closed it back and locked it. As Trout turned to go, Joe Pike said, "Trout, you may be a little *too* practical. You worry too much. Try to relax a little. Or failing that, try to find you a woman who's got a wild hair up her butt."

He came to himself standing in the Dairy Queen with Keats's hand on his arm. He was at the ice cream machine, hand on the lever, a cup beneath the spout. The cup was empty. Had he been asleep? No, just missing in action for a moment. He was long past fatigue, floating somewhere between wakefulness and a soft twilight.

"Let me do that," Keats said gently. She took the cup from him. "A shake?"

"What?"

"Were you making a shake?"

Trout tried to remember. It was like swimming through yogurt. "I think so."

"What flavor?"

He shrugged. Keats turned to the window, where a man dressed in wilted khaki work clothes and wearing an ACE PLUMBING cap peered in, frowning. Keats slid the window open. "What flavor shake did you order, sir?"

"Strawberry." He nodded at Trout. "Something wrong with that boy?"

"No sir," Keats answered and slid the window closed again. "Sit," she ordered Trout, pointing to a stool. He sat watching while she mixed up the shake, passed it through the window, and collected the man's eighty-five cents. There were several cars in the parking lot, an older couple at a picnic table, but for the moment, no one at the window. It had been a busy late afternoon, and if custom held, it would be a busy evening. Here in the grip of Georgia summer, the

Dairy Queen was an oasis, a moment's relief from heat and boredom for the locals and from road-weariness for the I-20 traffic. Business had never been better, Herschel said.

"Where's Herschel?" Trout asked.

Keats wiped the counter with a washcloth. "Gone to get a TV."

"What for?"

"It's almost six o'clock."

"So?"

"The news, dummy."

"Oh."

"Don't you want to see it?"

"Not especially."

Keats finished with the counter and hung the washcloth on the edge of the sink. She moved so efficiently about the cramped quarters of the Dairy Queen, you sometimes forgot that she was on crutches. "Well, I do," she said. "My daddy's gonna be on."

"So is mine," Trout said, making a face.

Keats leaned against the counter, a smile playing at the corners of her mouth. "Take fame where you can find it." She could really look nice when she smiled, Trout thought. It even made her eyes look softer, as if the smile muscles released a pigment that changed steel gray to a nice blue.

Herschel came in the back door then, carrying a small black-and-white television set. He set it on the counter, plugged it in and raised the rabbit ears. The picture from Channel 5 over in Atlanta was grainy and drifted in and out, sound disappearing with picture in a swarm of static. And just as *Eyewitness News at Six* came on, there was a rush of customers. But Herschel opened the window and called out, "Be just a minute, folks." And through hiss and snow, they watched as Gordon Goodnight, the anchorman, said, "It was quite a day in Moseley," and then showed them.

The reporter who had been in Moseley that morning had decided to take a somewhat lighthearted, tongue-in-cheek approach. He folded the three events — human remains, bulldozer escapade, and union movement at the mill — into two minutes of gee-whiz-you-won't-believe-this. There was Uncle Cicero presiding over the un-earthing of the skeleton; Joe Pike and Trout on the bulldozer as it plowed through the band shell; Uncle Cicero again, escorting Joe Pike to jail. The sound and picture faded just as he started to say, "No damn comment," so that they couldn't tell whether Channel 5 had bleeped out the "damn." But it returned in time to see pictures of Moseley Mill with Wardell Dubarry standing just outside the gate saying how the mill workers wanted "a decent wage and a fair shake" and had just today submitted a petition to the National Labor Relations Board for a union election. All but five of the workers, he said, had signed the petition. The holdouts, he said, were toadies for the Moseley family.

Trout didn't want to watch, but he was powerless not to. And he found himself, as the story unfolded, thinking of it as an out-of-body experience. He had read about such things: a man involved in a terrible wreck, dying but not quite dead, seeming to float above the scene watching medics work feverishly over his own broken body down below. The victim survives and lives on to tell how it was a detached, almost peaceful feeling. And then a sudden urge to return. To see what would happen next. Trout wished for a moment that he was a hundred years older, looking back on all this with historical perspective. Headline: TROUT MOSELEY DIES AT 116; SAYS IT WAS ALL A FART IN THE WIND.

The reporter signed off with another shot of the bulldozer destroying the band shell. It seemed to sum up everything. Then Gordon Goodnight launched into a story about a woman in Alpharetta who had set her husband on fire as he slept, and Herschel turned off the TV set and they went back to work.

At nine-thirty, when they had served the last customer and cleaned up and Herschel had turned off the red-and-white Dairy Queen sign on its pole out by the highway, Keats asked, "Can you take me home?" Trout hesitated. "It's okay if you don't want to. I can call Daddy."

"No," he said. "I'll take you."

They all left by the back door, and Herschel locked up and got in his car and headed for town. Then Keats said, "Want to talk?"

He hesitated again; but then he realized that he really did, that talking to somebody approximately his own age might be the sanest thing he would do this day. Everybody older seemed to have lost their minds.

They sat at one of the picnic tables beside the Dairy Queen and for a long time they didn't talk at all. It was warm and muggy, especially after having spent several hours in the air-conditioned Dairy

Queen, serving up frozen treats. Out on the Interstate, traffic barreled through the night. A carload of teenagers came up the road from town and turned into the parking lot. The windows were rolled down, the stereo throbbing with some Janis Joplin . . . *Oh Lord, woncha buy me a Mercedes-Benz* . . . Girls and boys inside, laughing. Then, disappointed to find the Dairy Queen closed, they made a quick U-turn in the lot and sped back toward town with a flurry of flying gravel. If they had seen Trout and Keats sitting at the picnic table, they paid no attention. The night settled back into stillness. Out on the Interstate, an air horn bleated. Maybe a regular customer, unable to stop tonight but sounding a howdy anyway as he passed the exit.

"Do you love your daddy?" Keats asked.

She was sitting about two feet away from him, but it was difficult to tell much about her face. The only light was a single bulb left burning inside the Dairy Queen.

"Sure," he said.

"I love my daddy too, but sometimes I think he's crazy as hell."

Trout didn't know what to say. Probably a lot of people thought Wardell Dubarry was crazy as hell. But he had never expected Keats to say it, much less think it. She seemed to be such a fierce defender of all that Wardell stood for. She seemed so sure of what she believed, while he, Trout Moseley, felt mostly baffled.

She read his silence for what it was. "You didn't expect me to say that."

"No."

"Neither did I."

"Why did you?"

"Because I had to say it to somebody."

He nodded wearily. "And I was convenient."

"No, I figured you'd understand. About a parent being crazy and all."

True, he did. Well, not crazy. Did clinical depression and acute theological angst qualify as mental illness?

"I wish he'd just walk away from it," Keats went on. "There's plenty of other jobs Daddy could do. We could move to Augusta, and he could go to work at the Army post. He's really good with his hands."

"A helluva painter," Trout said, then regretted it. Now was not the time for smartass remarks.

Keats let it pass. "I want to go to college and study art."

"Well, no reason why you can't do that. There's all sorts of loans and scholarships if you need 'em."

"It's not the money," she said bitterly, "it's this *place*." She stabbed angrily in the direction of town with one of her crutches. "It's like a big black hole with the mill and that pitiful little house and Daddy's anger. It's like it swallows you up, you know?"

"Yes," he said. And he did. She had put her finger precisely on the *problem*. Being swallowed up. Being sucked down by everybody else's circumstance, feeling that you had no power whatsoever to climb out on your own because you were weak and ineffectual and just a kid and at the mercy of people who should know better, act better.

"Your daddy's angry about" — he indicated her crutches — "what happened. I can understand that. I guess I would be, too."

"Maybe it started with that," she said. "But now, I don't know if he even knows anymore. He's all caught up in this union thing, like if he wins and the union comes in, he'll get his revenge."

"On Aunt Alma?"

"On the world. For shitting on him."

They sat for a while letting all that float in the warm sticky air, listening to the sounds of crickets in the high weeds at the edge of the parking lot and the bass rumble of traffic on the highway.

Then he said, "A couple of weeks ago you told me I ought to be pissed off. Are you pissed off?"

"Yes," she said. "No. I mean, you aren't supposed to be pissed off at your daddy, are you?"

"No, I don't think so. You can get" — he paused, searching for the word — "upset. But really pissed off? I don't think God would let you get away with that."

"God," she snorted.

"Don't you believe in God?"

"Sure. But I don't think He *lets* you get away with anything. Or *doesn't* let you. I don't believe all this crap about God running every little thing."

"When even a sparrow falls . . ." Trout remembered a verse from Sunday school.

"Yeah, I think He knows. But He doesn't worry with all the details. That would run Him nuts."

Trout laughed, but there wasn't any mirth in it. "You ought to talk to Joe Pike Moseley."

"Is he nuts?"

Trout considered again the concept of craziness. "No," he said thoughtfully, "just confused, I think. About himself. About Mama. But mainly about all the God business."

"But he's a preacher," Keats said.

"Yeah. That's the problem. He thought he knew, but now he's not sure."

"And where does that leave you?" she asked.

"About the same place it leaves you, I guess."

She reached out then and took his hand and the shock of her skin on his almost took his breath away. He realized that it had been a great long while since he had felt the soft, smooth touch of female flesh. It was part of that other life, eons ago, that had once been his. His fingers intertwined with hers, and she gave his hand a little squeeze. She didn't say anything for a long while, and neither did he. There didn't seem to be anything that particularly needed saying at the moment, and at the same time, everything to say and all of it with just the touch. He half expected to feel a rise of sexual excitement, but this was different. This was . . . He couldn't find a name for it, but it was at the same time both comforting and painfully sad. Sad to feel such a great, aching need that you couldn't even identify because you were too young and unformed and unwise.

Finally, she took her hand away and rose with a clank of her crutches. "I guess I better go home."

"Yeah," he said. "Me too. I need some sleep. I haven't had much lately."

She turned on him suddenly, a fierce edge in her voice. "Don't you think for one minute I'd do anything to hurt my daddy."

"Sure," he said. "Me too."

"It's just . . ."

"Yeah. I know."

She hesitated for a moment, then said, "I guess things have been pretty rough for you."

"A little." Then, "Maybe more than a little. I've found out it's not easy being a Moseley in Moseley. At least not right now."

"Because of the mess at the mill?"

Caution held his tongue. She was, after all, Wardell Dubarry's daughter. And Wardell Dubarry appeared to be on a rampage just now.

"I'm not trying to pump you or anything," she said, reading his mind. "I don't care if they have a goddamn union or not. They either will or they won't."

"Aunt Alma thinks that one of these days, I'm going to take over the mill. Run it. Me and Eugene."

She gave a snort. "You? Running that mill?"

"Well," he said defensively, "I guess I could if I had to."

"But you don't want to."

"No."

"What do you want to do?"

He sighed. What did he want? At sixteen, were you supposed to have the foggiest idea beyond food, drink, shelter, sex (in just about any form), and a new tennis racquet? "I kinda want to go hide."

"Well, you can't do that here. Not you."

"Then maybe I'd just like to have somebody tell me what to do. You know? I mean, that's really weird, isn't it? I always thought I wanted people to *stop* telling me what to do. But then they did, and . . ." He shrugged. "I guess they're all too busy trying to figure things out for themselves. Daddy's wrestling with God, Uncle Phinizy's sick, Uncle Cicero is busy, and Aunt Alma's pissed off." And scared, he could have added, but didn't.

"What about your mother?"

What a stupid thing to say, he thought. Maybe even mean, considering the circumstances.

But Keats wouldn't drop it. "Why don't you just pick up the phone and call her and ask her what to do?"

"She's sick," he said, spitting out the words.

"I know that. Everybody knows that. She's in the Institute in Atlanta."

"Yeah."

"Well, people call sick people all the time. Or go visit."

"Not there. Daddy says the doctors don't want her to talk to anybody for a while."

"Daddy says," she said with a touch of sarcasm.

Trout could feel the heat rising in his face. This was getting out of hand, and it made him angry. She was treating him like a little kid again. Damn her.

She waited. "Well?"

"It's none of your goddamn business," he said stiffly.

"Probably not," she said quietly. "But I hate to see you just sit there and take it. I keep thinking you'll get pissed off enough to hitch up your britches and do something for yourself."

It dawned on him that she sounded a lot like Uncle Phinizy. *Save your own ass.* But what did she know? Or Phinizy, for that matter? It wasn't their ass to save. "What about yourself?" he asked finally.

"What about me?"

"You don't sound like you're deliriously happy, either. Are you pissed off enough to do anything about it?"

"Not yet. But I'm working on it."

They sat for a while longer on the picnic table, but there didn't seem to be much else to talk about. So they got on the motorcycle and went home.

It was an hour or so later, as he teetered on the edge of sleep, that he thought of the dollar cup of vanilla ice cream Joe Pike had asked for. He thought of his father, sitting in the dark, hot, cramped little cell, knowing at this late hour that Trout had forgotten his one request, that there would be no ice cream this night. It might not be the greatest disappointment in his life, just the latest.

Trout began to cry, and at first he tried to stifle it, but he found that he could not. So he buried his face in the pillow and let the sobs come without struggle or protest. They were bitter tears and there was no comfort in them. Then he wondered, *Why this?* After all that had happened in the long hours since the sun had risen this morning, why was he crying over some stupid ice cream?

THIRTEEN

THE TELEPHONE WOKE HIM. He thought if he lay there long enough, it would stop, but it didn't. Someone pretty damned persistent was on the other end. So he gave up and padded back to the kitchen and answered it.

"Trout, can you come down here?" Uncle Cicero asked.

"Down where?"

"The police station."

"What's the matter?" Trout asked, suddenly alarmed.

"He won't leave."

Trout looked at the clock on the kitchen wall. It was nearly eight. "What do you mean, Uncle Cicero?"

"Your Aunt Alma got a judge out of bed at six o'clock this morning and posted bail for Joe Pike."

"She did?"

"Yes she did. And him a Republican, too. The judge, I mean. I reckon being a Moseley transcends party politics, huh?"

"Well, that's good," Trout said. "He needs to come home." Then what?

"But he won't leave," Cicero repeated. "He refuses to come out of the cell."

"Did he say why?"

"No, he just sits there. Staring at that damned traffic chart on the wall." There was a long pause. "I thought maybe you'd know what to do," Cicero said finally.

"Yes sir," Trout said. "I'm the practical one in the family."

True to Cicero's description, Joe Pike was sitting on the cot, his gaze fixed straight ahead. The cell door was wide open. Trout entered and sat down on the cot next to Joe Pike. Then he joined his father in studying the poster for a while, wondering if Joe Pike had perhaps found some answers up there among all those do's and don'ts. Stop, Yield, No Left Turn, Railroad Crossing. Low Shoulder, Steep Grade, Sharp Curve, Dead End Road. A vehicular minefield. Knowing all this, why would anyone ever drive?

"I'm sorry I forgot your ice cream," Trout said after a moment.

"I really need to stop eating so much of that stuff," Joe Pike said, startling Trout a bit with the sound of his voice. "I need to lose some weight. I have let myself get woefully out of shape and I imagine that I cut an abominable figure. Vanity of vanities. All is vanity, quoth the preacher."

"I saw the TV stuff," Trout said. "You didn't look all that bad."

Joe Pike gave a great sigh. "I suppose you've come to get me out of jail."

Trout didn't say anything.

"Well, I'm not ready yet."

"Why not?"

Joe Pike turned to Trout. "Because I am meditating. I have found a little peace and quiet back here and I am enjoying the contemplative life."

"Looking at traffic signs?"

"You can find all sorts of riches in symbols if you take long enough to think on them."

Trout looked at the poster, picked out one from the top row. "No U-Turn."

"Excellent choice," Joe Pike said. "Start with Thomas Wolfe: 'You can't go home again.' Then consider the lost magic of childhood. And think about the nature of wishes. Children wish for a BB gun from Santa Claus, a dollar from the tooth fairy. Pleasant things, mostly. When grown-ups wish, there's mainly pain involved: take away my arthritis; make my husband stop beating me; deliver me from evil.

Speaking of which, is there something in the nature of evil that is undeliverable? What of the sinner whose life is one dastardly deed after another, crying out with his last breath, 'Lord, I have sinned. Forgive me.' Does the Lord say, 'Of course.' Or does he say, 'Whoa just a minute, bubba. We got to have a little prayer meeting over this business you call a life.'" He paused, thought for a moment. "I could go on. The possibilities are virtually endless, but sooner or later you arrive back at the sign. No U-Turn. I thought about that one a good deal of the night. It's second from the left on the top, right after Stop, which I didn't. I have worked my way to the end of the first row and am ready to start on the second with Deer Crossing. I suspect there may be something there in the nature of nature."

Trout looked over the poster again. There were seven rows of traffic signs. About a week's worth of work at this pace. "Then will you leave?" he asked.

"I haven't thought that far ahead," Joe Pike said. There was something gently wistful in his voice. He seemed calmer than he had in days — a man poking about leisurely inside his soul. There was something to envy about that, Trout thought. Even a practical person could see that.

"Have you been to see Phinizy?"

"I haven't had time."

"Go," Joe Pike said urgently. "I think he's pretty sick."

"All right. Does he have any other relatives? A wife? Children?" Trout realized that for all of Phinizy's relating of Moseley history, he had revealed little of his own.

"No children," Joe Pike answered. "He did have a wife once upon a time. Married her in Italy after the war. But it didn't last. They fought like a couple of alley cats, to hear Phinizy tell it. So there's nobody but us."

Trout got up to go, and he started to say, *Can I bring you anything?* but he thought better of it. He might forget again, and that was so much unlike him, he didn't want to risk it. So he gave Joe Pike a hug and left.

"He won't leave," Trout told Cicero out on the sidewalk. "He seems pretty set on staying. Has he had anything to eat?"

"Oh yeah," Cicero said. "He's got a great appetite. I been toting stuff back and forth from the Koffee Kup since yestiddy."

"Maybe you should stop feeding him," Trout suggested. "Try to starve him out. Or yell, 'Fire!'"

Cicero looked down at the sidewalk. Trout could tell he was terribly tired. He sagged around the edges. "I don't know, Trout," he said, and Trout understood that he meant a great deal more than the Joe Pike problem. They were, all of them, much in need of mercy and grace.

"Maybe everything'll calm down for a while and you can get back to your project." Trout nodded to the vacant lot across the street.

Cicero gave a tiny shrug that didn't use much more than his eyebrows. "Grady come and got the bulldozer. Be a cold day in July before I get it back."

Phinizy looked like cannibals had gotten him. A shrunken head, brown and leathery and deeply creased, displayed upon a backdrop of white, nestled on a pillow with the bedsheet pulled up tight under the chin. A museum piece, that's what Great Uncle Phinizy was. Grotesque, aboriginal. Or maybe just original.

Fifteen minutes, they had told Trout at the front desk, and that only because he was a blood relative. He pulled up a chair next to the bed and sat watching Phinizy, noticing after a while the almost imperceptible rise and fall of his chest under the sheet, so little air being taken in and exhaled that Trout wondered that it could sustain life. The only sound, a tiny wheezing in his throat. A bedside cart stand held an oxygen bottle and mask, but Phinizy was apparently in no need of it at the moment.

Then all of a sudden Phinizy said in a raspy but perfectly clear voice, "The sonsabitches took my cigarettes and my pants and they won't bring me any whiskey." Nothing moved but his lips. Then his eyes fluttered open and he cut a glance at Trout. "What are you gonna do about it?"

"Me?"

Phinizy made a little farting sound with his mouth.

"I just came over here to see how you were doing," Trout said.

"Well, I'm just damn near dead. And I want to die in Moseley, not Thomson. I ain't got a thing against Thomson, but at least in Moseley I can smoke cigarettes and drink whiskey and wear my own pants."

Trout didn't know whether to believe him or not. Dying? From the look of him, that might well be the case. And if it were, Trout knew that it would make him indescribably sad.

"You look a mite taken aback," Phinizy said.

"Are you really . . ."

"Yes," Phinizy said, and there wasn't an ounce of self-pity to it. "They took out one lung five years ago and now the other one is as rotten as a month-old watermelon."

"I'm sorry," Trout said.

"Well, I'm not. Only thing I regret is, I ain't gonna be around to see how it turns out. I'll just have to use my imagination."

The door opened and a young nurse stuck her head in. "Time's up," she said. "Mr. Moseley needs to get some rest."

"Yes ma'am."

The door closed, and Trout got up and moved the chair back against the wall.

"Well?" Phinizy asked. "Are you gonna take me home?"

"Uncle Phin, I can't do that," Trout protested. "I'll go get Uncle Cicero or Aunt Alma." He didn't think it necessary to go into the business about Joe Pike.

"Cicero and Alma are the ones who put me in here."

"Wouldn't the doctors —"

"To hell with them," Phinizy interrupted. "There's not a damn thing wrong with me except that I'm dying, and I've been doing that for months. It could take me several months more. Those assholes just want to watch."

Trout thought of Phinizy as he had most usually seen him — nestled deep in the recliner with glass in hand, smoke curling about his head and disappearing into the pool of light from the reading lamp, holding court with the latest footsore pilgrim who wandered in. The place, for all its scruffiness, fit Phinizy. This place, this plastered and tiled and pasteled sterility with its hospital smells and mutterings, was no place to die.

But what to do?

"Go get your mother," Phinizy said. "She'll get me out of here."

"Mother?"

"She's the only one of the whole goddamned bunch that's got any sense."

"But she's . . ." *What the hell is going on here? All these people sud-*

denly invoking the name of my mother. Have they forgotten? Are they just trying to be nasty?

"Either get Irene or get me out of here yourself. I'm going home. It's your responsibility."

"What if the doctors won't let you leave?"

"Who the hell's gonna ask 'em? I'll just walk out. Go get the car. I'll meet you in the parking lot."

"I didn't come in the car," he said.

They had almost reached Moseley, taking the back way on two-lane roads, when the state trooper stopped them. Trout pulled the motorcycle over to the grassy shoulder of the road next to a thick stand of pine trees. He left the engine running and balanced the motorcycle with both feet on the ground. Not that Phinizy weighed all that much. Not even as much as Keats. The trooper got out of his cruiser and left the blue lights on top flashing and put on his Smokey Bear hat and walked up to the motorcycle. He was about thirty, Trout guessed, lean and crew-cut, creases sharp, leather and brass polished, the hat tilted forward on his head so that it shaded his eyes. A pair of sunglasses hung from one shirt pocket. Above the other was a small brass nameplate: SPENCER. He stopped a couple of yards from the motorcycle, studied things for a while, then walked all the way around and ended up back where he started. Finally he asked, "What in the hell is going on here?"

"I am an escapee from the Augusta Center for the Criminally Insane and Terminally Wealthy," Phinizy rasped. "I have commandeered this vehicle and have wired powerful explosives just under the gas tank. One false move, Officer" — he peered at the nametag — "Spencer, and I will blow all of us into the afterlife."

"He's just kidding," Trout said quickly.

"Try me," Phinizy snapped.

"Really," Trout rushed on, "he's my uncle. Well, my great-uncle. And he's been in the hospital over at Thomson and he's only got one lung and I'm taking him home to Moseley. There's no explosives or anything. Honest."

Officer Spencer didn't say anything for a long time. Finally, he reached out his hand, rubbed his thumb and two fingers together. "Your license."

Trout gave it over.

"What are you doing all the way up here?" Officer Spencer asked.

"What do you mean?"

"The address on here is Ohatchee."

"He's a runaway," Phinizy said.

"Dammit, Uncle Phin!" Trout exploded, turning with a jerk and almost toppling the motorcycle. "Will you just shut up." Phinizy gave a little shrug. Then Trout said to Officer Spencer, "We just moved to Moseley about three weeks ago."

"We?"

"Me and my father. He's a Methodist minister."

Officer Spencer studied the driver's license for a while, making small movements with his lips as he read. Then he nodded. "That one."

"Yes sir." He waited, but Officer Spencer didn't say anything else. "Can we go now? I need to get my uncle on home."

Officer Spencer gave Phinizy a careful looking-over. "His butt's showing."

That was, indeed, the case. Phinizy wore only the light-green hospital gown. Nothing underneath and a fairly wide swath of skin showing down the back. On a younger person, it might have been obscene.

"You can't ride around the state of Georgia like that," Officer Spencer said.

"What if I just take the whole thing off?" Phinizy asked.

"No sir." Then to Trout, "You'll have to cover his butt."

And so it was that Trout rode into Moseley bare-chested and Phinizy had Trout's T-shirt strategically placed at the rear of the hospital gown.

He pulled into the driveway of Aunt Alma's house and kept going to the foot of the stairs of the garage apartment. Then he helped Phinizy up the steps and into some clothes and onto the recliner. He fetched cigarettes and whiskey and volume three of Shelby Foote's history of the Civil War. Phinizy seemed tired but satisfied. "Now go away for a while," Phinizy said.

"Can you get up and down if you need to?"

"Of course."

"I'm going to tell Uncle Cicero," Trout said. "I don't care whether you like that or not."

"Doesn't matter," Phinizy said. "Thank you for everything, Trout.

You are a rather uncommon young man. You just don't know it yet. Come back later and we'll talk."

The rest of the week, to Trout's great surprise and relief, passed uneventfully.

Trout stopped by Phinizy's apartment several times a day, bringing meals from the Koffee Kup Kafe and checking on Phinizy's condition, expecting each time to open the screen door and find him peacefully departed in his chair with a half drunk glass of whiskey beside him and a cold cigarette stub between his fingers. But Phinizy seemed his old self — wry, grumpy, curious. His appetite was good, his relish for tobacco and alcohol undiminished. Trout suggested that perhaps Aunt Alma would be happy to hire a woman to come in occasionally and handle domestic duties. Phinizy wouldn't hear of it. "If I wanted a woman, I'm perfectly capable of hiring one myself. But I don't. I have had a singular lack of success with women all my life," he said. "I don't need to spoil the record now. I am completely comfortable with male orneriness and dissipation." He sent Trout to the library with a list of books, and Trout returned with the only one available, a thin volume of Robert Frost poetry. *And miles to go before I sleep.* They spoke no more of death.

Nothing more was said from either side about the union movement at Moseley Mill. Aunt Alma was silent on the subject, and from what Trout could tell, there was no particular agitation among the work force. Everyone seemed to be waiting on that score. To Trout's relief, Alma made no inquiry about the Dubarry family or goings-on in the mill village. Instead, she threw herself almost totally into cleaning up the house. A construction crew arrived to repair the fire damage in the kitchen. A professional cleaning crew came from Augusta and began to scrub walls and floors and carry off piles of clothing and linens to be dry-cleaned. Alma dogged their every step, making sure they handled the furniture and fixtures with care. She wanted everything back in its place exactly as before. Her greatest anguish was the draperies. They were simply rotten with age and came apart when the cleaners took them down. Alma sped off to Savannah with salvaged scraps of cloth, bent on finding exact replicas, or at least a close approximation. The house was a fixation. Nothing must change.

Alma made no more mention of Rosetta, but Cicero remarked that he had inquired at her house, hoping to learn more about the origin of the fire, only to find that she was visiting a sister in Detroit.

What Cicero did clear up was the mystery of the skeleton in the vacant lot. Dental records identified the remains as that of a wanderer from Birmingham, reported missing by his family several years earlier. As best the state crime lab technicians could determine, the man had somehow reached Moseley on a cold winter night, broken into the rear of the furniture store seeking a warm place to sleep, and had managed to start the fire. When the building collapsed, the body had been buried under the rubble. The initial investigation had blamed faulty wiring, so no one had imagined a human being was involved. Until now, when Cicero started digging up the past. Channel 5 Eyewitness News reported the new developments, but they did not send a crew back to Moseley. They simply replayed the earlier pictures of the crime lab technicians bagging the bones. Moseley's brush with notoriety had passed.

Joe Pike remained in the tiny cell at the rear of the police station. Trout visited daily, but Joe Pike seemed distant and preoccupied. By the end of the week, he was nearly to the end of the traffic signs on the poster, and the more he thought about, the deeper into himself he seemed to slip. Mayor Fleet Mathis came to call, gently suggesting that perhaps Joe Pike was needed elsewhere in the community. Joe Pike demurred. The preacher from the Pentecostal Holiness Church also showed up and spent several hours in prayer and meditation with Joe Pike. At the end, he seemed inclined to join Joe Pike on a more or less permanent basis, but Cicero hustled him out, reminding him that he had another job as night watchman at a poultry processing plant in Warrenton and a family to feed. Cicero brought Joe Pike three meals a day from the Koffee Kup Kafe. Dinner and supper included sweet potato pie. Cicero was keeping a tab, he said, and would present Joe Pike with a bill when and if he finally decided to give up his meditation and go home. The city would not pay to feed a man who wasn't supposed to be in jail.

Trout worked and rested. At the Dairy Queen, he settled into a routine, comfortable and proficient now with preparing any item on the menu. Herschel pronounced him satisfactory, ended his probationary period, and gave him a twenty-five-cent-an-hour raise.

With Keats, what had begun as a sort of truce passed at some point into something a bit more. They talked, stepping nimbly around the subject of their families and the nasty potential for conflict lurking in the background. Instead, they talked as teenagers — about music ("You like all that old stuff," she teased. "The Platters. Yuck. They're about as exciting as an organ recital."), movies (she had been to Augusta once to see a Zeffirelli film and pronounced it high art; his all-time favorite was an old black-and-white with Van Johnson and June Allyson, which turned up occasionally on TV), dreams (portents, she said; entertainment, he countered), and zits. The latter was the only thing they agreed on, but that was okay. Trout found himself lowering his guard, hungering for some normalcy. And so did she. There was no more physical contact, but he could still feel her cool touch on his hand. At night, in the silent dark of his room, he imagined more. In his fantasies, she was strong and unfettered, without limitation. Facing her at work, remembering, he stammered and blushed. There would, of course, be nothing more to it. They were too different in temperament, too bound by circumstance. She could still make him mad as hell.

He had the parsonage blessedly to himself. He ate mostly at the Dairy Queen, making do with orange juice and Froot Loops at breakfast. Nobody came to call. The community, particularly the Moseley Methodist congregation, seemed to regard the situation with the same kind of awed fascination as had the good folk in Ohatchee when Joe Pike replaced his wife with a motorcycle. Another wreck here, obviously not finished. You wouldn't want to get too close for fear of being struck by flying angst. So they stayed away.

Trout fell into the habit of peeling off all his clothes the minute he stepped in the door (though he always took them to the dirty-clothes hamper), remaining unclothed until it was time to leave the house again, except at night when he would sit naked on the back steps for an hour or so, letting the summer air bathe and soothe him. As he sat there on Friday night, thinking about nothing in particular, it began to rain. But it was a warm, soft rain, and he didn't move until it had passed.

He kept the parsonage neat, even spending one morning with the vacuum cleaner. There was something comfortingly satisfying about a simple task that took no thought to speak of and produced immediate results, much the same as preparing a banana split at the Dairy Queen. He mowed the lawn of the parsonage and church on Saturday with the same sense of satisfaction.

He watched TV, slept a lot, felt himself slowly edging up from the black hole of physical and mental fatigue. He found to his surprise that he was now in no hurry for Joe Pike to come home. He tried not to think about it.

He was sitting on the front steps (clothed in shorts and baseball cap) when the *Atlanta Constitution* arrived early on Sunday morning, delivered by a boy on a bicycle who flung the hefty rolled-up bulk from the sidewalk. It plopped with a thud onto the walkway. The delivery boy made a turn when he reached the business district and worked his way back up Broadus Street on the other side, dropping papers at Aunt Alma's house and those of her neighbors.

Trout would have let the paper lay where it landed, but he became curious about the Braves' score from the night before. They had played the Dodgers, and Trout had neglected to check the radio for results before he went to bed. So he barefooted out the walkway and picked up the paper and returned to his place on the steps. He removed the thick rubber band and spread the paper on his knees. And there it was. A large photo dominated the front page: a small crowd, mostly men and mostly young, proceeding along a downtown Atlanta street. GAY PRIDE MARCH, the bold letters above the photo read. And there in the middle of the throng was Eugene. He carried a placard that said, QUEERS HAVE RIGHTS TOO.

Trout studied the picture for a while and read the accompanying article all the way through twice. Then he said, "Oh, shit."

He looked across the street. Alma and Cicero's copy of the *Constitution* lay on the walkway beneath their front steps. Trout thought about going over there and getting it. But did he have any right to meddle? He had no idea what Alma and Cicero knew about Eugene's lifestyle and preferences. They hardly ever mentioned him, except for Alma's occasional insistence that he would one day, along with Trout, be responsible for the mill and the perpetuation of Moseley-ism. If they knew, this might be no great surprise. If they didn't, they soon would, one way or the other. Trout agonized over it for a while longer, and then Uncle Cicero saved him the trouble. He walked out in his bathrobe and fetched the paper with a wave to Trout. He disappeared into the house and Trout held his breath, half expecting an explosion.

None came. After a moment, Trout got up from the steps and put on a T-shirt and shoes and went to the jail.

At precisely eleven o'clock, just as Grace Vredemeyer was lifting her hands to launch the choir into an opening fanfare, the doors to the sanctuary swung open and Joe Pike strode in. Grace's hands froze in midair and she turned and watched Joe Pike (as did they all) as he marched down the aisle and up to the pulpit where Judge Tandy was standing, prepared to lead the service in the absence of the minister. They all saw that Joe Pike was wearing his cowboy boots under the billowing black robe. But it was the only thing even slightly scruffy about him. He was clean-shaven, freshly scrubbed, hair neatly combed. And there was a firmness to his face that Trout hadn't seen for some time — slightly less fleshy, more purposeful.

Joe Pike extended his hand and Judge Tandy, mouth slightly open, shook it. Then he glanced at Grace. "Y'all go right ahead," he said. And he sat down in the big high-backed chair behind the pulpit, crossed his legs, and waited.

Grace Vredemeyer glanced toward Aunt Alma, who was sitting in her accustomed front-and-center pew between Trout and Cicero. Alma had entered the sanctuary five minutes before Joe Pike, followed dutifully by Cicero. She had looked neither left nor right but had proceeded directly to her pew and sat down stiffly, smoothing out her clothing and then reaching for a hymnal. She gave Trout a thin, tight smile. She looked quite attractive, dressed in a navy blue summer suit with white piping on the sleeves and pockets and a simple strand of pearls. Her makeup was faultless, every hair in place. But if you knew what to look for, you could see the strain etched in thin lines around her eyes and mouth. If the sight of Joe Pike marching in abruptly had either surprised or nonplussed her, she gave no evidence of it. At the moment, with Grace Vredemeyer's eyes on her, she moved not a muscle.

Grace turned back to the choir and they sang the introit, and then the congregation rose as one and launched into the first hymn. "Blessed Assurance." Appropriate, Trout thought. He had heard the rumblings about updating the Methodist Hymnal, adding new material that paid respects to changing sensibilities and agitations, referring to God as a woman and all that. But to Aunt Alma, God — as He was represented at Moseley Methodist Church — was unchanging. She sang with a clear, strong voice.

Blessed Assurance, Jesus is mine
Oh what a foretaste of glory divine . . .

Cicero, at her side, chimed in off-key and an octave or so lower. Cicero looked weary and shopworn with bags under his eyes and a rather poor job of shaving. But he sang out bravely.

The sanctuary was packed, the largest crowd Trout had seen since they had moved to Moseley. Those who had not personally seen the front page of the *Atlanta Constitution,* he imagined, had at least heard about it. They had come, like the crowd that gathered uptown at the crime scene days before, to see its effect. Alma, to all appearances, bore it with great, calm dignity. Trout was moved. He was tempted to put an arm around her, but he refrained. She seemed, underneath that granite exterior, to be delicate porcelain.

When the hymn was finished, they all sat down, and for a moment, no one seemed to know what to do. Joe Pike sat musing in his chair, gaze fixed on the toe of one cowboy boot. Finally, Judge Tandy got up from his chair at Joe Pike's side and read some announcements and a few verses of Scripture and then prayed eloquently but vaguely. As he did, a few late arrivals straggled in and, finding no seats, stood self-consciously along the rear wall of the sanctuary. Ushers brought folding chairs from the educational building while the congregation stood and sang again. "Rescue the Perishing," one of Joe Pike's favorites. That, too, seemed to fit the occasion. After the hymn ended, Judge Tandy called the ushers forward and they passed the collection plates. The choir blessed the collection with song, Judge Tandy placed the stacked plates on the altar, and then he looked up at Joe Pike from the Communion railing.

Joe Pike stepped to the pulpit and peered down at the good judge. "Thank you, Judge Tandy. I'll take it from here."

Judge Tandy joined his wife, Myrtice, in his accustomed pew, and the congregation settled in their seats — quiet, expectant. Trout thought of Uncle Phinizy, sunk deep in the bunker of his overstuffed chair, celebrating Sunday with cigarettes, whiskey, and Plutarch. Trout had checked on him at midmorning and found him a bit weak but cheerful. "Ummmmm," Phinizy hummed when Trout showed him the newspaper. He studied the photo for a moment. "He has Leland's nose and eyes," Phinizy said.

"Was Grandaddy Leland gay?" Trout asked, not really knowing why.

"No. He was a prick. That's enough of a burden for a man to carry. Eugene got his only good qualities. The eyes and nose. He's a nice-looking young man."

Trout didn't know what to think about Eugene. He remembered the boy of his childhood, something of a fascination both because he was older and because he possessed a certain spark, a sense of modulated rebellion. He would not touch that sacred family heirloom, the old Packard, but there was a great deal he *would* do, including climbing out on the roof outside his second-story room and drinking black-berry wine filched from Rosetta's supply in the pantry. There had been nothing furtive or odd about Eugene, nothing to indicate he was anything but the most regular of boys. He seemed, even at that young age, to be satisfied with who he was. From the appearance of his smiling, somewhat defiant face on the front page of the *Constitution*, he still was.

Trout had actually never known anyone who was openly gay. There had been talk about the agricultural arts teacher at Ohatchee High School, whose eyes seemed to linger a trifle too long on some of the male students. Trout and his friends antagonized each other with jokes about their own maleness or lack thereof. Gayness was not something any of them personally knew anything about, or would at least admit. It was a condition, it was understood, to be avoided. But this was Eugene. His cousin. Openly and proudly gay. Trout needed some frame of reference other than the snide remarks of teenage boys. But Phinizy was no help. Phinizy went back to Plutarch and Trout went to church.

Where now Joe Pike stood towering over the deadly quiet of the sanctuary. There was not even a cough or the rustle of a petticoat, even among the scattering of children. He reached inside his robe and pulled out a small newspaper clipping. *Good grief,* Trout thought. *He's going to rip right into it.*

But he didn't. Joe Pike cleared his throat. "Maybe you saw this item in the paper a couple of weeks ago. I clipped it out because I thought it was sort of curious. It's about the Salem witch trials." His gaze swept the congregation, lingering now and then on a face. No one moved.

Trout cut his eyes over at Aunt Alma. Her forehead creased a bit, but that was all.

"You've probably heard the story. In Salem, Massachusetts, back in the seventeenth century, a number of young women were charged with practicing witchcraft, tried, and executed. The good people of Salem thought there was ample evidence. The young women had been acting strangely — speaking gibberish and the like. And in that unenlightened time, it was enough to convince the Faithful that the girls' bodies and souls had been possessed by the Devil. So, nothing to do but dispatch them summarily, to keep the evil from spreading and contaminating the entire community. Any reasonable person would do the same, don't you think?"

He waited, but there was no response. The congregation seemed in no mood to engage Joe Pike in Socratic dialogue this June morning. In fact, they seemed in no mood at all, only a state of expectant puzzlement.

"Well" — Joe Pike held up the clipping — "modern scientific thought and method have shed some new light on the Salem witches. In short, researchers have found good evidence that what actually happened was this: the girls ate some bread that was contaminated by a parasitic fungus. They became physically ill, and the illness manifested itself in part in disorderly behavior, delusions, and convulsions. In the Salem of the seventeenth century, that amounted to evidence of witchcraft. Ignorance, you say. How sad that twenty innocent young girls died because they ate bad bread."

Joe Pike folded the clipping neatly and tucked it back beneath his robe. Then he leaned forward on the pulpit, hands gripping its sides, and looked out across the congregation again. "Why do you think God made people who are different?" He waited for an answer. None came. None except from Aunt Alma. She stood up slowly, tucked her purse underneath her arm, and walked out. She had to climb over Cicero to get to the aisle. He sat there for a moment, looking very weary and sad. And he got up and followed Alma out the door.

In the pulpit, Joe Pike waited for a long while until the door to the sanctuary stopped swinging. Then he gave a sigh and plunged ahead. "Why did God make people who are blind or deaf or lame or retarded, people with horrible disfigurations — not because of accident or war, but from birth — little babies who emerge from the sanctity of the womb with arms and legs missing, with brains so ill-formed they have no hope beyond being vegetables. Why? Why?" There was true agony in Joe Pike's rising voice, at once a lamentation and a diatribe. He lifted both hands toward the ceiling. "Why? Why?" he thundered. "What the dickens are You up to?"

A shudder passed through the congregation. They held their breaths, watching Joe Pike's fists clench, seeing the raw, naked anger and grief that contorted his face, expecting the lightning bolt that might consume them all. They all, Trout included, shrank from his rage and blasphemy. But none moved. They were paralyzed, both by fear and fascination.

Joe Pike lowered his arms. "I don't know," he said wearily. "I just don't know. I don't know why the innocent suffer. I don't know why God creates or allows people to be so different that we hide our eyes in shame and shrink from contact and even make jokes to reassure ourselves and prove to the world that THANK GOD WE AREN'T LIKE THAT, and then secretly suffer agonies of guilt because we know in our hearts we've been cruel. I don't know why," he said, his voice sinking almost to a whisper, "God creates or allows a state of mind so bleak that a person cannot see beyond a curtain of despair. I don't know."

There was a long, painful quiet. Trout thought for a moment that Joe Pike might end it there, give a great bewildered shake of his head and retire from the field of battle. It seemed such a final, irretrievable sadness, an abject admission of failure. But he was not finished. He looked out across the congregation again, and when he spoke, they sat and listened in absolute stillness. "I don't know," he said, "and don't expect to. Ever. But there is one small thing I believe, and another that I guess. I believe that God's special grace is upon those who are different, that whatever temporal, earthly misery they endure is compensated tenfold when they stagger and crawl in their wretchedness to the gates of eternity. I believe they will be made whole and that they will sit on the right and left of God's throne and be His elect."

He smiled, and they could see that he took a small measure of comfort and peace from this thing he had come to believe. He went on. "I can only guess at why they have to endure what they endure. But is it possible" — he paused and looked upward again — "that God just wants to see how the rest of us will treat them?"

And with that, he did leave. And after he had gone, the congregation — drained and weak, as if they had been through Joe Pike's valley of shadows with him — got up quietly and went home. There seemed nothing worth saying.

It was a quiet Sunday night at the Dairy Queen. The afternoon traffic had been intense, long lines at both windows stretching out into the crowded parking lot, more people than they had ever seen in one blindingly hot stretch of summer day. Herschel and Trout and Keats worked frantically, filling the orders and passing them through the window and going on to the next and the next and the next. Finally, about seven o'clock, it ended abruptly. Trout shoved a cardboard container with a strawberry shake, two Mister Mistys, three foot-long hot dogs, and an extra-large order of fries through the window, along with change for a ten-dollar bill, and when the man who had ordered it all turned away, there was no one else. They hunkered behind the counter for several minutes like battle-weary soldiers, expecting another assault. But no one came. Finally Herschel said, "Sweet Jesus." It took another half hour of hard work to clean up the mess and litter, indoors and out. At eight, an hour earlier than usual, Herschel turned off the lights and they all headed home.

Trout dropped Keats off at the mill village, both of them exhausted beyond conversation. A minute later, as he passed the mill, he noticed the gate standing wide open, the Packard in Aunt Alma's parking space next to the office door, and the glow of a light from one of the tall windows of the mill itself. He was well past, turning onto Broadus Street toward the parsonage, when curiosity caught up with his work-dulled mind and he turned back.

When he pushed open the door to the weaving room, he heard the splash of liquid somewhere on the other side of the sprawl of silent machines. He followed the sound and found her, walking along the far wall and pouring kerosene on the floor. She looked up, saw him, but said nothing and went back to her work, walking slowly, tilting the can and letting the silver liquid gurgle from the long spout, leaving a reeking trail behind her. The last drops spilled out as she reached the end of the wall and she stopped and put the can down. She straightened and looked at him again. She was wearing the same blue suit she had worn to church that morning. Her hair and makeup were still perfect. But her eyes were now dull and lifeless.

"Aunt Alma . . . ," Trout said tentatively.

"It's finished," she said, her voice mechanical.

"What do you mean?"

"There's nobody left."

"Left to do what?" he asked.

Then she sank slowly down to her knees on the battered wooden floor, pitted and stained from all those years of grime and dust and oil, trod by the weary feet of generations of mill workers who had tended the machines. She spoke softly, almost to herself. "Did you see them today in church? Did you see how they looked at me, all there in their Sunday best, every seat filled to see the Moseleys brought down." Then her face shattered and she began to cry quietly. Trout went to her, stood awkwardly for a moment, then knelt with her. He put a hand on her shoulder.

"I was supposed to be the pretty one," she said. "Daddy said I was so pretty. I was supposed to dance and wear pretty things. Not" — she passed her hand through the stale, close air of the weaving room — "this."

She leaned against him then and sobbed into his shirt, and he held her and let her cry for a long time. And he understood how desperately lonely it had made her, quite beyond Cicero's love and devotion. It was a terrible thing, trying to live up to something, to have your life shackled by your history, or at least your notion of your history.

All of them, it seemed, were trapped in lives they no longer wanted, whether they had freely chosen them or not. Alma didn't want to be the keeper of the Moseley myth. Irene didn't want to be a preacher's wife. Joe Pike didn't want to be a preacher, not in the sense he had originally intended. And Trout didn't want to be sixteen, lost and wretched. Only Cicero and Phinizy seemed to have any peace about them. And even with them it seemed as much resignation as anything.

Finally, Alma pulled back from him. "It's over," she said.

"Why?" he asked.

"There's no one left."

"You've always said you're saving it for Eugene and me."

"Don't speak to me of Eugene," she said.

"Then me." And as he said it, he felt utterly crazy, knowing it was a lie, that if he stayed here that this would all devour him as surely as it had devoured Alma. But he lied to save . . . what? He wasn't quite sure, but he knew it shouldn't end as smoldering ruin and ashes. It had to be worth more than that.

"You?" she said. "You really mean that?"

"Of course."

She started to say something else, but fell silent. He helped her to her feet and took her back to her office. She leaned heavily on him like an invalid. He helped her sit in the chair behind the big desk, where she slumped, dull and vacant-eyed. And then he called Cicero.

An hour later, when he and Cicero had washed down the wall and floor where the kerosene had been poured and Cicero had taken Alma home, Trout went back to Keats's house. It was after nine when he knocked on the door and the porch light came on. He heard the clanking of Keats's crutches inside before she opened the door and peered out. When she saw who it was, she came out on the porch and closed the door behind her. They stood there looking at each other for a moment.

"Will you come with me?" he asked.

"Yes," she said without hesitation.

FOURTEEN

THEY FOLLOWED HIGHWAY 278 as it wandered through farm-land and pine forest and small towns — Crawfordville and Greens-boro, Union Point and Covington — traffic sparse in the towns, lights winking off in the farmhouses as they passed, Georgia drifting to sleep and girding itself for Monday.

Trout avoided the Interstate. It was no place to be late at night on a motorcycle with a girl hanging on behind and two aluminum crutches sticking out over the handlebars. He stuck to the older road because it was mostly two-lane and he knew that it led unerringly to Atlanta. He need only follow the signs. Stars overhead, the air cool but not uncomfortable at fifty miles an hour, the steady drone of the engine, the singing of the tires. There was a kind of hypnotic peace to it, a suspension of time in which the minutes folded back on one another in a rush of wind.

At first he tried to empty his mind of everything but the business of guiding the motorcycle. He was not yet in any sense a skilled rider, though he grew more sure of himself as miles passed without inci-dent. By the time they reached Madison, he was more confident, and his thoughts began to wander. He thought of Joe Pike, riding west on this same motorcycle, fleeing from one set of demons and pursuing another, with the Holy Ghost occupying the seat where Keats nestled now, her arms comfortably about his midsection. It had been less than three months ago, but it seemed a lifetime; and he felt a great deal older, if not wiser, than he had the Easter morning Joe Pike abandoned the pulpit in Ohatchee. Certainly not wiser, because things seemed more muddled than ever, questions more persistent, answers nonexistent. One great difference between Joe Pike's journey and his was that Trout didn't have to go so far. Atlanta might offer refuge, and that was all he asked for at the moment. Joe Pike was proof that you could ride a lot farther and not find any answers.

They stopped at a little crossroads grocery store outside Madison. It was closed, no lights on except a single bulb at the back of the store and a security light on a pole at one end of the building that bathed the small parking area and gas pumps out front in stark bluish white. Trout counted change from his jeans pocket. He had taken everything he had found in Joe Pike's pants while Joe Pike snored, oblivious, in his parsonage bed. He had a twenty and 6 ones in his billfold and enough change for a Pepsi from the soft drink machine next to the front door. They shared it, Trout leaning against a gas pump while Keats lurched about the parking area getting the kinks out of her legs and back, returning to him to take a sip and then clattering off again. There was an awkward grace to it, he thought. He remembered the first time he had seen her, blitzkrieging through the hallway at Moseley High School, blasting everyone and everything out of her way.

"What?" she asked now, catching him watching her.

A week ago he would have stammered and blushed. But things had changed, a subtle shift in wind direction. "How old were you when it happened?" he asked.

"Four."

"Do you remember much before?"

She balanced on the crutches before him. "I used to have a dream all the time. I'd be running across a field with Daddy, both of us holding on to a kite string. Then I'd let go and he would run on, faster and faster with me trying to keep up. And then I'd stop and look up, and the kite would be way up in the sky dancing from side to side. And I would start to dance like the kite. I don't know if it was something that really happened before I got hurt or if I just invented it."

"Do you still have the dream?"

"No. I guess I got over it."

He took another sip of Pepsi and passed her the can. She drank what was left, then tossed the empty can into a rusted oil drum that served for a garbage can. The clatter rang out in the stillness. "We aren't gonna get to Atlanta like this," she said.

Trout stopped again at a Jif-E Mart in Covington and filled up the gas tank. It took all of his one-dollar bills. Inside, he examined a Georgia road map tacked to the wall and saw that Highway 278 merged with I-20 just outside Covington. The thought of confronting I-20 spooked him. But the clerk showed him a couple of back roads he could take until he could pick up 278 again in Conyers.

They set out again, following the clerk's directions until they left the city limits on a narrow farm-to-market road that cut south and west from Covington into the countryside. It seemed that they had fallen off the end of the earth. They went several miles without seeing an inkling of life — only blackness ahead, pierced by the thin, timid beam of the headlamp, and to either side, trees growing close to the roadway, an occasional flash of fence posts, stretches of sheer emptiness. Keats's grip on him tightened.

And then the headlamp went out. They hurtled blindly into the pit of the night and Trout screamed, "Jeezus!" and fought the panic that seized him by the throat and made him want to brake the motorcycle with every ounce of his energy. Keats didn't utter a sound, but her arms were like a vise around him, squeezing his breath, the metal crutches biting painfully into his sides. He let up on the gas and tried to brake with a steady pressure. The motorcycle began to slow. He had no hint of where the pavement was and wasn't until he felt the bike slip suddenly sideways and lurch violently across grass and dirt. He had the sudden impression of a yawning void to his right and he fought to stay away from it, manhandling the motorcycle, almost losing it, summoning a surge of terrified energy and pulling it back to the left until finally it shuddered to a stop and the engine coughed and died.

They sat there unmoving, Trout's feet splayed to either side to keep the bike from toppling. Keats's grip on him eased and his breath came in great gasps. He felt faint. His heart was somewhere up around his ears, pounding like a rock band in heat. After a moment Keats said in a small voice, "That was interesting."

After a while, his eyes began to adjust to the darkness. There was a tiny sliver of moon low in the sky, and it provided just enough light to make out their immediate surroundings. He looked to his right. There was a ditch — not deep, as he had imagined, but deep enough to have caused a nasty spill if the motorcycle had hit it. They might both be dead, or at least badly hurt, lying helplessly in this godforsaken Georgia outback until someone stumbled upon them.

Trout's resolve and bravado — what there had been of it — deserted him. His shoulders slumped in defeat, his stomach churned, a wave of nausea hit him. "I can't do this," he said, his voice quivering.

Keats didn't say anything for a long while. Night sounds bubbled up around them — crickets, an insomniac bird, something small rooting about in the grass along the far edge of the ditch, the faint rustle of a breeze in what appeared to be a field of some kind of low-growing crop beyond the ditch. He felt utterly helpless.

"I've got to go to the bathroom," she said.

"What?"

"Help me off," she commanded.

A flash of rage took him. Damn her! It was all her fault, and if she hadn't said what she said in the first place, he would have never thought of taking off in the middle of the night on a motorcycle for Atlanta, much less with a crippled, tart-mouthed woman hanging on behind, goading him on without saying a word and now, when he was about to crap in his own pants, making him crazy with her goddamn bladder. It was a wonder she hadn't insisted on dragging along her goddamn sketch pad and stopping every now and then to scribble on it. She was maddening.

He lowered the kickstand with a vicious jab of his foot and climbed off and helped her slide off the back, making no attempt to hide his anger. She tottered off down the roadside without a word, and he watched her for a moment and then turned his back and kicked at the grass and heard the rattle of the crutches and then a hissing sound. After a moment she was back.

"Let's go," she said.

He turned on her with a jerk. "Go? Are you out of your mind?" he yelped.

"Yes," she said. "I'd have to be out of my mind to be out here in the middle of East Jesus with you in the first place. I can't believe I let you talk me into this."

"Me?" he yelped. "Talk you?"

"Who knocked on whose door?"

"Who opened it?"

"Why didn't you just take the Interstate?"

"Because I didn't want to get us killed."

They yelled back and forth in the semidarkness and whatever it was scratching about in the grass scurried away in fright.

"Well," she said with great finality, "I don't intend to be here a minute longer than I have to."

"Well, you're stuck," he said flatly.

"No I'm not," she shot back, and she clattered away up the road, putting a steady distance between them.

He stared in utter amazement. "Keats," he called, "don't act like an idiot."

She was perhaps twenty yards away now. She turned and looked back at him — a sturdy, if slightly askew figure, held upright by two thin pieces of aluminum. He could see her quite plainly, even in the weak light. "We can wait until daylight," he offered.

"No," she said, and turned again to go.

He started after her. "All right. Wait up." They wouldn't get far. For all her incredible stubbornness, she would tire quickly, and they would stop and let the rest of the night pass. In the morning he would find a telephone and call Joe Pike. No, Cicero. Somebody would come in a truck and fetch them and they would go back to Moseley and . . . what? The thought of Moseley made him ill. He had fled in panic and darkness, driven out by the sheer accumulated craziness of the place and everyone in it who mattered to him. No, Moseley would not do. But Atlanta? It seemed light years away and, at the moment, unattainable. And walking along a deserted rural road in the middle of the night seemed sheer folly. But what? He couldn't let her go off alone.

He had almost caught up with her when she tossed back over her shoulder, "I'd rather ride."

"The damn thing's broken."

"How do you know? Try it."

He threw up his hands and stalked back to the motorcycle. "All right!" he yelled. "You'll see! You're the most bullheaded, aggravating, two-faced person I've ever met, Keats! Just gotta have things your way! Can't admit for a second you're wrong! Get your jollies out of jerking people around!"

He was still yelling when he stomped down on the starter. The motorcycle roared to life and idled pleasantly. "Shit," he muttered to himself. He flicked the headlamp switch several times. Nothing. But that was all that was wrong. He slipped it into gear and rolled up to where she waited for him in the middle of the road, steadied the bike while he helped her climb on behind him and lay the crutches across the handlebars.

"I'm not two-faced," she said.

"Yes you are. One minute you seem almost normal. And the next you're pulling some kind of weird crap."

"I just know what I want, Trout. And right now I want to go to Atlanta."

He sat there straddling the motorcycle and fumed for a moment longer, then he calmed down a little. "I'll have to take it slow," he said. "I can't see very far ahead."

"Uh-huh."

"Keats, why are you doing this?"

"I'm not doing anything. You are. I'm just along for the ride."

"It's crazy."

"Trout," she said firmly, as if she were speaking to a knotheaded child, "if you don't do this, you might as well go home and dig yourself a hole and get in it and pull the dirt in behind you. Now, I *believe* you can do it. So get your ass in gear."

And so they rode on.

There was, incredibly, a light burning in the small, grimy garage in the tiny crossroads community. He fluttered toward it like a moth, and as the motorcycle drew closer, he could see an automobile inside, its rear hiked up in the air on jacks, and a pair of legs sticking out. The legs became a grease-smeared young man as the motorcycle pulled up to the yawning door of the bay. He sat on the concrete looking up at them, holding a wrench in one hand.

"Hi," Trout said tentatively.

"Evenin,'" the young man said with a little wave.

"Where are we?"

"Pacer," the young man said. "Georgia," he added. "Where y'all headed this time of night?"

"Atlanta."

"Damn. I wouldn't go to Atlanta even in broad daylight."

Trout glanced up at the sign above the garage bay: GLIDEWELL'S AUTO REPAIR.

"Are you Mr. Glidewell?"

"One of 'em."

Keats peered over Trout's shoulder. "Do you fix motorcycles?"

The young man grinned. "I can fix anything that don't eat."

His name was Elmer. He was working late because his daddy had torn the transmission out of the car racing on a dirt track near Macon on Sunday afternoon and needed it to go to work on Monday morning. Elmer quickly found the loose wire on the motorcycle and fixed it and sent them on their way, refusing payment, pointing the way to Conyers.

It was a powerful omen, he decided. But he kept that to himself. And Keats, blessedly, didn't say a word. As they bore on through the night, she nestled her head against his back and slept, keeping a firm hold on him. In an hour or so, the sky to the west began to glow softly with the lights of Atlanta. It was two o'clock in the morning when they reached Decatur and Trout pulled up to a telephone booth and called Eugene.

A shaft of light woke him. That, and the smell of coffee. He stretched his legs and arms and looked up for the source of the strong light. The condo had a skylight, something he hadn't noticed when Eugene had ushered them in. He hadn't noticed much at all, in fact. He was stupid with fatigue, butt gone completely numb. Yet his whole body hummed like a high-voltage transformer with the sensation of riding — the rush of wind and the vibrating rumble of the engine. Eugene had pointed Keats toward the spare bedroom while Trout collapsed on the living room couch. He closed his eyes and rode swiftly off the cliff of consciousness into the bottomless well of sleep, more profound than any he had ever experienced.

Now he was awake, stiff and sore but alert and remarkably rested. He was covered with a light blanket, his jeans and shirt hanging across a nearby chair, shoes tossed on the floor. He couldn't remember covering himself with the blanket or taking off his clothes. When? How? *My God. Did* . . . He searched his memory frantically. He could remember only utter exhaustion and then nothingness. He lifted the blanket gingerly and looked down at himself. Bare legs, Jockey underwear, his usual morning excitement. No sign of . . . what?

"Lost something?" Eugene asked, and Trout made an incredibly awkward attempt to cover himself, jerking the blanket up so that it left his feet sticking out. He looked around to see Eugene standing there with a cup of coffee in hand, barefoot, wearing jogging shorts and a MAKE MY DAY, KISS MY DERRIERE T-shirt, hair tousled, grinning, steam rising from the cup.

"I, ah . . . my clothes," Trout mumbled.

"Over there," Eugene said, pointing to the chair.

"Yeah."

"We thought you'd sleep better without them."

"We?"

"Keats helped me take them off. You were zonked."

Trout smiled sheepishly. "I guess so."

"I called Uncle Joe Pike and told him where you are," Eugene said.

"What did he say?"

"He said, 'I thought that's where he might be.'"

"Did you tell him Keats is with me?"

"Yes."

"What did he say about that?"

Eugene grinned. "Something about a woman with a wild hair up her butt."

"Oh. Yeah."

"Uncle Joe Pike said he'd call Wardell and tell him Keats is okay." Eugene headed for the kitchen. "Coffee's on."

Trout dressed and followed Eugene, who had a cup of coffee waiting for him on the kitchen table. He wasn't much of a coffee drinker, but he dumped in sugar and milk and found that it had a nice warm lift to it. Eugene poured himself another cup and sat down across the table from Trout.

"Keats still asleep?" Trout asked.

"I guess so. We stayed up pretty late talking."

"You did?" He tried not to sound too surprised.

"Keats and I go way back."

"You do?" Surprise won.

Eugene laughed, seeing the look on Trout's face. "I used to sneak over to the mill village and play with Keats and the other kids. Until Mom caught me and shipped me off to McCallie."

Trout realized how little he truly knew about Eugene. He had spent his junior- and senior-high years at prep school in Chattanooga, summers away at camps of one sort or another. When Trout made his infrequent visits to Moseley, Eugene was rarely there. He had gone to college at Vanderbilt, Trout knew that. But he had no idea what kind of job Eugene had or anything about his life. Or hadn't, until yesterday's *Atlanta Constitution.*

Eugene was studying him. "I hear the doo-doo really hit the fan," he said.

Trout shrugged uncomfortably, not having the slightest idea where to go with this. It felt incredibly odd, sitting here and knowing what he now knew about Eugene, knowing that he was supposed to recoil in horror at the thought of what Eugene *was.*

What on earth was he doing here, anyway? Well, admit it, he had been desperate, wheeling into Atlanta at two o'clock in the morning on a motorcycle with a crippled girl on the back and twenty dollars in his pocket, dead tired, no plan whatsoever. They hadn't even worn helmets. They could have been killed. Or, at the least, arrested and thrown in jail for violating the helmet law. Stupid! Stupid! He should have waited until today, found the keys to Joe Pike's car and some more money, left Keats at home. Then he could have driven to Atlanta without dragging along baggage and complicating everything to the point of near insanity. But no, he had to bolt like a frightened colt in the night and do it all wrong. He had damn near spent the night sitting in a ditch outside Pacer. And now here he was drinking coffee with his queer cousin, his asshole tightened up like a prune, and just wanting to get the hell out.

"Okay, let's talk about it," Eugene said.

"What?"

"Come on, Trout." Eugene gave him a long look. "Does it make you uncomfortable?"

"I guess so."

"Do you think I'm going to hit on you or something?"

"I don't know."

"Well, you're not my type," Eugene said with a smile. "And I'm not a pedophile; I'm gay. It's entirely different."

"It is?"

"Yes. So you don't have anything to worry about. Okay?"

Trout nodded. Eugene took another sip of his coffee. "So, ask me. Anything."

Trout went blank. There were a million questions, of course, but none of them in words. This was something you never ever talked about, not in any way but a snide joke, for fear that somebody would think you were . . . *that*. Talk about football, girls, hunting, zits, the Braves, dumb teachers, even jerking off. Anything but *that*. He blurted, "Do you have a roommate?"

Eugene smiled. "Roommate. Well, I *had* a lover. His name is Jason. But we broke up a month ago and he moved out. It was," he sighed, "every bit as painful as your breaking up with a girl."

"Oh." Then he added after a moment, "I'm sorry."

"I'm getting over it. Jason wouldn't pick up his underwear. I try to remember that, not the rest of it."

Trout laughed, and it made him feel a little better.

"I am who I am," Eugene said easily. "I've known for a long time that I'm gay. It's not something I'd have wished for if I'd known how it can complicate your life. But then, it's not something you wish or don't wish. It just is. I am what God made me. And like I heard Uncle Joe Pike say one time, God don't make no junk."

Trout could feel his anxiety easing. This was just Eugene — not much different, really, from the boy Trout remembered. Just older, more mature, but with the same stubborn streak of independence. The same Eugene who had thrown down his horseshoe and walked away from Grandaddy Leland's backyard game years before because he could see that it was rigged and dumb. Eugene seemed at peace with himself. Just playing the hand that he had been dealt.

Trout felt a sudden rush of both envy and self-loathing. He was disgustingly pliable, eager to please, running along behind other people and picking up after them. Especially Joe Pike. He hated that part of himself. And he hated what he believed to be a deep-rooted cowardice that let him simply go with gravity and current. On the one hand, he craved some notion of control over his life, self-determination, self-knowledge. All the things Eugene seemed to have. On the other hand, if and when he truly figured out who he was, it might scare the hell out of him. It may have, he realized, scared the hell out of Eugene at one point in the past. But he had gotten over it.

"Do Uncle Cicero and Aunt Alma know?"

"Dad, yes. God bless him. It was a shock when I told him, back when I was at Vandy. But he got over it. We talk. A lot. He's incredible." He ran his hand roughly through his hair. "Mom? Not, I'm afraid, until yesterday. I tried to drop hints. I even took Jason home with me last Christmas. But she just wouldn't see. Didn't want to see. You know how she is."

"Yeah." And then he told Eugene about the Sunday that never seemed to end, Alma's marching out of church and Joe Pike's sermon and then Alma's trying to burn down the mill. Recounting it, he was struck by how nightmarish it seemed now, by how profoundly the earth had shaken in Moseley, Georgia, in the space of one day. He realized in the telling that it sounded like Eugene had brought down the temple on everyone's head with one photograph on the front page of the paper. But it wasn't so. The fault lines had been there all along. All it took was a nudge.

"I didn't know about the thing at the mill," Eugene said, staring into his coffee cup. "Dad didn't tell me that."

"Aunt Alma talks all the time, or used to, about you and me running it one of these days."

Eugene didn't say anything for a long time. His finger traced a circle around the rim of his coffee cup. His brow furrowed. Finally, he looked up at Trout. "It's all gone," Eugene said quietly. "You realize that, don't you?"

"Gone?"

"The mill hasn't turned a profit in five years," Eugene went on. "Maybe longer. But Mom just kept on running it full-tilt and selling stuff at a loss and using up the cash reserves. She plowed ahead like nothing was wrong, sending everybody in the family their checks, keeping up appearances, holding it all together somehow. Until now."

"The union . . ."

"Wardell and the rest of them are just chasing their tails," Eugene interrupted. "There's nothing to unionize. The cash is gone and the only way to keep going is to borrow. And no Moseley ever borrowed a dime. It's an article of faith. Mama's darn sure not going to borrow money to pay for a union." He paused, then shook his head. "Funny. Wardell wants a union because he thinks things are so bad. Well, they'd be a darn sight worse if Mama hadn't kept the mill running like she has. Wardell's about to find out what 'bad' is."

At first, Trout was stunned. And then lights went on, bells rang, pieces fit. *Watch and listen*, Phinizy had said. Trout had, and he realized that he had known more than he thought. The pained, frightened looks in people's eyes, the fierce clutching at myth and symbol. What it amounted to, he could see now, was desperation — the acts of people trying to save themselves. *Save your own ass,* Uncle Phinizy had said. Well, that's what all the rest of them were doing, whether they knew it or not. Phinizy, Joe Pike, Alma, even Cicero, with their hauntings and agonies and dreams. Maybe Wardell Dubarry and his daughter, too. Everybody scrambling for the lifeboats.

"Who else knows about all this?"

"Dad. Judge Tandy, probably. He does all the legal work."

"My dad?"

"I don't know. Uncle Joe Pike's got his own problems, I suppose."

"Yeah. Uncle Phinizy?"

"Not all of it, I don't think. But he suspects a lot."

"Yeah."

"And now, Keats."

"You told her?"

"Yes."

"What's going to happen?" Trout asked.

"I suppose they'll lock the door and turn out the lights. Mom and Dad will be okay. Dad's done really well. Real estate, stocks and bonds. People have no idea."

No they didn't, Trout thought. He wondered what might happen now to Cicero's Do-It-All, to the notion of economic transformation in weary, down-at-the-heels Moseley, especially with the mill and its wages gone. It seemed the height of futility.

Cicero had obviously known all along what was going on with the mill and the Moseley family money. Had he bought into the charade simply to keep peace? Or had he loved Alma enough that he was unwilling, even unable, to hasten the inevitable. Surely, what Alma had done had been foolish — clutching at blind hope and some terribly warped notion of what it meant to be a Moseley, letting the ghosts of Moseleys past run her life. Surely, Cicero could see it. But he had either ignored or helped stave off the inevitable. To confront it would have meant admitting that the temple was rotten and crumbling. And that would have broken her heart, as Trout had seen it broken last night in the mill. Cicero might be something of a fool for doing what he did. But a man would be a fool for a woman. Trout Moseley knew that. And it stood to reason that a woman might also be a fool for a man. He just hadn't seen that side of it yet.

Eugene stood. "Well, I've got to go to work."

Trout realized he didn't know what Eugene did for a living. "Where?" he asked.

"The studio."

"Are you an artist?"

"Film and video production."

Then he remembered — he and Eugene, playing TV station years before. Eugene organized everything. He combed Trout's hair and put some of Alma's pancake makeup on him. He made a camera from a cardboard box with an old toilet paper tube as a lens. Then Eugene manned the camera while Trout read articles from the newspaper. When Eugene eventually grew up and went off to college, Aunt Alma insisted he major in pre-law. But in the end, Eugene had obviously done what he wanted.

Trout indicated the condo. "I guess you're doing okay."

"I'm having fun." Eugene smiled down at him. "You ought to try it, Trout."

He turned to go, but stopped in the doorway. "Keats is a neat kid. If she has half a chance, she'll make something of herself. She's got a lot of spirit."

"Yeah. She does."

Eugene studied him closely. "She likes you a lot. I guess you know that."

He woke Keats an hour later with a cup of coffee. She was nestled like a burrowing rodent in the double bed in the spare bedroom. She sat up quickly, startled from sleep, and stared at him uncomprehendingly. She was wearing one of Eugene's shirts.

"Hi," he said.

She took the coffee cup without speaking and drank several sips. Then she said, "Hand me my crutches."

He watched as she tottered off unsteadily to the adjoining bathroom. Bare legs, a sliver of white panties showing beneath the hem of the shirt. She came back after a moment and sat on the side of the bed next to him, propping the crutches next to her, looking much improved. She drank more of the coffee.

"I'm a good sleeper and a bad waker," she said.

"Have you called your folks?"

"No."

"Are you going to?"

"No."

"Why not?"

She looked down at her hands. "Because I'm scared." It was, he thought, an incredibly naked confession for someone like Keats Dubarry.

"Scared of what?" he asked.

She looked at him harshly. "Do you know what's going to happen? Do you have any idea of the kind of pain and agony that's coming?" He didn't answer. "No, I guess you don't," she said with a sneer. "You folks up there in the Big House, you'll do just fine. Us po' white trash down in the mill village are out on our butts. No jobs, no place to live, no nothing. Can you imagine what this is going to do to my daddy?"

"But you said he ought to get out of there and find another job," Trout reminded her. "You said he's good with his hands."

"It's losing," Keats said. "That's what he won't be able to stand. Losing to the Moseleys. Every time he looks at me, a little bit of what's good and kind about him dies. And a little more hatred for the god-damn Moseleys takes its place." She turned away from him with a jerk, quivering with rage. He thought for a moment she might cry, but then he knew she would not. She had learned from Wardell Dubarry that anger would keep you going when nothing else could.

"Keats," he said after a while, "I'm sorry. I really am. I don't want anybody to be hurt. Not you, not your family, not my family. I just don't know what to do."

She turned back to him then and gave a weary sigh. "I know."

Impulsively, he put his arm around her shoulders. He didn't know how she might take it, but she looked at him strangely for a moment and then she rested her forehead against his and slipped into the crook of his arm and he put his other arm around her, encircling, protecting. He closed his eyes, and the two of them sat that way for a long time, and there was no sound but their breathing. Then he opened his eyes and saw her legs, bare below the shirt. They were firm and strong and smooth. Whatever damage the truck had done, it was not there. He felt a rush of blood to his face and his breath quickened and his head spun and his stomach did little dipsy-doodles. "I'm really glad you came," he said hoarsely.

Her lips were incredibly soft. He disappeared into them, like falling from a great distance into a cottony cloud, and he only faintly heard the clatter of the crutches as they fell to the floor. He fell and fell and the cloud that was Keats caught him and held him and then they fell together, through rain and then sun, crying out to each other like winged things. And when they landed finally, entwined and enthralled, the earth swallowed them in all its soft, lush greenness.

They huddled together like puppies, sharing warmth and security, not speaking for a very long time. Trout was astonished. That was the only word for it.

So that's what it was. That's what everybody made such a big deal about. Well, he thought with a smile, it was indeed a very big deal. It was not just the joining. That happened so quickly, so awkwardly, it was almost embarrassing. No, it was what the joining meant. You truly stepped out of yourself for the very first time in your life and entered a communal space where you willingly gave up something of your innermost self and were given to in return. It was, he realized, something you could never adequately explain to a friend, even one who had engaged in the same kind of act. Because it wasn't just an act. It was . . . astonishment.

She stirred in his arms, flesh on flesh. He felt immensely tender, almost to the point of tears. He kissed her hair and she raised her head from the crook of his arm where she nestled.

"Did you . . ." he started.

But she put her fingers quickly over his mouth. "No questions," she said.

And they slept.

It was almost noon. She sat up in the bed and moved away from him a bit, and when he finally opened his eyes, she was sitting cross-legged, studying him. Every inch, head to toe and back again, seeming to absorb the minutest detail. Her eyes stopped just below his waist and lingered there and it was almost like a touch. He stirred. She smiled.

"Well, now you know," he said, returning the smile. He should feel incredibly self-conscious, he thought, should make some frantic move to cover himself. But he didn't feel that way at all. He felt freer than he had in a very long time — perhaps ever. He felt that he was letting go of a lot, easing out from under the peddler's sack of stuff he had been carrying around. He reached for her, but she gripped his wrist and stopped him.

"Let me draw you," she said.

"Will it make me feel famous?" he asked.

She smiled again. "Of course."

FIFTEEN

IT WAS A light, cheerful room with the walls painted a pale yellow, bright floral print curtains at the window and a matching bedspread, pictures of birds and woodsy scenes on the walls. There was a night-stand by the bed, a chest of drawers, a small table that served as a desk. The stack of books on the desk included a couple of novels (she was partial to Anne Tyler and Walker Percy), a typing manual similar to the one Trout had used in class at Ohatchee High, and a volume on organic gardening.

The desk also held a portable typewriter and beside it, a thin stack of typed sheets. He thought of reading them while he waited, but decided against it. Whatever she had written, it was private. And in a place like this, your private thoughts would surely be intensely per-sonal and even painful, part of whatever it was they did here to help you save yourself. There was much he wanted to know, but he didn't want to find out that way. It would be, in a way, dishonest. So he stood instead at the window looking out at the shaded grounds, the long oak-lined driveway that led to the main building across the way, where the motorcycle was parked and where Keats waited inside.

Keats. He tried not to think about her, because this — this room and what it meant — was why he had come. But he couldn't *not* think about her. Every nerve ending tingled with the feel and smell and taste of her, and he felt light, floating, helium-filled, strangely abstracted.

He shook his head, trying to rid himself for a little while of the images. There would be plenty of time for that.

Back to the room. She might not come. They had told her that Trout was here, but she might decide not to see him. It wouldn't be because she didn't love him, but because she just wasn't ready yet. And if she did come, what to say? What to tell? What to ask? He was afraid it would all rush out in a great blur of words, all the wrong ones as well as the right ones. He might frighten her. Or bring on one of the great black silences that had so frightened him in the days before they took her away.

It was so quiet, he could hear his heart pounding. He turned on the clock radio on the bedside table. It was tuned to the Atlanta oldies station. Patti Page sang "Old Cape Cod," and he thought suddenly of the beach. He must have been two or three — spooked by the waves that pounded the sand and swirled up around his legs. He cried, and Joe Pike picked him up and held him and then walked into the water to show him it was all right. But every time a wave broke, Joe Pike, unthinking, turned his back and Trout got a face full of salt water that stung his eyes and made him bellow with terror. And Irene had come to rescue him.

He heard the door open behind him, but he was unable to move — stricken suddenly by the fear of what he might see, what she might be. *Oh God* . . .

"Trout," she said softly. He turned slowly and saw that she was small and beautiful and filled with light, even if there were tiny lines etched around her eyes and mouth that hadn't been there before. She was as he remembered, as he had hoped, only different. But not so much that it mattered. And then she took him in her arms and rescued him again, if for just a little while.

"You know? All of it?"

"Yes," she said.

"How?"

"Cicero. He calls just about every day."

Trout was stunned. Cicero had never mentioned Irene except in the most oblique and offhand way. But all the while, he was giving her a link with the world she had escaped.

"And Phinizy calls sometimes," she added. "Mostly just to see how I'm doing and to tell me about something he's been reading."

"They let you talk on the phone?"

"Of course, honey. It isn't a prison."

They sat together on a concrete bench in the shade of a tree just outside her cottage. The afternoon was warm, but her touch was cool as she smoothed his hair and caressed his cheek.

"Dad said the doctors didn't want anybody to come see you."

Her face clouded. "What they tell you here is that you have to take responsibility for yourself. You can't depend on anybody else or blame anybody else. You have to wrestle with who you are and come to grips with that." She hesitated, searching his face for some sign of comprehension. "Do you understand that?"

"I guess so."

"I'm wrestling. And it just seemed better to do it by myself." She smiled. "But I'm glad you came. It was time."

"Are you well yet?"

She pondered that for a moment. And then, without exactly answering his question, she told him about her long pilgrimage — medication, electroshock therapy, a lot of talk, the gradual return of awareness and interest. It was like being a baby chick inside a shell, she said. She hadn't wanted to come out for a good while. The world was too fierce and demanding. But then one day, almost by accident, she had pecked at the shell and a splinter of light had broken through and the journey began. It was painful, often terribly so. "Honesty," she said with a rueful laugh, "really sucks." There were setbacks, days when the old curse returned. But there were fewer and fewer of those now.

"When can you come home?" he asked tentatively.

"I don't know, Trout."

Don't know when? *Or don't know* if? "Can I come stay here with you?"

"No, honey," she said gently. "They wouldn't let you do that." She looked away, out where the sun, almost directly overhead, splattered stretches of grass between the trees with a bright, hot light. It was quiet here, sheltered, the noises of Atlanta beyond the grounds of the Institute only a faint murmur.

"Dad needs you," Trout said tentatively.

She looked back at him. "Dad needs . . ." But then her voice trailed off and she was lost in thought. It dawned on Trout that whatever great chasm of need that existed between them might be unbridgeable, maybe even unknowable. *I am,* Joe Pike had said, *part of the problem. Maybe most of it.* Trout felt a hollow sickness at his core, a dawning awareness that things might never be a great deal better, that she might never come all the way back and that Joe Pike might spin off like a runaway meteor into nothingness. And he, Trout Moseley, sixteen years old and ancient in his battered soul? What? What?

"Mama," he said, his voice small and distant. "I've got to know. Was any of it my fault?"

She pulled him close, pressed his head against her chest and held him for a long time. He could hear the beating of her tiny heart, a bird's heart. He felt hollow. And pointless. She might never tell him. She might not be able.

But after a while she said, "I've had a lot of time to think about what happened, honey. You think about everything, all the possibilities. I wondered if it was just that I didn't want to be a mother, didn't want the responsibility. I wondered if I was a coward. But then I thought of how much I love you. How could I not want to be your mother? You are the most precious thing in the world to me, Trout. No, sweetheart, none of it is your fault. I may have failed as a mother, but you didn't fail as my son."

"You didn't fail, Mama," he protested.

"I left. It's a kind of failure."

He raised up and looked her in the eye. "But why?"

She thought about it for a moment, closed her eyes, sighed, opened them again. "I left because I just couldn't handle things anymore." She paused again, searching for words, for a beginning, perhaps. "Has Dad ever told you anything about his father?"

"They didn't get along. I learned that much."

"Leland Moseley went for an entire year without saying a single word to his son. The year Dad was a senior in high school. They sent him off to the military school, but he ran away and came home and insisted on going to high school in Moseley. And his father refused to speak to him or even acknowledge that he existed."

"Just because Dad wouldn't mind him?"

"I suppose so."

"But that was way back, Mama. What . . ."

"So Dad went off to college in Texas, and that's where he met me. His father showed up, quite unexpectedly, at graduation. And he told Joe Pike it was time to come home and take over the mill."

"But he didn't."

"No. He went on to seminary and became a minister. I think he had God and Leland Moseley confused. He wanted to please Leland, but he couldn't bring himself to go to the mill. So he turned to God, and Leland couldn't argue much with that. Only later, he began to figure out that he turned to God for the wrong reasons."

"And you?"

"I never wanted to be a preacher's wife. It's very hard. People are always watching you, pulling and tugging on you, asking for things and expecting things you can't give. Your dad" — she paused, again trying to find the right words to describe something that may be indescribable — "wants people to love him."

Images flashed through Trout's mind: Joe Pike on the parsonage lawn, surrounded by the remnants of his distant past, pulling them to him, enveloping them with his smile and his great arms, soaking them up hungrily; and Joe Pike at summer camp, lumbering to the swimming beach draped with laughing kids.

"I love him," Trout said tentatively. He waited.

"So do I, honey. But that wasn't enough. And there came a time when I began to ask myself, 'Why am I putting myself through this? Why is he?' And I suppose that's when I started to run away."

Trout could see the pain of it in her face, and he realized that it was pain, as much as anything else, that had permeated their lives all these years. That was the worst thing about the silences. The pain. For all of them. Pain, disappointment, and finally exhaustion. Bending under the great weight on your shoulders, the weight of being who you were, or at least who you were supposed to be. Eventually, you might have only two choices: run or die. *Save your own ass.* But in doing so, it was an admission of failure. It was a word Joe Pike had used, and now Irene. They had all lost a lot. Much of it was irretrievable.

He crumbled then. "I miss you, Mama." She searched his face and then put her arm around him while he cried unashamedly, burying his face in her lap, a lost and bewildered little boy, for one last moment the child he would never be again.

It was midafternoon when Trout called Joe Pike and told him they were leaving Atlanta. They got on the motorcycle and headed out, finding Highway 278 in Decatur and retracing the route they had traveled the night before. The towns and crossroads — Conyers,

Pacer, Covington — and the ribbons of winding rural road that connected them seemed strange and unfamiliar in the daylight, like territory fought over and conquered in some long-ago night battle, filled with sound and fury.

They said little to each other until they stopped for a foot-long hot dog and a shake at the Dairy Queen in Covington. It had a small covered patio that shaded several picnic tables, and they sat alone and ate ravenously.

"I'll bet Herschel's mad as hell," Trout said.

"Yeah. We should have told him, I guess."

"Do you think he'll fire us?"

"Probably. Then hire us back. At least me."

"Why you?"

"Well, he can't do without me."

The Dairy Queen seemed somehow strange and distant, something he had known long ago. Everything was changed now. What to do? Who could tell him? It was still only mid-June and the summer stretched ahead like an unending highway, the horizon shimmering with heat phantoms. There was, at least, Keats.

When they had finished, Trout took all their trash to a nearby can and then sat down again across from her, and they looked at each other for a long moment.

"I don't know what to say," he said finally.

"About your mother?"

"About anything. Us."

She looked away from him.

"I didn't mean to . . . I mean, I wasn't trying to . . . it just happened."

She looked back. "Look, Trout. Let's don't spoil it, okay? Let's leave it where it is."

"Damn it!" he said. "Stop making me feel like a little kid!"

"If you feel like a little kid, that's your problem."

"I love you!"

Her eyes softened then, and she reached for his hand and held it. "It was the sweetest thing that ever happened to me," she said gently. "I want to keep it that way."

"But what about . . ."

"I don't know. That's all I can say. I don't know." She raised his hand to her lips and kissed it lightly. "Right now, I just want to go home."

It was late afternoon when they reached Moseley. And as they rolled in from the west, Highway 278 becoming Broadus Street, he was struck by how small and dowdy it looked. Even Aunt Àlma's house seemed to sag under its own weight and he noticed, for the first time, that paint was beginning to flake from the fascia board above the front porch. The Packard was parked under the porte cochere, but the Buick wasn't there. And across the street at the parsonage and church, there was no sign of life at all.

The park looked almost normal, except there was no band shell. You had to look closely to see where the gash the bulldozer had made was now sodded over.

The rumble of the motorcycle engine echoed hollowly off the downtown buildings as they rode through. It was mostly deserted, everything except the Koffee Kup Kafe closed for the evening, long shadows swallowing the storefronts and making them even more somber and drab than ever. The vacant lot where the furniture store had been was an open red sore. The slab of concrete that had un-earthed the skeleton was a dirt-covered scab at the middle of the lot. Across the street there was nobody in the police department, or at least not visible in the front room. Trout wondered if Joe Pike had gone back to his cell, back to contemplation of the rules of the road. Then he remembered that Joe Pike had answered the telephone in the parsonage when Trout called. But where was he now? Maybe at the Dairy Queen.

They passed the city limits sign on the east side of town, and that's when he got his first glimpse of the commotion in front of the mill. As the motorcycle drew closer, he could see that the gate was closed and a big crowd was milling about in front of it. A couple of hundred people, men and women, black and white, a sprinkling of kids. It looked like the entire population of the mill village. Joe Pike's car and Cicero's police cruiser sat at the curb, well back from the crowd. As he turned onto the mill street, he could see Alma's car parked inside the fence next to the office door. The crowd at the gate seemed agitated, and as he got nearer, he could hear its angry buzz and he could see Wardell Dubarry towering over the rest of the mill workers, one hand on the gate, shaking it furiously. It was padlocked. Then he saw Joe Pike and Cicero and Calhoun standing next to the police cruiser. The driver-side door was open, and Cicero was standing next to it, talking on the radio, while he kept an eye on the crowd.

"Damn!" Trout said. Why couldn't they all just be quiet for a little while?

He could feel Keats craning her neck to see around him, seeing what he saw, her body tensing. About the same time, Joe Pike spotted them. His eyes and Trout's met and Joe Pike shook his head vigorously, warning him away. Trout turned to give the crowd a wide berth, and then Keats yelled, "Stop!" He kept going. "Stop, Trout! Dammit, stop!"

"I'm taking you home," he yelled back. "You might get hurt."

"Let me off!" she bellowed. "Let me off!" She started beating on his back with one of her fists, holding on to him with the other hand and digging her fingers painfully into his side. At the rear of the crowd, people turned to look at them. And then Keats stopped hammering on his back and began to slip backward off the motorcycle. Damn! She'd kill herself! He slammed on the brakes and she lurched hard against him, and then as he fought to keep the cycle from toppling over, she scrambled off, an incredible flurry of crutches, arms, and legs. She left him there struggling with the bike and plunged into the crowd, disappearing in the general direction of Wardell.

Trout got the motorcycle under control and turned around and headed for Cicero's police cruiser. As he pulled in behind it, Joe Pike pointed a no-nonsense arm toward the parsonage. "Go home, Trout."

Trout glanced at the crowd, pressing up hard against the locked gate. Wardell was rattling the gate furiously and the noise level was rising. This was not a placard-carrying crowd, not some well-organized protest. It was a nasty-looking spur-of-the-moment mob. And Keats was somewhere in the middle of it. Trout killed the engine, kicked down the kickstand, climbed off the motorcycle and headed toward Joe Pike and Cicero. "Did you hear me?" Joe Pike barked.

But just then there was a roar from the crowd, and they all looked and saw Aunt Alma emerge from the mill office. "Open up!" Wardell bellowed. Alma paid them no attention. She got into her Buick and sat there for a moment.

Cicero turned to Joe Pike. He looked grimly alarmed. "I told her we should have called the state folks an hour ago!"

"What's going on?" Trout demanded.

"Go home!" Joe Pike ordered again.

"No!" he shot back, standing his ground. "What happened?"

"Alma closed the plant."

Another roar from the crowd. Alma was backing out of her parking space now, turning and easing toward the gate. The noise was deafening. Cicero turned and said something to Joe Pike, but Trout couldn't hear what it was. He handed the radio microphone to Calhoun and yelled something to him. Then Cicero headed toward the crowd, hitching up his gun belt as he went, Joe Pike close on his heels. Trout followed, slipping in behind them as Cicero lowered his shoulders and waded into the crowd. They edged along the fence, Cicero and Joe Pike shoving people out of the way as they struggled toward the gate. Trout was bumped and jostled. He almost went down, but he grabbed on to the back of Joe Pike's belt. Joe Pike whirled angrily, then saw who it was. "Get outta here!" But it was too late now. Bodies pressed in around them — yelling, pushing, pressing toward the gate in a heaving mass. "Hang on!" Joe Pike yelled, and pushed on.

Through the fence, Trout could see Alma's car stopping, Alma getting out, walking up to the gate, unlocking it. "The plant's closed!" she cried. "This is private property! Get off!"

"Well, if we ain't coming in, you ain't coming out!" Wardell yelled back. The noise exploded, drowning out everything for a moment until the gun went off. POW! Then bedlam. A panic in the other direction. Joe Pike staggered, almost losing his feet, and Trout was bounced roughly against the wire fence. He held on and suddenly they burst free and he looked around Joe Pike's great bulk and saw Cicero and Wardell, faced off like two bulls, Cicero's arm holding his police revolver high in the air. Cicero kept his eye on Wardell, but he yelled through the fence to Alma, "Get in the car!"

"Yeah!" Wardell screamed at her back as she retreated from the gate. "Get in the car, Alma! Turn tail and run! Go see that faggot young'un of yores in Atlanta!"

Joe Pike lunged forward and Trout lost his hold on the belt and almost fell. He grabbed the fence to steady himself, just in time to see the powerful movement of Joe Pike's right shoulder and hear the sickening crunch as his fist collided with Wardell Dubarry's face. Suddenly, all sound ceased — except for the sound of Wardell's body slamming backward into the gate and dropping with a thud to the ground. Nobody moved. Cicero stared at Joe Pike, then Wardell, an astonished look on his face, his gun still high in the air.

Joe Pike stood over Wardell, massive and unmovable. "Get up, Wardell," he said. "Get up and apologize to my sister."

But Trout could see that was quite impossible. Wardell was out cold.

Then from somewhere off to Trout's right there was a horrible scream and then an explosion of motion as Keats came slashing through the crowd, yelling incoherently, scattering people with her crutches. She lurched up to where Joe Pike stood over Wardell, her face contorted with rage. "Goddamn you!" she screamed. "Get away from him!" She smacked Joe Pike's shin with a crutch. He didn't say anything, but he backed away a couple of steps, and Keats collapsed on the pavement next to Wardell, covering him with her body. She sobbed against his ashen face while they all stood, stunned and unmoving, watching her. It was pitiful. Trout took a step toward her, but she looked up and saw and stopped him with her savage voice. "Goddamn you! All you goddamn Moseleys!"

And Trout knew that she was quite beyond comfort.

He tried, just once. It was just after six the next morning when he knocked on the door of the Dubarry house. After a moment, Keats opened it and stood there, staring at him as if he were an apparition. She was calm, but there was a fierce hardness to it. After a moment she said, "You're crazy, coming over here."

"Can I see your daddy?" he asked.

"No," she said, and started to close the door. But then Wardell was there, standing just behind her and peering out. When he saw who it was, his eyes bulged with rage and he made a ragged gargling sound through the wires that held his jaw together.

"Mr. Dubarry," Trout said, "I came to ask you to drop the charges against my daddy so he can get out of jail and preach Uncle Phinizy's funeral."

Wardell just glared at him, stunned at the audacity of it, then turned away from the doorway in disgust.

"You'd better leave," Keats said.

Trout heard a screen door slam somewhere behind him and turned to see a shirtless, barefoot man standing on the porch across the way, arms folded across his chest, eyes narrowed. Then he saw more people on other porches, some of them drifting down into their yards, moving slowly in the direction of the Dubarry house. The hostility hit him like a hot wave.

"Don't come back, Trout," Keats said. Her voice was absolutely flat and emotionless. "Ever."

He was stunned. "Keats. Don't. After what happened . . ."

"Nothing happened," she said.

"Yes it did!" he cried.

"You're just like a little puppy. You want somebody to hold you so you'll stop whining. Grow up, Trout."

"No," he cried. "Don't do this, Keats." It was something he had to hold on to, something that was just his. She couldn't take it away. She couldn't.

"Forget it," she said. "It doesn't matter."

"I'll never forget it," he said, his voice barely a whisper.

"Okay, don't. But leave me alone. Don't ever come back here. If you do, I'll hang pictures of you all over the high school. Use your imagination."

He knew, with a sickening sense of helplessness, what she could do if she wanted. She knew every line and angle of his body, had committed them to paper and memory, and she could bend them into any shape or act her imagination could conjure up.

He felt helpless. Betrayed. But then he looked into her eyes and saw that it was the same with her, only worse. She was a small wounded animal, snarling at the thing that had hunted her down and cornered her. It was not really him. It was all the other. And she had only her crutches and her anger to hold her upright. That, and the gift of her talent. Maybe she would use it to find her way out. But if she did, it would be on her own. She was beyond his reach, perhaps always had been. There had been one brief, exquisite moment when he had thought there might be such a thing as grace and redemption and, yes, love. But it existed now only in his memory. Another loss, perhaps the most profound of all.

He sat on the back steps of the parsonage in the twilight waiting for the sun to dip below the treeline so it wouldn't blind him as he rode west. The motorcycle leaned on its kickstand at the edge of the house, the small duffel bag strapped to the passenger seat with a piece of rope he had found in the garage.

As he waited, he looked about the yard. The grass needed mowing. The storage shed needed painting. Next to it, the small plot of plowed-up ground was becoming clotted with weeds. Joe Pike had never gotten around to planting a garden. It was too late now.

Joe Pike still languished in the tiny cell at the rear of the police station, guarded by Calhoun, the new police chief. Joe Pike appeared somewhat at peace. But with him, it was hard to tell. It might be just exhaustion. They were all exhausted. He hadn't had much to say to Trout. Things were a trifle uncertain, he said. The Bishop would be in Moseley tomorrow to see to things at the Methodist church. And then there was the judge to consider. Joe Pike was reading Aeschylus now. And Heidegger. Trout had brought him the books from Phinizy's apartment, along with an enormous tub of Dairy Queen ice cream.

At graveside, there had been just the family — Trout, Alma, Cicero — and two fellows from the funeral home in Thomson. The four men carried the casket from the hearse. It didn't weigh much.

It was early, before nine, and the June sun angled through the tall pines that shaded the Moseley family plot. It had rained during the night, and the grass underfoot was spongy and the freshly dug earth was soft and ripe-smelling. There was the faintest of breezes, just enough to make the pines whisper.

Aunt Alma looked rather pretty. She was dressed in a mint green summer suit, silk maybe, something that clung to her figure. She had a nice figure. She, too, looked at peace. Or at least relieved.

The four men placed the casket on the metal stand over the open grave and then they all stepped back and stood there for a moment, no one quite knowing what to do next.

Then Cicero cleared his throat and spoke up. "Phinizy was a good listener," he said. "People went trooping in and out of his place at all hours of the day and night with all manner of baggage, and he always had time to listen. He had what some folks might call some bad habits, but I don't think they really amount to much in the big picture."

They pondered that for a moment, then Trout opened the Bible he had brought and read the passage from Job that Joe Pike had suggested. *"With the ancient is wisdom; and in the length of days understanding."*

"Amen to that," Cicero said. Then he turned to Alma. "Anything you want to say, hon?"

"I wish I had known him better," she said simply. "I wish I had . . ." Then her voice trailed off.

They all stood there for a while longer and then one of the men from the funeral home said, "Y'all want to stay while we finish up here?"

"No," Cicero said. "We've got a plane to catch."

"I'll stay," Trout said.

As he walked home later, he found himself thinking about Great Uncle Phinizy and smiling. Phinizy had seen the wreck and it was a doozie.

Cicero and Alma would be in Bermuda by now. They would probably stay for a good while, Cicero had said. Would Trout be okay while they were gone? Of course, he assured them. He was used to fending for himself. There were chicken pot pies in the freezer. And of course there was the Dairy Queen. He didn't want Cicero and Alma to worry.

When he returned to the parsonage from the cemetery, he changed into jeans, packed a few things, and made his call.

"Sure," Eugene said without hesitation. "Come ahead. For as long as you like."

It would be dark again as he rode. But that was all right. This time, he knew the way.

HOME FIRES BURNING

"Stands head and shoulders above the crowd.... The best small-town Southern novel since *To Kill a Mockingbird*."
— *Atlanta Journal-Constitution*

"A wonderful novel, filled with characters who live and breathe and hurt and cry and who come to seem like friends."
— *Morganton* (N.C.) *News Herald*

"A beautiful work, tough and bittersweet, funny and frightening, just terrific."
— *Philadelphia Inquirer*

OLD DOGS AND CHILDREN

"A remarkable saga of the South . . . a magnificent storyteller."
— *Chattanooga News–Free Press*

"A parade of vivid characters and immediate, gripping scenes."
— *Seattle Times–Post Intelligencer*

"Storytelling at its best.... Through the eyes of a spirited lady, Robert Inman celebrates the beauty and battles of a family and a region."
— *Atlanta Journal-Constitution*

DAIRY QUEEN DAYS

"A remarkable and profound novel.... A joyous addition to our Southern literature."
— *Nashville Banner*

"Inman deserves a place on any list of the best contemporary Southern writers. Make that a high place, even on a short list."
— *Winston-Salem Journal*

"Inman captures perfectly the nuances of small-town life."
— *Chattanooga Times*